SECOND FLIGHT: BACK TO THE VORTEX II

THE UNOFFICIAL AND UNAUTHORISED GUIDE TO DOCTOR WHO 2006

SECOND FLIGHT:
BACK TO THE VORTEX II

THE UNOFFICIAL AND UNAUTHORISED
GUIDE TO DOCTOR WHO 2006

J SHAUN LYON

First published in England in 2006 by
Telos Publishing Ltd
61 Elgar Avenue, Tolworth, Surrey, KT5 9JP, England
www.telos.co.uk

Telos Publishing Ltd values feedback. Please e-mail us with any comments you may have about this book
to: feedback@telos.co.uk

ISBN-10: 1-84583-008-3 (paperback)
ISBN-13: 978-1-84583-008-3 (paperback)
ISBN-10: 1-84583-009-1 (hardback)
ISBN-13: 978-1-84583-009-0 (hardback)

Internal design, typesetting and layout by Arnold T Blumberg
www.atbpublishing.com

Printed and bound in England
Antony Rowe Ltd, Bumper's Farm Industrial Estate,
Chippenham, Wiltshire, SN14 6LH

1 2 3 4 5 6 7 8 9 10 11 12 13 14 15

British Library Cataloguing in Publication Data.
A catalogue record for this book is available from the British Library.

TABLE OF CONTENTS

For Matt Dale, John Molyneux and Jason Knight
and memories of travels far and wide.

FOREWORD

I have enjoyed the company of Shaun Lyon at many conventions in both the USA and England. I have found him to be both bright and amusing – and a fan of *Doctor Who* – not mutually inconsistent qualities, I hasten to add.

Despite the pleasure always to be found in his company, I did not for a second suspect that he might be capable of producing such a detailed and meticulously researched work as this 'Unofficial and Unauthorised' Guide to what we are all learning to refer to as 'New Who' ('If you knew *Who*-oo, like I knew *Who*-oo …') as opposed to the last century stuff I contributed to briefly – now charmingly referred to as 'Classic Who'. Just like 'Classic Cars', all that really means is that you can't get the parts any more. Sigh.

If you want to know what David Beckham thinks of *Doctor Who*, what Christopher Eccleston said to David Tennant or what the former may or may not have been doing with Renee Zellwegger – then this is the book for you. The first third of this generous work will give you every available piece of information about the way in which the media embraced the return of a former favourite, as it re-established itself as the 'must see' programme for families across the UK – and beyond. From the *South Wales Echo* to the *Belfast Telegraph*, from the *Sunday Herald* to the *Daily Bugle* (all right I made the last one up) – *Doctor Who*'s timely return was fêted and fed upon across the British Isles.

I can easily imagine this book being a point of reference for decades to come, such is the volume of information that Shaun has somehow contrived to unearth whilst residing on the other side of the Earth. No mean feat. If you want to know what the third assistant director said to the relief driver who brought the Face of Boe's beautician out to location, I would not be surprised if you found the answer in these pages.

The body counts, the faux pas, controversies and gossip all jostle with hard fact and creative detail. Each new episode and each story is dissected with a loving but critical eye by several well-chosen reviewers and, indeed, the editor himself.

No *Doctor Who* fan – or indeed no Doctor – should be without this book. And I suspect, however Unofficial and Unauthorised it may be, it will become an indispensable point of reference for all involved with the making and enjoying of our favourite programme.

Ten out of ten from six out of ten!

Colin Baker
October 2006

INTRODUCTION

'Did you miss me?'

There's a moment in 'The Christmas Invasion' that could very well be a seminal event for a generation of *Doctor Who* fans. Rose Tyler is on her own, facing down the leader of the Sycorax with only her wits and her recent experiences to guide her, but she's in far over her head: a third of the Earth's population stands on the brink, literally, and it looks like all hope is lost. Then, with a hint of magic as the TARDIS begins translating the Sycorax leader's words into English, the doors to the ship open and out steps our hero.

The Doctor is back, and he's taken charge... and nothing will ever be the same again. *Doctor Who* is at its most successful when the viewer is taken along on a journey with the one person in the universe who truly knows what's going on and how to deal with it. He's the quintessential hero in this day of anti-heroes and shades of grey; he's never cruel or cowardly, as his mantra was once stated, and he is always fair and true. Far too often we find our television icons taking missteps, turning them into fragile creatures of circumstance... and there's nothing wrong with that, so long as we know that in *Doctor Who* we will enjoy the company of the one person who will *never* let us down.

Welcome to *Second Flight*. Like its predecessor, *Back to the Vortex*, this book is a trip alongside the Doctor in his travels facing evil and danger across the cosmos – this time during the 2006 season, with a new actor in the lead and a ramping-up of the drama and adventure. It's not a nuts and bolts behind the scenes book, nor was it written with any insider information; it's a voyage purely from the fan perspective, covering the highs and lows, the press coverage and the media reaction and, yes, the happenstances of fans watching from the sidelines.

That's part one; part two examines the series in depth, its plot points, its themes and continuing storylines (like the first book, perhaps going a bit further than one might expect on the details!) along with an international panel of reviewers from the United Kingdom, the United States, Canada, Australia and New Zealand. It's all pretty much as it was for *Back to the Vortex*, with only a few changes; notably, the two short reviews per panellist we featured in the first volume (one thematic, one general) have been eliminated in lieu of a larger general episode commentary/review by each. This gives us more space for specific critique and analysis, which I hope works more favourably in this volume.

If you're looking for a tell-all, you're going to be disappointed; that's not what *Second Flight* is about. Instead, it's a loving look at a year of *Doctor Who*, the year David Tennant took the role and made it his own; the year Billie Piper got a chance to really shine and say farewell; the year the Cybermen were on the march. It's all here... Queen Victoria, the Ood, the Abzorbaloff, Sarah Jane Smith and K-9, Cassandra, the Sycorax, the Isolus, the Clockwork Men, the Wire... oh, and those pesky Daleks, too.

Join us now for a second flight into space and time... as the trip of a lifetime continues.

J Shaun Lyon
July 2006

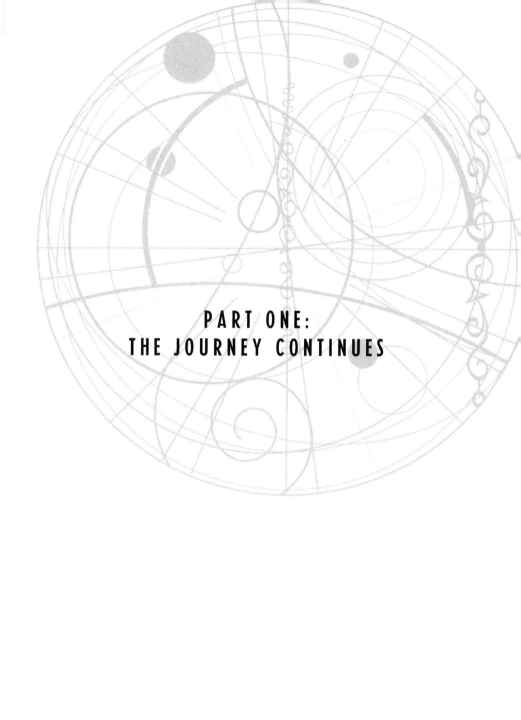

PART ONE:
THE JOURNEY CONTINUES

CHAPTER ONE:
THE MORE THINGS CHANGE...

'New teeth. That's weird. So where was I? Oh that's right... Barcelona!'

Two years before its long-awaited return in 2005, *Doctor Who* was considered to be a relic, a television icon from an era long past. In hindsight, perhaps no-one could have expected that when it returned, it would do so with such unprecedented force as on that March evening, when Christopher Eccleston and Billie Piper made their first trip together in the magical, bigger-on-the-inside blue box called the TARDIS.

It had been, to borrow the tagline associated with the programme's first new series in 16 years, *the trip of a lifetime*: the Doctor and his companion Rose Tyler pitted against villains such as the Daleks, the Slitheen, the Gelth, the Mighty Jagrafess of the Holy Hadrojassic Maxarodenfoe and a sheet of skin called Cassandra; facing the scourge of the Reapers over a crack in time; and welcoming the aid and support of Captain Jack Harkness, Mickey Smith, Jackie Tyler, Adam Mitchell, Jabe the tree person, the servant girl Gwyneth, Lynda Moss, the orphan mother Nancy, Pete Tyler, and even Charles Dickens. They'd visited Cardiff in the 1860s; stopped nuclear Armageddon in present-day London; and taken several glimpses into Earth's far future. They'd faced adventure, and fun, and danger, and tragedy and, all the while, looked inside themselves for strength and absolution.

But Christopher Eccleston decided to leave the programme at the end of its first new series, a fact that was to be kept quiet over the course of its broadcast... until an untimely leak (one of many) caught the world of *Doctor Who* unawares. In those last few moments of the closing episode, nestled within the relative safety of the TARDIS, the Doctor bid Rose goodbye – in fact bid all of *us* goodbye – with his trademark smile and a wink and a bright flash of light.

And then, as quickly as it had begun, the Eccleston era was over. The David Tennant era was soon to begin, *Doctor Who* had left its innocence behind, and all eyes were on the future.

DAVID TENNANT IS... DOCTOR WHO

David Tennant had been a *Doctor Who* fan all his life. 'I grew up loving *Doctor Who* and it has been a lifelong dream to get my very own TARDIS,' said Tennant to the world in a BBC press release on 16 April 2005, the day his official pronouncement as the next incarnation of the Doctor was made. 'I am delighted, excited and honoured to be the tenth Doctor! Russell T Davies is one of the best writers television has ever had, and I'm chuffed to bits to get the opportunity to work with him again. I'm also really looking forward to working with Billie Piper, who is so great as Rose. Taking over from Chris is a daunting prospect; he has done a fantastic job of reinventing the Doctor for a new generation and is a very tough act to follow.'

David Tennant was first mentioned as the lead candidate to play the tenth Doctor on 30 March 2005 in a story reported by the *Daily Mirror*. Fresh from his appearances in the lavish costume drama *Casanova* and at the time soon to appear in BBC4's live recreation of *The Quatermass Experiment*, Tennant was already known to *Doctor Who* fans. He'd taken a small role in the official BBC *Doctor Who* website animated serial *Scream of the Shalka* (2003), despite not originally being a member of the cast. He had been recording a radio play in a neighbouring studio, and when he discovered what was being recorded next door he managed to persuade the director to give him a cameo role. He had also taken roles in various Big Finish

Productions audio CD dramas, including several characters for their *Doctor Who* and *Dalek Empire* lines and headlining their adaptation of Bryan Talbot's *The Adventures of Luther Arkwright*. Tennant himself commented briefly on the rumours to the *Mirror*, noting that '[the Doctor] would be a great role to play.'

Christopher Eccleston's sudden and startling departure from the role – an official BBC announcement was prompted by the *Mirror*'s leak of the news – had taken viewers by surprise, but it soon became clear that the production team had already faced this issue and had taken steps to ensure a smooth transition. Indeed, by the time of the official announcement, everything was 'go' for a sequence bridging the two seasons, an official handover of the torch from Doctor to Doctor, more commonly known as a regeneration. On 15 April, the BBC made a formal announcement that Tennant would indeed step into the role, debuting officially in the forthcoming 2005 Christmas special but appearing briefly at the tail end of the season finale, 'The Parting of the Ways'.

David Tennant was born in West Lothian and trained at the Royal Scottish Academy of Music and Drama in Glasgow. He began his career on the stage, performing as part of the Royal Shakespeare Company, including in such roles as Touchstone in *As You Like It* (1996), Romeo in *Romeo and Juliet* (2000), Antipholus of Syracuse in *The Comedy of Errors* (2000) and Captain Jack Absolute in Sheridan's *The Rivals* (2000), as well as appearing at such venues as the Young Vic, the Edinburgh Lyceum, the 7:84 theatre company and Dundee Rep. Tennant had been nominated for a 2003 Laurence Olivier Theatre Award for 'Best Actor of 2002' for his performance in *Lobby Hero* at the Donmar Warehouse and the New Ambassador's Theatre. By the time of the announcement, Tennant had also already undertaken his first official role with the production: he narrated *Doctor Who: A New Dimension*, a half-hour special that had aired on BBC1 prior to the transmission of the debut episode, 'Rose'. His many film and television roles included *Jude* (1996 – sharing a scene with Christopher Eccleston), *Bite* (1997), *Holding the Baby* (1997), *Duck Patrol* (1998), *LA Without a Map* (1998), *The Last September* (1999), *Love in the 21st Century* (1999), *The Mrs Bradley Mysteries* (1999), *Being Considered* (2000), *Randall and Hopkirk (Deceased)* (2000), *Bright Young Things* (2003), *Posh Nosh* (2003), *Spine Chillers* (2003), *The Deputy* (2004), *Blackpool* (2004) and *Harry Potter and the Goblet of Fire* (2005). Tennant was already quite well known when his name came up; his relationships off screen had been subject to tabloid press comment, including a rumoured pairing with *Cutting It* actress Sarah Parish and, later, his more public romance of actress Sophia Myles (after her appearance in the episode 'The Girl in the Fireplace').

Recalling the hype surrounding the change in *Doctor Who*'s lead actor from decades before, and its impact on the British public, Tennant's casting in the role was the subject of the day on 16 April in the press and on the morning television programmes. Two days later, attending the annual awards show of the British Academy of Film and Television Arts (BAFTA) – an experience he would repeat the following year, for the show he was about to work on – he told *BBC News* that 'the expectations are fierce.' He would give no specific time for how long he planned to remain on *Doctor Who* or what he'd signed up for, but he told *Hello* magazine, 'Let's get through one at a time. I'd love to do 100 years, but they might sack me.' The press reporting around his casting was also not without controversy; the *Daily Mail* said on 19 April that his salary would be half what Eccleston's had been, a story that led to further speculation about Eccleston's reasons for departing the series. Details about Tennant's costume, his relationship with his co-stars and the like would all be subjects for later discussion; at the time of this intense press scrutiny, Tennant had yet to even record his first scene. (That would come on 21

April, as Tennant would record the closing moments for 'The Parting of the Ways' with the production's second unit; it would later be merged with Eccleston's previously recorded final scenes.)

On 15 June, just days before the transmission of 'The Parting of the Ways', executive producer Russell T Davies and BBC Head of Drama Jane Tranter had announced that a third series of the programme had been commissioned, including a second Christmas special. Also revealed at the time was the title of the forthcoming Christmas special that would be Tennant's first full episode, 'The Christmas Invasion', as well as the fact that Billie Piper would return for the entirety of the second series. Despite all this good news, there was also speculation as to the third series. 'Doctor Who could face yet another regeneration for the show's third series, after the BBC revealed it has still not signed a deal with its new Time Lord actor David Tennant,' said Broadcast Now on 23 June. 'Tennant and co-star Billie Piper have both been confirmed for the second series,' they continued, 'but the BBC admitted that no contract has been signed with either actor for the third series, announced this week. "We're still in discussions with David Tennant and Billie Piper. The third series has only just been announced, so it's still early days," said a spokeswoman.'

Shortly after broadcast of 'The Parting of the Ways', the Daily Mirror said on 20 June that it expected Tennant's Scots accent to be integrated into the series. 'New Dr Who David Tennant will speak in his Scots accent in the next series of the show,' they reported. 'Scottish fans were shocked to hear the Paisley-born Tennant speaking in posh English tones during his debut as the Doctor last Saturday. It was all the more surprising because Tennant had said he hoped to give the role a tartan flavour. The accent sparked an outcry among Scottish Who fans, and now producer Russell T Davies has hinted Tennant will be speaking naturally come his first full adventure at Christmas.' At the time, it was expected that the upcoming Christmas special would carry a reference to this accent confusion, though an appearance by Tennant's natural accent would have to wait for the forthcoming series' second episode, 'Tooth and Claw'.

Of course, not everyone was celebrating the casting of Tennant; after all, Eccleston's performance in the first series had met with considerable acclaim. So, too, would his departure be greeted by some measure of sadness... as would the end of the run. The New Statesman of 20 June said: 'Davies has, as has been much remarked, reinvented the phenomenon of families gathering around the electronic hearth and, thanks to Doctor Who's extermination of ITV1's Celebrity Wrestling, helped kill off ITV's reliance on the celebrity genre... Just as the police box once represented the presence of the state in every high street, Davies's TARDIS became a symbol of public-service quality in the Saturday-night schedules. And that makes three cheers in all.' And the Daily Record asked on 23 June, 'Anyone else feel like they lost a friend on Saturday night? Since watching the last episode of Doctor Who, I've been at a loss over just what to say... Saturday saw the climax of a love story, a tragedy, a comedy, an end, a beginning and a satisfying culmination to the most successful TV return since, well, Lassie Come Home. Everything – the music, the sets, the effects, the characters, the aliens, the acting (Billie Piper excelled in the final episode) worked brilliantly. Between Casanova and Doctor Who, Russell T Davies better take a big bag with him to the next BAFTAs.' And so he would, but that's a story for later...

DOCTOR WHO WILL RETURN...

Even though 'The Parting of the Ways' had just been transmitted on 18 June, Doctor Who devotees – and the people behind the series – were already looking to the future. 'A Christmas special this year, another series of 13 episodes in 2006, followed by another Christmas special and then 13 more episodes in 2007, which is very exciting,' said executive producer Russell T Davies in an interview with *CBBC Newsround* the very next day. While Series One had made the headlines, Series Two promised so much more. 'Some famous old monsters called Cybermen will be coming back and they are equally scary as the Daleks,' continued Davies. 'Lots of new villains too, and one or two favourite characters from this year as well. But at the same time, the Christmas special has a brand new monster to fight, and that's gonna be good!' In fact, the wait time between the previous series and the next would be relatively short; *Doctor Who* was returning in only six months' time. '*Doctor Who* will return in "The Christmas Invasion"' promised the tag – in the style of the closing credits of the old James Bond films – at the end of 'The Parting of the Ways', suggesting that the adventures of the past 13 weeks would soon be revisited in style. In fact, BBC television was itself quick to celebrate the series and the prospect of its return. Within a couple of hours of the conclusion of 'The Parting of the Ways', a one-minute trailer aired on BBC1; a compilation of iconic moments from the previous 13 weeks. Ending with the regeneration and the new Doctor's beaming smile, the trailer announced: 'The countdown to "The Christmas Invasion" starts now ...'

Doctor Who was, by now, a known commodity, not for its past but for its present and future. As explained by the BBC in-house weekly journal *Ariel* in late June, marketing *Doctor Who* had been a challenge eventually overcome: 'It was, after all, a much loved brand. Its return was researched among families with children... Its heritage could be a help and a hindrance. For guidance, the team looked to Hollywood, to see how it trails movies such as *Spiderman* and *Batman*. They discovered that there is often no explanation of the hero's back story. Moreover, making references to returning characters – as in 'he's back' – alienates the younger audience. So instead of reinterpreting *Doctor Who* for both children and parents, the marketing emphasised the fantastic adventure element, a journey on which we are invited to travel. In trails [for the season] Christopher Eccleston asks if you want to follow him on the trip of a lifetime. Billie Piper, who plays Rose, lent the show credibility to a younger audience. But there was still a fine balance to strike – the trails had to look exciting and thrilling to people of all ages.'

So, too, was Russell T Davies now a known commodity to fans and viewers worldwide. Now firmly in charge of the direction of *Doctor Who*'s future, he was no longer merely an interested producer with a fondness for what was now known as the 'classic' series, but instead boasted a long-term vision. Davies, however, considered himself more a storyteller than a producer. 'I don't think I'm remotely famous,' he told the *Western Mail* (as quoted by the icWales website on 25 June). 'I have got a gay hook, a Welsh hook and now a *Doctor Who* hook. It has given me greater visibility and it is that which helps my career. *Queer as Folk* opened a lot of opportunities for me, but I think people would prefer writers to go away and shut up.' Davies' reference to what was his most famous work prior to *Doctor Who*, the landmark gay drama series *Queer as Folk*, perhaps put the past year in perspective: no longer a potential suitor to the crown of *Doctor Who* producer, he was now *the* man at the helm. Julie Gardner, his fellow executive producer, herself now familiar to audiences as well thanks to regular appearances on *Doctor Who Confidential*, remained at his side. The two had been accompanied throughout much of the first year by Mal Young, who had elected to leave the position of Head of Continuing Series, and the BBC, late the previous year. Series Two would instead bear the stamp of Davies and Gardner, and the team they had assembled. 'It's going to be 60 minutes long,' Davies continued in his *CBBC Newsround* interview, referring to 'The Christmas Invasion'. 'It's the first story of the new Doctor played by David Tennant. I remember when I was young, it's very strange when a new Doctor comes along, and that's exactly how Rose feels. Her mum gets involved again, but beyond that I can't give anything else away.' But this would not be just any *Doctor Who* adventure. 'It's as Christmassy as can be. It's got reindeer, it's got sleigh bells, it's got the works.'

There were however some concerns about the direction the series would take. While the first series had boasted a lavish special effects display, some had disliked the fact that the Doctor and Rose had remained on or near Earth during every televised adventure. 'I'm the one who has stopped us going off Earth,' explained Davies, 'because I think you see an awful lot of shows, expensive, good ones like *Enterprise* and *Angel*, where they go to another planet or dimension and it looks rubbish, it looks like California in the sunshine with a funny rock. I think it's the hardest thing to do, and I'm very wary of [it] looking... rubbish, because I think the moment the programme looks rubbish people point at it and laugh in a bad way.' The Earth-bound storytelling, and more importantly the series' newfound reliance on the city of Cardiff not only as a production base but as a dramatic focus, bothered others, such as former BBC Director General Greg Dyke, who addressed an open letter to the BBC in late June. 'As a lifelong *Doctor Who* viewer, I don't believe the series was without flaws. Given that the Doctor is a time traveller, able to go anywhere at any time, he did end up on Earth a disappointing number of times during the 13 episodes and, even worse, he kept turning up in Cardiff. I haven't got anything against the capital of Wales, but if I could land anywhere in the universe at any time, would I really go to Cardiff more than once? Of course, any connection with the fact that the series was made by BBC Wales, and that for the production team, Cardiff was a cheaper location, is purely coincidental.' A spokesman for BBC Wales answered the charge: 'It is clear that viewers felt that praise applied especially to the two episodes set in Cardiff as they attracted tremendous average audiences of eight million people.'

Likewise, there were concerns in the press over David Tennant's thick Scottish accent, which Davies answered in the *CBBC* conversation with a play on his own dialogue, right out of 'Rose': 'Well, every planet has a Scotland. You'll have to wait and see, there are big revelations on the way, and I can't say any more than that.' And there was quite a fervour when Davies announced that the second series would contain a story arc not unlike the first year's 'Bad Wolf' theme; in fact, it would be based around one word. 'Yes, there is, and that word has already been heard on screen. And that's all I'm saying. You'll have to go back and trawl through 13 episodes to realise what I'm on about. You'll hear the word in the Christmas special though.' That word would turn out, of course, to be 'Torchwood'...

The high on which the series had bowed out could not be overstated. 'They said it couldn't be done,' commented the *Daily Express* on 20 June. 'But *Doctor Who* did it. Helped by the gorgeous, pouting Rose, a murderous army of Daleks, assorted scary monsters and scripts that were out of this world, BBC1's Time Lord triumphantly regenerated a life form that everyone thought was long extinct; a family audience. For 13 weeks, whatever ITV hurled at the show, be it *Celebrity Wrestling* or blockbuster movies, fell through a ratings black hole.' Christopher Eccleston's contribution to the first series was also emphasised by Davies, speaking to *BBC News* a day earlier; Eccleston's performance, he said: '... turned around the reputation of *Doctor Who*... Chris, as one of the country's leading actors, by being willing to step up to the line and take on that part has proved himself to be magnificent and has turned it around. So now you get actors like David Tennant who is the next generation and just about one of the best actors in the world. David himself says he wouldn't have touched this part if Chris hadn't done it, because the part had become a joke. But Chris has salvaged it and made it new, and now we get to do one of the most famous parts of *Doctor Who* folklore – the moment when the Doctor regenerates and becomes a new person and yet stays exactly the same man.' Eccleston himself spoke briefly to *Newsbeat* at a Mencap charity event in mid-June, saying: 'The best thing about *Doctor Who* for me has been the response I've had from children, both in the street and the number of letters and drawings of me and Daleks, which are all over my wall at home. In all the 20 years I've been acting, I've never enjoyed a response so much as the one I've had from children, and I'm carrying that in my heart forever.' With the end of Series One, however, Eccleston's brief relationship with the programme was severed, and the comments the actor made at the charity affair were some of the last words spoken by the actor to the press about his time on the series.

With a new leading man coming aboard, Billie Piper's role as Rose Tyler would end up serving as a buffer between the two eras. Said Davies, 'We've been talking to Billie for months now, and Billie Piper is in every single episode next year. We have got a Christmas special coming up and then 13 episodes, so we are going to make 14 in total and she is in all 14 episodes.' It was quite a change from the year before, when Piper's association with *Doctor Who* had been considered by some commentators a potential liability for the forthcoming series; now, Piper was a celebrated *Doctor Who* veteran lauded with critical acclaim and would serve as an anchor between successive eras of the show.

Creating the role of Rose Tyler, 'a *Buffy*-style female sidekick... a modern action heroine' for the new series, Billie Piper had been announced to the news media on 24 May 2004. 'Billie Piper is confirmed to play Rose Tyler, companion to Doctor Who, it was announced today by Julie Gardner, Head of Drama, BBC Wales,' said the original press release. Brought up on a Swindon housing estate, Leian Paul Piper (her first name was changed to Billie when she was seven months old) had begun taking dance lessons at the age of five; by seven, she was filming soft-drink commercials in America and at 13 she had a brief film role as an extra in *Evita* (1996) starring Madonna. She won a scholarship to the Sylvia Young Theatre School in London in her teenage years and moved to London to live with her aunt and uncle. While she filmed several commercials and even had a bit part in *EastEnders*, her first true big break came when she starred in a commercial for *Smash Hits* magazine, becoming a 'spokesmodel' for a year until she was scouted by the head of Virgin Music's Innocent label. 'Because We Want To' was her first hit, topping the charts in 1998 – making her the youngest female vocalist to hit the exalted top position since Helen Shapiro in 1961. She followed her success up with promotion of her first album, *Honey to the B* (1999), which went platinum; over the next two years, she produced two additional chart-topping hits, 'Girlfriend' and 'Night and Day'. Her second album, *Walk of Life*, came out during the summer of 2000. Her career then started cooling off, with rumours running rampant that her record label would soon drop her. Late in 2000, after an appearance on his radio show, she began dating DJ and entrepreneur Chris Evans and, in May of the following year, despite a 16 year age gap, they married in Las Vegas. After the wedding, Piper vanished from the music scene. She eventually turned back to acting, and in 2003 starred in *Canterbury Tales: The Miller's Tale*, following this with several film roles, in *The Calcium Kid* (2004), *Bella and the Boys* (2004), *Things To Do Before You're 30* (2004) and *Spirit Trap* (2005).

But it was the first series of *Doctor Who* in 2005 that brought Piper to front and centre in the public eye. She possessed a natural chemistry with Christopher Eccleston, and press and public reactions were largely effusive. Her performance as Rose was described as 'superb' (*Radio Times*, 10 May 2005), 'perfect' (*BBC Ceefax*, 14 May 2005) and the series' 'principal strength' (*The Times*, 4 May 2005); and *icCroydon* noted on 15 April that her casting had 'brought a whole new angle to the story of the regeneration of the show.' Co-star Camille Coduri (Jackie) told the *People* in April 2005 that Piper: '... really shines. She's one of the leading actresses of her generation – divine, funny and witty.' Former *Doctor Who* stars Sylvester McCoy and Colin Baker also offered their own insights; McCoy told the *Daily Record* on 28 April: 'I think Eccleston is terrific, but it's Billie Piper as Rose who steals it.' Baker meanwhile wrote in a column piece for the *Bucks Free Press* (March 2005) that Piper was: '... an unexpected revelation [who] has made the perfect start.'

But, besides the addition of Tennant to the cast and the departure of Mal Young, there would be other changes afoot for year two. One of the first year's script editors, Elwen Rowlands, had elected to depart for the BBC's new time travel series *Life on Mars*, and had been replaced by Simon Winstone, who had enjoyed success behind the scenes on *EastEnders* but who also had spent a time editing *Doctor Who* fiction at Virgin Publishing in 1997. There would also be changes in the wardrobe and make-up departments, with Lucinda Wright, Davy Jones and Linda Davie all electing to depart for other projects. Some directors would opt not to return, or would not be asked back; however, both Euros Lyn (whose work on 'The Unquiet Dead' in the Swansea and Monmouth location shoots had been much admired by the production team) and James Hawes (who had directed perhaps the most critically acclaimed first season story, the two-parter 'The Empty Child' and 'The Doctor Dances') would be asked back to direct early in the season. Meanwhile, Graeme Harper was asked to join the production to direct four episodes of the new season. Harper had first worked on *Doctor Who* on the 1971 Jon Pertwee serial 'Colony in Space' and had later directed two critically acclaimed stories: 'The Caves of Androzani', the landmark 1984 serial that marked Peter Davison's departure as the Doctor; and 'Revelation of the Daleks' for Colin Baker's Doctor.

Perhaps the biggest surprise came with the revelation of two further people who were rumoured to be working on the second series. First, comedian/writer Stephen Fry, according to a report from *BBC News* on 24 June, was in talks with the BBC about writing an episode, though he would not be appearing in the said story. Fry, who had only recently starred in 'Death Comes To Time', a *Doctor Who* audio serial produced by Fictionlab and released initially through the series' official website, would eventually be confirmed as one of the original Series Two writers; later it would be announced that his episode had been postponed to Series Three for budgetary reasons and then dropped entirely due to Fry's other commitments. Secondly, Elisabeth Sladen, fondly remembered for her portrayal of the savvy, sophisticated Sarah Jane Smith from the 1970s-era of *Doctor Who*, was rumoured to be returning to reprise her role. Last seen in televised *Doctor Who* in the 1983 twentieth anniversary special 'The Five Doctors', Sladen had gone on to star as Sarah in a spin-off series of audio adventures released by BBC licensee Big Finish Productions, though a television return for any of the series' original cast had long been considered unlikely. In public appearances throughout the year in the UK as well as at a reunion with several former castmates at the *Gallifrey 2005* convention in Los Angeles in February, Sladen had kept quiet regarding any discussions she might have been having with the production team at the time. Nevertheless, while both stories at the time remained unconfirmed, they were certainly further proof that an attachment to *Doctor Who* – any attachment, even rumoured – was grist for the media mill.

The status of first-series semi-regular John Barrowman was also the subject of speculation. Fresh from a five-episode stint in the show's debut series as Captain Jack Harkness, a fan favourite and media target for controversy due to the character's implied (and, albeit slightly, displayed) bisexuality, Barrowman had been seen bidding the TARDIS an unexpected farewell in the concluding minutes of 'The Parting of the Ways'. Barrowman continued a public relationship with the production team that had, in essence, kicked him out of the TARDIS – he recorded DVD commentaries alongside Gardner, Piper and producer Phil Collinson – and there were rumours that he would return mid-way through the second series, or perhaps toward the end. Few suspected at the time, however, that Davies had other plans for the wayward adventurer, as the spin-off series *Torchwood* reared its head later in the year.

WORLDS APART

While *Doctor Who* was taking its summer break from original adventures transmitted in the United Kingdom, the series' impact was felt elsewhere in the world. On 3 July, the official *Doctor Who* website confirmed that Canada would definitely see the second series in 2005. 'Following the success of the first series,' stated the website, 'the Canadian Broadcasting Corporation have agreed to screen series two and the Christmas special. "We're delighted to have the CBC on board for another season," said Russell T Davies. "They have been the perfect partner on *Doctor Who* – sharing the editorial vision at the outset, then running a strong campaign from sexy posters to slick, witty trailers, and best of all having the confidence to schedule the series in a big, showy prime time slot." Davies suggested that Canadian viewers would be among the first beyond the UK to see 'The Christmas Invasion', a suggestion confirmed later in the year when the adventure was broadcast a day after its UK transmission. (Canadian fans would, however, be disappointed with the delayed transmission of Series Two a year later.)

Early July was also the start date for the series in New Zealand; the show would once again be transmitted on the Prime TV network. The *New Zealand Herald* on 3 July said that the series had given Piper: '... a new lease of life... Billie Piper, Serious Actor. Who knew? Many people in the television industry, it seems.' In another article in the paper, the *Herald* suggested that the series' return would: '... recapture the popularity it achieved at its height when the *Daily Sketch* called it "the children's own programme that adults adore."' The *Herald* focused additional coverage on memorable *Doctor Who* villains from the past, as well as addressing the 'Inside the TARDIS' convention tour that would soon travel through the nation (at the time making its way through neighbouring Australia) with several of the series' original cast including Sylvester McCoy and Colin Baker.

Australia was, in early July, already familiar with the show's return, the series having been successfully launched on the ABC network. The *Australian* had choice comments about the most recent episode broadcast as the month had opened, Rob Shearman's 'Dalek': 'It's George Orwell meets *The Matrix* on *Deep Space Nine*.' The paper also commented on the recent release of the first batch of episodes on DVD: 'Previous series of *Doctor Who* were notable for their crummy effects, monsters made of mop heads and Royal Academy of Dramatic Arts types slumming it for pin money. But you get the sense, watching this uncanny new incarnation, that more money has been spent on each episode than on entire seasons previously... Without a doubt, these are the Time Lord's finest hours.'

Terrestrial and satellite channels in English-speaking countries weren't the only sources for *Doctor Who*'s first season. British Airways began showing 'The End of the World' on its flights equipped with video-on-demand services, as Thomsonfly Airlines had done earlier with screenings of 'Rose' as part of its in-flight entertainment. British Midlands Airlines also announced it would carry 'selected episodes' of the series on its overseas flights, while VoloTV, the television service on the First Great Western Railway, also acquired rights to screen the series. Telewest Broadband announced plans to carry new video-on-demand services to their cable subscribers, which would include recent UK series such as *Doctor Who*, while the show continued to be sold to foreign markets as well; on 14 July there was an announcement that the RTLKlub Network in Hungary would carry the series, and a day later an announcement that Denmark had picked up the show.

British fans meanwhile were given several treats on the collectibles front. *SFX* Magazine released a special booklet, *The Art of Doctor Who*, which showcased 'loads of concept drawings and production art from the first season of the new show.' Character Options announced a new batch of *Doctor Who* tie-in toys; the range would include a 12-inch standard Dalek from the previous season's episodes, walkie-talkie figurines of the Doctor and a Slitheen, a sonic screwdriver, and even a talking TARDIS money box! (Press reports at the time suggested considerable consternation from the retailers that several of the items being released bore the image of Christopher Eccleston, but licensees had discovered at the same time as the rest of the public that the actor had chosen to leave.) For the grown-ups, *The Complete First Series* DVD released in November would include commentaries from the producers, writers and actors. Of rather curious interest a bit later on was a 27 July report in the *Daily Mirror* that one of the people who would be buying the DVD boxed set was none other than Queen Elizabeth II. 'She has become a huge fan of the hit BBC show starring Christopher Eccleston – and she was hugely disappointed when the actor quit after his first stint as the Time Lord,' the article claimed, noting that Her Majesty: '... is also a fan of the Daleks and she intends to while away August evenings watching the series at her Scottish residence. A Buckingham Palace source said: "The Queen loves the programme and has requested a full set of DVDs. She has asked the BBC to send her copies so she can watch the series again during her stay at Balmoral."'

UK viewers also had the opportunity to watch the first series again from the beginning, with a screening on the digital channel BBC3 beginning on Sunday 17 July with 'Rose', followed by the cut-down version of the first episode of *Doctor Who Confidential*; the rest of the series would continue on subsequent Sundays and Fridays, ending in mid October. The UKTV Gold cable and satellite channel also announced it would begin televising the first series later in the year, starting in late October.

THE SLOW CLIMB

After the tumult that late June had brought, whispers of the impending start of production on the second series began in early July 2005. The Outpost Gallifrey website reported on 3 July that at least one retailer in downtown Cardiff had been approached regarding recording outside their shop, with the likely date of production being 1 August. As the retailer noted, 'We will be required to put a Christmas display in the window. As far as I know, they will only be filming outside the store. It's in a place called The Hayes, in the city centre. It just so happens it's across the road from the department store that was used for Henricks [sic] in "Rose".'

Speculation had begun in earnest. The *People* had some thoughts about the salaries of both Billie Piper and David Tennant, noting in its 3 July edition that Tennant's salary (as reported by a 'source') was far less than Piper's reported take, and suggesting that Tennant had already signed a contract for a third series... while Piper had not yet done the same. But Piper's continued presence was yet to be questioned. 'It's great news that Billie is staying,' the source told the *People*. 'Her deal is what she deserves, as she's a favourite with fans.' And speculation wasn't limited solely to the two actors whose commitment to the second series was assured. '*Doctor Who*'s famous canine companion looks set to make a comeback,' reported the *Newsquest* media group (a syndicated news feed reported in various print newspapers) about the possible return of K-9, the fan-favourite mechanical companion originally part of the series in the late 1970s and voiced by actor John Leeson. *Newsquest* commented that such a return was: '... to the delight of its Bridport creators... David Martin and his script-writing partner Bob Baker... Now, BBC chiefs are understood to be planning a return for the Time Lord's faithful four-wheeled friend in the next series. This week Mr Baker confirmed that he was meeting with the show's producers to discuss K-9's future role. "It is not confirmed yet, but I am sure he will be in the new series, although we have to discuss how to use him."' The BBC had no comment, although an appearance by K-9 wasn't implausible; the recent reports that Elisabeth Sladen might return suggested that her mechanical pal, last seen alongside her in the series' twentieth anniversary special 'The Five Doctors', wouldn't be far behind.

The reality was that production was ramping up, with recording scheduled for later in July. David Tennant, interviewed in an edition of *TV Times* magazine released as the month opened, said he was 'absolutely terrified' about the prospect of playing his new role. 'It's so daunting, the amount of attention it gets, the amount of expectation it has. And the fact that Christopher Eccleston has been so bloody good at it is really annoying from my point of view, because now I have to try and equal that!' Rather non-committal on the subject of his involvement in the third series at this point, Tennant noted that he would: '... wait and see what happens. The BBC might sack me – I might get replaced by [BBC newsreader] Moira Stuart. Who knows?' Across the Atlantic only weeks later, Tennant spoke briefly in Los Angeles at an autumn press preview event for the BBC America channel; appearing in connection with the channel's announced acquisition of *Blackpool* (retitled *Viva Blackpool!* for the US market), he said of *Doctor Who*, 'It's very exciting and fantastically daunting that you come to LA and everyone here knows about it as well... It's very scary right now, because I haven't started.'

TV Zone magazine, released in the last week of June, featured an interview with producer Phil Collinson, who noted that in the new season Rose would have to: '... learn to trust [the Doctor] all over again – and that's going to be an interesting dynamic through the early episodes – but they'll still be fighting monsters and saving the world, and above all they'll still be enjoying each other's company.' Collinson stated that the second series would follow: '... the template of Series One. A little London filming but the majority being filmed in Cardiff... Quite frankly I'm amazed and delighted that so many of the wonderfully committed and brilliant team from Series One are coming back.' *Time Out* magazine, meanwhile, reported that ex-Soft Cell singer Marc Almond wanted a cameo in the series. 'I can't act, I'm wooden and self-conscious but I could just about manage a cameo role,' he said. 'I'm still getting over the new Doctor dancing to "Tainted Love". I've always been a huge fan of the show, so when Christopher Eccleston danced to "Tainted Love", I got texts from everyone... I remember thinking, "It can't get much better than this."'

BBC audience research for the first series demonstrated significant successes for the channel, with the first episode of the now-completed series, 'Rose', claiming both the second highest-rated launch of a new *Doctor Who* season (behind the 1979 season) and the highest-rated launch for a new actor in the role of the Doctor. More importantly, the series had averaged over its first year a stunning eight million viewers and a 40 percent share of the audience watching television during the hours of its transmission. Its demographics suggested the new series was particularly popular both with children and with the 35-44 age bracket. Nearly 90 percent of the viewers polled by the BBC thought *Doctor Who* was 'good family viewing' and 82 percent would be 'very likely' to watch the second series. BBC Wales was, naturally, pleased with the results. '*Doctor Who* led BBC Cymru Wales to one of its most successful 12 months ever during 2004–05,' stated a 13 July press release from the BBC Press Office. Noted *BBC News*, 'The high spot for Drama was undoubtedly *Doctor Who*.' In the pages of the BBC Wales Annual Review for the past television year, the introduction lauded *Doctor Who* as being: '... a galaxy away from the Saturday night entertainment of a generation ago... Now the Daleks can even climb the stairs. Their return, and the return of the Doctor, has proved hugely popular with audiences on BBC1... It is a vivid demonstration of what we can achieve in Wales.' Also of interest was the possibility that *Doctor Who* could be at the forefront of new technologies in television itself; *Media Guardian* said on 18 July that the BBC might consent to soon sell its programmes over the Internet, including to overseas users. 'New technology makes it possible for the BBC... to identify exactly where its internet users are coming from,' the article stated. 'While it is unlikely that straightforward online news coverage would be accompanied by advertising, other elements of the bbc.co.uk site could be accompanied by ads if viewed from abroad.' At the same time, it was reported that the BBC's Cult service – a collection of BBC websites that covered classic cult television from *Buffy the Vampire Slayer* to *The Hitchhiker's Guide to the Galaxy* – would soon be shutting down, but that the *Doctor Who* portion would be saved and moved to its own sub-domain in anticipation of the start of Series Two.

The ITV-sponsored National Television Awards 2005 included *Doctor Who* on its nominations list, with Eccleston and Piper receiving nominations for Most Popular Actor and Actress respectively, and the show itself being listed in the Most Popular Drama category. Meanwhile, Russell T Davies was listed at number 14 on the *Media Guardian* top 100 list of the most powerful people in UK media; of the listing, his co-executive producer Julie Gardner wrote that Davies: '... has extraordinary talent as both a writer and a producer. As a writer, he is a masterful storyteller, able to juxtapose effortlessly humour and tragedy whilst creating engaging, real characters that an audience can care about. As a producer, Russell is an inspiration – he is hardworking, ceaselessly enthusiastic and able to make people believe they can achieve the impossible.' Jane Tranter, the BBC Head of Drama whose faith in the concept, alongside that of former BBC1 Controller Lorraine Heggessey in 2003, had led to the show's revival, was also listed on the chart at number 79.

In late July, the children's magazine show *Blue Peter* gave kids across Britain the chance actually to contribute to *Doctor Who*, running a contest for those aged 15 and under to design a *Doctor Who* monster. The winner would have his or her design brought to life by the *Doctor Who* team in an episode to be shown in the second series, and would also be able to spend a day on the set. On 22 July, there was further promotion on *Blue Peter* for the contest; along with an array of clips, a Slitheen, the Auton Bride and a Dalek prop were in studio and were joined by monster designer Neill Gorton, who gave viewers tips on entering the competition... and gave presenter Liz Barker a 'monster makeover'. Barker herself would later gain a closer attachment to the series as one of the co-hosts of CBBC tie-in show *Totally Doctor Who*.

As the launch of production approached, *Doctor Who Magazine* filled in some of the blanks still remaining. The editors confirmed in the issue released the third week of July that talks were indeed under way with Elisabeth Sladen but could not comment further on the recent reports that K-9 would also be featured. Producer Phil Collinson noted that the second and third series had been commissioned but that Jane Tranter and Julie Gardner: '... had forgotten to tell Russell and me about the second Christmas special! We didn't know until it was announced from the stage!' Davies himself commented that he would be able to take advantage of the ability to plan both Series Two and Three at the same time, including by moving a plot thread from the former to the latter. (This was in fact the great 'secret' that the Face of Boe would ultimately neglect to tell the Doctor in the Series Two opener, 'New Earth.') The magazine also announced four new episode titles: 'Tooth and Claw', the second episode, written by Davies, who would also pen episode 12, 'Army of Ghosts'; 'School Reunion', the third, penned by writer Toby Whithouse; and 'The Satan Pit', at that time suggested to be the title for episode eight, written by Matt Jones. (Episode eight would later be retitled, with 'The Satan Pit' being used instead for episode nine, the story's second half, also written by Jones.) An order of writers was also suggested in the magazine, ultimately reflecting the precise order of the series; only episode 11 was yet to have an author officially attached to it, although this was the likely spot for actor/writer Stephen Fry's submission. Returning director James Hawes, meanwhile, would take the helm of 'The Christmas Invasion' as well as Whithouse's episode and the series two opener, while Euros Lyn ('The End of the World') would direct episodes two and four, and Graeme Harper would take the reins for episodes five and six. The magazine also announced that Louise Page, whose previous credits included *The Wedding Date* (2005) and *The Young Indiana Jones Chronicles* (1999), would replace out-going costume designer Lucinda Wright, while Sheelagh Wells, who had received a credit on the classic *Doctor Who* series for the four-part story 'Mawdryn Undead' (1983) and had worked on the third series of *Blake's 7* in 1980, would be the series' new make-up designer.

The same week, actors Noel Clarke (Mickey) and John Barrowman (Captain Jack) appeared at the *Invasion V* convention sponsored by the Barking-based retailer 10th Planet. Both actors noted on stage that they would return to the series, although Barrowman was hesitant on when this would occur (perhaps cheekily inferring his status headlining the forthcoming, but still yet unannounced, *Torchwood* series). Clarke announced he would be joining Tennant and Piper for the production of 'The Christmas Invasion', implying that his character would be developed significantly. Barrowman also commented that, as he had understood, several endings had been planned for the prior season's finale, 'The Parting of the Ways', some before it had been known for sure that Eccleston would be leaving the series, including one allowing for the death of Rose Tyler, in case Billie Piper elected not to return.

Clearly, the start of work on the next chapter of *Doctor Who* was just around the corner... but, surprisingly, it was only a few days prior to the start of production that fans would be sure of the exact timing. The word came from the fan websites first: Friday 22 July would see the *Doctor Who* production team and BBC Wales gather together to set off for a second series of adventures with the Doctor and Rose. And then, Series Two would become a reality.

CHAPTER TWO:
LIGHTS, CAMERA...

The second series of *Doctor Who* officially started production on Friday 22 July 2005, not with a grand battle sequence but with a photo call. David Tennant, heir apparent to the *Doctor Who* throne, stepped into the limelight in full costume: a long brown overcoat and pinstriped suit and tie. 'I think we've come up with something distinctive that's both timeless and modern,' Tennant told the official *Doctor Who* website, 'with a bit of geek chic and, of course, a dash of Time Lord!' He added, wryly, 'Most importantly, Billie tells me she likes it – after all, she's the one who has to see me in it for the next nine months!' *BBC News* noted that the latest Doctor: '... is kitted out in high fashion. Flamboyant. Garish. Bizarre... The type of man Kate Moss might date, kitted out in a brown pinstripe suit, white shirt – unbuttoned at the collar – a loose tie and scruffy white Converse trainers. The ensemble, put together by a freelance costume designer, is finished off with a long brown trench coat, a cross between an old hack's mac and flasher attire. The suit is skinny and crumpled – much tighter and Norman Wisdom will be demanding copyright. The look is just-got-out-of-bed, dragged-through-a-hedge-backwards, only-thing-I-could-find. It's Franz Ferdinand cum Kaiser Chiefs.' The *Guardian* said that Tennant had: '... wisely ditched the leather jacket, a garment loaded with embarrassing "rocker dad" connotations, and kitted himself out in a charming tweedy suit with white trainers.'

The tabloids, the genre press and the official *Doctor Who* website all confirmed that production was ramping up, with the official press call for Tennant and his co-star Billie Piper taking place that Friday evening, along with some initial recording, and that the following Monday, 25 July, would be Tennant and Piper's first day together on set playing their characters. Tennant's co-star seemed effervescent, as she always did in interviews, commenting to the official site that she was: '... thrilled to be stepping back into the role of Rose. We plan to make Series Two even bigger and better and challenge the viewers' imaginations like never before. Wait until you get a load of the new Doctor!' Executive producer Russell T Davies was also effusive. 'We were delighted and honoured by the first series' success, and we can promise new thrills, new laughs, new heartbreak, and some terrifying new aliens.' Davies confirmed that it would indeed be 'The Christmas Invasion' going into production first – logically, since it would be the first episode screened, three months before the rest of the series.

Piper and Tennant were spotted by some of the press leaving the studio in Newport on the evening of 22 July after the press call. While the paparazzi focused on the duo, a unit at Newport's Tredegar House were already recording the special's initial scenes with Penelope Wilton, returning to *Doctor Who* as Harriet Jones, MP for Flydale North, as seen in the first series' 'Aliens of London' and 'World War Three', and now, as predicted by the Doctor in those episodes, Prime Minister of the United Kingdom. Her presence in the series was officially confirmed by the production team on 25 July, as was that of Elisabeth Sladen, returning as rumoured to the role of Sarah Jane Smith for the series' third episode. Much more surprising was the announcement of a guest appearance by Anthony Head, a fan favourite from his long-time role of Rupert Giles in the series *Buffy the Vampire Slayer*, and himself no stranger to the *Doctor Who* mythos, having been heard in the BBC's online miniseries *Death Comes to Time* and in Big Finish Productions' *Excelis* mini-series in 2002. Head's participation in the series would be in a role as yet unannounced; it was speculated at the time (correctly, it turned out) that Head would be in the same story as Sladen, 'School Reunion', due to be recorded in Newport in August, potentially at Duffryn High School, where initial location scouting appeared to have taken place several weeks earlier. Another actor whose presence would be needed fairly soon, it was confirmed, was Adam Garcia, an Australian whose films included *Coyote Ugly* (2000) and *Riding in Cars with Boys* (2001), and who would appear in the Christmas special.

Also confirmed at this point was the return of Camille Coduri and Noel Clarke as Jackie Tyler and Mickey Smith respectively. Both Coduri and Clarke had become inextricably linked to *Doctor Who* the previous year, each appearing in half a dozen episodes of the first series and creating what Davies had referred to early on as Rose's – and the Doctor's – 'anchor' to Earth. Both Coduri and Clarke would be seen in the forthcoming 'The Christmas Invasion'. Davies told *Newsround* on 23 July that 'The Christmas Invasion' would involve a new monster as well as all the Christmas trimmings 'including reindeer and snow'. More accurately, Davies also mentioned that Rose would be finding it difficult to come to terms with the new Doctor.

THE DOCTOR AND ROSE RETURN

As David Tennant joined Billie Piper for their first day together in their roles on Monday 25 July, they were spotted by several paparazzi photo services in costume and in the rehearsal trailers. Pictures of several eerily-masked Santa Clauses that seemed bent on their destruction subsequently appeared in the press alongside these shots of the two leads. The next day, location recording took place on the Brandon Estate, where *Doctor Who* had realised the Tyler residence and its surrounding areas in the previous series, and continued during the remainder of the first week of production, with mostly preliminary location dressing and rehearsals taking place on that Monday. Martin Hoscik of the *UNIT News* website was present when recording started, noting that the production team had decked out the courtyard with seasonal decorations. Camille Coduri was there for the start of recording, later joined by Noel Clarke – on 26 July, the two would be threatened by the lower half of a TARDIS prop spinning above their heads, and some pyrotechnics designed to resemble the crash landing sequence later seen in the teaser for the episode. Between recording scenes, both Clarke and Coduri mingled with local residents and children as well as a fans who had heard about the start of production and wanted to see it first hand. Tennant and Piper arrived some time later in the evening.

The next day, the Brandon Estate was pummelled by snow – artificial snow, mixed in with the light rain. Tennant, Coduri, Clarke and Piper were all present for the recording during that day, which included Jackie and Mickey's first sight of the new Doctor. Wrote Hoscik, 'The paparazzi were out in force today, but the crew were pretty adept at dealing with them – especially during the night time shoot when highly technical anti-paparazzi tactics were employed. Real efforts were made by the team not to disrupt those who wanted pictures for fansites or personal collections whilst minimising access for the uninvited professionals.' A brief relocation to central London took place on the Thursday, and then the production crew returned to the Brandon Estate for their final day's work there for the episode. Visiting the set with his children on the Friday was none other than Peter Davison, the man who had played the fifth Doctor. Davison's presence on the set caused considerable speculation that he might somehow be associated with the episode. In fact, Davison had been invited along to meet Tennant, and the 'two Doctors' shared a few moments together; Tennant, long a *Doctor Who* fan himself, was said to enjoy the experience. Tennant later left, after which Piper, Coduri and Clarke recorded a brief outdoor sequence together.

The following Monday, there was a location shoot in Cardiff, in a section of the city used in the previous series called The Hayes (which, along with Working Street, another location used during Series One, was closed to the public for two nights). Fan John Williams told the Outpost Gallifrey website, 'Filming was taking place today (and has been since the early hours apparently – we were there just after 3 pm) right opposite an ice-cream parlour, in the former bistro bar/restaurant under Signor Valentino's Italian Restaurant. We approached the Bay from the direction of the Millennium Centre. My suspicions and excitement were first roused when to the left, in front of the Pierhead building (red church), we spied an open-backed rental van containing all sorts of standard furniture, lighting equipment, and two large police-box sized colour prints of the TARDIS interior (presumably interior rear wall prints for the TARDIS prop). As we made our way round towards the bistro area and Terra Nova bar where "Boom Town" was filmed last year, huge blackout screens had been hung from the railings around Signor Valentino's, obscuring everything in the building beneath. Despite our best efforts, we were unable to glimpse anything within. However, when we arrived, there was quite a scary looking character wearing a black hooded cloak with a whitened face and dark eye sockets outside the screen waiting for his cue. We were then rewarded further when both Billie and David came out at that moment to take a break.' Williams also noted: 'We chatted up the guy closest to us, who happened to be the location manager. We spoke about the Duffryn High School shoot, and he confirmed it for us as being for *Doctor Who*. He was then called away to choose a TARDIS landing spot, just as Billie and David broke out from the screens again... A red Volvo estate had already reversed up, and they both dashed over to it and jumped in the back, apparently off to a late lunch.'

The recording of 'The Christmas Invasion' continued throughout the following week and into the next Monday, where fans were again in attendance. Paul Mount told Outpost Gallifrey: 'Afternoon preparations continue into the early evening, and by around 7.30 pm Howell's store has once again been transformed into Henrik's (the location of "Rose") courtesy of a well-placed banner covering the Howell's sign and with posters advertising the Henrik's Christmas sale. Out on the pedestrianised area outside the store a huge Christmas tree – 30 feet or more high – is being carefully adorned with coloured lights and tinsel. Clustered around the tree are a number of market stalls selling Christmas paraphernalia, and, curiously, a newspaper hoarding for the *Evening Standard* proclaims "Soccer Star's Divorce Shock" or words to that effect. Christmas lights stretch between the buildings, a congestion charge sign has been erected in the adjoining Wharton Street where an illuminated "Merry Christmas" sign hangs between Howell's and its neighbouring building. For a while not a lot is happening – production crew are hurrying to and fro and there are security guards and police aplenty. There's a noticeably large crowd gathering – dozens of people, many clearly hardcore fans, others families with young children, others just new fans drawn to the first new series.' Mount noted later: 'The action moves to Wharton Street. Several scary burly men in Santa costumes take position outside the door to Henrik's. A red London bus is manoeuvred into position in the perilously narrow street and a coach disgorges what seems like a hundred extras dressed in their best winter clothes. Some of them are laden with Christmas parcels. Billie Piper and Noel Clarke, who were apparently on set earlier rehearing an action scene... are back, getting on brilliantly as they repeatedly rehearse a scene where the bus crawls along Wharton Street and Billie and Noel walk hand-in-hand through the throng of shoppers. It's midnight and the scene is repeated until director James Hawes is satisfied. Billie is delighted to spot an old friend at the edge of the set and she spends a few minutes animatedly chatting to him. Producer Phil

Collinson watches the action from a nearby monitor. Over-enthusiastic photographers are distracted by a huge arc light shone in their direction, and one photographer with a particularly long lens balanced on a tripod is thwarted by two production members who block his view by holding up two huge white boards!'

Wrote fan Rob Stickler, 'All I really saw happening was extras getting off a red London bus and Mickey and Rose walking down the street, looking quite chilled. Lots of market stalls and a big Christmas tree. There were some Santas hanging about but I didn't see them do anything. Did see Noel and Billie rehearsing a scene where they darted off like they were being chased. No sign of Tennant... Someone at Waterstones must have... forgotten to take the *Doctor Who* novels out of the window. I happen to know that they were specifically asked to make sure they weren't visible.'

According to fan Matthew Spencer, 'At one point, the special effects team were seen to be testing out some form of flame thrower, and a member of security told me that they were going to blow up the Christmas tree! Later, during the setting up of another scene, a few gas canisters were brought onto set (along with fire extinguishers, and there was a fire engine standing by). I spotted one crew member carrying what seemed to be a trombone with a small gas canister attached to it – in an earlier scene the three "Santas" were playing musical instruments, stood outside the front of Henrik's. The next scene involved Mickey and Rose walking around by the Christmas tree amongst the crowd of extras. Then Rose screamed something, followed by a few bursts of flame and some small explosions as the crowd scattered. At the end of filming, the special effects team warned us that they were about to test out some pyrotechnics, and a very large bang and a flash followed (a much bigger explosion than those that had happened during filming – perhaps for use in the next night of filming).'

Of the activity the following night, 9 August, John Williams noted: 'We were treated to a lot more action, as filming began at around 10.30 pm. The first shot involved many extras dressed in heavy winter clothes, carrying Christmas shopping bags and presents. Before shooting, we were warned that the scene involved a series of explosions, and the police were asked to call HQ to warn them... Blocked mainly by the Christmas tree, the scene began shooting. Extras ran in terror, with Rose and Mickey running through the stalls hand-in-hand, explosions going off around them. One of our less than courteous drunken neighbours shouted during the scene and was promptly marched away by the police once "cut" was called. Both Phil Collinson and James Hawes seemed more than happy with the result though, and the scene wasn't reshot. We watched several more scenes being shot, most of which involved explosions from different camera angles. During one shot, an explosion went off just as Noel Clarke ran past it. He was thrown to the ground and the crew rushed over to him. Fortunately he seemed only to have sustained a ringing in his right ear, although it continued to aggravate him for some time afterwards. As we called it a night again at 12.30, the next scene was to include four largely built Santas brandishing deadly brass instruments!'

LOOKING IN

Fans were turning up regularly to watch the location recording of the series, as they had done the previous year. And as had happened in 2004, this led to a statement on the official *Doctor Who* website from the production team asking for noise to be kept at a minimum, and flash photography to be halted. '*Doctor Who* is now filming – it may even be in your area, as we speak,' wrote producer Phil Collinson on the official site. 'If you find out that *Doctor Who* is filming near you, and plan on turning up to watch, then can we ask that you respect the wishes of the cast and crew and follow any instructions that are given to you by security and staff on set? The most important request is please don't take photographs during an actual take. Filming last week was disrupted by cameras with flash.' Fans swiftly reacted on Internet forums, with many who had been present during the previous week's recording noting that it had been the paparazzi, not the fans, who had used flash photography – the same situation as had occurred the previous year. The *Daily Mirror* reported in the first week of August that 'Doctor Who fans are wrecking the new series by turning up on set with their own special effects,' suggesting that fans were ignoring the pleas by the production team not to use flash photography.

On 11 August, the *Western Mail* reported: 'Santa Claus is coming to town for *Doctor Who*. It may be the middle of summer, but Cardiff has been decked out in its Christmas finery as *Doctor Who* returns. Billie Piper ditched her summer gear for winter warmers yesterday to film the *Doctor Who* Christmas Special in the middle of [the] summer sunshine. Shop windows were given a Christmas makeover and a giant Christmas tree was installed near the Central Library. The Doctor's pin-up sidekick pulled on a fur-lined jacket despite the balmy August weather. She was filmed in the city centre, which was turned into a winter wonderland with Christmas trees and fairy lights. Billie and Noel Clarke, who plays her on-screen boyfriend Mickey, recorded several scenes in Cardiff's shopping centres... An onlooker said, "It was a warm night but Billie was wrapped up for winter. They filmed right through the night and Billie seemed to be really enjoying herself. She looked stunning even if she was just in jacket and jeans".

By mid-August there were plenty more stories about the forthcoming second series. *Doctor Who Magazine* noted that John Barrowman would *not*, after all, return for this series, while actor Shaun Dingwall commented that he would be back in the role of Pete Tyler at some point during the year. Even Billie Piper's former husband, Chris Evans, might make an appearance, according to the *Daily Star*. The radio DJ was to appear as the Devil in 'The Satan Pit', the paper claimed. An unnamed source told the *Daily Star*: 'We've already got some great celebrities lined up for the next series, but having Chris Evans would be the icing on the cake. Having him as Satan would be a hoot, and we're sure he'd relish the role. And we know Billie would find it a giggle.' There were also rumours that the role played by Anthony Head in 'School Reunion' would be the Master, a renegade Time Lord, and that 'Torchwood', mentioned in the episode 'Bad Wolf' during the first series, would be the mysterious word Davies referred to in his *Doctor Who Magazine* Production Notes as the basis of the second series' story arc. Of these, the Evans and Master stories would prove untrue, as would rumours that the first episode of the new series would be called 'The Sunshine Camp'. *Doctor Who Magazine* did however confirm, in its mid-August issue, that Adam Garcia would play the role of Alex Klein in 'The Christmas Invasion' alongside other newly confirmed cast members, while crewmembers on the second series would include Llinos Wyn Jones (script supervisor), Jon Older (first assistant director), Julian Barber (camera operator) and Simon Fraser (sound recordist). The issue noted that work on the second series had begun with rehearsals on 18 July, which included David Tennant and Billie Piper and future guest stars Anthony Head and Elisabeth Sladen, and that the production start date was officially 22 July.

David Tennant, it was announced, would make a live appearance on *Blue Peter* on 17 August to announce the winner of the 'Design a *Doctor Who* Monster' competition. On the day, it was revealed that the competition had received 43,920 entries, apparently the best response to a *Blue Peter* competition since 1993. Footage was shown of Davies and the team judging the contest and a Dalek visited the studio along with Tennant, who answered questions posed from the audience, noting that he'd watched *Doctor Who* as a child and that his favourite part of the series to date was the regeneration sequence where he'd taken over the role. The winner of the competition, nine-year-old William Grantham from Colchester, spoke to Tennant on the telephone, while prosthetics supervisor Neill Gorton was on hand to discuss how he would realise the design of Grantham's monster, the Abzorbaloff, described first as a 'hairy Sumo'; the monster would ultimately feature in the episode 'Love & Monsters' during the second series. Later the same afternoon, Tennant joined the CBBC website for a 15-minute live chat.

Recording continued on the Christmas special, but away from the public eye: the production spent a week in mid-August inside Clearwell Caves shooting sequences for the story's climax, followed by several days' work at the Millennium Stadium in Cardiff, which served as the UNIT headquarters seen in the episode. The Stadium shoot was seen at a distance by some fans. 'The set is dressed up like a "James Bond" style office with posh chairs and tables,' recounted Ian Golden. 'A video screen is showing a loop of a satellite broadcast of the Earth and there is a big Union Jack in one corner... There's loads of extras, all dressed in black riot gear. No David or Billie today but maybe tomorrow. *Doctor Who Confidential* was filming there today as well.' After recording at the Stadium, the production would return to the studios in Newport to continue work on 'The Christmas Invasion' as well as the first two episodes of the second series sent into production, 'School Reunion' and the opening episode, still untitled as far as the public was concerned. Meanwhile, the official *Doctor Who* website brought back its 'WhoSpy' feature, briefly continuing the behind-the-scenes photo selections from the first series of the show.

On 24 August, the BBC Press Office announced that John Leeson would reprise the role of K-9, confirming rumours that had spread for months. 'Today David Tennant, the tenth Time Lord, will be reunited with two of his favourite and most iconic companions – Sarah Jane Smith and the faithful robot dog, K-9,' said the press release. 'K-9, who was the loyal friend to Tom Baker's Doctor between 1977 and 1981, joins Sarah Jane Smith, the Doctor, Rose and Mickey in a fight against the evil Krillitanes. John Leeson, the voice of K-9, says: "I am delighted to have been invited back on board the series – and a little gathered rust is no object to a fully functional K-9!" Producer Phil Collinson adds: "It is great to be welcoming K-9 back to *Doctor Who*. A whole generation fondly remember him as an ever-faithful companion and best friend to Tom Baker's Doctor. I hope the new generation of viewers will fall in love with him in the same way. I'm sure he's going to prove an invaluable help to the Doctor in the fight against intergalactic evil."' Said Sladen, 'I am so thrilled to be back and I feel so empowered by the affection that [the whole team] have for Sarah Jane Smith and for the programme. Toby Whithouse's script is wonderful – it's an absolutely truthful progression of Sarah. I just hope I can live up to their expectation, and I hope I can still run as fast after 30 years!'

On the tie-in front, BBC Books announced that it would reprint Justin Richards' hardcover from the previous year with slightly revamped content and title, as *Doctor Who: The Legend Continues*, while Panini, publishers of *Doctor Who Magazine*, would bring out the *Doctor Who Annual 2006*. A *Doctor Who* Interactive Electronic Board Game was also announced as being in preparation, while the *Daily Telegraph* reported on 30 August that the stock of the Character Group merchandisers had jumped recently after they'd unveiled plans to launch a *Doctor Who* range of toys. The recent BBC Books ninth Doctor hardcover novels had, it transpired, been a huge commercial success; according to a BBC press release, 'The three tie-in novelisations of *Doctor Who*, published as hardbacks and profiting from the attractions of Christopher

Eccleston and Billie Piper on their jackets, occupy numbers four to six on the fiction tie-in chart for the period with combined sales of nearly 50,000 copies.' The BBC also announced it would have security labels attached to licensees' *Doctor Who* merchandise to prevent counterfeiting. 'Obviously counterfeit *Doctor Who* merchandise would damage legitimate sales and tarnish the brand's image,' said BBC brand protection manager Rick McEwen. And in Canada, Buzzworthy Licensing + Entertainment announced that it had signed to become the merchandising agent for *Doctor Who* in that country. Said Buzzworthy's Kevin Durkee, 'We've seen *Doctor Who* enjoy decades of awareness in Canada and are therefore thrilled to be part of the ongoing development of such a terrific brand... We're excited to be working with BBC Worldwide, who recognise the importance of managing this business locally.'

BBC Radio 2, meanwhile, announced that it would tie in the transmission of 'The Christmas Invasion' with another *Doctor Who* radio documentary. *Doctor Who: Regeneration* would assess the impact that the new series made when it returned to BBC1, featuring interviews with the cast and crew. The documentary would also consider how the production team dealt with the need to regenerate the character of the Doctor after just 13 episodes. Interviews would take place throughout the following month. *Broadcast* magazine also noted in an August issue that *Doctor Who* might be one of the first BBC shows to be recorded in High Definition television format. HD 'is a priority at the BBC, where commissioners are urging programme suppliers to shoot future productions in HD, especially for flagship programmes such as *Doctor Who*,' said BBC Corporate Strategy Controller Simon Walker. *BBC News* reported that the BBC's channels might also appear on the Internet... eventually. 'We believe that on-demand changes the terms of the debate, indeed that it will change what we mean by the word "broadcasting",' said BBC Director General Mark Thompson. 'Every creative leader in the BBC is wrestling with the question of what the new technologies and audience behaviours mean for them and their service.'

THE FLOODGATES OPEN

As *Doctor Who* returned to production, so came the expected onslaught of press coverage of the series and its stars. 'The Time Lord clutches the hand of assistant Rose Tyler, played by Billie Piper, as they film on a South London council estate,' said the 29 July issue of the *Sun*, noting that Tennant had 'donned a natty pinstripe suit for one scene with Billie... before changing into a leather jacket.' The *Daily Star* asked, 'Who else but the Doctor could conjure up wintry scenes like these slap-bang in the middle of summer? While Britain lurches from heatwaves to tornados, the Doc's sexy sidekick Rose is wrapping up warm... Piper looks chilled to the bone as she shoots a special festive edition of the sci-fi smash... These new shots of the Doctor clasping hands with Rose seem to show that things are set to pick up where they left off.' *BBC News* reported on the start of production: 'New *Doctor Who* star David Tennant said it was "pretty daunting" to play the sci-fi character, as filming of new episodes began in Cardiff. Ex-*Casanova* star Tennant, 34, said it was an intimidating role because "the series is so huge. I'm aware of all that but I try to keep it in my back pocket and just get on with the job," he added.' The *Irish Examiner* and the Manchester Online website both noted the start of production and commented on 1 August that 'the makers of the hit TV series took over a restaurant in the Mermaid Quay area of Cardiff Bay for a morning shoot.'

CBBC Newsround also interviewed Tennant and Piper on 1 August. 'Morphing out of Christopher Eccleston, I don't think it's possible to get a stranger entrance than that,' Tennant told the programme. 'It's a very unusual way to begin a job, but fantastic! I mean, you know, you couldn't ask for a finer entrance really... It's pretty daunting because it's kind of everywhere; you know, *Doctor Who* as a concept and also just the show itself is... so big!' Piper, meanwhile, said of her co-star, 'I've only been working with him for about two weeks now, but he's absolutely adorable and just perfect as the Doctor.' Both BBC1's *One O'Clock News* and BBC Radio 4's *PM* programme carried a location report and interviews with Tennant and Piper as well, including a mention that the production was recording at a Chinese restaurant in Cardiff on the Monday, standing in for a futuristic nightclub. The BBC's news channel News 24 featured Antony Wainer of the *Doctor Who* Appreciation Society stating that *Doctor Who* 'was all about change' when asked if the series would remain as popular with Tennant, while later in the evening, actor Nicholas Courtney (the Brigadier from the classic *Doctor Who* series) was live in studio talking about the programme's new success. Casting details were also slowly emerging; actress Zoë Wanamaker's own fan club e-mail list was the first to report that the actress would be returning during the second series, possibly in the first regular episode.

Some of the press coverage was focused solely on Billie Piper, whose career had been strongly boosted by the critical success of the show in its previous season. The *People* on 8 August said: 'Her turn in *Doctor Who* as Rose got better and better as the series went on. She's really become a good actress. And with time, she'll probably get better at rejecting utterly rubbish movie scripts, too.' The article referred to Piper's appearance in *Spirit Trap*, a new film soon to debut, which was receiving less than stellar reviews. 'This one's a teen-horror movie that'll have you cowering in terror afterwards in fear you might accidentally end up watching it again,' said the *People*. 'It's all a bit of a misfire, but I do like Billie. So she gets a couple of rashers by herself. It's the ratings-system gift that every girl wants.' The *Daily Mirror* noted on 2 August that the producers of the film could not get her to attend its premiere, forcing them to scrap: '... the glittering opening night... Director David Smith and the cast are said to be angry and upset after Billie would not be pinned to a date in London. A film source said: "Billie has lots of commitments but that's cold comfort to her co-stars, crew and director. If she can't make the premiere, there's no point." Some insiders fear Billie... wants to distance herself from the film because of weak reviews.'

On the same day, the *Daily Star* discussed Piper's transformation into an action figure. '*Doctor Who* babe Billie Piper left toy bosses panting when they were ordered to make a doll of her. They spent hours working out the shapely star's measurements so the toy version of Rose Tyler looks just like the real thing. Show bosses have lined up a series of special moveable models of Rose and the Doc in time for the Christmas rush... Workers at Character Options, who had the task of making a model of 22-year-old Billie, had the best job of all. One joked: "Let's just say the sculptors particularly enjoyed creating Rose. I can't think why!"'

The album *The Very Best of Billie Piper* was released by EMI Gold on 8 August, containing 15 of the songs Piper had performed in her earlier music career, including all the hit singles.

Amongst all this media coverage, the *Daily Star* even claimed that Piper: '... looked close to a breakdown as she felt the pressure of her punishing work schedule for the hit show. [Billie] is filming from 11 pm to 5 am every night as sexy sidekick Rose Tyler while the streets of Cardiff are deserted. But the strain showed on Billie's face yesterday as she took a rest... An insider said: "Billie is sleeping all day and working all night. She was fine for a couple of nights but it gets to you."'

With so much attention focused on the series, the ITV network – which had suffered a dramatic ratings turnaround in the spring as *Doctor Who* had trounced each of its Saturday night offerings – announced that it was planning its own comeback, with a pantomime featuring cast members from the long-running soap *Coronation Street*, hinting that it might air opposite 'The Christmas Invasion'. Said the *Daily Star* on 27 July, '*Corrie* bosses are planning to zap *Doctor Who* this Christmas. The cast have been told they will be recording a panto for ITV1. And it could go out in competition with the BBC's special. But the plan has met with a mixed reaction. A source said: "Some stars are a bit miffed. They are not allowed to do panto independently when they're working on *Corrie*. People have missed out on huge salaries in the festive season."'

The prominence of the new *Doctor Who* series, in fact, led it to be judged the Best British Fantasy TV Show by the readers of *SFX* magazine, covered by *BBC News* and a variety of online and print journals. 'The sci-fi drama, which began in 1963 and became a hit with a new audience when it was recently revived, beat comedy *Red Dwarf* into second place... *SFX* magazine polled 4,000 readers, and editor Dave Bradley said *Doctor Who* was "a great British institution which has entertained people for generations. There has always been great affection for *Doctor Who*."' *BBC News* also reported on 28 August that BBC1 and BBC3 had taken the terrestrial and digital 'channel of the year' prizes respectively at the Edinburgh Television Festival; among the accomplishments mentioned were both *Doctor Who* and the documentary series *Doctor Who Confidential*. Davies' production of *Casanova* (starring David Tennant), however, lost out to Channel 4's *Jamie's School Dinners* in the programme of the year category.

The general affection for the show, and its personalities, was reflected throughout the press. *BBC News* asked on 4 August why science-fiction and fantasy were hard to escape from at the moment: 'The films are tops at the box office, the books dominate the best-seller lists and on the TV the revived *Doctor Who* has pleased old fans and won a generation of new ones. Science-fiction is booming and the British writers are leading the pack. For the first time in its 63-year history, all the writers nominated for the prestigious Hugo award for the best novel are British.' The *Herald* on 15 August profiled John Barrowman ('Growing up in Illinois, I used to get bullied a lot for being Scottish. Other kids would shout things like, "You wear a dress", and they thought we lived in mud huts. Most of all, though, they made fun of the accent.'). *Newsquest Media* reported that Christopher Eccleston 'has found something to keep him busy after leaving *Doctor Who* – trying to save Manchester's historic Victoria Baths.' The *Independent* on 19 August ran an article about Billie Piper: 'For the past couple of weeks, Piper has been going to work when most other people are going to bed. She is resuming her role as Rose Tyler, the effervescent sidekick of *Doctor Who*... Tennant following Christopher Eccleston's rather abrupt departure at the end of the first series. Despite much tabloid speculation that Piper herself was also quitting the show – for movies, for Hollywood, for wraparound superstardom – the truth is that she is staying precisely where she is. For now, at least. "Well, I've not heard any rumours of me being killed off," she says. "So as far as I'm aware, I'm around for the entire second series."' The *Sunday Mirror* on 23 August discussed recent sightings of Billie Piper on the town: 'She's apparently been filming from 11 pm to 5 am every night in Cardiff, which means her days are often spent in bed catching up on sleep, so it's no wonder she hit the pub at the first opportunity.' The 30 August *Daily Star* said that Piper 'blooms in sexy black,' and illustrated this with some shots reprinted from a photoshoot the actress had done for *Arena* magazine earlier in the year : 'It seems the show's famous TARDIS is now about to transport our Billie to global superstardom... Her gorgeous curves and sexy pout have helped win the cult sci-fi show a whole new generation of fans – and earned her plenty of hot offers from telly and film bosses.' *BBC News* on 11 August interviewed Mike Collins, the artist drawing the regular comic strip in *Doctor Who Magazine*. 'Christopher

Eccleston's decision to leave *Doctor Who* may have shocked most of the show's fans, but it also meant a pile more work for artist Mike Collins,' said the article. 'I had just got to the stage when I can draw Christopher Eccleston quite comfortably,' Collins told the magazine, 'but I have no problems, he has made a decision that was interesting for the show. It is a fresh new broom – David Tennant has a great face, and I have to get it right as he is a big fan and is going to read it.' Davies announced he'd attend September's Cardiff Mardi Gras Fringe Benefit evening, while Barrowman appeared with Rob Lowe in *A Few Good Men* on Broadway.

Late in the month, David Tennant was the subject of the cover and an interview inside the latest issue of *Dreamwatch*. 'It's not like any other acting job,' he told the magazine about his new role in *Doctor Who*, 'just with the amount of attention that it gets. I've done all sorts of different things. That's all been great fun, but suddenly I get cast as Doctor Who and it was on the news!' Tennant noted he was approached for the role because: 'I was working with Russell T Davies, the main writer and creative head of it, on *Casanova* at the end of last year. I knew him through that. Unbeknownst to me, that was my audition.' Tennant added that when he was told that Tom Baker, the fourth Doctor himself, had endorsed him for the part, he was: '... completely thrilled. That's really lovely. I haven't actually confirmed it. I've only heard it third-hand, and of course I never believe anything I read in the papers. I hope it's true. I'm choosing to believe it's true.' The *Scotsman* on 7 August wasn't as impressed with Tennant's casting: 'Eccleston had quit because he did not want to be typecast – too late, Christopher – and BBC Cardiff had found a replacement. And who did we get to play the greatest alien in the universe? The being we need to save Earth? The son of a former Moderator of the Church of Scotland better known for playing Andy Crawford, the wimpish sidekick of Dixon of Dock Green in the radio revival of the cosy 1950s police series. Yawn.' The paper featured a 9 August reply by fan David Bickerstaff: 'Having been a lifelong devotee of *Doctor Who*, I am absolutely thrilled that an actor of his standing has accepted the role. He has a real passion for the character and will, I am sure, give it 101 percent commitment. As for the costume, perhaps George Kerevan should look around at the dress sense of today and see that the Doctor mirrors the fashion sense of society... Mr Tennant's costume is a mish-mash of all that is smart in our fashion-conscious male.'

It was, simply, everywhere. *Radio Times* ran a television advertising campaign that started in August featuring a *Doctor Who* slant. Near the end of the advert, with passengers stuck in cars at road works, one of them notes, 'Did you know that there have been ten Doctor Whos?' *BBC News* reported that three people hid in Brighton's *Doctor Who* exhibition after escaping an immigration department raid. The *Evening Times* on 25 August mentioned that there was a new version of *Doctor Who*'s classic police box on the streets: 'It looks like it has landed from outer space, but this hi-tech box is the latest crime-busting device used by police in Glasgow. The city's new police box would not look out of place in an episode of *Doctor Who*, but the "TARDIS" will remain at St Enoch Square. Sitting prominently near the entrance to the subway station at the bottom of Buchanan Street, the box will be a vital tool in solving crime in the city centre and will be used by officers across the division.' Meanwhile, the *Blue Peter* series online poll voted David Tennant's appearance on the programme as their favourite moment of the month, while *Doctor Who* was first on the CBBC's favourite TV programme poll.

AROUND THE WORLD

Doctor Who continued to air on television in Australia and in New Zealand throughout August; Steven Moffat's two-parter 'The Empty Child' and 'The Doctor Dances' was shown in

Australia in mid-July, with 'Boom Town' debuting at the end of that month. The reactions were not always unequivocally positive. The *Age* on 21 July reviewed the episode 'Dalek' from several weeks prior: 'I never thought I'd see the day when a Dalek – one of the Doctor's most bloodthirsty adversaries – would turn into a kind of namby-pamby existentialist... It is an uneven production that wears its heart on its sleeve... Eccleston makes you feel that the years of time travelling have messed with his head and that deep down this Doctor is sad, lonely and jaded. Saving the universe from alien tyrants has come at a substantial personal cost. It all gives this series an emotional clout the old programme never had... The problem lies with the scripts. The plotting of the episodes is wildly uneven... The real marvel of this venerable programme is not that the Doctor is able to regenerate; the real miracle is that the programme itself has regenerated and found a fresh audience more than 40 years after it all began.'

Not everyone was critical of the show, though. Far from it, in fact; the *Sydney Morning Herald* said of 'The Doctor Dances', 'Stand by for a delightful finish as the Doctor gets In the Mood.' The *Herald* also praised 'Boom Town', asking, 'Was *Doctor Who*, before this revival, ever quite so humorous? Annette Badland is brilliant as the conniving and vicious Slitheen, occupying the body of Margaret Blaine.' The *Age* also reviewed the episode on 28 July: 'Make the most of *Doctor Who*, because he's not long for this world. Christopher Eccleston, that is, the man who has breathed new life into the first genuinely intergalactic TV brand. Soon we'll have David Tennant, and, like me, if you've been grateful to old jug-ears – as he almost gets called in tonight's episode – then wallow in his over-acting for a few more weeks... Russell Davies, the man behind this new incarnation of *Doctor Who*, has a lot of fun with this episode... [with] all sorts of weird and very wonderful devices, including a pan-dimensional surfboard. Every surfer should have one. See you at Bells Beach in the year 3000?' The *Sunday Herald Sun* said of the episode, 'This engaging and witty series seems to reach new heights each week.'

The *Age* on 2 August described John Barrowman as 'a man's man... a new kind of hero with a flexible sexuality.' Writer Tim Hunter wrote, 'The new series of *Doctor Who* has grown up... It is also a lot more sophisticated than the classic series and not just in terms of effects and technology. There's a great deal of cleverness in the scripts, in the humour, the characters and their relationships. You need not look any further than the Doctor's new companion, Captain Jack Harkness, for evidence of that.' The official website of broadcaster ABC noted: 'John Barrowman was better known as a Broadway and West End darling when he was given the role of 51st Century time agent Captain Jack Harkness in the new series of *Doctor Who*. As an American actor based in London, John never expected this chance to feature in one of his favourite childhood shows, but as a long-time fan of the Doctor, he was overjoyed at the news.' The *Sydney Morning Herald* also featured a profile of the recent 'Inside the TARDIS' official *Doctor Who* tour, quoting original series actor Sylvester McCoy as saying, 'I have been all over the world with *Doctor Who*. I've done conventions, I've done cruises, I've done everything. It has changed my life. I love travelling, and it has enabled me to do so.'

The *Sydney Morning Herald* on 10 August said of 'Bad Wolf': 'With just two episodes to go, a series' worth of loose ends are about to be tied up – but before that, writer Russell T Davies is going to have some fun... Australian viewers might not appreciate how spot-on these send-ups are, as our versions of the shows are subtly different. The *Big Brother* spoof uses the real music and logo and the android hosts of *The Weakest Link* and *What Not to Wear* are voiced by the actual people. There are plenty of sly digs at reality TV here, but Davies is not about to bite the medium that feeds him.' The *Age* on 11 August said of 'The Parting of the Ways' that the finale: '... features the best devices of the series in spades. It's overflowing with deadpan one-liners – among the best, Rose's exclamation "He's fighting for us, for the whole planet, and I'm just sitting here eating chips"... And let's not forget the salty élan Eccleston brings to the title role. This isn't his finest work since Michael Winterbottom's *Jude*, but it's a pity he's pissing off now that episodes one to 13 have taken care of the mortgage... Trainspotters – and boy, this show does attract them – will have a ball analysing subtle contradictions and inconsistencies in this episode and the fact that the denouement comes via a near-perfect example of the *deus ex machina*. But who cares? It's *Doctor Who*, not Chekhov.'

Meanwhile, in New Zealand, the series had become a huge ratings success. 'Cult Classic *Doctor Who*... in only its fifth week on screen [has] placed the network in third place amongst the four commercial channels for the 7.30 pm time slot.' Broadcaster Prime TV noted that it had 'scheduled series two of *Doctor Who* to screen in Winter 2006.'

Norwegian public broadcaster NRK announced it had bought the rights to run the episodes starting in September, while Singapore Airlines would air the series throughout August on their 747 planes. South Korea also completed its run of the first series, while back at home, broadcaster UKTV Gold confirmed its plans to repeat the first series from 23 October.

In fact, while the new episodes of *Doctor Who* were several months away, the show's presence was being felt throughout the UK and far beyond. Perhaps nothing demonstrated that more than the *Blue Peter* annual children's prom at the Royal Albert Hall, where the *Doctor Who* theme was played by the orchestra, accompanied by a roaming Dalek threatening to exterminate the musicians. A far cry from the days when the series had languished in relative obscurity, it was now firmly back in the limelight.

CHAPTER THREE:
THE CALM BEFORE THE STORM

PRODUCTION CONTINUES

As September began, production on *Doctor Who*'s second series continued. Location work on 'School Reunion', the third episode, was completed at the Duffryn High School on 2 September; recording had taken place there, as well as at the neighbouring Fitzalan High School, from 22 August. Other Newport locations for the episode included a restaurant called Da Vinci and the nearby Belle Vue Park. Fans had spotted the park location, with one correspondent, under the alias Myrrdinthemage, writing on the Outpost Gallifrey message board, 'They were filming as I came back from Royal Gwent Hospital and I almost walked straight into shot... As I walked past they were filming something just outside the TARDIS, which had landed on a sort of upraised bandstand/flowerbed effect. (It's the one nearest the tennis courts for those who know the park.) Some girl – I would have said it was not Billie as she had long dark hair) was getting a hug from someone in the shot I saw. The TARDIS was set up with a silver backdrop on the far side, so the interior will be composited in by the looks of it.' As readers would later discover, 'some girl' would turn out to be Elisabeth Sladen, recording the final scene of the episode as Sarah Jane says goodbye to David Tennant's Doctor. Meanwhile, Davies confirmed at his appearance on 6 September at the Mardi Gras Fringe Benefit that 'School Reunion' would feature an 'ex-wife meets girlfriend' type of encounter between Sarah Jane and Rose. A young actress named Lucinda Dryzek, who had played the younger version of Keira Knightley's character Elizabeth in the film *Pirates of the Caribbean: The Curse of the Black Pearl*, was reportedly cast as a schoolgirl in the episode.

The first leak of the second series' first episode's title, 'New Earth', came in the pages of *Starburst* magazine in the first week of September. The magazine reported that the episode, to be transmitted in the spring, would feature the rumoured guest appearance by Zoë Wanamaker, confirming the news her fan club had previously revealed. *Doctor Who Magazine* soon confirmed Wanamaker's role in the first episode, and its title; the magazine stated that, unlike her voice-only role in the previous series' 'The End of the World', Wanamaker had actually visited the 'New Earth' set to appear in person alongside Tennant and Piper. The issue also noted that Euros Lyn would work on two additional episodes of the forthcoming series, and confirmed additional cast members for the first and third episodes. *Doctor Who Confidential* was reported to be having additional production time during its second year; up until now, there had been speculation, but nothing concrete in print, that the documentary series would return.

Dreamwatch magazine published an interview in early September with concept designer Bryan Hitch, who confirmed that one additional room inside the TARDIS would be seen in the second series (referring to the wardrobe seen at the end of the year in 'The Christmas Invasion'), and that while K-9 was going to look pretty much as he had in the original series, the redesign of the Cybermen would be drastic. At a *Red Dwarf* convention, visual effects consultant Mike Tucker, now working freelance after the shutdown of the BBC's own Visual Effects Department, noted that his new company would be working on the effects for the second series. Writer Steven Moffat also made public comments about his episode, which was rumoured to be entitled 'The Girl in the Fireplace' and was likely to air in fourth position, stating that it would feature Madame de Pompadour and would reveal 'a side to the Doctor you haven't seen, or not seen a lot.' He added; '[It's] quite a personal story, about someone he meets and his effect on her life.' By 29 September, the website of actress Sophia Myles had confirmed that she would be taking this role, and that the title of the episode was indeed 'The Girl in the Fireplace'.

Repeat episodes of Series One continued to be transmitted throughout early September on BBC3, while three new novels were released by BBC Books featuring the ninth Doctor (Christopher Eccleston's incarnation) and Rose, along with the popular character Jack Harkness: Gareth Roberts' *Only Human*, Justin Richards' *The Deviant Strain* and Steve Lyons' *The Stealers of Dreams*. John Barrowman confirmed on *BBC Breakfast* on 2 September that he wouldn't be back as Captain Jack for the second series but would be seen again in the third. However, during an appearance at the Invasion convention in early September, the actor noted that his character 'might have something going on' during the series – taken at the time to be a hint of potential cameo appearances, but later revealed to be an oblique reference to the (yet to be announced at that time) *Torchwood* spin-off.

On 16 September, the *South Wales Evening Post* reported that the BBC Wales crew would 'descend on the Gower coast in Swansea this weekend' for new series recording, specifically for work on 'New Earth'. While the report noted that the production team did not want the precise location to be revealed to the public, devotees of the series did discover the *Doctor Who* crew over the 23 and 24 September weekend at Rhossili on the Gower Peninsula, west of Swansea, which coincidentally was hosting its first-ever *Doctor Who* convention, Regenerations. The sequences recorded on Monday 25 September, for example, were for the post-opening-credits sequence in 'New Earth'. Wrote fan Ruth Gunstone on the Outpost Gallifrey board, 'I found Rhossili, parked my car, and walked out toward the Worm's Head, a spectacular outcrop of land joined to the headland by a causeway, which can be walked at low tide... Walking around the cliff path, I noticed a group of people on the skyline, one of whom was holding a boom-mic... The day was windy, *really* windy, and Billie and David were having trouble with their costumes. Billie's hair was being blown about, as was David's long brown coat. The shot seemed to consist of the two of them lying on the ground (almost as if sunbathing!), and after some conversation, getting up, David putting on his coat, and the two of them walking off toward the TARDIS. David seemed to have real problems putting on his coat as the wind kept threatening to take it (and David!) over the cliff edge!' Later, Gunstone noted: 'Shooting... recommenced, but now the action was immediately outside the TARDIS, and involved a scene with Rose and the Doctor emerging from the TARDIS, and the Doctor telling Rose where and when they had landed... I did manage to overhear something along the lines of, "This is the year five billion and twenty-five, and it's the galaxy..." The Doctor and Rose then laughed, and ran along the cliff-top, hair and clothes being pummelled by the wind.'

Only days later, what would become the second episode of the forthcoming season was in full production, an hour north of Cardiff in central Wales at Gelligaer Common. Fan Steve Gerrard wrote, 'First of all, there was a black carriage – originally my dad thought it was a hearse – with some horses reined to it. There were some officious, and rather gallant-looking, foot soldiers with rifles pointing them at the Doctor and Rose. The sergeant atop the lead horse asked the Doctor who he was... [Later] there were more soldiers, given directions to look as if they "meant business," and they all stood pointing their guns at the Doctor and Rose. Those two intrepid travellers walked up to the coach and a coachman opened the door. Blow me down with a feather!! Inside was Queen Victoria! Again the Doctor shows his psychic paper. Queen Victoria leans forward and takes it from him... There were numerous takes of this scene – first of all were the rehearsals, then the filmed rehearsals and finally the filming itself. Most ran very smoothly, apart from when one of the horses decided he'd had enough and almost fell asleep, causing the carriage to judder violently, and shaking ol' Queen Vic and the camera crew up considerably. There were multiple takes of close-ups, medium close-ups, wide shots, etc. The actor playing the sergeant had to walk behind the camera crew and then step up a ladder so that his voice – off-screen – could be heard, to give the other actors [something] to act against. All through this set up, the extras stood around, looking rather stoical, including earlier some as Buddhist monks looking rather cold with their shaven heads nicely catching the sun's rays.' Gerrard later asked Tennant, in an off-duty moment, if he'd been having a good time. 'I'm having a whale of a time', Tennant told him. 'My ears are freezing... I've never experienced anything like this before!' That wasn't it, either, for public locations; at Tredegar House in Newport, fans noted, 'BBC Wales were building the TARDIS in the basement, but no-one was allowed to see it', while at the Headlands School in Penarth on 29 September, service vehicles were spotted at the car park, and blank gunfire shots were heard in town.

True to form, reports of recording attracted not only fans but the press as well. The *South Wales Echo* on 28 September said, 'The *Doctor Who* team have been spotted out and about filming one of the latest episodes for the sci-fi series. A desolate spot on the mountainside at Gelligaer Common, in between Bargoed and Merthyr, was where the stars and the... crew starting setting up from dawn yesterday. New *Doctor Who* star David Tenant and actress Billie Piper were reported to have been on site – and the famous TARDIS could be seen in the distance. A carriage and horses were also seen from the road, which was blocked off by two police officers while the cameras rolled. Traffic was stopped while action was being filmed about quarter of a mile from the narrow winding road leading to Bedlinog.' A day later, the *South Wales Evening Post* discussed the Gower sequences: 'David Tennant, who plays the latest incarnation of the Timelord from Gallafray [sic], was joined by Billie Piper, who plays companion Rose, on the cliff-tops overlooking the stunning sweep of Rhossili – to the delight of passers-by. One visitor, Viv Richards of Port Eynon, was there with her grandchildren. She said: "They are great fans of *Doctor Who*, so they were delighted to be able to see the filming... They seemed really nice people."'

As expected, there was very little news coming out of the production team itself about the specific contents of the Christmas special or the second series. They had in fact made a great deal of effort to tighten up the security of information on the series, so that little escaped barring the occasional snippet gleaned from public recording (which was, after all, unavoidable). 'Spoiler' leaks were now becoming less commonplace. However, there were still stories breaking, mostly controlled through official releases to BBC *Doctor Who* licensees and through the series' own website – its editors now moved to Cardiff and firmly under the auspices of the production team – and *Doctor Who Magazine*.

That said, the press was quite happy to scoop the official sources whenever it could. Such was the case with the revelation of the casting of Pauline Collins as Queen Victoria in the 3 October *Sunday Mirror*. Collins, who nearly 40 years earlier had played the role of Samantha Briggs in the *Doctor Who* serial 'The Faceless Ones' starring Patrick Troughton, and at the time had been under consideration to become a series regular, was well known to British audiences for her role in the television drama *Upstairs, Downstairs* and the film *Shirley Valentine* (1989). 'Pauline found it amusing that she played a fashionable young woman in the '60s, but now she's playing a very wrinkly Queen Victoria', the *Mirror* quoted an insider as saying. Collins was to star in the new season's second episode, 'Tooth and Claw', which would be written by Davies and feature a trip into Earth history, not unlike the previous season's 'The Unquiet Dead'. Producer Phil Collinson, appearing at a charity dinner, was reported to have said, 'If you thought Simon Callow was good, wait 'til you see Pauline Collins.'

The recording of the episode would receive quite a bit of local attention. 'A year after shooting snowy scenes in the centre of Monmouth', reported the *Newsquest Media* wire service in early October, 'BBC's *Doctor Who* has returned in the TARDIS to film another episode in the Wye Valley. [Tennant] and actress Billie Piper, who returns as Rose Tyler, were among the cast and crew spending a day at Treowen House in Dingestow last week... The episode is set in a Victorian castle in the Scottish Highlands. [Programme]-makers said Treowen House, a 17th Century Grade I Listed building owned by brothers John and Dick Wheelock, had been chosen as one of several locations in South Wales perfect to fulfil the role.' The episode's location manager, Gareth Lloyd, told *Newsquest*, 'We specifically required an ornate staircase to film a chase sequence, and our designer Ed Thomas suggested Treowen after a colleague got married there. I went down to take some photographs and the director loved them. After that, we looked to see what else we could use. We filmed scenes in the entrance hallway and one of John's reception rooms, which doubled as the corner of a study.' The production crew arrived at the location on 4 October.

Doctor Who Magazine, released in the middle of October, gave further casting information for both 'Tooth and Claw' and 'The Girl in the Fireplace', confirming both story titles. At the time the magazine was released, the production team were, according to producer Phil Collinson, 'editing the first episodes, filming Block Two and prepping Block Three.' Following the pattern from the previous year, the production team had chosen to divide the production into a number of 'blocks', each helmed by one director, to minimise clerical and technical complications. Block One recording – that is, for the episodes 'The Christmas Invasion', 'New Earth' and 'School Reunion' – was completed on Saturday 8 October, save for a second-unit night shoot in London that would be scheduled for early November; it included an 'extended action sequence' from 'New Earth' as well as several missing shots for 'The Christmas Invasion'. Block Two, Euros Lyn's production block on 'Tooth and Claw' and 'The Girl in the Fireplace', started around 1 October. Block Three, the forthcoming four-episode block of Cybermen episodes directed by Graeme Harper ('Rise of the Cybermen' and 'The Age of Steel' as well as the two-part season finale, 'Army of Ghosts' and 'Doomsday') would go into production in early November. The stories in the other three production blocks for the 2006 series – Block Four ('The Idiot's Lantern' and 'Fear Her'), Block Five ('The Impossible Planet' and 'The Satan Pit') and Block Six ('Love & Monsters'), the latter shot concurrently with Block Five – would be recorded early in 2006.

NEW HEIGHTS: THE NATIONAL TELEVISION AWARDS

While production continued on location in Wales, as well as in the studios in Newport, the relative calm of the *Doctor Who* off-season was broken by news on 11 October that the series, nominated in three categories during July for the 2005 National Television Awards (see above), had been shortlisted in all three. These awards, created in 1995 and sponsored by the ITV network, demonstrate the mood of the British public at the time; while the BAFTAs are considered more prestigious industry awards, the National Television Awards reflect the 'people's choice.'

At the star-studded presentation ceremony on 25 October, *Doctor Who* was the big winner, beating such competitors as the American drama series *Desperate Housewives* and the home-grown *The Bill* and *Bad Girls* for the Most Popular Series award. Billie Piper, Noel Clarke and Camille Coduri accepted the award on behalf of the programme; and all three were rather speechless when the announcement that the series had won was read out. Taking the stage as the now-familiar *Doctor Who* theme tune played, the three seemed genuinely enthusiastic, and

Piper nearly giddy as she spoke: 'I'd like to thank the viewers, everybody that voted... I know this means so much for everybody back in Cardiff, and it's so great to have [the programme] back. Thanks to Russell T... he's just genius,' she added, as the ITV camera pointed toward Davies, ebullient and overjoyed at *Doctor Who*'s win.

Both Eccleston and Piper beat stiff competition to win their respective awards as well, demonstrating exactly how far *Doctor Who* had come in the public eye even since it had returned to television only seven months earlier. Eccleston was not present to collect his award for Most Popular Actor – a fact that subsequently led to a good deal of speculation that his departure from the series had been less than amicable – though Davies read a statement on his behalf: 'I'm very sorry that I can't be there tonight. A heartfelt thank you to the British public for their encouragement over the past 17 years. I'd like to dedicate this award to the memory of a little boy who loved *Doctor Who* and loved life, Kieran Wynne.' Eccleston's agent later explained that the actor had met the boy before he died but could give no other details, noting that Eccleston had planned to attend the awards but had been struck down with flu and also felt ill after having vaccinations in advance of a forthcoming trip abroad. Eccleston's award had been presented by *Dynasty* actress Joan Collins, and the co-nominees included Nigel Harman (*EastEnders*), Martin Clunes (*Doc Martin*), Bradley Walsh (*Coronation Street*) and Shane Richie (*EastEnders*).

The presentation of the award for Most Popular Actress was made by *CSI: Crime Scene Investigation* actor Gary Dourdan, and was preceded by clips of Piper as Rose in 'The Parting of the Ways' and of Piper's co-nominees: June Brown (*EastEnders*), Caroline Quentin (*Life Begins*), Jessie Wallace (*EastEnders*) and Sally Lindsay (*Coronation Street*). Piper was again shocked to have won the award, saying how much it meant to her. She thanked Davies, Julie Gardner, Phil Collinson, Eccleston for being 'such a fantastic Doctor' (although some early press reports would wrongly state that she'd neglected to mention her co-star), her agents, her 'lovely family', her boyfriend and 'Mr E' – referring to her husband Chris Evans, to whom she was still legally married, although they were separated. (Evans and Piper had split up some months earlier, but remained very good friends throughout their break-up.) Piper was 'genuinely quite touched,' said BBC Radio Five Live, adding that she later told journalists, 'Chris is not here this evening, I don't know why,' and saying of new co-star David Tennant, 'He's a lot lighter on his feet and I am sure you will all be thrilled.' Piper also told Five Live that it was the first award she'd won since she was adjudged Most Fanciable Female in Pop at the *Smash Hits* Poll Winners' Party several years before. *MediaGuardian* reported on 26 October that Piper was also very forthcoming about the contents of the forthcoming Christmas special: 'It's got scary Christmas trees,' said the actress, 'Santa attacks, there's an invasion, and the Doctor stays in bed for a long, long time. I am carrying most of the show.' She also praised her new co-star: '[Tennant] is a bit more childlike and dances around a lot. I'm sure you will like him.'

The press bought into the celebratory air of the whole affair, with the following day's *Daily Mirror* featuring Piper on its front page, and the *Daily Star* proclaiming that she seemed to have 'dressed down for the awards.' The *Sun* headlined 'Hip Hip Who-Ray: TV Gongs for Dr and Daleks.' ITV, however, downplayed the awards; still perhaps reeling over their ratings losses on Saturday nights earlier in the year, when *Doctor Who* had knocked *Ant & Dec's Saturday Night Takeaway* out of the first place slot, the ITV website heralded the awards programme and their own winners, neglecting to mention a single BBC entry. 'You can understand why ITV might be a bit miffed,' wrote *Media Guardian* on 26 October, 'after the BBC gate-crashed its National TV Awards last night and made off with the best actor, actress and drama awards for *Doctor Who* and the best soap gong for *EastEnders*. But still, it seems a tad churlish for ITV.com's report on the bash today not even to mention the BBC winners. Instead, ITV.com leads on '*X Factor* cleans up at TV Awards' – although to be fair, the talent show did win two gongs – and goes on to list all the other ITV winners. ITV.com – first with the news. As long as it's about ITV.' The *Sun* on 27 October featured a cartoon by Paul Sutherland in its print edition, which took a look at 'How Russell T Davies turned the Doctor from axed laughing stock to award-winning pride of the Beeb.' The paper praised Tennant, saying, 'For this timeless hit programme, the future looks brighter than ever.' The *Daily Mail* the same day wondered if Piper had received a touch of cosmetic surgery: 'For as Billie Piper collected an acting award, onlookers couldn't help commenting on her apparently fuller lips. "I could hardly concentrate on what she was saying," said a member of the audience. "Even Angelina Jolie's lips aren't that luscious."' BBC Wales Radio noted that producer Phil Collinson said he was pleased with the awards, and that the prize for Most Popular Drama would be kept in the BBC Drama Department's offices in Llandaff. He also mentioned that they were halfway through recording the new series, and were looking for it to return to the screen at Easter time.

TORCHWOOD AND CHILDREN IN NEED

In the middle of October, less than a week after the National Television Awards were presented, the BBC made another stunning announcement: *Doctor Who* would be spun off into a separate series starring John Barrowman as Jack Harkness. *Torchwood* would be launched the following year, and was described by executive producer Russell T Davies as a 'British sci-fi paranoid thriller, a cop show with a sense of humour.' Davies stated that he was just starting work on the scripts for the show, which would be set in modern-day Cardiff and would segue from events seen in the forthcoming *Doctor Who* Christmas special and second series. In fact, the BBC press release for *Torchwood* confirmed for the first time that the second series of *Doctor Who* would feature stories involving Torchwood, which it described as 'a renegade group of investigators'.

The announcement of the spin-off wasn't the only surprise; fans then learned that they wouldn't have to wait until Christmas to get a glimpse of the tenth Doctor, when the BBC announced that Davies was penning a special *Doctor Who* mini-episode to be aired during the annual BBC *Children in Need* appeal. While rumours flew in cyberspace as to the precise content, it was soon confirmed that the mini-episode would be set directly between 'The Parting of the Ways', the previous series' finale, and 'The Christmas Invasion'. The short, only the second *Doctor Who* segment to be made and broadcast as an exclusive *Children in Need* presentation (the first being the 1993 two-part special 'Dimensions in Time', featuring members of the cast), would be televised on Friday 18 November. Terry Wogan, who hosted the appeals programme, mentioned on his Radio 2 show *Wake Up To Wogan* on 26 October that the segment would be 15 minutes in length, although ultimately on transmission, the item was approximately seven minutes long.

To help celebrate the *Children in Need* event, David Tennant and Billie Piper attended a *Doctor Who* charity dinner in mid-October, which raised over £20,000 for the appeal. Said *BBC News*, 'Money raised through the *Doctor Who* Galactic Dinner will help improve the lives of children and young people. Writer and executive producer Russell T Davies presided over a special auction of coveted *Doctor Who* memorabilia. Guests bid up to £4,000 for some of the items, which are destined to become valuable collectors' items.' The event, at Cardiff's Macdonald Holland House Hotel, was attended by over 250 people. As Tennant told *BBC News*, 'We always knew it was going to be a fantastic event, but it exceeded all our expectations.' Menna Richards, Controller of BBC Wales, said: 'The *Doctor Who* team made a fantastic contribution towards raising a huge sum of money for *Children in Need*. But they couldn't have done it without the amazing support of all those *Doctor Who* fans who bid for prizes and gave so much money to the event.'

THE AUTUMN PRESS

While *Doctor Who* maintained a busy production schedule, much of it was set apart from the eyes of the media and watchful fans. Nevertheless, the press onslaught that had marked much of 2005 continued well into September and October.

Christopher Eccleston's win at the *TV Quick/TV Choice* Awards on 4 September was widely reported; the award, voted on by readers of the two magazines, was in spite of the fact that he'd quit the show the previous spring. The *Sunday Telegraph* on 4 September reported that BBC1's ratings over the summer had plummeted towards an all-time low, but noted that, according to BBC Controller Peter Fincham, ratings weren't the sole measure of success; in fact, websites like the official *Doctor Who* site get millions of hits nowadays. *TV Fodder* said of 'The Regeneration of *Doctor Who*' on 4 September, 'The key to the success of *Who* lay in the clever invention of the main character's ability to regenerate... Enter Christopher Eccleston as the Doctor and Billie Piper as his assistant, Rose: the two main ingredients in the resurrected *Doctor Who* series that recently finished airing its first season. The special effects are a lot better than in the classic programme, and the episodes tend to move along at a more accelerated clip... The new series is every inch a chip off the old block. Season one is over now, and so is Eccleston's stint as the renegade Time Lord. But there's no sign that the programme is in any danger of fading out.' On 5 September, the *Evening Gazette* quoted as new Billie Piper's comments in the *previous* summer's tabloid press that 'I was always struggling with my weight... I was brought up on bread and butter as a kid and have at least two slices [of bread] every meal – no wonder I had weight trouble at school.'

The BBC Gloucestershire website recapped August's recording inside Clearwell Caves for the Christmas special on 5 September: 'Scenes for the forthcoming *Doctor Who* Christmas special have been shot at the popular Forest tourist attraction, and although its plot remains a secret, it's a safe bet that extra-terrestrials are involved.' Said Jonathan Wright of Clearwell Caves, 'They wanted the largest underground cavern that they could find in this part of England. [We're] quite surprised at the scale of it; it's taken up the entire car park.' *Round Table*, the BBC Radio York current affairs discussion programme, covered *Doctor Who* on 9 September. New Zealand's PrimeTV network reported a 'dramatic increase' in audience levels during its broadcast of the current *Doctor Who* season in their target demographics of ages 25–54: 'Taking into consideration the previous programme in this time slot was *Wife Swap USA*, it appears Prime's audience was crying out for a change.'

Andrew Marr, speaking to *The Sunday Times* on 11 September, discussed his appearance in the previous series: 'I loved doing *Doctor Who*. I was presenting a news report about an alien invasion. They took hours and hours to light it, which was bizarre, because they were mimicking something I normally do in five minutes with one cameraman.' *The Times* also noted, in its 'Biteback' column, that it: '... felt [the series] had too many episodes set in the UK. I gather Stephen Fry has written one of the 13 episodes of the next series, and it is likely to be set in 1930s England.' John Barrowman spoke to *BBC News* the same day about 'why he swapped *Doctor Who* for a role in West End play *A Few Good Men* alongside Hollywood star Rob Lowe' and confirmed that he wouldn't be back in Series Two but would be for the year after. *Dreamwatch*, released on 10 September, featured an article by former *Doctor Who* star

Colin Baker, who praised the series, calling the two-parter 'The Empty Child' and 'The Doctor Dances' his favourite story, and proclaiming Annette Badland and Florence Hoath to be the season's best guest actors. 'It was great to sit down and watch the new *Doctor Who* from the very first moment, knowing I was not in it', wrote Baker. *BBC News* on 10 September noted that Russell T Davies would be appearing during the weekend at the Cardiff gay and lesbian Mardi Gras, alongside such notables as singer Charlotte Church. icWales reported on 11 September that retailers were concerned they wouldn't be able to keep up with the demand for *Doctor Who* merchandise this year. 'We have people coming in two to three times a day asking about when the new toys are going to come out', said Alan Vaughan of Cardiff's Comic Guru Presents shop. 'Everyone's waiting for them. When they come in, we expect them to start flying out the door. In between now and Christmas, that's what everyone will be wanting... Even if you haven't watched it, you know what a Dalek looks like.' Demand for *Doctor Who* products had, according to retailers, increased by 15 percent over the previous year.

The *Sun* on 14 September revealed that K-9 would be killed off in the forthcoming series, destroyed while saving the Earth, but there was a silver lining: the paper quoted a series insider as saying, 'A new K-9 appears. He has been assembled and sent by the Doctor. Everybody loves K-9 – we couldn't really kill him off.' The BBC Press Office issued a press release announcing: 'As part of this year's *Children in Need*, BBC Radio Wales is offering two lucky people the chance to be wined and dined in the company of the time-travelling lord Doctor Who and his companion... This amazing prize will consist of a pair of tickets to the dinner, overnight accommodation at the Holland House Hotel and the chance to mix with the cast of the hit drama *Doctor Who*.' *BBC News* reported on a Brighton television conference and said, 'Writers have praised BBC1 hit sci-fi series *Doctor Who*... in a call for more funding for UK TV productions. It showed there was "still an audience for quality family entertainment".' *Drum Media* on 14 September said, 'Before David Tennant was announced as the BBC's new *Doctor Who*... a number of actors were linked with the role in the media, all of them white. Sure, there has been the odd black name in the frame for these parts in the past, but it has always been reported in the media as a semi-novelty item.' The writer of the article: '... visited four of the Internet's most popular *Doctor Who* and *James Bond* fan-sites and left near identical messages on each of their discussion forums. Posing as a "lifelong fan, but first-time poster," I very gently suggested that maybe it would be "cool" to have a black Bond or Doctor... *Doctor Who* fans seem to fall into the same pattern of debate – a majority who simply state that "the Doctor is white" and generate any number of convoluted and impossibly obscure plot-related reasons why this is an unalterable fact, and a minority who support the idea and are able to respond using their equally encyclopaedic knowledge of the *Doctor Who* universe in their defence.'

Doctor Who Magazine reported in mid-September that there was uncertainty over the future of the *Doctor Who* exhibition in Brighton after its seasonal closure in November; said Lorne Martin of Experience Design, '[We are] looking at other ventures in other areas, whereby the exhibitions can grow... The fact that the show is already signed up for Series Three [means that] we can go and talk to more venues about making an even more thrilling experience.' *SFX* magazine asked on its website, in conjunction with a new contest, 'What do you reckon [the Cybermen] should look like when they stride across our screens once more? We reckon you'll want to bin the moon boots and cricket gloves, but how far would you go? Should they have fleshy bits showing?' Paul Abbott, who had been rumoured to be a potential writer for the first series, was quoted by the *Guardian* and *The Times* on 16 September saying that 'too much television drama is under-ambitious, predictable and needlessly boring' but that

Russell T Davies' series *Second Coming* was 'a television masterpiece.' The *Stage* on 19 September noted: 'West End star John Barrowman looks as if he is going to be a busy boy this Christmas... After all, the *Simply Musical* star made a recent TV appearance as time-travelling Captain Jack Harkness in the new series of *Doctor Who* and it seems that he will be employing some sort of TARDIS-like device (perhaps draped in tinsel?) to travel between Wimbledon and the West End on a daily basis for the beginning part of the festive period. Either that, or some unfortunate punters are going to be watching an understudy somewhere along the line.' On 20 September, the *Sentinel* reported: 'Pupils invited a special time traveller... to see their school's TARDIS. Year six children from Belgrave Primary, in Longton, were treated to a drama workshop with Alan Ruscoe, who played a mannequin-like Auton in the last series.' Lifting an interview answer from *Doctor Who Magazine*, the *Daily Mail* said on 21 September, 'Despite being an early favourite to play *Doctor Who*, Richard E Grant never really had a chance – writer-producer Russell T Davies loathes the *Withnail And I* star. He says: "I'm not a fan. He was never on our list to play the Doctor. Never."'

icWales kicked off October with an announcement: 'The BBC are filming 18 episodes for the new series. And the action, which also features *Coronation Street*'s Todd Grimshaw, aka Bruno Langley, will see the heroes battle new and familiar foes including Cybermen and an evil race of Catwomen.' This led to speculation that Langley, who had been seen as Adam in the first-series episodes 'Dalek' and 'The Long Game', would be in the second series, which was later determined to be false, as was the number of episodes the report claimed. *Popbitch*, a gossip column/online magazine that had reported many rumours in the past, said: 'Tom Baker *is* putting [an appearance] in during Season Three (and maybe Two) – [voiceovers] only, as 'voice of the Time Lords'. He would have appeared but only if they cast him as an alien woman (or the Master), which was rejected.'

Alan Davies was interviewed by the *Sunday Telegraph* on 2 October, and discussed considering the lead role in *Doctor Who*: 'When it was mooted, I thought it was going to be six half hours, like it used to be. And then when I heard it was 13 hour-long episodes and they were going to be in Cardiff for 10 months, I thought: Oooh. Then they worked Christopher Eccleston into the ground, he quit and the BBC put it about that he didn't want to be typecast. The truth was they just overworked him and he was exhausted.' The *Mirror* took these comments as gospel, reporting that Eccleston had quit the series because he was: '... overworked and exhausted. Actor pal Alan Davies said the BBC worked Eccleston "into the ground" before he quit as the famous Time Lord.' Eccleston himself replied to the *Mirror* on 16 October, and was quoted as saying, 'Alan should keep his nose out of my business. I rang his agent and told him he had no right to say what he did.' Meanwhile, Eccleston headed up 11 October's *Pride of Britain Awards* on ITV1, alongside such celebrities as Catherine Zeta-Jones, Bono, David Beckham, Bob Geldof and the Duchess of York, while it was announced in the *Scotsman* that David Tennant would appear at the fortieth anniversary gala for the Royal Lyceum Theatre Company in January.

Writer Mark Gatiss ('The Unquiet Dead') appeared on the Jonathan Ross radio show on BBC Radio 2 on 1 October along with his *League of Gentlemen* co-star Reece Sheersmith; Gatiss confirmed he would be writing episode seven for the forthcoming season and it would be an historical adventure, and commented that writer Steven Moffat's son was apparently upset that David Tennant's new costume 'isn't like the old *Doctor Who*.' The 'Green Room' column in the 4 October *Metro* mentioned that Charlotte Church apparently wanted a guest role in the forthcoming series, quoting her as saying, 'It's filmed in Cardiff so I can do the accent, but I'm really rubbish at acting.' The US-based magazine the *Simon* said of the BBC America network on 4 October, 'Hell, how you haven't taken up Russell T Davies' brilliant re-invention of *Doctor Who* is beyond me.' The *Off The Telly* media website called the 2005 series the fourth greatest Saturday night television series ever broadcast: 'It seems simple now, but what the new production team obviously realised was that if *Doctor Who* was going to survive on Saturday nights in 2005, it had to face its audience head-on and ask for no concessions... Prior to the announcement of [Eccleston's] casting it had been difficult to differentiate the revived *Doctor Who* from the countless other remakes and niche cult programmes floating about. But the choice of Eccleston as the Doctor demanded that the series receive the same type of media coverage as *Casualty* and *EastEnders* (rather than *Hex* or, dare we say it, *Buffy*). In the course of only 13 episodes, *Doctor Who* 2005-style immediately gained a place at the top table of Saturday night programming.' The official *Doctor Who* website on 11 October also announced the availability of a collection of sounds and photos for readers' mobile phones, and confirmed the involvement of Pauline Collins as Queen Victoria and of Sophia Myles in the series' fourth episode.

The Times on 12 October profiled Billie Piper, in conjunction with her forthcoming lead role in BBC1's *Much Ado about Nothing*, a take on the Shakespeare play but set in modern times. 'So unnerving was the launch [of *Doctor Who*], she went into hiding. "It scared the hell out of me, if I'm honest. But then, when the first one was out and it was just part of Saturday-night viewing, it felt a bit more real." As Rose Tyler, street-smart companion to the titular Time Lord (aged 953), Piper has been integral to the show's success... There was talk that she might jump TARDIS along with Christopher Eccleston... But no, it was just tittle-tattle.' Ten days later, the *Daily Record* also looked at *Much Ado about Nothing*, noting that Piper: '... plays weathergirl Hero. She causes a storm when she dresses up as Monroe for a fancy dress party.' The *Sun* on 17 October sparked some controversy when it reported: 'TV chiefs are plotting a showdown between Doctor Who's most fearsome foes the Cybermen and the Daleks. The Timelord's robot enemies will confront each other for the first time... We can also disclose that [the Cybermen] are making a surprise reappearance during the last two episodes as well. And in those shows – called "Army of Ghosts" – the Daleks turn up too. An insider said: "It's going to be an explosive end to the series and the fans will love it. It's war."'

SFX released a feature interview with Russell T Davies late in the month, in which the executive producer noted that the forthcoming second series would have: '... a whole different feel, with David now at the centre of things – a different energy, a different Doctor, which makes it a different show. But at the same time, it's still good old *Doctor Who*.' He was exuberant about the appearance of Elisabeth Sladen: 'I thought Stephen Fry was going to faint... And it was the same, walking on set, seeing her with David and Billie. And it's a hell of a ride, cos one minute you're remembering the past, but as soon as Toby Whithouse's blistering dialogue rips out, then you know immediately that this isn't nostalgia, it's a great, new story to tell about the Doctor's life. Then you add Anthony Head, who's just brilliant.' Davies confirmed Cassandra would be appearing: '... partly to shore up the show and ease the changeover of Doctor. At the same time, there's only a fleeting mention of her escapades on Platform One, so brand new viewers can start from scratch. But actually, the most powerful reason for bringing Cassandra back is that I thought she was the most amazing piece of CGI, voiced by one of the UK's best actors and, crucially, I thought of a brand new story for her.' As for the third series, Davies was wry: 'I was just talking to Julie Gardner this morning, and we realised that we've probably got about ten of next year's episodes nailed down already. Including that episode in Nobby's Circus Tent with the talking gay elephants. I think we'll transmit that live.'

Meanwhile, the *Daily Star* on 22 October flagged the appearance of David Tennant in the comedy series *Rab C Nesbitt*, airing on Channel 5's *Greatest Before They Were Stars TV Moments*, in which Tennant had played the role of transsexual barmaid Davina. Tennant's personal life was also under scrutiny; the *Mirror* reported the same day that he had split from his actress girlfriend Keira Malik, with a source telling them, 'Work commitments were keeping them apart for longer and longer periods of time. It's very sad things didn't work out. In the end, though, they both agreed that it was better if they just split.' The *South Wales Evening Post* on 23 October profiled series production designer Edward Thomas, who explained that he: '... knew [*Doctor Who*] was going to be enormous, but I don't think anything could have prepared me for the immense success... Initially the biggest challenge was to get the TARDIS done both on the inside and the outside. I was racking my brain – because it's not a space ship, it's a time machine.' The *Metro* said that, because of *Doctor Who*, an entire third of Britain's population now believed time travel was possible, according to a UKTV poll: 'It is just one example of how science-fiction has helped people believe some concepts are science fact.'

ITV1's *This Morning* revealed on 26 October that actress Tracy-Ann Oberman – best known to British audiences as Chrissie Watts on *EastEnders* – would guest star in the forthcoming second series, and the *Daily Mirror* the next day added that this would be in the role of the villainous Yvonne Hartman. The *Mirror* also announced the casting of Roger Lloyd-Pack, the actor best known as Trigger in the BBC comedy series *Only Fools and Horses* and soon to be seen playing Barty Crouch – father of Barty Crouch Junior, played by David Tennant – in *Harry Potter and the Goblet of Fire*. Lloyd-Pack would play John Lumic, a human who becomes the Doctor's opponent in several episodes with the Cybermen. CBBC presenter Andrew Hayden-Smith announced on air that he'd been cast as a guest star as well; the actor, who played Ben in the CBBC drama *Byker Grove*, would take the role of Jake Simmonds in the two-part Cybermen story that would enter production a week later. 'I am so excited about joining one of the most famous programmes on TV,' said Hayden-Smith in a statement. 'It's an absolute dream job for me.' David Tennant and Billie Piper, it was reported, would switch on the 2006 Christmas lights in Cardiff, with the official *Doctor Who* website saying, 'Santa has an early present.' The Dark Horizons website interviewed Adam Garcia on 24 October; the actor, who had finished recording his scenes for the forthcoming episode 'The Christmas Invasion', told the site, 'I have been a fan of *Doctor Who* since I was little... You know, just getting to read the scripts is amazing, because they keep them all secret.' Anthony Head, who would appear in 'School Reunion', guested on the Jonathan Ross show on BBC Radio 2 on 24 October, praising Tennant in the role of the Doctor and implying that he was playing a schoolteacher who isn't nice, but isn't necessarily the villain, either. BBC Radio Cornwall reported that an actor named Spencer Hawken would appear in the second series as 'an evil Time Lord', which later proved to be untrue. And Christopher Eccleston would open in the play *Night Sky* by Rachel Wagstaff at the Old Vic Theatre in London on 30 October; an appearance that would receive a great deal of attention in the newspapers.

Doctor Who merchandise also continued to be promoted and sold in huge quantities approaching the Christmas season. With the three new ninth Doctor novels published in September and selling strongly, three more volumes – which would be the first to feature David Tennant on their covers – were announced for the following April. Panini, the publishers of *Doctor Who Magazine*, released the *Doctor Who Annual*, which managed to overtake the three new novels on the Top 20 TV Tie-Ins Chart published by the *Bookseller*. Several unofficial books about the series were also released during September: Mark

Campbell's *Dimensions in Time and Space*, the analysis book *Back In Time: A Thinking Fan's Guide to Doctor Who*, and the first volume of *Back to the Vortex*, the latter accompanied by a press campaign that included coverage on over a dozen regional BBC Radio stations across England. The first series' DVD box set release was scheduled for November. Although it had previously been thought that *Doctor Who Confidential* would not appear on DVD, in part because of the likely difficulty of gaining clearance for the contemporary music tracks featured liberally in the programmes, rumours now abounded that the set would actually incorporate the 'cut down' versions of the documentaries. These rumours proved true. In addition, it was announced that the box set would feature an exclusive edition of *Confidential* previewing 'The Christmas Invasion'. The first series was also released in the UMD (Sony Playstation/PSP) format from October. Character Options, the toy manufacturer whose items were expected to dominate the Christmas market, announced it would be releasing several new figures in the spring, including a tenth Doctor action figure, Rose and K-9 models, a Sycorax, the Lady Cassandra and others.

And *Doctor Who* itself stayed in the public eye throughout the early autumn, with BBC3 showing reruns of the series with excellent viewing figures and UKTV Gold putting out publicity (including a billboard campaign featuring the Daleks and the tagline, 'Watch *Doctor Who* Week or Die!') in advance of *its* screening of the episodes starting on 23 October. BBC Radio 2 announced a new documentary special, *Doctor Who: Regeneration* for December. New Zealand's PrimeTV also confirmed the record ratings improvement in the time slot they'd used to broadcast *Doctor Who* in that country throughout July, August and September. Germany acquired the rights to show the first series on its Pro7 network, and BBC Worldwide Canada announced a 'major licensing deal with CBC Television for the second series of the latest *Doctor Who* adventures' after the network had seen its own enormous amount of success with the first series, as well as early reports that BBC Video would release the series in that country on DVD. The deal stipulated that 'The Christmas Invasion' would be hosted by Billie Piper exclusively for CBC viewers to air on Boxing Day, 26 December... the day after it was very likely that the BBC would choose to air the special itself.

With the promise in Britain of the *Children in Need* special in November and a full-length episode for Christmas Day, *Doctor Who* was likely to be on everyone's minds over the festive period.

CHAPTER FOUR:
CHRISTMAS COMES EARLY

While *Doctor Who* had taken the summer off – at least from the public eye – there had been a slow but steady trickle of news, press commentary and gossip. As the holidays approached and the series made its way back to television for its much-vaunted Christmas special, however, the onslaught of media attention would begin again in earnest. This time, there would be no mistaking it: *Doctor Who* was part of the public consciousness again.

PARALLEL WORLDS

In early November, the *Sun* confirmed that Shaun Dingwall would be returning to play Rose's father, Pete Tyler, in the two-part Cybermen story, which was now entering production in various locations in London and Cardiff. In fact, the story that would eventually air in the new year as the fifth and sixth episodes was being recorded in tandem with the two-part season finalé; Davies eventually explained this to *Doctor Who Magazine* as a necessity due to the limited schedules available to the guest cast (many of whom, including Dingwall, would appear in both stories).

Recording of the mid-season Cyberman story included a two-day excursion to London, where sequences were shot on the Embankment, at Lambeth Pier and at Battersea Power Station, as well as a sequence for 'Army of Ghosts' at the Brandon Estate, home of Jackie Tyler. Martin Hoscik of the *UNIT News* website watched the recording and explained that David Tennant, Billie Piper and Camille Coduri were: '... on-set for the filming of one scene involving the Doctor's reaction to an unseen entity. After the leads finished their scenes, a number of shots of extras were filmed. These involved two sets of extras also reacting to the (same?) unseen force. Filming of one set of extras involved a large green screen, suggesting that elements will be added in post production.'

Another viewer, known as 'Fleetboy', posted at Outpost Gallifrey, 'A colleague of mine went out jogging at lunchtime and excitedly announced on his return that they were filming *Doctor Who* on the Albert Embankment, adjacent to Lambeth Bridge, diagonally opposite from the Houses of Parliament... [Tennant] was in his long fawn coat and brown suit; Billie in black trousers and a red top. Also in attendance was Noel Clarke and [director] Graeme Harper... The next interesting thing that caught my eye was the poster display board not displaying its usual South Bank arts posters – instead three other posters were in prominent position, two relating to the 'Cybus Corporation'. One indicated 'Cybus Property – world leaders in commercial and residential development', the second advertising 'Cybus Finance – Life package'. But most interesting was the subject of the third poster – none other than Pete Tyler! Pete was dressed in a wide boy suit holding a bottle and displaying a cheesy grin. The advertising hook was "Trust me on this... New Cherry and Vitex Lite". Obviously excitement levels grew at this point.' Later in the day, Fleetboy wrote: 'The activity first of all centred on scene dressing – mainly hosing down the path to make it look like it had been raining. My eye was next caught by the arrival of none other than Shaun Dingwall – resplendent in a suit. The other noticeable thing about him was his close-cropped hair. My eye was next caught by [producer] Phil Collinson reviewing the rushes of the day so far. The scenes consisted of a shot looking up at the TARDIS with Lambeth Palace in the background, a scene of David, Billie and Noel jumping down from the raised grass area (obviously exiting the TARDIS) and picking up the *Evening Standard*, and the scenes centred on the poster display board... [Later] the first scene was Billie hugging Pete – looks like a tear-jerker, possibly a farewell scene... The last scene I was able to catch before I was forced to leave was what appeared to be a farewell scene with Mickey, with David playfully tapping his face in an endearing way.' Also spotted on set were co-executive producer Julie Gardner and actor Andrew Hayden-Smith, whose participation in the series had been announced only a week earlier.

SFX Magazine, released on 3 November, confirmed the appearance of Dingwall and made note of the possible inclusion of Mickey Smith among the TARDIS crew – albeit on a limited schedule, as it was known by now that he wouldn't be appearing in the entire series. A title, 'Parallel World', was also quoted as potentially being the name of one of the Cybermen episodes; though denounced as made-up rumour at the time, it was in fact the working title of the first two-parter, as proposed by Davies in his initial pitch of Series Two to the BBC.

Only a week later, *Doctor Who Magazine* was the first to reveal that, following transmission of the Christmas special, viewers would 'be invited to "press their red buttons" to join the Doctor on a new adventure', referring to an additional special 'episode' to be made available over the BBC's digital services. The episode would be written by Gareth Roberts – whose previous involvement with *Doctor Who* included writing several novels for the BBC and Virgin Publishing ranges in the 1990s – and directed by Ashley Way and produced by Sophie Fante 'in conjunction with the *Doctor Who* production team'. Said Julie Gardner, 'This is being treated as a full-blooded, sophisticated production, with a brand new alien villain... and brand new sets. Viewers will even be able to use their remotes to fly the TARDIS!' The name of the special would later be revealed in *Radio Times* in early December: 'Attack of the Graske'. (The same issue of *Radio Times* would also unveil the titles of two episodes of the second series – Mark Gatiss' 'The Idiot's Lantern' and the series finalé, 'Doomsday', written by Davies.) The magazine also revealed that the series was shortly to debut in France, on the new digital channel France 4, while it was announced later in the month that Belgium too would see the series on the Een (One) network, with subtitles rather than dubbed voices, while Showtime Arabia would be screening it in the Middle East.

The new design of the Cybermen was at last revealed by the BBC Press Office on 10 November. A photograph of a menacing Cyberman – reminiscent of its counterpart from the earlier series but updated with a slightly art-deco feel – was issued along with a press release, noting that production of the two-part story that would reintroduce the familiar villains was currently under way in Cardiff (the production having returned to that city after the two-day London shoot). 'The first two-parter of series two, written by Tom MacRae (*Nine Lives*, *School's Out*), sees the Doctor and his companions battle against a new, more deadly breed of Cybermen who are out to convert humanity into their own kind,' read the release. Producer Phil Collinson stated: 'The villainous Cybermen are as much a part of *Doctor Who* heritage as the Daleks, and so it's a huge personal thrill to see them back. I hope that the evil silver giants will terrify a whole new generation of viewers as they confront the tenth Time Lord.' The press release verified the appearances of Roger Lloyd-Pack, Andrew Hayden Smith and Shaun Dingwall in the episodes, as well as noting that Camille Coduri and Noel Clarke were also appearing. Nothing was said at the time, however, about the concurrent filming of the two concluding episodes of the season; the fact that they were being shot in tandem with the mid-season two-parter was information carefully concealed until well into 2006. Later in the month, news of two additional pieces of casting leaked out: Don Warrington, who had appeared as the Time Lord historical figure Rassilon in Big Finish's series of audio plays, was rumoured to be playing 'the President', while actor Nicholas Briggs (who had voiced the Daleks and the Nestene Consciousness during the first series) told *BBC Wiltshire* on 22 November that he was returning to voice the Cybermen. The press covered the news of the return of the Cybermen extensively; said *The Times* on 12 November: 'Viewers, while terrified, could not help noticing in the past that the low tech Cybermen appeared to be 70 percent Bacofoil with a car lamp stuck on their helmets. They have been redesigned by the same experts who reinvented the Daleks and previously worked on films including *Hellraiser II*.'

Production on the two-part Cybermen story continued throughout November. Around 15-16 November, fans were treated to more location recording in Cardiff. 'The set was under a railway bridge and involved a burnt-out car, which they are setting alight when it gets dark, some soldiers in modern (I think, but I am no expert!) cammo, sand bags and a barrier, some old looking street lights and Mickey', wrote fan Melanie Hill to the Timeless fan group. 'I overheard that the bridge above and the backdrop will be CGI'd to show the toffs' part of the city. On the fence next to the burnt-out car is a sign saying 'Cybus Industries', and underneath it says 'commercial properties to let'. The sign has a logo for Cybus on it; it is a stylised 'C', in grey, with a circle around it... On the set I was lucky enough to have a good chat with Julian Luxton, who [worked on] eight episodes of the first season [as assistant director], and is apparently doing ten this season! He has confirmed that David Tennant will *not* have a Scottish accent!' Several press outlets reported the names of episodes five and six as 'Nine Lives' and 'School's Out'; in fact, these were the names of other series that writer Tom MacRae had written for.

A day later, on the evening of 17 November, the stars of the series took time out for a special event in Cardiff. David Tennant and Billie Piper were in the downtown area to switch on the city's Christmas lights, an event that had been announced nearly a month before. Fireworks marked the occasion, while Tennant and Piper joined BBC Wales broadcasters Derek Brockway and Sara Edwards on stage, along with a replica TARDIS and a montage of first series clips that demonstrated the recording done in Wales (but omitted any appearance by former star Christopher Eccleston). Tennant, when asked how he was finding being the tenth Time Lord, replied, 'I'm having a ball. I get my own TARDIS. I get my own sonic screwdriver. I get to hang out with Billie Piper. I'm having a great time.' He described the forthcoming Christmas episode as being: '... the perfect thing for Christmas Day. Sit down with a big lump of turkey, put on a paper hat, pull a cracker and you'll have a great time.' He also mentioned that the Doctor and Rose would face a werewolf... and that he even got to play a woman in one episode. The lights were then turned on and fireworks went off, as Billie and David wished the crowd Merry Christmas in perfect Welsh ('Nadolig Llawen'). *BBC News* reported: 'Piper revealed to the crowd that other dangers the pair face in the sci-fi series, the second made by BBC Wales, include a werewolf as well as the Cybermen. Speaking from the stage moments before switching on the city's festive lights, she confided that the enemy in next month's episode is a Christmas tree.' The article also noted that 'The Christmas Invasion' did not yet have a firm time slot on 25 December: '[Russell T Davies] said he did not yet know what time the *Doctor Who* special would be broadcast, but viewers should expect to be frightened. He said: "It's scary. That's why we can't show it after the Queen."' Footage of the event at the lighting ceremony was later made available online by BBC Wales on its website and on the series' official site.

WILL SHE STAY OR WILL SHE GO?

Back in May 2005, shortly before the end of transmission of the first series, *Dreamwatch* magazine had reported that Billie Piper was to leave the series during its second year. 'She's not doing the full season,' the magazine quoted Piper's agent as saying, indicating that she could appear in as few as three to seven episodes. The UK press immediately picked up on the story; the departure of Christopher Eccleston announced in March had made front-page headlines across the country, and the prospective departure of the series' other principal star provoked equal noise. The BBC, compelled to address the rumours, issued a press release on 28 May: 'The BBC today confirmed that Billie Piper – who plays Doctor Who's companion Rose – will return for the second series on BBC1.' However, at the time, the press was quick to point out that this wasn't *exactly* a denial...

In fact, as discovered later, Piper *had* informed producers of her intention to leave at some time during the second series. Davies' initial submission document, later revealed in the *Doctor Who Magazine: The Doctor Who Companion: Series Two* magazine, indicated that at various times the production team had faced uncertainty as to whether Piper would be staying for the whole year or only for part of it. A June press release from the BBC indicated that Piper had been signed for all of the second season... yet there was still an ominous air to the story, as if no-one wanted to talk about a third season. Generally speaking, the BBC were keeping as quiet as they could about Piper's plans.

The *Daily Mirror* had no such inhibitions. On 11 November, the paper reported that Piper: '... told producers she did not want to become typecast as they begged her to stay for a third run of the hit show. A source said last night: "Her mind's made up... She wants to strike while the iron's hot and make a big name for herself while she's so popular. She feels her profile will go down if the series isn't as big the third time around. The BBC are auditioning other girls to take over. They want to have the next actress all lined up when they announce Billie's departure."' The BBC declined to respond to this report. 'We are not commenting on the third series', said an unidentified BBC spokesperson in a further press release. 'We are still working on the second series. Rose has a whole new journey and a fantastic set of adventures to go on with the brand new Doctor, starting in the special on Christmas Day.' Again, many readers noted that this wasn't actually a denial of the truth of the story. The *Daily Record* the same day quoted another source, saying: 'The casting people have been conducting secret auditions with a very small number of actresses and keeping it very, very quiet. They are calling girls in for screen tests one at a time and making sure they never bump into any of the other candidates. They've told all of them that if any names leak, they'll be struck off the list.'

Only days later, however, on 14 November, the *Daily Star* reported that Piper had 'laughed off' reports that she was quitting, quoting her as saying she would never let Davies or the show down. The article quoted a 'friend' of Piper who said that she was already under contract for a third series. However, the *Mirror* stuck by its story, reporting on 17 November that Piper was: '... at the centre of a tug-of-love between the BBC and ITV... Since quitting the hit sci-fi show, 23-year-old Billie has already been snapped up for two major new projects, one with each of the main channels.' The *Mirror* reported that the BBC had a 'secret project' waiting for Piper, while ITV had acquired her talents for a new adaptation of Jane Austen's novel *Mansfield Park*. Piper didn't even address the topic when she appeared on 21 November's instalment of her husband Chris Evans' new chat show *OFI Sunday*, where she instead bantered with Evans about their impending (amicable) divorce, her dissatisfaction with the Rose Tyler action figure that had been recently released ('Because I look like Master Splinter... you know, the giant rat from the [*Teenage Mutant Ninja*] *Turtles*, and I know I've got big teeth but this really takes the mick') and her happiness working on *Doctor Who*.

The usual rumours and Internet gossip followed, but, as the Cardiff Christmas lights ceremony and the *Children in Need* special had become more prominent *Doctor Who* story topics, speculation about Piper's career plans almost completely died down. In contrast to the previous year's sudden announcement of Eccleston's departure, the secrecy around Piper's decision would remain until well into the following year.

THE CHILDREN IN NEED SPECIAL

It would have been unusual if the BBC had not featured its flagship show during one of the biggest events of the television year. The *Children in Need* telethon, a mainstay of British television since 1980, had become one of its most prestigious charity events, raising money for charities working with children in the United Kingdom.

The appearance of *Doctor Who* as part of the appeal was nothing new; in 1983, the twentieth anniversary special 'The Five Doctors' had been broadcast as part of the telethon, and in 1993 there had been a two-part mini-story 'Dimensions in Time'. The 2005 telethon was scheduled for 18 November, and the *Doctor Who* segment was set to be broadcast shortly after 9.00 pm.

On 10 November, director Euros Lyn appeared on BBC Radio Jersey, noting that the segment would be 'a real episode that links the last series to the new one' and that it would be considered part of the second series, along with 'The Christmas Invasion'. The subject matter was, at the time, unknown. On the same day, the BBC started running trailers for the telethon, including excerpts from the *Doctor Who* sequence. 'The first shows the Doctor, evidently right after the regeneration still standing in the same position as we last saw him, assuring Rose that "I'm the Doctor!"' wrote Paul Hayes to Outpost Gallifrey. 'The second, later in the trailer, has Rose leaning over the console as an alarm bell sounds. She asks what it is, and the Doctor leans in next to her and exclaims in delight: "We're going to crash land!" before laughing manically. Tennant is, as expected, using an English accent as heard at the end of "The Parting of the Ways" rather than his native Scots one.' Meanwhile, the BBC also announced that the special would be available for viewing on the Internet for a short time. This would be only the second instance of an Internet broadcast of a televised *Doctor Who* episode; in April 2005, the episode 'Dalek' had been simulcast over the web as a test for new BBC internet technologies, the URL link accidentally being leaked to the public. (Additionally, the Comic Relief skit 'The Curse of Fatal Death' was streamed over the web for a short time in 1999.) *Doctor Who Magazine* indicated in November that the special would be considered 'a proper piece of *Doctor Who*': 'It's not a spoof, or an interview, or a preview of the Christmas episode, or a look behind the scenes. It's genuine new *Doctor Who*,' noted Davies. 'We've been planning this for months.'

The special was transmitted at approximately 9.09 pm on 18 November 2005, although viewers of BBC Scotland had to wait another quarter of an hour to see it. Presenter Terry Wogan introduced it as something he'd been 'looking forward to all night', and it was met with steady applause from the studio audience. David Tennant and Billie Piper taped several appeal messages that went out with local and regional broadcasts as well as with the Internet version, while the previous Doctor, Christopher Eccleston, also taped voice-overs for the evening (though linked to the charity appeal rather than to the *Doctor Who* special). Though media reports and promotion for the telethon had suggested that K-9 would be in the studio, he was nowhere to be seen. Also surprising (at least to *Doctor Who* fans) was the lack of an on-screen title for the mini-episode, which Davies would later nickname 'Pudsey Cutaway', a joke that combined the name of the *Children in Need* telethon mascot bear Pudsey with the title 'Dalek Cutaway', used in some 1965 production paperwork to refer to the one-shot episode 'Mission to the Unknown'. Bizarrely, this joke was seized on by some fans as the 'official' title of the *Children in Need* scene, although, as the *Doctor Who Magazine: The Doctor Who Companion: Series Two* magazine later confirmed, Davies's script had specified that there would be no title.

The scene ran just short of seven minutes, and contributed to the final take for the *Children in Need* appeal of over £17 million. This included an auctioned prize for two fans to visit the *Doctor Who* set the following March to meet the cast and watch recording. Said BBC News the following day, 'The BBC telethon *Children in Need* raised more than £17.2 million during the fund-raising campaign on BBC1. The total is slightly higher than last year and is expected to grow to more than £30 millioin when all donations are in.' The telethon 'attracted a big audience on Friday night', according to *Media Guardian* on 20 November, 'with a peak of more than 11 million viewers'.

NOVEMBER IN THE PRESS

The press barrage leading up to the *Children in Need* special and 'The Christmas Invasion' continued throughout November. Billie Piper was a principal focus of many of the stories: ITN reported on 2 November that she was: '... apparently putting herself in the frame to become the next Bond girl. The *Doctor Who* star is said to be taking a few days off filming to meet producers, currently gearing up to shoot *Casino Royale*... A source told a newspaper: "She's very excited about making it to the big screen."' Piper's role in BBC1's *Much Ado About Nothing* landed her a *Radio Times* cover in early November, as well as a feature interview: 'I was thrilled to find out that Hero, in this version, makes such a liberating choice in the end... She starts out very green, very young, but in the course of the play, she becomes more certain of who she is. The original Hero just wouldn't sit happily in the 21st Century, for the simple reason that it's acceptable and expected now for young girls to be their own people.' *BBC News* reported on 3 November that presenter Chris Evans was: '... suing a national newspaper for libel over a story about his split with wife Billie Piper. The BBC Radio 2 DJ's solicitor has begun proceedings against the *Daily Star* newspaper. It claimed Mr Evans gave it an exclusive interview where he blamed the BBC series *Doctor Who* – in which Ms Piper stars – for the break-up. Mr Evans said the story was "completely fabricated".'

On 2 November, icWales talked about Davies's signing of the first series *Shooting Scripts* book in Cardiff. 'TV Studies student Ross Garner, 22, of Eclipse Street, Adamsdown, was one of those in the queue outside Waterstones, in The Hayes, hoping to get some advice from the award-winning scriptwriter. "I'd like to get into writing in one shape or form, maybe even on *Doctor Who* itself," he said. "I have a few ideas and want to ask Russell for a few tips."' *People and Planet* the same day reported that Christopher Eccleston was supporting a pledge to help reduce Manchester's greenhouse gas emissions by 20 percent before 2010, as part of a city-wide campaign on climate change. The *Norfolk Eastern Press* covered Roger Lloyd-Pack's casting in the new series, mentioning other actors who had appeared in both *Doctor Who* and *Only Fools and Horses* including John Challis. Daniel Radcliffe of *Harry Potter* fame spoke with *SFX*, mentioning David Tennant, who appeared in the new *Harry Potter* film: 'I'll tell you what – I wish there was more of David Tennant in *Goblet of Fire*... He's only got a few scenes and he's brilliant in all of them. He is so absolutely, fantastically watchable. I think he'll be a good Doctor Who.' Tennant himself was reportedly accompanied to a show by Sophia Myles, while the *Daily Record* said: 'Billie Piper admits glamour doesn't come naturally – because of her huge hands and feet', as she posed for a photo set in December's issue of *Glamour* magazine: 'I have extremely wide feet, which means all those stilettos are a no-no.' The *Sun* wondered:

'Where the ecc was he? I hope Christopher Eccleston had a bloody good excuse for not showing up at the National TV Awards to pick up his gong as Best Actor... I accept that he has quit the role, but he played a huge part in the success of the series and it would have been gracious of him to turn up and thank his fans.'

On 6 November, the *Doctor Who* Exhibition at Brighton Pier closed its doors in order to move to the National Space Centre in Leicester, an event planned in conjunction with the airing of the Christmas special. *BBC News* the same day covered the world premiere of *Harry Potter and the Goblet of Fire*, which Tennant attended; *CBBC News* called Tennant one of the night's 'biggest crowd-pleasers'. The *Sun* also focused on Tennant, with a picture story about the recording that had taken place the day before in London; a 'BBC insider' was quoted as describing the chemistry on-screen between Tennant and Piper as 'explosive'. *Sky Showbiz* also concentrated on the recording, with new photographs: 'Frankly we can't get enough of this new version of the Time Lord, complete with his baseball boots. Sure, he's not a conventional Brad Pitt-style handsome... but there is something highly fanciable about Mr Tennant in his long brown tweed coat.' The *Bookseller* reported that Panini Books' *Doctor Who Annual 2006* had already spent three weeks in the Top 20 Children's Books. The *Sun* on 7 November called Billie Piper's new Shakespeare foray *Much Ado About Nothing* its Best Drama of the evening, while the Arts section of the previous weekend's *Daily Telegraph* said Piper 'has the nation's heart in her pocket', ahead of her appearance in the Shakespeare reworking. Of her part in *Doctor Who*, the *Telegraph* said, 'Piper is perfect in the role of Doctor Who's sidekick Rose Tyler, conveying a winning mix of streetwise pluck, cool glamour and a kind of been-there, done-that savvy.' The *Sunday Mail* on 6 November said: 'Writer Steven Moffat is working on the new episodes starring David Tennant as the Doctor and says petrified viewers will once again be peering out from behind the sofa. This is bad news for the parents whose complaints about the last series forced the BBC to issue a warning it was not suitable for children under eight.' icWales reported on the shortage of new series merchandise from Character Options; stock had been reaching UK high street and online retailers in very limited numbers over the previous several weeks, and always selling out immediately. Retailers in the icWales report commented: 'Every year there's always one toy that they don't make enough of, and this year it's definitely the remote-controlled Daleks.' Character Options, the report continued, 'said deliveries were being made to shops on a daily basis, but they could not guarantee stock would reach all the shops in time for Christmas ...' The *Manchester Evening News* reported on 7 November that Christopher Eccleston was 'getting back to his roots', noting that the actor had narrated a documentary about the Working Class Movement Library on The Crescent. Meanwhile, the Manners McDade Artist Management group revealed that their client Murray Gold was 'currently working on the music for the second series of *Doctor Who*, which will be recorded by the BBC National Orchestra of Wales, as well as writing the music to the third series of *Shameless*.'

The *Stage* revealed on 10 November that the ITV network had developed a £6 million science-fiction series to rival *Doctor Who*. 'The six-part series, with a working title of *Primaeval*, will follow a team of scientists who travel into prehistoric times and other worlds through black holes.' The *South Wales Echo* reported on the return to Cardiff for the *Doctor Who* production team for the two-part Cybermen story; a BBC spokeswoman said of the recording along the banks of the River Usk near the Riverfronts Arts Centre, 'We wanted a location that looked like a stretch of the Thames in London.' Stephen Fry addressed his participation in the second series in an interview with *Scotland Today*: 'I've never done anything quite like it; I've written an episode of *Doctor Who*. We are bound by all kinds of secrecy, [but] I can tell you that it deals with a well-known British legend that has alien origins rather than just folklore origins. And that one of the most exciting moments of my life was starting the first page and writing "Exterior – The TARDIS. The TARDIS materialises on the surface of a strange planet." You write that and you think, "I can't believe I have just written that". *Media Guardian* on 12 November reported: '*Little Britain* star David Walliams wants to ditch his "laydee" clothes and step into the TARDIS once David Tennant has finished his tenure. "I'd like to take over as Doctor Who. I promise not to make it camp."' The *Bookseller* on 11 November noted that there would be a *Doctor Who* book release in May 2006 as part of the Department for Education and Skills' Quick Reads initiative.

The *Daily Star* reported on 14 November that *Doctor Who* fans in England: '... want to exterminate show bosses over the Time Lord's new Scottish twang. English websites have been bombarded with complaints over claims the new Doctor, Scots-born David Tennant, 34, speaks in his native accent in the next episodes... One fan wrote: "*Doctor Who* can't keep changing his accent."' The *New Statesman* discussed Billie Piper's foray into Shakespeare: 'Now Piper has become the star turn in the first instalment of the BBC's new Shakespeare project... Piper plays her with fetching non-virginal innocence and then, having been given a rather stronger fifth act than the one Shakespeare gave his boy-actresses, turns on her two suitors. This Hero is a truly modern heroine, whose happy ending is to refuse to go up the aisle with anyone.' *Ultimate DVD*, in an issue published on 15 November, interviewed participants in the commentary recordings for the forthcoming boxed set DVD of the first series, including Christine Adams (Cathica from 'The Long Game') and Bruno Langley (Adam from 'Dalek' and 'The Long Game'). *The Pink Paper*, the UK's long-standing free gay and lesbian community newspaper, interviewed Davies and producer Phil Collinson, about the new series and about why *Doctor Who* has so many gay fans.

On 17 November, the *Sun* featured an 'exclusive' about football star David Beckham, whose passions apparently included *Doctor Who*: 'Victoria Beckham has splashed out on a book of *Doctor Who* screenplays for soccer star hubby Becks – as he is "completely obsessed" with the Time Lord... An insider said: "They were in Harrods for a couple of hours. She had a good rummage and found the *Doctor Who* book. Staff were expecting her to spend a fortune on designer gear – but she only bought the Russell T Davies scripts."' *SFX* Magazine, published the same day, interviewed Anthony Head about his guest starring role in the new season: 'It was fantastic. And he's a blinding Doctor, David Tennant. For the first time in a long time, it's effortless... He's literally born to play the part.' Head also appeared on London's Capital Radio, where he said that Tennant was the 'best Doctor since Patrick Troughton' and that he was natural at the role but was 'steely when needed'. HeartFM Radio claimed on 18 November that Ross Kemp (Grant Mitchell from the BBC soap *EastEnders*) would be a guest star in the new season; a report later proved false. On 19 November, the *Sunday Mail* said: 'The new Doctor Who has stunned fans by transforming into a Cockney. Tennant sounds like mockney Dick Van Dyke in Mary Poppins in sneak previews of the new series. And the BBC were last night forced to admit that David, 34, had dumped his native accent to star as the Time Lord.' Former *Casualty* star Claire Goose – soon to be one of Tennant's co-stars in the ITV drama *Secret Smile* – told the *Mail*, '[Tennant is] going to be a fantastic *Doctor Who*... He is one of those people who loves his job. He's really enthusiastic.'

The *Daily Mirror* on 24 November featured its own 'exclusive', spoiling some of the action in the forthcoming Christmas special: 'Earth is invaded by a gang of evil Santas in a *Doctor Who*

Christmas special – but the hero can't help as he is in the middle of regeneration into the new Doctor. Actor David Tennant is flat on his back and barely conscious as he makes his debut... Tennant joked: "I'm getting there and I'm coping with it. So far I'm doing a damn fine job of being unconscious – I'd say it's my finest work.'" Tennant, meanwhile, headed *Broadcast* Magazine's Hot 100 list: 'Landing the role of one of TV's most iconic characters has propelled Tennant into the big time. As yet, we've had only the briefest glimpse of him as the Doctor, but if you missed his exuberant, charismatic, detailed performance as the eponymous hero in *Casanova* – where were you?' The *Daily Record* the same day featured an interview with Tennant, in which the actor noted, 'My life hasn't changed. But I get invites to premieres, which I never used to. I've never done the career plan. My ambition goes from one project to the next.' Meanwhile, 24 November's *Daily Star* noted: 'Of course, the big one everyone's talking about for Christmas Day is BBC1's *Doctor Who*: "The Christmas Invasion". The *Sun* said that Billie Piper was: '... a huge fan of Christmas specials. "It means so much to me that our show is going out when families will be sitting down together, eating copious amounts and drinking sherry. I think I'm going to need a few sherries before I watch it."

The *Independent* on 26 November said: 'Of all the planets, in all the galaxies, Doctor Who and his assistant Rose (aka David Tennant and Billie Piper) had to pick the Welsh capital' for the Christmas lights ceremony. 'They should have hired... Billie, a couple of Cybermen and Chris Evans. Now that we'd like to see.' The *Observer* on 27 November opined: 'The best British actors, writers and directors are putting inventive drama back on the small screen... The *Doctor Who* effect suggests it might [be worthwhile]. No-one is claiming Russell T Davies's self-referential crowd-pleaser will have Ken Loach looking over his shoulder, but it's about as close to memorable as the Saturday family slot is ever going to get, and it's proved to the execs that, at its best, drama can trump both light entertainment and reality pap in the ratings.' Also reported in several papers that day was a retort at Davies from the website of Online Recruitment: 'Russell T Davies goes on record in an interview with the BBC stating that he would never cast a Doctor over the age of 45... Something is obviously wrong. Not only will he be in direct contravention of the new age discrimination laws due to come into effect in October 2006, but he's also lost much of the radicalism presented by the original series.' icWales reported: 'A life-sized replica of *Doctor Who*'s TARDIS came to Cardiff city centre as protestors campaigned to re-establish a city hospital. Scenes of the hit BBC sci-fi series were filmed in the empty wards of Cardiff Royal Infirmary. And protestors calling for a hospital to be re-established on the site took the TARDIS to Queen Street yesterday ...' And *London 24* said it had been a great 12 months for David Tennant, who had 'rocketed from relative unknown to a household name.'

The 27 November *Sunday Times* reported that Stephen Fry's episode was to be delayed to the third series. 'More intrigue at *Doctor Who*, where Stephen Fry's episode may be delayed. My mole in the TARDIS assures me it is "good" and "very Stephen Fry", but that it needs so many special effects, it could prove to be too expensive, at least for the next run.' The *Sunday Mail* revealed a school essay written 20 years prior by a young David Tennant: 'The 14-year-old sci-fi nut was so obsessed with the show he got his gran to knit him a long, multi-coloured scarf – just like his favourite Doctor, Tom Baker. The scarf featured regularly in his essays until English teacher Moira Robertson warned him to "exterminate" the references or he could end up failing his exams.' *Radio Times* for the week commencing 3 December interviewed Tennant, who said he considered himself: '... the dullest actor ever to have played the Time Lord... I've no hobbies or pursuits. I live in north London and drive a Skoda. I'm afraid that's as interesting as it gets.' *CBBC Newsround* ran a competition to 'Meet Doctor Who!... We're looking for one Press Packer to report for *Newsround* from the premiere screening of the Christmas episode.' And the *SF Crows Nest* site interviewed science-fiction writer Robert J Sawyer, who said that the previous season of the series was: '... absolutely terrific. I've got a total crush on Billie Piper, who I gather is a pop star in the UK. I'd never encountered her before the new series started airing. And I'm really sorry that Christopher Eccleston has left; I thought he was great.'

BBC Video announced that they would release the first series on DVD in both Canada and the United States; as far as the United States was concerned, this was a reversal of a previous policy decision that the series would be released there only after a broadcaster had transmitted it. On 1 December, the US Sci Fi Channel website's Sci Fi Wire reported: 'The BBC made the unusual decision to release the DVD in the United States before the show had found a broadcast outlet there.' A BBC representative was quoted as saying: 'This is a unique situation, really, because there are so many fans of *Doctor Who*... already out there, and we were just finding [that] people were getting... second-hand copies or copies from the UK.' The official *Doctor Who* website, meanwhile, reported that there were several problems with the series one boxed set in the UK, including an authoring fault affecting the episode 'World War Three' that cut out several minutes unless 'Play All' was selected; BBC DVD were quick to offer replacement DVDs to affected customers. Times Online reviewed the release on 26 November, saying: 'Your £70 buys irresistibly cheesy TARDIS packaging and five hours' worth of extras... Four stars.' *DVD Times* commented of the release: 'Video-wise, the print appears to be identical to the previous bare-bones releases and it's exceptionally clear at that... There is also an exclusive special featurette containing behind the scenes footage of "The Christmas Invasion", which is sure to fascinate any fan counting down the days until David Tennant's first proper episode as the tenth Doctor... Some of the video diaries are a little drawn out and repetitive in places.'

Writer Mark Gatiss appeared on the Simon Mayo show on BBC Radio Five Live and appeared to confirm that Stephen Fry's series two episode would be delayed for budget reasons, though there was no final decision reported. icWales reported on the National Orchestra of Wales's recent recording sessions for the new series' incidental music: 'The Cardiff orchestra recorded the music in closed sessions this month at the BBC studios in the city. Conducted by Ben Foster, the sessions were produced by the programme's composer Murray Gold, who also arranged the new version of the *Doctor Who* [theme].' The week's *Radio Times* featured a listing of the 20 most eagerly awaited Christmas programmes; *Doctor Who* came in at Number 2 (behind *Little Britain*), described as: 'Eagerly anticipated Christmas Day special, with David Tennant as the new Doctor, and Billie Piper. Real family viewing.' The magazine also presented its review of the year's broadcasting, and the show featured heavily.

The same day, the BBC launched the 2005 Drama Awards where viewers could vote online for their favourite dramas of the year. The official *Doctor Who* website commented, 'With categories including Best Actor, Best Actress, Best Villain and Most Desirable Star, we're hopeful that *Doctor Who* might be up for a couple of awards.'

In fact, *Doctor Who* would soon see a season of awards and accolades as 2006 approached, with transmission of the Christmas special now drawing ever nearer.

CHAPTER FIVE:
'DID YOU MISS ME?'

As 2005 drew to a close, the focus was all on the long-awaited Christmas special. From the moment the ominous but enticing caption 'Doctor Who will return in "The Christmas Invasion"' had appeared at the start of the closing credits for 'The Parting of the Ways', there had been ample speculation about what the episode might contain. An atypical *Doctor Who* adventure, surely, but with a Christmas theme? Or merely broadcast at that time of year? Davies had been quite mischievous, telling tales of evil Santa Clauses throughout the year. 'I love the title,' he commented to *SFX* magazine in November. 'What else could you call it? It will be a great adventure that's really big in scale. It will be Christmassy – there's nothing I like more than a Christmas special set at Christmas!'

A DECEMBER TO REMEMBER

BBC One repeated its 'Countdown to Christmas' promotional trailer in late October, but it wasn't until 3 November that the channel confirmed that 'The Christmas Invasion' would actually air on Christmas Day. According to the *Sun* that day, the episode would be sandwiched between two hour-long episodes of *EastEnders* 'to complete a three-hour telly fest'; the *Mirror* meanwhile reported that the episode would be broadcast against two specials from the popular ITV soap opera *Coronation Street*. The BBC and ITV, after all, were traditional rivals, battling for their share of the television audience on Christmas Day. True to form, the BBC Press Office started releasing press releases about their December offerings in late November, with a full preview of the *Doctor Who* special within their Christmas release issued on 22 November. Quoted in this release, David Tennant was ebullient: 'It was funny, when I first got asked [to play the Doctor,] I just laughed! I found it hilarious and impossible! And I remember Russell, very perceptively, saying: "Don't say anything now, because I know the experience is quite a weird one". But it's such a great job! I [mean], I get to play a Time Lord and have a TARDIS: you can't knock that!' Billie Piper said: '[Winning at the NTA awards] was the most amazing feeling. I was so terrified and really thought one of the soap actresses would win. But when they said it was me, I was just amazed. It was such a strange, wonderful evening. I felt like I was having an out of body experience.' Another press release, on 6 November, for the BBC's winter/spring 2006 season highlights, omitted Stephen Fry's name from the list of writers for series two, effectively confirming rumours that his episode, said to be heavily reliant on special effects, would be moved to series three; ultimately, the episode would be indefinitely postponed. Instead, a new name was listed: Matthew Graham, among whose credits included writing scripts for *Hustle, Spooks, EastEnders, This Life* and *Byker Grove* and co-creating and writing for the at-the-time forthcoming series *Life on Mars*. The release also noted that in the series to come, 'The Doctor and Rose travel through time and space, battling a host of new and returning aliens and monsters, including the dreaded Cybermen, an evil race of Cat Women, the sinister Krillitanes and maybe even a Dalek! The new series, which promises to be even scarier than the last, sees the welcome return of two of the Doctor's favourite and most iconic companions, Sarah Jane Smith (Elisabeth Sladen) and his faithful robot dog, K-9.'

Radio Times announced it would feature the year's third *Doctor Who* cover with the issue that went on sale on 3 December. Two days later, ITV announced the nominees for the annual *South Bank Show* Awards, for which *Doctor Who* was nominated in the TV Drama category and Billie Piper for the '*Times* Breakthrough Award'. The *Norwich Evening News* reported that shoppers had 'been fighting tooth and nail to get their hands on this year's must-have Christmas gifts' and quoted a retailer as saying: 'Anything related to *Doctor Who* has been really big this year, especially the remote control Daleks. We sold out but we have just had a new delivery of them and we are putting them on the shelves today and tomorrow'. The *Daily Express* also noted: 'Christmas toy shoppers could miss out due to a shortage of Daleks. Customers have been snapping up the radio-controlled *Doctor Who* models as soon as they hit stores.'

Early previews of the Christmas special were seen by various journalists. The 5 December *Daily Mirror* said: 'It clearly takes a while to get the hang of piloting the TARDIS. But a regenerated Doctor Who still looks a bit embarrassed in the flying police box after his crash-bang-wallop landing on Earth.' *Doctor Who Magazine* confirmed that the 'red button' episode – the interactive story to air on BBC digital services following the transmission of 'The Christmas Invasion' – would be produced by Sophie Fante, who told the magazine that the viewer would be able to fly the TARDIS, 'fight the Graske on the planet Griffoth' and 'hunt the Graske in Victorian London' – the latter 'an authentic Dickensian Christmas scene, complete with snow'. The magazine announced that Jimmy Vee, who had played the Moxx of Balhoon in 'The End of the World', and the 'space pig' in 'Aliens of London' the previous year, would return in the story. Also reported in the *DWM* issue were several other series two casting confirmations including Colin Spaull and Helen Griffin, who would both be in the Cybermen two-parter, and former *Crossroads* actress Freema Agyeman, who would appear in the final story of the year.

On 6 December, actress Tracy-Ann Oberman appeared on the *Richard & Judy* show and said that the *Doctor Who* production team was 'more secretive than the *EastEnders* team', noting that she would play a villain in charge of a large organisation in the forthcoming series. David Tennant was profiled in the 7 December *Independent*; asked about his accent, Tennant said, 'I'm used to doing English accents... I don't feel any great nationalistic need to be Scottish.' The *Daily Mirror* reported on a Billie Piper sighting: 'She emerged from a North London branch of Waterstones with her face hidden deep inside a fur-lined hoodie and obscured by a big pair of specs... "She looked like she was in a really bad mood," said an onlooker. "Billie obviously didn't want to be recognised. Still, what did she expect wearing such a conspicuous jacket?" Never a hood idea, love.' Manchester Online on 8 December previewed *Secret Smile*, a series that Tennant had recorded prior to the start of production on this season of *Doctor Who*: 'Fans of the Scottish thespian can catch him in action in this two-part drama based on Nicci French's novel. But, rather than play a likeable soul, the actor for once goes against type by portraying a charmer without a heart of gold.' Days later, *Media Guardian* suggested that Tennant was responsible for the ratings success of the drama. The *Guardian* opined: 'Slightly predictable, but Tennant makes a terrifically deranged villain, just in time for panto season.' 'I can't imagine many blokes, other than the supinely married, watching much beyond the first ten minutes,' said the *Scotsman*. *Sunday Life*, though, commented: 'Personally, I reckon [Tennant's] Oscar material. It surely can't be long now before Hollywood discovers yet another British leading man who, as well as having great camera presence and being particularly toothsome, is blessed with the best pair of lamps in the business.'

Tennant was interviewed on BBC Radio 4's *Front Row* on 8 December, saying that taking the role of the Doctor was: '... surprisingly difficult ... It's a show that I always loved... Suddenly you are asked to do something like this and the scale of it is quite grand.' Tennant noted that he didn't yet have a lot of recognition on the street. Childrens' magazine series *Blue Peter* featured a Dalek in studio for a 'Christmas Invasion' preview on the same day. *Broadcast* said on 9 December that the BBC's efforts to sell the new series to American networks were ongoing: 'The Corporation is thought to be holding off making a long-term sale in the hope of attracting a mainstream cable operator after the success of the first series on major Canadian broadcaster CBS [sic].' The report confirmed that BBC America remained 'keen to acquire the series' and was 'currently in discussion' with BBC Worldwide. The *Observer* interviewed Tennant on 11 December: 'I know that in *Casanova*, Russell wrote a lot of that stuff where the character's thoughts change very quickly, so you're still finishing off one thought as you catch up with the next, and he's written the Doctor in the same way,' said the actor. 'I think that's very attractive to watch in a character, when they're plucking all these extraordinary thoughts down and you have to race to catch up, kind of like *The West Wing*.' On Piper: '[Billie's] just perfect, she was so welcoming and easy to work with, and I was nervous about that, because it's nine months and a lot of stuff to do together and that relationship has really got to work... I really think she is a brilliant actress, too: in every take she's got something new, she makes it look effortless.'

The *South Wales Echo* on 12 December reported that the city of Cardiff would be hosting a new, free exhibition based on the series starting late in the month: '*Doctor Who Up Close*, based at the Red Dragon Centre in Cardiff Bay, celebrates the success of the latest series filmed in the capital with an exclusive behind-the-scenes look. The experience... links into areas such as modern story-telling, script-writing, acting, costume design, sound and music, special effects, set construction and creative thinking.' The event was scheduled to run until February but would end up continuing throughout 2006. The *Sydney Morning Herald* in Australia awarded the show's return for its first year with an 'honourable mention' in annual TV 'awards' given by their TV critics on 12 December; *Casanova* starring Tennant also won Best Imported Miniseries/Telemovie. The *Hornsey & Crouch End Journal* reported that Tennant had found time to join opposition to plans for the construction of a concrete factory; a Crouch End resident (when not in Cardiff), Tennant had joined a number of other local celebrities in the campaign. *Media Guardian* reported a 'possibility of a *Doctor Who* live show at some point in the future', according to a BBC press official.

The *Independent* said that 'the Doctor will save the world... and join the protest [against] the war in Iraq' in the Christmas special, causing an enormous controversy. 'Tony Blair may prefer to ride out Christmas Day's *Doctor Who* special by sheltering behind the No 10 sofa. For one of the highlights of the BBC's festive schedule will contain a pointed anti-war message and raise the suggestion that the Prime Minister is a poodle of the US President.' Davies said that the story 'absolutely' included an anti-war message: '... because that's what I think. It's Christmas Day. Have you read the Bible? It's a day of peace.' The US-based magazine *American Thinker* later reacted to the news by saying: 'The once-respected BBC is using a Christmas Day broadcast of a science-fiction series to bash America... And this from a government-owned broadcaster.' The latter statement was of course inaccurate: the BBC is not government-owned. *BBC News* reported: 'Christmas comes once a year, except in Cardiff, where it has already been and gone. Back in July, shoppers in the city centre found themselves walking past a giant Christmas tree, a late-night festive market and Santa lookalikes. It was as if the Welsh capital had somehow been flung into a different dimension. And in a way, it had been.' *BBC News* also reported in the same story that former Doctor Christopher Eccleston had been invited by the British Red Cross to visit the Indonesian province of Banda Aceh as part of relief efforts for the previous year's devastating tsunami. The US-based *MSNBC* network wondered what famed director Peter Jackson (*The Lord of the Rings*, *King Kong*) would do next, and offered up *Doctor Who* as a thought: 'Nobody's made a feature-length film spinoff of the series since Peter Cushing starred in two forgettable *Doctor Who* movies in the mid-1960s. Jackson would find an excellent match for his talents in *Who's* mix of slam-bang action, creepy horror and thought-provoking science-fiction.' *Irish News* reported that Billie Piper was among a list of celebrities behind a new event in aid of a Belfast-based victims support group, Art Wave.

The *Sun* reported on 15 December that 'Stephen Fry's *Doctor Who* script has been postponed', confirming with its own sources what was already suspected. 'Our TARDIS insider reveals: "Stephen's script is in its third draft and it's so ambitious that Russell T Davies decided it fitted in better with the next run. It will give the team more time to sort out all the special effects and prosthetics." Blimey.' *BBC Radio Wales* announced it would feature a new documentary in their *Back in Time* series that had run with the first season. The *Daily Telegraph* interviewed Penelope Wilton, who was soon to be seen in 'The Christmas Invasion': 'He has the most wonderful sense of humour,' said Wilton of Davies. 'So when he asked me to play Harriet Jones, MP for Flydale North, I said, certainly. Unfortunately power goes to my head a bit in this. I keep saying "Harriet Jones, Prime Minister," to which a lot of people say, "Yes, we know who you are."' The *List* magazine, a listings publication for Edinburgh and Glasgow, named David Tennant number one in its list of 'Scotland's hottest creative talent of 2005', while according to *Newsquest*, Tennant had not had any contact from predecessor Eccleston. And *Inside Housing*, of all places, featured a report about recording at the Brandon Estate in London: 'Many council tenants complain about noisy neighbours and anti-social behaviour. But they've had it easy. One south London estate has been invaded by the army and was nearly crashed into by an alien spaceship... How do you film on an estate populated by hundreds of people and not cause chaos for the tenants? Some disruption is inevitable but it can be mitigated with a little bit of help from the residents' association.' The *Daily Star* also reported that there might be a cameo appearance in the series by football star David Beckham; the tabloid claimed that Davies had said, 'I have heard Becks is a big fan of the show. Well, I'd love him to be in it. I am looking at ways we can write him into an episode.'

Then, just two weeks prior to the transmission of 'The Christmas Invasion', the *Sun* – confirming rumours that had been posted to the Outpost Gallifrey website – revealed that it was likely the new series would appear during the Easter weekend in 2006. Even with an impending holiday special, viewers were already looking forward to the events of the new year.

SOMETHING'S COMING...

The first *real* glimpse of the Christmas episode came on Friday 2 December. A BBC website exclusive was made available of a short teaser of a spinning Christmas tree and the ominous words 'Something's coming ...' The teaser was then shown regularly on BBC television throughout the following week. It was, in fact, the start of a grand parade of festivities that would culminate in the 25 December transmission of *Doctor Who's* first Christmas special. A second teaser, ten seconds of menacing Santas, was again premiered online on the official website on Friday 9 December, as was the first full trailer two days later. The latter, 50-second trailer gave viewers their first glimpse of the Sycorax spaceship and, like the two teasers, was subsequently broadcast extensively on the BBC's television channels.

With photographs appearing in major newspapers including the *Sun* and the *Daily Mirror* of renegade Santa Clauses and terrifying alien countenances – and photos of David Tennant in a dressing gown, accompanied by Billie Piper, Noel Clarke and Camille Coduri – anticipation was high. Perhaps the first real indication of the surprises in store, however, came following a 12 December press screening hosted by BBC Wales in Cardiff; a prestigious affair that brought out the series' stars, its executive producers and the news media. The reaction to the episode shown at the press conference was ebullient. Said the *Sun*, 'Killer Xmas trees, slaying Santas and a sackful of sexual chemistry – the *Doctor Who* special is the best gift fans could hope for. Best bits are the PM scrapping the Queen's Speech in an alien invasion, the Doc being revived with a cuppa, and his regenerating hand. Just don't let the evil Sycorax put you off your turkey!' *TV Zone* magazine said: 'It's hard to believe the Christmas special only lasts an hour; it manages to pack a feature film's worth of incident into its short running time, with visuals to match. There are one or two moments when the effects waver a little, but on the whole, this blockbuster TV movie is a worthy substitute for the traditional Christmas film – certainly, the sight of the Sycorax battleship looming over Nelson's column easily beats watching yet another bloody wedding in Albert Square.' *Heat* magazine gave the special five stars, while interviewing Tennant: 'I'm continually surprised by the number of trendy teenage girls and middle-aged mums who come up to talk to me and who genuinely love the show. That's what's extraordinary and unique about it. I doubt I'll ever do anything that attracts such a varied audience again.' *Star* magazine said of the adventure, 'The usual, really, with a festive seasoning of extra campery.' *Closer* magazine simply commented, 'Prepare to be enthralled.'

The *Daily Mirror* reported more of the story details, and ended on a speculative note: 'BBC bosses seem to have nailed Tennant down to a third series of the show, avoiding a repeat of Eccleston's sudden exit. Few fans will be left remembering – let alone regretting – the departure of the one series wonder. Not bad indeed.' *Media Guardian* pursued a story about Tennant's refusal to sign a few autographs at the screening: 'Last night eager fans gathered outside the screening of the *Doctor Who* Christmas special in London's Soho, hoping to get his signature. Alas, Tennant sniffily told them he was having a "no autographs" day.' But the trailer for Series Two at the conclusion of the Christmas special led much of the press coverage down another path. *BBC News* said: 'The new series will feature a brief kiss between the Doctor and Rose. "There is a lot more of that to come, but we don't like to give anything away," said Mr Davies.' The *Sunday Mail* reported Davies as saying, 'The story between the Doctor and Rose is basically a love story without the shagging. That's certainly something we will continue to explore. But it's still absolutely celibate. I think that's very important. As soon as there's nookie in the TARDIS, it would all go wrong.' *Sky News* asked, 'Who is Billie snogging? Could her next challenge with the Doc be a more lusty one, as the romantic temperature on the TARDIS gets steamy...? Will they? Won't they? Well, when it comes to a good session of tonsil-hockey, apparently they will.' Manchester Online reported that Davies had been asked at the event if he would like to make a film of the series: 'Wouldn't that be marvellous?' That response also featured in BBC Radio 1's *Newsbeat* coverage of the press screening, with an apparently bewildered David Tennant responding to questions about a possible film by saying that this was the first he'd heard of any *Doctor Who* movie. The *Ain't It Cool News* website, which the previous year had some of the very first – and some of the most negative – reviews of 'Rose', from early leaked copies of the episode, had a much more positive review in 2006: 'In the end, it's the characters and not the action set pieces that make "The Christmas Invasion" work... As a holiday special that also introduces the new Doctor, "The Christmas Invasion" is a thoroughly entertaining hour of television that will definitely whet viewer appetites for the upcoming season.' The *Manchester Evening News* said, 'Not sure what's funnier – that *Who*'s now so valued a property it gets an Xmas special or that ITV have bottled it completely and avoided scheduling any competition.'

CBBC's *Newsround* on 13 December featured the participation of 12-year-old Calum Klek, winner of the CBBC Press Packer competition, with his televised report on the press screening. 'I've just got back from the premiere screening of the Christmas episode of *Doctor Who*, "The Christmas Invasion". It was screened in London for the cast and press and, as a *Newsround* Press Packer, I got to see the Christmas special first with all the other journalists. David Tennant is the tenth Doctor Who and I got to meet and interview him! He gets regenerated in this episode and it looks as if he could be the best ever.' The official *Doctor Who* website launched a British Rocket Group spin-off website for the special, while it was also reported that digital channel BBC3 would repeat the first series from Boxing Day before screening the Christmas special on New Year's Day.

Over the following weekend, the press was booming, not just about the episode but about the forthcoming series, which was now back front-and-centre. The *Sun* reported that Roger Lloyd-Pack, soon to be seen in the two-part Cybermen adventure: '... fell down the stairs at his home in Camden, North London. The accident happened just days before Roger, 61, was due to start filming the new series of the BBC sci-fi show... so scriptwriters have made Roger's character wheelchair-bound.' The inference proved false, since the Lumic character had been written as a wheelchair user in the first place. The *Western Mail* interviewed Tennant, who commented on his forthcoming reunion with an old companion: 'Okay, [regeneration] might have been filmed in a warehouse in Newport, with special effects put in later on, but that was the first moment I thought to myself, "This is something special." And those moments keep coming every day. Just being in the TARDIS, for example. And getting to act opposite Elisabeth Sladen as Sarah Jane, a veteran *Doctor Who* sidekick who returns in the next series. I used to watch her when I was a kid, eating beans on toast and a cup of Irn Bru. She looks the same and sounds the same! It's mad, it's crazy – how unreal is this?' The *Herald* also featured comments from Tennant: 'There are moments in this series that are... well, sexual would be the wrong word, but they explore that side of things possibly more than we've seen before... You can be saving the universe and then talking about fly-fishing, but you've got to play it for the truth of the situation. You've got to believe that this guy can be talking about tangerines and then suddenly save the world.' The *Herald* also interviewed Davies, who said: 'Nobody is more excited than me about the Christmas special. I am a fiend for Christmas television.' The *Independent* commented: 'Christopher Eccleston made Saturday evenings on BBC1 a must-see again by breathing new life into an old character... and then promptly walked away. If he doesn't regret it, I certainly do. He was, quite probably, the best Doctor yet – writer Russell T Davies and Eccleston's replacement, David Tennant, will have a hard act to follow.' The *Guardian* noted, 'The consensus view was that reality television had peaked and some new hot genre would emerge in the course of the year. But what no-one predicted 12 months ago was that the story of broadcasting in 2005 would be the return of family entertainment... *Doctor Who*, *Strictly Come Dancing* and *The X Factor*.' The report went on to say that it was notable that the first two of these were 'clever reimaginings of concepts originated several decades ago.' The *Independent* on 17 December said that the following weekend's special: '... which sees skull-headed Christopher Eccleston replaced by bug-eyed David Tennant is bound to cause a stir... My guess is that *Doctor Who* will reveal that Santa Claus has been Davros disguised in a wig all along.'

In the week leading up to the special there were additional broadcasts and interviews, such as the BBC Radio 2 documentary *Regenerations*, which revealed that the first episode of the two-part Cybermen story would be called 'Rise of the Cybermen' and that the Face of Boe – last seen in the previous season's 'The End of the World' – would return in the second year. A new 50-second trailer was first seen on BBC1 on the evening of 19 December and then throughout the week up to Christmas, showing clips of Harriet Jones (Penelope Wilton) appealing to the Doctor for help via television, and of Rose telling the Sycorax to 'leave this planet in peace'. Davies was interviewed on the day's *Wales Today* programme, looking back enthusiastically on a successful year and happily predicting that children watching on Christmas Day 'will remember it when they're 70!' David Tennant appeared on BBC1's *Breakfast* on 21 December; a few clips were shown, and the actor noted that his castmate Billie Piper: '... is hanging around. Despite what you may have read in the tabloids, Billie's hanging around.' Tennant also appeared later in the week on *Friday Night with Jonathan Ross*. As well as making similar comments about Piper 'hanging around', he told the presenter: 'As long as I don't get the sack, I'll do another series. It's a bit of a gamble. The danger is that you get stuck with it, but the only other option is you don't do it. I didn't want to be that guy.' On BBC Radio 1's *Colin and Edith Show* on 23 December, Tennant mentioned the cutting of a line of dialogue about the Doctor's accent and said that the production team would be resuming recording on 3 January, working through until April and then taking a break before beginning recording Series Three in July. The same day, Camille Coduri and Noel Clarke also appeared on *GMTV* in a morning interview in which both professed their fascination that so much media attention was centred on the weekend's forthcoming special.

Indeed, the press seemed intensely interested both in the holiday special and in the full series to come in the spring. Political magazine *Prospect* on 20 December named the return of the Daleks in the previous series as one of the ten highlights of 2005: 'This is partly about nostalgia. But even new viewers respond to the strange mix of pure evil ("Exterminate!") and absurdity (creatures with silly voices who want to take over the universe but have only just learned to climb stairs and always lose).' The *Scottish Daily Record* listed David Tennant at number one on its 100 Hottest Scots chart. *The Times* asked, 'Was it the special effects that made the new *Who* so memorable, or the scripts by Russell T Davies, or the acting of Billie Piper and, in particular, Christopher Eccleston?' The *Financial Times* however, wasn't that impressed with the hype: 'A TV-deprived childhood has left me impervious to *Doctor Who*... This is kids' TV, for heaven's sake, not a breakthrough in biological ethics.' *Contact Music* reported that frontman Ricky Wilson of the band Kaiser Chiefs had claimed, tongue in cheek, that he was offered the role of the Doctor before David Tennant: 'The BBC offered it to me but I was so busy they got a lookalike.' The *Sun* wondered if '*Doctor Who* may pull in as many viewers for BBC1 tomorrow as the *Only Fools and Horses* festive shows. Bosses hope 15 million will tune in. A source said: "With Kat and Alfie's departure from *EastEnders* and *Doctor Who*, we hope to have viewers hooked to BBC1 – harking back to when *Only Fools* was watched by the entire nation."' *The Times* noted that booking agents SkyBet: '... have cut [the odds on] *EastEnders* to 2-5 (from 1-2) to be the most-watched television programme on Christmas Day. *Doctor Who*, another runner for the BBC stable, is quoted at 2-1, with *Coronation Street* being friendless at 4-1, having initially been offered at 11-8. The Queen's Speech is a 100-1 chance.' The *Scotsman* and *UTV* both reported that, for the broadcast, Tennant 'will watch his Time Lord debut after tucking into Christmas dinner with his parents, if he can escape his busy schedule.'

Perhaps the greatest accolade came when the Christmas edition of *Radio Times* was released around the start of December. As usual, this was a double issue, covering the two weeks over the Christmas and New Year period, but unusually – in fact, for the first time since 1986, when *EastEnders* was featured (In 2000, the Christmas *Radio Times* cover had also been partly given over to promoting a 'Harry Potter Day', consisting of an unabridged reading by Stephen Fry of the first *Harry Potter* novel, transmitted on BBC radio on Boxing Day) – a specific television programme was featured on the front cover, rather than a generic Christmas image. That programme was *Doctor Who*. The cover depicted a TARDIS within a festive snow globe, flanked by a snow-Dalek and a snowman wearing a long, multicoloured scarf.

On 24 December, television previewer Charlie Brooker wrote in the *Guide* section of the *Guardian* that the Christmas special was: '... the greatest Christmas episode of any programme ever... Wildly anticipated because a) *Doctor Who* was the best show of 2005 by about 16 billion parsecs and b) it's our first proper chance to see David Tennant in action. Thank God, then, that this doesn't disappoint in the slightest.' *Newsquest* wondered if the Doctor could 'help the BBC to achieve its usual Christmas Day ratings high.' The *South Wales Echo* said: 'At an exclusive preview yesterday, a small group of fans viewed the props and scenery at the exhibition. Adam Jenkins, nine, of Canton, Cardiff, who won a place at the event by entering a competition in the *Echo*, said: "It's good. You recognise everything from the television and it is really cool." Jessey Sanders, nine, of Llanrumney, Cardiff, who was with brother Zarren, ten, said: "I liked the Daleks the best." Zara May, ten, of Tremorfa, Cardiff, said: "Rose is my favourite. She is very brave."' The *Western Mail* noted: 'The stunning success of *Doctor Who* means the series has become part of the tourist campaign for Wales'. The *Scotsman* meanwhile looked back at *Doctor Who*'s previous Christmas Day episode: 'In 1965, the Doctor took time out from an epic battle with the Daleks to partake in an odd 25-minute run-around which saw him in a silent film-style encounter with the likes of Charlie Chaplin and the Keystone Kops. As if that wasn't bizarre enough, at the end of the episode the Time Lord – then in his first incarnation, played by William Hartnell – caused many a viewer to choke on their turkey by suddenly turning straight to camera and addressing the TV audience across the land. "Incidentally," he chuckled, "a happy Christmas to all of you at home!" Four decades on, and for only the second time in the programme's long history, the TARDIS is once again materialising onto our TV screens on Christmas Day.' The *Times* said simply that Tennant was: '... a damned good actor, whose fine work comes from the right blend of talent and unswerving determination. Enjoy.'

'THE CHRISTMAS INVASION'

On Christmas Day, at 7.00 pm, *Doctor Who* made its return to the screen with the broadcast of 'The Christmas Invasion'. 'It's hard to believe it is less than a year since the Beeb brought back this cult classic,' said the *Sun*. 'But the Time Lord's battle against the ugly Sycorax really was the jewel in the BBC's crown... From the moment the TARDIS hurtled out of the sky and crash landed in a council estate, you knew you were in for something special.' The paper raved: 'New Doc David Tennant has not just stepped into Christopher Eccleston's impressive shoes, he jumped into them at full pelt – not an easy feat... his comic timing was one of the best things about the Christmas special... David brings back the humour and is not as menacing as Eccleston, while Billie Piper was a real jingle-belle as she tried to stand up to the aliens. But the Christmas special is a tribute to writer Russell T Davies, who masterminded the *Doctor Who* revival and whose words crackle and spit hotter than a roast turkey dinner. If this is anything to go by, roll on the next series ...' The *Times* also had positive things to say: 'This sense of finally getting your hands on your idols, and making things go the way that you have always dreamt of, is why every episode of the new *Doctor Who* series has a moment that makes the *Doctor Who* fan simultaneously shivery and tearful. Obviously you'd have to go a long way to beat the last episode of the last series... but Christmas Day came pretty close.' The *Independent* said that 'I think even the Queen may have enjoyed the joke about the Royal Family, up on the roof of Balmoral and prepared to jump to their death after the mass hypnotism of the human race.' The *Daily Record* said, simply, 'Thank you David Tennant!'

Perhaps inevitably, not every reviewer was as complimentary. The *Belfast Telegraph* described the episode as: '... a lot of inglorious hokum, if you ask me, and high time they got rid of the police box TARDIS. No one under 60 knows what on or off Earth the thing is.' The *Scottish Herald* said that the special 'began by putting itself in danger of becoming an ultra-camp parody of itself, complete with spinning Christmas trees and zombified Father Christmases'. It added that Tennant's first real outing as the Doctor: '... got off to a shaky start. But, for a show that will always have its history weighing it down, it doesn't do badly in settling for being entertainingly dichotomous. So, we're saying it's nonsense then. Just cleverer nonsense than pretty much anything else.' The *Daily Record* reviewer found heself: '... warming to it a little bit. Maybe it's the scripts, or the rubbery monsters, or the fact that Billie Piper can act (a bit). But no, if I'm being honest, it's none of these things. It's because finally, after 30 years of bug-eyed uglies in long scarves, *Doctor Who* is hot. Yes, the famous Time Lord has finally regenerated into something us ladies can really get to grips with, and if David Tennant ever fancies taking me off to the distant galaxy of Buggerlugs 5, then I'm quite happy to hold his sonic screwdriver for him while he takes the TARDIS up to warp factor 11.'

The broadcast of 'The Christmas Invasion' concluded with a trailer featuring images from the first six episodes of the new season, including the Cat People, Pauline Collins as Queen Victoria, guest stars Anthony Head and Andrew Hayden-Smith and Elisabeth Sladen as Sarah Jane Smith alongside the robot dog K-9. While viewers could also tune into 'Attack of the Graske' on digital services – and join Tennant fighting off the villainous Graske – the official *Doctor Who* website featured an audio commentary track to accompany any re-viewings a fan would undertake of the Christmas special, with Davies and Julie Gardner and Phil Collinson commenting on the episode. The website, not unexpectedly, also offered 'Attack of the Graske' online from mid January, providing viewers with a rich source of *Doctor Who* gratification after the holidays. Canadian fans also benefited from the Christmas cheer: 'The Christmas Invasion' aired on the national CBC network on 26 December, with Billie Piper appearing in previously-recorded segments to introduce the episode and thank the viewers for making the previous series a success.

BBC News reported that while *EastEnders* had been the most watched television programme in the UK on Christmas Day, *Doctor Who* had placed an impressive second, peaking at nearly ten million viewers according to the initial overnights and managing a strong 42.7% share of the viewing audience. ITV's *Coronation Street* lost out to *Doctor Who*, something that had been considered all but impossible even a year earlier. Said a BBC1 spokesman to the *Daily Mail* on 27 December: 'We are delighted that the audience turned to the BBC to be entertained this Christmas. It has been a wonderful climax to the year for *Doctor Who*.' Changing times, indeed.

The Times said: 'Science-fiction has overtaken reality shows as space-and-time travel becomes the new hit formula on TV... Senior BBC figures were sceptical about *Doctor Who*, believing a revival would fail to reach a mass audience despite a much bigger special effects budget for the £13 million series. In fact there is a large international audience for British sci-fi. The new *Doctor Who* has been sold to 12 countries, including South Korea and Australia.' *The Times* also noted that a 'pre-Christmas mini-revival that pushed ITV1's audience above BBC1 has not stopped Britain's leading commercial broadcaster losing viewers this year, denting its prospects of pulling in advertising in tough conditions.'

Doctor Who ended 2005 on many successful notes. The *2005 TV Moments* awards, voted for online by the viewing public, saw the series win not only its category (May to June), but also the top award of Golden TV Moment of 2005 for a scene from 'The Doctor Dances'. Billie Piper accepted both awards, thanking cast, crew and viewers, with Phil Collinson and Steven Moffat also in the celebrity audience. There were several other clips from the series shown in various highlights compilations, including the first appearance of the Dalek, the climax of the series, and scenes from 'The Christmas Invasion'. There was a nomination, too, for the Tennant-starring *Secret Smile*. Also mentioned (and shown) was the interruption of the first transmission of 'Rose' by an erroneous voice-over from *Strictly Come Dancing* presenter Graham Norton, who talked briefly about the incident with the awards host, Jonathan Ross. Meanwhile, Tennant himself made a guest appearance on *The Big Fat Quiz of the Year 2005* on Channel 4 on 26 December. And the *Guardian's* 'Guide' section included reviewer Charlie Brooker's statement about the year, concluding that 'the Best Overall Show Of The Year was clearly, obviously and undeniably *Doctor* Bloody Brilliant *Who*.'

Perhaps the truest summation of the power of *Doctor Who* was in the *Northern Echo* the day after transmission of the special. '"The Christmas Invasion" was quite rightly given centre stage in the schedules by the BBC [and] contained all the elements that made the revival of the sci-fi series so successful last year. Tennant has a hard act to follow, as Christopher Eccleston made the role his own even though he only hung around for one series. The signs are that the new Doctor will be just as good.' David Tennant had made *Doctor Who* his own, it seemed, in the eyes of the press, the fans and the general viewing public; series two, four months down the line, now seemed like an eternity away.

CHAPTER SIX:
THE SECOND TIME AROUND

'The Christmas Invasion' ended 2005 in style, and 2006 was poised to cement *Doctor Who*'s success. In contrast with the uncertainty at the start of 2005, when the series was still an unknown commodity and had yet to debut, 2006 would begin with its fortunes on the rise; both a ratings and critical success, the show was now firmly part of BBC's family line-up, and by Easter, anticipation for the debut of the second series was running at a high.

ON THE MARCH

At the centre of the revival was Russell T Davies, now an established powerhouse of British television entertainment. The *Stage* honoured the executive producer at the beginning of 2006, awarding him highest position on its annual Top Ten Movers and Shakers list for the world of theatre and light entertainment: 'Hats off to Davies, the clear winner of this year's poll. The man has achieved the almost impossible and transformed *Doctor Who* for a cynical 21st Century audience and made them fall in love with it again. He wrestled Saturday nights out of the hands of Ant and Dec and revitalised family drama.' The journal went on to note that the Christmas special had 'gone down a treat' and that fans were anxiously awaiting Series Two, as well as calling Davies the head of 'the holy trinity' of British scriptwriters, alongside Paul Abbott and Jimmy McGovern. David Tennant was voted number six in the same poll, the *Stage* commenting that he'd had a 'tremendous year', culminating in *Doctor Who*'s Christmas special. 'His transformation into the tenth Time Lord has made the nation sit up, take notice and ask, "Christopher who?"' Not to be outdone, Billie Piper was voted *Doctor Who*'s sexiest assistant by the *Sun* on 29 December, with companion actresses Louise Jameson (Leela), Wendy Padbury (Zoe) and Nicola Bryant (Peri) also mentioned. The 4 January edition of *Broadcast* magazine confirmed the series' popularity in statistical terms, noting that *Doctor Who* was sixth in the chart of the UK's top-performing television series of 2005 with its 26 March broadcast of the first episode, 'Rose', while the *Guardian* on 3 January awarded the series first place in its 'favourite television series of 2005' readers' poll.

In the wake of the Christmas special, all eyes turned to the second series. 'The Doctor's enemies have their claws out for him in the new series,' said the *Daily Record* on 2 January. 'Evil Cat Women are just one of the alien races the Time Lord... and Rose... will face when the new series of *Doctor Who* starts in the spring... Writer and producer Russell T Davies said: "We can promise new thrills, new laughs, new heartbreak and some terrifying new aliens. The Doctor and Rose are destined to meet Queen Victoria, an evil race of Cat Women and the dreaded Cybermen – 2006 is going to be scarier than ever." Producer Phil Collinson added: "The villainous Cybermen are as much a part of *Doctor Who* heritage as the Daleks, so it's a huge personal thrill to see them back. I hope that the evil silver giants will terrify a whole new generation of viewers."' The *Observer* also noted that the Doctor and Rose 'go farther into the future than they've ever gone before, zip back for an appointment with Queen Victoria (Pauline Collins) and confront returning terrors the Cybermen.' As yet, however, no date had formally been announced for the start of the second series, although Easter was still hotly rumoured.

To compete, ITN suggested that the Saturday night duo Ant and Dec would front a revival of the hit 1980s game show *Bullseye*, which ITV1 would pit against *Doctor Who* in the spring (although this challenge ultimately failed to materialise). The *Sun* also reported that ITV1 would soon be transmitting the drama *Eleventh Hour* starring Patrick Stewart and written by novelist Stephen Gallagher, the channel launching a 'sci-fi offensive' against the BBC and its popular series. The story also mentioned the debut of *Primaevil*, ITV's other science fiction series, created directly as a response to *Doctor Who's* success. Even reality television would soon get a boost, it appeared, with *BBC News* reporting on 4 January that Series One star John Barrowman and classic *Doctor Who* actress Bonnie Langford were to feature as contestants on ITV's *Dancing on Ice*, to begin a few weeks later.

Everyone wanted to get in on the act. Manchester Online reported on 3 January that TV medium Derek Acorah had been cast in the series: 'I've just filmed *Doctor Who*,' he told the paper. 'It's a bit of a mickey-take. The Doctor finds that spirits and ghosts have invaded the whole of the galaxy, so he gets me along to see what we can do about it. It's only a small part, but there's a bit of fun to it.' *Doctor Who Magazine* in mid-January confirmed new guest stars including Mona Hammond and Raji James in the Cybermen episodes, as well as the return of David Warwick in a brief role; Warwick had played Kimus in the story 'The Pirate Planet' and later became the partner of Louise Jameson. Others were less successful: the *Sun* on 5 January reported that glamour model Jordan was: '... hoping to bag herself a role in the new series of *Doctor Who* as a baddie. She is hoping that she could play a killer model who kills people with her [cleavage]... Says Jordan, "I could be a baddie who doesn't speak but kills with my ample charms."' These hopes were to remain unfulfilled.

January would see a number of developments, including the 18 January revelation that there would be a new 'children's magazine-style programme, specifically related to *Doctor Who* and aimed at older children', later to be confirmed as *Totally Doctor Who*; the availability the same day of the BBC digital episode 'Attack of the Graske' on the official BBC website, in another test of their broadband services aimed solely at UK viewers; and a welcome gift for *Doctor Who* fans in the country hosting the largest potential audience outside the UK...

THE AMERICAN FRONT

Doctor Who had enjoyed critical and demographic success in four of the five English-speaking countries that had comprised the bulk of its fan awareness throughout 2005 – the United Kingdom, Canada, Australia and New Zealand – but one country had remained unrepresented, as broadcasters in the United States had been unable to work out a deal to show the first series. While many fans had been able to watch the series through less-than-official means (swapping tapes and DVDs with friends in the UK, as well as more dubious file-sharing activities online), the likelihood of a formal US transmission seemed increasingly distant, especially when BBC Video announced that it would release the series in North America on DVD on 14 February. While it had never been formally stated as such, unofficial statements from representatives at BBC America had made it clear that there had previously been a policy not to release the series on DVD prior to a television broadcast. The fact that a DVD release was now to go ahead was seen by some as a tacit admission that BBC America had given up on securing a broadcast deal altogether.

This situation was soon to change, however. As the planned release date for the DVDs approached, eagle-eyed fans began to notice that there was no information about them on the Warner Home Video distributor site – Warner being the series' US licensed DVD distributor. Then, on 11 January, both the Outpost Gallifrey and TV Shows on DVD websites reported that, according to their individual sources, the US DVD release had been cancelled, although the Canadian release was apparently still going forward. TV Shows on DVD noted that according to a BBC public relations representative, there were 'complications' with the set that prevented the US release.

The answer came the next day. On 12 January, the official *Doctor Who* website announced that the American science fiction network Sci Fi had picked up the series for broadcast starting in March, the week after the season finalés of its current original programming, *Battlestar Galactica*, *Stargate SG-1* and *Stargate Atlantis*. The press release issued by Sci Fi noted that the channel had been granted first-run rights for the first series, with an option for Series Two (which it would later execute, to broadcast the second series towards the end of the year). 'The Doctor's made all sorts of journeys in time and space, but this is one of his most exciting yet!,' said Davies in the release. 'I'm a huge fan of the Sci Fi Channel, and I'm delighted that *Doctor Who* is appearing on a channel that supports and enhances the entire genre.' Julie Gardner also noted how it: '... just really felt like the right people [to air the show]. They really did get it. They were happy with how British it is, they really liked the humour. They really, really got it. And that was the most important thing.' Sci Fi subsequently announced its schedule on 30 January, confirming that the first episode, 'Rose', would air on Friday 17 March 2006.

Reactions on the Internet from *Doctor Who* fans in America were very positive. *TV Guide* columnist Matt Roush wrote of the acquisition, 'I'll be honest. I'm far from a *Doctor Who* expert or even a fan. The few times I ever tried watching the earlier incarnations of the show on PBS or wherever, I was underwhelmed. But I doubt I gave it much of a chance. Now that I'm more invested in the genre, especially since *Farscape* rekindled my passion for space fantasy and *Battlestar Galactica* confirmed it, I'll approach this series with an open mind. It certainly seems to be arriving with a fair amount of buzz and hype, so I can't imagine why this wouldn't work to Sci Fi's advantage.'

In conjunction with the announcement, the press release also mentioned the delay of the US DVD release of the first season, rescheduled later for release on 4 July 2006 to follow the final broadcast of the show's first series. Late the following month, a promotional trailer appeared on the network, featuring the words 'Who Is ...' then showing clips from the series and culminating in the phrase ... coming in March.' The channel also announced at this time that it would double-bill the first two episodes of the series, with 'Rose' and 'The End of the World' airing together on 17 March instead of the first episode alone. In addition, it launched a mini-site about the series with an accompanying chat forum. A new, 30-second trailer was then shown on the channel in mid-March. Noting that the Doctor was 'over 900 years old' and was 'a legendary adventurer through space and time', the trailer went on to say that his 'limitless power fuels an endless quest for... the perfect vacation. The British smash hit comes to Sci-Fi.'

Meanwhile, after a few false starts and confusing signs, Canada would still see its 14 February DVD release – good news for Canadian fans of the series, but quite surprising considering that the standardisation of DVD format between the two countries would allow anyone who wanted to buy it early to purchase from cross-border vendors such as Amazon.com. Still up in the air at the time was the status of American broadcasts of the classic *Doctor Who* series, which had been stalled for nearly a year and a half while BBC Worldwide had attempted to sell the series as a package deal, the original and the new, to broadcasters. Fans in Canada, meanwhile, were told by *TV Guide* Magazine that the next season would hit their airwaves in 'fall 2006'.

RETURN TO PRODUCTION

Production on the second series of *Doctor Who* restarted after its Christmas break on 3 January, with work continuing on block three, comprising the four Cyberman themed episodes. While much of the first week consisted of studio recording, Cardiff location work would soon be seen by fans and the press as the production team took to the streets the following weekend, with Tennant and Piper joined by Shaun Dingwall (Pete Tyler). Recording in Mount Stuart Square on Saturday 7 January was watched by fans such as Paul Mount, who reported seeing: 'A built-up area of civic buildings and businesses. Filming at one end of the road. Extras dressed as soldiers. The basic scene being rehearsed and filmed this morning was a street scene – business people, shoppers, people milling about. The Doctor and Rose are walking amongst them – in full costume (Billie in a red/pink top and black trousers, the Doc in full regalia). Suddenly everyone stops still – apart from the Doctor and Rose. Our heroes wander around them, trying to get some response. Rose's mobile starts to download information – weather reports, lottery numbers, etc. The Doctor examines it, mentions something about it being a product of "Cyber-technology" and then tosses the phone casually back at her. They walk off.' John Campbell Rees wrote on Outpost Gallifrey, 'Basically it was a street scene with about a dozen extras, filmed old style with multiple cameras. One camera was mounted on a boom and followed one man, in a long brown coat, who was sitting on a bench. He appears to read a text on his mobile, and he gets up and crosses the road. The camera on the boom tracks him, and when he hit a mark, the cue was given and everyone in the scene stopped and stood still as a statue. They were all wearing Cybus Corporation headsets in both ears, all with flashing blue LEDs. After a few seconds, another cue was given, and all the extras turned to face the same direction, and then on a third cue, they all marched out of shot.'

'The crew set up another shot further up the road round the corner,' contributed David Shaw, 'and between takes David and Billie put on padded coats and drank cups of coffee, to escape the bitter cold weather. The second shot lasted only a few seconds; it was rehearsed and recorded a few times and involved a crowd of extras: some of the soldiers, policemen and many in contemporary dress. I recognised Graeme Harper, the director, and everyone seemed to be in good spirits. A separate camera was filming for *Confidential* and someone was interviewing Harper... In the alleyway with us was a crew member, and you can imagine our surprise when Russell T Davies ran into the alley (he had just arrived). He had a few pleasant words with the guy from the crew and then I was able to shake his hand and congratulate him on the return of *Doctor Who*. My daughter told him she'd enjoyed "The Christmas Invasion" and he asked if she likes the Sycorax (yes, she does). He was really kind and it was wonderful to chat with the man who's brought back our favourite show.'

Location work was also spotted throughout much of the following week. 'Womanby Street in Cardiff, behind the Gatekeeper public house, is currently being dressed for filming,' wrote Rees about production on 11 January. 'Lots of Cybus Corporation signs around, so it looks like it is still the Cybermen story.' Wrote Ian Golden on 12 January, 'They were filming a scene from the Cybermen two parter. David Tennant, Billie Piper and Shaun Dingwall were all present and very involved. The action contained four Cybermen stomping out from a passageway attacking the trio mentioned plus one unknown guest star, then a shot was filmed with the four all running away. Finally, more Cybermen walking shots were filmed. All this plus set up took around four hours... During a break in filming, I walked up to David Tennant and said, "There's a five-year old boy over there who would love to meet the Doctor, and if the Doctor has a minute, would he be able to come over?" David was delighted to. He asked [the boy] if he'd watched the Christmas special and even held Sam for a photo.' Simon Watkins watched the recording on 14 January: 'We were lucky enough to clearly view the last two shots of the day, which had the Cybermen marching around. The final shot had four Cybermen marching from halfway down Womanby Street near Wetherspoon's right up to the corner near The City Arms, and was completed with one take... Up close the Cybermen were very impressive. The Cyber suits seemed to be quite flexible, latexy rather than metallic, but still quite shiny when lit correctly. They made a heck of a noise when they were stomping down the street.'

icWales on 14 January said, 'Drinkers would have been forgiven for spilling their pints when they saw a troop of Cybermen marching outside a pub. But the only thing the streets of Cardiff were under attack from was a film crew... Fans looking through the windows of The Gatekeeper yesterday evening were able to see all the action taking place on Womanby Street, parts of which were closed off to the public... The metal robots, which have caused countless children to hide behind sofas, didn't seem quite so scary when the actors playing them were seen in anoraks.' Two days later, the same news service reported that the production team was about to return to the Millennium Stadium, where they had recorded 'Dalek' the previous season. 'There were members of the production team taking pictures and having a look around,' an onlooker told icWales. 'They were hoping to film at the stadium when there was a game on, [but] they decided it was too much hassle and now they're just looking at using it. They wanted the Doctor to be running up and down stairs and filming in the BBC commentary box.' Meanwhile, the *Sun* claimed a photo exclusive from the recent production, with a photograph headlined 'Cyber binmen' showing a large colour shot of two of the Cybermen from behind, approaching two large wheeled waste bins. 'Our exclusive picture shows the sinister silver robots coming face to face with a couple of wheelie bins,' reported the paper. The *South Wales Echo* also reported happenings on the set, noting: 'A young fan was starstruck when he came face to face with his hero – and a few villains. Sam Hill, five, was with parents Andy and Melanie watching the new *Doctor Who* series being filmed. And when there was a break in the action, which saw Cybermen marching up Womanby Street, he had the chance to meet David Tennant... [Tennant] picked Sam up and posed for a picture, asking if he'd seen the Christmas special. Sam was so thrilled and carried the picture around with him all day.'

JANUARY IN THE PRESS

While production on the series continued at full speed, the media were still looking back to the recent airing of 'The Christmas Invasion'. *Newsquest Media* on 4 January discussed the recording of the episode at Clearwell Caves in the Forest of Dean. 'The location was chosen because the programme's designer Edward Thomas remembered filming a horror film [entitled] *Grim* at Clearwell, in 1995, and he decided that the caves were capable for the transformation to enable the Doctor to fight the evil Sycorax. The caves remained open to the public while the set was being prepared and filled with glowing eggs and tortured aliens along with a host of other special effects.' The right-wing magazine the *Spectator* in its January issue, meanwhile, had choice words about the Christmas episode, saying – perhaps somewhat tongue in cheek – that it showed: '... worryingly peacenik tendencies... Our wussie new Doctor was outraged by this underhand behaviour, but it seems to me that the Prime Minister was only doing her job. What guarantee had these hissing, slimy, alien creatures provided that they would never try to conquer Earth again? None at all. I hope the nation's kiddies were sensible enough to see through Davies's dangerous pacifist propaganda.'

Billie Piper's future in *Doctor Who* was again the subject of press attention as 2006 began. The actress was reported to have landed a prime role as Sally Lockhart in a BBC adaptation of author Philip Pullman's popular trilogy of novels (*The Ruby in the Smoke*, *The Shadow in the*

North, The Tiger in the Well), and there was some speculation that this might mean that she had already left *Doctor Who*. The *Daily Express* on 8 January said: 'Billie's success will further fuel speculation that she is about to quit *Doctor Who*... Billie will start work on the first Sally Lockhart story – *The Ruby In The Smoke* – in May. "The Sally Lockhart episode is being shot in between Series Two and Three of *Doctor Who*, so it doesn't mean Billie couldn't shoot Series Three," a BBC spokeswoman said.' The *Express* did note, however, that other television 'insiders' thought it unlikely that Piper would return to *Doctor Who*, quoting an unidentified drama producer: 'She has made a terrific impression in *Doctor Who*, and for a young relatively inexperienced actress to hold her own against Christopher Eccleston [in Series One] was no mean feat.' The *Daily Record* on 3 January featured astrological predictions for various celebrities including Piper, saying: 'We all know she isn't going to be the Doctor's assistant for much longer... She may return to music or a project she shelved to take up the role of Rose in *Doctor Who*. But one thing is sure. She will have to give her choices some thought, as illusion is all around her working life.'

The Times the next day argued for Piper to be viewers' pick for the forthcoming *Times/South Bank Show* Breakthrough Award, saying: 'Much of the series' success has to be credited to Piper. She confidently held her own against Christopher Eccleston's showboating, and by being everything from petrified to spunky to heartbroken, she has succeeded in making Rose every bit as central to the show as the Doctor himself.' Piper guest hosted Channel 4's *The Friday Night Project* on 6 January, while *CBBC Newsround* looked at the year's 'rising stars', including Piper's co-star David Tennant: 'His performance on Christmas Day suggests he's going to be a quirky but lovable Doctor, and a *huge* heart-throb.' *Doctor Who Magazine* artist Mike Collins was interviewed by icWales about his work on the magazine's comic strip to capture Tennant's likeness: 'I had just got to the stage when I could draw Christopher Eccleston quite comfortably,' Collins said. 'David Tennant has a great face, and I had to get it right as he is a big fan and is going to read it.' *Toy News* for January 2006 put *Doctor Who* on its cover, focusing on the Character Options company and its new licensed toy products for the series, including action figures of the new Doctor and Rose. The official *Doctor Who* website interviewed Murray Gold about the song used at the end of 'The Christmas Invasion': 'It's called "Song for Ten" in honour of David Tennant being Doctor Ten. James Hawes mentioned in passing, while I was writing the score for "The Christmas Invasion", that he might need a song or two... If you think it does have a Phil Spector way about it, I'm happy, because I adore him.'

Radio Times for the week starting 14 January interviewed John Barrowman about his forthcoming appearance in ITV1's *Dancing on Ice* and asked Davies about the Sycorax language from 'The Christmas Invasion'. 'Sycoraxic was completely invented,' said Davies. 'I just made it up! But I did try to give it some logic, so that the same word always meant the same thing: "Soo chack chiff!" means "You're going to die!", which tends to get said a lot in *Doctor Who*.' The Dark Horizons media website interviewed Sophia Myles on her appearance in *Doctor Who* later in the year: 'It was fantastic, I did one episode... When you get asked to do *Doctor Who* it is a bit like being called to jury service – you can't really say no. I mean, it runs through the veins of the British public and it *is Doctor Who*.' The issue of *TV Zone* magazine out that week interviewed Davies about the unprecedented success of the show: 'Who'd have thought, this time last year... it's just inconceivable. You've seen BBC launches; you don't get the Controller of BBC1, you don't get the Controller of Drama standing up and giving a speech at the beginning. It's quite extraordinary; that's how much they're behind it.' The *Daily Snack* reported: 'Billie Piper has revealed how she got a real beast of a Christmas surprise when a friend gave her two cows. Billie... sneaks off to visit the pair in between filming for the smash hit show. The 23-year-old blonde fell in love with the heifers, so they are stopping at a friend's farm instead of heading to the slaughterhouse.'

On 16 January, bbc.co.uk reported that *Doctor Who* had won its online drama 'Best of 2005' survey, with a staggering 56 per cent of the vote; Christopher Eccleston had featured first in the Best Actor category on the site, while Billie Piper achieved the same feat for Best Actress. icWales reported on a charity auction at the Fusion Restaurant in Cardiff, the prize for which would be to spend the day on the *Doctor Who* set. *NewsWales* noted that more than 30,000 visitors had passed through the doors to the free *Doctor Who* exhibition at Red Dragon Centre. The 17 January *Daily Star* said that Billie Piper was: '... the ultimate comeback kid. Just three years ago, beautiful Billie was more likely to be found propping up the bar of her local pub with husband Chris Evans than in a TV studio. But today entertainment bosses are fighting over the gorgeous blonde thanks to her outstanding performance as Doctor Who's sexy sidekick Rose.' The *Guardian* reported that Tennant would soon be seen in a BBC4 drama about Lady Chatterley. Meanwhile, according to *EntertainmentWise*, Tennant had been ordained 'sexiest man in the universe' by gay voters: 'Tennant was gob-smacked to receive the *Pink Paper* Awards accolade and commented: "I'm surprised to be thought of like that. Casanova is the only role I've played where you had to look good. But that particular Casanova didn't have to be an Adonis. He was more of a cheeky chappie."' One of Tennant's predecessors, meanwhile, was sold on the new series, according to the *Daily Express*: 'Colin Baker, who had the keys to the TARDIS for two years from 1984, is full of praise for the show's latest incarnation and current Doctor David Tennant... and can't understand why people hark back to earlier shows. "I have been astounded when [some] diehard fans have expressed a preference for the old series," he says. "It's hard to imagine how the [new] series could be bettered."' A week later, Baker had more to say on the subject, in his regular column in the *Bucks Free Press*: 'If you had told me a couple of years ago that the flagship programme on Christmas Day might one day be *Doctor Who*, I would have suggested that you seek specialist medical help immediately. But building on the excellent series transmitted last year, the special festive episode introducing David Tennant as Doctor number ten was the undoubted success amongst what was a predominantly lacklustre batch of offerings this holiday. In fact, it was the only programme that tempted the Baker family away from the delights of enjoying each other's company.'

Doctor Who picked up a nomination for best drama series at the Celtic Film and Television Festival Awards according to *Broadcast Now* on 19 January. *BBC News* also reported that the staff of a South Wales brewery: '... had to make sure they had not been transported to another dimension when the cast of *Doctor Who* turned up for filming. Billie Piper, who plays the Doctor's assistant Rose Tyler, 50 extras and the... crew spent the day at Magor Brewery, near Newport, to shoot scenes. The production of thousands of bottles of lager was halted while filming took place in two areas of the site. Brewery bosses said they were asked to help when another location cancelled.' The *Financial Times* looked back on the Christmas special, noting: 'For one delicious moment... I actually thought the new Time Lord on the block was going to emerge as a kind of Austin Powers-meets-Pete Doherty Doctor... The new hero was shown rifling through a rack of clothes, consciously deciding what kind of profile he wished to present to the world. This is when the promise of a 1960s-style rocking Doctor was tantalisingly hinted at. Tennant fingered a regimental military Sergeant Pepper-style jacket, as worn by Doherty in the Libertines, and by Mick Jagger and the Fab Four before him. I reckon he'd have looked great in it, possessed as he is of a cheeky McCartneyesque physiognomy and mod-style fringe.'

Billie Piper was honoured on 28 January at the *South Bank Show* Awards: '... an awards ceremony for her successful breakthrough into an acting career. Piper... impressed audiences with her portrayal of Rose, the Doctor's sidekick... Daniel Radcliffe, the star of the Harry Potter movies, handed Piper her prize – *The Times* Breakthrough Award.' Piper told *The Times* that she was dedicated to acting. 'I care so much more about acting than I do for music. I'm having the time of my life at the moment and this [prize] just makes it even better.' The series itself won Best Drama Series or Serial at the 2006 Broadcast Awards sponsored by *BroadcastNow*, announced the same day. Maureen Lipman herself confirmed rumours that she would appear in *Doctor Who* this season in her column in the *Guardian* on 28 January: 'I did six hours as an alien on *Doctor Who*. This will probably earn me my entire year's worth of street cred. We filmed it at the old studio in Alexandra Palace, in north London. It was very cold and the wind blew up my evening dress and rattled my pearls.' The *Daily Star* mentioned that Tennant and Piper had been seen quite often together, and remarked on: '... just how friendly they've become during a break from filming the hit sci-fi show in Cardiff. Gorgeous Billie, 23, gazed adoringly at David, 34, before they tenderly hugged each other. And he kept a close eye on the babe, who plays the Time Lord's assistant Rose Tyler, as she burst into a fit of the giggles.'

The 29 January *Sun* said that Tennant was: '... joining a starry line-up for a cartoon flick by *Shaun of the Dead*'s Simon Pegg. David, 34, will voice Hamish in *Free Jimmy*.' *The Times* claimed that the paparazzi were everywhere, mentioning: 'The highest single-value picture we've sold so far was of the new *Doctor Who* monster, Sycorax. A *Doctor Who* fan was watching the filming in June in the Forest of Dean, and this monster came out of the dressing-room trailer, so he took a photograph of it. Then the security men came out and said, "no pictures" and closed the set down. We got the picture and sat on it.' And the *Daily Express*, asking 'Is the bloke making a comeback?' opined, 'Who brought *Doctor Who* into the 21st Century? Christopher Eccleston, rough and rough-spoken, a world away from the cut-glass William Hartnells and Patrick Troughtons, time travellers when time travel was more genteel.'

DEVELOPMENTS BEHIND THE SCENES

Doctor Who Magazine released at the very end of January revealed that James Strong, whose previous directing credits included BBC1's *Rocket Man* and episodes of *Casualty* and *Holby City*, would direct two episodes of the fifth recording block ('The Impossible Planet' and 'The Satan Pit'), and that the guest cast for block four ('Fear Me' and 'The Idiot's Lantern') would include long-time television character actress Edna Doré and *Teachers*' Nina Sosanya. The cameo appearance by TV psychic Derek Acorah was also mentioned. As the magazine had gone to press, block three (the four Cybermen episodes) had been nearing completion, and Phil Collinson confirmed that one episode of the series – comprising a single-episode block six – would be 'double-banked', i.e. shot concurrently, with the fifth; this was later realised to be 'Love & Monsters', which worked around the schedules of the leads by simply recording much of its action without them. Star David Tennant, it was announced, had also agreed to do readings for CD releases of three BBC Books *Doctor Who* novels, *The Stone Rose*, *The Resurrection Casket* and *The Feast of the Drowned*, for release in May.

The *Radio Times* Covers Party, an annual celebration of the magazine's cover stars over the previous year, was held at the Savoy on 1 February. Hosted by television presenter Graham Norton, the party's guests included Stephen Fry, Ricky Gervais, Sir Bob Geldof, Dame Vera Lynn, Charles Dance and Dame Helen Mirren, as well as many *Doctor Who* personalities. With *Doctor Who* having had such a strong presence in the magazine over the previous year, it was no great surprise to find that Tennant, Piper and Davies were all in attendance... though Tennant appeared on stage to collect a *Casanova* framed cover. As Davies went to collect his cover, the lights dimmed and a Dalek – a genuine BBC model voiced by series actor Nicholas Briggs – appeared from the wings, crossed the floor and threatened him. A later issue of *Radio Times* featured photos from the event, with Helen Mirren, pictured with a Dalek, commenting 'I just had to be photographed with it,' and Anna Maxwell-Martin (who had played Suki in 'The Long Game' the previous season) appearing alongside Tennant and Piper. Piper spoke briefly to the magazine, saying, 'I honestly don't think my career will get any more exciting. [*Doctor Who* has] done the most amazing things for me both personally and professionally.'

While British fans were informed by *Radio Times* that 'The Christmas Invasion' was soon to see a BBC3 repeat, Australian fans were wondering when they'd get their first chance to see the special and the subsequent series. On 7 February, Australia's ABC Network confirmed via e-mails sent to enquiring fans: 'The ABC has secured the rights to broadcast the second series of the (new) *Doctor Who* and "The Christmas Invasion". A broadcast date has not been set. Please check your local television guide on a regular basis for scheduling information.'

Mid-month, there were more casting updates; the *Daily Mirror* reported on 13 February that, according to an 'insider', UK television chat show icon Trisha Goddard would appear in an episode entitled 'I'm In Love With A Ghost'. 'Television chat queen Trisha Goddard is to star in *Doctor Who*... as herself. The Time Lord, played by David Tennant, will discover that Earth is overrun by ghosts in the new series before stumbling upon Trisha's show... Trisha asks, "Can you trust him if he's always appearing and disappearing?" It's hilarious.' In fact, Goddard had already taped her appearance, which was simply a cameo hosting her chat show, which the Doctor watches on television in 'Army of Ghosts'. The official *Doctor Who* website also had a piece of casting news, announcing on 23 February that Will Thorp, 'best known for his role as heroic paramedic Woody in *Casualty*, will play Toby in two-parter "The Satan Pit."' Explaining why Thorp was chosen for the part, Davies told the site: 'This two-parter is just about as tense and scary as *Doctor Who* can get, so we needed a stellar cast to grip the audience. Will's proved his popularity with audiences... but if he thought Holby General was dangerous, then we can guarantee that we're about to throw him into some truly terrifying situations.'

Another issue of *Doctor Who Magazine* – accidentally sent to subscribers over a week before its official release date – confirmed much of the cast of 'The Idiot's Lantern' and announced that Dan Zeff, who had previously worked on *Linda Green* with Phil Collinson, would direct the tenth episode. In addition to announcing the official title of episode six, 'The Age of Steel', the issue also noted that April was now the 'most likely start date' for Series Two to debut, and that it would be accompanied by 'dozens' of fictional tie-in websites, according to BBC *Doctor Who* website producer James Goss: '[It's] not an enormous in-joke for fans – it's a game. Each week you've got a mission. Perhaps it's Mickey needing help after he's accidentally switched off the Earth's satellite defence system ...' The magazine also announced that mobile phone users would soon be able to download 'exclusive additional content' before each episode aired. Vortext – the project's working title – would feature scripts by Gareth Roberts, and contain 'exclusive footage, state-of-the-art special effects and new material directly linked to the following episode'. Davies revealed in the magazine that this new material was 'being shot alongside the regular crew' for each episode, while Roberts said that these would be 'proper, full-on productions', made by the team responsible for the BBC digital programme 'Attack of the Graske'. The Vortext title, however, would soon be changed to TARDISode. These mini-episodes would be promoted widely during the Series Two broadcasts.

Late in the month, the *Sun* reported: 'Doctor Who is to land in *EastEnders* – and be served pints in the Queen Vic by Peggy Mitchell.' The 24 February article stated: 'Landlady Peggy – 68-year-old actress Barbara Windsor – will pop up behind the bar, while other *EastEnders* stars could also appear.' The *Sun's* source said that Windsor was: '... thrilled. She's a very big fan of *Doctor Who* and feels very honoured.' However, unlike the *Doctor Who/EastEnders* 'crossover' in the 1993 *Children in Need* special 'Dimensions in Time', this would turn out to be – like Trisha Goddard's cameo in the same episode, 'Army of Ghosts' – merely a cameo, with the Doctor viewing a short, specially-recorded *EastEnders* segment on television, with no actual interaction. The *Sun* on 26 February followed up on the report that Nina Sosanya – who had appeared with Tennant in *Casanova* – was soon to be seen in the show, playing 'the mother of a key character', also mentioning the casting of Will Thorp in the mid-season two-parter and Jamie Foreman in 'The Idiot's Lantern'.

THROUGH THE IDIOT'S LOOKING GLASS

In early February, *Doctor Who* fans had another opportunity to watch the recording of an episode of the series, as the production team moved back out onto the streets of Cardiff for 'The Idiot's Lantern'. While the BBC had never made public any of their plans for recording, eagle-eyed fans and the paparazzi were always on the look-out for signs of production; usually it was a case of putting disparate clues together and figuring out where the crew would next turn up. On 7 February, one of those fans, Emma Sandrey, spotted the signs: 'So I arrived about 12-ish. A few of the girls from the Cardiff Uni HP society... said they had earlier filmed scenes where the Doctor aka David Tennant was riding a moped into the TARDIS. Thrilling stuff. The security guys were for the most part very helpful and even gave us guidance on where to stand so that we could see stuff but also be out of the shot and out of the way. Florentia Street was decorated with loads of Union Jack flags. Rose aka Billie Piper was wearing a bright pink skirt and what looked like a blue denim top and the Doctor was in his usual suit [but] with a '50s hairstyle... We mainly saw three scenes. One [was] where someone was being pushed into an old fashioned Rolls Royce. Another was of the Doctor and Rose making what looked like a getaway on the aforementioned moped. The rehearsal of this was particularly funny, because it was sans moped, so Billie kind of jumped onto David's back.'

The same day, John Campbell Rees noted: '... the props van out of shot on Gower Street, and the anachronistic recycling bags hidden from shot. The HP Sauce poster and the George VI postbox are props for the series. All the modern streetlighting had Union Flags hung on [it] to disguise the modern lamps. The whole of the street was decked out with red, white and blue bunting, and... the factory at the end of the street (whose car park was being used as the temporary base for filming) had a patriotic mural chalked on its side... The first thing I saw after arriving on Tuesday was Billie Piper in a huge, fluffy pink circular skirt with layers of petticoats, a blue denim top and a pink ribbon in her hair. David Tennant was sitting on a Vespa scooter, wearing a white crash helmet. Just to show that he was getting into the spirit of the era they were visiting, when the helmet was removed, it revealed that the Doctor will be sporting a teddy boy style DA hairstyle in this episode. Earlier, scenes of the Doctor riding the Vespa out of the TARDIS against a green background stapled to the interior of the prop had been filmed. Once Euros Lyn, the director, was satisfied with the shot of Rose taking a pink crash helmet from the Doctor, climbing onto the back of the Vespa and riding off, the action moved further up Florentia Street. A long segment, [lasting] roughly two and a half minutes, ... was then rehearsed, in which, having parked the scooter,... Rose and the Doctor [walk] along the [street] and [talk] to the locals... Despite the fact that David Tennant reportedly had lessons last week, most of the long shots of Rose and the Doctor aboard the Vespa were done with stunt doubles.'

Recording continued the following day. 'The sunshine was deceptive, as it was bitterly cold all afternoon,' wrote Rees on 8 February. 'The extras were all dressed for a summer's day in the 1950s, so were visibly shivering between takes, and they would quickly don thick, padded coats to keep warm. The door of 44 Florentia Street has a modern white uPVC plastic door. In later scenes, ... this was covered by a more authentic-looking fake red wooden door. On the road is a coating of gravel to hide the contemporary road markings. This was regularly damped down to prevent it slipping and to help it blend in with the existing tarmac surface of the road. To help the actors get into the party mood, Lonnie Donegan's hit "Rock Island Line" was played over the loudspeakers during takes.' Meanwhile, Emma Sandrey reported, 'David Tennant was filming a scene... It involved the Doctor talking to a man while a couple of kids ran up and down the street. I should mention that the road had tables lined down it, obviously set up for a street party. They suddenly stopped and the Doctor looked forward (in our direction) and shouted "Run!" while bolting down the street, right at us... Several other scenes were rehearsed/filmed during the day. The next featured a man sat at one of the tables in the road while the same couple of kids played in the background. They were then called inside by... I assume... their parents. This scene was repeated about four times, during which a black Rolls Royce drove past ominously in the background.' Paul Robinson was also watching the recording: 'The scene was a street party with Rose and the Doctor walking up the table, the Doctor grabbing cakes and eating them along the way. A boy of about 12 stood between them for a couple of lines before Billie patted him on the shoulder and he went off to join the dancing. The Doctor picked up two glasses of orangeade, gave one to Rose, they clinked them in a toast and that was it!' Later in the evening, said Rees: 'The final thing to be recorded at the end of the week's [work] at this location was what appeared to be a night-time establishing shot, showing what is meant to be Florizel Street in Muswell Hill, North London on a dark, rainy night. This involved a camera on a crane, and a curious rig with six sprinklers on an arm suspended 50 feet above street level pumping out gallons and gallons of water to the ground below. Only in show business is it necessary to fake rain in a city that receives between 75 and 80 inches of the stuff naturally throughout the year.'

'Today's filming was in Pen-y-Lan, Cardiff, on the corner of Kimberley Road and Blenheim Road (which seemed to have been renamed Mafeking Terrace and Ladysmith Road respectively)', noted Philip Dore on Friday 10 February. 'It all seemed to revolve around a 1950s electrical shop entitled Magpie Electricals, with people leaving the shop and getting into a charabanc-style van.' Emma Sandrey expanded on this: '... and on the corner there was an old-fashioned shop set up, called Magpie's, selling radios and TVs. The scene first filmed involved Tommy [the boy seen coming out of the TARDIS with the Doctor on a previous day] and the Doctor talking outside of the shop and then going in. Sounds fairly ordinary, but the dialogue, and more importantly the delivery of it by David Tennant was, to quote [Eccleston], fantastic... This was done about five times. Julie Gardner arrived on set during one of the last takes and began talking with David. Another short sequence was filmed by the shop involving a man in a trench coat exiting the shop, smiling. No idea what that was about. That was done about four times. Then, while the crew were setting up for a different shot, a class from a local primary school arrived. It was pretty funny seeing David Tennant being mobbed by a bunch of eight year olds. The kids were even asking for autographs from the crew, some of whom wound the kids up by pointing to random people and saying "He's famous!"'

On 10 February, icWales reported: 'Residents of a city street were faced with a blast from the past when they opened their curtains to see *Doctor Who* being filmed outside. Florentia Street, in Cathays, Cardiff, has been decked out with bunting and turned into a scene from the 1950s. Vintage cars were parked on the street and on a wall was an old advert for HP Sauce. Curious passers-by were amazed to see the television series stars Billie Piper and David Tennant, and the TARDIS itself made an appearance. Evan Chapman, 39, of nearby Tewkesbury Street, who works at the National Museum and Gallery, said: "I didn't know what was happening so I came down for a look. I'm surprised to see all the bunting; I'd presumed the road was closed for the gas board. It will be curious to see the area on television."'

Two days later, the same press agency reported: 'Pupils from Marlborough Junior School couldn't contain their excitement when they saw actor David Tennant filming scenes for the TV series near their school in Penylan, Cardiff. Deputy head teacher Robert Cook, who brought the group to watch, said: "Lots of the children are big fans. Ever since they found out it was being filmed here, they've been unable to talk about anything else."' Both articles noted that Florentia Street had been retitled Florizel Street, which knowledgeable fans noted was the original working title for the long-running soap *Coronation Street* – a fact also picked up by the *Western Mail* on 12 February. 'It was the original name for *Coronation Street*, but was rejected for sounding too much like a disinfectant. Now, 46 years later, Florizel Street will finally make an appearance on our screens as the setting for an episode of *Doctor Who*. In a nod to the classic ITV soap, Welsh writer Russell T Davies, who briefly worked as a storyliner on *Coronation Street*, changed the name of Cardiff's Florentia Street for filming the new time-travelling series... Arrangements were made for diversions around the newly-christened street and nearby Monthermer Road to avoid catching modern cars in shot, while all traffic in the area was made to stop for a minute at a time to avoid the sound or sight of modern vehicles. Local residents received scant warning that they were about to be taken back in time.'

Recording of 'The Idiot's Lantern' then moved indoors for a few days, returning to Florentia Street on 16 February. 'It was dark, but not so cold as the previous week's shoot for the same episode,' wrote Timothy Farr. 'The presence of a large crane light shining down into the street alongside the supermarket gave away the exact location. In many of the earlier Florentia Street location photographs there can be seen a large board with a pale blue background depicting a textless illustration of children playing in bright colours. It's an advertisement for Spangles, a popular confection last century. This wall is part of a street that forms a T-junction with the southern end of Florentia Street. This was where the day's filming was taking place. The Spangles ad had been removed. The camera was near the back wall of the western arm of the T-junction, pointing east. A large, dark green period lorry with words something like B D Casey & Sons was parked at an angle across most of the eastern arm of the junction, obscuring from camera view some 21st Century cars and the traffic roaring back and forth along the busy Crwys Road further off. The road markings were covered with straw. An abandoned wooden handcart containing tall metal milk churns and other period produce containers stood to one side. This street is mostly anonymous brick walls, although there is an anonymous metal gated yard along the wall of the western arm of the T-junction. This yard had been lit from within, light spilling into camera view... When they were ready to resume recording, a very simple shot was rehearsed and then recorded. Not far from the handcart, a member of the crew held the dark blue Vespa scooter steady from behind. David Tennant in the tenth Doctor's pin stripe suit and wearing a pale crash helmet sat astride the scooter and the engine was started. The crew member pushed the scooter forward and moved quickly out of camera view. The scooter glided slowly towards the camera and Tennant stopped it only a very few feet from the camera lens. Although his stand-in was also present in a matching costume, it had to be the man himself for this shot, as it plainly ended on a close up of his face.'

New magazine summed up the feelings held by many fans and members of the general viewing public alike: 'Billie Piper and David Tennant get to rock around the TARDIS in the next series of *Doctor Who!* The pair were filming an episode in which their TARDIS lands in the 1950s, where they battle aliens who travel though TV airwaves. Filming took place in a residential street bedecked with bunting, retro adverts and lined with vintage cars, while diversions were in place to stop modern-day cars being caught on film. The new series is expected to air in April. We can't wait!'

FEBRUARY PRESS COVERAGE

Though the second series' transmission date was drawing ever nearer, February was perhaps not unsurprisingly light on press coverage; the same effect had been seen the previous year, ramping up only a few short weeks before the debut date. Much of the focus on *Doctor Who* was aimed at its 40-year-plus legacy, as well as its long-time stars; former lead Tom Baker, for example, had signed to become the voice of BT's home text service, while former companion Bonnie Langford was battling new series celebrity John Barrowman in *Dancing on Ice*.

However, there was still some information to be gleaned from the newspapers about the forthcoming series. *This is Plymouth* on 4 February interviewed Jessica Atkins, the 11-year-old actress from Looseleigh who would play the young Reinette in 'The Girl in the Fireplace'. 'Everything was really cool and fun,' the actress told the paper. 'At first it was a bit nerve-racking meeting all the stars. But David Tennant was lovely. He showed me around, we had a long chat and he was really friendly. Mum was more scared than I was anyway. When David took me on to the set, Mum was walking behind us just speechless.' This article was the first to mention (through Atkins' revelations of her days on set) that Noel Clarke (Mickey) would appear in the episode. *Doctor Who* was featured on the ITV show *100 Greatest Websearches* on 7 February; Tracy-Ann Oberman, guest starring in the final episodes, talked about her expectations of the series coming back without Christopher Eccleston, noting that she'd worried it might not be done well. The show also discussed *Doctor Who*'s 'cyberspace life', mentioning the multitude of websites devoted to it. *New Woman* magazine featured David Tennant at number 20 on the list of the world's 100 Sexiest Men. On 10 February, the *South Wales Evening Post* wrote: 'Eight youngsters have become the envy of their friends after going on a journey with *Doctor Who*. They are all taking part in the highly-anticipated second series of BBC Wales's smash hit... Youngsters from Neath and Port Talbot will be able to watch themselves on screen in the second series, now being filmed. But despite being understandably excited about their big break, the youngsters cannot say much about it.' (The children were probably part of the crowd scene in 'The Idiot's Lantern'.) *Metro* asked *EastEnders* actress Michelle Ryan if she was going to be *Doctor Who*'s new assistant, if the rumours about Billie Piper leaving were true: 'Everyone's been rumoured to be up for that. The media speculate as to who they'd like to see in the role, but as far as I know, no offers have been made. I'd consider it if it came up, though.'

Noel Clarke was achieving some buzz, and notoriety, as the writer of *Kidulthood*, an independent film to be released in early March. The *Observer* of 12 February called Clarke one of its 'ten on the verge of big success'. Clarke himself discussed the film in *RWDMag*, released the next day, and explained: 'Sometimes you get scripts, you know, and you read them and think, I can do better than this. But that was never my job. I'm an actor, so I thought you just let the writer do his job. Basically it all started with a case of sitting down in front of the computer and writing it. The reason I started was, I feel in terms of a lot of things that are happening today in society (with young people) – I didn't think things were being told right. I wanted the film to be something that people haven't seen before.' The 19 February edition of the *Independent* said that the film: '... shows what children really get up to when Mum and Dad aren't looking... It promises to be the most controversial British film of the year.' The *Daily Telegraph* on 22 February reported: 'There's a new kids' film on the block. Hardly a scoop – barely a week goes by without the release of another movie featuring some plucky youngster battling good and evil with their pals. *Kidulthood*, out in a fortnight, is no exception: it follows 15-year-old Trife and his school friends getting up to all sorts of adventures one day in December. But *Harry Potter* it ain't... It's a shocker all right, and intentionally so.'

Maureen Lipman appeared on *Wogan Now and Then* on UKTV Gold on 14 February, briefly discussing her appearance in the episode 'The Idiot's Lantern' and commenting that she'd recorded her part separately from the main cast, at Alexandra Palace. The *Sun* on 16 February profiled Pauline Collins, soon to star as Queen Victoria in the episode 'Tooth and Claw', complete with photos. The *South Wales Evening Post* ran an article on the Craig y Nos castle, which the previous September had been used for the recording of 'Tooth and Claw': 'Most of the filming was done over three days in the outer courtyard of the castle. The appearance of the castle façade needed changing to give it a bleak, period feel, and security lights and other modern fittings had to be camouflaged. Martin Gover, managing director of Selclene, the domestic cleaning agency which now owns the castle, said: "The highlight of one of our overnight hotel guest's stay turned out to be the moment Billie Piper accidentally trod on her dog's tail between scenes."' The *Post* also mentioned a young actress, Lara Philippart, who had recently recorded scenes for *Casualty* and who would be an extra in 'The Idiot's Lantern'. *BBC Good Food*, meanwhile, featured an interview with Pauline Collins during the month, in which the actress noted that if she had a TARDIS, she would 'travel forward 2000 years and have dinner with H G Wells, eating stardust sundaes.'

The *Daily Star* on 16 February reported: '*Doctor Who* bosses have gone monster mad after a script for the new series was left on a park bench. The top secret document was abandoned by someone who works on the BBC hit... And the script for a forthcoming episode called "The Idiot's Lantern" could already have been read by passers-by and even posted on the internet.' A BBC source apparently told the *Daily Star*, 'They were stunned that anyone could just leave a secret script just lying around for all the world to see. These things are sacred because so few are given out, and the ones which are often have the names of the cast or crew member printed on the top. The last thing we want is leaks on the internet.' The *Daily Record* noted that David Tennant was backing a fundraising drive for a cash-strapped Scots hospice in his home town of Paisley: 'The Accord Hospice have just six weeks to buy their buildings from Argyll and Clyde Health Board. Tennant has stepped in to give the buy-a-brick campaign celebrity backing.' Director James Hawes told *Broadcast* magazine that he 'wants to be reincarnated as a Time Lord,' and said that the cruellest thing he'd ever done was 'use an air rifle to shoot holes in my sister's David Soul album.' *Yahoo News* noted that Tracy-Ann Oberman, fresh from recording her appearance in the series finalé, was moving on to the BBC's new comedy-drama *Sorted*. icWales on 21 February said that 'fans will be spending more time getting up close and personal with *Doctor Who*,' reporting that the *Doctor Who Up Close* exhibition in Cardiff had 'proved so popular that it will now be open to the public for longer than its planned two-month run'. There were new displays to be placed in the exhibition as well. The *Financial Times* on 24 February used the fact that Tennant's Doctor was not wearing a scarf to introduce a feature on scarves (illogically headlining the piece 'The scarf-clad *Doctor Who* era dawns again').

Perhaps the best indication, however, that the series was no longer just a niche interest came from Canada's *National Post* on 27 February, which said that the recent DVD release of the first series there had missed a golden opportunity: since the Queen had recently been revealed to be a fan of the programme, the discs could have been labelled 'Official purveyors of DVDs to Her Majesty Queen Elizabeth II.' While it was not to be, it was every indication that *Doctor Who* was a passion shared by a far wider audience than the children and science-fiction fans of today.

CHAPTER SEVEN:
FURTHER THAN WE'VE EVER GONE BEFORE

At long last, the launch date for *Doctor Who's* second series was fast approaching; but there were a few details still to be worked out. Meanwhile, the American debut of the series was also nearing, and there was still some life left in the old TARDIS publicity machine for the British public.

BIGGER, BETTER

Though the new series would not officially premiere until April, the month of March 2006 saw some important developments and surprises that continued to bring it to the public eye. On 2 March, *Doctor Who* was nominated for five Broadcasting Press Guild Programme Awards, with the series one of only two nominees (the other being *Bleak House*) for Best Drama series, and Davies up for the writers' award for both *Doctor Who* and *Casanova*. Piper, Eccleston and Tennant all received nominations for their work on *Doctor Who* as well.

With *Doctor Who* still in production on its second series and *Torchwood* waiting in the wings, it seemed improbable that the BBC would want more, yet the *Sun* on 3 March reported that the characters of Sarah Jane Smith and K-9 – soon to appear in the series' third episode 'School Reunion' – would appear in their own spin-off series. 'We told how BBC bosses are bringing back K-9 for an episode in the Time Lord's new series,' said the *Sun*. 'Now it has emerged that the pooch and Sarah Jane, played by Elisabeth Sladen, will also star together in their own children's series. An insider said: "It would have been a shame to put K-9 back in his kennel, so we've come up with an idea for another drama. It's early days, but K-9 and [Sarah Jane Smith] are inseparable characters. There are loads of things we can do with *Doctor Who*. It's one of the most popular shows on TV and viewers can't seem to get enough of it."'

The same day, the official *Doctor Who* website revealed further details about the children's programme *Totally Doctor Who*, which would accompany the broadcast of Series Two. The series was: '... recruiting cadets for a Companion Academy. Eight Cadets will be picked, but only the best will make it through the gruelling physical and mental challenges of the Academy. The prize? A day on the *Doctor Who* set.' It also noted that, if fans thought they were the 'biggest *Who* brainbox around', they could: '... take the Who-ru challenge. Stump the *Totally Doctor Who* studio guests with your *Who* knowledge and you'll walk away with some serious prizes.' The series was initially said to be airing on BBC2 in mid-April, with repeats following on the BBC's children's network, CBBC. Also announced at roughly the same time were new acquisitions of the first series on SKAI, the Greek television channel to launch in early April, and Russian station STS TV.

Casting developments abounded in early March. Peter Kay was confirmed on 8 March to be appearing in an episode of the series, said to be playing the 'cold and powerful Victor Kennedy'. Davies noted that this was 'not a comedy turn' and pointed toward Kay's experience as a versatile actor in Paul Abbott's *Butterfly Collectors* and *The Secret Life of Michael Fry*. A report on 14 March about Kay's casting, in fact, contained the first official word of the title, 'Love & Monsters'; this report, again in the *Sun*, also noted the casting of Danny Webb in the two-parter concluded by 'The Satan Pit'. On 20 March, the *Sun* further reported that Shirley Henderson, best known as Moaning Myrtle in the *Harry Potter* films, would appear in the series' tenth episode; a BBC insider was quoted as saying: 'Shirley is a massively talented actress with a long and respected CV. She was fantastic in *Harry Potter* and we knew she would be great in *Doctor Who* too. It was just a matter of finding some space in her schedule and getting her to sign on the dotted line.' That day's *Daily Mirror* reported that Marc Warren would appear in the same episode: 'Marc plays Elton Pope, who becomes embroiled with the Doctor as he takes on Victor Kennedy, played by Peter [Kay]. Marc thought the first series was great and can't wait.' And TV presenter Alistair Appleton revealed on his own website that he would appear in the series 'in quite the most exciting TV job he's ever done.'

Doctor Who received nominations for three Hugo Awards on 22 March, all in the Best Dramatic Presentation – Short Form category, for 'The Empty Child'/'The Doctor Dances' (which would eventually win) by Steven Moffat, 'Dalek' by Rob Shearman (which would come second) and 'Father's Day' by Paul Cornell (which – completing a clean sweep for *Doctor Who* – would come third). While many of the awards and nominations that *Doctor Who* had received to date had come on the strength of votes from the British public or critics, the Hugo Awards, given out by the science-fiction community and presented at each year's annual World Science Fiction Convention, represented many countries and science-fiction fans worldwide.

Late in the month, *Doctor Who* would also be shortlisted for the prestigious British Academy of Film and Television Arts (BAFTA) awards, to be announced in May; *Doctor Who* received 14 nominations in all, dominating the lists with nods in the categories for Best Drama Series/Serial, Best Actor (Eccleston), Best Actress (Piper), Best Director (James Hawes for 'The Christmas Invasion'), Best Screenwriter (Davies), and others.

Doctor Who Magazine officially announced the start date of transmission for Series Two in late March; confirmed what was by this point a somewhat poorly-kept secret, it stated that the first episode would go out on Saturday 15 April. It also announced the final previously-unconfirmed episode titles for the season, with 'The Impossible Planet' being the first of the two-part story concluded by 'The Satan Pit', and 'Fear Her' being the title for *Life On Mars* writer Matthew Graham's submission. The issue also confirmed that the publicity campaign for Series Two would include posters and special TV trailers, while *Blue Peter* would continue its association with the series with studio guests from *Doctor Who* appearing on several instalments. Details such as the contents of the TARDISodes, the official *Doctor Who* website tie-ins and even a special *Doctor Who* night on BBC3 the weekend prior to transmission were revealed. And new guest actors were confirmed including Shaun Parkes, Claire Rushbrook, MyAnna Buring and Ronny Jhutti to appear in 'The Impossible Planet' and 'The Satan Pit', which was being recorded throughout March and into early April.

As recording on the series *Doctor Who* came close to wrapping – it would be completed in early April with studio-bound work, including a visit to Pinewood Studios for an underwater sequence for 'The Impossible Planet' – fans had one last opportunity to see the production crew in action. Wrote Emma Sandrey to Outpost Gallifrey on 25 March: 'Yesterday I was lucky enough to see some filming just outside the Maelfa shopping centre in Llanedeyrn. Camille Coduri and the newly announced Marc Warren were doing a rather tense scene. It seems the Maelfa area was doubling-up as the Powell Estate – St David's cars had been turned into Powell Estate Motors – and graffiti and posters were put up all around to create a run-down effect. It also looks like it's set in autumn, because leaves were being thrown around everywhere.... The scene involved Jackie confronting Elton Pope about a photo of Rose that he'd taken and she had found... The scene was repeated about ten times so they could get different angles. There was a lot of noise because of traffic (the buses go by every seven minutes; possibly the worst place to shoot).' Wrote Paul Mount: 'Made my way to the area behind / alongside the Central Railway

Station in Cardiff. A number of the usual vans and lighting rigs and a couple of large arc lights fully illuminated. Not much sign of life but some people lurking near the vans... At first I thought they were just curious members of the public watching what was clearly filming for *Doctor Who*, despite the absence of anything discernibly recognisable... until I saw a technician in the background walking about with an Auton prosthetic mask in his hand!... More rehearsing of people running and screaming, unmade-up Autons amongst them (including the Auton bride). A taxi with a Henrik's livery was manoeuvred into place, then a motorbike. Cue the smoke, burning debris, *Hustle's* Marc Warren dodging amongst the chaos and nearly getting run over by the taxi. After a few rehearsals, the Autons were sealed into their masks (they still don't join up at the back) and the attack scene was filmed again. Looks like those who weren't impressed by the Auton break-out in "Rose" might be a little happier this time.'

THE AMERICAN DEBUT

The middle of March saw the debut of the first *Doctor Who* series on the Sci Fi Channel in America. The long-awaited US debut – opening up the series to its largest potential market outside the UK – was met with considerable press attention. The large-circulation television periodical *TV Guide* called the series one of its '21 Shows You've Gotta See!' in its 13 March edition, saying, 'The culty classic gets a slick update for the *Battlestar* generation when Christopher Eccleston checks in as the ninth Doc to do the time warp.' In a review of the start of the series, *TV Guide* said that, 'Unlike the old *Who* serials, which were shot largely on videotape and hamstrung by cheap F/X, this version of the venerable series... consists of self-contained instalments produced entirely on film. Nevertheless, these 2005 stories... remain as engaging as those of Eccleston's predecessors.' (*TV Guide's* note about the series being entirely on film was nonsense, as in truth it was shot entirely on videotape; but it made for a good story!) Another widely circulated periodical, *Entertainment Weekly*, noted: 'When *Doctor Who* makes its triumphant return to the United States on the Sci Fi Channel March 17, the average American's reaction will likely be: It was here before? A science-fiction staple of British TV for over 40 years, *Who* achieved only cult status in the US when the show was imported to PBS in the late '70s... While it's airing on Sci Fi's Friday line-up, don't expect things to be nearly as grim as, say, *Battlestar Galactica* – especially when the good Doctor hangs out in a futuristic *Big Brother* house.'

The media website *Monsters and Critics* said the series was fifth on its list of 'top ten reasons to watch in 2006', writing, 'Eccleston combines an impish sense of mischief with a ruthless dark side that always keeps you guessing as to how he'll react... A must for science-fiction fans.' *Eclipse* magazine said of the series, 'The sets no longer wobble; the SFX, while perhaps not as stellar as those of US science fiction shows, aren't exactly shabby; the writing is witty and intelligent; the stories [are] full of fun and menace with a delicious British eccentricity.' The *Long Island Press* on 14 March wrote, 'Unless you're one of the two million nerds Googling the online version of this article, you've probably not had much exposure to the classic British science-fiction series *Doctor Who*... Little has changed since the show's last official season in 1989, aside from the marked improvement in wardrobe, hairdos and dental work... Even though the show has failed numerous times to capture an American audience, I think the new series has the best shot by far of becoming a minor hit.' A writer for the *San Antonio Express News* commented, 'To be honest, the series with cheesy special effects and fairly cardboard characters never quite became my cup of British tea. Then the remake arrived and my opinion radically changed. This 21st Century version of *Doctor Who* is terrific, a sci-fi show that everyone, fan or not of the genre, can enjoy. It's fast-moving, meaty and funny, with three-dimensional characters who tug at your heart and tear ducts.'

Not all comments were positive; on 14 March, the *Village Voice* from New York wrote, 'Although this remake attempts to add tragic depth to the Doctor, it lacks true darkness. The early series overcame skimpy budgets to conjure the uncanny; this was cosmic horror as HP Lovecraft would have understood it.' The *Voice* complained that the true disappointment of the series was structural: 'Instead of stretching a storyline across a whole season, each adventure is resolved within a single episode, making this closer to your average detective series. The thrill-filled cliff-hangers of yore are gone, taking with them the child's urge to watch TV from behind the sofa, breath bated.'

The *AZ Central* of Arizona, by contrast, felt that, for 'good old fashioned' escapism: '... *Doctor Who* is the trip of a lifetime. Here's hoping audiences on this side of the Atlantic will think so, too.'

In the days leading up to the premiere on 17 March, the Sci Fi Channel ran several additional trailers for the series, one of these noting, rather curiously, that the Doctor is: '... not here to save the universe... He's just enjoying it while it lasts.' The channel's website featured a web-only video featuring interview clips with Russell T Davies, Julie Gardner and Phil Collinson, some of which were shot on the TARDIS console room set. The channel's Sci Fi Wire website, itself a major science-fiction media news feed, said that the timing was 'right' for the series to return. 'I think the BBC had their eye on it as a very good property that could be resurrected,' Davies told Sci Fi Wire. 'And the Drama Department as well as the Controller of BBC1 wanted to work with me, which sounds very arrogant, but it's the truth. They'd been asking me to write all sorts of things; every year, they'd phone up and say, "Do you want to adapt *A Tale of Two Cities*?" or "Do you want to write another series about gay men?" Or something like that. And every year I quite confidently (and cheekily) sat there and said, "No, I just want to do *Doctor Who*!"'

Finally, on 17 March, the series made its debut, with the first two episodes – 'Rose' and 'The End of the World' – aired back to back. The critical reaction was quite extensive. 'Forget the slow pacing and the not-so-special effects of the previous versions – this is not your father's *Doctor Who*!' said *TV Guide*. 'Like so much British science-fiction... this *Doctor Who* has a goofy, homemade quality,' opined the *New York Times*. 'It's less interested in gizmos than in characters... The familiar blue police box doesn't seem much revamped, either; it appears to run on pneumatic tubes, and there is no sign of a computer on board. The Doctor, on the other hand, almost quivers with energy.' The *Hollywood Reporter* wrote, 'This latest revamp of the by-now infamous *Doctor Who* is silly, sophomoric stuff that is sure to please its television audience... [Davies] has a good thing going here, even if it does seem absurd at times for monsters and other such horrific creatures and events to spring out of nowhere.' The Knight-Ridder news service said, 'The good news for long-time fans is that [Davies] hasn't mucked around with the quirky essence of *Doctor Who* that much, while giving it a more polished look.' The *Los Angeles Daily News* said, 'You needn't know anything of past series to become quickly addicted to this series' seemingly endless quirky charms.' The *Seattle Times* noted: 'While most space sagas drag a comet-tail's worth of back story behind them, *Doctor Who* is instantly accessible. Maybe that's because the series at heart is an old-fashioned romance in the dashing, 19th-Century sense.' The *Chicago Tribune* said, 'Despite a few missteps, there's much to recommend this fast-paced edition of *Doctor Who*... Christopher Eccleston has a cheeky, spiky charm and more than a dash of sex appeal. As the Doctor's companion, Rose Tyler, English pop star-turned-actress Billie Piper brings a winning combination of dogged sincerity and working-class irreverence to her role.' The *Tampa Tribune* said, 'The new incarnation of this classic character captures the charm of the original. The series has decent special effects while maintaining the campy, slightly cheesy appeal that made the original a hit in the 1960s and '70s.' The *Deseret News* commented, 'This isn't *Star Trek* or *Battlestar Galactica*. It's a decidedly British sensibility that mixes some state-of-the-art effects with stuff that looks, well, decidedly cheesy. And it's an odd combination of action, adventure and wackiness – an odd combination that somehow works... It will make fans out of people who are new to the franchise.' The *North Adams Transcript* noted, 'In its current incarnation, the show is accessible and fun, with just enough darkness to add to the tension and intrigue... *Doctor Who* is clearly one of the smartest TV shows around, but it doesn't decrease its enjoyment level through heavy-handedness. There are still plenty of aliens and monsters and space ships – and, in the Doctor, we oddballs still have a hero we can believe in.'

Davies told Sci Fi Wire on 20 March that he thought the series had found its footing very quickly. 'I think the learning experience is overstated by fandom,' said Davies. 'I think it's very much fandom's attitude to sit there with [Series One] and say, "Ah, well, they're learning!" Frankly, we hit the ground running and were a success right from the start, so there's truly not a single episode that I'm not proud of.' *TV Guide*, in the first of its 13 'water cooler' segments that covered new episodes of most series the day after airing, said, 'The ho-hum plot – the Autons want to wipe out the human race, again – served as salad dressing for the episode's real function, which was to reintroduce us to our favourite Time Lord... I will be around for *Doctor Who* for as long as Sci Fi continues to air it, and I hope that will be for a very long time. Welcome back, Doc!' *Slate.com* said: 'The pilot of *Doctor Who*... combines themes from all kinds of media experiences: the chick lit of self-actualisation, the Kim Cattrall vehicle *Mannequin* (1987), and Norman Mailer's patented rants against plastic... Billie Piper brings limitless pluck to her portrayal of Rose. She's on equal footing with Christopher Eccleston, who plays the Doctor as a notably alienated alien, a sweetheart full of secret sorrows. Yes, the show tells its fan-boy audience, there's a plump-cheeked gal out there for you. The two of you can talk about the end of time until the end of time. This is geek love.' The *Hartfort Courant* said: 'The stories may seem a little silly (the first foes are mannequins that come to life) but it's fairly lively and fun.' The *Capital Times Wisconsin* said, 'It's really quite a hoot, faithful to the goofy charm of the original series while doing the serious upgrading and improving that was so desperately needed.'

Ratings for the first night were surprisingly good, with over a million and a half viewers tuning into the broadcast – well above the channel's normal ratings in the time slot during what was considered 'repeat season'. (Sci Fi traditionally airs its original series in two slots, the second ending in early March.) Audience ratings would be strong enough over the course of the 12-week run that Sci Fi would later announce the pickup of Series Two, to run from the end of September.

MARCH MADNESS, REDUX

Even with a month (or longer) to go until the second series' debut date, March – like the same period the previous year – was rife with media commentary. Series star David Tennant told the unofficial website david-tennant.com that he and Billie Piper: '... are on set together all the time, so she's my constant pal. We get on really well, she's very funny and we have a real laugh. It obviously helps to be working with someone that you get along with so well.' *TV Zone* magazine on 3 March profiled Julie Gardner, who said of the series' production in Wales, 'There's a determination [at the BBC] to do more out-of-London production. There is an absolute determination to represent as many areas of the UK as possible, which is absolutely right for a public service broadcaster. From where I sit, I think the most important thing is the stories that writers want to tell, and the confidence that I hope they now feel in coming to me with ideas that sound quite mad, or quite bold.'

Christopher Eccleston made a surprise appearance on the final of *Junior Mastermind* on BBC1, his first public appearance in connection with *Doctor Who* since his departure; in a pre-recorded insert, he was seen chatting to a boy named Sam, who had chosen *Doctor Who 2005* as his specialist subject. Describing himself as an 'unemployed Time Lord', Eccleston said that the best thing about being in *Doctor Who* had been 'the response from children.' Eccleston also appeared in a special called *The Best Ever Muppet Moments* on 11 March, while an edition of *Life Style Extra* three days later linked him to actress Renee Zellweger (*Chicago, Bridget Jones' Diary*) when it said: 'The stunning actress – who is in England filming a Beatrix Potter biopic – asked the hunky star to take her on a traditional English date.'

'It was so cool to be part of *Doctor Who*,' said Jo Joyner, who played Lynda Moss in the previous series' finale, to the *Sunday Mercury* on 6 March. 'If I do nothing else in my life, I can always say I was exterminated!' In the *Scotsman*, Zoë Wanamaker said of her role as Cassandra, which would be seen in the coming series, 'It's such fun! It's such a credit to Russell T Davies and the producers. I think what they've achieved is brilliant. I think Cassandra's a naughty, naughty girl. That's what's such fun about her. She's cheeky. She's not evil, she's just naughty... That's the best thing about science-fiction, it's really basically fairy stories come to life, but they're great fun.' John Barrowman told *Eclipse* magazine on 14 March, 'It was like a childhood dream, because I'd grown up watching the show. I've loved the show even from when I lived in Glasgow.' Tamsin Greig, from the previous year's 'The Long Game', told the *Sunday Times* on 13 March that her appearance on *Doctor Who* was: '... one of the most terrifying experiences. Trying to remember lines when you can't remember to wash. And some of the lines have sci-fi words like introspike in them.'

Doctor Who came up empty handed at the Royal Television Society Awards on 15 March, leading former BBC Director-General Greg Dyke to write the next day in the *Independent*, 'So what happened to *Doctor Who*? Why didn't it win the RTS award for the best drama series at the ceremony last week? Of all the difficult things to pull off in television, radically re-launching a much-loved series is just about the hardest to do, and the BBC team who made *Doctor Who* did it brilliantly. So why didn't they win? Could it just be that snobbery came into it and the judges couldn't bring themselves to give the award to a drama that was so obviously populist?... Meanwhile, we wait to find out if BAFTA will give *Doctor Who* the award it so surely deserves.'

The *Watford Observer* on 21 March profiled two schoolchildren taking part in the *Totally Doctor Who* series: 'Tom and Tony, who both go to Sir William Ramsay School, Rose Avenue, Hazlemere, are so crazy about the scarf-wearing Time Lord that they shoot their own *Doctor Who*-style films on a video recorder, taking on the roles of the aliens the Doctor encounters.' The *Daily Star* said: '*Doctor Who* star Noel Clarke is set to enjoy a kinky threesome on the show – with Billie Piper and her TV mum. The hunky actor, who plays Rose's boyfriend Mickey Smith, says his character has been "sexed up" for the new series, which starts next month.' In comments lifted unaccredited and out of context from a *Doctor Who Magazine* interview, Clarke was quoted as saying, 'You know, I think he's secretly giving [Jackie] one. It's his plan. It's like a fantasy thing – having a mother and daughter at the same time. He's working up to it slowly.' The *Daily Record* said that David Tennant 'has no plans to pen his autobiography', quoting the actor as commenting: 'Never say never, but I don't think that I have a particularly interesting life. I think people would be very bored of me. Maybe when I'm 75. I don't really know. Ask me again then.' The Harrods department stores, meanwhile, were using Billie Piper in their latest poster ads, which could be seen on the London Underground.

American broadcasts of the first series continued, with *TV Guide* saying of 'The Unquiet Dead' on 24 March, 'The coda was perfect. Dickens runs through the streets shouting yuletide greetings. But what else can we expect from the new *Who*, a mind-bending adventure with a heart amidst the delicious rapid-fire dialogue? This is as good as sci-fi – and Sci Fi – gets.' Meanwhile, *Doctor Who* received two Spacey Award nominations from the Canadian SPACE: The Imagination Station network, which had previously shown *Doctor Who*; the programme was up for Favourite TV Show, while Rose Tyler was nominated for Favourite New TV Character.

But leave it to *Radio Times* to kick off the true anticipation: 'The Countdown Starts Here!' proclaimed the issue of the TV listings magazine released at the end of March, covering early April. 'It's not long now...' began the feature, illustrated with a full-length shot of David Tennant; it included an interview with Phil Collinson, and promised future features on the Cybermen, Sarah Jane Smith, K-9, 'cat nuns... and much more!'

THE PRESS LAUNCH

On 28 March, the press launch for Series Two took place at the Millennium Centre in Cardiff, with a screening of 'New Earth' for the assembled press and various dignitaries; among the celebrities in attendance were Tennant, Piper, Clarke and Coduri, director Graeme Harper and various writers and producers. *BBC Wales Today* briefly covered the event in news reports that evening, and featured a clip along with interviews with Tennant and Piper the following morning. However, due to a press embargo of materials from the event, there wasn't much other coverage until 30 March, when *BBC Breakfast*, with more from the same Tennant/Piper interview session and clips from the episode, launched a day of tremendous press attention.

The UK Press Association said: '[David Tennant] has signed up for the third series of *Doctor Who*, it was disclosed today. Speaking about the final episode of the second series, portentously entitled "Doomsday", Billie Piper, who plays the Doctor's sidekick Rose Tyler, told reporters she would be returning for Series Three. "There are lots of places for Rose to go," she said. Tennant... appeared more circumspect about his contract, saying: "Mine's not as simple as that..."... Asked if there were any nerves about the kissing scene, Piper joked... "We did not do tongues."' The feature also noted that Piper was 'shocked' by the final episodes of the series, which, she said, 'completely blew my mind'. The Press Association's news wire also noted that Davies: '... said he would not rule out reincarnating the Time Lord as a woman. Mr Davies said he would "have the nerve" to have a woman playing the role. And he said it would also be possible to have a Welsh Doctor, such as the actor Michael Sheen, whom he described as "brilliant".' Asked if he had a wish-list of talent for the series, Davies apparently commented, 'I would love to get a gripping American star like Sigourney Weaver.'

BBC Wiltshire featured extensive coverage including video interviews with cast and crew, as well as a question and answer session with Tennant and Piper. 'The worst bit of that was before we started,' Tennant said, 'all the hoo-ha that comes with this show. The fact that everyone is so fascinated by it. Obviously that partly makes it the most wonderful job in the world, but it also makes it the most terrifying job in the world. When I finished my first day of filming, I remember going home to collapse, because of the amount of nervous energy that had been building up in the months previous to getting going. I suppose it could have been awful, but I've been so welcomed by this extraordinary crew.' BBC Radio Wales featured audio interviews with Tennant and Piper; among the comments, Tennant noted, 'It's such a joy to be filming here – everybody here has been so enthusiastic and so indulgent of us that we have a really lovely time. So I'd like to thank the people of Cardiff for putting up with us blocking their roads and asking them to go round the long way while we film scenes!' On television, Davies spoke to CBBC's *Newsround* on the morning of 31 March, while GMTV on ITV1 featured a special look at the press function, including clips from the series.

The *Daily Mirror* continued its insistence that Piper was soon to leave: 'It looks like Billie Piper is basking in a golden glow of happiness with everything going her way. Although she confirmed she is quitting *Doctor Who*, she denied plans to head for Hollywood. The 23-year-old star said when viewers see her character Rose Tyler leave the BBC1 show, she wants to try other TV roles.' 'It's *Doctor Who* and the Bra-Dis,' proclaimed the *Sun*, illustrating a half-page piece with a photo of Piper wearing a see-through top as she 'cosied up to' Tennant. *Hello Magazine* said: 'Billie Piper is fond of describing herself as low-maintenance, but at the press launch for *Doctor Who*'s second season the actress was looking decidedly sexy in a combo of a sheer taupe-coloured top and white trousers. Her co-star, gorgeous Scottish actor David Tennant, had likewise gone for casual chic in a trendy jacket and jeans.' *Media Guardian* featured podcasts on the *Guardian* website of interviews with the series' stars and producers, while its print edition focused on Davies's supposed anger at the 'snobbery' of the Royal Television Society and BAFTA for the relative lack of nominations for *Doctor Who*. 'You watch a Charles Dickens adaptation and you're clapping [at] all those antique lace collars, but if you watch a bird woman from the 57th Century you don't imagine that someone put two weeks' thought and work into it.' The *Daily Telegraph* was concerned that the Doctor and his companion: '... are being forced into silly roles... This is the latest in a long line of ludicrous adjustments forced on our favourite characters by PC modernisers; fans of the series must be feeling betrayed by a kiss'.

Fan Caleb Woodbridge, writing for the Cardiff student paper *Gair Rhydd*, said of the press evening, 'One sign of *Doctor Who*'s success was that the launch for Series Two wasn't just ten journalists and a sausage roll. No, a whole crowd of reporters and journalists turned up, eager to cover the event... Russell T Davies once again captures the sheer joy of the Doctor's travels. From the opening moments, it's clear that the Doctor and Rose love travelling the universe and also each other. Just platonically? Well, the more squeamish fans can keep telling themselves that, but decide for yourself!'

As March closed, a new trailer for the second series was expected on 1 April in the early evening, while the BBC's Press Office issued a release about the launch of the series and its first episode, 'New Earth', with one possible problem: no official broadcast time. The press release stated that the episode was 'unplaced' on the schedule, but it was almost certainly not to be 7.00 pm; *Strictly Dance Fever* was listed as running from 6.15 to 7.15 pm that night on BBC1's schedule. It seemed that, despite nearly a year of production, everything was really waiting for a last-minute confirmation this time around.

GET READY, GET SET...

The first trailer for Series Two debuted on 1 April on BBC1 and lasted one minute. It was then repeated numerous times over the next couple of weeks in two abbreviated versions: a 40-second version and a 20-second edition. There was also a 15-second trailer for the TARDISodes and two 30-second trailers for the children's series *Totally Doctor Who*, soon to debut on CBBC. The return of the series and the TARDISodes were also heavily promoted on the bbc.co.uk homepage, while on 7 April, digital television viewers could press the red button to see a CBBC Extra show on BBCi: a 12-minute looped video package promoting *Totally Doctor Who* and 'New Earth', featuring interviews with show presenter Barney Harwood and with David Tennant and Billie Piper, contributions from children, and extensive clips from the first episode. The official *Doctor Who* website creators unveiled several new tie-in spin-off websites and games. Another new 20-second trailer debuted on 12 April, including specific sequences from 'New Earth' that had not appeared in previous promotional packages or previews, such as Cassandra commenting 'The Sisters are hiding something,' and the Sisters of Plenitude themselves saying, 'One of the patients is conscious – we can't have that.' The voiceover stated that the Doctor was back 'in a hospital with a dark secret.' The next day, digital television viewers could access a looped, three-minute selection of preview clips from Series Two, comprising scenes or images from episodes two to nine and 12, though the majority were from 'Tooth and Claw', 'School Reunion' and 'The Girl in the Fireplace'. This was adapted from a press preview compilation. A slightly shorter edit subsequently had regular airings on BBC1 throughout the first few weeks of the series' run.

By now there was confirmation of a new time slot for *Doctor Who*: the episode 'New Earth' would start at 7.15 pm on 15 April, while the BBC3 documentary series *Doctor Who Confidential* would kick off at 8.00 pm. The BBC's Press Office confirmed this information in the same release that announced broadcast details for 'Tooth and Claw', the series' second episode. Guest star Pauline Collins was quoted as saying that: '... having seen David Tennant in action, I believe he is going to be the best Doctor ever... He seems to combine authority and humour and quirkiness which, in a way, is an amalgam of all the very best Doctors. He's terrific in it and I think he'll be great.' A press release for the third episode, 'School Reunion', a week later would reveal that while the first two episodes of the season would be shown at 7.15 pm, the series would return to its expected 7.00 pm time slot for the third.

A bearded David Tennant appeared on ITV1's *This Morning* on 12 April, to be interviewed by stand-in co-host John Barrowman. Billie Piper's absence from the same programme was attributed to illness, with Tennant commenting that the end of a long and intense job often brings on ill health, and had for him too. *GMTV* announced forthcoming *Doctor Who* guests for the same day, although these ultimately did not materialise. Tennant was heard on *The Christian O'Connell Breakfast Show* on Virgin Radio, however, and both he and his father appeared in a pre-recorded segment on BBC2's *Ready Steady Cook*, with the actor showing a special flair for creating square oranges. 'Tennant has revealed his scariest TV moment – an on-screen cook-off with his dad,' the *Daily Mail* wrote mid-month.

In the last couple of weeks before transmission of Series Two, the media frenzy continued. Two new broadcasters of the series were announced – Dutch station NOS and TV Ohjelmapalaute in Finland. Back home meanwhile, the *Sun* on 1 April said that presenters Ant McPartlin and Declan Donnelly (aka Ant and Dec): 'were not so pleased... after *Doctor Who* went head to head in the telly ratings with their *Saturday Night Takeaway* show [for ITV] last year. The boys hope to exterminate the Beeb with their new series.' On the subject of a possible *Doctor Who* feature film, Davies told icWales: 'We would not have time to do a movie at the moment. Maybe if it was all over and still popular, but I would not be desperately keen to work with BBC Films myself. I'm not supposed to say this... but I can't bear them! I am in no rush to work with them whatsoever personally, but I suppose the BBC could have a go.' The 2 April *Sunday Mirror* noted: 'The man who revived *Doctor Who* says the inspiration behind his most ghoulish alien character was film star Nicole Kidman. Writer Russell T Davies says he got the idea for villain Lady Cassandra... after watching the stick-thin beauty arrive at the Oscars.' icWales commented: 'David Tennant may be the housewives' favourite, but it's Billie Piper who gets sent knickers in the post!' Said Piper, 'I have had some ladies knickers in the post.' Tennant was quoted as responding: 'I can only dream of women's knickers in the post!' *Media Guardian* asked, 'Has *Doctor Who* lost out to snobbery?... On this week's MediaGuardian podcast Davies and Jane Tranter complain about how *Doctor Who* is being treated by awards juries... Serious stuff, and no doubt there is something in what they say about the attitudes of fellow professionals. But what this little outburst really illustrates is something about the BBC in general and the Drama Department in particular.' The weekend's *Daily Star* proposed 'some female candidates for the Doctor we'd like to see on screen', including Charlotte Church ('*Voice of an Angel* would be a sound hit in the TARDIS'), Sigourney Weaver ('Russell T Davies has already admitted he's a fan'), Angelina Jolie ('Would definitely give the ratings a massive boost. Brad could have a role'), Davina McCall ('A bit of a disaster with her chat show, so maybe she would like a trip in the TARDIS'), Keira Knightley ('Hottest young Brit actress would become an even bigger star') and even Billie Piper ('It would stretch the imagination a bit, but maybe Rose could somehow morph into the Doc').

The 2 April *Sunday Telegraph* featured a piece by the father of a young *Doctor Who* fan who had visited the set with his son: 'Transported five years into the future (by fearful imagination rather than the TARDIS), I am wondering whether my newly truculent teenage son will remember that his father once took him to the set of *Doctor Who*, and so hate me that little less for helping bring him into the world... Tennant appears to be that most precious of beings, the wholly unactorly actor who is entirely at ease with obsessive fans.' The *Telegraph* opined: 'There was a time not so long ago when the only British television programmes Americans knew or cared about were *Monty Python's Flying Circus*, *The Benny Hill Show* and the occasional costume drama shown so late at night that only insomniacs watched. But now, judging by the column inches currently devoted to British television in serious newspapers, there's a big chunk of America that's as au fait with British TV as we are. My favourite [question], "Is the new *Doctor Who* [as played by Christopher Eccleston] really gay?"' icWales noted that Wales: '... has become a beacon for new film and television projects... *Doctor Who* star David Tennant said Wales was a perfect alternative to overused locations like London. "In London, people are so hacked off with film crews, they've no time for them," he said. 'But one of the great things about filming in Wales is everyone is so pleased to see us."'

Even though 'New Earth' hadn't yet aired, some papers were looking forward to the second episode, 'Tooth and Claw', thanks to the press release and an early April preview screening in Scotland, with the *Sunday Herald* on 8 April noting, 'On-set in Cardiff, Tennant is nervous energy personified. While waiting to film a scene, he jumps up and down on the spot and waggles his fingers, then attempts the dance routine from the latest Rachel Stevens video... He's wearing the brown pinstripe suit that is his *Doctor Who* outfit ("Jarvis Cocker had this look 10 years ago"), and leaning up against the scenery. There's a deer skull screwed to the wall above him, and a candelabra nearby. One woman has the job of keeping the candles lit, which is bad news for Billie Piper – Rose in the show – who sets her hair on fire while running past, but quickly pats it out.' The *Western Mail* commented of the werewolf creature to be seen in 'Tooth and Claw': 'With its speed, thirst for blood, menacing eyes and evil looking teeth and claws, this is the enemy the Doctor must face in one of the scariest episodes ever.' The UK Press Association said: 'Tennant has spoken of his joy at getting to play a Scot in one episode of the new series. The star was in Glasgow for a preview of episode two from the second series... The 34-year-actor ditched his Scots accent to take on the role of the Doctor at the request of writer Russell T Davies. But he gets to use his own accent in the new episode as he pretends to be a doctor trained in Edinburgh.' The *Evening Times* discussed an appearance that week by Tennant and Billie Piper in Glasgow, promoting the second series debut: 'Tennant, the Paisley boy who attended the Royal Scottish Academy of Music and Drama in Glasgow, proved as enigmatic as the iconic television character he is playing... He was a little guarded about the fact he doesn't use his own accent when playing the Doctor.'

On 9 April, the *Independent* interviewed Davies, who said he believed British drama to be in genuinely good health. 'If there's a paucity, I think it's the fault of the writers, because the commissioners are desperate for good material,' Davies told the paper. 'The greatest censor at work is the writer sitting at home saying, they'll never accept that on BBC1 or ITV.' Davies also discussed the forthcoming episode 'The Girl in the Fireplace': 'Stephen Moffat has written what is practically a love story for the Doctor in episode four. That's never been seen. It's very understated, very beautifully done, but it's nonetheless a Time Lord falling in love, and Rose's reaction to him falling in love with someone else.' The *Sunday Mirror*, meanwhile, said that Davies: '... has banned ex-Time Lords from appearing on the show. The writer has vowed former Doctors will never come back for the sci-fi drama's anniversary specials as they have done in classic BBC episodes. It means that Tom Baker, Peter Davison, Colin Baker, Sylvester McCoy, Paul McGann and Christopher Eccleston won't return to the show.' According to the newspaper, Davies said, 'I don't like past Doctor adventures. I've never liked it when Doctors met other Doctors because I think it's an actors' parade. You're not watching the Doctors, you're watching party pieces – so it won't happen.' The *Mirror* also noted the same day: 'If *Doctor Who* sidekick Billie Piper had a real-life time-travelling TARDIS, she'd probably spend some more time with her boyfriend. Poor old Amadu Sowe. His gorgeous girlfriend spends nine months of the year in Cardiff [making] one of Britain's most popular TV shows with a desirable young actor, and he sees her about as often as the viewing public will do – once a week.'

Radio Times for the mid-April week featured a fold-out cover depicting the Doctor, Rose and the TARDIS, Sarah Jane Smith and K-9, a Sister of Plenitude, a clockwork robot and a Cyberman, with a caption in the series' brand typeface, Deviant Strain. A 16-page pull out section featured an article by Davies, who revealed: 'If you watch the Doctor and Rose very closely, there's an overconfidence at times that could well be their downfall.' The issue also included an episode guide to the forthcoming series, with extensive comments from Davies and other members of the production team accompanying a 20-strong selection of previously unseen photographs. *SFX* magazine meanwhile interviewed Sophia Myles, who said: 'When my agent called me and said "You've been offered an episode of *Doctor Who*," I thought, brilliant! I'm going to meet the Daleks! "No, you're going to be in a corset in Versailles!"' Billie Piper was featured as the cover model for *InStyle* Magazine in April, saying in an interview inside: 'I'm very trusting and that's often my downfall. I don't ever think anyone is going to be horrible. But I'd rather get burnt than become cynical.' icWales commented that David Tennant had 'turned his sex symbol status on its head by admitting he wore saggy Steptoe thermals while filming in Wales!' The service also reported that: '... the days of wobbly sets and cardboard aliens on *Doctor Who* are long gone. Instead, kids really will have a reason to hide behind the sofa when they see this snarling werewolf in the new series of the sci-fi drama.' Sci Fi Wire on 10 April asserted that the second series would 'build on the strengths of Season One,' and Davies told them: 'The temptation of the format is to keep being too different, but it's easy to forget that for a lot of people, it's a brand-new series. Even for the oldest, most dedicated fan, it's a new series. So we've got some new elements, and some new elements that I want to become regular elements, including what I call the "celebrity historical". *Doctor Who* always did historical stuff, so last year, we met Charles Dickens, and this year, we meet Queen Victoria.'

Broadcast interviewed Mill TV's Will Cohen, who said that the previous year's tally of 1,300 visual effects shots over 13 episodes was to be matched this year, with approximately 600 effects shots completed at press time. The magazine also noted that the group BDH had created the title sequence for *Totally Doctor Who*. The *Daily Star* suggested that the Gelth would be making an appearance in the series, though this was another case of the press recycling unfounded fan rumours. The *Sun* featured a two-page colour spread on David Tennant as part of a series of features marking the show's return that Saturday, noting how he'd predicted while a youngster at school that he would one day play the Doctor, and interviewing his former English teacher, Moira Robertson, who said she still held a copy of a story, called 'Intergalactic Overdose', that he had written when he was 14. *Televisual* interviewed BBC Drama's Jane Tranter, who said that the two shows she was most proud of were *Life on Mars* and *Doctor Who*. *This is Wiltshire* profiled a biographer soon to release a book about Billie Piper. The *Rutherglen Reformer News* said that Davies had admitted: '... he was gutted [in 1980] when he heard that fan Andrew Smith, from Rutherglen, had got to write for the series after speculatively submitting a script. Originally entitled "The Planet That Slept", the [story] was renamed "Full Circle", and was shown... as part of Tom Baker's final year in the part.'

Shortly before the new series launch, crew members on *Doctor Who* were nominated for four awards in the BAFTA Craft Awards, which BAFTA described as honouring 'the unseen heroes of television, those who tirelessly work behind the camera.' The nominations for *Doctor Who* production personnel included Joe Ahearne (Best Director), Jo Pearce and Andrew Whitehouse for 'Attack of the Graske' (Best New Media Developer), Russell T Davies (Best Writer) and production designer Edward Thomas (Break-through Talent). The *Stage* noted that the series had 'missed out on nominations for its costume, make-up and special effects at the BAFTA Craft Awards, a result that will anger creator Russell T Davies, who recently hit out at the "snobbery" surrounding the awards system.' IT Wales, meanwhile, said: 'Welsh interactive agency Sequence has been commissioned by BBC Wales to develop a suite of interactive games for the new *Doctor Who* series... The contract was awarded to Cardiff based Sequence, after stiff UK wide competition as part of the BBC's commitment to outsource the design and development of some of its online content.' New Zealand fans were delighted when Prime TV announced on 13 April: '*Doctor Who* with David Tennant will return, [although] not until the middle of the year. As it is one of our biggest shows, we want to give it a really good launch.'

On Sunday 9 April, BBC3 aired its *Doctor Who* Night in anticipation of the following weekend's premiere; the evening featured the debut of the second series of *Doctor Who Confidential* with an opening chapter entitled 'One Year On'. The special, featuring links by American actor Corey Johnson, who had played Henry van Statten in the previous year's episode 'Dalek', reintroduced the public to the series, highlighting the previous series that had starred Christopher Eccleston and Billie Piper. 'The Christmas Invasion' was rescreened, along with a repeat of the 2003 documentary special *The Story of Doctor Who*. BBC2, meanwhile, in honour of the impending return, went back into the archives for a reshowing of the 1960s Peter Cushing film *Dr Who and the Daleks* on 13 April, just as it had 12 months earlier. CBBC launched *Totally Doctor Who* on BBC1 on 13 April. A children's magazine show complementing the new series, this was presented by Liz Barker and Barney Harwood and featured in-studio guests and a variety of special content designed exclusively for younger viewers. (See Appendix C for full details.)

The TARDISode for 'New Earth' had made its online debut on 1 April on the official BBC website and on mobile phones across the UK, just as the television trailers were beginning to be broadcast; it featured a glimpse of the New Earth Hospital and a patient suddenly erupting in terror.

On the morning of 15 April, a simple ten-second trailer aired on BBC1: 'The one to watch, tonight,' said the accompanying voice-over. 'Brand new *Doctor Who*!' CBBC went '*Doctor Who* Crazy!' with hosts Matt Edmondson and Anne Foy hosting while dressed as the Doctor and Rose, 'building up the excitement to the big event'. The BBC homepage for Saturday simply proclaimed *Doctor Who Returns!*... a short, simple proclamation that the adventure of a lifetime was finally back.

MID-APRIL: 'NEW EARTH', 'TOOTH AND CLAW'

At long last, Series Two had begun, with the first regular episode, 'New Earth' airing as scheduled at 7.15 pm on Saturday 15 April. In anticipation of the debut, some of the press had released early reviews. The *Sun* called the episode's cat-nuns: '... purr-fect villains... feline foes who provide the opposition for Doctor Who as the Time Lord returns to our screens. At first they look cute, but fans soon discover these weird kitties aren't your average housecats – they are deadly.' Charlie Brooker wrote in the *Guardian*, 'My anticipation gland was bursting as I settled down to watch the series opener... It left me a bit... well, a bit down. For starters, there's a bit too much going on... but there's also a lot of messing about with supporting characters who feel superfluous to the main storyline, diffusing your attention... Watch with a forgiving eye, because the predictive chart I'm preparing indicates a steep upturn in quality from here on in.' Another preview, in the *Guardian*, said: 'Anyone who thinks that television no longer unites the nation should peer into living rooms across the country at 7.15 pm tonight... Just over a year ago, reviving *Doctor Who* seemed like a mad geek's gamble, now it's the toast of the town.' The *Scotsman* wrote: 'Television has changed since the old days of *Doctor Who*. The performance style of shouty acting, which has its roots in theatre, has begun to die off. It has gone in most of the comedy and in some of the drama... As a fan of both Christopher Eccleston and David Tennant, I was excited when they each got the part. But neither of them are at home with the new laddish thing. Weren't Ross Kemp or Jeremy Clarkson available?' The *Hollywood Reporter* called it: '... silly and clever stuff, and the sets and CGI are all just good enough. The BBC promises more series, and it seems that Tennant and Piper, who have terrific chemistry, will be around for a few eons more. Long may they travel.' *Closer* listed the episode as one of their 'choices' of the day: 'Weird aliens, check. Rose Tyler's dodgy Cockney accent, check. A crush on the new Doctor, David Tennant, check. Yes, the new series of *Doctor Who* is here.' *Heat* gave the episode a maximum five stars: 'This first episode is every bit as giddily ambitious and entertaining as anything we saw last year... Let's just say that David Tennant is clearly shaping up to be the sexiest Doctor ever, and that the lack of a BAFTA nomination for Billie looks even sillier than it did before we saw her bravura work in this glorious story.' The official *Doctor Who* website brought its 'Fear Factor' feature – a gathering of children viewing and assessing the scariness of the episode – with the group giving 'New Earth' a 'chilling' four out of five.

The next day, the Sunday morning papers weighed in with a mixed batch of reviews. 'Back like lightning in a bottle, *Doctor Who* returned last night with David Tennant taking over from Christopher Eccleston as the quixotic spaceman in the plywood phone booth,' said the *Daily Telegraph*. 'Less promising are Tennant's efforts to keep pace with Piper's street-girl backchat: his estuary English sounds decidedly off, halfway to slummed-down Ben Elton.' The *Herald* wrote: '*Doctor Who* is, and has always been, intended for children... Still, say this for the show: in the time-warp known as Easter weekend TV, it more than held its own. Russell T Davies knows his way around a script, and the production values are, by the old standards, out of this world.' The *Guardian* on 17 April described the episode as: '... scary sci-fi, camp humour and warm family viewing all in one... And it's wonderful. Tennant turns out to be a splendid Doctor – likeable, funny and sexy. Piper continues to be brilliant and gorgeous.' The *Lancashire Evening Telegraph* said, 'I think the Doctor is in need of a bit of a tonic. Clearly all that rejuvenating has left the Time Lord feeling a little lacklustre, or at least that was the indication after the first episode... After all the hype, where was the substance?... David Tennant was all wild-eyed stares and ill-fitting suit.' The *Independent* said, 'Shock, horror, then that there was a full-blown snog between the Doctor and his young sidekick... albeit that Rose's body was being inhabited at the time by an old foe of the duo's, the vampish Lady Cassandra.'

The *Daily Express* said: 'At the risk of receiving death-threats from *Doctor Who* extremists, I'd like to say that David Tennant is the best TARDIS captain in the history of the universe. Or at least the last few decades.' The *Northern Echo* wrote, 'Tennant has swiftly settled into the Doctor's skin and will, I reckon, make as good a Who as his predecessor.' The Times Online website opined: 'Billie Piper... showed a real skill for comedy – like Lucille Ball, but with the teeth of a wolf. David Tennant, meanwhile, wore an extremely fetching pair of spectacles, and continued to project the aura of a phenomenally great lay with access to a TARDIS – in other words, the first Timephward.' The *Daily Mirror* said that the episode was: '... the TV event of the week by a million miles – by a billion light years... It was imaginative, energetic, high impact, completely bonkers good fun – amusing, original entertainment that, uniquely for television these days, could appeal equally to viewers from eight to 88, although the chase scenes drag a bit.' The *Daily Star* said: 'This has become a strangely sexy series for a Saturday teatime, hasn't it?' The *Leicester Mercury* was rather direct in its disapproval, though: 'Forgive me, dear reader, if today's review has the feel of a first draft. It's sunny outside, and I quite fancy nipping off to the pub, but the weather's not actually... After all, if submitting a script that seemed half-done is good enough for [Davies] and the BBC, well, then it's good enough for me. Like my kids, I was looking forward to this first episode of this new series. Like my kids, I was a bit underwhelmed.'

The overnight ratings for the first episode's debut on BBC1 were high, placing it ninth in the week's top ten, but were also the subject of controversy. The *Daily Mail* on 17 April said: 'The first episode of the second series of *Doctor Who* drew around eight million viewers on Saturday night – nearly two million less than for last season's debut. Despite the promise of the Doctor and his sidekick Rose sharing a passionate kiss, numbers were also down on the show's Christmas special, which drew ten million.' This widely syndicated report featured a spokesperson for the BBC stating that the ratings figures were 'still among our highest for drama this year.' *Broadcast* said that the episode: '... managed to grow its audience over time and hit a high... in the final 15 minutes.... The BBC1 show had no problem having the upper hand over ITV1's film premiere of *Harry Potter and the Chamber of Secrets*.' The *Western Mail* also featured its own BBC source, who told the paper, 'Saturday's *Doctor Who* peaked at 8.3 million, which we are really pleased with. *Doctor Who Confidential* on BBC3 got an audience of 729,500 – again, fantastic viewing figures. This is a brilliant start for the new Doctor, and is the best drama audience figure so far this year.' The report in the *Western Mail* also took a look at how the episode was playing to fans: 'The reaction from *Doctor Who* fans on website Outpost Gallifrey was similarly mixed, although most predicted an enjoyable series. The following reaction was typical: "What we've got here is a fast paced, enormously entertaining and surprising episode, leaving you feeling short-changed only because as a two parter it could have been so much more. It is a confident and stylish opener, rich with performances and special [effects] and is more than enough to keep the kids happy."'

The *Sunday Mirror* on 16 April, however, decided to play a different angle, focusing on ratings abroad to show how the series was faring: 'Millions tuned in to BBC1 last night to see Billie make her return as Rose Tyler in the second series of the new *Doctor Who*... But pretty Billie, 23, is being bashed in the US ratings by beautiful blonde former model Tricia Helfer [*Battlestar Galactica*]. The first series of the revived *Doctor Who* – starring Christopher Eccleston as the Time Lord – is currently being aired on America's Sci-Fi Channel. But since its Stateside debut last month, the time-travelling series has proved a ratings loser.'

The official BBC website featured a companion episode commentary for 'New Earth' in MP3 format with Tennant, Gardner and Davies, while over the Easter weekend BBC1 twice aired the full three-minute trailer for the following episodes of the season. CBBC, meanwhile, was celebrating nearly a million viewers for the previous Thursday's premiere of *Totally Doctor Who*. When the audience appreciation index (AI) figure for 'New Earth' became available, it showed that the episode had received a rating of 85 – higher than that achieved by 'The Christmas Invasion' and all but the last two episodes of Series One.

In conjunction with the debut of Series Two, the week's media featured a number of *Doctor Who*-related stories. Billie Piper told Radio Wales, '[Rose] is a bit feistier this time round and very jealous, which I love playing. She feels that at any given moment he can be taken away from her. And I don't think she ever considered that before.' Elisabeth Sladen, to be seen in 'School Reunion' at the end of the month, told 18 April's *Daily Mirror*: 'Sarah Jane plays a much more integral part in the story [than in the original series]. The new show is much more realistic. I am thrilled that the BBC realises the companion has an effect on the ratings.' According to the *Sunday Mail*, Sophia Myles admitted to carrying a *Doctor Who* action figure in her bag to comfort her when she missed her boyfriend Tennant: 'BBC bosses sent Sophia... two of the coveted Time Lord dolls, complete with sonic screwdrivers. The dolls, one wearing a long coat and one in a pinstripe suit, were launched this month by BBC Toys. Sophia was sent hers when she said in a magazine interview that she planned to buy one.' The *Daily Record* reported that Jimmy Vee, who played the Moxx of Balhoon in the previous season's 'The End of the World' and the title villain in the digital episode 'Attack of the Graske', had: '... his sights set on an even bigger role. Scotsman Jimmy, who plays an assortment of aliens in the new series with David Tennant, says he'd love to fill the shoes of the Doctor himself, eventually.' As Vee told the *Record*, 'You never know what might happen in one episode. I'm slowly but surely moving up the ladder and getting more in to my characters. I'd love to play the Doctor at some point. Maybe I could take over from David Tennant one day.' Actor Simon Greenall told the

News and Star about his forthcoming turn in the episode 'Love & Monsters': 'He's a lonely little man who forms a group with other people who want to find the Doctor. Peter [Kay]'s character joins the group but we don't know he's a monster, who's also trying to find the Doctor, until he eats us all!... [Tennant and Piper] are hardly in this episode – it's quite daring – the Doctor is only in it at the beginning and the end.'

The *Daily Telegraph* said: 'He has defeated Daleks and Cybermen but Doctor Who has now achieved possibly his greatest victory yet – attracting tourists to South Wales. The BBC's decision to film the series around Cardiff and Swansea has been credited with breathing new life into the region's tourist trade.' The *Sun* said that 'a recent poll found one in five visitors to Cardiff had decided to go after seeing the Welsh capital on TV' on *Doctor Who*. 'But it is tricky for viewers to spot the sites as the Beeb uses props and special effects to transform locations, making them appear as if they are in London.' The *Daily Express* commented: 'The new series of *Doctor Who* has only just warped into action but this has not stopped Time Lord David Tennant from nominating his replacement when he parks his TARDIS for good. He would like *League Of Gentlemen* comedian Mark Gatiss to take over the Dalek-fighting duties.' Said Tennant to the paper, 'Mark would be great and would be keen to do it, too, I think.' The BBC Press Office announced that Camille Coduri (Jackie) would be one of the stars of a new six-part drama for BBC3 called *Sinchronicity*, while *Media Guardian* reported that David Tennant 'is to film a 90-minute BBC1 drama in which he plays the victim of a car crash who suffers a debilitating brain injury' – a production called *Recovery*, to be screened in the autumn.

Attention later in the week turned toward the second episode, 'Tooth and Claw', for which the TARDISode, showing a werewolf attack on the moors of Scotland, had debuted on 15 April. *Radio Times* previewed the episode with a warning on its cover – 'Beware the werewolf!' – and photos from the episode, which it described as: 'Preposterous but terrific fun... After last week's comparatively thoughtful opener, here's a full-on action adventure, packed with chases, fights and a huge, hungry werewolf.' The *Daily Express* noted: 'The Doctor lands his TARDIS at Balmoral Castle [sic] in Queen Victoria's time and tackles the terrifying creature. But historical accounts show a "wolfman" did stay in a cave on the royal estate. Local author Sheila Sedgwick said a "wild boy" was raised by wolves on the mountain Lochnagar in the 19th Century.' The *Scotsman* said that David Tennant's long-awaited Scottish characterisation would be seen in this episode: 'Held at gunpoint by a procession of 19th-Century Scottish soldiers, [Piper] tries out a pitiful "hoots mon" and is quickly shushed by the Doctor, who then proceeds to converse with the soldiers as if he were one of their own. Which in real life, of course, he is. Indeed it is perhaps one of the only times in the new series that viewers will get a hint that the latest Doctor Who hails from Paisley, rather than the distant planet of Gallifrey.' *Heat* gave the episode five stars, saying: 'There's surely no other show on TV right now that manages to be as funny, scary and giddily entertaining all at the same time. Except for maybe *Deal Or No Deal*.' *Reveal* previewed the episode by calling it: '... extra spooky... Scarier than Pete Burns without any slap on!' Burns is the cross-dressing, collagen-lipped lead singer of '80s pop group Dead or Alive.

The *Daily Record* on 20 April said: 'When Glasgow actor Derek Riddell dies in *Doctor Who* this weekend, it's at the hands of a man-sized Teletubby. The *No Angels* star, who last night brought the curtain down on the hit Channel 4 comedy-drama, switches to BBC1 on Saturday playing a Scottish nobleman who meets a grisly end fighting a giant werewolf.' Riddell told the paper, 'The werewolf was a guy in an all-in-one Lycra bodysuit with a pole attached to the top of his head. I just needed an eye-line, something the right height, so it looked like I was acting with a werewolf, which was all done with computer-generated imagery (CGI). That was a challenge – I had to look scared of a student in a body stocking.' Newsquest website said: 'This Saturday night the eagled-eyed residents of a Monmouth village will be glued to their television screens to try to catch a glimpse of their leafy home on *Doctor Who*. BBC Wales... crews were in Dingestow last October filming scenes at Treowen House for the second episode of the new series... But residents may be disappointed to find that only footage filmed inside the historic building has been used.' Pauline Collins, returning to *Doctor Who* after nearly 40 years, told Manchester Online, 'One of the great things that Russell has really taken up in this reincarnation of *Doctor Who* is once you unleash the imagination of writers, it can go anywhere. He's kind of set us off on a rocket into the universe in a way. That's the appeal and that's why it's timeless. It can catch up with whatever is available to us scientifically, or in our imaginations, whatever the era is.'

The day of the episode's broadcast, the possibility of it being delayed or even postponed weighed on the minds of fans, owing to the fact that it was scheduled after a Liverpool v. Chelsea live football match; however, BBC sports presenter Gary Lineker assured viewers that the episode would follow 'even if the match goes to penalties'. 'Tooth and Claw' did in fact air as scheduled at 7.15 pm on 22 April. Initial overnight ratings were stronger than those for 'New Earth', with a gain of nearly a million viewers. Once again, ITV1 proved no match for *Doctor Who*, managing less than half of that for the programmes in the same time slot. *Doctor Who Confidential*, meanwhile, continued to pull in hundreds of thousands of viewers to BBC3 at 8 pm Saturday over the two weeks, both episodes ranking in the top five for non-terrestrial channels.

The morning-after reactions to 'Tooth and Claw' in the press were again mixed. 'So *Doctor Who* is an Ian Dury fan,' wrote Garry Bushell in the *People* on 23 April. 'Good man. Unfortunately the Blockheads could be writing his scripts. Let's be honest about Russell T Davies:... He's great at thinking up/nicking striking images... creepy cat nuns, killer monks, zombies with rice crispy-blitzed faces.... But no amount of flash computer images can disguise the pot-holes in his plots.' Bushell did note, however: 'As with last series, the best stories will be written by others. David Tennant... is a great casting, though: fun, upbeat, and his relationship with Rose is far less creepy than Chris Eccleston's was.' Said the *Sunday Mirror*: 'This Tennant guy is really scary-looking. The werewolf was pretty frightening. But nowhere near as spine-chilling as demon-faced Dave. In a big improvement on the half-baked first episode... What *did* happen to Tennant's accent? Why did Scotsman Dave decide that the latest Time Lord ought to speak mangled "Mockney" – like Dick Van Dyke in *Mary Poppins*? I mean, gor blimey gov'nor. It's proper 'orrible.' Newsquest called the episode 'another pacy, funny, exciting, scary rollercoaster ride.' The *Liverpool Echo* asked: 'What has happened to *Doctor Who*? Last time I checked, the acting was almost as plastic as the Time Lord's adversaries. But Saturday's romp in Victorian Britain was gladly lacking in rubber masks and Lycra leggings... So far, Tennant's Doctor has been much too lightweight, with a repertoire of clownish expressions and a laddish demeanour ill suited to the role of a being with enough years of existence on the clock to have learned how to grow up.' The *Daily Express* marked the episode as their 'Critic's Choice': 'The TARDIS delivers the Doctor and Rose back to 1879, where it turns out things aren't all they appear to be in the Scottish Highlands. This is partly because the programme is actually filmed in Wales and they're hoping nobody will notice, but mostly it's thanks to the presence of some rather sinister monks, blatantly up to no good. Oh, and there's a sort of werewolf-type thing on the rampage, which doesn't help. The Queen herself comes across as a tiny bit less stern and grumpy than you might expect.'

The *Evening News* of Scotland interviewed Ruth Milne, who played Flora the maid in 'Tooth and Claw': 'Everyone that I have ever met seems to know that I'm in *Doctor Who*... I'm so nervous about watching it, because I haven't had a chance to see the finished episode yet... I was absolutely thrilled [at being cast], because at the time, everyone was watching the first series and thought it was really good.' Dave Houghton, the visual effects supervisor on the episode, was interviewed by Sci Fi Wire in the US, saying: 'Our modellers and animators have worked on films like *Harry Potter*. So they were very well aware of what they could achieve in the time allowed, and we planned the episode accordingly... I think our werewolf is the best creature we've done for the show so far. It's fantastic.' Meanwhile, the *Sun* wondered if the previous weekend's debut episode had really been the 'television event of the year' as the BBC had implied. 'You don't think BBC1 over-sold it just the teeniest little bit, do you?... At the very least, you'd expect Series Two to open with a dynamite episode and maybe some Daleks or Cybermen, wouldn't you? But oh no. Instead? We have a huge letdown, from the moment David Tennant's pop-eyed, Mockney Doc took aim at the entire universe... and ended up back in a field full of cowpats in south Wales... Because what's happened here is that, at best, someone (probably Russell T Davies) has chosen the wrong opening episode. Or, at worst, we're in for a lousy series. Hopefully it's the former.'

It was far too early to see if there would be a backlash this year, as so many other returning television series had experienced over the years (a phenomenon often referred to in the USA as a 'sophomore slump', with a perceived drop in quality for a series riding the waves of press attention). There were, though, signs that the public – and the television industry – still held the series in high regard, when *Doctor Who* won five categories on 22 April at the BAFTA Cymru Awards, the BAFTA ceremony for television and film made in Wales. *Doctor Who* picked up the award for Best Drama Series as well as awards in direction, costuming, make-up and photography, and Davies was also presented with the Sian Phillips Award for Outstanding Contribution to Network Television. The critics might be addressing perceived faults with the second series, but the production team was riding high.

CHAPTER EIGHT:
RIDING THE WAVE

At long last, the second series of new *Doctor Who* was back on television. 'New Earth' and 'Tooth and Claw' had both enjoyed very high ratings and high audience appreciation figures from the audience and, at the end of April 2006, while the series sped onward, it was time to take a few steps back into the past.

LATE APRIL: 'SCHOOL REUNION'

In the lead-up week to the debut of the series' third episode, 'School Reunion', there was not only the usual press hype about the episode, but a few developments off the screen to go along with it. *Blue Peter* was joined on 24 April by actress Elisabeth Sladen, who arrived in the show's own TARDIS to discuss her forthcoming appearance. Sladen spoke to the presenters about her character, Sarah Jane Smith, and how David Tennant had the qualities that make a good Doctor 'in spades'. Sladen then appeared on 26 April on BBC1's *Breakfast* show, with clips shown from both her original series run and the approaching episode. She also gave a video interview to BBC Norfolk, available on their website. *The Times* announced on 24 April that K-9, the robot sidekick from the original *Doctor Who* series soon to appear alongside Sladen in 'School Reunion', would subsequently be making a further return to television in his own series. This spin-off was being worked on by one of the character's creators, Bob Baker, and had been commissioned by the Jetix Europe children's entertainment channel. 'Doctor Who's faithful robotic assistant, who will be reunited with his master on Saturday in a special guest appearance on the revived BBC show, will become a star in his own right – equipped with a lethal blaster – in a computer generated series made in partnership with the Walt Disney Corporation.' Details would later emerge that the series, originally announced as animation, would instead be a mix of live action and computer-animated imagery.

The newspapers and magazines for the several days prior, meanwhile, featured the usual episode previews. 'Welcome back, Sarah Jane and K-9!' read the *Radio Times* cover, with the inside marking 'School Reunion' as 'An episode to relish'. Sladen, Anthony Head, effects consultant Mike Tucker and The Mill's Will Cohen were interviewed for the magazine. The *Sunday Times* said in their episode preview, 'Old-school *Doctor Who* fans might well feel a particular frisson of adolescent excitement tonight... There are old scores to settle and Rose has a chance to find out how following the Doctor round will affect her life long-term.' *Heat* said of the episode, 'It's always a nervous moment when you get an episode of *Doctor Who* not written by its new supremo Russell T Davies. Not that many of them ever turn out to be anything other than top-notch, it's just that Davies sets the benchmark so high.' *Closer* said 'Diehard *Who* fans are in for a treat,' while *Inside Soap* called K-9 the 'Telly Hero of the Week'. *Sneak* chose the episode as Saturday's 'pick of the day', writing, 'Will the never-ending sexual tension between the twosome finally crack? Just get a room!'

The *Southland Echo* interviewed writer Toby Whithouse, who told the paper: 'It's the first thing I have ever written that [my kids] could possibly watch. They loved it. My son's very proud... I started writing it before the first series went out. I found out [that Tennant was to play the Doctor] on the news when I was about halfway through writing the episode. Nobody knew how David was going to do his Doctor. With Christopher Eccleston, I knew what his Doctor was like. David had just been on TV in *Casanova* and I'd watched that and thought he was fantastic. I thought I'd write it as if he was playing that character – without all the sex! That seemed to do the trick.' *Sci Fi Wire* also spoke to Whithouse, who commented: 'I could probably name all the Doctors in the right order, and maybe four monsters, so I thought that made me quite a big fan – until I met the other writers and realised that I knew absolutely nothing!' He went on to say that he: '... actually remembered a little more than I thought I did, and the producers sent me tapes and DVDs of Sarah Jane episodes, which is really what I needed a refresher on. But, as I say, because Russell had reinvented the series, I don't think anyone would have thanked me if I had written a story too much like the previous *Doctor Who*, because the way it's done now has changed so radically. I think it was more important that I got that right.' The *Herald* spoke to Elisabeth Sladen, who said that she had some collectibles from the series: 'I've got a Dalek [model], because my husband, Brian Miller, was the voice of one. I've also got a figurine of Sarah Jane Smith and a TARDIS. It's a nice remembrance. But some of the merchandise in the 1980s was so awful. I actually wrote to complain.' Sladen told the UK Press Association that when she got the call from the new series' production team, 'I thought they might be asking me to come back for just one small jokey scene, in a little homage to the old programme. I was actually thinking, "How can I turn this down? My agent will kill me," because I wouldn't have wanted to have done anything like that... I suppose I just thought it was a really good opportunity, and also a challenge to see if we could get it to work.' Guest star Anthony Head told the *Mirror*, 'The script is great and I liked the idea of being able to do a character part, rather than a romantic role. Billie is absolutely adorable, a genuinely lovely person. She's cute as hell, but I don't find her sexy. She's half my age. I wouldn't go there.' Director James Hawes told Sci Fi Wire, 'I think it's going to surprise a lot of people. There's so much going on... From the relationship between the old assistant [Sladen] and the now-assistant [Piper] to the menacing sparring between Anthony Head's character and the Doctor. So you've already got two separate character journeys going on. And then you've got the "spare part" Mickey, a metal dog, and I haven't even got to the aliens yet.' He added: 'There was a moment when K-9 first came out, and I knelt down to give him notes! I fell so completely under his spell that I literally forgot there was an operator I needed to be talking to.'

Radio Times reported that the start time for the episode, originally expected to be 7.00 pm, would be moved back 20 minutes to 7.20. As had been done for both the previous episodes in the run, BBC1 promoted 'School Reunion' as 'The One to Watch Tonight' on its debut day, with a ten-second trailer running between programmes throughout the day. The trailer used the scene where the Doctor uncovers and introduces 'K-9!' Early overnight ratings reports suggested a drop of nearly a million viewers from 'Tooth and Claw', though this was due to the episode debuting once again on a bank holiday weekend; all of UK television had experienced a drop in ratings that weekend, though *Doctor Who* was once again in first place on Saturday's charts of all UK networks by both audience numbers and by share.

'Following a minor setback with this year's series opener, my love affair with *Doctor Who*... is firmly back on,' wrote Charlie Brooker in the *Guardian* of 30 April, the morning of the episode's transmission. 'Tonight's episode... brought tears to my eyes. Perhaps I'm losing my mind, or perhaps I'm just a sucker for a bit of bittersweet nostalgia, especially when it involves a ludicrous robot dog.' The *Scotsman* said: 'David Tennant seems to have settled into the Time Lord's shoes and is starting to have fun with the role. Not quite as much fun as Tom Baker had, perhaps, but then it'd take a lot to convince me that the first Baker wasn't the best Doctor ever... Just like the TARDIS, *Doctor Who* manages to be more than it first appears.' The reviewer in the *Lancashire Evening Telegraph* wrote: 'Sarah Jane back with the Doctor; K-9 firing his red laser and wagging his metal tail. Suddenly I became an eight-year-old all over again. I don't know about Doctor Who being a time traveller, [but] I suspect that actress Elisabeth Sladen must know something about defying the years, as she didn't look any different from when she first appeared in the series back in the '70s. After a shaky start, the second series of the new *Doctor Who* is getting back on track.' The *Herald* said: 'Doctor Who struck a far more acerbic comedy note – at least, it did when it wasn't coming over all grief-stricken for the transient nature of humanity. Heavy stuff for a Saturday tea-time, and all the more engrossing for it... Profoundly good, *Doctor Who* is.' The *Times* opined: 'Every Saturday, one wonders, can *Doctor Who* get any better? Surely it couldn't, without in some way hurting us? And yet, every week, it does get better... I was one year old when Sarah Jane originally left *Doctor Who*, so I didn't have a danny who she was, really, but even I was blubbing by the end. I can't believe something this good is a kid's show. Children raised on this stuff are going to be light years ahead of the rest of us. We'll probably be their chimp-gimps by 2012.'

The *Western Mail*, on the other hand, was a little less enthusiastic: 'Reunited with the regenerated Doctor, there was genuine pathos as [Sarah Jane] described the pain of falling in love with a Time Lord who never returned her calls. But at least she got custody of the dog – just a shame it was K-9, a robot so tiresome he made Metal Mickey seem scintillating company.' The Blogcritics website said: 'Overall, this was a good reunion of an old guest star to the show. In terms of the quality of the episode, it was only fair. Perhaps when the Cybermen come along later this season, the writers will finally use their full abilities to make a classic episode. That's one of the conditions in being a fan of a show: you stick with it even in the dark times.' And the *Leicester Mercury* summed it up quite succinctly: 'It was a hoot.' Interestingly, there was very little in the press about the change in status for Noel Clarke; no longer merely a guest star, he was actually now in the thick of things, being a regular part of the TARDIS crew. However short-lived that ultimately might prove.

ON BOTH SIDES OF THE SCREEN

While *Doctor Who* continued its second series, as April ended and May began there were a number of developments and a lot of press attention. *Doctor Who Magazine* continued its run of exclusive announcements by revealing several members of the third series' writing team in its issue released at the end of April. The first of two returnees would be Steven Moffat (whose second series episode 'The Girl in the Fireplace' would be seen within the week), who would contribute an episode he'd thought of during his work on the first series (though, he wryly promised, it would 'not be as good as "The Empty Child"'). The second would be Paul Cornell, whose first series episode, 'Father's Day', had been a hit with many viewers; he would contribute a two-part story. Two new faces – that is, new to writing episodes, rather than contributing to *Doctor Who* in other capacities – would be Gareth Roberts, long-time *Doctor Who* novelist who had also penned the interactive adventure 'Attack of the Graske' and scripted the mobile-unit TARDISodes, writing one episode, and Helen Raynor, series script editor and *Torchwood* writer, contributing a two-parter.

Sky News on 27 April, in an interview with the Duke of York, stated: 'The Duke revealed details of family life during his childhood when he would rollerblade in state apartments, race in miniature cars with his brother Prince Edward and watch the BBC show *Doctor Who* with the Queen.' During the interview the Prince said that he was 'a child of the original *Doctor Who*'. The same day, the *Stage* claimed that Billie Piper was 'in talks' to play Fanny Price in an ITV adaptation of *Mansfield Park* and stated that she would 'return for a third series of *Doctor*

Who – although she is expected to bow out early in order to juggle other projects'. The *Edinburgh Evening News* reported: 'David Tennant has helped out his father's former church in Edinburgh by donating his copy of the script from the Time Lord's latest adventure... Sale organisers are consulting *Doctor Who* memorabilia experts before setting a price on the script, which has also been signed by David's co-star Billie Piper.' The *Daily Mirror* profiled effects designer Mike Tucker, noting: 'When Dalek maker Mike Tucker received his BAFTA nomination letter, he was gutted. It's not that he's got anything against being honoured for his TV model-making work, it's that in the same post he received his redundancy notice from the BBC. But at least he could prove he was good at his job – which helped him make the decision to set up his own effects business.' Tucker told the *Mirror*, 'It certainly sweetened the pill a little. I knew I wasn't being got rid of because my work was rubbish!' The *Daily Star* reported, inaccurately: '*Doctor Who* fans have been turning up to secret filming locations in Cardiff after being tipped off about the crew's whereabouts. And surprisingly the tips came from the BBC's own website, leaving bosses fearing for the cast's safety.' A BBC spokesperson told the *Daily Star*: 'Fans were turning up on set in Cardiff and we couldn't work out how they knew where we were. Eventually one person was quizzed about how he discovered our whereabouts and we were stunned when they told us it was our own website. People were posting sightings of Billie (Piper) and David (Tennant), giving details of their locations within minutes.' In fact, fans were not able to discover these details on the BBC website.

On the subject of the show as a whole, Ian Hislop, the editor of *Private Eye* magazine and a regular panellist on the topical television news game *Have I Got News For You*, told *The Times*: 'I'm a huge fan. If Russell T Davies wanted me to appear, I'd be there... I think it's time for Davros to be back, isn't it?' Media Blvd's reporter said he was: '... sceptical when I learned of the planned return of this iconic programme. Other remakes or renewals of classics had failed to impress me – some had downright infuriated me –and I had little hope for the new *Doctor Who* being any different. I was nervous and sick to my stomach: was my childhood memory about to be destroyed forever? I expected to hate the new *Doctor Who*... [but] I was pleasantly surprised!... As Season Two begins in the UK, with yet another Doctor to get to know and love, my daughter and I will sit huddled together on our sofa (and my sister and her children will be on theirs), and once again, the cushions will be fought over as the scary aliens appear. And maybe, just maybe, a new generation of sci-fi lovers will be born ...' Worldscreen website noted that Billie Piper was at Lake Lucerne, Switzerland, at the end of April for an award given for her appearance on *The Friday Night Project* at the international entertainment television Rose d'Or festival.

May began with the news that Piper had signed a six-figure deal to write her autobiography. 'The 23-year-old will tell all about her marriage to Chris Evans and her journey from teen pop singer to award-winning actress,' said the *Daily Mail*, noting that the book would be published this autumn by Hodder & Stoughton. 'It may sound ridiculous,' Piper commented, 'being just 23, but I've a few good stories I'd like to share.' (An unofficial biography, meanwhile, was announced in late May and was published in August, and the probability is that it was this book, written by Chris Stevens and published by Michael O'Mara Books, that prompted Piper to sell her own autobiography.) Camille Coduri told the *Sun* of 2 May: 'This series is certainly scarier and darker than the first one, and I know there have been concerns. But I don't think they should have a warning beforehand or anything like that.' Two days later, the *Sun* reported Coduri as saying: 'I think David [Tennant] is the sexiest Doctor I have ever seen. I didn't think he was so sexy until I saw him at a screening of the show, then I realised that he's gorgeous. He is 110% sexier in real life, and he's great to work with.' Andrew Hayden-Smith, soon to be seen in the two-part Cybermen story, told the BBC's *It's Hot* magazine, 'I really wanted to do a good job. I'm pleased with what I've done. Everything about *Doctor Who* is great, the stories, the actors, the effects – the whole team behind it are great too. There's nothing else like it on TV.' *BBC News* interviewed Roger Lloyd-Pack, who would also appear in these episodes: 'The Cybermen are definitely more scary than they were. I am limited about what I can tell you. But I can say that I'm a baddie and I have a factory in which I capture people from London and upgrade their brains to Cyberman status.'

Newsquest website reviewed the DVD release of the first two episodes of the year, 'The Christmas Invasion' and 'New Earth', saying: 'Somehow managed to slip through quality control. The special effects are polished and there are loopy leaps of imagination but the scripts lack character development and taut plotting.' icWales on 4 May echoed earlier reports that *Doctor Who* had made Cardiff a tourist destination: '*EastEnders* is eternally linked with London, Morse epitomised Oxford, and Bergerac is synonymous with Jersey. Now Cardiff has its very own TV series that is attracting thousands of tourists... Now one city centre hotel is offering a special *Doctor Who* package, especially for visitors who want to experience the locations where the Time Lord battled with the Cybermen and defeated the Daleks. The Park Plaza Hotel is charging... for visitors to stay in the centre of the action.' The Newbury Today website profiled Sam Storey, age 10, who had appeared on *Totally Doctor Who* alongside Noel Clarke the previous week: 'Sam won on the day and walked away with a whole host of *Doctor Who* goodies. Had the hours of watching the show, which is seen by around nine million viewers each week, and reading the books not paid off for the Brockhurst school pupil, Sam would have been forced to part with his prized possession – a Reading football shirt.' The *Hackney Gazette* on 5 May said, 'From the moment Billie Piper as a possessed Rose Tyler looked at herself in the mirror and exclaimed, "Oh my God, I'm a chav," you just knew that Saturday night TV had at last moved out of the mundane... With *Doctor Who* now working on so many different levels it's compulsive viewing of a quality normally reserved for big boy's telly such as *Messiah* and *Cracker*.' The *Paisley Daily Express* reported: 'Stunned regulars at a town centre pub couldn't believe their eyes when Doctor Who strolled in for a surprise visit. David Tennant, who plays the Time Lord in the hugely popular BBC TV series, turned heads when he walked through the doors of the Bull Inn, in New Street, Paisley sporting a hairy new look.' The *Daily Express* on 5 May quoted original series companion actress Bonnie Langford as saying, 'I love the new series. I think both David and Billie are marvellous.' Sci Fi Wire interviewed Steven Moffat, whose second series episode was to air the next weekend and whose episodes 'The Empty Child' and 'The Doctor Dances' would air in May in the US: 'I didn't know the story was going to be as powerful as it was, and I certainly had no idea there would be kids saying, "Are you my Mummy?" So that was all very exciting.'

DOCTOR WHO GOES TO THE BAFTAS

On 7 May, *Doctor Who* confirmed it had won the respect that it so richly deserved – and that many critics said was long overdue – as it won both the awards it was nominated for at the British Academy of Film and Television Arts (BAFTA) awards: Best Drama Series and the Pioneer Audience Award for Best TV Programme of 2005. In addition, the Dennis Potter Award for outstanding writing for television went to Russell T Davies. Davies, Piper and Tennant were all on hand for the ceremonies.

A clip from 'The Parting of the Ways' was shown before the announcement for Best Drama Series; Piper, Collinson, Gardner and Davies came on stage to accept the award, with Tennant applauding from back at the show's table. Gardner gave an acceptance speech on behalf of the series, thanking Christopher Eccleston, Piper and particularly Davies as well as the entire production staff. The group was startled by the sudden arrival of a jet-black Dalek, which, voiced by Nicholas Briggs, announced: 'All BAFTAs will be surrendered to the Daleks!' (This turned out to be a spoiler for the series finale, since the black Dalek was supposed to be a surprise element of the concluding two-parter.) Presenter Kevin Whately foiled the Dalek's plans by putting a hand over its eyestalk. Gardner admitted that they wouldn't have been there *without* the Daleks. Sir David Jason presented the Pioneer Audience Award, comparing *Doctor Who* to *Strictly Come Dancing*: 'One,' he said, 'is about a spry but eccentric one-million-year-old man and his sexy sidekick [referring to *Strictly* presenter, veteran variety entertainer Bruce Forsyth], the other is about a flying police box.' Piper accepted the award on behalf of the programme, grinning and describing it as 'a treat!' Piper enthused about how much the award meant to the cast and crew and how grateful they were.

David Tennant, in full kilt regalia, came onto the stage to present the Dennis Potter Award. Noting that he was proud to count Davies as a boss and a friend, he outlined Davies's career and achievements to date, highlighted by clips of his work and remarks from colleagues including Gardner, actors Nina Sosanya and Matt Lucas (*Casanova*), Anthony Cotton (*Queer as Folk*) and Lesley Sharp (*Bob & Rose* and *The Second Coming*), Nicola Shindler of the Red Production Company, David Liddiment (former Director of Programmes at ITV) and Piper. 'Dennis Potter understood that television was an art form that was new and unique,' Tennant said. 'Any writer who gets a BAFTA presented in his name has to be something very special indeed.' Taking the stage, Davies thanked the Academy for 'an honour beyond words'. He gave special thanks to a friend, Sally Watson, who once asked him, 'Why don't you write like you?', when he worried about comparing himself to other writers; Davies claimed it was the best piece of advice he had ever been given.

The BAFTA awards were televised a day later, on Monday 8 May, on ITV1. BBC News 24 and BBC1's evening news programmes on 7 May, meanwhile, both covered the event, including clips of the Dalek's arrival at the ceremony. The news reports that evening (with actual clips from the programme to be televised) featured interviews with Tennant, who said that the series had 'cross-nation appeal... unlike anything else I've ever been involved with'. The *Guardian* made *Doctor Who*'s win front-page news, noting '*Doctor Who* finally materialises on red carpet as TV series scoops drama prize' and focusing on a supposed previous lack of industry awards for the series discussed in the press by Davies (omitting the fact that the series had won several other industry awards). It also noted that Anna Maxwell Martin, who had won Best Actress for BBC1's *Bleak House*, had been a guest star in the first series of *Doctor Who*. Later in the month, it would be announced that Mike Tucker, who had worked on both *Doctor Who* series, had won a Visual Effects BAFTA for his work on the BBC1 documentary *Hiroshima*.

At last, *Doctor Who* had some of the respect it had long deserved; with such a huge win at the BAFTA awards, it was no longer a Saturday night fluff piece but held the honour of being one of the UK's flagship drama series.

EARLY MAY: 'THE GIRL IN THE FIREPLACE', 'RISE OF THE CYBERMEN', 'THE AGE OF STEEL'

The same weekend that *Doctor Who* made such a splash at the BAFTA awards, the series presented its fourth episode, 'The Girl in the Fireplace', by Steven Moffat. Though *Radio Times* had no mention of the episode on its cover – the first time in six weeks that this had been the case – there was still plenty of coverage of the episode inside, including an interview with Moffat in which he said, 'I wouldn't say this episode is as sinister, but there's an opening sequence that might frighten children.' Moffat himself posted online on the Outpost Gallifrey forum shortly before the release of the issue stating that the *Radio Times* article contained 'story-killing' spoilers. Writer Alison Graham wrote in the magazine that the episode was 'terrific family entertainment.' The issue also predicted *Doctor Who*'s huge win at the BAFTAs: 'It's got to be *Doctor Who*, worthy though the others are. Russell T Davies's joy, enthusiasm and vision suffused every episode of a series that revitalised Saturday family viewing and introduced a new generation to one of TV's most enduring heroes.' *Heat* said: 'This week's episode, as well as being funny, ambitious, mysterious and as scary as we've come to expect, also functions as a superb showcase for Tennant. He switches brilliantly from action scenes to comedy and, most importantly, to intense romance in this intriguing story... This is Tennant's episode all the way.' *Closer* asked viewers: 'Sit back and enjoy quite possibly the most surreal *Doctor Who* yet.' The official *Doctor Who* website featured new video diaries from the making of the episode, and uploaded a new commentary featuring Moffat and actor Noel Clarke. Young guest star Jessica Atkins also appeared on *Totally Doctor Who*.

'The Girl in the Fireplace' was, however, overshadowed by the approach of the highly anticipated two-part story that would bring back the famous Cybermen to the series, an event widely covered in the British press over the previous year. On 2 May, a press screening of the two-parter was held at the Apollo West End Theatre in London, with members of the production team and the writer and director present (though not Tennant and Piper, who were back in Cardiff). *Radio Times* for the week starting 13 May featured *Doctor Who*'s fifth cover in just over a year, a close-up of the Cyber-Controller, while inside the issue were photos of the new Cybermen design and several interviews. 'We wanted to bring the Cybermen into the 21st Century... and give them a uniformity that they didn't have previously,' said prosthetics man Neill Gorton. 'Davies was adamant they had to look like steel... We ended up doing it as "cold-cast metal": you take a powdered metal, add it to a resin and brush that into your moulds, then put fibreglass behind that.' Production designer Edward Thomas revealed: 'The whole design concept of the episode was that it was going to be art deco, so we kept the very art deco lines [for the Cyberman design]... It all has to feel as if it clips together.' Actor Paul Kasey told the magazine: 'It took about half an hour [to put it all on], the first time. By the end of the shoot, I'd got it down to about ten minutes.' Writer Tom MacRae said that the two-part story has gone 'to the root of what's scary [about the Cybermen], which is that they come and they take you and they don't kill you, but they turn you into one of them.' Meanwhile, television and radio trailers focused during the week on the Cybermen, and many newspapers issued story previews as usual. *Heat* magazine said: 'We've been lucky enough to have nothing but one-off eps so far this series, but now we have to cope with one of those cliffhanging two-parters that make us every bit as frustrated as they did when we were kids.' *Closer* commented: 'The monsters in this series of *Doctor Who* have been a bit namby-pamby so far. So... it steps up a level.' The BBC's in-house magazine *Ariel* featured an article written by MacRae but disguised as an interview with John Lumic, the villain of the story.

Other mentions of the series – and the mythos – were popping up in the press. The *Guardian* compared revelations about Liberal Democrat MP Mark Oaten's private life to Sir Robert's situation (specifically his wife being away) in 'Tooth and Claw': 'If only Mr Oaten had cared to name the psychiatrist he has been seeing for all these years, I would call him and moot the possibility that the MP and his family were in the thrall of some terrible evil – possibly lupine – and advise him to flag down the TARDIS without delay.' Broadcast Now website called BBC1 'the UK's most creative channel', because its 'dominance in the drama series category is fuelled by hits such as *Doctor Who* and *Bleak House*.' *Media Guardian* reported that ITV1 had suffered the worst audience share in its history due to the broadcast of 'Rise of the Cybermen' and other programmes that Saturday. A BBC spokesperson told *BBC News*, 'We are delighted that the thrilling FA Cup Final and the Cybermen's return to *Doctor Who* proved a winning combination to BBC1 viewers.' *BBC Wales Today* featured a story about the National Orchestra of Wales recording Murray Gold's new arrangement of the title theme for the series.

Doctor Who once again featured on *Blue Peter* on 15 May, with presenter Gethin Jones – who appeared in the two-parter as an extra inside one of the Cybermen suits – remarking on how much mail the programme had received from children with the return of the series. A pre-recorded segment showed Jones's visit to the set shooting the episode, as well as brief chats with Andrew Hayden-Smith, Tennant and Piper. The segment was made available on *Blue Peter's* website. Jones later followed up the piece with a segment the following week on the inspiration for the clockwork monsters of 'The Girl in the Fireplace'. Meanwhile, BBC1 announced yet *another* time change to the *Doctor Who* schedule: 'The Age of Steel' would go out on 20 May at 6.35 pm (the *Doctor Who Confidential* segment then airing on BBC3 from 7.25 pm) due to the *Eurovision Song Contest* broadcast that evening. Noel Clarke appeared on *GMTV* on 19 May to discuss the second episode of the two-parter, while new trailers were broadcast that Friday and the morning of transmission. A brief sketch about the series appeared on *Dead Ringers* on 22 May. BBC3 also announced that it would start repeating the already-broadcast episodes of Series Two, starting on 22 May at 7.00 pm.

Radio Times once again selected 'The Age of Steel' as its 'drama of the week', calling it 'very possibly the best episode yet'. *Heat* magazine's reviewer wrote: 'You won't be too shocked to learn that the gang survive last week's cliff-hanger. With Trigger from *Only Fools and Horses* poised to take over the city via his earpods (imagine what he could do with an earpod nano), the Doctor infiltrates his robofactory – formerly known as Battersea Power Station – while Mickey literally has a word with himself and bucks up enough to finally do something useful.' *Closer* said: 'It's a tough episode for Rose too as she suffers not one, but two, heartbreaking goodbyes.' The episode saw the farewell of Noel Clarke as a short-lived regular, although he would return briefly at the end of the season.

LATE MAY: 'THE IDIOT'S LANTERN'

May's *Doctor Who* broadcasts were concluded on 27 May with the airing of 'The Idiot's Lantern' by Mark Gatiss. *Heat* magazine said: 'If you've been wondering why a Time Lord with access to all the places in the universe and the whole of time to choose from keeps ending up on Earth within a two-century range of history, blame series producer Russell T Davies – he likes to keep the Doctor close to home so that the kiddie viewers can be frightened by familiar things.' Guest star Maureen Lipman was interviewed on *Sunday AM* by Andrew Marr; the two discussed the poor state of TV drama, but singled out *Doctor Who* as one of the bright spots. Lipman also wrote a comment about her hairstylists in the *Guardian*: 'I'm normally very happy with my hairdressing arrangements... But I shall have to grovel next time I go, or pretend the make-up girls did it on the set of *Doctor Who* to make me look more alien.' *BBC News* reported a week later that Lipman had praised the series as 'giving hope for family drama on television.' According to the report, Lipman told the Hay Festival, 'I think Billie Piper and David Tennant are wonderful and the writing is so good, it gives me hope that these writers are writing for families.' She also noted, regarding her role on screen, 'My children seemed to think that was quite normal. It was very difficult, I didn't see a soul, I was trapped in a TV set in Alexandra Palace, with a director and producer. It was like doing a Joyce Grenfell sketch. I had to imagine what was being said to me.' Jamie Foreman, playing Eddie Connolly in the episode, appeared on the *Paul O'Grady Show* on 26 May, saying: 'The costumes are fantastic... It's like watching a Spielberg movie.' The official *Doctor Who* website featured a commentary for the episode – this time with Ron Cook, who had played Magpie in the episode, costume designer Louise Page and make-up designer Sheelagh Wells – and a game called 'Defeat the Wire!' The Welsh-language *S4C News* programme spoke to fans on location at the recording of the episode, with a Welsh-dubbed Tennant and Piper speaking to the audience.

The *Guardian* said the episode: '... attracted 6.3m viewers, the lowest of the year to date. I'm sure it is no coincidence that it was also the worst episode of the year thus far – a satire of the brain rotting properties of television set in 1953 during the Queen's coronation. It exhibited all the worst attributes that have been turning the series into a smug pantomime... At least the villainous Wire on the weekend, played by Maureen Lipman, was a proper evil baddie.' *CBBC Newsround* said that it was 'a very different episode', noting: 'It rattles along well enough, but unfortunately doesn't have the energy that previous episodes have had. It has a slightly clumsy sub plot about equality between men and women, and a villain who's never really satisfactorily explained – I much prefer us to understand more about their background.' The report did, however, say: 'It's good to see Rose well entwined in the nastiness that's going on.'

Ratings for the episode had indeed continued a slight downward trend, as the *Guardian* had reported, partly due to the *Soccer Aid* charity event but mostly thanks to a public holiday and good weather at the end of a week-long school break. *Media Guardian* on 29 May asked prematurely, 'Where have the viewers gone? BBC1's *Doctor Who* revival has been lavished with critical praise and awards, but there are signs midway through its second series that viewers may be tiring of the time travelling sci-fi drama.' *Media Guardian* said that the episode was the lowest-rated yet, but also remarked that the show's haphazard scheduling – with episodes starting first at 7.15 pm, then at 7.00 pm and 'The Age of Steel' airing even earlier – might be causing confusion. It also noted the stiff competition from live events, including the upcoming BBC1 World Cup coverage. Yahoo News quoted a BBC spokesperson as saying, 'The series is proving to be incredibly popular with audiences and has continued to outperform strong competition from its competitors week on week. However, episode seven did transmit over a bank holiday weekend when more people are likely to be away.'

Rumours abounded across the Internet of two new pieces of casting: Gabriel Woolf, who had played Sutekh in the 1975 *Doctor Who* serial 'Pyramids of Mars', and Bella Emberg of *The Benny Hill Show* and *Russ Abbot's Madhouse*, who had previously made two uncredited appearances in the series in the early 1970s. Their casting was confirmed in *Doctor Who Magazine* released on 26 May, which also noted that the final edits for the rest of the series had been concluded by the magazine's press time, and that both writer Matthew Graham and director Euros Lyn would work on series three. (Graham's other commitments would later lead him to pull out.) *Heat* magazine and other periodicals featured photos of Peter Kay's character in the upcoming episode 'Love & Monsters', while the This Is Lancashire website said: 'This is Bolton comedian Peter Kay as you have never seen him before. The *Phoenix Nights* star has swapped Brian Potter's wheelchair for green skin and pointy ears as he plays a new Jabba-the-Hut style villain in *Doctor Who*.' *People* interviewed Camille Coduri, who said, 'You don't need to get your bra off to prove yourself. A lot of these young actresses who do it are really beautiful and talented and I just think... "Have a bit of dignity."' *Casualty* veteran Will Thorp told the UK Press Association, 'I would have said "yes" to whatever [the part] was,' referring to his appearance in the next two weeks' episodes. The *Independent* asked, 'What era can we be said to have entered when it is no longer possible for a single person to have consumed every text bearing the *Doctor Who* logo? This month, the tally of new material includes four episodes of the new Saturday night series on BBC1, four instalments each of the cable spin-offs *Doctor Who Confidential* and *Totally Doctor Who*, one issue of *Doctor Who Magazine*, two issues of the *Doctor Who Adventures* comic, two audio-only dramas on CD, three hardback novels, one paperback novella, seven mass market non-fiction books and one academic study by the Professor of Film at Leicester University. So to participate completely in the cultural practice of *Doctor Who*, you would have to devote every waking hour to it.' The icNewcastle website spoke to fan John Paul Green, who had appeared as an extra in the Cybermen two-parter: 'The hardest thing was keeping it a secret from everyone... People commented "that looks a lot like you", and then the penny dropped. They were all utterly shocked and couldn't believe I'd managed to keep it from them.' The *Evening Express* said, 'I know a Time Lord who is desperately in need of treatment. To describe the second series of *Doctor Who* as "disappointing" is a bit like describing the Titanic as a wee mishap at sea... The only tortured souls now are those of us who wish we had a TARDIS to bring back the Doctor who breathed magic into the character.'

EARLY JUNE: 'THE IMPOSSIBLE PLANET' AND 'THE SATAN PIT'

June began with the year's second double-header: Matt Jones' 'The Impossible Planet' and 'The Satan Pit'. The two-parter, set on an alien planet trapped in the orbit of a black hole, introduced the nightmarish-looking Ood, which *Radio Times* said 'might put you off eating spaghetti bolognaise ever again'. Davies told *Radio Times*, 'I loved inventing the Slitheen and Raxacoricofallapatorius and then I thought, "Why don't I just call something the Ood?" They're the most brilliantly made monster in the world. I love them.' Neill Gorton, explaining the prosthetics brief to the magazine, said, 'There's always a brief description in the script, and for this story it was "bald albino things with tentacles like a sea anemone rather than a mouth."' *CBBC Newsround* said of the story, 'This is a seriously scary episode featuring a growing menace, there are lots of shocks and it leaves us on a great cliff-hanger... Presumably one of the reasons we haven't featured alien planets before is the relatively cheap cost of filming Earthbound episodes. This story certainly doesn't seem any cheaper than others, and in fact the effects are some of the best seen so far.' The *Forester* reported, 'Clearwell Caves boss Jonathan Wright and his children won't dare hide behind the sofa on Saturday when they hear the *Doctor Who* theme tune. They will be glued to the screen to see the tourist attraction get prime time BBC1 coverage. Scenes for the episode... were filmed in the bowels of the caves.'

The *Guardian* said of the first episode, 'The Impossible Planet', 'Oh, but this is fantastic – it's *Alien* plus *The Matrix* divided by *The Exorcist*... Thank God for *Doctor Who*.' The *Daily Star* wrote, 'Having lost the TARDIS in an earthquake on a planet at the rim of a black hole, [the Doctor and Rose] wondered what the rest of their lives would be like. For just a second they considered a life together then, as if reading each other's minds, started to blush and splutter. Yes, it was tongue-in-cheek, but not much less convincing than some of the scenes our soap operas dish up as serious drama.' Overnight ratings for the episode were down again, though *Doctor Who* remained one of the top-rated shows of the week and the audience share was significantly higher; the start of summer was having a direct impact on the viewers across UK television.

Of the follow-up, 'The Satan Pit', *CBBC Newsround* regular reporter Lizo Mzimba said: 'When I first heard the name of this episode a few months back, I wasn't really paying attention and thought that it was called "The Santa Pit" and that it was the name of this year's Christmas Special. I couldn't have been more off the mark... All in all an outstanding episode that's all that *Doctor Who* should be – the stuff of legend.' The *Daily Star* commented that Rose 'shows she can shoot from the hip with a space gun.' The *Guardian* noted the marketing of the episode: 'While today may be plain old 6 June to most of us, to some it's 06.06.06. That gives it a whole new level of significance, for it becomes the day of the beast, the birthday of the Antichrist – who is known by the number 666... Even *Doctor Who* is getting in on the act. He has a date with the devil this Saturday teatime.' Four days later, the *Guardian* also commented, 'Let's be honest: Series Two, so far, has been a bit of a bumpy ride. Even the Cybermen failed to rise to the occasion, and Chris Eccleston's tenure already feels like the halcyon days. Simply, this is no longer essential Saturday night viewing, and that's just wrong. So storylines like these are as welcome as a monogamous, straight-talking politician... More like this please, and quickly.' *Heat* said: 'When you call your episode "The Satan Pit", it had better live up to the title. So it's with relief that we report that the Doctor has not only to keep the Ood's planet from tipping into the black hole, but, if he can fit it into his schedule, stop the entire universe from being devoured by the Beast.' The *Cambridge Evening News* asked, 'What would the late Mary Whitehouse (God rest 'er) have made of last week's *Doctor Who* episode? – surely the most terrifying thing seen on TV at 7 o'clock on a Saturday night since Chico did the Time Warp [on televised talent contest *The X-Factor*]... Television as thrilling and imaginative as this – British television at that (think how many hours your little 'uns spend soaking up American "cultural values") – can only be a good thing. They should put *Doctor Who* on the national curriculum.'

In Australia, meanwhile, there was news of a debut date for Series Two of *Doctor Who*: the ABC Television Audience and Consumer Affairs Department began contacting enquiring fans on 1 June to let them know that Saturday 8 July at 7.30 pm was the newly scheduled premiere slot. Later, ABC began promoting the forthcoming series using the tagline 'Do you fancy a Christmas in July?', referring to the start of the series with 'The Christmas Invasion'. Meanwhile, Canadian fans were told that CBC Television had acquired rights to Series Two, which would start on 9 October at 8.00 pm; the series had been delayed for so long, after 'The Christmas Invasion' had aired in the country almost immediately after its UK transmission, to make way for sports coverage throughout the summer. (In fact, while Canada had received the first series directly after the UK, it would be beaten this time by the United States, where the second series would debut over a week earlier, on 29 September.) The Nederland 3 channel in the Netherlands meanwhile started transmitting the first series on 10 June, YLE2 in Finland announced that it would also start showing it from 10 September.

The series concluded its first year run in America on the Sci Fi Channel. Ratings for the debut season had hovered between 1.0 and 1.5 million viewers weekly for the Friday night first-runs, not far behind those for the channel's broadcasts of its other science-fiction series, *Stargate SG-1*, *Stargate Atlantis* and *Battlestar Galactica*, which were all on season break. Fans were doubtful if, on this showing, the series had done well enough to persuade Sci Fi to pick up the second series, although Sci Fi Wire, the channel's news service, said on 14 June, 'The new, updated *Doctor Who* boosted Sci Fi Channel's ratings on Friday nights by double digits.' The Futon Critic website, a respected source of industry and media news also noted 'the double-digit ratings growth this quarter on Fridays from 9 pm to 10 pm versus the time period last year', referring to the fact that *Doctor Who* was a broadcast original for the network in a time period (March to June) when it normally shows reruns. A pop-culture website called ICV2 stated: 'The second season will kick off in the US on Sci Fi Channel in October.' This report appeared at the time to be speculative, but the channel itself announced in August that the series would indeed return for a second year, on 29 September.

Back in the UK, the *Dead Ringers* series included a one-minute sketch in which the tenth Doctor accurately predicted lines and events based on his reading of spoilers in the *Radio Times* and in preview clips on *Totally Doctor Who* and *Doctor Who Confidential*. Actor/writer Stephen Fry meanwhile said in a chat hosted by the Douglas Adams Continuum website, 'Ah, now, unfortunately, I've had to pull out of the *Doctor Who* gig,' referring to his series two script that had recently been pushed to series three, but now appeared off the table altogether. 'Lack of time. I just couldn't find three minutes to string together. Barely enough time to go to the lavatory these days, let alone take on new projects.' Julie Gardner told attendees at the BBC Worldwide Licensing Showcase event held in St Albans, 'We're in pre-production on *Doctor Who* [Series Three]. We'll be filming for 34 weeks, beginning with a Christmas special.' Gardner then went on to say that the TARDIS would be travelling into the future during the third series: '... and into the past, where we will meet Shakespeare – and why wouldn't you?!' The *Mirror* reported that Tennant was the reason behind the change from the first season 'Doctor Who' credit for Eccleston, to his own 'The Doctor' credit at the end of each episode: 'As a kid, it always bothered me – obviously it's the name of the show, but he's not called Doctor Who.' The *Daily Express* reported on 2 June that guest star Peter Kay: '... fancies his chances as the Time Lord himself. Kay is a massive fan of the classic sci-fi show and is keen to take the lead role when David Tennant eventually hands in the keys to the TARDIS.' Said Kay to the paper, 'I think the Doctor should come from Bolton next time. He's always been a bit posh for my liking!' A reviewer for the *Evening Chronicle* wrote, 'I can't even put into words how superior David Tennant's Doctor is to that grinning, gurning fool who went before him... although Billie Piper is starting to grate on me. I can't help but wonder if in the first series all of my negative energies were so focused on Christopher "I'm a serious actor don't you know" Eccleston that she slipped under the radar. I think it's her strange Cockney accent that bothers me the most. Or the fact that she's gone a bit smug.'

Piper was presented with *Glamour* magazine's UK TV Actress of the Year award in early June, and the BBC Radio 1 website on 8 June featured a photo from the event, captioned, 'As if these two don't see enough of each other, David Tennant presents Billie Piper with her award. On style, Billie says she's inspired by Kate Moss, Nicole Ritchie and Marilyn Monroe.' The *Daily Star* quoted actress Shirley Henderson, from the forthcoming 'Love & Monsters', as saying about her co-star Peter Kay, 'Peter is the funniest man I've ever met. I couldn't stop laughing at him. It was such a joy working with him.' Actor Tom Baker, who had played the fourth Doctor from 1974 until 1981, told the *Daily Express*: 'I think the new fellow, David Tennant, is excellent. My only disappointment is that they didn't ask me back to play [renegade Time Lord] The Master. He and the Doctor are like Holmes and Moriarty: two sides of the same man. That would turn a few heads.' Lancasters Armourie on 7 June announced they would auction off the original prototype of the Sycorax sword they'd created for 'The Christmas Invasion', in aid of the Great Ormond Street Hospital for Children. The *Evening Herald* on 10 June profiled young Catherine Roberts, who would appear on *Totally Doctor Who* the next week: 'Catherine was going mental just to get the phone call from the BBC to interview her,' said her father Mike Roberts. 'Despite being told that she'd have to wait until they interviewed other fans, they were back on the phone in about five minutes saying she would be on the programme.' The same paper also reported: 'Being killed by a Cyberman was a dream come true for a Plymouth sci-fi fan who featured in the latest series of *Doctor Who*. Jules Burt has been a fan of the series since he was a boy, so was overjoyed to be offered a walk-on part in the episode "Rise of the Cybermen", which was aired on BBC1 in May. A dealer in sci-fi memorabilia, the 36-year-old from Lipson says acting is only a hobby.' Said Burt to the paper, 'We filmed at midnight and it was very atmospheric. Eleven Cybermen crashed through sugar glass windows and more filled the doorways. I had to duck between them and try to escape. I had to pinch myself. I kept thinking "I'm really in *Doctor Who*". It was a once in a lifetime experience.' ITN reported that Tennant had given his opinion about the World Cup: 'I don't get football; it just leaves me cold. It's got nothing to do with England, Scotland, anyone else, I just don't get it. I know there's the traditional Scottish thing that you can't support England, but I've lived here for 12 years, so I've got to try.' And a New Zealand tabloid called *Sunday News* offered up its own ludicrous news report: 'Lucy Lawless is hot favourite to take over the TARDIS and become the first female *Doctor Who*. Current stars Christopher Eccleston and David Tennant are both relinquishing their Time Lord status after one series and the cult show is now considering the idea of "guest Doctors". Landing Lucy for the role would be a major coup for the BBC.'

The *Daily Mirror* meanwhile said of Billie Piper's career, 'Just two years ago, she spent her time downing pints of lager in the pub, piling on the pounds and looking like she'd just rolled out of bed. But Billie Piper's down and out days are well and truly over.' The paper reported on the actress's part in the film *Things To Do Before You're 30*, which opened on 2 June. 'She was a complete knockout,' producer Marc Samuelson was quoted as saying. 'In the first meeting, she'd read the script, she was completely focused, very serious, very nice. She's perfect for the role. It's nice to discover that we knew exactly what we were doing.' The BBC Press Office issued a report about Piper's starring role in the forthcoming BBC1 adaptation of Philip Pullman's *The Ruby in the Smoke*, while the *Sun* of 12 June reported that she wanted: '... to take time out from her acting career to backpack around India and Africa. The *Doctor Who* actress is keen to explore more of the world – and doesn't want to do it in five star style.' Quoted from an interview in *OK!* magazine, Piper said: 'I definitely need a couple of months off, which I'm looking forward to. I want to allocate a considerable amount of time to travelling and then come back and hopefully get a job.' Not unsurprisingly, this report led to a resurgence of fan speculation about Billie's status as a regular in the series. Only a few days later, however, the world would have its answer.

FAREWELL, BILLIE PIPER... HELLO, FREEMA AGYEMAN

Confirming rumours that had been on the table for nearly a year, on 15 June BBC Wales issued a press release announcing that Piper was giving up her role as Rose Tyler. 'Billie Piper who has played Rose Tyler, the feisty young companion of both the ninth and tenth Doctors, will leave *Doctor Who* in a nail biting series two finale.'

'Rose and I have gone on the most incredible journey with Russell T Davies and the cast and crew of *Doctor Who* over the past two years,' said Piper in the press release. 'It has been an amazing adventure, and I can confirm it comes to an end, for now at least, as series two climaxes. I am truly indebted to Russell for giving me the chance to play Rose Tyler, and to all the *Doctor Who* fans old and new who have been so supportive of me in this amazing role. Thank you so much.' Davies himself was quoted as saying: 'It has been a wonderful experience working with Billie – we will miss her – and wish her all the success in the world for her future.

However, the *Doctor Who* team have had a whole year to plan this final scene and have created a stunning exit for Rose Tyler.'

With this announcement, it became clear that – despite the official denials that had been issued at the time – *Dreamwatch* magazine had been correct when it had first broken the story that Piper would be leaving and had quoted the actress's own agent as having spilt the beans. Some news outlets, including the *Sun*, now began to report that Rose would be killed off, perhaps picking up on the press release's question: 'Does saving the world mean the death of Rose Tyler?' Rumours were also posted on various web forums that Piper had only recently decided to leave the series, or that her departure had been prompted by a disagreement over money.

Naturally, attention turned toward the question of who would be Piper's successor as the Doctor's main companion. The *Sun* was early to join the fray on 16 June, getting it exactly right: 'Former *Crossroads* stunner Freema Agyeman was last night revealed to be the front-runner to replace Billie Piper in *Doctor Who*. Freema, 26, will appear in the final two episodes of the BBC1 sci-fi's current series playing the character Adeola... Insiders say Freema will join the Doctor in the TARDIS full-time in the third series after her appearance in the episodes called "Army of Ghosts" and "Doomsday"'. (Agyeman would, in fact, appear only in 'Army of Ghosts'.) A BBC source reportedly told the *Sun*, 'Freema is a fantastic actress. She is great in the final episode. And she is more than capable of stepping into Billie's shoes to play the Doctor's new cohort. No-one knew Billie could act before we gave her the job – and she has proved to be a sensation.' BBC spokespersons refused to comment on this report; meanwhile, other papers suggested that names possibly linked to the series also included Michelle Ryan (*EastEnders*) and Nikki Sanderson (*Coronation Street*).

Only three weeks later, on 4 July, 27-year-old actress Freema Agyeman was officially confirmed as joining the cast of *Doctor Who*, in the new role of Martha Jones – a different character from the one she had played in 'Army of Ghosts'. Agyeman, who had been seen as seductress Lola Wise in *Crossroads* in 2001 and had also appeared in such shows as *Casualty* (2004), *Silent Witness* (2005) and *The Bill* (2006), was introduced via a BBC press release in which Davies said, 'The search for a new companion had been underway for some time when I first saw Freema Agyeman. She had come in to audition for the part of Adeola in Series Two. Watching her during filming confirmed what an exciting new talent she was, so under cover of darkness we called her back in to audition with David for the role of the new companion. It was an immediate and sensational combination, and her range, presence and charm blew us all away.' Davies said that Tennant and Agyeman were 'terrific together' and noted that the first scripts had been written. He also confirmed that Martha would *not* be seen in the forthcoming Christmas special, but would instead be introduced in the first regular episode of the third series. Agyeman herself told the BBC Press Office: 'I've been keeping this secret from my friends for months – it's been driving me mad! Auditioning with David in secret down in Cardiff was unbelievable, but I never in my wildest dreams thought I'd actually become the new companion.' Agyeman also noted: 'Billie rightfully built up an amazing fan base and she will be missed, but I hope the fans are willing to go on new adventures with me.' Tennant said that Agyeman was: '... a joy to work with in episode 12 of the current series. She is not only very talented and very beautiful, she's [also] great fun, and I'm delighted she's coming on board the TARDIS full time.'

When Agyeman's role was confirmed in early July, the *Guardian* featured quotes from Sophie Aldred, a former companion herself from the series in the late 1980s: 'Most importantly, wear sensible shoes (I always wore Doc Martens) because you're bound to be going into a quarry at some stage. I always found myself in quarries, and I've noticed Rose Tyler has too. (I was pleased to see she was wearing sensible shoes.)... Also, don't wear jewellery that rattles. One of these days, you'll be hiding somewhere, your bracelets will jangle and before you know it, a monster will be coming for you... There was never any mention of romance with the Doctor in my day, but now that's a distinct possibility. The Doctor, in his current incarnation, is extremely handsome, so don't snog anyone else – stick with him.' icWales asked, 'How can Freema fill Billie's boots?... For one thing, she is not nearly as famous, having never reached number one in the music charts, married a DJ twice her age, or gone through a public divorce. Freema is also an actress by trade – albeit not yet enormously established in the TV world.' *The Independent* asked, 'Does colour matter? Would we be so interested in *Doctor Who*'s new sidekick if she was white?... It shouldn't be necessary to dwell on the fact that Freema is black, but it is.' The *Sunday Mirror* asked, 'Can Martha be Dalektable too?... Does Freema have what it takes to fill brilliant Billie's shoes? Because you get the feeling that without the incredibly popular Ms Piper, *Doctor Who*'s comeback would never have been such a triumph. Now it's up to Martha to prove that a Rose by any other name can smell as sweet!' The *Sunday People* simply noted, 'The real story about *Doctor Who*'s new assistant is not that she's black, but that she's won the role despite appearing on *Crossroads* – usually the kiss of death for any actress.'

LATE JUNE: 'LOVE & MONSTERS' AND 'FEAR HER'

The shock of Billie Piper's announcement in mid-June was not unlike that experienced by viewers and fans the previous year when news of Christopher Eccleston's departure became public, though it came considerably later in the year. While a replacement in Freema Agyeman would not be confirmed for several weeks, the end of June saw two additional new episodes, the one-episode stories 'Love & Monsters' and 'Fear Her', receiving their debut transmission.

'Peter Kay joins *Doctor Who* as the 'orrible Abzorbaloff!' said *Radio Times* for the week, illustrated with photographs of Kay being made up as the sinister creature created by young *Blue Peter* viewer William Grantham. The magazine featured an article on the 'Design a Monster'competition, noting that during his set visit, Grantham's reaction to the creature was, 'Oh. It was supposed to be the size of a double-decker bus.' Davies reportedly responded to William: '[You] didn't actually say that on your bit of paper'. Davies was also quoted as saying that the episode would be: 'Very different: different style, different feel. It's an experimental script. Not so experimental that people will run away screaming from Saturday-night BBC1, because you can experiment too much.' The *Observer* wrote, 'Forget those who would try and tell you that *Doctor Who* is for kids... Davies wrote the episode himself, and it is shot through with that humorous, self-referential charm [that has] made the series such a gem.' The *Sun* called the episode a 'monster munch... as *Doctor Who* dangles a big steak in front of his latest foe.' Reviewer Lizo from *CBBC Newsround* said: '"Love & Monsters" is the most bizarre episode since the series returned last year... It might sound like a bit of a mess, but thanks to Russell T Davies's sparkling script, it ends up as a hugely enjoyable show about *Doctor Who*, rather than a straight *Doctor Who* adventure.' The *Times* wrote that the episode was: '... essentially ephemeral. It was a bit of slapstick with Peter Kay as a vile Abzorbaloff – a lascivious green blob of what appeared to be the expanding foam that you inject into cavity walls, which was sporadically sprinkled with tufts of disturbing black hair, much in the manner of greasy spoon macaroni. Kaye, fairly understandably, appeared to be having a ball... Even when playing with the loveliest toy a scriptwriter ever had, Davies is hard as nails.' The *People* said: 'Oddly, Peter [Kay] seemed even stranger as [the Abzorbaloff's] alter-ego, sinister Victor Kennedy, who could have passed for Burl Ives. Burl sang about the Big Rock Candy Mountain. Victor looked like he'd eaten it.' The *Scotsman* said: 'Now here was an episode of *Doctor Who* with a difference... By the time the TARDIS arrived to half-save the day, I could almost hear the dismayed chatter of shell-shocked former fans. It's true, this episode came close to being a spoof, but it was actually quite nice to have a rest from the Doctor. Even saving the world gets boring sometimes.'

The following weekend saw the screening of Matthew Graham's 'Fear Her'. The BBC Press Office quoted Graham as saying that the episode was 'really quite a creepy story, which hopefully will tap into psychological fears a bit like "The Empty Child" did'. *Heat* awarded the episode five stars, writing: 'We'd love to be a fly on the wall at the *Doctor Who* production meetings as Russell T Davies punts ideas around, and says stuff like, "Wouldn't it be good if the Doctor and Rose ended up in London in 2012 to see the Olympics?"... Some moments are silly or cheesy or plain ridiculous, but no other show on TV has this level of commitment to letting the imagination run gloriously, giddily free. No other show takes these risks.' The *Guardian* called the episode 'great' and noted: 'It's absolutely terrifying: kids must be a lot more robust these days than they were in my day. I'm watching it from behind the sofa and I'm 41.' The *Financial Times* on 24 June said: '*Doctor Who* continues to be a wondrous thing, Russell T Davies and his collaborators having managed to retain the playful spirit of the original while creating storylines consistently smarter and even more inventive than previous incarnations of the show'. Ratings for both episodes took an upward turn, as BBC1 began to step up its trailers for the show again in the run-up to the end of the series.

In the midst of what was to be the calm before the storm of the two-part season finale, a number of other developments occurred. The official *Doctor Who* website reported that first assistant director Susie Liggat would become the series' new producer for one recording block while Phil Collinson took a much-needed month-long holiday. *Doctor Who Magazine* interviewed writer/editor Justin Richards, range consultant for BBC Books, who informed them that the new series hardcover novels had been outselling the earlier paperbacks 'by a factor of ten'. New Zealand fans discovered that the series had been picked up for a second year by Prime TV, scheduling the series' debut on Thursday 6 July. Outpost Gallifrey revealed that the television trailer campaign for the series would be stepped up further with the two-part finale approaching. Overseas, DR1 in Denmark started airing the first series in late June, as did the People+Arts Channel in Mexico and Latin America and the ASTRO network in Malaysia; and it was announced that Japan's BS-2 cable service, owned by the Japanese public broadcaster NHK, would transmit the series starting in the autumn.

The media also turned toward the approaching finale. Tracy-Ann Oberman, soon to guest star in 'Army of Ghosts' and 'Doomsday', was interviewed by the *Stage* for its issue published in the final week of June, saying that she had: '... always been one of this rare breed of women who is a massive sci-fi fan... David Tennant and I sat around on set talking about sonic screwdrivers, and there was a very special moment when I saw the TARDIS for the first time.' Oberman said: 'I've been a lifelong fan, a proper "Whovian" as we call ourselves. They told me to be really hush-hush about the scripts – even more so than with *EastEnders* – but I can say that my character, Yvonne Hartman, is a very strong human villain. She's almost a match, intellectually, for the Doctor.' The *Daily Star* said: '*EastEnders* landlady Peggy Mitchell is horrified to discover Dirty Den's ghost haunting The Queen Vic... The bar boss, played by

Barbara Windsor, is... trying to get rid of the spirit... The Doc is horrified to see the apparitions popping up everywhere – including on the telly. Even chat show host Trisha Goddard, 48, is in on the act.' The Lancaster Today website profiled another *Totally Doctor Who* participant, nine year old Olly Kay, whose mother told the paper, 'He knows everything about it, and thanks to my husband he knows all about the old *Doctor Who* stuff too. They were very impressed with his knowledge.'

ENDLESS SUMMER

As the finale approached, the media hype surrounding the series once again hit crescendo. Billie Piper's impending divorce was the subject of a media story about her financial arrangements with her husband and friend Chris Evans. 'I'm not taking a penny from him,' Piper told *Radio Times*. 'I think that's disgusting... Chris and I found each other when it could have gone badly for both of us, and we saved each other from our worlds of madness.' Drawing from the *Radio Times* interview, the *Daily Mirror* also reported Piper as saying, regarding speculation that she might move to Hollywood: 'There are lots of great movies coming out of the US, but it's not something I'm ever really interested in. I'm happy in the UK. I absolutely love it, and I've finally got a great group of friends. I've got a lovely little flat and my work's here.'

Down under, the second series was preparing to make its debut in Australia and New Zealand on the ABC and Prime TV networks respectively. The *Sydney Morning Herald* on 8 July discussed the series' impending return by profiling the people behind it, including its writers. 'They're the best writers you could possibly want, and if the scripts are good, then the battle is half won already,' David Tennant was quoted as saying. The *Herald* commented of the first episode, 'The Christmas Invasion': 'Tennant looks like being a fabulous *Doctor Who*. He is funny and sarcastic. And sexy. He retains the cocky, slightly disconnected aura of Christopher Eccleston while bringing a spiky vulnerability to the character... Tennant's delivery and his chemistry with Piper augurs well for the rest of the series.' *The Advertiser* on 5 July said: 'After 2005's botched premiere date, which meant the rest of the world saw the sci-fi classic's revival before we did, ABC has its chronometers in tune... Thankfully, it's a lag well worth watching... The future of *Doctor Who* is well and truly in good hands, and the new series will only get even better from here.' The *Sunday Age* the weekend of transmission wrote: 'Instead of letting Tennant quickly build the brand for his own Doctor and prove to us we will soon get over quirky Eccleston, we're back in Rose's old council flat with her noisy mother and passive, stay-at-home boyfriend Mickey. This show is a bit of a curate's egg: some tasty comic snippets, some sniffy anti-Blair references, and some distinctly old gags.' The *Sunday Herald Sun* quoted Tennant as saying, 'I got a text message from Tom Baker the other day, which I got ridiculously over-excited at.'

The *New Statesman* on 7 July reported rumours that Davies might soon make for greener pastures: 'The dynamic writer... has been widely credited for the sci-fi show's remarkable resurrection. But I understand that he could be preparing to hand over the baton (or should that be the sonic screwdriver?) to someone else.' *BBC Wiltshire* interviewed voice artist Nicholas Briggs, while *BBC Breakfast* featured an interview with Tracy-Ann Oberman about her work on the *Doctor Who* set. The *Mirror* also interviewed Oberman: 'For some actors, walking into the Queen Vic is their dream job and the ultimate moment, but for me, walking onto the *Doctor Who* set and seeing the TARDIS was a childhood dream come true. *Doctor Who* had a family feel; it's only 12 episodes as opposed to *EastEnders* which goes on year after year. So it was a luxury doing five scenes a day rather than 25.' The *Daily Mail* reported that Tennant: '... looks to have been spending rather too much time in the TARDIS. When he ventured onto the beach for the first time on a Mediterranean break with his girlfriend, the actress Sophia Myles, it looked like the first time his skin had seen the sun in years.' The *Hornsey and Crouch End Journal* reported that Tennant had: '... landed in the playground of Ashmount Primary School, Hornsey Lane, Archway, to open the school's summer fair... Pupils, parents and *Doctor Who* fans who had been tipped off about the visit had queued outside the school from early morning. Once the door opened, the two parents manning the official merchandise stall were besieged by a queue eager to buy autographed memorabilia being sold to raise cash for school funds.'

Brand Republic said that the Cybermen would: '... invade central London for a DVD campaign. The BBC is to promote the release of the forthcoming *Doctor Who* Series Two: Volume Three DVD with a sequence of five-second animated LCD screen ads in central London. Two separate ads created by Grand Visual will appear inside Tottenham Court Road tube station.' Yahoo News reported: 'The writers of *Doctor Who* are auctioning themselves off on website eBay in a bid to raise cash for sufferers of Crohn's disease. Steven Moffat and Paul Cornell are offering a night out with dinner and drinks for the highest-bidding fan and one guest, as well as a signed script and filming schedule.' Davies, meanwhile, was handed 'an honorary fellowship from the Royal Welsh College of Music and Drama', according to the *South Wales Evening Post*. Said the RWCMD principal Edmond Fivet, 'We are delighted to have such high-calibre people accepting fellowships from the College.'

The *Independent* commented sardonically on BBC newsreader Huw Edwards' cameo appearance in 'Fear Her': '... cast wilfully against type as a newscaster. I won't dwell on his performance when required to sound astonished at the sudden disappearance of the entire crowd at the 2012 Olympics, let alone suggest that he doesn't give up the night job. But I trust it's clear to all Huw fans that apart from reading the script, he also wrote it, produced and directed the entire episode, designed the set, coached David Tennant and Billie Piper, and took K-9 for a long walk on Clapham Common. That's the thing about Huw, as he is always too bashful to point out.' The *Independent* meanwhile noted that it was: '... more gloomy about the disappearance of Billie Piper from *Doctor Who* than [about] England's defeat in Germany [in the football World Cup]... Raise a glass to this sassy lass, who really is worth it.' Piper was voted number one in the *OK! Magazine* Celebrity Chart in the second week of July: 'A nation mourns England's Rose as the Doctor's ultimate companion checks out of the TARDIS ...' Piper later told the *Daily Star*, 'I've been trying to persuade both [Christopher Eccleston and David Tennant] to do a cameo appearance in one of my new projects, so fingers crossed.' And icWales reported that the BBC was inviting 100 people to see the season finale of *Doctor Who* for free in Cardiff Bay.

EARLY JULY: 'ARMY OF GHOSTS' AND 'DOOMSDAY'

At long last, the two-part season finale – 'Army of Ghosts' airing on 1 July and 'Doomsday' on 8 July – had come. 'Sadly, the end is in sight for this series of *Doctor Who*,' wrote *CBBC Newsround* reporter Lizo on 29 June. 'Like last year, it ends with a two part story... The focus is on Rose from the very start, and there's no doubt that what she has to say will shock many of you. And then things come full circle.' The *Stage* called 'Army of Ghosts' a: '... tense contest, full of drama, tears, adversity and two powerful forces coming face to face in the ultimate battle. And that was just the Cybermen and the Daleks popping up... Doctor, please don't go away. Your country still needs you!' The *People* said the episode: '... had a lot in common with *EastEnders*. Set in East London, there was a whopping great hole in the fabric of reality, hostile aliens were everywhere and a huge spherical object hovered around uselessly. But enough about [*EastEnders* character] Charlie Slater ...'

After the airing of 'Army of Ghosts', the BBC ran a daily series of six teaser trailers for 'Doomsday', also carried on the BBC's website. The series finale prompted *Radio Times* to give unprecedented promotion to the show including two covers, one featuring a Dalek and another featuring a Cybermen – which oddly sparked a minor controversy over spoilers in some letters columns, complaining that the presence of the Daleks was supposed to have been a surprise, despite their appearance at the cliff-hanger to the previous week's episode. The *Radio Times* reviewer called the final episode 'an epic battle on a truly intergalactic scale' and the week's recommendations described 'a nail-biting climax'. The *Observer* commented: '[The] evil, evil people at the BBC didn't give us any preview tapes for this episode despite it being one of the most awaited finales in the show's history. For which they are to be both admired and cursed.' The *Sunday Times* noted: 'You can blame Queen Victoria. If she hadn't had the brainy idea of founding the Torchwood Institute after her hairy encounter with the Doctor, none of this might have happened.' *Heat* magazine pleaded that Rose shouldn't die in the finale: 'We bloody hope not. Because, more than both the new Doctors, Billie Piper's performance has summed up the feisty, no-holds-barred, giddy joy for the whole *Doctor Who* revival. And whether she's killed off at the end of tonight's final episode of this current series or just slinks away mysteriously, we know for sure that we are bidding a reluctant farewell to her huge contribution to the *Who* phenomenon.' The *Daily Star* warned that the episode would be: '... a real tear-jerker. No previous Doctor has ever faced such a difficult and painful dilemma as he tries to put his personal feelings aside.'

As the episode aired on 8 July, the *Guardian*'s Charlie Brooker wrote, 'When it was first announced that the revived Doctor's travelling companion was to be played by Piper, a former kiddywink pop star, I rolled my eyes so violently I found myself staring backward into my own skull... How pitifully wrong I was. Anyone who thinks she's been anything other than excellent is a brick-hearted stump of a being. Effortlessly balancing feistiness and charm, vulnerability and goofiness, Billie Piper out-acted almost everyone else on television.' The *Daily Express* said, 'In the midst of the public mourning over Rose's departure, spare a thought for her boyfriend, the ever-faithful Mickey. Not only did he put up with her being absent for several centuries, he also refrained from thumping the Doctor, even though the bloke had blatantly pinched his girl from under his nose.' *The Times* said: 'Despite the moving efforts of David Tennant and the quite glorious Billie Piper, [the final story has] been a disappointment. Indeed, it's been the worst kind of disappointment – something that promises to be absolutely mind-blowing, and then fizzles out at the last minute, like a wet firework.' A writer for the *Daily Mail* commented: 'I don't think I've seen anything so affecting outside the movies of Joan Crawford or Ingrid Bergman. Rose and the Doctor met on a Norwegian beach to say goodbye, but she was not allowed to touch him. Remember the lump in the throat when Bergman had to say farewell, forever, to Gary Cooper in *For Whom The Bell Tolls*?... Having lost Christopher Eccleston as one Doctor, and now Rose, can the next series possibly rise to similar heights?'

Both episodes saw substantial increases in ratings, beating most of the soaps during that fortnight and making *Doctor Who* second only to the World Cup football. *BBC News* reported: 'In a good weekend of ratings for the main BBC channel, more than 8 million viewers tuned in to see Billie Piper's final appearance in *Doctor Who* on Saturday.' *Media Guardian* noted on

10 July: 'Billie Piper's departure from *Doctor Who* pulled in a peak audience of 8.3 million viewers on Saturday night... This beat the final episode of last year's series, which pulled in an average of 6.1 [sic] million viewers.'

icWales featured a collection of children's comments on the finale, with notes ranging from 'I thought Saturday's episode was brilliant – the best episode yet,' to 'It was amazing. It was even better than the episodes with my favourite monster, the Ood, in [them].' The *Herald* said, 'Farewell then, Billie Piper. With your curiously alien rhomboidal face. And those eyebrows of yours that – in an almost supernatural way – never matched the colour of your hair. You done been gone. TARdisappeared. Poor Billie. But didn't you sign off in style?' The *Lancashire Evening Telegraph* opined, 'We've been starved of classic TV moments recently, but I have to say that the final episode of *Doctor Who* was up there with the best. However you look at it, the Time Lord saying goodbye forever to Rose Tyler was brilliantly done. As someone who wasn't convinced at first by the arrival of David Tennant as the Doctor, I was completely won over by the end. And Billie Piper has been a revelation as his spiky sidekick... It's a shame she won't be around for the next series.' And the *Independent* simply called it: 'The end of an era.'

Even viewers who had surmised that Rose *wouldn't* die at the end of the episode – despite her demise having been apparently predicted by the Beast in 'The Satan Pit' – were nevertheless in for a surprise in the form of a twist ending to 'Doomsday'. Actress/comedienne Catherine Tate, in a carefully kept secret, made a brief appearance in the episode's closing moments, credited only as 'the Bride'. Tate, who was best known for her comedy series *The Catherine Tate Show*, appeared out of nowhere, confronting David Tennant's Doctor with as much shock as he expressed himself... quickly followed by the familiar sting of the *Doctor Who* theme and the news that the series would return at Christmas (in '170 days', according to BBC1's continuity announcer) with an episode entitled 'The Runaway Bride'. Tate would, in fact, bridge the second series and the forthcoming Christmas special, although she wasn't expected to go beyond that, as Freema Agyeman would join Tennant in the third season's first regular episode. *BBC News* reported that Tate, famous for her catchphrase 'Am I bovvered?', would 'play Donna, a runaway bride, alongside lead actor David Tennant'. Tate told *BBC News* that she was 'honoured and delighted' to join the show. 'I was holding out for summer season at Wigan rep, but as a summer job this'll do.' Davies told *BBC News*, '*Doctor Who* and Catherine Tate is just the most irresistible combination, a genuine treat for Christmas viewing. After two years of travelling with Rose, the TARDIS is in for a bumpy ride with Donna on board.'

ONWARD

With its second series now firmly behind it, *Doctor Who* entered production on 'The Runaway Bride', its 2006 Christmas special, at the end of June, with location recording beginning in early July. 'You can see them filming on the top of 76 Shoe Lane fairly clearly from Ludgate Circus, looking up St Bride St,' reported an anonymous contributor to Outpost Gallifrey. 'I could make out Tennant from his silhouette – he wasn't wearing the coat... and you could see a woman in a white dress – I'm pretty sure it was a wedding dress.' Added fan Alistair Moore, 'I did have a nice chat with one of the production crew. Apparently they've been filming in London for three days, though today was the last. The TARDIS had been erected on the roof last night and left there overnight covered by a sheet. The roof has a helipad and is where some of the BBC idents were filmed a few years ago. As the TARDIS exterior pieces were being loaded into the truck this evening, the cast were already in cars heading back to Cardiff for TARDIS interior set shooting tomorrow.'

Series Three had barely begun production, and already the rumours were flying. The *Daily Star* reported that the episode would feature the Doctor and his new friend Donna coming face to face with a Cyberwoman played by *Footballers Wives* actress Caroline Chikeze. Other false rumours in the tabloid press suggested that Elisabeth Sladen and original series actor Sylvester McCoy would appear in the special. The *Daily Mirror* reported on 5 July that another classic alien race from the original series – the Ice Warriors – would appear in the coming episodes, though this was later denied by Davies. BBC Radio 1 even reported that Billie Piper herself might be back once again in 'one form or another'; the *Sunday Express* contacted a BBC spokesperson who said, 'I can't confirm or deny that story about Billie Piper. What I can say is there are lots of surprises in it. It is *Doctor Who*, after all. There is already a lot of speculation about the Christmas episode; you can make your own conclusions.'

There was, however, some more tangible news. Gary Russell, producer of the *Doctor Who* audio range at Big Finish Productions, announced he was leaving the company to work on other projects; it was later revealed that he would join the series' production team as a trainee script editor, overseeing the various fiction ranges associated with the show. In the meanwhile, he would complete writing duties on *Doctor Who: The Inside Story*, a hardcover book focusing on the production of the series' first two years. John Barrowman told the assembled crowds at a London convention early in July that he'd signed a contract to appear in the third series, after his work was completed on the first year of *Torchwood*. (*Doctor Who Magazine* later confirmed that Barrowman would take part in the third series' finale.) The official *Doctor Who* website announced that Murray Gold's soundtrack for the first two series would soon make its way onto CD. *Doctor Who Magazine* released in mid-July reported that Series Two make-up designer Sheelagh Wells would soon depart, to be replaced by Barbara Southcott (*Born and Bred*), while the director for the first block of the new series would be Charles Palmer, who had previously helmed episodes of Channel 4's *Ghost Squad* and had worked with Phil Collinson on *Linda Green* in 2001. At this point, Stephen Fry and Matthew Graham were confirmed as having dropping out of the third series' writing line-up because of other commitments, though Davies suggested 'everything's in place' for replacement scripts. *Doctor Who Magazine* also printed Freema Agyeman's first interview. The actress told the magazine that at press time she was expecting to see her first script 'any day now' and dropped hints that there might be an explanation of her appearance as a different character in 'Army of Ghosts'.

Clearly, *Doctor Who* was riding the wave of another successful year... varied in critical acclaim but still incredibly popular among the masses. In July, it was once again up for Best Drama on the nominees list for the National Television Awards, with Tennant and Piper nominated for Best Actor and Best Actress respectively. Although the winners weren't due to be announced until November, it was already apparent that *Doctor Who* would be *the* series to beat this year. And a great deal of the credit could be laid at the doorstep of Russell T Davies, whom *Media Guardian* on 17 July said had single-handedly revived family TV drama. 'We were told that bringing it back would be impossible, that we would never capture this generation of children,' Davies was quoted as saying. 'But we did it.'

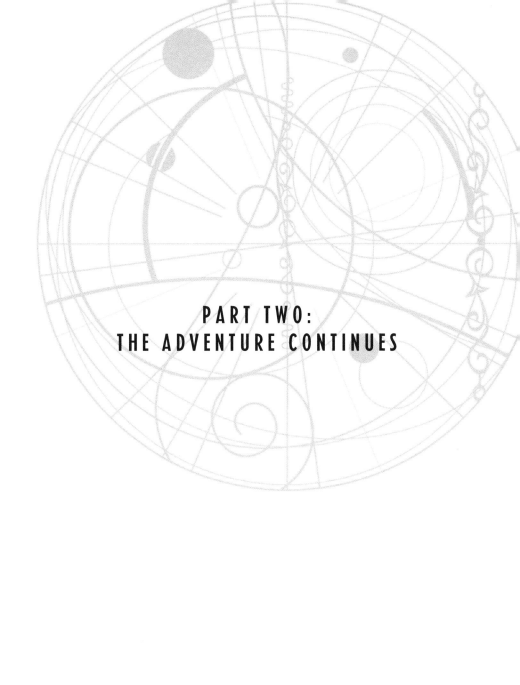

PART TWO:
THE ADVENTURE CONTINUES

EPISODE BY EPISODE: A GUIDE TO THE ADVENTURES

The following section covers the second series of *Doctor Who* series in depth by story, with both technical analysis and review:

Untitled *Children in Need* Special	199	18 November 2005
The Christmas Invasion	200	25 December 2005
Attack of the Graske	200-A	25 December 2005
New Earth	201	15 April 2006
Tooth and Claw	202	22 April 2006
School Reunion	203	29 April 2006
The Girl in the Fireplace	204	6 May 2006
Rise of the Cybermen	205	13 May 2006
The Age of Steel	206	20 May 2006
The Idiot's Lantern	207	27 May 2006
The Impossible Planet	208	3 June 2006
The Satan Pit	209	10 June 2006
Love & Monsters	210	17 June 2006
Fear Her	211	24 June 2006
Army of Ghosts	212	1 July 2006
Doomsday	213	8 July 2006

As in the first *Back to the Vortex*, we have adopted the notation popular online, which is series number – ie 2 – followed by the episode number; hence 'New Earth' is episode 201 and 'Doomsday' is episode 213. 'The Christmas Invasion,' preceding 'New Earth' but still produced as part of this year's episodes, is referred to as episode 200. (Two exceptions: the untitled *Children in Need* special, produced as a preamble and falling immediately prior to 'The Christmas Invasion,' is noted as 199; 'Attack of the Graske', regarded as not truly a part of the series proper, is noted as 200-A.)

Each episode is broken down into (some or all of) the following categories before being further explored in specific sections:

WHERE AND WHEN: The date and fictional locations that each story is set in.

THE STORY UNFOLDS: Major plot elements and story threads revealed during the course of the episode.

THE DOCTOR AND ROSE TYLER: Information about, and developments concerning, the two main characters.

CHARACTER BUILDING: Significant information about other major characters.

TORCHWOOD: The unfolding of the second year's story arc.

BODY COUNT: Who dies and where.

THE DOCTOR'S MAGICAL SONIC SCREWDRIVER: Places where the Time Lord's trusty tool comes into play.

REALITY BITES: References to and connections between *Doctor Who* and the 'real' world.

LINKING THEMES: Links between the episodes, or between the classic and current *Doctor Who*.

SCENE MISSING: Unexplained events and unanswered questions, including pieces of the puzzle that the viewer must put together on his/her own; there may be answers to all of them, but this deals specifically with what is presented in the story on screen.

ALTERED STATES: Items that changed at any point prior to transmission that we know about.

BEHIND THE SCENES: Clues about where each story was recorded, and important factual information or developments in the production. Also real-world items germane to the episode, such as spinoff websites.

DULCET TONES: Details about music heard in the episodes.

OFF THE SCREEN: Where to look out for some of the actors, directors and other important contributors in other projects.

TECHNICAL GOOFS: The usual, unavoidable *faux pas* and errors made along the way.

CONTROVERSIES: Subjects of concern and debate.

INTERNAL CONSISTENCY: An analysis of each episode's internal timing, as extrapolated from visual and verbal clues in the episode.

PANEL REVIEWS: Our nine panellists' short takes on each story. These were written shortly after each episode was transmitted, rather than after the whole season had gone out. In contrast to the first book, where panellists were asked to contribute two reviews (one thematic, one general), this time they were asked instead for a single, more detailed review, covering aspects of their own choosing.

EDITOR'S REVIEW: A final thought on each story.

199: UNTITLED CHILDREN IN NEED 2005 SPECIAL

The Doctor settles into a new body... but can Rose ever accept him?

FIRST TRANSMISSION: UK – 18 November 2005.
DURATION: 6'54"
WRITER: Russell T Davies
DIRECTOR: Euros Lyn
CREDITED CAST: David Tennant (The Doctor), Billie Piper (Rose Tyler).

WHERE AND WHEN: Inside the TARDIS, immediately following the events of 'The Parting of the Ways' and prior to 'The Christmas Invasion'.

THE STORY UNFOLDS: After his hasty regeneration following the destruction of the Daleks, the Doctor is taking Rose to Barcelona (the planet, not the city); he sets the coordinates to arrive at 6 pm on a Tuesday in October 5006. He changes course during this mini-adventure to London, the Powell Estate, 24 December (most likely 2006 to take place after the events of earlier episodes) to tie into the opening of 'The Christmas Invasion'.

The Doctor says that he and Rose once visited a planet where they spent time hopping for their lives. He hasn't used a particular switch on the TARDIS console (as yet unidentified) in years.

THE DOCTOR: He's delighted that he has hair ('big hair', in fact) and isn't bald, that he has sideburns (or 'really bad skin'), is thinner than his previous incarnation, and that he has a mole between his shoulder blades. ('Love the mole!') He has a slight weakness in the dorsal tubercle on his right hand. He says he's changed his body, every single cell, but it's still him. He remembers the word he told Rose when he first met her (in 'Rose', he said 'Run!') and tells her he can't change back. His regeneration, for some reason, goes awry – perhaps an after-effect of the time vortex energy (some of which he appears to breathe out at one point) – and this makes him very manic.

ROSE TYLER: Rose at first doesn't believe the evidence in front of her, that this is the same Doctor in a different body. As in previous episodes, she pronounces Slitheen as 'Sliveen.' The Doctor decides to give her the choice as to whether she wants to return home or not. She smiles slightly when the Doctor makes fun of her mother.

BODY COUNT: None, although Rose thinks the Doctor has 'exploded', and still considers him to be dead even when she begins to realise the truth.

THE DOCTOR'S MAGICAL SONIC SCREWDRIVER: No use by the new Doctor yet.

LINKING THEMES: The Cloister Bell is sounded throughout the TARDIS. The gong-sounding chime is used several times in the original *Doctor Who* (making its debut in 'Logopolis', 1981, and featuring most recently in the TV movie, 1996) as a sound of great impending danger for the vessel; here, it's heard when the TARDIS is about to crash on Earth.

Rose mentions transmat (a teleportation system used often during the original *Doctor Who* series as well as in 'Bad Wolf'), nanogenes ('The Empty Child'), the Gelth ('The Unquiet Dead') and the Slitheen ('Aliens of London'). The Doctor recalls the shop window dummies (Autons) Rose was being attacked by when he first met her ('Rose') as being a long time ago.

The Doctor recalls Jackie Tyler (Rose's mother) without much fondness, questioning her mental stability (referring jokingly to 'nut loaf' as a dinner item for Christmas!)

Captain Jack is currently on Earth rebuilding it, as the Doctor tells Rose, which is why they can't go back for him. However ...

SCENE MISSING: How does the Doctor know that Captain Jack is rebuilding the Earth? Though the ninth Doctor and Rose never saw him die ('The Parting of the Ways'), we are led to think at the end of that episode that the Doctor believes everyone on the Game Station to be dead. It is possible, however, that the Doctor knows a bit about Jack's future history, or that he took some of Rose's recent memory during the 'magic kiss.'

BEHIND THE SCENES: The *Children in Need* special was recorded in a five-hour block (11 am to 4 pm) on 3 November as a stand-alone mini-adventure, never intended to be part of 'The Christmas Invasion'. By this time, Tennant and Piper had already recorded the Christmas special and the first three episodes of Series Two.

The title sequence was updated to remove Christopher Eccleston's name and include David Tennant's. There is actually no on-screen title for this 'episode' (in fact, the title sequence is clean after the *Doctor Who* logo, except for the *Children in Need* phone number in the corner on the original broadcast) and there is no end credit sequence, it being replaced by a caption '*Doctor Who* will return in "The Christmas Invasion"'. Davies would later nickname the episode 'Pudsey Cutaway', a joke that combined the name of the *Children in Need* telethon mascot bear Pudsey with the title 'Dalek Cutaway', used in some 1965 production paperwork to refer to the one-shot episode 'Mission to the Unknown'.. However, this was intended as a joke, not a serious suggestion.

The pre-credits sequence was composed entirely of scenes from 'The Parting of the Ways', including a recap of the regeneration sequence, and there was almost exactly five minutes of original material in the episode.

The episode was hosted live during the *Children in Need* broadcast by Terry Wogan, though it was time-delayed in Scotland. The version that was hosted online ended with several different appeals from David Tennant and Billie Piper for the charity. In one, the two introduced themselves using the names of actors Letitia Dean and Nicholas Lyndhurst; in another, Tennant introduced himself as Piper and vice-versa.

In November 2006, the special was made available on the DVD boxed collection, *Doctor Who: The Complete Second Series*, despite earlier rumours that it had not been cleared for release.

TECHNICAL GOOFS: Billie Piper's hairstyle and eyebrows, along with David Tennant's sideburns, do not match their states at the end of 'The Parting of the Ways', as this was recorded several months after that story. Similarly, Rose's white top can be seen slightly over her cleavage in this story, but was not visible at the end of the 'The Parting of the Ways'. (Perhaps she pulled her zip down a couple of centimetres during the opening credits?) These minor points aside, the production team have done a fantastic job of matching the costumes and accessories (specifically Rose's rings and various bracelets) across the break. The lighting in the TARDIS also differs somewhat, especially in the use of a fluorescent green reflected upon the beams of the TARDIS interior. Due to the change in recording techniques, not only is there a change in 'look' between shots in the pre-credit sequence but the sharpness changes once again for the rest of the 'episode'. As the Doctor tells Rose to 'consider it a Christmas present,' she steps towards the console and places her left hand on it, then there is a view of the vortex, and when we return, she makes exactly the same move again.

CONTROVERSIES: The fact that the first real glimpse of the new Doctor and Rose's incredulity over his regeneration are seen in a one-off special instead of in the main body of the series, has been controversial amongst some *Doctor Who* fans, as has the lack of an on-screen title.

INTERNAL CONSISTENCY: This 'mini-episode' dovetails exactly between 'The Parting of the Ways' and 'The Christmas Invasion', with no interruption of continuity.

200: THE CHRISTMAS INVASION

A run-of-the-mill Christmas holiday is interrupted by an alien invasion: the Sycorax have come to Earth to enslave mankind. The world stands on the brink, and it needs a hero... but unfortunately, the Doctor is nowhere to be found.

FIRST TRANSMISSION: UK – 25 December 2005. US – 29 September 2006. Canada – 26 December 2005. Australia – 8 July 2006. New Zealand – 6 July 2006.
DURATION: 58'57"
WRITER: Russell T Davies
DIRECTOR: James Hawes
CREDITED CAST: David Tennant (The Doctor), Billie Piper (Rose Tyler), Camille Coduri (Jackie Tyler), Noel Clarke (Mickey Smith), Penelope Wilton (Harriet Jones), Daniel Evans (Danny Llewellyn), Adam Garcia (Alex), Sean Gilder (Sycorax Leader), Chu Omambala (Major Blake), Anita Briem (Sally), Sian McDowall (Sandra), Paul Anderson (Jason), Cathy Murphy (Mum), Sean Carlsen (Policeman), Jason Mohammed (Newsreader 1), Sagar Arya (Newsreader 2), Lachele Carl (Newsreader 3)

WHERE AND WHEN: London, including the Powell Estate, near Henrik's department store, and the UNIT control bunker, 24 and 25 December 2006. Also on board the Sycorax ship.

THE STORY UNFOLDS: The Sycorax are an alien race of scavengers with a voodoo cult-like culture. They wear large, bony helmets that disguise their true appearance: humanoids with exoskeletal bones and exposed musculature. They speak Sycoraxic; in their tongue, they call the Earth's occupants 'cattle' who 'belong to' them, and state that they, as a people, 'rock'. Their ship – an organic-looking craft, or possibly a hollowed asteroid – causes a sonic wave that shatters glass in the vicinity as it hits the atmosphere. They can detect the TARDIS, and it is implied that the Doctor's residual regeneration energy is what calls them to Earth.

Making their way to Earth also are what the Doctor calls 'pilot fish' – advance scouts – which can 'smell' the Doctor's energies; their job is to weaken the Earth's defences, and the implication is that they are mechanical beings who can 'run their batteries on' the Doctor's energies for years. They've sent Jackie a Christmas tree, which she believes was ordered for her by Rose but is in fact a remote-controlled weapon.

The 'Guinevere One' space probe is the British government's first apparent Mars space probe (see Linking Themes), sent to the Red Planet to herald what some call 'the dawn of a new age' for the country. It loses contact with Earth shortly before final approach. Expected to show pictures from the Martian surface, its communication system instead transmits the image of a Sycorax face to Earth, which (according to the BBC News 24 crawl) causes 'global panic.' Once the transmission occurs, global responsibility for dealing with the threat is transferred to the British branch of UNIT, which has a command and control bunker somewhere within the confines of (or perhaps below) the Tower of London.

The Sycorax use a process called blood control; having found a sample of blood carried aboard 'Guinevere One' as a symbol of humanity, they can control the minds of those whose blood is of the same type as the sample, which is type A-positive. The blood control causes the affected people to walk up to the tops of buildings and prepare to jump. Fully one third of the planet's population (two billion people) are affected, including UNIT analyst Sally Jacobs and operatives Luke Parsons and Geoffrey Baxter; the Sycorax's terms are that either half the Earth is sold into slavery, or one third of the population dies. The Doctor reveals blood control to be a 'cheap bit of voodoo', like hypnosis; survival instinct being too powerful, one cannot use it to hypnotise subjects to death.

Time Lords can regrow appendages, apparently, during the first 15 hours of their regeneration cycle (due to residual cellular energy). The Doctor loses and regrows a hand, which happens to be his right hand, the one he complains about (as having 'a slight weakness in the dorsal tubercle') in the *Children in Need* special.

The TARDIS translates alien languages inside its occupants' heads; Rose determines that the Doctor must be 'broken', because she can't understand Sycoraxic, but realises he has returned when she begins to understand the Sycorax leader. '*Crannak pel cassackree salvack*' apparently means something very insulting in Sycoraxic.

Queen Elizabeth II is the current Queen in the *Doctor Who* universe at this time (as her photograph sits on Jones's desk), but her Christmas address this year has been cancelled due to the crisis. The Royal Family is apparently all of blood type A-positive as 'They're on the roof.'

THE DOCTOR: The Doctor has freshly regenerated into his tenth incarnation, and his face has changed considerably, to the confusion of Rose, Jackie and Mickey. He appears disappointed that he's not ginger-haired. He doesn't know what kind of man he will be (obviously referring to the disparate facets of his previous personalities), but notes that, like other incarnations, he's 'certainly got a gob'. He has two hearts as usual (for his species). His new outfit consists of a white collared shirt with paisley tie, brown pinstriped suit coat and, occasionally, tan overcoat and spectacles. His regeneration goes awry at first, and he spends some time recuperating, asleep, in Jackie's flat; Rose awakens him too soon, he says, as he's still bursting with energy and has a neuron implosion. Later, a 'superheated infusion of free radicals and tannins,' from a thermos of tea spilt by Mickey helps heal the synapses and allows him to recover. He's not afraid of the Sycorax, and recognises their blood control for what it's worth; later, he stands as Earth's 'champion'. He loses his hand (but regrows it); his new hand is 'a fightin' hand!' He compares Christmas to going through presents and finding a satsuma. He eventually realises he's a 'no second chances' sort of man.

ROSE TYLER: Rose feels betrayed by the Doctor's sudden regeneration, as if she no longer knows him, and she has to remind herself that the Doctor is an alien. She thinks he's abandoned her, but her faith in him is restored when he returns to life. She isn't sure at first, however, if the Doctor wants her to continue travelling with him. The ability to fly the TARDIS has been wiped from her memory 'like it's forbidden'. She speaks for Earth after the Sycorax recognise superior technology in the TARDIS. Her cousin Mo lives in the Peak District.

CHARACTER BUILDING: *Harriet Jones* – Harriet Jones, MP for Flydale North, has now also become (as the Doctor predicted in 'World War Three') the Prime Minister of the United Kingdom – having won a landslide election majority – and 'Britain's golden age' has come to pass. She still identifies herself in roughly the same way, holding up her ID badge and introducing herself as 'Harriet Jones, Prime Minister.' There is an Act of Parliament banning her autobiography (presumably due to her experiences with the Slitheen the previous year). She addresses the public on television, with a last-ditch message to attempt to contact the

Doctor. She tells the Sycorax that she represents the planet, and is teleported aboard their ship along with Major Blake, her assistant Alex and Llewellyn. She accepts the Doctor's new persona after he refers to her need for her mother's safety. She isn't supposed to know about Torchwood, but does; she later decides, to the Doctor's extreme displeasure, to have them destroy the Sycorax vessel. In retaliation, the Doctor attempts to have her removed as Prime Minister by saying six words to her assistant, 'Don't you think she looks tired?', causing a press scandal, the reports describing her as 'unstable and failing fast'.

Mickey Smith – Works in an auto mechanic's shop within walking distance of the Powell Estate. He's happy to see Rose but comments sarcastically that he 'loves hearing stories about the TARDIS', suggesting that he's still very jealous of her attachment to the Doctor. He suggests his mate Stan might put them up after he and Rose are attacked, but Stan's flat is only two streets away. He still knows how to access UNIT's computer system ('World War Three'), monitoring the approach of the Sycorax vessel toward Earth. He thinks drinking a cup of tea while the world comes to an end is 'very British'.

Jackie Tyler – While she's bought Rose a Christmas present, she remains unsure if her daughter survived the events of 'The Parting of the Ways' (after she helped Rose regain control of the TARDIS) until the TARDIS returns. She's incredulous about the Doctor's twin hearts and wonders if there's anything else he has two of. She borrows a stethoscope from 'Tina the Cleaner' (or rather, the latter's medical student lodger) by just taking it. She's £18 (per week) better off due to Harriet Jones's economic policies, but apparently keeps very little in the refrigerator (as she sends Rose out to get food – the alternative being, as she tells her friend Bev, for Rose to have 'a Christmas dinner of meat paste'). She has neighbours named Sandra and Jason (the latter of whom is affected by the blood control). Her solution 'to everything', says Rose, is a cup of tea. Someone named Howard (from 'the market') has been spending time at her flat for the last month, which explains the pair of pyjamas she has. (He 'gets hungry late at night,' hence the apple and, later, the satsuma in the pocket.)

Daniel Llewellyn – Project Manager of the 'Guinevere One' space probe mission for the British Rocket Group, a mission he first deems to be 'an unqualified success'. He is startled by news that the Sycorax aren't the first alien species Earth has encountered. He believes himself to be responsible for what's happened, because it was his decision to have 'Guinevere One' carry an A-positive blood sample as a memento of humanity. The British Rocket Group tie-in website (see Reality Bites) says that 'Daniel studied at Swansea University, gaining a Masters in Areology' and is 'the UK's foremost expert on Mars'.

Alex – A UNIT employee. Harriet Jones describes him as her 'right hand man'. He announces that all those affected by the Sycorax mind-control are blood related. Alex also, apparently, betrays her trust later (by, it is implied, repeating the Doctor's six words to bring down her government).

Major Blake – A UNIT officer assigned to the bunker where Prime Minister Jones comes to deal with the alien invasion. He obviously knows all about the Torchwood project (surprisingly, considering that, officially, UNIT isn't supposed to know about it; presumably this is because he is also a British Army officer).

FANTASTIC!: As an homage to his previous incarnation (for whom this was his catchphrase), the Doctor says 'It's gonna be... fantastic!' to Rose on their imminent journey through space and time.

EPISODE 200

TORCHWOOD: The second mention of Torchwood (the first being the question about the Torchwood Institute in the first series episode 'Bad Wolf') starts off a season of references.

Torchwood has access to a super-secret weapons project, adapted from alien technology on a ship that fell to Earth ten years earlier. The project is secret – even the Prime Minister isn't supposed to know about it – and is designed to protect the world from alien invasion. While the victorious Doctor tells the Sycorax ship to go away – that Earth is defended – Harriet Jones nevertheless authorises the use of the weapon – which destroys the Sycorax vessel, turning it into a rain of ash that falls on London. The weapon fires from five locations around London, shooting a green beam of energy into space.

BODY COUNT: Daniel Llewellyn and Major Blake are both killed by the Sycorax leader using an energy whip; the Sycorax leader is also killed at the end.

THE DOCTOR'S MAGICAL SONIC SCREWDRIVER: Rose doesn't know how to operate it, but one whisper into the comatose Doctor's ears of the words 'Help me,' and he wakes up briefly to use it to stop the rampaging Christmas tree (perhaps interrupting the remote control, resulting in the tree tearing itself apart). He also uses it to threaten the 'pilot fish'.

REALITY BITES: When Rose and Mickey are picked up by a London taxi, the inspiration for the *Doctor Who* logo is clearly visible: the orange-and-yellow, eye-shaped taxicab logo above the windscreen. (The taxicab licence plate reads WIO4 RWS.) Also seen briefly is a Routemaster bus; while the Routemasters are now out of commission, a small number remain on London streets as tourist attractions. The 'Gherkin' building in the financial district of London is also seen for the first time in *Doctor Who*; this building at 30 St Mary Axe opened in 2004.

The name Sycorax is taken from the William Shakespeare play *The Tempest*.

A pilot fish is a small horse mackerel that exists in a symbiotic relationship with sharks, both feeding upon the sharks' leftovers and cleaning away fragments of food from between sharks' teeth. It was long believed that pilot fish would guide sailors' journeys back to port, although in the context of this story it is implied that the 'pilot fish' are advance scouts for an invasion fleet. (Mickey researches pilot fish and comes to the conclusion that they will precede the 'sharks' coming to invade.)

NATO is the North Atlantic Treaty Organisation, an alliance of Western governments in existence since the end of World War II and spearheaded by the UK, the United States, France and Germany. The Doctor, on seeing Rose, Mickey and Harriet Jones, refers to *This Is Your Life*, a long-running series on both sides of the Atlantic, which featured a star guest confronted by people from their past saying nice things about them. A 'gob' is British slang for mouth, used here when the Doctor suggests that he is very talkative.

UNIT taps into the Hubble Space Telescope, here referred to as the 'Hubble Array'. This large orbital telescope was launched in 1990 and was named after famed American astronomer Edwin Hubble.

LINKING THEMES: The opening sequence – the panoramic shot from the Moon through space and down to Earth – is lifted directly from the opening moments of 'Rose' the previous season (where it served as an homage to the first colour *Doctor Who* serial, 'Spearhead from Space', which opened the same way). Rose and Mickey pay a visit to a shopping district right outside Henrik's department store, where the opening action in 'Rose' took place.

The sequence toward the end where the Doctor picks out his wardrobe is an homage to several classic *Doctor Who* stories (including 'Robot', 'Castrovalva', 'The Twin Dilemma', 'Time and the Rani' and the 1996 TV movie) in which previous incarnations did much the same. Items visible in the multi-tiered wardrobe (with a spiral staircase and a full-length mirror) include: a jacket similar to those worn by David Tennant in *Casanova*; a smoking jacket and frilly cravat reminiscent of the clothes typically worn by the third Doctor (Jon Pertwee); the straw hat and cricket bat used by the fifth Doctor (Peter Davison); a Hawaiian shirt (perhaps in honour of late *Doctor Who* producer John Nathan-Turner, for whom they became a sort of 'trademark'); a full coat of armour and pith helmet (an homage to the UK children's cartoon series *Mr Benn*); a striped pullover identical to the one worn by the first Doctor's companion Steven Taylor (Peter Purves) in the 1966 story 'The Celestial Toymaker'; and various dresses. Also included was a scarf reminiscent of that worn by the fourth Doctor (Tom Baker); this was loaned to the production by producer Phil Collinson, and had been made as a replica *Doctor Who* scarf for him by his grandmother during his childhood. According to the production team, costumes reflecting those worn by all nine previous Doctors were included in the wardrobe scene, but most are not visible on screen. This is the first glimpse of any part of the TARDIS beyond the control room since the series' 2005 revival.

UNIT – the United Nations Intelligence Taskforce, an international paramilitary force and a staple of the classic *Doctor Who* series for many years – returns in this story after a brief glimpse of the organisation in 'Aliens of London' and 'World War Three'. Major Blake is in operational authority here. He refers to Martians as looking 'completely different' from the Sycorax (proving they aren't from Mars), likely referring to the title villains introduced in the *Doctor Who* story 'The Ice Warriors' by Brian Hayles in 1967 and later seen in 'The Seeds of Death', 'The Curse of Peladon' and 'The Monster of Peladon'. Jones asks Major Blake if UNIT has had a 'Code Nine'; 'Aliens of London' established this as an alert that the Doctor's whereabouts are known. Blake calls the Doctor the 'stuff of legend'. Mickey first learned the password into the UNIT website in 'World War Three'.

The mention of the British Rocket Group is an allusion to the organisation featured in the BBC's *Quatermass* serials of the 1950s; it was also referenced in the *Doctor Who* story 'Remembrance of the Daleks' (1988). (Coincidentally, David Tennant co-starred in the 2005 BBC live broadcast remake of *The Quatermass Experiment*.) According to the original series, the first space probes sent to Mars were just before the third Doctor began his exile on Earth. He later helped with the recovery of Mars Probe 7 in 'The Ambassadors of Death' (1970).

In addition to the regular and semi-regular cast and the return of Penelope Wilton (Harriet Jones), actress Lachele Carl briefly reprises her role as the American network AMNN's newscaster from 'Aliens of London' and 'World War Three', reporting on the initial Sycorax transmission.

St Stephen's Tower, including the clock (known colloquially as Big Ben), is still under reconstruction following its partial destruction by the crashing Slitheen vessel in 'Aliens of London'; there is scaffolding up to the top of the tower. The Doctor refers to singer Elvis Presley and the character Arthur Dent from Douglas Adams' landmark science-fiction satire *The Hitchhiker's Guide to the Galaxy* (calling Arthur 'a nice man' and spending much time in a dressing gown, as did Dent in the TV version of Adams' radio serials), and quotes the opening song from the film *The Lion King*, an animated feature produced by the Walt Disney Company, the song itself being written by Elton John and Tim Rice. Rose mentions 'Article 15 of the Shadow Proclamation', 'the Slitheen parliament of Raxacoricofallapatorius', 'the Gelth Confederacy', 'the Mighty Jagrafess' and the Daleks in an improvised speech to the Sycorax leader, referring to these entities from the previous season while attempting to reproduce the Doctor's authoritative demand to the Nestene Consciousness in 'Rose' (and mangling it in the process). Harriet Jones refers to her cottage hospital plans ('Aliens of London') in a speech; it is also noted in the BBC News 24 television crawl. Her destruction of the retreating Sycorax ship mirrors that of the Argentinean cruiser *ARA General Belgrano* on 2 May 1982, a controversial incident during the Falklands War.

Jackie's comment regarding whether or not there is anything else the Doctor has two of (in addition to his hearts) mimics a piece of dialogue cut from the transmission of the 1996 *Doctor Who* TV movie, and also a line from the recent film version of *The Hitchhiker's Guide to the Galaxy*. Jackie also asks, 'Doctor who?' – an obvious homage to the series' title.

The Doctor's questions to Rose about his appearance are fairly redundant, considering he'd asked her the same questions in the *Children in Need* special. Possibly, however, his memory of events in the special was affected by his subsequent regeneration trauma.

The Doctor's (and his people's) ability to reform and regrow the body during the first 15 hours of a regeneration cycle could perhaps be said to explain, indirectly, a long-time *Doctor Who* mystery: why his former travelling companion, Romana, herself a Time Lord, could change her appearance selectively before settling on the form of actress Lalla Ward in 'Destiny of the Daleks' (1979).

SCENE MISSING: Why are the 'pilot fish' Santa Clauses attracted to Rose and Mickey (apart from the fact that they know the Doctor)? In fact, what are they doing at the shopping centre in the first place? Rose assumes they are after the Doctor, but why then was the Christmas tree delivered to Jackie's flat? If they know the Doctor is at the flat, why go to the trouble of attacking Rose and Mickey?

The Doctor stated in 'World War Three' that Harriet Jones was to serve three terms as Prime Minister; however, by the end of this episode, he has clearly attempted to bring her government down. Either the Doctor has changed history, or Harriet's career in politics is far from over...

The 'Guinevere One' space probe collides with the Sycorax vessel with nothing more than a slight bump; assuming that the probe is travelling at velocities considered normal for space missions to Mars, then the Sycorax ship must be moving backwards in the same direction and at *almost* the same speed, or the probe would have burst into bits the second it impacted. This seems implausible. How convenient, also, that the probe contains a sample of human blood (and it's highly doubtful that Llewellyn, chief designer of the probe, would have selected a blood type that *wasn't* his; he is, after all, a human being, and human beings have egos).

On the subject of 'Guinevere One'... Britain's space technology seems to have taken a massive leap backwards from the original series. The probe is said to be Britain's first major spacecraft, but what of the manned Mars probes of 'The Ambassadors of Death' (transmitted in 1970 and set in 1969/70) and the XK5 in 'The Android Invasion' (transmitted in 1975 and set in 1973)? One could also ask, if the British Rocket Group is more than an homage to the *Quatermass*... serials and is in fact linked to them, what of the manned spaceships seen in *those* serials, dating back to the 1950s? Another *Doctor Who* historical fact ignored: why does a photo of Queen Elizabeth II sit on Harriet Jones's desk when 'Battlefield' (1989) establishes there is already a King (presumably Charles) on the throne?

How does UNIT's 'translation software' work so quickly, considering that they've just met the Sycorax? Of course, if the Doctor had anything to do with giving them the technology during his tenure as scientific advisor, this could explain a lot... but not how the Sycorax understand the humans. (They seem to do so, perfectly; however, they speak 'only Sycoraxic' as their leader describes, saying he would never 'dirty' his tongue with their 'primitive bile'. But this poses a problem – why would space conquerors who want to dictate terms of Earth's surrender, and who obviously understand English, refuse to communicate in a human language?)

Also on the subject of language, how do Alex and Harriet, neither of whom has ever been in the TARDIS, utilise the ship's translation method? The automatic translation is a 'gift' the Doctor shares with his friends, after all, and at this point, at least, he's not even met Alex, nor is he aware Harriet is there. Unless, that is, he has checked the scanner screen before emerging from the ship, as seems quite likely.

Why would the government of the United Kingdom and the Historic Buildings Trust allow a top-secret UNIT base to be constructed beneath the Tower of London? Would this not attract attention, with all the chauffeur-driven and military vehicles coming and going at all times of day?

How does the Doctor recognise 'human blood, A-positive, with just a dash of iron' just by tasting it on the tip of his tongue? Is this just a previously-unmentioned Time Lord ability? Why does Alex, Harriet's assistant, know about Torchwood, when even *she* isn't supposed to know about it?

The TARDIS returns to a location somewhat different than it was transported from, but Jackie seems to know exactly where to find it. Perhaps she hears the materialisation noise from a distance, as at the start of the story?

It's been established for decades that the Doctor and his TARDIS have an innate connection. But how does Mickey spilling tea into the TARDIS circuitry help the Doctor? It gives off smoke, which the Doctor breathes in... but would that not just be burning residues? Also, it's a bit of a minor quibble, but how does the Doctor grab hold of the Sycorax energy whip with relative ease, when it's just killed two men after touching them?

Why does this incarnation of the Doctor appear to need glasses? Perhaps they're just for looks... On the other hand, at least some of the previous Doctor's incarnations – notably the first and the fifth – were seen to need reading glasses too, so maybe there were already glasses of the correct strength stored in the TARDIS wardrobe.

ALTERED STATES: While the opening credits sequence otherwise remains identical to the previous year's, David Tennant's name has replaced Christopher Eccleston's (obviously).

The usual editing process prior to transmission removed a scene that would have explained the tenth Doctor's accent. According to an interview with Tennant for BBC Radio 1, a line of dialogue would have explained that, after his regeneration, the Doctor mirrored his new persona's accent on the first he heard, specifically Rose's, 'like a chick hatching from an egg'.

The character Alex was originally referred to as 'Alex Klein' in pre-broadcast publicity, including in *Doctor Who Magazine*. Sean Gilder was noted as appearing in the episode but was not identified as the Sycorax Leader until the release of the *Radio Times* television listings. Major Blake is given no first name in the episode or any other pre-release press; however, the 'secret area' of the BBC's UNIT tie-in website (www.unit.org.uk) lists his first name as Richard. Various news reports prior to broadcast misspelled the name of the actor who played Blake as 'Ornambala' instead of 'Omambala'.

EPISODE 200

BEHIND THE SCENES: The Cardiff metropolitan area once again doubled for London as it did in 'Rose', with the sequence with the 'pilot fish' attacking Rose and Mickey taking place outside Howell's department store (once again redressed as Henrik's). Brief location photography was completed outside the Tower of London for the sequence in which the cars approach the UNIT HQ. The HQ interior was created not on a soundstage but, in fact, in the loading dock of the Millennium Stadium in Cardiff, where the previous series' 'Dalek' was also recorded. The British Gas building and Baltic House in Mount Stuart Square, both in Cardiff, were used for exterior shots where the blood-controlled hostages ascend the staircases. Harriet Jones's office, ostensibly in 10 Downing Street, was a room at Tredegar House in Newport. A section of the Clearwell Caves Ancient Iron Mines historical mining site in Gloucestershire was dressed to become the interior of the Sycorax spacecraft. A site near Barry Docks in Wales was also used, dressed with false walls to become the exterior of the Sycorax craft (which was completed through the use of special effects). Scenes at the end of the episode were recorded at Wallis House in Brentford, across the street from where location work was done for the *Doctor Who* serial 'Invasion of the Dinosaurs' decades before.

The production also returned to the Brandon Estate in Southwark, London, from 25-29 July 2005 to record the sequences taking place outside Jackie Tyler's flat; among the visitors to the set that day were actor Peter Davison (the fifth Doctor) and family. On set security was provided by C & M Locations Limited of Essex.

'The Christmas Invasion' was the first *Doctor Who* story to make its first-run premiere nationally on a Sunday (though episodes had been screened before on Sunday in various regions). One day later, the episode was aired on the Canadian network CBC, hosted by Billie Piper. (Christopher Eccleston had done the honours for the season prior.)

Following broadcast of this episode, digital subscribers were invited to participate in 'Attack of the Graske' (see separate entry), a fully-produced featurette starring David Tennant as the Doctor. A commentary track similar to those issued on DVD releases was uploaded to the official *Doctor Who* BBC website; participating were executive producers Russell T Davies and Julie Gardner and producer Phil Collinson. Also included at the end of this episode was a 'coming soon' trailer featuring clips from most of the episodes of the second series.

This was the first time the title character was credited as 'The Doctor' since the final transmitted episode of the classic *Doctor Who* series, episode three of 'Survival', in 1989.

The BBC's online service created a new spin-off website for this episode, www.guinevere.org.uk, supposedly dedicated to the launch of the 'Guinevere One' space probe and run by the British Rocket Group. It states that the mission was launched on 31 October 2006, arriving at Mars in less than two months – quite a bit quicker than the most recent 'real world' Mars probe, Mars Reconnaissance Orbiter, which took seven months – and was intended to land on Christmas Day 2006. The unsuccessful conclusion of the 'Guinevere One' mission mirrors that of the real-life ESA probe 'Beagle 2', which was intended to land on Mars in 2003 but was lost during descent; that probe carried with it a recording of music by the UK band Blur, including a special piece containing elements of the theme tune from... *Doctor Who*!

Updated from the first series, meanwhile, is www.whoisdoctorwho.co.uk, ostensibly run by Mickey Smith, which continues his blogging about the Doctor and discusses the fact that the 'Guinevere One' website seems to concentrate on the question of talking to aliens. The site is now called 'Defending the Earth!' On the BBC homepage and the official *Doctor Who* website during the broadcast of 'The Christmas Invasion', the banner stated, 'Harriet Jones Says: Switch this website off for Britain.'

The *Radio Times* released a special edition on 3 December 2005 with a *Doctor Who*-themed cover. This was the first time that the series had been featured on the cover of a Christmas edition of the magazine, and the first time that any programme-specific (as opposed to general Christmas) image had been used on the cover of such an edition for some 16 years. Inside the magazine was an article by Russell T Davies; the capital letters beginning the paragraphs of this article, when assembled together, spelled out the words 'A cup of tea.'

'The Christmas Invasion' was the first special Christmas Day episode of *Doctor Who* since 'The Feast of Steven' in 1965. (In the latter, the festivities had even extended to the Doctor wishing a merry Christmas to viewers at home.) It was repeated one week later, on New Years Day.

DULCET TONES: 'Song For Ten' – Written by Murray Gold and sung by Tim Phillips. The song played during the end sequence as the Doctor picks his wardrobe and enjoys dinner with Rose, Jackie and Mickey. It was written specially for this episode and was the first original song (with lyrics) composed for the series since 'The Ballad of the Last Chance Saloon', heard in the 1966 story 'The Gunfighters'. Also heard: the Christmas carols 'Jingle Bells', which plays while the Christmas tree spins (though in a more ethereal and scary rendition than the traditional), and 'God Rest Ye Merry Gentlemen', performed by the Santa 'pilot fish'.

With this broadcast, the *Doctor Who* theme was altered slightly during the opening credits, and significantly during the closing credits: the section of the traditional *Doctor Who* theme known as the 'middle eight', missing during the first series, was restored. The score was rearranged by Murray Gold, continuing on from his first year with the series, and was performed by the BBC National Orchestra of Wales, which received a credit at the end of the episode (and, indeed, on all subsequent Series Two episodes). The music over the end credits of the Canadian broadcast was a slightly different arrangement.

Gold reused in this episode several themes he had created for the first series, most notably the music from the end of 'The End of the World' for the concluding moments; however, there was also plenty of new material composed for the story.

OFF THE SCREEN: Australian actor Adam Garcia co-founded the dance troupe that went on to become the internationally acclaimed Tap Dogs, and was nominated for a 1999 Laurence Olivier Theatre Award (1998 season) for Best Actor in a Musical for his performance in *Saturday Night Fever*. He also achieved notoriety as stripping bartender Kevin in *Coyote Ugly* (1999) and has appeared in *Agatha Christie's Marple*: 'The Body in the Library' (2004), *Confessions of a Teenage Drama Queen* (2004) and *Riding in Cars with Boys* (2001) and as the voice of the title character in the film *Kangaroo Jack* (2003). Daniel Evans has appeared in episodes of *Spooks* (2004), *To the Ends of the Earth* (2005), *Dalziel and Pascoe* (2006), *The Vice* (2001) and *Doctors* (2000). Sean Gilder has appeared in episodes of *The Bill* (1999, 2004), *Shameless* (2005, 2006), *Casualty* (2003), *Murphy's Law* (2004), *Our Friends in the North* (1996) and *Soldier Soldier* (1996), as well as the films *King Arthur* (2004) and *Gangs of New York* (2002), and as Boatswain's Mate Styles in several instalments of the series of *Hornblower* television films from 1998. Chu Omambala has appeared in episodes of *Judge John Deed* (2006) and *Holby City* (2004) and in the TV movie *Doomwatch: Winter Angel* (1999). Anita Briem has appeared in several productions in her native Iceland and on UK television in *The Evidence* (2006) and *Doctors* (2004). Cathy Murphy has been in *Holby City* (2005), *The Vice* (2003), *About a Boy* (2002), *Doctors* (2000), *Casualty* (1999), *EastEnders* (1997, 2005), *The Bill* (1997),

Men Behaving Badly (1994) and *She Wolf of London* (1990). Sian McDowall has gained credits in episodes of *Casualty* (2003). Sagar Arya has appeared in *Life on Mars* (2006) and *Casualty* (2006). Sean Carlsen has had roles in many *Doctor Who* audio plays from Big Finish Productions, most notably as Coordinator Narvin in the *Gallifrey* miniseries, and been seen in episodes of *The Bench* (2001), *Casualty* (1998) and *Tiger Bay* (1997). Lachele Carl has appeared in *A Kiss Before Dying* (1991), *Batman* (1989) and *Star Cops* (1987) and in the first series *Doctor Who* episode 'Aliens of London' (see Linking Themes, above.)

Biographies of actors Camille Coduri, Noel Clarke and Penelope Wilton and director James Hawes were included in the first *Back to the Vortex*.

TECHNICAL GOOFS: At one point, Project Guinevere is spelled, on a computer screen, as 'Guinivere'. Also, editing continuity: when the Doctor first spies his new clothes his mouth is open, but in the next shot, as he reaches up for them, his mouth is closed. His hair is different as well.

CONTROVERSIES: The American President insists (via Major Blake) that Harriet Jones turn control of the situation over to him, but as she notes, 'He's not my boss, and he's certainly not turning this into a war.' This is apparently a loosely-disguised dig by the writer at the current Prime Minister Tony Blair, the US President George W Bush and the conflict in Iraq. It caused a minor media stir when first reported.

INTERNAL CONSISTENCY: The dating of the story to Christmas 2006 is based on the fact that 'Aliens of London' is specified on screen as taking place in March 2006, and 'Boom Town' is set 'six months later' (September). It is very likely that the Earth-bound segments of 'The Parting of the Ways' and this story take place within the next few months, especially since it seems at the onset that this would ostensibly be Jackie's second Christmas without Rose (the first having been during the year she was 'missing' between 'Rose' and 'Aliens of London'). The story takes place from late afternoon Christmas Eve to early evening (right about dinner time) on Christmas Day.

At one point, the Doctor says that he's still within 15 hours of his regeneration. However, it is difficult to see how this can be the case. The TARDIS materialises intially while it's still quite bright outside on Christmas Eve, obviously before 5.00 pm. Sunrise the following morning would likely be between 12 and 13 hours later, and it's obvious that some time has passed since sunrise when the scenes take place on the outside of the Sycorax ship, as it seems to be mid-morning; therefore it's very likely that it's been longer than 15 hours. (The date itself also seems anomalous, for the simple fact that the trees appear to be carrying full sets of leaves... just as they would in July, when this episode was recorded.)

REVIEWS

After a triumphant return to television and an amazing first series, *Doctor Who's* first-ever Christmas special is 60 minutes of pure joy, and visible evidence of a production team kicking up its heels and revelling in its success. And to help celebrate, they give fans the one thing we missed with the debut of Eccleston's ninth Doctor – a thrilling, proper regeneration story that recalls classic elements of the old mythology while giving us a chance to meet a new Doctor all over again. It's the ultimate Christmas present, a cinematic-level adventure on the small screen that owes more than a little to big budget romps like *Independence Day* and *The Empire Strikes*

Back. What an embarrassment of riches! And what a Doctor the new guy is! Right out of the gate, David Tennant's incarnation is exuberant, ecstatic, and above all, downright Tom Baker-ish in his over-the-top glib charm, mixing some of the breathless energy of Davison's fifth with the slight obnoxious edge of Colin's sixth (but more on that later in the series). No wonder Rose looks so happy; her would-be boyfriend just got even sexier and more excited about simply being alive. Piper also steps up to the plate and takes command for most of the story, and she does a superb job. True, Tennant may be trying a bit too hard to capture that trademark lunatic enthusiasm, but then again, this is a debut story, and he has plenty of time to settle into the role. Tennant only really emerges in full force in the final act, but once he's on screen, he owns the show, no question. As befits a Christmas story, there are gifts aplenty hidden within for fans both new and old, from references to UNIT and the forthcoming spin-off *Torchwood* to plot inspirations lifted from 'Spearhead From Space', 'Doctor Who and the Silurians', and 'Castrovalva' to a marvellous look at the TARDIS wardrobe, which offers a glimpse of outfits from every previous Doctor's era – yup, even Steven's pullover! But there are plenty of logical gaps in the somewhat threadbare plot, from the nonsensical preliminary attack of the 'pilot fish' aliens – a spinning Christmas tree, I ask you – to the somewhat shaky invasion plans of the Sycorax themselves. And then there's that whole moral dilemma at the end, with the tenth Doctor playing Jon Pertwee's third Doctor to Harriet Jones's Brigadier. But whether you agree that Harriet was justified or not in her actions – I say she was – her possible political downfall may have introduced the new show's first glaring continuity glitch. After all, wasn't she supposed to preside over Britain's 'golden age'? So now the Doctor can just arbitrarily rewrite history any time he likes? We need the High Council of Time Lords back, and pronto. But why focus on flaws when we're having so much fun? With the Christmas invasion thwarted and the tenth Doctor taking Rose off to all new adventure, firmly leading the way with his brand new 'fightin' hand', there has never been a better time to be a *Doctor Who* fan. 'The Christmas Invasion' is a spectacular slice of holiday magic served up with love for the present, appreciation for the past, and hope for the future. If this one-hour extravaganza is any indication, that future is going to be... 'fantastic.' – *Arnold T Blumberg*

The Doctor's transformation at the end of 'The Parting of the Ways' may well be the most important *Doctor Who* regeneration since William Hartnell changed into Patrick Troughton almost 40 years ago. The series was well established and familiar to the viewing public in the '70s and '80s, when the majority of the Doctor's nine lives came and went. In 2005 it was essentially a new show. A popular show. And it had been on for only a year. How would a new generation of viewers take to a new Doctor? Well, I can't speak for an entire new generation of fans, but I absolutely loved Christopher Eccleston's Doctor, and yet after watching 'The Christmas Invasion', I was saying 'Christopher who?' The first 15 minutes or so of 'The Christmas Invasion' are a sort of warm-up act – as though Russell T Davies couldn't think of very much to do with a Christmas theme. Fortunately things quickly change gears, as if Davies has parachuted in a better script he has already written for the rest of the story, and 'The Christmas Invasion' starts resembling his earlier work *The Second Coming*, in that it turns into a story about giant, incredible events happening around totally ordinary people. All this is reinforced by some haunting images (particular the crowd shots of people leaving their suburban homes). Director James Hawes was absolutely the right man for the job. Noel Clarke and Camille Coduri are wonderful, but the only character who really gets short shrift here is Rose, which is surprising as Billie Piper and Penelope Wilton (fabulous, as always) virtually carry the majority of the episode. Her despondence and pessimism are perhaps realistic but seem completely out of character. The reason this doesn't work is that, ultimately, it's not the real agenda at work here. What Davies wants to do is cleverly reintroduce the Doctor. And he picks the most cunning way of doing it: by having the Doctor out of the picture for most of the episode. By giving us something that neither Harriet, nor Earth's defences nor even Rose can handle, they (and by extension the audience) don't need to *learn to trust* the new Doctor anymore, but rather they just *need the Doctor*. And when the Doctor does finally show up, we're treated to one stand-up-and-cheer moment after another as he exposes the baddies (Sycorax and human) and stops them in ways that are totally satisfying and even unexpected. That's just genius. David Tennant makes his mark on the character immediately, in spite of having very little screen time. He's smart. He's charming. He's sweet. He's cunning. And, most fascinating of all, he's *tough*. Bringing down Harriet Jones's government with just six words is one of the best moments in the new series (and doesn't break continuity, by the way: the British electoral system is such that Jones's three-term 'golden age' could still happen later, this being just a false start where she needs to learn some humility) and, I think, signposts an exciting, dangerous time in *Doctor Who*. – Graeme Burk

Hey, *Doctor Who* is back! We haven't had a new adventure for... okay, well, just over six months. (It loses its kick when you can't use the phrase 'years and years' anymore.) But the excitement is back, because we have a new Doctor for the first time in forev– wait, never mind. Having our cake and eating it really takes the fun out of fandom, don't you think? Seriously, though: the interesting thing about 'The Christmas Invasion' is that what we have here is completely more of the same of what we had last year, and yet not, all at once. Rose is, again, the main focus, but the Doctor is finally allowed to swoop in and save the day, adventurer-style. We're back for an invasion of Earth with Mickey, Jackie and Harriet Jones, but the story couldn't be less like 'Aliens of London' if it tried. There are silly bits, there are funny bits, and there are exciting bits, and for once, it seems to work. Maybe it's the magic of Christmas. Maybe, and more likely, it's a simple understanding going in that a Christmas special is always fluffy and fun and a little bit pointless. What if, though, this is a sign of things to come? I can't say I like everything about 'The Christmas Invasion', because I don't. I think the over-advertised 'pilot fish' make very little sense (why do they come in familiar Christmas forms?) and have even less relevance to the main Sycorax plotline. There's an emotional moment that Billie Piper hideously overacts, the 'Harriet Jones, Prime Minister' gag gets a little tired, and the whole thing about the Doctor's new hand is easily the most ludicrous addition to his mythos since Sylvester McCoy learned to knock people unconscious with a single touch. What I do like, however, is significant. I love that this new Doctor is active, funny, adventurous, and above all a hero – something Christopher Eccleston, even in his best moments, never quite managed. David Tennant may be a bit young for my taste, but he has a 'Doctorishness' that bodes very well. His chemistry with Billie Piper is good, and heavens above, Noel Clarke redeems himself, too. I think it's perfectly acceptable for a Christmas special to be irreverent and silly and hinge on a cup of tea and a satsuma; I might not forgive it so easily during the regular season, but it seems completely appropriate here. Best of all, I love that what seems so fluffy and forgettable at first becomes, at the end, completely serious. The Doctor facing down Harriet Jones is a great moment – and the final scene amongst the ash storm is really good, too. 'The Christmas Invasion' is fun, frothy, and hugely enjoyable. Is it perfect? No, but it makes me all the more anxious for the new season to begin. The Doctor is a completely new man – and I think I like him just that little bit more. – *Sarah Hadley*

What you typically want out of a British television Christmas special is something big, flashy, maybe even a little over-the-top. That's why the soap operas always roll out their most melodramatic and often ludicrously contrived plotlines on Christmas day, and why, aside from them, dramas rarely get a look-in – aside from the occasional specially commissioned one-off such as 2001's BBC1 centrepiece *The Lost World*. Channel controllers tend to go for more broadly appealing and easy-going fare such as light entertainment spectaculars, sitcom specials or blockbuster movies – something with a broad base of appeal and a bit of sparkle. How fortunate for BBC1 Controller Peter Fincham come Christmas 2005, then, that he had in his pocket a festive episode of a series that had delivered such popular appeal and 'special event' quality on pretty much a week-in, week-out basis earlier in the year. Was there any doubt that 'The Christmas Invasion' would, on that basis, be British television's Christmas event of the year? The amazing thing is that with all the hype of Series One's success, its coveted position in the schedule and the introduction of a new leading man to live up to, the episode actually delivers on the expectation, and in spades. While the Series One two-parters 'The Empty Child'/'The Doctor Dances' and 'Bad Wolf'/'The Parting of the Ways' are perhaps still my overall favourite new series stories, I would go so far as to say that I believe 'The Christmas Invasion' may well be the most successful single episode of the resurrected *Doctor Who* to date. Russell T Davies has provided a script that, while fun and lightweight in places, has enough genuine drama and epic quality to it to give the episode some real backbone and status. Added to that, James Hawes' welcome return to the director's chair gives the whole thing an astoundingly Hollywood look – as Hawes himself has said, it's questionable if anything this epic has been seen in a British television production before, and certainly not in science-fiction terms. The special effects work from The Mill is stunning, and Murray Gold's opportunity to utilise a full orchestra for his luscious, symphonic score also gives the episode a much bigger feel than any other *Doctor Who*. It's perhaps particularly impressive that in all this, the excellent performances of the cast are not overshadowed. Piper, Coduri and Clarke are all on fine form, as is the excellent Penelope Wilton, but the episode really belongs to Tennant. He gets a big build up, and it's a brave decision to wait so long before giving the new Doctor a proper entrance, but it makes him seem all the more heroic when he does finally appear, and from thereon in he owns the episode. I'm not completely sold on all aspects – I didn't take to the magically regenerating hand, for example, although that is perhaps forgivable as it led to the excellent 'Witchcraft!' 'Time Lord!' exchange, and the 'fightin' hand!' exclamation. It was also rather sad to see Harriet Jones turn out as she did, although again this was a brave decision to take with such a popular and likeable character. Overall, then, a fine curtain-raiser for the tenth Doctor's era, and one of the finest things there's been on Christmas Day television in the UK for many a long year. – *Paul Hayes*

Although expectations for Series Two were running high – that'd be Phil Collinson's constant 'raising the bar' comments, no doubt – I moderated my hopes slightly given that this was a BBC1 Christmas special, which tend to be immense fun to watch, but ultimately lightweight. 'The Christmas Invasion' was far from lightweight, but was flawed. Leaving the newly-regenerated Doctor out of action for three-quarters of the story isn't new, unexpected or even unwelcome, especially if it gives the rest of the cast a chance to shine, as in 'Castrovalva' (arguably!). But they have to be carrying an impressive storyline: sadly, despite a few flashes of deeper characterisation than usual for Jackie and Mickey, the actions of the Powell Estate Three lack sufficient interest to distract from the Doctor-shaped hole in the plot. I understand that Davies was trying to show that people are 'rubbish' without the Doctor, but Rose has just seen – and saved – the universe. Would she really crumple like that? Have her travels with the Doctor had so little effect? As for the threat of the week... not convinced. Sorry. I got lost somewhere around the murderous Santas who seem to have been shoehorned into the storyline just for the hell of it, and then some Faction Paradox rejects crop up with a plot straight out of 1960s *Batman*. Sending everyone to the roof? Be off with you! Thankfully, the Doctor's old friend tea has completed his regeneration, so we are finally introduced to Doctor Number Ten... and thankfully, he isn't a disappointment. Pulling off the impressive achievement of hitting the ground running – consider even Tom Baker's lacklustre first performance – Tennant demonstrates his ability to switch instantly between Mockney wideboy to 'The Last of the Time Lords™' and shows the potential to be the first Doctor since Tom Baker to truly embody the series' twin themes of humour and horror. 'No second chances' – this is a Doctor who isn't afraid to trade on his reputation and abilities. However, after the battle-scarred Eccleston, is this Doctor just a little too full of himself? This isn't to say that 'The Christmas Invasion' doesn't push the right buttons: Harriet Jones is superb, and the appearance of UNIT and mysterious whisperings about Torchwood both satisfy and intrigue. No-one can criticise any of the effects, from the deadly Christmas tree to the shattering of the Gherkin to the Sycorax ship itself, and it did live up to the definition of a BBC1 Christmas special. But I can't help thinking it could have done so much more with its 60 minutes. 'The Christmas Invasion' really touches the high-notes of Series One only at the end. From the confrontation with Harriet Jones – my god, this Doctor could give the seventh a run for his money on the righteous anger and manipulation front – to the wonderful wardrobe room scene and 'Song for Ten', to the scenes of this Doctor 'doing domestic', there's a warmth and a cuddliness that only the very best in the series can provide. Not a classic, but a fun, camp Christmas romp that hints at something far, far darker down the line. – *Craig Hinton*

Perhaps thrown-together a little too hastily in the wake of the success of the new *Doctor Who*, this hour-long 'special' has the feel of a 45 minute season-opener, designed to get over the regeneration hump for an audience that has forgotten how the convention works, with a 15-minute Christmas-themed prologue tacked on to make it suitable for holiday broadcast. (Note how none of the three billion mind-controlled A-positive humans is wearing a paper hat or a naff new jumper given by a granny.) The Sycorax feel a bit too much like several previous Davies capitalist villain races for comfort and the *Day the Earth Stood Still* grand gesture gambit is ridiculous when you think about it. We see people on top of the Coliseum or near the Eiffel Tower, but what happens in flat regions of the globe, prisons, planes in flight, etc? What chaos is caused by one-third of all essential service personnel leaving posts when they're undermanned for a holiday everyone now forgets until the coda? Wouldn't roofs collapse under the added weight or people fall off when they are freed from mind control and overcome by vertigo? Meanwhile, a global crisis boils down to the key cast being beamed up to the Sycorax ship where one single alien (Sean Gilder) does all the talking as serried ranks of minions cheer on his every evil pronouncement but do nothing at all to help. Davies keeps sparking ideas, like the breakdown of the TARDIS's auto-translate mechanism while the Doctor is comatose (with the Sycorax's subtitled snarling turning into English as he gets better off-screen), but also defaults to hoary business like a single combat challenge that can overturn a whole society. The fillip at the end, after one of Davies's patented defiant heroic speeches ('It is defended'), is that the Prime Minister uses a reverse-engineered alien zap beam to destroy the fleeing Sycorax ship just as Thatcher torpedoed the Belgrano, prompting the Doctor to one of those indignant tirades ('I should have told them to run, because the monsters are coming, the human race') that Jon Pertwee gave voice to in 1970 or so. The point would be better taken if the Sycorax hadn't already shown his sworn word was worthless by trying to stab the Doctor in the back after the duel was over and he had supposedly yielded. Tennant's first stab at the Doctor isn't that impressive – he was better in the minute or so at the end of 'The Parting of the Ways' – as he free-associates in what threatens to be a nerdily geekish manner (which extends to referencing Arthur Dent), grins way too much, quotes Eccleston's signature expression ('fantastic') weakly, spends most of the story laid up and fussed over by Rose's frankly played-out supporting characters, and doesn't really get enough material to make a strong first impression. The closing trailer montage promises K-9 – suggesting a shark is about to be jumped. Let's hope it's a one-off aberration. – *Kim Newman*

The new *Who* never shows blood. 'The Christmas Invasion' contains an extreme example, when the Doctor has his hand sliced away by the Sycorax leader's sword, but he thankfully fails to do an impression of *Monty Python and the Holy Grail*'s Black Knight, or indeed anyone from *Kill Bill*. (Compare and contrast the gory crushing of Lytton's hands in 'Attack of the Cybermen'.) Curiously, 'The Christmas Invasion' also contains a rare – if not unique – sighting of blood, in the clinical context of the blood control device. The Doctor even gives it a taste. One bottle of *his* blood, Rose reminds us, could change the future of the human race. 'I keep forgetting he's not human,' she confesses, bewildered and distressed by the Doctor's regeneration. Presumably, back on Gallifrey, the process was more like childbirth: for one thing, you could get expert help and pain relief, and for another, you saw it coming. The Doctor gives birth to himself, with only first aid in the form of bed rest and tea. Like a woman in the grip of her body's program of dilation and contractions, the Doctor is temporarily overwhelmed by his own body's involuntary actions and needs. Even that ubiquitous marker of his alienness, his double heartbeat, is reduced to a single mortal pulse. The 'pilot fish' would have gone a step further, and reduced him completely to meat. Unlike, say, Cassandra, they have no use for his intelligence: all they want is the energy physically blazing through him. Now this is not something you can do to a *person*. On Earth, just for being born human, the law gives you the right not to be reduced to a body: not to be enslaved, or tortured, or locked away like an animal. Major Blake is outraged when the Sycorax leader kills Daniel Llewellyn on the spot: 'That man was your prisoner! Even your species must have articles of war forbidding ...!' They're his last words. Now, the invaders' society has laws of its own: I'll bet the leader couldn't have got away with reducing a fellow Sycorax to smoking bones at a whim. Killing 'cattle' is a different matter. The Doctor holds the Sycorax leader to his own rules: when the leader breaks his word, he's instantly satsuma-ed. Minutes later, the Doctor does the same thing to Harriet for the same reason: she has broken Earth's own articles of war. He doesn't look back, not at either of them. (By the way, watch Harriet when the Sycorax are enraged by the detection of hidden alien technology on Earth: surely she thinks they've found Torchwood's big gun.) In the midst of all these failures of compassion, Jackie Tyler – of all people – stands out. When Rose finally breaks down, her mum is there to hold her. She watches over the Doctor like he's some sort of ill child ('Are you really better?'). Inadvertent as it is, she's the one who brings him back to life. Jackie can't save the Earth – but she midwives the Doctor's rebirth, and he *can.* – *Kate Orman*

An invasion of red-clad Santa robots... talking Christmas trees... Rose sings... the Doctor dances (again)... I think I've been listening to far too many fan rumours! None of the above happened in the Christmas special and yet I'd read that they would. So my reviews will sometimes discuss what I thought was going to be in the episode and compare it to what was in the episode! And more importantly, did the real version stack up to my imagined version? When I saw the first photos of the three deadly Santas, I had visions of thousands of them marching against familiar London landmarks, just as the Daleks and Cybermen had been seen to do in years past... Sadly, this was not to be... As a bit of silly Christmas Day fluff, 'The Christmas Invasion' delivered precisely what it said on the gift-wrapping. It had pretty much everything that *Doctor Who* does so well: an invasion of Earth, ugly monsters, space-probes, the military machine gone mad, lots of silly puns... But beneath the surface of these safe and familiar trappings, 'The Christmas Invasion' is a bit of a mess – all style over substance. Even after a couple of viewings, I'm still totally perplexed as to the purpose of the 'pilot fish' killer Santas subplot. And the bit that everyone in the production team seemed the most proud of – the deadly Christmas tree – was illogical and pointless. They're further examples of one of the main problems I had with the first series; incoherent plot elements that serve no purpose other than to look good on screen. It seems like Series Two is going to continue this 'tradition'. If these plot-holes were apparent to me as a viewer, surely the production team should have detected and addressed them at the script stage? Or did they think that by 7 pm, viewers would have already had too much Christmas good cheer to even notice or care? Of course, the reason most people tuned in was to see David Tennant's take on the role. (The 'bound for Barcelona' *Children in Need* doesn't really count.) Despite his all-too brief screen time, Doctor Ten stole the limelight with his infectious cheeky grin. He has almost pitch-perfect comic timing, and I'm sure I'm right in saying the way he changes context mid-sentence ('No, hang on, that's *The Lion King* ...') will become a personality trait. But it's early days yet – after all, we don't judge the entire Tom Baker era based upon 'Robot', do we? We've still got 13 episodes ahead of us, so it's rather unfair to pass judgement on Mr Tennant right now. If he hasn't won me over by, say, the fourth episode, then I doubt he ever will. My favourite tenth Doctor moments are the sublime image of the jim-jam clad Doctor defeating the villain (we missed out on Tom doing battle with the giant robot still wearing his UNIT-issue nightgown); and secondly the Doctor in the TARDIS choosing his new garb, accompanied by Murray Gold's simply beautiful 'Song for Ten'. (Where's that soundtrack album?) Despite some rough bumps, the Doctor Ten-nant era is off to an average start... – *Jon Preddle*

As if *Doctor Who* regeneration stories don't have enough inherent iconography in them anyway, here we have a lot of Christmas icons decorating the walls of the episode's structure as a bonus – tinsel, trees, Slade(!), not to mention Santas with machine guns. You don't get many of those in *It's a Wonderful Life*. The slow first half of 'The Christmas Invasion' actually works as an effective mood-piece, establishing tone and metre, before the second half picks up the slack and sees an impressively dominant debut 15 minutes with the new Doctor. Amid some fairly serious themes (mass suicide, the ethics of warfare), comes a series of political comments marginally more subtle than those of the first year (though one or two seem crass and hammered in simply to court controversy). And, just to remind us that, hey, it's Christmas, some rank – and not a bit out-of-pace either – frivolity. It's, therefore, perfectly in keeping that next to the seriousness of an alien invasion that line about the Royal Family being 'up on the roof' should work with such charm and wit. There's a gentle warmth to the dialogue and set-pieces in 'The Christmas Invasion', a fundamental core humanity, which is one of the things that has always set *Doctor Who* apart from the colder and more clinical end of science-fiction. Here is a show in which a cup of tea, literally, saves the world. Where the hero's response to a bullwhip-wielding aggressor is casually to note, 'You could have someone's eye out with that.' In which a Doctor with mannerisms that sometimes echo those of Kenneth Williams and Tommy Cooper can end the episode as Errol Flynn, swashbuckling his way to victory and then telling the nasties to leave Earth alone because, magnificently, 'It. Is. Defended.' Sure the Torchwood stuff is laid on a bit thick (hark, is this a spin-off I see before me?), the Sycorax ultimately turn out to be the intergalactic equivalent of Madagascar and there's that odd (yet curiously affecting) coda that feels so much like padding but, actually, isn't. Forget all that and concentrate on a Doctor who doesn't know, quite, who he is yet, but has just taken a very big step towards finding out. – *Keith Topping*

EDITOR'S REVIEW: I knew from the first moment I saw him on screen in the *Children in Need* special that I was going to like David Tennant playing the Doctor. That beaming smile, the wicked eyes, the sense of 'to heck with the danger, we're here to have fun', immediately captured my attention, far more than had Christopher Eccleston (a wonderful actor, I admit, but never quite right, for me, for this particular role).

Which is why 'The Christmas Invasion' seemed so strange at first, because Tennant was barely in it. This struck me in the most unusual way, highlighting just what it is that makes this show special, and how utterly lost it is without the Doctor. *Doctor Who* is not a concept series in the strictest sense; you can say that it's about a guy who fights monsters and travels through time in a police box, but you can't capture the essence of what *Doctor Who* really means until you accept the character for who he is: the Selfless Hero, the absolute good in good versus evil. He may have his foibles, but the Doctor is the heart and soul of the show. As good an actress as Billie Piper has become – and have no doubt, she's one of the best things about modern *Doctor Who* in every sense – she simply cannot carry this series.

To soften the blow, I imagine, we were granted audience with some familiar faces, including Mickey (not so much the idiot anymore), Jackie Tyler (who's been transformed from irritating to plucky), the old *Doctor Who* staple UNIT, and even Harriet Jones, in a most welcome return for one of Series One's finest. It's now Christmas, and there are all the trappings of a Russell T Davies Yuletide spectacle: killer Santa Clauses and deadly Christmas trees galore. Meanwhile, David Tennant's Doctor lies asleep in a bed... almost a Christmas parable in reverse, the world's Messiah slowly dying while lying in swaddling clothes, while the forces of darkness gather storm outside. And somehow, it all seems hollow.

That is, until that wonderful moment – perhaps, in my mind, one of the finest moments in the series' long history – when, as all hope seems lost and the Earth seems doomed to slavery and destruction, out steps this man from his blue box. 'Did you miss me?' he asks with a smile, and suddenly *Doctor Who* is back... not just the character, but the episode and the series itself. Up until now, Rose, Mickey and Harriet Jones have been unable to stop the tide of destruction the Sycorax have wrought; we know that the Doctor, with merely a wink on the sly, has the power to change things. And suddenly, Doctor Who the archetype returns: the Selfless Hero, come to set the world to rights. Tennant gives a smashing performance – some of it even improvised, apparently (that impersonation of the boorish Sycorax leader is priceless) – and never once fails to make you believe that it's really him inside, all of him: the Doctor, the historical personage, the man from Gallifrey who has led ten lives over a thousand years. If it had been anyone else – Rose, Harriet, or just about anyone, really – who had defeated the Sycorax with the rather timely discovery of a satsuma, we would scoff and shake our heads with disdain. This is the Doctor, however, and we instantly know the impossible has become the possible.

Of course, with the Selfless Hero, anyone else pales in comparison. I'm rather unhappy, therefore, that the author chose to rewrite the role of the Noble Innocent; that would be Harriet, who stands as our representative from Earth, first watching the events unfold throughout the crisis, then making her brave stand aboard the Sycorax ship. There is a world of difference (and a world of difference of opinion) between the Harriet Jones who greets the Doctor with her genuineness and her 'Landslide majority' guffaw, and the sad-faced Harriet Jones the Doctor basically tries to ruin at the end. Yes, there must always be shades of grey, but for a series that tends to present its good and evil in absolutes, I must ask why Davies and company seem so bent on darkening every character (other than the Doctor and Rose) that they touch. Surely someone else could have fired at the Sycorax ship, after all. I think a few hearts bled when our Harriet – the woman who faced down Slitheen at Downing Street and never faltered – suddenly was on the opposite side of the fence from our Selfless Hero. Oh well.

For a fairly standard alien invasion/deadly danger story, 'The Christmas Invasion' can boast that, for its first 40 minutes, it manages to cope with the loss of the Doctor at least passably. We don't doubt that the Doctor will return, of course, a fact that sustains our interest, but it does tend to become a bit bogged down in the details. (Was the whole blood control, which in fact is nothing but a cipher, really necessary? Why not just avoid the whole affair and have the Sycorax threaten to, say, blow up Europe. There's your third of the world's population without pages and pages of exposition.) We deal with two rather meaningless deaths (okay, the poor chap who's responsible pays the price, but does *anyone* really care that Major Blake turns into smoking embers?) and watch the next incarnation of the 'MP, Flydale North' running gag play itself out again, and again, and again, before we really get to that moment we're waiting for. Then, when it does, our fears are shattered; mine certainly were, as I suddenly believed that the Doctor, in the hands of this wonderful new actor in the role, could duel like Errol Flynn, banter like a seasoned politician, or get his moralisms mixed up and suddenly start quoting Disney films. Because in a sense, that's really what – or rather, *Who* – it's all about. Welcome back, Doctor; I've missed you. – *Shaun Lyon*

200-A: ATTACK OF THE GRASKE

The sinister Graske have started taking captives from all over the galaxy, creating duplicates in their place that obey their commands. It's up to the Doctor... but he's on his own, and needs the help of a new companion to save the day.

FIRST TRANSMISSION: 25 December 2005 (BBC digital services) following 'The Christmas Invasion'.
DURATION: 13'36" (approx)
WRITER: Gareth Roberts
DIRECTOR: Ashley Way
CREDITED CAST: David Tennant* (The Doctor), Lisa Palfrey (Mum), Nicholas Beveney (Dad), Mollie Kabia (Girl), James Harris (Boy), Robin Meredith (Granddad), Gwenyth Petty (Grandma), Jimmy Vee (Graske), Roger Nott (Older Man), Ben Oliver (Urchin), Catherine Olding (Young Woman)

* David Tennant is not listed in the closing credits of the episode; the only credit he receives is the opening titles (in which the character is not named).

WHERE AND WHEN: Somewhere in Great Britain, Christmas Day 2006; the same day in 1883; and a base on the planet Griffoth, as well as in the TARDIS.

THE STORY UNFOLDS: The Doctor invites the viewer into the TARDIS, as if whisking him/her off on one of his adventures. The viewer is then able to witness and shape events as they unfold... using the TV remote control to play an interactive game with a series of puzzles to be solved. Rose is absent; the Doctor has dropped her off at an ABBA concert at Wembley Arena in 1979.

A Christmas family gathering somewhere in Britain is invaded by a diminutive alien called a Graske, who has replaced the mother with a duplicate under its control; the creature soon does the same to the father using a small portable device. The same thing happens to a boy in Christmas 1883 on a street corner.

The Graske's homeworld is the legendary planet Griffoth, where the Graske keep alive original forms of the people they've kidnapped. The victims are eventually teleported home after one of the Slitheen family breaks out of its container (assuming the viewer does everything right!)

The TARDIS console has a dimensional stabiliser (a crank), a vector tracker (two dials) and a vortex loop (a hand pump). Queen Victoria is mentioned when the TARDIS arrives in 1883.

THE DOCTOR: He reiterates that he takes only the best on his adventures, and says that he's been watching some of the viewer's adventures himself. He thinks he might like opera and doesn't know if he likes mangoes. He says he may pick up the viewer one day (assuming they've chosen all the right answers!)

TORCHWOOD: No reference in this story.

BODY COUNT: None; the Graske's evil plot is foiled and everyone is sent home. Unless the player chooses 'stasis', in which case he/she ends up permanently stuck on Griffoth and the Graske's duplicates stay on Earth.

THE DOCTOR'S MAGICAL SONIC SCREWDRIVER: The Doctor aims it at the viewer to 'link' to his/her DVD remote controls; this will supposedly enable the viewer to control events through the remote. He tells the viewer he will guide him/her through the Graske's base with the sonic screwdriver. Later, he uses it to 'disconnect' the viewer's remote.

REALITY BITES: The Doctor says the Graske base has 'as many doors as Jim Morrison', referring to the legendary singer and his band, the Doors. ABBA did indeed play Wembley Arena in November of 1979 over an unprecedented six sold-out performances.

The Doctor tells the viewer at the end that there's a risk of the galaxy imploding if they turn to ITV that night. The ITV network is the traditional rival to the BBC for Christmas viewers. In one variation, the Doctor refers to advocaat, a Dutch liqueur made from eggs, spirits, sugar, brandy and vanilla.

While it is implied that the family Christmas in the present day takes place in London, there is no direct *evidence* to suggest this is the case; in fact, going by the Welsh accents of the family members, it could take place in Cardiff or somewhere else in Wales.

LINKING THEMES: A camera descent toward Britain is seen, very much like the one used at the opening of 'Rose' and 'The Christmas Invasion' but going down not quite as far; instead, the viewpoint hovers above Britain at night to start one of the puzzles, then moves down into London for another.

The beggar boy says he's collecting pennies to save up for a satsuma; a satsuma was in the Doctor's pocket in 'The Christmas Invasion', and was instrumental in the defeat of the Sycorax leader. One of the victims on Griffoth is a Slitheen ('Aliens of London'/'World War Three'/'Boom Town') – or rather, one of the Raxacoricofallapatorian race of which the Slitheen family are a part.

SCENE MISSING: How does the Doctor know that one of the people at the Christmas party is an alien impostor? Why does he follow the Graske back to its base and then not go out himself to find out what's going on? What is the Graske's purpose in duplicating people? (Yes, we know this is supposed to be a bit of Christmas *fun*... but, after all, finding story gaps is the purpose of this section!)

DULCET TONES: Portions of 'Rockin' Around the Christmas Tree' can be heard during the first puzzle sequence. The song was penned by Johnny Marks, the American popular music composer who also wrote 'Rudolph the Red-Nosed Reindeer' and a host of other successful Christmas rock 'n' roll singles released during the '60s, and made young Brenda Lee – whose recording career had started only two years previously – an international star. It was recorded on 19 October 1958 and released on vinyl on 17 November the same year.

A 30 second section of Gary Glitter's 1984 song 'Another Rock and Roll Christmas' is used in the final family scene – but only if the viewer is successful in his/her mission! The flamboyant Glitter (real name Paul Gadd) was a household name in the '70s and had a previous brush with *Doctor Who* when one of his songs ('Rock and Roll Part 2') was sampled by the KLF, under the guise of the Time Lords, for use on their track 'Doctorin' the TARDIS', which topped the UK charts in 1988. Glitter's original track appeared on a great many Christmas compilation CDs between 1984 and 1999, but virtually disappeared from such releases thereafter following Glitter's conviction for possessing indecent images of children. (He has since been found guilty of further child sex-related crimes in Vietnam.)

OFF THE SCREEN: Jimmy Vee appeared in two roles during the first series of *Doctor Who*: as the Moxx of Balhoon in 'The End of the World' and as the alien pig in 'Aliens of London'. Roger Nott appeared in the role of a prisoner in the *Doctor Who* story 'The Twin Dilemma' in 1984, and has also been seen in *Silent Cry* (2002), *Darklands* (1996), *The Professionals* (1982), *Softly Softly* (1973) and *Dixon of Dock Green* (1970). Lisa Palfrey has been seen in *The Bill* (2004), *Casualty* (2002) in the recurring role of Melanie Collier, *Soldier Soldier* (1997) and *The Englishman Who Went Up a Hill But Came Down a Mountain* (1995). Nicholas Beveney was in *Sahara* (2005), *Holby City* (2003), *Jack and the Beanstalk: The Real Story* (2001), *The Bill* (2000) and *Pie in the Sky* (1997). Robin Meredith has been seen in *Love Soup* (2005), *Goodnight Sweetheart* (1999), *Only Fools and Horses* (1996), *As You Like It* (1992), *Pennies From Heaven* (1978), *Father Brown* (1974) and *The Merchant of Venice* (1973). Gwenyth Petty was in *Other People's Children* (2000), *Mortimer's Law* (1998) and *A Mind to Kill* (1995).

Writer Gareth Roberts is the author of nine *Doctor Who* novels for both Virgin Publishing and BBC Books – including 'The Highest Science', 'The Romance of Crime', 'The English Way of Death', 'The Plotters', 'I Am a Dalek' and 'Only Human', the latter two based on the current *Doctor Who* series – and co-writer (with Clayton Hickman) of two *Doctor Who* audio plays for Big Finish, 'Bang-Bang-a-Boom' and the critically acclaimed 'The One Doctor'. His television work includes writing for *Swinging* (2005), *Swiss Toni* (2003), *Randall & Hopkirk (Deceased)* (2001), *Brookside* (1999-2003), *Springhill* (1996), *Coronation Street* (1997) and both writing for and story editing *Emmerdale* (1998-1999). Roberts also penned the teleplays for the TARDISodes seen throughout this series, and will be one of the featured script writers for *Doctor Who* Series Three and *The Sarah Jane Adventures*.

Ashley Way's directorial credits include *Casualty* (2005), *Hoodlum & Son* (2003), *Belonging* (2000) and *Filligoggin* (2000); he has also served as a first assistant or second unit director on *The Sorcerer's Apprentice* (2002), *Berserker* (2001), *Glory Glory* (2000), *Dazzle* (1999) and *The Last Leprechaun* (1998), and as writer and associate producer of *Askari* (2001).

BEHIND THE SCENES: 'Attack of the Graske' was recorded in early November in a private home in Penarth, at Mount Stuart Square (the exterior sequences in 1883) and at Enfys Television Studios in Cardiff, concurrent to the start of production of the four-episode block of Cybermen episodes directed by Graeme Harper.

The episode was originally transmitted on the BBC digital service on 25 December 2005 and was repeated on 1 January 2006. It was also later made available on the official *Doctor Who* website, though restricted to UK residents.

Among the options in the episode that the viewer has to choose from are: which of two camera positions to view from in the modern-day family's home at Christmas (one from inside the television, the other from a video camera held by the daughter in the family); which of the six members of the family is the Graske duplicate; which control to operate on the TARDIS console; where the Graske is located on a TARDIS scanner map of first Britain and then London; where the Graske is hiding in the Victorian segment; which key to use to break into the Graske base; and finally whether to teleport the Graske's prisoners away or freeze them forever in stasis.

Unlike in all other televised episodes of the new series to date, Billie Piper receives no onscreen credit at the beginning (she does not appear); David Tennant's is the only name seen prior to the *Doctor Who* logo. This episode was presented in the more traditional 4:3 aspect ratio and not the newer 16:9 standard used by almost all broadcast stations in the UK today. Each repeating transmission of the episode was preceded by a countdown sequence, with the 'numbers' resembling the Gallifreyan designs seen in the Doctor's TARDIS.

201: NEW EARTH

In the distant future, humanity has resettled in another galaxy on the planet New Earth, where a terrible secret is harboured within the confines of a famous hospital. But the Doctor and Rose, it seems, are not the only ones trying to discover that secret... and someone who by all accounts should be dead is very much alive.

FIRST TRANSMISSION: UK – 15 April 2006. US – 29 September 2006. Canada – 9 October 2006. Australia – 15 July 2006. New Zealand – 13 July 2006.
DURATION: 44'03"
WRITER: Russell T Davies
DIRECTOR: James Hawes
CREDITED CAST: David Tennant (The Doctor), Billie Piper (Rose Tyler), Camille Coduri (Jackie Tyler), Noel Clarke (Mickey Smith), Zoë Wanamaker (Cassandra), Sean Gallagher (Chip), Dona Croll (Matron Casp), Michael Fitzgerald (Duke of Manhattan), Lucy Robinson (Frau Clovis), Adjoa Andoh (Sister Jatt), Anna Hope (Novice Hame), Simon Ludders (Patient), Struan Rodger (Face of Boe).

WHERE AND WHEN: New Earth, a planet in the galaxy M87, the year 'five billion and twenty-three... further than we've ever gone before' according to the Doctor. Also, many years earlier (date unknown) at a party, location unspecified.

THE STORY UNFOLDS: Some time after the destruction of the Earth by the sun's expansion, the human race, spread across the stars, gets nostalgic for its home world and starts a revival movement. This leads them to New Earth, a planet of the same size and with the same orbit as the original. New Earth is a pastoral planet with rolling green apple grass hills and blue lakes, and is home to a futuristic city called New New York, which has towering skyscrapers and hovercars. (New New York is apparently the fifteenth since the original, making it 'New New New New... York' – new many times over.)

The hospital is run by the Sisters of Plenitude, a group of feline-faced aliens; they take life-long vows to heal. (It is implied that they are either the original inhabitants of New Earth or else were settled here before humanity arrived.) They dress in white robes (reminiscent of Catholic robes crossed with nurses' uniforms). Their slogan is 'Hope, harmony and health' and, according to their literature, the one thing they cannot cure is old age. However, their hospital hides a dark secret: a massive 'intensive care' chamber of specially-grown clone human test subjects, infected with every known disease all at once, functioning as a giant laboratory or human farm. Upon being released from their containers, the test subjects can impart their diseases (and, later, the cures) by touch.

A green moon is the universal symbol for hospitals. New Earth has a 'pleasure gardens' centre (which at one point is announced as taking visitors carrying green or blue identification cards); cuttings from the gardens are not permitted. Viruses, like humans, have apparently evolved. Petrifold regression turns a person to stone, but the cure will not technically be invented for a thousand years beyond this time.

The hospital uses disinfectant devices in the elevators, which spray water and other liquids and powders over visitors and then dry them as they ascend. Among the procedures the Sisters perform are blood washes, cell-washing cascades and incinerations (the latter usually a standard procedure for test subjects who speak or demonstrate sentience). The cured lab subjects are later referred to by the Doctor as a new form of life, 'new humans', and the Sisters are arrested by the police (from the NNYPD, or New New York Police Department).

Those infected with Marconi's Disease should take years to recover, but a patient in the hospital recovers in two days. Paladome Pancrosis kills in two days – again, except in this hospital. One of the Sisters of Plenitude, Sister Corvin, wrote a thesis called 'The Echo of Life' on the migration of sentience. A subframe can apparently be unlocked with the installation protocol.

THE DOCTOR: He doesn't like hospitals (they give him the creeps) and is dismayed that this one doesn't have a shop. When Rose's body is taken over by Cassandra, he almost immediately picks up on the fact that she is not quite herself (mostly because she has a grasp of the high-tech and speaks with a strange form of Cockney). Cassandra enjoys slipping inside his body (and admires his various body parts, many of which are 'hardly used'; she describes his the two hearts as 'beating out a samba'). His plan involves mixing all the various cures together; after all, as he says, 'I'm the Doctor, and I cured them.'

ROSE TYLER: Rose is the only pure-blood human left in the universe at this time. She tells the Doctor she loves travelling with him, and thinks she'll never get used to the idea of different planets. ('Different ground beneath my feet, different sky,' she exclaims; while this is obviously not the first alien planet she's been to, as she's mentioned others, it's the first one in the televised series.) Cassandra, in her body, thinks she's a 'chav', but quite curvy ('Like living inside a bouncy castle').

CHARACTER BUILDING: *Cassandra* – Although her skin-sheet was destroyed by the Doctor in 'The End of the World', her brain survived in its suspension tank, and her blue eyes were salvaged from the bin; her new skin was taken from the back of her original body. She tells the Sisterhood that she wants money, and later opens the test subject containers in an attempt to escape. A party she attended years earlier – a drinks reception for the Ambassador of Thrace – was the last occasion on which anyone told her she was beautiful (though it turns out that it was actually she who told herself this, while in Chip's body). She calls Rose a 'dirty blonde assassin' and thinks their reunion is predestined. She speaks some French. She has a psychograft (illegal on every civilised planet in the galaxy) and a suspension field in the basement of the hospital and uses these to trap Rose with the aid of energy filaments, and then to place her own mind into Rose's body. She thinks the Doctor is a hypocrite for criticising this when he has changed his face, and later knocks him out with an aerosol spray. Her attempts at Cockney dialect are in one way laughable, but in another quite impressive for someone so far removed from the 20th Century. Placing her consciousness into one of the test subjects changes her outlook about the situation, and later, when inside Chip's body, she realises it's time for her to die... but not until after seeing herself from years before, one last time.

Chip – Cassandra's manservant (she refers to him as her pet), who is devoted to her; he is not a proper life form, but a force-grown clone modelled on her favourite pattern. He brought her to the hospital in secret and now brings her medicine. He gives up his body as a permanent home for Cassandra's mind – she refers to his body as 'a walking doodle'.

The Face of Boe – A massive alien head suspended in a smoke-filled tank; he is at least several thousand years old. The Doctor has come to New Earth after receiving a message on psychic paper; he later learns it is from the Face of Boe, whose message is 'Ward 26... Please Come'. The rest of his kind are extinct. Novice Hame can sometimes hear him sing in her mind, 'such ancient songs'. Legend says that the Face of Boe has watched the universe grow old; there are many superstitions around, including one (that turns out to be true) that before his death, he will tell his secrets to a wanderer, 'the lonely god', the man without a home. While the Face of Boe is dying at the outset, the Doctor's actions cause him to gain a new lease of life; 'dying can wait', he says. He says he's grown tired of the universe, but the Doctor has taught him to look at it in a new way. He has a great secret that 'can wait'; as he says, he and the Doctor will meet again for the third, and last, time.

Duke of Manhattan – Having spent a lifetime of 'charity and abstinence', he is now suffering from petrifold regression. The public may look at him only with written permission of the Senate of New New York; statements he makes may not be made public without clearance. He helps keep the test subjects out of the medical ward.

Frau Clovis – The Duke's assistant. She is more concerned with etiquette than anything else and refuses to die in the hospital. She believes that if she contacts New New York, they can send a private executive squad.

The Sisterhood – Matron Casp and Sister Jatt, who appear to be the two in charge of the hospital, both perish at the hands of the test subjects (and their infectious diseases). Novice Hame, the nurse that the Doctor encounters the most, is led away in handcuffs by the NNYPD.

TORCHWOOD: There are no references in this episode.

BODY COUNT: Various patients and members of the Sisterhood are infected with toxins from the test subjects' bodies via touch, and die horribly. Technically, Cassandra's old body is dead, and Cassandra herself perishes while contained within Chip's body (leaving Chip a casualty, too). The Face of Boe is expected to die, but doesn't.

THE DOCTOR'S MAGICAL SONIC SCREWDRIVER: The Doctor uses his screwdriver on the high-tech computer console to gain access to the 'intensive care ward'. He later threatens Cassandra with it after demanding she leave Rose's body, and then again uses it to open the lift door. He also uses it to disassemble one of the medical scanners (later to be used as a winch in the lift shaft).

REALITY BITES: Cassandra attempts to imitate Rose's Cockney dialect, using rhyming slang such as 'I can't Adam and Eve it' – meaning 'I can't believe it'. She also refers to Rose as a 'chav', a pejorative slang word referring to people with an uncultured, 'lower class' background who dress ostentatiously.

The phrase 'inside a bouncy castle' has been used on other productions written by Russell T Davies, most notably *Queer as Folk*.

LINKING THEMES: This episode is a direct sequel to the previous year's 'The End of the World', set a short time in its future; Cassandra's spider-robots are seen at the beginning, spying on the Doctor and Rose, while later the villainess herself returns. This is the first adventure seen in the new series that takes place entirely away from Earth and its solar system. Platform One (the location of 'The End of the World') is mentioned. Rose's original reference to

Cassandra being a 'trampoline' is repeated.

The Doctor notes that he met the Face of Boe only the once, although the ancient being was also seen briefly on a monitor screen in 'The Long Game'. This is the first time, however, that he has demonstrated the ability to communicate.

Petrifold regression is a major theme of the BBC *Doctor Who* novel 'The Stone Rose' by Jacqueline Rayner, which also references talking cats. There were cat people (called the Cheetah People) in the story 'Survival'.

The inscription 'BAD WOLF' (from 'The Parting of the Ways' the previous season) is still visible on the pavement at the Powell Estate, though it is slightly faded. Rose's cousin Mo is name checked at the start (following the mention in 'The Christmas Invasion'). Rose refers to Chip as Gollum, after the tragic character in the novel (and now film) series *The Lord of The Rings*. New New York is also a city in Matt Groening's science fiction cartoon series *Futurama* and could be an homage to that show.

SCENE MISSING: The situation with the human test subjects is very disturbing, and confusing. Why would these test subjects possess rudimentary speech and language skills when they've been isolated in their containers for so long? How would their motor skills function; would they even be *able* to walk? Why would they have been infected with every disease known to science? Moreover, and perhaps the most pressing question, if the cures are easy to locate (the Doctor finds them very easily), why did the Sisters not release the subjects from their anguish by curing them already?

Also, how does the cure that the Doctor fashions actually work? Surely the various medicines must be introduced intravenously, as they are taken by the Doctor from the hospital ward in IV bags? It seems implausible, to say the least, that simply mixing them together (even if in certain specific proportions) could cause them to work as effective external treatments for *every* disease known to man, and that their curative effect could then be passed on by touch. What about drug interaction complications? Also, would not some of the diseases be airborne, and therefore infecting everyone else including the Doctor? Perhaps even more troubling, from a moral standpoint, is this question: if the Doctor really can concoct, with remarkable ease, a cure for every human illness, why has he not done so before, and why does he not take steps to disseminate the cure as widely as possible, to relieve human suffering throughout the ages?

When did the Doctor *actually* receive the Face of Boe's message? Was it when he and Rose were in London? It's possible, after all, that the Doctor takes his companion 'further than we've ever gone before' directly *because* he received the message. But if so, how did the message travel back in time? How could the Face of Boe locate the Doctor throughout the time vortex? And just how old *is* he? This story takes place around the year five billion; 'The Long Game' in which the Face of Boe was also seen, on a television screen, was set in the year 200,000. As there is no indication that he is a time traveller, this would appear to suggest that he is almost inconceivably ancient.

Cassandra has a film projector, and footage is taken of her at the party; why, in the year five billion plus, would someone be using such 20th Century technology? (Perhaps for nostalgia purposes, as per her 'iPod' in 'The End of the World'; but where would she get spare parts to fix it when it aged?) Speaking of Cassandra, why does she react so strongly (and positively) to being a male, while inside the Doctor's body, when it has been noted elsewhere (for example, in Justin Richards' BBC book *Monsters and Villains*) that Cassandra, in fact, used to be a male?

In the lift tube, the Doctor uses a makeshift winch, which seems to be modified very conveniently from a small IV-fluid winch to one that can support the weight of two people plunging dozens of levels downward. And why don't his trousers burn, while his legs are grasping the cable during this descent? The hospital has at least 26 floors, and yet the lift shaft seems to be much longer (or is part of a massive hospital underground?)

How does Matron Casp locate the Doctor and Rose (Cassandra) in the lift shaft? She was in the intensive care ward, and yet seems to appear from out of nowhere in the shaft behind them, between them and the test subjects.

Why does the Duke of Manhattan's assistant, Frau Clovis, wear glasses? Surely in the year five billion plus, they'd have been able to solve retinal issues without subjecting one to years of wearing spectacles?

Why is the hospital located outside New New York on an unspoilt stretch of beach, with no other construction around it? Surely, ten million people confined to a relatively small area (the city itself) would very likely have something to say about that. And if so, why is the whole episode called 'New Earth' when it's set in the one building, the hospital?

ALTERED STATES: The working title for this episode was reported to be 'The Sunshine Camp', although this was denied in the pages of *Doctor Who Magazine* as early as August 2005. The title 'The Sunshine Camp' was discovered in a meta-tag in the code for one of the pages for the episode on the official *Doctor Who* website. Davies, in his production notes for the second series, referred to this episode as 'Body Swap'.

BEHIND THE SCENES: The exterior sequences for 'New Earth', the lush rolling hills, were recorded on the Gower Peninsula, near Swansea, at Worm's Head, Rhossili. Fan photographs taken while the recording was in progress demonstrate that the script originally intended some of these sequences to be included at the end of the story (as they show David Tennant, Billie Piper *and* Sean Gallagher as Chip approaching the TARDIS).

The interiors of the hospital were shot in various locations besides the *Doctor Who* studios in Newport; these included the Wales Millennium Centre in Cardiff Bay (used for the large, open main foyer area of the hospital), the basement of Tredegar House near Newport (which doubled as the basement of the hospital where Rose first encounters Cassandra) and a disused paper mill in Grangetown, Cardiff (the intensive care unit or test labs), which was also used in 'Rose' as the Nestene lair. The sequence at the party at the episode's conclusion was shot at the Ba Orient restaurant in Cardiff Bay, with black drapes used to block sunlight from the windows.

In the hospital sequences shot at the Wales Millennium Centre, when the Doctor points toward a spot where he would put a shop, he points toward the location of the actual Portmeiron Shop inside the Centre. The shots of the lift car seen near the beginning as Rose descends to the basement level reuse material from 'Rose'.

The official *Doctor Who* website made a commentary available online; this one featured David Tennant, producer Phil Collinson and executive producer Russell T Davies. Tennant noted in the commentary that, at the beginning of the episode, the TARDIS has moved from where it was last seen in 'The Christmas Invasion', and that it no longer looks like Christmas outside; he speculates that some time has elapsed, and that maybe the Doctor and Rose have left and come back in the meantime. Davies states that Cassandra, in creating Chip, likely patterned him after the man who appeared to her at the party – in essence creating a temporal paradox, since Chip is based on Chip himself.

Davies noted in an interview with *Radio Times* that he had promised Billie Piper a comedy episode in which Rose would be funny, so this was written with that in mind.

With this episode, the format of the producer and director credits changes slightly; the credit is in lower-case and the name itself in upper-case, a reversal from the previous series. This was due to a suggestion made by *Doctor Who Magazine* editor Clayton Hickman, after noting that the previous scheme suggested the title had more prominence than the person doing the job.

OFF THE SCREEN: Sean Gallagher has appeared in episodes of *Clocking Off* (2005), *Murder Prevention* (2004), *Linda Green* (2001), *Earth: Final Conflict* (1999), *Noah's Ark* (1997), *Murder Most Horrid*(1994) and *Peak Practice*(2003). Doña Croll (here credited as Dona Croll) has appeared in *Holby City* (2004), *The Bill* (1997, 2004), *William & Mary* (2003), *Gimme Gimme Gimme* (1999-2001), and *Brothers and Sisters* (1998). Struan Rodger has done voice-over work and has appeared in *Distant Shores* (2005), *Sea of Souls* (2004), *An Unsuitable Job for a Woman* (1997, 2001), *The Vice* (1999), *Moll Flanders* (1996), *Highlander: The Series* (1996), *The Madness of King George* (1994), *Lovejoy* (1994), *Bergerac* (1990), *Chariots of Fire* (1981), *Return of the Saint* (1979), and as Detective Inspector Brush in *Rumpole of the Bailey*. Michael Fitzgerald was in *Kingdom of Heaven* (2005), *Love Actually* (2003), *Charlotte Gray* (2001), *Wilde* (1997), *The Choir* (1995) and *Prime Suspect 2* (1992). Lucy Robinson appears as Pam Draper in *Suburban Shootout* (2006), and has also been seen in *Donovan* (2006), *Brief Encounters* (2006), *Holby City* (2005), *Bridget Jones: The Edge of Reason* (2004), *Cold Feet* (2003), *Casualty* (2002) and *Peak Practice* (2001). Adjoa Andoh has been seen in *Dalziel & Pascoe* (2005), *The Bill* (2004), *Casualty* (2000-2003), *Jonathan Creek* (1999), *The Brittas Empire* (1994), *Waiting for God* (1992) and *EastEnders* (1991). Anna Hope was in *Macbeth* (2005) and *The Long Firm* (2004). Simon Ludders was in *My Family* (2004), *The Bill* (2004), *Casualty* (2003), *I'm Alan Partridge* (2002) and *Shakespeare: The Animated Tales* (1994).

A credits listing for Zoë Wanamaker appeared in the first *Back To The Vortex* book.

TECHNICAL GOOFS: After the psychograft transference procedure, Cassandra's original 'body' (the trampoline bit) is suddenly missing from its frame. Rose exits the lift into the sub-basement in a different lift shaft from where she started (she was in the left-side lift on the main floor, and the right-side lift down below.) After quarantine starts, the lift shafts are stopped, but on external shots of the hospital during this time, they're still moving.

CONTROVERSIES: Cassandra's reappearance, so soon after her debut the previous year (and after her very visible death), caused some controversy, as did the sometimes frank dialogue involving the character and the reference to Rose being a chav. Also, the question was asked: why does the new Doctor, who in the previous story made such a big deal about not being a man to give second chances, here give Cassandra a second chance and return her to see her old body one last time? There's also the ridiculousness of the IV spraying, and the 'pass it on!' method of curing thousands.

INTERNAL CONSISTENCY: The episode is probably set very shortly after 'The Christmas Invasion'; Rose says goodbye to her mother and Mickey, obviously meant to follow on from her statement in the prior episode that she wanted to continue travelling with the Doctor. However, the TARDIS has moved within the Powell Estate to a slightly different location.

Either they've stayed in London for a while, despite the general notion at the end of the previous episode that the new Doctor is about to whisk Rose off on an amazing series of adventures, or they've already been on further adventures and are just back. Either way, from Jackie and Mickey's perspective, it has to be very soon after – 'Rise of the Cybermen' is set in February, 'School Reunion' therefore likely taking place in January, and this very shortly before that. (One might then ask where the snow is that's supposed to be on the ground, but why quibble...)

TARDISODE #1: An advert for the New Earth hospital, with a representative of the Sisters of Plenitude beckoning viewers to come and be cured, just like a happy, smiling patient presented on screen... but after the screen goes dark, there is an ominous scream for help. The speaker in the first TARDISode is Anna Hope (as Novice Hame), while very brief clips from the episode (hospital locations and Sisterhood members) are shown. The patient suffers from Portray's Syndrome, a terminal disease, which has been cured here. Hame says that they never lose a patient, and that donations are welcome.

REVIEWS

Our first regular episode with the tenth Doctor takes us to a distant planet with flying cars, gleaming edifices and stunning creatures. From the first scene, you can see how ecstatic the Doctor and Rose are to be in each other's company. At first I thought the romantic subtext might be best left behind with the Doctor's regeneration, but Tennant's incarnation seems more suited to pursuing something meaningful with Rose than Eccleston's brooding, battle-damaged version, and I can't help but be swept away by their chemistry, so let's just go for it – maybe we'll get a snog or two before the series ends. If there's one thing I would say to Tennant though, it's 'Calm down, you got the job!' He's got what it takes to be a Time Lord, but his flashes of righteous indignation and victorious celebration are uncomfortably over the top. We've heard that over-confidence may lead to a major fall for the Doctor and Rose this year, so perhaps it's all part of the plan that this Doctor is proactive to the point of recklessness and ready to bask in the glow. As for Piper, her seductive turn as the villainous Cassandra is inspired. Coquettish, scheming, and even more beautiful than before, CassandRose almost makes me wish the Doctor took her up on her request to let her keep Rose's body. I know I'd ask to keep that nice 'bouncy castle'. For a show that's spending money in some areas – the cat nuns are just fantastic! – it's visibly cutting corners elsewhere. The top of that hospital elevator looks suspiciously like a department store lift from five billion years earlier, and while I really like Murray Gold's recurring musical themes from the first series, most of this episode's score is obviously recycled. Kudos though for the Face of Boe's plaintive melody, a lovely reworking of the middle eight passage of the *Doctor Who* theme. The 'Terminus'-lite plot also suffers. Cassandra's presence is a bit forced, and the Doctor's last-minute resolution has so many holes, the script pages must have looked like a piece of Swiss cheese. How exactly do a dozen bags of intravenous solutions sprayed haphazardly on the skin instantly heal the subhumans, and just how quickly are they able to spread the cure to everyone by contact alone? And why does Cassandra's skin disappear completely when she first possesses Rose? We have a new possible recurring theme – the Doctor as 'lonely god' – as well as a sentimental coda out of left field. Who would have thought we'd shed a tear for Cassandra? The meeting between her future Chip-inhabiting self and her past self is quite touching... if a bit troubling, given this Doctor's comfort level with potential paradoxes. It really looks like the post-Time Lord universe is one of complete and utter chaos, with only the Doctor deciding what should happen and what shouldn't. Not sure these are choices that should be left up to this unstable guy in the pinstripes. A decent but not adrenalin-pumping start to the series that once again borrows from movies, like *Coma* and *28 Days Later*, while also lifting some motifs from classic *Who* stories such as 'The Hand of Fear' (Cassandra *must* live!) and 'Survival'. But, with luck, things can only get better from here. – *Arnold T Blumberg*

One of the hardest things for adult fans of television and movies is the discovery that some things just aren't made for them and their age group. I remember the first time I made this discovery when I took my then seven year-old goddaughter to see *Star Wars Episode I – The Phantom Menace* and discovered to my horror that she adored a film I was completely bored and annoyed with. (To add injury to insult, she was bored during a screening of the 1977 original a week later!) It made me realise: *Star Wars* is first and foremost a series of children's films that has all-age appeal, and the fact that George Lucas' work had connected with this generation's seven year-olds was more important than whether or not it had connected with a member of the audience whose life was changed by it as a seven year old two decades before. I say all this because I was prepared to write off 'New Earth' as a lightweight, undemanding fluff-fest that really was designed just to kick the season into gear – nothing more, nothing less. Even though Billie Piper was wonderful, it was otherwise too camp, too silly, too... well, everything really. And it had a plot that really seemed more written on the back of a packet of crisps. But then I watched it (and the next three episodes) with my now 13 year-old goddaughter. She loved the CGI thrills of Peter Jackson's *King Kong*, so I thought she might like 'Tooth and Claw' best. She also loved Sarah Jane and K-9, so maybe 'School Reunion' would be at the top of the pack. To my utter astonishment, she told me her favourite of the first four episodes of the season was in fact 'New Earth'. When I asked her why, she said it was exciting, funny, had great monsters and it even had Cassandra for good measure. 'New Earth' might fail for old farts like me. But *Doctor Who* isn't being made for old farts like me – or at least, no more than it was in, say, 1977 or 1965 – it's being made to delight and amuse kids and, like with *Star Wars* and *Harry Potter*, adults can come along for the ride. It's clear that Russell T Davies is savvier than I am at what entertains kids. And I'm really not bothered by that at all. – *Graeme Burk*

It took me a long time to review this episode, and I think I've finally pegged down the reason. It's not that I felt it was truly horrible, because I didn't; and neither did I feel it was particularly good. In fact, it didn't leave me feeling much of anything at all. My whole family sat down with great excitement to watch the episode, saw it through to the end, looked at each other, and said, 'Well, that was a bit lame, wasn't it?' And then we went on, and never really said anything about it again. That's the kind of episode this was. The fundamental problem with 'New Earth', in my opinion, is it wants to be so many different things, with strangely opposing elements propped up to try and support each other in a sort of scriptwriter's Jenga. Sure, Billie Piper's impression of Zoë Wanamaker is dead-on, and her early scenes in front of the mirror are the highlight of the episode. Yet the Cassandra B plot never really seems to gel with the main, plague victim A plot, and even though it's the more interesting of the two it ends up feeling remarkably shallow. It's there because the A plot isn't strong enough to stand on its own, which is too bad, as the issue of humans used as medical guinea pigs has a lot more to offer. The humour – some of it clever, some of it poor – simply tips the balance of the story too far, and produces something that isn't a comedy, isn't a tense action thriller, and isn't a meaningful drama. It's a mess, really: a glossy, shiny, vaguely amusing mess. The ending compounds every problem and makes it worse. Cassandra goes from being desperate to live to accepting death in approximately 30 seconds; the plague victims are suddenly cured by a shower of supposedly intravenous fluids; the Face of Boe plays hard-to-get; and it's all dealt with like someone's ticking off the little boxes on a checklist. There's no time for depth and there hasn't been time to earn any of the emotional investment the story so desperately wants from the viewer. Everything comes across as half-solved and quickly disposed of. Readers of last year's volume will recall that I didn't much care for 'The End of the World', either, so perhaps it seems natural I wouldn't like the sequel. Whatever problems I had with that episode, however, I certainly cared about those characters – so much so, in fact, that the ending left me angry and upset. I did not care about the characters of 'New Earth' one itty, bitty bit. There is no single, strongly-identifiable theme to the episode, no powerful dramatic climax, nothing solid enough to even begin to grab on to. At the end of the day, what do I remember most? 'It's like living in a bouncy castle.' It's amusing, sure, but short shrift for what wanted to be – and should have been – a big, pacey season opener. – *Sarah Hadley*

'New Earth' makes for a reasonable but unspectacular start to the second series of *Doctor Who*, with some lovely moments and very good performances, but never quite gelling as a whole, and ultimately proving a little below par. Certainly there is a lot to enjoy in the central performances of Tennant and Piper, with the former showing he can do both authority and levity as the Doctor with the best of them, and the latter clearly having a ball during the sequences in which Rose is possessed by the Lady Cassandra. Sean Gallagher provides worthwhile support as Cassandra's lackey, Chip, and even manages to evoke some sympathy for Cassandra when he's playing Chip possessed by her at the very end. Aside from these three, however, nobody else in the guest cast, even Zoë Wanamaker, gets very much to do, and this gives the episode the feeling of being rather smaller than it ought to. Visually it's a similar mix of the very good let down by a few less impressive elements. The transformation of a windy day on the Gower Peninsula into a stunning New Earth cityscape is some of The Mill's best work yet, and the prosthetics and make-up of the cat nurses are similarly impressive. But then there are irritating features such as the obvious re-use of both a lift shot and the paper mill location from *Rose*, which draw you out of the drama and give the episode a slight feeling of cheapness, which isn't good for a season premiere. Despite the good make-up job on the army of plague victims, their lumbering zombie army theatrics are unimpressive, as is the nonsense pseudo-science of the Doctor's cure, which gives the ending of the episode the let-down feel that perhaps accounts for some of the negative reaction towards it. Listening to the download commentary from the BBC website, one gets the distinct impression that this episode was a difficult and disjointed one to make, and unfortunately this does come across in the finished product. I'm glad they brought back the Face of Boe, however – I rather like him, and look forward to eventually learning his mysterious secret. It's still an enjoyable slice of adventure television, and certainly still stands out from anything else in the schedules of the BBC or any other British broadcaster, but with a whole year's worth of experience at making the show behind them, you'd have hoped they could have made a better start to the season than this. But the only way is up, and with Tennant and Piper on top form and a cracking next episode trailer, the signs for the rest of the season are looking more promising. – *Paul Hayes*

Oh God, not the Powell Estate again? I fully understand RTD's rationale about needing to ground the series, but the pre-titles for 'New Earth' are simply a repetition of the scene from the end of 'World War Three', and really add nothing to the proceedings. How much better to have begun with the money shot of New New York, to show the nay-sayers that *Doctor Who* can actually hold its own, effects-wise? Once we're away and five billion years in the future, the plot suddenly starts to hurtle along with a pace and a regard for dialogue that RTD has sadly lacked in some of his previous episodes. Here, everything flows together, relentlessly adding to the storyline as we meet some of the series' most wonderful grotesques, both old and new. The cat-nuns are simply creepy, with prosthetics to rival Hollywood. The Face of Boe promises much, but since he was the driving force behind the Doctor's arrival, his 'textbook enigmatic' departure at the end – 'I feel better, I'm off, tell you the next time, which will probably be really important to the season as a whole, bye!' – just seems a bit of a waste and a cop-out. Boe's words had better be worth the wait! But the star turn this week is the return of arch-bitch, Cassandra. Not only is Zoë Wanamaker superb (as both Cassandras), but Billie Piper and David Tennant are obviously having a riot playing her in their bodies. *Doctor Who* rarely gets this camp, but sometimes it's worth it for sheer entertainment value. But does it succeed? Almost. It's easy to be seduced by the make-up and effects, but there are some irritating plot-holes that could have been plugged with just a few lines of dialogue. The logic of the Sisters' plan – humanity as a group of lab rats being experimented on by animals – may look great on the surface, but look deeper and it's a mess. If they've solved all the galaxy's illnesses, why are they still breeding humans? And if the drugs are intravenous, how do they work on contact? And we saw thousands of 'zombies' – all with lovely hair and clean-shaven – escape. Are we to believe that the few the Doctor cured managed to spread the cure to all of them? But that's always been the curse of this new series: over 45 minutes, the plot too often has to take second place to the pacing and the characterisation. Talking of characterisation, I am getting the first twinges of concern about the Doctor and Rose. The unresolved romance that added a frisson to Series One has now turned them into giggly teenagers, laughing their way through all manner of horrors and heartache. Is this building to a payoff, or is it the new status quo? As for the Doctor's claim that 'there is no higher authority'... ooh, get her! This isn't the Time Lord-liness of the Fourth Doctor, though. This suggests that the tenth Doctor realises – and relishes – his role in the universe, which is a very worrying development. The Doctor has always fought authority – what happens when he becomes the ultimate authority? Couple that with the 'no second chances' of the last story, and I suspect this is going to be the underlying theme of the series. There's no doubt that we're off to a decent start. 'New Earth' may not be a classic, but it's far from disappointing. Maybe the bar has been raised too high? – *Craig Hinton*

After successfully reinventing *Doctor Who* for the new millennium in the 2005 season, Russell T Davies is threatening to regenerate into John Nathan-Turner. This season-opener has exactly the kind of ramshackle plotting and careless tone that made *Doctor Who* hard to sit still for in the late 1980s, with a great deal of running-about to skip past half-formed ideas and situations that might have had potential but are on and off screen so quickly they barely register. Only a year into the relaunch, and Davies is doing sequels – indeed, he began this with the previous season's weakest episode, 'Boom Town' – and here we pick up after 'The End of the World' with humanity re-established on an Earthlike planet and the return of two alien characters from that story. It's a slight switch in that Lady Cassandra *isn't* the major heavy this time, but the actual villains – who might be vaguely well-intentioned, but don't get enough screen time to fix their character one way or another – are reduced to plot devices. An apparent B story about Rose being possessed off-and-on by Cassandra takes over the show, allowing Billie Piper to be scattily funny but also breaking frame by employing slang like 'chav', which I suspect will be obsolete by the time the programme is on DVD let alone millennia from now. The possession plot allows for a fan-fictionesque smooch between Rose and the Doctor, but Davies lazily rejigs his own creation – surely, the Cassandra we met in 'The End of the World' would consider the curvy Rose to be disgustingly obese as a host body, and a moment of poignancy for the character at the end requires we forget that she's a mass murderess and not just a comedy soap bitch. David Tennant is fast finding himself in the sorry quandary of Sylvester McCoy – giving every indication that he could play the Doctor if he were given half a chance but persistently getting shoved out of the way by the supporting cast and stuck with the worst lumps of exposition and a magical fix-it plot solution that prompts head-scratching rather than elation. It doesn't even matter that we've seen the apparent-utopia-with-a-nasty-secret gambit often before, but it's a shame it's so easy to stumble over and furthermore is so dramatically inert. Given that the Cassandra-Rose plot shows mind transference is possible, couldn't the Sisters of Plenitude have the rich, ill clients of the hospital just possess the vat-grown clone bodies? It's not really credible that manufacturing people to keep them sick would somehow (don't think about it too much) enable the Sisters to pull off miracle cures. And one *Austin Powers* cut-from-a-swearword-to-a-near-homonym gag was enough. On the plus side, the cat-nun-nurses are well-realised alien creatures and Davies can still manage tiny moments of whimsy, satire and affecting drama in between the hectic fudge. Major improvement is required if this show is to survive... – *Kim Newman*

Fans have long considered the Doctor to be like Sherlock Holmes: 'I am a brain, my dear Watson, and the rest of me is a mere appendage.' This is wishful thinking. For all his ways of cheating death, the Doctor eats, he weeps, he bleeds, he can be poisoned. No wonder he finds hospitals creepy: nowhere else are we more aware of being bodies. Endlessly punishing her body, like a model addicted to surgery, Cassandra has made herself the perfect anorexic, as a magazine cover, just a flat sheet with a computer-generated face; she is as totally dependent as any patient in intensive care. Cassandra clearly enjoys Rose's stolen body, with its thick and juicy curves. But neither scalpel nor psychograft can remove Cassandra's self-loathing; she brings it with her, and is picking at her new body within seconds. 'I must get the name of [the Doctor's] surgeon. Could do with a bit of work.' By contrast, the Doctor's body is source of glee: he has a ball with the disinfectant, he teases Cassandra to 'live a little' before their adrenal plunge down the lift shaft. Cassandra/Rose's furious kiss ruffles his mind as much as his hair. Perhaps death-defying stunts – and telling others it's time to die – are easier when you've got a good chance of surviving death yourself. Cassandra's entry in the book *Monsters and Villains* gives her an outrageous biography of identity switches. She has a remarkable presence throughout the story, even though Zoë Wanamaker is physically absent until the story's last moments. Born Brian Cobb, the Lady Cassandra would have learned to speak and move like a boy, then learned to speak and move like a woman – much as we can assume her posh manner is learned. Even more than a woman making up for a night out, or a drag queen making up for a show, Cassandra is entirely made of performance. To become her, the actors put on mincing femininity and snobbish mannerisms, much as others will put on makeup and masks to become plague carriers and cat people. Cassandra has ruined her own body and become a predatory mind. At the other extreme are the plague carriers, clones whose minds and bodies are so tightly joined that thanks to 'migration of sentience' they can think and speak. It seems likely the Sisterhood of Plenitude genuinely wanted, and had, mindless research subjects. Novice Hame makes a sincere argument that the 'lab rats' have 'no proper existence' – I think she genuinely has no idea that some of them are literally 'conscious'. She makes a sharp distinction between the 'the flesh' and the human beings whose lives and health the Sisterhood have saved. The other Sisters know this distinction is false, but choose to ignore the suffering they're causing. Ultimately Cassandra is caught by the same false distinction. Unlike the Face of Boe, her fellow head-in-a-tank who's quite happy to pass away, she imagines she has infinite control over the flesh. It's a little unclear in the story why she comes to accept death. I think she's just tired of the fight. – *Kate Orman*

Let's see – finally an adventure set on an alien world, but it's Earth again, sort of... what a swizz! 'New Earth' was flawed in many ways, but it was nevertheless hugely entertaining, despite very few of the rumours ('The Sunshine Camp', anyone?) having any truth in them... I'm beginning to get the hang of RTD's style of *Doctor Who*. Great dialogue and bizarre characters, lots of humour, all within multiple set pieces merged together, but not necessarily entirely successfully. We have the cats and the hospital, the Face of Boe, Cassandra's revenge – and a disinfecting lift. The elevator was genuinely funny in a *Red Dwarf* sort of way (well, I laughed), but when you stop and think about it, it was nonsensical – I mean, this was supposed to be a futuristic hospital! True, it did provide the pay-off at the end, but come on! Wet sets aside, David Tennant and Billie Piper were clearly having a ball, relishing the opportunity to camp it up in the latter half. Ah, yes, the old body-switch, a science-fiction cliché that *Doctor Who* had, prior to this, surprisingly never attempted before. But it was handled and pitched at just the right level, with Billie Piper demonstrating her versatility and range by adopting a totally different body language and speech pattern. As for David Tennant's Julian Clary impersonation... In a way, it's a pity that the swap-shop situation was resolved at the end, as I'd quite like to have seen Piper doing 'Rose possessed by Cassandra' for a couple more stories. As a production, 'New Earth' was glorious. The Cat-nun make-up was superb – just compare them to the woeful Cheetahs in 1989's 'Survival' to see how far make-up techniques have progressed in 16 years. And bizarre as it may sound, I was rather attracted to Anna Hope's hauntingly beautiful eyes and voice... It's rather a shame that the cats weren't featured more. What was their origin? Were they native to the planet? Davies has hinted that he's far from finished with this time period, so can we expect more of the Face of Boe, the cats, and New New (New New ...) York in Series Three? As the first episode of the season proper, 'New Earth' was a simple, fun, harmless 45 minutes of *Doctor Who*... Now, I have a theory regarding a plot-point in this episode, one that concerns Rose, that I think will pay off in episode 13. I'm calling it my Guns 'n' Rose theory... Stick with me on this... – *Jon Preddle*

Humanist and human – two key words that run throughout *Doctor Who*'s history and that crop up again, forcefully, in this episode. 'New Earth' (a basic sequel to last year's 'The End of the World') has its share of aesthetic disappointments but, ultimately, delivers on an unexpected theme, guilt and redemption. The irony of a very pointed critique of the ethics of animal involvement in the drug experimentation process will, I presume, not be lost on the audience when it's a race of cat nuns doing the experimenting on humans. Not all the satire is that sharp, of course, and some elements flat out don't work – in some ways, the story itself is too big, too ambitious to be contained within a single 45 minute episode. 'New Earth' is

visually stunning – a couple of dodgy pussy-gets-infected effects aside. And, whilst some of the images are not the most original in the book (*The Matrix*, *The X-Files* movie and *Masque of the Red Death* being just three of more obvious influences), that's a very minor complaint in the overall scheme of things. Where 'New Earth' succeeds is in its humour ('Still got it!' notes the Doctor after Rose/Cassandra has snogged him breathless), in Billie Piper's finest 45 minutes in the Rose role to date and in, again, its essential humanity. The ending – criticised in some fan circles as a *deus ex machina* – is, with hindsight, clearly signposted by earlier hints and allusions. First, another 'everybody lives' moment to rival last year's 'The Doctor Dances' and, secondly, Cassandra's dying revelation. There are *Doctor Who* stories that are born great, there are some that achieve greatness and there are some that have greatness thrust upon them. 'New Earth' falls into the latter category and it picks up the load and carries it to the finishing line.
– *Keith Topping*

EDITOR'S REVIEW:

I didn't care for 'New Earth'. Good, I've gotten that out of the way... Believe me, it pains me to say it as much as it probably does you to read it, but it's the only episode of the season I've had such an antipathy toward, almost like an allergic reaction; I've watched it a number of times in preparing this guide, and unlike other experiences I've had with this show, it just goes downhill from there. Let me start, though, by saying that there *are* a few positive aspects I want to point out. Billie Piper, for one, demonstrates that she's not just good *as Rose* but as an actress in general; it's a rare skill in these sorts of 'body swap' stories (and there have been a lot of them, in practically every science-fiction series I can name) for the actor to so completely change his or her mannerisms, speech patterns and aura to resemble another person, and yet everything about Piper's performance here just screams 'Cassandra'. Tennant shows further potential here – but I'm not convinced, yet (read on) – and the technical aspects of the episode (the visuals, the make-up) are all first rate.

So what happened? The *Doctor Who* producers know full well that it takes good writing, and not just the trappings of a sci-fi parable, to tell a good story, and for the most part, over two years, they've succeeded. 'New Earth', however, fails *because* of its script, not in spite of it; it's shallow and unconvincing. To whit: resurrect a monster (or in this case, a shallow bitch) that really didn't need to come back or be explained further, put the Doctor and Rose in danger using an inconsequential and silly problem (the plague rats), solve the problem by way of the dumbest solution ever (spray them with gel), and then make the lacklustre monster a misunderstood and wayward soul.

That, there, is something I don't understand: why Cassandra does her startling about-face at the end. Yes, okay, she sees the world through someone else's eyes, but it seems far too forced; this is a woman who, after all, was ready to murder a bunch of people she'd only just met in 'The End of the World' for money. Greedy people can rehabilitate, yes. But attempted mass murderers accepting their own death for inauspicious reasons, becoming sympathetic characters virtually overnight? Sorry, I don't buy it.

Now, I'm not unsympathetic to the need to tell very basic, simple stories about hope and redemption and having a good time. I think that I was simply expecting a lot more from the first full episode of what was, for all intents and purposes, a reboot of Series One. (We *Doctor Who* fans tend to look upon the series in its 'eras', marked primarily by the terms of its lead actors; why should this be any different?) David Tennant gives it his best shot, but it's obvious that he hasn't quite settled into the role here yet (surprisingly, considering how on the mark he was in 'The Christmas Invasion'), whereas Christopher Eccleston was his incarnation of the Doctor as soon as we saw him in 'Rose'. And he certainly wasn't as silly...

Perhaps that's the rub, then: last season we saw a very serious Doctor with a slightly silly side (and that only in patches, such as the makeshift dance in 'The End of the World' or his banter with Jack at the onset of 'Boom Town'), while here we're presented with a silly Doctor who might take a moment to be serious. Naturally, one should give Tennant the benefit of the doubt, and for the most part he does tend to tone this down in later episodes, but the boyish 'I'm the Doctor and I cured them' at the end of this episode doesn't inspire much confidence. Still, there's enough here to assume that things will get better, and Tennant is obviously a very capable actor.

I'd rather they had kicked off the season with 'Tooth and Claw', a far better and more convincing episode, than 'New Earth', which simply doesn't work. – *Shaun Lyon*

202: TOOTH AND CLAW

There are legends whispered by the people of 19th Century Scotland that, on a night when the moon is full, a man will lose his humanity and take the form of a wolf. But legends sometimes have a basis in fact, as the Doctor and Rose will soon discover – as will one of the most powerful rulers in history.

FIRST TRANSMISSION: UK – 22 April 2006. US – 6 October 2006. Canada – 16 October 2006. Australia – 22 July 2006. New Zealand – 20 July 2006.
DURATION: 44'31"
WRITER: Russell T Davies
DIRECTOR: Euros Lyn
CREDITED CAST: David Tennant (The Doctor), Billie Piper (Rose Tyler), Pauline Collins (Queen Victoria), Ian Hanmore (Father Angelo), Michelle Duncan (Lady Isobel), Derek Riddell (Sir Robert), Jamie Sives (Captain Reynolds), Ron Donachie (Steward), Tom Smith (The Host), Ruthie Milne (Flora)

WHERE AND WHEN: Scotland, 1879, on the road to Aberdeen and within the estate at Torchwood House.

THE STORY UNFOLDS: Over 300 years earlier, in 1540, an alien intelligence fell to Earth. The alien being, who keeps itself alive by taking over the bodies of other people, has been stranded, and legends about it have cropped up over time: once in a generation, a boy will vanish from his homestead and be taken over by the soul of another creature. According to drawings and woodcarvings of the creature, it has the appearance of a werewolf, and takes wolf form during a full moon.

The wolf creature, which the Doctor calls a 'lupine-wavelength haemoveriform', seems to be impervious to bullets. Mistletoe (*viscum album*), the Doctor says, is bursting with lectins and visco-toxins; the wolf has been trained to believe it is susceptible to it. The book the Doctor finds about the werewolf's arrival contains a picture of a falling star, along with the words, 'In the Year of our Lord 1540 under the reign of King James V, an almighty fire did burn in the pit.'

The Torchwood Estate has as its centrepiece a grand mansion owned by Sir Robert MacLeish and his wife, Lady Isobel, inherited from Robert's father, an eccentric scholar of science and storyteller as well as a dear friend of Queen Victoria's late husband, Prince Albert. Albert's fascination with stories of wolves in the area (reminiscent of stories from his childhood in Saxe-Coburg, Bavaria) led to a similar interest by Queen Victoria, and a relationship with Sir Robert and his family. Sir Robert's father believed the werewolf tales were actual fact, and said that he eventually learned what the creature's purpose was by communing with it, and discovered a way to stop it. Meanwhile, a group of monks at a monastery in the Glen of Saint Catherine opposed his work, becoming worshippers of the wolf.

Among the trappings of the house is a large telescope, built by Robert's father in his final years, which the Doctor notes has too many prisms inside. In fact, the telescope is a weapon, built by Robert's father and Prince Albert together as a trap to be used against the werewolf creature. The weapon uses the Koh-i-noor diamond to focus a beam of energy that destroys the creature.

Queen Victoria carries with her the Koh-i-noor diamond, given to her as the spoils of war. Prince Albert was never happy with the diamond, and kept having it cut down from its original size, 40% larger than it is currently; as an annual pilgrimage after her husband's passing, Victoria is taking it to the royal jewellers, Hellier & Carew at Hazelhead, to have it recut again. Albert died with the diamond unfinished, suggesting to the Doctor that Albert was on a mission. Victoria also notes she was *en route* to Balmoral Castle when a tree fell on the rail line between London and Aberdeen.

The Doctor, in the course of piloting the TARDIS, hits several items on the console with the rubber mallet first seen the previous year. The first antigravity Olympic Games apparently take place in Rose's future, while the Torchwood Institute will apparently be waiting for the Time Lord at some point in his.

The monastery's brethren, a group of shaven-headed men in red robes led by Father Angelo, come to the Estate to capture Queen Victoria in order to allow the alien creature to enter her body and take control of the planet and bring about 'the Empire of the Wolf'.

THE DOCTOR: He's not fond of ex-British Prime Minister Margaret Thatcher but loves *The Muppet Movie*, and was partially responsible for Skylab falling to Earth in 1979 (an event that nearly cost him his thumb). He's a fan of Ian Dury and the Blockheads (see Dulcet Tones, below); based on his musical tastes, Rose believes this new incarnation to be a punk at heart (with a bit of rockabilly thrown in). He has a natural-sounding Scottish accent, which he drops during the crisis, piquing Victoria's suspicions about him. He is mesmerised by the telescope in the house. He has brief fits of rudeness ('The Christmas Invasion') and is impressed by the werewolf ('That's beautiful!') Queen Victoria knights him Sir Doctor of TARDIS, but then banishes him and Rose from the British Empire for their part in the affair.

He says he has a doctorate from the University of Edinburgh (with 'proof' offered in the form of his psychic paper) and trained under Dr Bell. His 'credentials' state that he has been appointed by the Lord Provost as Queen Victoria's protector.

ROSE TYLER: She can't do a Scottish accent, or dialect, well at all. The Doctor and later Queen Victoria describe her as a 'timorous beastie', referring to the poem 'To A Mouse' by Scottish poet Robert Burns. She bets the Doctor ten pounds that she can get Victoria to say 'We are not amused', a phrase historically attributed to the Queen. (She eventually succeeds, but under different circumstances than she expected.) The Doctor jokes that he bought Rose for sixpence in Old London Town, though he could have bought the Elephant Man instead. Victoria dubs her Dame Rose of the Powell Estate.

CHARACTER BUILDING: *Queen Victoria* – Ruler of the United Kingdom of Great Britain and Ireland (See 'Reality Bites'). She's had five daughters, so Rose's 'nakedness' means nothing to her, and says she's quite used to staring down the barrel of a gun. She'd had six attempts on her life by 1879, according to the Doctor. Since the death of her husband (whom she misses deeply), she has developed what she calls a 'taste for supernatural fiction' but believes the dead stay silent. After the many attempts on her life, she's learned to carry a gun, which she uses to kill Father Angelo (though she tells Sir Robert that Captain Reynolds did it, perhaps to avoid losing her air of ladylike supremacy). The wolf cuts her before it is destroyed, possibly passing along its genetics to the ruler and explaining several curiosities about the Royal Family for the next century. She banishes the Doctor and Rose because they consort with stars and magic, and later heralds a new organisation, which she dubs the Torchwood Institute after the house, to defend against Britain's enemies.

Sir Robert MacLeish – Owner of the Torchwood Estate, he is persuaded (by the kidnapping of his wife and staff) to commit treason by bringing Queen Victoria here. He later recants, helping the Doctor and Victoria to escape. The Doctor questions his sexuality at one point. He gives his life to buy the Doctor time.

Father Angelo – Once a man of God, one of (perhaps the leader of) the brethren of the monastery at St Katherine, he now worships the wolf (*lupus dei*, Latin for 'Wolf of God', is his chant). He invaded the Torchwood Estate on the orders of the alien creature; apparently, he has been waiting a long time for Victoria's plans to coincide with a night with a full moon.

Lady Isobel MacLeish – Initially mesmerised by the werewolf creature, she eventually takes charge of her maids to create a defence against it using mistletoe. Later, having lost her husband, she is asked by Victoria if she intends to stay at the house.

Captain Reynolds – Captain of the guards for Queen Victoria and fiercely loyal to her. He hasn't dined very often with Her Majesty. He is later killed by the wolf while he attempts to buy the Doctor, Rose and Victoria time to flee.

Flora – A young maidservant in the household who escapes the initial attack by Father Angelo's people; she hides in a closet in one of the bedrooms and is found by Rose. She and Rose are later abducted by Angelo, but then freed by the Doctor.

The Host – The werewolf creature inside him states that he was once a 'weakling, heartsick boy' born ten miles from the Torchwood Estate, stolen away at night by the brethren. The energy beam from the telescope weapon destroys the creature inside him, but the young man, apparently aware of what has happened, asks the Doctor to kill him.

Steward – A servant of Sir Robert, he's the first one Angelo attacks at the Torchwood Estate, is imprisoned along with Lady Isobel, and is later killed by the wolf.

TORCHWOOD: 'Tooth and Claw' is a lynchpin in the Torchwood storyline; it is Queen Victoria herself who apparently causes the founding of the Torchwood Institute on the site of Sir Robert and Lady Isobel's former home, the Torchwood Estate.

BODY COUNT: Father Angelo is shot by Queen Victoria, the Steward is ambushed by the wolf after believing he'd killed it, and Captain Reynolds sacrifices his life so that Victoria can escape the wolf's attack. Sir Robert later gives his life so that the Doctor and Rose can prime the telescope weapon. The Host also presumably dies after the alien entity inhabiting his body is released by the moonlight refracted through the telescope and the diamond.

THE DOCTOR'S MAGICAL SONIC SCREWDRIVER: He uses it to lock (or perhaps jam) a door to the cellar, in an effort to trap the werewolf.

REALITY BITES: The Doctor says that 1979 was 'a hell of a year' and mentions China's invasion of Vietnam, the rise of Margaret Thatcher, the fall of Skylab to Earth, and a concert by Ian Dury and the Blockheads at the Top Rank club in Sheffield on 21 November. Also out the same year, *The Muppet Movie*, the first film featuring Jim Henson's popular anthropomorphic puppet creations that spawned a merchandising empire, is name checked. In addition, there are mentions of the Battle of Trafalgar (21 October 1805) and Julius Caesar's crossing of the Rubicon river (49 BC). The Doctor and Rose joke about the Royal Family, saying that the wolf encounter might explain its secrecy. (Princess Anne is name checked.)

Her Majesty Queen Victoria, Empress of India and Defender of the Faith (born 24 May 1819, died 22 January 1901), was the monarch of the British Empire for more than 63 years – the longest reigning monarch in the nation's history – including through the height of the industrial revolution. She was a carrier of haemophilia – she didn't suffer from it herself – (an affliction some called the Royal Disease), but her parents weren't; perhaps the encounter with the wolf explains this.

The Koh-i-noor diamond was once the largest diamond on Earth, mined (possibly in the 16th Century) in India before it was given as a gift of tribute to Queen Victoria. Legends surround the crystal that it will bring death or misfortune to any male who carries it. (Victoria's concern about the legend in this episode is misplaced; women are said to be immune to its effects.) It is currently housed in the Tower of London.

Prince Albert (born 26 August 1819, died 14 December 1861) was Queen Victoria's husband and was addressed as the Prince Consort. Ian Dury (born 12 May 1942, died 27 March 2000) was a popular singer and songwriter who led his band, Ian Dury and the Blockheads, and later became an ambassador for UNICEF. Dr Joseph Bell (1837-1911) was the personal physician to Queen Victoria whenever she was in Scotland; the character Sherlock Holmes is said to have been loosely based on him. Balmoral Castle, near Aberdeen, was originally purchased by Albert as a summer estate and is still owned by the Queen.

The Doctor claims he hails from the township of Balamory, from the children's programme *Balamory* (2002) set within a fictional local community on a Scottish island.

The title 'Tooth and Claw' is an allusion to the line 'Nature, red in tooth and claw' from the poem 'In Memoriam AHH' by Alfred Lord Tennyson, written in 1850. The poem is said to have been a favourite of Queen Victoria's. The same title was previously used for a comic strip story in *Doctor Who Magazine*, issues 257-260.

LINKING THEMES: At gunpoint, the Doctor uses the name Dr James McCrimmon. This is a nod to one of the Doctor's longest-serving companions, Jamie McCrimmon, a Scottish Highlander from the 18th Century played on television by Frazer Hines opposite second Doctor, Patrick Troughton, from December 1966 ('The Highlanders') to June 1969 ('The War Games'). He also cameoed in 'The Five Doctors' in 1983 and made a return appearance in 'The Two Doctors' in 1985. The character travelled widely with the Doctor until the Time Lords returned him to his own era, in the aftermath of the battle of Culloden in 1746. Queen Victoria is the second role that actress Pauline Collins has taken in *Doctor Who*, the first being that of Samantha Briggs in the 1967 serial 'The Faceless Ones', also starring Troughton. (See 'Off The Screen', below.) Also, in another *Doctor Who* story of that era, 'The Moonbase', the Doctor informed one of his companions that he had earned a medical degree in Glasgow, 1888, from Joseph Lister, who also worked at the University of Edinburgh.

The Doctor mentioned in the 1972 story 'The Curse of Peladon' that he'd attended Queen Victoria's coronation; this is, perhaps, the reason he identifies her so quickly here (besides the familiar countenance and the fact that she's travelling with guards, of course!)

The Host looks at Rose and sees 'something of the wolf' inside her; this is possibly a reference to the previous year's Bad Wolf story arc.

SCENE MISSING: It is never made clear exactly what sort of influence has affected Father

Angelo and his henchmen, or whether or not their abilities (which are very like those seen in otherworldly combat sequences from such films as *Crouching Tiger, Hidden Dragon*) are supernatural in nature. They do, however, apparently feel they are serving God (Angelo asks God for forgiveness), even though they are later worshipping the wolf. More important than the uncertainty surrounding their belief system, though, is the unanswered question of why they suddenly give up at the end of the story. After the Doctor defeats the wolf-creature, the monks are suddenly gone. Did they know the beast was dead? Were they aware that Father Angelo had been killed? (And of course, although Angelo was clearly shot, we don't know if he really *was* dead ...)

Has the Doctor really not encountered werewolves before? On television, he met a were-being in Mags, the Captain's assistant, in the seventh Doctor story 'The Greatest Show in the Galaxy' (1988), while BBC-sanctioned tie-ins from Big Finish Productions ('*Loups-Garoux*') and BBC Books (*Kursaal, Wolfsbane*) have also featured the creatures. In a related note, within one of the official tie-in novels for this series, Justin Richards' *The Clockwise Man* published by BBC Books, the subject of the Royal Family's haemophilia is addressed (and Rose acts as if she knows nothing about it).

The Doctor and Rose step out of the TARDIS at the beginning of the episode... and right into the middle of Queen Victoria's travelling party. Did no-one notice the police box materialising on the Scottish moors? Only a few seconds appear to pass between the TARDIS's arrival and their exit from it, and by the time they emerge, Captain Reynolds and company have their weapons drawn. Also, why does the Doctor's psychic paper state that he will be part of Victoria's guard entourage when he himself seems ignorant of this fact?

When does the Doctor come clean about his true identity? At the onset, he is Dr James McCrimmon of Balamory, and at the end he is Sir Doctor of TARDIS.

And... why has the Doctor never heard of Torchwood (except during the end of 'The Christmas Invasion' from Prime Minister Harriet Jones)? If the organisation was indeed created by Queen Victoria after 1879, surely he would have heard *something* about it before now? Even if one accepts that it was a top secret organisation – a point diluted in 'Army of Ghosts' – the fact that, in 2006, UNIT officers know of its existence suggests that the Doctor would have heard of it... especially given the fact that he's already in on the greatest secret of all: the existence of intelligent, and sometimes hostile, extraterrestrial life. (Then again, as the Earth was invaded countless times during the original series but the general public seem to be unaware of the existence of real aliens until the invasion of the Sycorax in 'The Christmas Invasion', the lack of continuity of information seems to be more of a running joke than a real problem.)

BEHIND THE SCENES: 'Tooth and Claw' relied on extensive location photography, including on the hills of Gelligaer Common, near Fochriiw, Merthyr, in South Wales for the shots of the Scottish moors; at Craig-y-Nos Castle, within the Brecon Beacons, which served as the front and courtyard of Torchwood House; at Penllyn Castle in Cowbridge, which was used for additional courtyard scenes; and at a disused school in Penarth, used for interior sequences here as well as for the previous year's 'The Unquiet Dead'. Tredegar House, seen in several *Doctor Who* stories, was the location of the kitchen, the library, and additional exterior shots, while Treowen Manor in Dingestow, Monmouth was used for the stairwell, parlour and entry hall. Additional sequences, including those set in the observatory, were recorded at the BBC's *Doctor Who* studios in Newport.

Performance artist Josh Green served as body double for the werewolf; the animators at The Mill replaced him with the CGI-created creature in post-production. (Actress Pauline Collins stated in an interview that there were two performance artists, but *Doctor Who Magazine* gave Green the sole credit by for the job.) Four members of the Korean Kick-boxing Association of Wales and the United Tae-Kwon-Do Association of Wales, David Jennings, Rob Taylor, Richard Carpenter and Sam Stennett, played members of the brethren; in the episode's commentary on the official *Doctor Who* website, director Euros Lyn noted that such films as *Crouching Tiger, Hidden Dragon* (2000) – the obvious inspiration for the opening sequence – were studied to research the action.

'Tooth and Claw' was not in the original synopsis for Series Two that Davies presented to the BBC; in its place was the episode that would eventually become 'The Girl in the Fireplace'. Davies later took the commission for the episode, after another writer was unable to fulfil the brief to his satisfaction, and at one point considered promoting it to season opener.

David Tennant was able to use his natural Scottish speaking accent for some scenes in this episode. According to an interview he gave to BBC Wiltshire, his parents attended the episode read-through, reading the parts of Captain Reynolds and Lady Isobel because actors Jamie Sives and Michelle Duncan were unable to attend.

Derek Riddell (Sir Robert) suggested a change in the script's dialogue, altering the Queen's reference to his character as 'my Sir Francis Drake' to 'my Sir Walter Raleigh'. Riddell had recently portrayed Raleigh in *The Virgin Queen* (2005), and knew that the reference to Drake was historically inaccurate.

Script editor Simon Winstone notes in the episode commentary that mistletoe was used not only to ward off werewolves but also as an anti-convulsant; in the episode, the Host suffers convulsions as he transforms into the werewolf. Also included in the commentary is a brief discussion addressing the fact that the knighting ceremony at the episode's conclusion is factually inaccurate (as women were not proclaimed with a sword, and nor did titles include 'of *wherever*' in them).

The BBC opened up a spin-off website, visittorchwood.co.uk. The site proclaims, 'Torchwood House is one of Scotland's architectural treasures. Owned by the MacLeish family since the 1500s, it was purchased by the Crown in 1893. Famed for its beautiful grounds and stunning Observatory, the house was opened to the public in 1981. A real jewel of the Highlands, it has received over a million visitors since opening.' The site includes a game revolving around the house's observatory. It also fills in several blanks from the episode, including naming Sir Robert's father (Sir George MacLeish) and giving some further details of the house's history: Isobel apparently sold it to the Crown and later passed away in 1893. Also of note: many members of the MacLeish family suffered tragic deaths, including one, Sir Edward, who apparently passed away in 1746 at Culloden. Meanwhile, on the whoisdoctorwho.co.uk website, Mickey Smith (Noel Clarke) appears in a taped message about Torchwood, while the site redirects to visittorchwood.co.uk to enter a secret code to play a game about accessing Torchwood satellites.

Another tie-in website is that for the fictional Leamington Spa Lifeboat Museum, at leamingtonspalifeboatmuseum.co.uk. The location itself never appeared in the second series of *Doctor Who*, but the site makes reference to a family killed by a 'mad wolf' and to Queen Victoria having opened the museum. At the same time, the millingdaleicecream.co.uk website was launched. This was for the Millingdale's Ice Cream company, which again was not referenced in the series. The site contains details of several 'themed' flavours of ice cream though.

DULCET TONES: The story opens with a 0'44" clip from Ian Dury and the Blockheads' 1978 track 'Hit Me With Your Rhythm Stick', as the Doctor prepares to take Rose to a Blockheads gig (setting this story before the events of 'Attack of the Graske' – here Rose acts as if going to a historical gig is a new concept, whereas during the events of the prior story she was at an ABBA concert). He seems to have an unusual edit of the track, shortening the instrumental and jumping straight to the chorus. The track was released as a 7" and 12" single (Stiff Records BUY 38) in November 1978; it also appeared as a B-side on the later single 'Reasons to be Cheerful Part 3' in 1979. A 12" single of Paul Hardcastle remixes of the track was released (BUY IT 214) around 1985, with a different remix released on 12" and CD single in 1991. The song appeared as a bonus track on the 2004 CD reissue of Ian Dury and the Blockheads' 1979 album 'Do It Yourself'. The scene was originally to have featured the Lene Lovich track 'Lucky Number' from 1978 and referred to a Lovich concert date, but was hastily altered when it proved impossible to gain the necessary clearances for the track. (With a line about insanity – 'It's nice to be a lunatic', lunatic literally being someone affected by the moon – tying in with the werewolf storyline, 'Hit Me With Your Rhythm Stick' was arguably the better choice.)

OFF THE SCREEN: Actress Pauline Collins marked her second appearance in a principal *Doctor Who* guest role in this story, the first having been as Samantha Briggs in the serial 'The Faceless Ones' broadcast in 1967. Collins was at one point considered as a potential replacement for outgoing series stars Michael Craze and Anneke Wills, but opted not to take a regular role on the show. (The job later went to Deborah Watling as, coincidentally, a girl named Victoria.) Collins has appeared extensively on television in such productions as *Bleak House* (2005), *Little Grey Rabbit* (2000), *Forever Green* (1989), *Wodehouse Playhouse* (1975), *Upstairs Downstairs* (1974), *Softly, Softly* (1967) and *The Saint* (1966) and in the films *Mrs Caldicot's Cabbage War* (2000), *Paradise Road* (1997), *City of Joy* (1992) and, in the title role, *Shirley Valentine* (1989). Ian Hanmore has appeared as Judge Roberts in *Outlaws* (2004) and in *Vital Signs* (2006), *No Angels* (2005), *The Deal* (2003), *Monarch of the Glen* (2001) and *Two Thousand Acres of Sky* (2001). Derek Riddell has also appeared in *No Angels* (2005) as well as in *The Virgin Queen* (2005), *Clocking Off* (2002), *Spooks* (2002), *Casualty* (2002), *The Book Group* (2001), *Taggart* (2000) and *The Bill* (1997). Ron Donachie's credits include the recurring role of DCI Andrew Ross in *The Bill* (2002-2004) and parts in *Taggart* (2006), *The Golden Hour* (2005), *Where the Heart Is* (2005), *Heartbeat* (2005), *The Genius of Mozart* (2004), *Auf Wiedersehen Pet* (2002), *Monarch of the Glen* (2003), *Titanic* (1997), *Ivanhoe* (197), *Cracker* (1995) and *Rab C Nesbitt* (1990). Michelle Duncan has appeared in *Driving Lessons* (2006), *Sugar Rush* (2005) and *Sea of Souls* (2005). Jamie Sives has been seen in *To the Ends of the Earth* (2005), *A Woman in Winter* (2005), *On a Clear Day* (2005), *Wilbur Wants to Kill Himself* (2002), *Ultimate Force* (2002), *Taggart* (2000), *The Bill* (1999) and *Holby City* (1999). Tom Smith has appeared in *Casualty* (2005), *The Bill* (2005), *Attachments* (2002), *Monarch of the Glen* (2000), *Midsomer Murders* (1999) and *Taggart* (1992); he also, according to the episode's online commentary, studied with David Tennant at drama school. Director Euros Lyn's credits were given in the first *Back To The Vortex* book.

TECHNICAL GOOFS: The telescope weapon appears to be able to function purely on a vertical axis yet perfectly aligns with the moon on this one night. And at the end of the final action sequence, as the werewolf disintegrates, the moonbeam suddenly disappears, for no apparent reason. (This is very much akin to the beam of light shining on the TARDIS and disappearing when it dematerialises at the end of the previous season's 'Rose'.)

CONTROVERSIES: Probably the biggest controversy revolved around the realisation that the entire plot was fundamentally the same as that of the 1977 *Doctor Who* story 'Horror of Fang Rock' by Terrance Dicks. In that earlier adventure, the Doctor and companion (Leela) arrive at an isolated dwelling (a lighthouse) and battle an alien that can shape-shift (the Rutan). As all the humans in the dwelling are killed off one by one, so the alien chases the Doctor and Leela to the top, where the threat is ultimately defeated by focusing light through a large diamond.

INTERNAL CONSISTENCY: The episode takes place over the late afternoon and evening of one day and into the early morning of another, in 1879, obviously summertime (as this is when Victoria made her yearly pilgrimage to the Royal Family's summer home at Balmoral). In view of the relatively warm weather, it is likely that this episode is set during the later part of the summer, perhaps July or August.

TARDISODE #2: A burning streak of light, perhaps a spaceship, approaches and crash-lands on Earth. Three hundred years later, a bearded old man is attacked by a vicious wolf-like creature.

The TARDISode uses what is known as a Wilhelm scream, a stock audio piece heard in countless television shows and films.

REVIEWS

The cinematic special effects and set design, superb direction, atmospheric lighting and gothic style make for a very impressive, terrifying episode with a truly great werewolf – the visuals do *not* disappoint. Unfortunately, there are still a few minor but noticeable flaws. The resolution is set up well enough, even if it is a bit of a smoke-and-mirrors light show, and there are some delightful character touches, especially Queen Victoria's pensive recollection of her husband, but the whole thing seems about one episode short. Oh, for the breathing room of a two-part slot! And is there any reason for the crucifixion parallel in the climactic sequence? Are we suddenly supposed to care about a cold-blooded creature that spoke of cleaving a young boy's heart? This is the first time that I have felt that Billie Piper is off kilter in her performance. Strangely glib and childish, Rose seems wildly out of character, pestering the Queen to utter an apocryphal phrase on a bet with the Doctor even after people had been savagely killed. Rather than keep her on the point, the Doctor actually seems to be encouraging her inappropriate attitude! Overall, though, Tennant is nearer the mark, exhibiting the Doctor's trademark enthusiasm and his devotion to knowledge as the ultimate weapon. In particular, his otherwise bizarre decision to lick the wall to deduce something about its composition is a cute quirk that seems just right for his incarnation. Nevertheless, he too comes off as disturbingly dismissive when the Queen banishes the time travellers, and indulges in some very juvenile jabs at the Royal Family with Rose while ignoring Victoria's warning about the way they toy with death and danger. Is this more of that supposed plot thread about the Doctor and Rose's blithe overconfidence, setting up a dramatic downfall later on? Perhaps, but even if so, it still feels as if the leads are being made deliberately and uncharacteristically oblivious of the consequences of their adventures in order to justify some horrific later twist. I hope this doesn't adversely affect their portrayal in future episodes; I already miss the Rose we met in the first series. The guest cast, thankfully, are uniformly excellent, with standouts Pauline Collins as a predictable but effective Victoria, Derek Riddell as the noble, courageous Sir Robert and Tom Smith as a very eerie Host/Werewolf. In fact, he wins my vote for the most blood-curdling line in *Doctor Who* history: 'I carved out his soul and sat in his heart.' Ooh, shivers! As for the episode's coda, in which the story grinds to a halt and Queen Victoria stares out at the audience, proclaiming with sledgehammer subtlety that she has a great idea for a spin-off series, I almost expected a graphic to flash on the screen right across her face: 'Be sure to watch *Torchwood* when it debuts later this year!' There *had* to have been a less obvious way of setting this up; I have a horrible feeling these Torchwood references are going to get more annoying, and we've already been through this once before with the whole Bad Wolf business. At the very least, this plot thread should lead to a more satisfying dramatic pay-off. And ultimately, the werewolf here is light years away from Mags' less impressive turn in 'The Greatest Show in the Galaxy'. – *Arnold T Blumberg*

'Tooth and Claw' is one of the best ghost train rides *Doctor Who* has ever presented. There are so many incredible set pieces – the delightful running gag of getting H M Victoria to say she isn't amused; the eye-popping opening with the monks storming Torchwood House; the Host circling the library, trying to get in – all assembled at dizzying speed (and directed with verve by Euros Lyn). The whole story is about keeping the pace going, keeping the excitement up and the viewer off-balance, finding a new twist to take it to the next level. That's the core of all good suspense writing, and Davies excels at this. At the same time, however, I can't help but think it could use a little more personal dynamics, a little more of the Doctor and Rose's relationship. There is too much of a feeling of larking about, especially after the two have been banished by Queen Victoria. I feel somewhat churlish making this complaint. In every other respect, 'Tooth and Claw' works for me. It's a great little gothic horror story, and as with the Hinchcliffe/Holmes years, Davies has found a clever way to bring a popular legend – the werewolf – into the *Doctor Who* universe. The performances are superb, especially Pauline Collins' Victoria, who uses the royal façade to hide more cold-blooded tendencies. And David Tennant is so delightful when he gets to use his own accent that it's a shame when he reverts to received pronunciation. If Davies really did write this to demonstrate he could write horror, he more than succeeded. 'Tooth and Claw' is an early highlight in the latest season.– *Graeme Burk*

Although *Doctor Who* is traditionally seen as a science-fantasy series – occasionally managing to delve successfully into harder science-fiction – it is generally at its best and most effective when it turns to horror. The images burned in our memories from the original series owe far more to a heritage of gothic thrillers, schlocky monster movies and *The Twilight Zone* than anything with the word 'star' in the title, so it shouldn't really come as a surprise that this episode is very nearly a complete success. And yet, I was surprised. Why is that? 'Tooth and Claw' has all the right elements: famous historical figure, spooky gothic setting, clever supernatural/alien threat. To be honest, though, a writer's credit for Davies never exactly inspires my confidence. As I said last year, his scripts seem largely made up of interesting ideas and great characters that never quite gel into a coherent story. Here, though, we have absolutely classic *Doctor Who* – by-the-numbers, sure, but classic all the same. It has a deft balance of scares and laughs, great performances from everyone involved (with special praise for Pauline Collins and Tom Smith), and absolutely amazing werewolf CGI. Euros Lyn's superbly atmospheric direction returns to the series, and what you end up with is an excellent and superior companion piece to last year's 'The Unquiet Dead'. I couldn't dislike it if I tried. There are a few small problems – the last scene is about as subtle as a sledgehammer, and I'd really like to know what happened to those completely superfluous kung-fu monks – but the main complaint I could level against the story (if I so wished) is that it isn't exactly deep. I generally watch each episode two, three, sometimes even four times before I sit down to review it, but viewing 'Tooth and Claw' even a second time seemed unnecessary; I could feel it even as I watched. The last time I had that experience was with – you guessed it – 'The Unquiet Dead'. Is that a bad thing? Not really. They are both meat-and-potatoes stories, and you wouldn't want them every week, but for what they are, they're tremendously entertaining. 'Tooth and Claw' works because it's the kind of thing that's going to appeal to just about everyone, from the youngest kid quivering behind the proverbial sofa to the hardened *Who* fan of the '60s or '70s halcyon days. It's the complete opposite of something like 'New Earth', which was so overstuffed it actually hurt. This is the one that should've opened the season, but either way, it's definitely the one the kids will remember. In 20 years' time, they'll be talking about 'the one with the wolf' – and all of us who remember the giant maggots, the robot mummies and the killer shop window dummies will sit there and smile, knowing just how it feels. – *Sarah Hadley*

Shaky hand-held camerawork? Pauline Collins? A 19th Century setting? It must be *Bleak House*, surely? Well no, but like that much acclaimed 2005 BBC1 adaptation of the famous Charles Dickens novel, 'Tooth and Claw' seems to be an example of the BBC's new approach to the sometimes staid genre of the costume drama. Just as that literary adaptation was an attempt to break away from the norm with its all-star cast, very modern style of direction and half-hour instalments, so 'Tooth and Claw' responds to BBC Head of Drama Jane Tranter's note to the *Doctor Who* team to give the historical episodes 'a kick up the arse' by employing a fresh and invigorating style. This contrasts greatly with last year's '19th Century with a famous person' episode, 'The Unquiet Dead', which is quite impressive when you consider that both were helmed by the same director, Euros Lyn, now establishing himself as one of the new show's leading lights behind the camera. It's not just Lyn who excels himself here, however. Davies delivers one of his tightest and most effective scripts for the show, displaying that he can do historical settings just as well as he can present-day or future ones. Let's hope he allows himself another step back in time in the next series. Allowing David Tennant to use his natural Scottish accent in this episode was a good decision, and indeed represents something of a 'what if?' for me, as when his casting was originally announced, I always imagined that he would play the role with it. I feel it gives him a bit more gravitas; and given that Davies seems keen to set the Doctor up as the last authority in the universe, the 'lonely god' and so forth, that might have been more appropriate for the character. The other performances are equally good, although Piper is given comparatively little to do this week, and most of the guest cast are completely overshadowed by Pauline Collins' excellent portrayal of Queen Victoria, which manages to be quirky and individual and not strained under comparison with the likes of Judi Dench. Perhaps the episode could have stood to be a little longer to allow more time for the other guest characters to get their chances to shine, but the production team were caught between a rock and a hard place here – there's not enough story for a two-parter without a lot of padding, so they probably made the right call by deciding this was a single-episode storyline. It doesn't all come off brilliantly – the kung-fu monk fight at the start is rather ridiculous and very difficult to take at all seriously – but it's a well thought-out adventure with great pace and verve, it generally looks very good and has an intriguing ending. A less-than-subtle trailer for the spin-off, or setting up events to come later in the season? Just how clunky or not the final scene actually is may not be known for several episodes yet. – *Paul Hayes*

Doctor Who and Victoriana go together like Ant 'n' Dec. Ask a fan, and 'The Talons of Weng-Chiang' or 'The Evil of the Daleks' will usually pop up in the top ten stories, and let's not forget 'The Unquiet Dead'. But 'Tooth and Claw' shows what happens when the director is given his head and allowed to indulge himself and lift it above the Sunday serial. All the trappings are here, as wonderful as any BBC costume drama, but Euros Lyn has applied the modern techniques that made *Bleak House* such a hit, and in doing so has turned 'Tooth and Claw' into something quite special. This is obvious from the pre-title sequence, which is possibly the most breath-taking intro to a story ever. I once had a Virgin Missing Adventure proposal rejected because of the presence of Ninja nuns. But now we have kung-fu monks! And quite splendid they are too. You can't tell me that this wasn't a deliberate homage to the BBC1 station idents! All the characters are beautifully delineated, from the flawed Sir Robert to the simply magnificent Queen Victoria, with Pauline Collins showing a side of the Queen that few save Dame Judi Dench have managed. All the characters... except the Doctor and Rose. Their juvenile asides – the 'We are not amused' joke fell very flat with me, I'm afraid – are now starting to annoy me. I was very much on the Queen's side when she initially chastised them, given the amount of death that they'd already seen. The werewolf itself is an SFX tour-de-force, but all the pixels in the world can't make up for a weak story: thankfully 'Tooth and Claw', while not perfect, is far from weak. Plotting is fairly tight, especially compared with the string bag that was 'The Christmas Invasion', and the action starts the moment the story does. 'Tooth and Claw' can never be regarded as deep, but that was obviously never the aim: the production team were asked to 'Tarantino-ise' the pseudo-historicals, and they've definitely succeeded. I'm not 100 percent convinced by the climax. The idea of a trap within a trap is a good one, but the leaps of logic that Sir Robert's father and Prince Albert (how the production team resist making a joke about his name I'll never know!) made to identify the threat, followed by the Doctor coming to the same conclusion, are too far-fetched to be entirely believable. And if Victoria is *en route* for another cutting of the Koh-i-noor in accordance with her husband's wishes... how does it work in the moon laser thingie? Still, at least the Doctor is now playing an active part in the resolution of the stories, in contrast to his background presence in Series One. Given my feelings towards the Doctor and Rose's smug attitudes thus far, seeing them knighted (except that factually that was so wrong!) and then banished from the country did give me a degree of pleasure, but it didn't stop them giggling away on their way to the TARDIS with their illogical insinuations about the lycanthropy of the Royal Family. But if anything lets this episode down, it has to be the heavy-handed foreshadowing of *Torchwood*. Victoria might as well have said 'Coming this Autumn on BBC3' with John Barrowman ice-skating behind her! 'Tooth and Claw' has a lot going for it. Unlike the majority of episodes from both series, it doesn't bear repeated scrutiny. But it is a brave, and not completely unsuccessful, experiment in directing the series with an edge. – *Craig Hinton*

After two duff episodes, it'd be easy to over praise 'Tooth and Claw' – but there's no denying that it's fun, if unambitious, horror TV, and the story makes sense on its own terms and as part of the overarching thread this season is pursuing. It perhaps has to move a little too fast to fit all its ingredients into a cramped 45 minutes – most of the second half is one long, computer-game-like chase-with-puzzle – but David Tennant at last gets to put his stamp on the Doctor, even using an off and on Scots accent, and playing up a quixotic, free-associating enthusiasm that meshes well with Billie Piper's gushing tourist-in-time-and-space. Actually, this reading of the Doctor and Rose gets perilously close to suggesting they are having too much fun in the midst of yet another massacre (bantering terrible private jokes between them), which is why the coda is surprisingly satisfying, following a corny bit of old-fashioned wish-fulfilment as the Doctor and Rose are ennobled by Queen Victoria (Pauline Collins, very good) only for the Queen to cast her famously cold eye on those she is obliged to be grateful to and order them off her world. It may be doing long-term spadework for the *Torchwood* spin-off, but this is another of Davies's effective, why-hasn't-it-happened-before bits. In many earlier endings, the Doctor shyly backs away from overwhelming appreciation and dematerialises during a victory celebration – here, everyone is so shell-shocked and grief-striken that they half-blame the Doctor for what's happened and really would like never to see him again, while he and Rose are so wrapped up with joking about the Werewolves of Windsor that they don't even notice how shattered the people left behind are. As to the actual story, it is it a bit like a greatest hits compendium: a historical figure reimagined to fit into the *Who* universe; a CGI gothic monster with a (tiny) science-fiction element; an unstoppable monster scything through supporting characters (cf 'Dalek'); a cleverly-contrived monster-destroying gadget. Davies still has a weakness for feeble jokes (that running 'We are not amused' gag is almost defiantly poor, as is the suggestion that Rose's outfit is tantamount to nakedness) and cramming in cool stuff whether it fits or no (why are Scots werewolf cultists into Shaolin stick-fighting?), but this at least has a blasted heath atmosphere, a monster on a par with the CGI wolfmen of *Cursed* or *An American Werewolf in Paris* (not hard, admittedly), some surprisingly credible bits of history (Queen Victoria has been done so often as a caricature that it's refreshing to see her credited with some wrong-headed backbone) and a few moments of proper horror to recommend it. As the author of *Anno Dracula*, I found some elements of the monster's long-term plans to infect the Queen and the Empire with a supernatural curse a tad familiar – though I went with vampirism rather than lycanthropy. – *Kim Newman*

Rose is not being well-served by the second series of the new *Who*. Sidelined by other characters (Reinette and, oddly, Cassandra), she has less to do: her courage and compassion are still present, but are sometimes overshadowed by the less attractive side of her character, such as her continuing mistreatment of long-suffering Mickey. In 'Tooth and Claw', she comforts a petrified maid and organises an escape, but contributes little else. While Rose sometimes comes across as a shallow girl – in this story, she is even dressed like a little girl, a 'feral child' – there are meatier roles for women in their fifties and sixties. Prime Minister Jones was decisive and authoritative; Queen Victoria no less so. If anyone (like me) came into this story expecting a stuffy paperweight they would have been shocked not only by her authority but by her humour and energy. This old Queen shoots an assassin, runs from a werewolf, and can shut the Doctor up – no mean feat. But with such powerfully physical adversaries, our heroes have only their wits to save them. Bullets can't stop it, nor can the blade: but brainpower can. You can almost imagine the ghosts of Sir Robert's father and of Prince Albert urging the Doctor on to puzzle out the clues they've left for him. You don't need to be a scientist to use your smarts: Rose offers the obvious alien a way home, Lady Isobel puts two and two together and cooks up her own weapon. (Speaking of science, we have to assume the Doctor was just teasing Rose about the Royal Family's haemophilia: almost every word he says is nonsense.)

Under pressure, characters reveal themselves. Sir Robert is a hero, not a traitor. The Doctor and Rose give themselves away as fakes, cheeky adrenalin junkies who fit badly into a world of rules and protocol, where a soldier's duty may be to guard a jewel with his life. The most naked of all is the nameless werewolf, who strips off first his clothes and then his skin. With this revelation, Queen Victoria's world has shown itself to her: her Empire is just a tiny island in a huge ocean of the unknown. Like Hadrian, or indeed Harriet, she hopes to preserve it within a wall; like Harriet, she considers the helpful Doctor no less an 'alien threat' than the werewolf itself. His merry attitude is going to return to bite him. – *Kate Orman*

On location in Wales, staff-wielding warriors monk, a Scot called James McCrimmon, Victoria, a stronghold under threat by a great hairy beastie... . Right, that's enough reminiscing about 'The Abominable Snowman' (1967); we're here to talk about 'Tooth and Claw'. A werewolf... Queen Victoria... kung-fu monks. Probably the weirdest script shopping list that one could imagine, but this is what RTD wanted, and this is what he got! 'Tooth and Claw' has it all – dark, foreboding and creepy. And that is just the Doctor! Let's face it: werewolves are pretty boring. There is only so much you can do with them – unless you inject some sort of twist into the traditional mythology (*à la* the recent *Underworld* film franchise). Davies has done this by making this particular lycanthropic affliction extraterrestrial in nature. Surprisingly, *Doctor Who* has never done proper werewolves before (with emphasis on 'proper' – the Lukoser in 'The Trial of a Time Lord' and Mags in 'The Greatest Show in the Galaxy' are too divorced from the concept to count). As for the realisation, werewolves in film and TV are usually stuntmen in badly fitting hirsute jumpsuits, or CGI. I think the BBC took the very wise decision to go all CGI. A consistent look onscreen helps to suspend any disbelief. (Imagine how so much better 'Aliens of London' would have been if the Slitheen had been rendered entirely in CGI.) While Davies may have (unconsciously?) been inspired by the aforementioned Troughton serial, he and director Euros Lyn also seem to have been watching *Alien3* recently; a number of visual cues are near carbon-copy moments from David Fincher's underrated second sequel: bald 'monks', lots of wood, POV of the monster, running through corridors, people snatched upwards from the ceiling. Even the Doctor/werewolf face-off (with door between them) is very suggestive of the classic Ripley/Queen pose. And Davies seems to have copied much from 'Ghost Light'; even the alien's motive to seize power through Queen Victoria is virtually the same. But then, of course if you set a story in Victorian times, and feature the Queen, comparison to 'Ghost Light' is unavoidable. A stunning production of exemplary set design and a top-notch guest cast playing it absolutely straight (Pauline Collins is quite superb as Queen Vic). Top honours however must go to director Euros Lyn, one of the best directors, if not the best, working on the new series. The 'flying monks' choreography was clearly inspired by the *Matrix* films, and I'm grateful that Lyn resisted the temptation to use bullet-time, a visual effect that's already (yawn) rather passé now. But I do have one request – Mr Tennant please slow down with your delivery of important expository dialogue! It's unusual for *Doctor Who* to have a pre-credits teaser as well as a tag scene with only the secondary characters. It's a pity that any potential mystery or shock value to come from the Queen's closing proclamation is rendered somewhat ineffective by the fact that we've already seen Torchwood in action in 'The Christmas Invasion'... Despite being derivative in places, 'Tooth and Claw' – even without the rumoured flying monks and haunted castle – is wonderful stuff. Unlike the Queen, we are definitely amused. – *Jon Preddle*

Doctor Who's never done a proper honest-to-god werewolf story before. Oh, sure, changeling tales like 'Inferno', 'Planet of Evil' and 'The Seeds of Doom' ticked many of the right boxes, but the missing element was, always, the inherent Byronesque tragedy of the classic werewolf *oeuvre*. Missing Ian Dury and the Blockheads by a hundred years and Sheffield by a couple of hundred miles, the Doctor and Rose instead find themselves as the unlikely protectors of a rather charmingly three-dimensional Queen Victoria facing treachery and kung-fu monks in a bid to stop 'the Empire of the Wolf' with only the Koh-i-noor diamond as a weapon. 'Tooth and Claw' rather bites off more than it can chew in terms of mystery. 'There is something of the wolf about you,' the Host tells old Bad Wolf herself, but this potentially fascinating avenue is never followed as the episode descends into a series of stock horror movie clichés. All of which would be a bit rubbish if it weren't for the fact that 'Tooth and Claw' also features great direction, great acting (Pauline Collins and Ron Donachie head a fine support cast), great dialogue ('You're a big old punk with a bit of rockabilly thrown in!') and truly incredible special effects. One questionable element, much discussed at the time of the episode's broadcast, is the somewhat smug and grinning flippancy of the Doctor and Rose throughout much of this (and, indeed, the previous) story. There is a sense watching 'Tooth and Claw' that here are a couple of intergalactic backpackers for whom the thrill of the experience and the adventure therein are, perhaps, beginning to take an edge off their (here's that word again) humanity. There certainly seems to be something being pre-empted here with regard to how casual and, even, indifferent both the Doctor and Rose appear to some of the horror that's going on around them. It's something the Queen spots quickly and acts upon in an unexpected little coda that cuts through the *faux-naïf* chummery of a traditional *Doctor Who* ending. The controversial anti-Monarchy riff at the end and the heavily signposted references to *Torchwood* are further elements that some have used as sticks with which to beat both the episode and its author. But, ultimately, 'Tooth and Claw' stands or falls by the effect that its monster had on eight year olds. And, on that score at least, it's this season's first, genuinely flawless, 105.602-metric-carat classic. – *Keith Topping*

EDITOR'S REVIEW: Now *that's* more like it. *That's* the *Doctor Who* I know and love and remember... The Doctor riding the time waves into Earth's past, taking his faithful companion on a historical adventure against nasty alien monsters that threaten to disrupt and rewrite history and allying himself with a historic personage to boot. Yes, we got that with 'The Unquiet Dead', but it was all a little distant; *Doctor Who* is often at its best when it deals with the familiar, and not unlike that episode last season, here we have a trip to Scotland in the presence of Queen Victoria. From the moment the TARDIS arrives, it's quite obvious that the production team are having the time of their lives; the giddiness from Billie Piper in particular is overwhelming.

Pauline Collins was a marvellous casting choice to play the Queen; she demonstrates just the right amount of both Imperial haughtiness and nervous aloofness to suggest a woman who should instinctively know everything going on in her kingdom but is also aware that she knows far less. While Rose's attempts to get her to say 'We are not amused' tend to wear a bit thin later on, the relationship between Victoria and the Doctor is quite priceless. She's barely met this man, after all, but senses that he's firmly in charge; in fact, she downright proclaims it at the end, when banishing him and Rose from Britain forever. (One must ask why, then, does the Doctor get away with helping Earth all those times in the original series... but of course, time travel doesn't make much sense any way you look at it.)

The supporting cast merit our attention; Ian Hanmore is absolutely chilling as Father Angelo, Derek Riddell shows sensitivity and pathos as Sir Robert (as well as demonstrating the needed yellow stripe up his back) and Jamie Sives could have been a British captain for all I know, because he is absolutely convincing in the role. The rest of the cast are equally good, although I don't quite get the point of the whole *Crouching Tiger, Hidden Dragon* monkfest that we see at the opening; for some strange reason, the monks just seem to disappear at the end, which doesn't exactly fit in with what we know about them.

Most especially, as with 'The Unquiet Dead', the production team have succeeded in recreating the period setting with skill; it truly *feels* like we're in Victorian times, most especially in the sequences recorded inside the castle (interestingly, the one aspect for which they *didn't* use an authentic period location; much of that was done in studio). I wouldn't call myself a fan of period drama, but I'm beginning to think that this is what the people in charge of *Doctor Who* right now do best – they seem to capture historical eras, be it Dickensian Cardiff or wartime Britain last year, or Victorian Scotland or 1950s London this season, as well as a BBC period drama ever could. This wasn't always the case with the original series – Renaissance Italy seemed to look just like the woodlands of present-day Britain, for example (for obvious reasons). One thing that would be nice, though, is an actual overseas trip like those John Nathan-Turner arranged in the classic show's latter years; the only time the new show has really ventured outside Earth-bound Britain (beyond its trips off planet) has been in 'Dalek' when the Doctor and Rose arrived in 2012 Utah, and then we never even saw the place.

The only real quibble I have is with the story's ending: after such a great, atmospheric little tale, we have that epilogue tacked on as if as an afterthought proposed by the BBC marketing team. 'Yes, we shall create an institute, and it shall be called Torchwood!' Yes, I know those aren't the exact words spoken by Queen Victoria, but they might as well be, because it's truly silly and obviously designed to plug the *Doctor Who* spin-off series. A classic sequence from *The Hitchhiker's Guide to the Galaxy* closely mirrors this; Deep Thought announces that it will design the ten-million-year computer, 'and it shall be called *the Earth!*' And one of the attendants mutters, 'Oh, what a dull name.' I swear, I could've heard that same line whispered behind Queen Victoria. Ah well.

But a lovely episode nonetheless; definitely the season's first real winner. – *Shaun Lyon*

203: SCHOOL REUNION

Something is not right at Deffry Vale High School; teachers have resigned, students have disappeared, and UFO sightings plague the area. It's a mystery, and every good mystery attracts notice – but this time, it's not just the Doctor and Rose who are on the case...

FIRST TRANSMISSION: UK – 29 April 2006. US – 13 October 2006. Canada – 23 October 2006. Australia – 29 July 2006. New Zealand – 27 July 2006.
DURATION: 44'11"
WRITER: Toby Whithouse
DIRECTOR: James Hawes
CREDITED CAST: David Tennant (The Doctor), Billie Piper (Rose Tyler), Noel Clarke (Mickey Smith), Anthony Head (Mr Finch), Elisabeth Sladen (Sarah Jane Smith), Rod Arthur (Mr Parsons), Eugene Washington (Mr Wagner), Heather Cameron (Nina), Joe Pickley (Kenny), Benjamin Smith (Luke), Clem Tibber (Milo), Lucinda Dryzek (Melissa), Caroline Berry (Dinner Lady), John Leeson (Voice of K-9)

K9 originally created by Bob Baker & Dave Martin

WHERE AND WHEN: Deffry Vale High School, England, in the spring of 2007.

THE STORY UNFOLDS: Deffry Vale High School has been invaded by the alien Krillitanes. An amalgam of conquered races, the Krillitanes take on physical aspects of their victims. The Doctor says they're definitely bad; the last time he saw them, they looked more or less human 'but had really long necks'. In their current form, they are bat-like with large wings, a form they've held for nearly ten generations, acquired from the planet Bessan (whose people had 'some rather lovely wings'); a million of Bessan's population were wiped out in a single day. The Krillitanes sleep in the school (in the Headmaster's office), upside-down like Earth bats. They know of the Time Lords, and are aware that the Doctor is the last of that race. The Krillitanes have come to Earth to become gods, by using the children's brains to crack the Skasas Paradigm. Finch, aka Brother Lassar, is their leader and took over the school as its Headmaster; he brought with him seven new teachers, four dinner ladies and a nurse, a total of 13 Krillitane invaders. They now use morphic illusions to present themselves as human. Their plot involves the use of advanced computer systems and the mental abilities of the children, controlled by the use of headphones.

The Skasas Paradigm, also known as the 'God-maker', is the universal theory that involves equations that control the building blocks of the universe. Finch tells the Doctor that if he allies himself with them he will have the opportunity to change the universe; he can teach the Krillitanes wisdom and help save all the civilisations that have fallen, including the Time Lords and the planets Perganon and Ascinta.

Krillitane oil is a conducting agent that, when consumed by humans, makes their brains function on a higher level, in essence making them smarter; the children have been given Krillitane oil in order to help the invaders' plan, because the God-maker 'needs imagination to crack it' and the Krillitanes are using the children's very souls to find the equations. The chips at the school are cooked in the oil; there are signs in the school saying 'Eat More Chips', obviously to entice the students. The vat of Krillitane oil brought into the kitchen has alien symbols written on it (probably in the Krillitane language itself). The oil is poisonous to the Krillitanes, and the Doctor concludes that this is due to the fact that they have changed forms so many times.

Sarah Jane Smith's investigation of the school is under the pretext of a newspaper column she's writing for the *Sunday Times* about Finch. Finch has recently brought about major change at the school, including the provision of free (but compulsory) school dinners, but controversy has arisen from the fact that the children are being worked very hard – many pupils have become ill. The menu at the school was designed by Finch. The day after he arrived, half the staff got the flu and their positions were filled with hand-picked replacements.

Mickey discovers vacuum-packed rats in one of the kitchen cupboards, possibly the Krillitanes' food source (when they're not eating children). The Krillitanes all appear to be male, despite human genders. (Finch addresses them as 'brothers'.)

The school has been fitted with a security system, controlled from Finch's office, that locks everyone inside.

There's a sign on the wall of the Internet café, 'Because Friends Stick Together'. The small café that the Doctor, Sarah, Mickey and Rose visit is the Da Vinci Coffee House. Mickey notes that over 40 UFO sightings have occurred in the area of the school before the Doctor's arrival.

THE DOCTOR: He has got himself employed at Deffry Vale High School as a substitute physics teacher after hearing of the UFO sightings and of record results at the school. He replaced a teacher who won the lottery two days earlier, despite the fact that she never played. (A winning ticket was posted through her door at midnight – obviously the Doctor's doing.) He is overjoyed at seeing Sarah Jane Smith again, though at first he doesn't tell her who he is; instead he uses the pseudonym John Smith. He's regenerated 'half a dozen times' since they last saw each other, he says. He has trouble calling Rose and Mickey a 'team', 'gang' or 'comrades'. The meeting of Sarah and Rose gives the Doctor, as Mickey calls it, 'a reunion of the missus and the ex'. He says that he always leaves his companions behind (eventually) because he can't bear the idea of watching them wither and die. He says he's old now (in this incarnation) and 'used to' have a lot more mercy in him. He still strokes bits of the TARDIS and explains things as if his companions know what he's talking about (a joke Rose and Sarah share together). He has encountered the Krillitanes before.

ROSE TYLER: Employed as a dinner lady in the school, she's not very happy with the role she's taken, though she loves the chips. She thinks it's wrong seeing the school at night; when she was young, she thought the teachers slept there. She takes an immediate dislike to Sarah (and the feeling is probably mutual) and feels jealous of her place in the Doctor's life, but later comes to respect her. Mickey warns her to 'go easy' on the chips, considering her rivalry with Sarah. The Krillitane oil in the chips briefly makes her smarter at maths. Sarah tells her to look her up one day, if she needs to, when she finally comes home.

CHARACTER BUILDING: *Sarah Jane Smith* – A freelance journalist who is ostensibly writing a piece for the *Sunday Times* but who has in actuality been drawn to Deffry Vale school to investigate a mystery. A former long-time travelling companion of the Doctor, she felt abandoned when he left her behind. She breaks into the school, where she realises that the Doctor is present after seeing the TARDIS in one of the disused storage rooms. She says she has got old while the Doctor looks incredible, and that she thought he had died after they parted company. She's jealous of Rose's relationship with the Doctor and says that he was her life; she had to cope with the aftermath of seeing amazing things and then being dropped back on Earth. She never got married or had children. She turns down the Doctor's offer to rejoin him, finally able to move on with her life, and asks him to say goodbye to her properly this time.

K-9 – A mobile computer, the Mark III version of the original. The first two K-9 units travelled with the Doctor for some time; the Mark III was a gift from the Doctor to Sarah. He was designed around the year 5000 using 'cutting edge' technology (that Rose thinks looks 'disco'). One day he just simply stopped functioning. Sarah hasn't had him repaired because the technology is so advanced that it could rewrite human history. The Doctor still has great fondness for him. K-9 still refers to the Doctor as 'master' and to Sarah as 'mistress'. He has a 'maximum defence mode'. He saves everyone (after Mickey brings him into the school) with his frontal laser; he later shoots the bins of Krillitane oil and thereby blows himself up, taking the kitchen and the Krillitanes with him. Later, he is rebuilt by the Doctor, his systems much improved 'with new omniflexible hyperlink facilities'.

Mickey Smith – The Doctor still refers to him as Rose's 'boyfriend' (a pejorative used in the previous series). He is still investigating mysteries and brings this one to Rose's attention; every time he sees Rose nowadays, he says, it's an emergency. He styles himself as an expert at 'infiltration and investigation', but he's terrified of rats and bats. Though he initially calls himself the Doctor and Rose's 'man in Havana', i.e. confidante/informant, he then likens his status to that of the 'tin dog', the useful but otherwise unimportant sidekick. He eventually rescues the children by breaking into the school and pulling the plug on the computers. At the end, he asks the Doctor and Rose if he can join them (in response to which Sarah says that the Doctor 'needs a Smith on board'); he's tired of being the 'tin dog' and wants to see the universe.

Headmaster Finch – Headmaster of Deffry Vale High School; in reality, Brother Lassar of the Krillitanes. Unlike the rest of his brethren, who use morphic illusions to appear human, he actually has taken human form ('a personal favourite'). He always thought the Time Lords to be pompous and frightened of chaos.

Kenny – A withdrawn student at Deffry Vale who suspects something strange is going on. He investigates noises and is the first to see a Krillitane (in this case, Mr Wagner) in his proper form. He stays behind when the children return to class, suspicious of Wagner. He helps Mickey get inside and later is assumed to be the one who 'blew up the school'.

Mr Wagner – Science teacher at the school, and apparently Finch's main henchman.

The Students – Milo is a student in the Doctor's physics class; his ready answers to very technical questions (for example knowing that FTL travel is achieved 'by opening a quantum tunnel with an FTL factor of 36.7 recurring') provide the Doctor with clues as to what's really going on. Mr Wagner later says Milo has 'failed' him; his fate remains unknown. Melissa is another student, whom Mr Wagner 'moves up' to the top class after Milo's disappearance. Nina is a student without parents who lives in Ambrose Hall, a children's home. The Headmaster, in his original Krillitane form, devours her (because, as he says, there is no one to miss her).

TORCHWOOD: Mickey's online investigation into the UFO sightings brings up a screen on his Internet café computer: 'Torchwood – Access Denied'.

BODY COUNT: Nina probably dies, as do several of the teachers of the school when the

Krillitanes devour them. K-9 Mark III makes the ultimate sacrifice (though there's always another model!).

THE DOCTOR'S MAGICAL SONIC SCREWDRIVER: The Doctor uses it to repair K-9, and later gives it to Sarah to open the computers in the school. Sarah has trouble using the latest model. Later, the Doctor uses it to investigate the computer, to no avail; the sonic screwdriver can open anything except a 'deadlock seal', which locks both the computers and the vats of Krillitane oil.

REALITY BITES: The Doctor says he thought the school would be full of 'Happy-slapping hoodies with ASBOs and ringtones'. 'Happy-slapping' is a term coined to describe making physical attacks on people and recording them on mobile phones for later 'enjoyment', while 'hoodies' are youths, often seen as troublemakers, who wear hooded tops that can be used to prevent identification (by the hood being drawn over the top of the face). 'ASBO' is an acronym for 'Anti-Social Behaviour Order', a measure designed to curtail behaviour that 'causes or is likely to cause harassment, alarm or distress to one or more people who are not in the same household as the perpetrator', to quote the UK Home Office. Such behaviour can include painting graffiti, using intimidating and abusive language, vandalism, being drunk in the street, making excessive noise, and dealing in drugs. The Orders, granted by courts at the request of the police, usually have a string of conditions attached. These conditions can include a curfew and can also stipulate that the person who is the subject of the Order should not associate with named other people (i.e. other troublemakers) and should stay away from certain shops, buildings and areas.

The Doctor uses the word 'correctamundo' (and then chides himself, hoping to never do it again). This is a 1950's-like slang term similar to those brought to prominence by the Fonz (played by Henry Winkler) in the long-running sitcom *Happy Days*. (A similar phrase is used in the BBC Books novel *The Feast of the Drowned*, as the Doctor says 'Ace-a-mundo'.) He also asks his classroom, 'Are we sitting comfortably?', a reference to the BBC Radio series *Listen with Mother*, which started each broadcast with those same words (also used later in Series Two in 'The Idiot's Lantern').

LINKING THEMES: This episode presents the first true tie-in to the Doctor's past with the reintroduction of Sarah Jane Smith and K-9. Smith (Elisabeth Sladen) travelled with the Doctor for some considerable time before being left behind on Earth (in 'The Hand of Fear'); she didn't recognise the place where she was left. Sarah's story continued in the spin-off *K-9 and Company*, in which the Doctor left her a gift, the metal robot, and again in the special 'The Five Doctors', where she joined the third Doctor on an adventure on Gallifrey. (It is very likely, however, that she doesn't remember this; see 'Scene Missing'.) K-9 has since broken down and she still dreams of the days when she travelled the universe. The Doctor says that, after he and Sarah parted company, he lived but 'everyone else died'. While it didn't happen straight away, he's probably referring to the death of the Time Lords; the Doctor was *en route* back to his homeworld when he dropped her off. The Doctor says that 'in those days' (when he left Sarah's company) humans weren't allowed to come to his home planet, meaning that this rule was eventually dropped (before, of course, the planet was destroyed); both Leela and Nyssa in were later allowed on-planet.

During an argument between Sarah and Rose, Sarah refers to her encounters with mummies

('Pyramids of Mars' (1975), robots ('Robot' (1974) amongst others), Daleks ('Death to the Daleks' (1974) and 'Genesis of the Daleks' (1975)), anti-matter monsters ('Planet of Evil' (1975)), dinosaurs ('Invasion of the Dinosaurs' (1974)), and the Loch Ness Monster ('Terror of the Zygons' (1975)), while Rose mentions she's met ghosts ('The Unquiet Dead'), Slitheen in Downing Street ('Aliens of London'/'World War Three'), the Dalek Emperor ('The Parting of the Ways'), gas-masked zombies ('The Empty Child'/'The Doctor Dances') and werewolves ('Tooth and Claw').

A long-time *Doctor Who* mystery is solved in this episode: where was Sarah Jane Smith left when the Doctor dropped her off in 'The Hand of Fear'? He had intended for it to be her home in Hillview Road, South Croydon; after the TARDIS departed, she noted that he had blown it (again), and bet that the unfamiliar territory she was in wasn't even South Croydon. It was, in fact, Aberdeen. (The Doctor jokes, 'That's next to Croydon, isn't it?')

The Doctor initially gives his name to Sarah as 'John Smith'; this was a pseudonym he used extensively in the original series (especially during the third Doctor's era). Sarah refers to the Doctor's companions as 'assistants', which doesn't sit well with Rose. She also references the events of 'The Christmas Invasion', having witnessed it (like the rest of the planet) on television and been fairly sure that the Doctor would be up there in the Sycorax ship.

This episode is very difficult to reconcile with the continuity established prior to the series by BBC Books, which ran from 1997 to 2005. In *Bullet Time* by David McIntee, the seventh Doctor encounters Sarah in 1997, while in Lawrence Miles' two-part novel *Interference* Sarah has been married to Paul Morley and encounters the eighth Doctor. She also turns up alongside the seventh Doctor in the comic strip 'Train Flight' published in issues 159-161 of *Doctor Who Magazine*. However, in the officially licensed audio series produced by Big Finish with Sladen as Sarah, none of this is referred to; instead, Sarah is a sort of private investigator in the early part of the decade, which can theoretically be dovetailed into these latest developments.

Two original K-9 props were used in this episode, one for scenes involving him moving and one for when he is stationary; however, the insides are different. Also used from the original series is his laser-beam effect (visual and sound). Sarah refers to spare parts for K-9 being as hard to acquire as those for a Mini Metro; she drove a Mini Metro in *K-9 and Company*.

The Skasas Paradigm seems similar to Block Transfer Computation from 'Logopolis' (1981). Rose says that she's been to the year five billion (referring to 'The End of the World' and 'New Earth'). She name checks her friend Shareen (first mentioned in 'Rose'), and says that the two fell out once, over a man. The Doctor briefly ponders being able to stop the Time War, which destroyed the Time Lords (as addressed in Series One). The motto 'Because Friends Stick Together' on the café wall also appears on Mickey's website (see 'Behind the Scenes').

SCENE MISSING: The big question for long-time *Doctor Who* fans: why is Sarah Jane Smith so surprised that the Doctor is alive? In the *Doctor Who* mythos, Sarah has had at least two encounters with the Doctor and his legacy – the gift of K-9, left for her in the spin-off special *K-9 and Company* (1981) in a box in the attick of her Croydon home, and her kidnapping and subsequent adventure on Gallifrey in the anniversary special 'The Five Doctors' (1983). The latter is easily explainable: the Time Lords probably erased the memories of everyone who took part in the adventure (save perhaps the 'current' Doctor and companions at the time, Tegan and Turlough, as it occurred in their 'present'). Such a happenstance has a precedent: at the end of 'The War Games' (1969), the Time Lords erased the memories of companions Jamie

McCrimmon and Zoe Heriot. It is certainly plausible that they did the same thing again in 'The Five Doctors', not just with the bystanders (including Sarah) but also with the past versions of the Doctor himself. The former, however, presents a problem: why would Sarah wonder if the Doctor had died after their parting, when only a few years later, she received a gift from him? Sarah would not assume that it's a 'past' version of the Doctor (at that point, in *K-9 and Company*, she's only ever encountered one version of the Doctor at a time, and never out of chronological order). Obviously, that would count as a sign that he was somewhere safe.

Also, why does Sarah carry around the broken down K-9 in the boot of her car? If he was partially functional, then he could still provide her some measure of use, but he's gone completely dead. Perhaps he's been there for a while, including when he was still barely functional, and she's never got around to taking him out, but there doesn't seem to be a proper explanation. (Nor is there one for the fact that, the next day, K-9 is out of the car boot and in the back seat.)

Why is Mickey operating from a cyber café instead of his home computer? (Perhaps because he's breaking into government websites; but surely if they were on to him, he'd be a lot easier to capture in public.) In addition, why would he – but not the government – make a connection between the UFO sightings and the school? (What happened to the UFOs? Did they just drop off the Krillitanes, or are they still out there somewhere?) According to the TARDISode, Mickey finds the information in the Government's mainframe, complete with a section that's classified (with a 'Torchwood' moniker on the warning notice); they've obviously got some interest in the subject as well.

Which then makes one wonder... why would Finch, who's the leader of an alien invasion using the resources (and children) of Deffry Vale High School for a secret master plan, consent to a profile in the *Sunday Times*? Surely he's trying to keep a low profile and not attract attention, especially with mysterious disappearances of both students and teachers?

Also, why would Finch think, just because Nina lives in a foster care home, that no-one would miss her? Surely that would cause further concern to the local police? Also, is it feasible that he could introduce a new curriculum into the school when others in the country have to follow a national plan?

Why do the Krillitane dinner ladies transport a vat of dangerous chemicals (dangerous to them, anyway) without a lid? Why not have children or other staff members move it? Why does Kenny not have to eat the 'compulsory' meals? (Is it because he needs a diet?) And speaking of Kenny, since all the children now believe he blew up the school, what about his future? Is he now considered an arsonist? (No doubt the Doctor would have intervened, but honestly...)

A minor continuity glitch. In the classic *Doctor Who* series, the Doctor more often than not referred to his companion as Sarah, not Sarah Jane. (She even introduces herself as Sarah to Tegan in 'The Five Doctors'.) Here, however, he calls her Sarah Jane.

Why *couldn't* the Doctor go back for Sarah, all those years ago? He's hesitant to answer here (and is interrupted anyway), and doesn't provide a real reason. Why has the Doctor parked the TARDIS inside the school, and later, how does he get it outside into a garden without anyone noticing? Also, is the TARDIS's next destination Jackie's house, perhaps? Surely Mickey will want to tell his boss that he's leaving, not to mention Jackie herself? (The last time someone disappeared – Rose's year in space as noted in 'Aliens of London' – there was a year-long manhunt and Mickey was a murder suspect. Jackie asks where Mickey is in 'The Age of Steel', so she obviously knows he's gone with the Doctor and Rose.)

Finally, how in the world does an entire Krillitane computer project run off one power socket?

ALTERED STATES: The character played by Anthony Head was originally credited as 'Headmaster'. Fans at one point speculated that the character would be the Master, a villain from the original series. However, this was never the plan for Finch. The character's first name is never given on screen, but script editor Helen Raynor mentions in the episode commentary on the official *Doctor Who* website that it is Hector. Head himself also revealed in an interview that this was originally to have been the name, but noted that it was changed when BBC researchers discovered that there was a real-life headmaster called Hector Finch. The Deffry Vale High School tie-in website (see below) says his first name is Lucas.

The story was originally planned with the title 'Old Friends' (and at one point may have born the name 'Black Ops'), and featured the Doctor and Sarah being reunited during the investigation of an army base and an isolated village nearby. However, Davies decided to change the setting to a school.

An excised scene featured the character Milo, who disappears after the classroom scene with the Doctor and is later mentioned by Wagner as having 'failed' him. The scene depicted Milo collapsing on his desk after having his brain scrambled.

BEHIND THE SCENES: Duffryn High School in Newport was the location used for much of the episode; various scenes were recorded in the school foyer, classrooms, staff room, headmaster's office, corridors and dinner hall. A false wall was built onto the front of the school for the sequence in which Mickey crashes the car through the door. A green screen was placed inside several rooms for effects work. Dozens of children who attend the school were used as extras in the episode. Fitzalan High School in Canton, Cardiff, also doubled as the high school in this episode; areas featured included the kitchen, the swimming pool where Fitch and the Doctor confront each other and the gymnasium. The sequence at the end where Sarah and the Doctor say goodbye was recorded in Belle View Park on Cardiff Road in Newport. Da Vinci's Coffee Shop on the High Street, Newport, featured under its own name in the episode.

The BBC created several tie-in websites for this episode. The 'official' website of the school is deffryvaleschool.org.uk, which includes: a message from the headmaster, Lucas Finch (see 'Altered States'); a section on the school's security system; the school menu; and details of several staff members, including 'Mr Smith', aka the Doctor. (Curiously, it says that the Doctor replaced a 'Ms Barrat' but congratulates a 'Ms Mehru' on her recent lottery win, even though they're supposed to be the same woman according to dialogue in the episode.) It notes that the Doctor previously taught physics in Shoreditch, site of the Coal Hill School from the first episode of *Doctor Who*, '100,000 BC: An Unearthly Child' (1963). Also included on the website is a game based on the Skasas Paradigm. Another website created was www.deffryvale.co.uk, the 'official' website of the town of Deffry Vale. This gives information on the town, on travel by bus and train and on local social groups ('a diverse borough as well, with one of the oldest Mosques in the country, and a real Polish tea room on Tarrant Road'). It also features a 'news story' about a teacher, Victoria Nehru, winning the lottery, and one on the recent UFO sightings; and a number of links, including one to 'The Parsons Family Project' at www.cheapserve.co.uk/members/09032, the fictitious website of teacher Bob Parsons who dies during the episode, and one to the website of a 'David R' at www.cheapserve.co.uk/members/7974; the latter has been mysteriously 'discontinued' but links to the Who Is Doctor Who?

website previously run by Mickey...

The BBC also registered sarahjanesmith.org.uk and deffryvale.com but never used them.

DULCET TONES: 'Song For Ten', the piece written by Murray Gold for the episode 'The Christmas Invasion', is heard instrumentally at no fewer than three points during this episode: the chorus section is heard over the first lunchroom scene as the Doctor and Rose speak, and then later again at night as the Doctor and Rose discuss the situation in front of the Da Vinci Coffee House. The full verse of the song is then played at the end over the Doctor's and Sarah's final goodbye.

'Love Will Tear Us Apart' by Joy Division is playing in the Da Vinci Coffee House when the Doctor, Rose, Mickey and Sarah are there. This track was first recorded in November 1979 for a BBC Radio 1 John Peel show session (later released on assorted Peel compilations), then in Paris in January 1980 in a live version (eventually issued as the B-side to 'Atmosphere', 1988), then finally in March 1980 in studio for an A-side produced by Martin Hannett, reissued as a single in 1995 (London/Polygram: 850 129-2, with 12" and cassette alternatives) with remixes by Don Gehman and Arthur Baker. The studio version was later included on the compilation albums 'Substance' (1988, currently available on a 1999 CD re-issue) and 'Heart and Soul' (1997). It regained fame again shortly afterwards when used in a key scene in 2001 indie film *Donnie Darko*, and was included on the second release of the soundtrack in 2004.

OFF THE SCREEN: Elisabeth Sladen is arguably one of the most popular *Doctor Who* cast members to appear throughout its long history. Having made her debut in December 1973 as the new companion opposite third Doctor Jon Pertwee in the story 'The Time Warrior', she was present at the transition to the fourth incarnation, Tom Baker, to whose era she is inextricably linked. Sladen stayed with the series until October 1976, when she bowed out in the concluding moments of the story 'The Hand of Fear'. She later returned to the fold in 1981 to headline the *K-9 and Company* special, with John Leeson as the voice of K-9, then again in 1983 for the twentieth anniversary *Doctor Who* special 'The Five Doctors', where she was reunited with Jon Pertwee. She also reprised the role of Sarah in the 1993 *Children in Need* charity skit 'Dimensions in Time', and in the 1995 independent Reeltime Pictures video drama *Downtime*. In 2002, Sladen returned to the character once more for the first of two series of *Sarah Jane Smith* audio CD dramas for Big Finish Productions. The second series was released in 2005. Outside her *Doctor Who*-related work, Sladen has also appeared in *Faith in the Future* (1996), *Peak Practice* (1996), *The Bill* (1989), *Dempsey & Makepeace* (1985), *Take My Wife* (1979), *Z Cars* (1972), *Doomwatch* (1972) and *Coronation Street* (1970).

John Leeson was first heard in *Doctor Who* as the voice of K-9 in the 1977 story 'The Invisible Enemy' (in which he also played the voice of the Nucleus). He remained in the role through the remainder of the series' fifteenth and sixteenth seasons. In the story 'The Power of Kroll', broadcast in December 1978 and January 1979, he made his first (and so far only) *Doctor Who* appearance in front of the camera, playing Dugeen. The following year, Leeson took a break from playing K-9. The role then went temporarily to actor David Brierley, until Leeson returned for the eighteenth season. K-9 was written out of the show in January 1981 in the story 'Warriors' Gate', though Leeson later had the opportunity to reprise the role in the 1981 special *K-9 and Company* and the 1983 special 'The Five Doctors'. He also provided an unrelated background voice in the 1988 serial 'Remembrance of the Daleks'. In 1995, he took an in-vision role in Reeltime's independent *Doctor Who* spin-off *Downtime*. He later recreated the role of K-9 in several audios for BBV Productions, and later again for Big Finish Productions alongside his one-time *Doctor Who* co-stars Louise Jameson, Lalla Ward and Mary Tamm. Leeson's career has also included appearances in *Doctors* (2001), *Bugs* (1995), *The Bill* (1993), *Allo Allo!* (1989), *Oscar* (1985), *Sorry!* (1981), *Blake's 7* (1978) and *Dad's Army* (1969).

Anthony Head, also known as Anthony Stewart Head, first came to prominence in a series of coffee commercials on British TV, but is perhaps best known for his portrayal of Watcher Rupert Giles in the cult television series *Buffy the Vampire Slayer* (1997-2003). He has had two prior *Doctor Who* roles, both on audio: in the BBCi webcast serial 'Death Comes to Time' (2001) and in a series of Big Finish CD dramas collectively entitled *Excelis* (2002). He played the Prime Minister in the series *Little Britain* (2004) and has appeared in *Hotel Babylon* (2006), *Rose and Maloney* (2005), *MIT: Murder Investigation Team* (2005), *Monarch of the Glen* (2004), *New Tricks* (2004), *My Family* (2003), *Fillmore!* (2002), *Spooks* (2002), *Manchild* (2002), *Silent Witness* (2001), *Jonathan Creek* (1997), *NYPD Blue* (1995), *VR.5* (1994), *Highlander: The Series* (1993), *Pulaski* (1987), *A Prayer for the Dying* (1987), *Howard's Way* (1985), *Bergerac* (1981) and *Secret Army* (1979). In addition, he unsuccessfully auditioned for the role of the Doctor in the 1996 *Doctor Who* TV movie. Rod Arthur has appeared in *Bleak House* (2005), *55 Degrees North* (2005), *Doctors* (2004), *Silent Witness* (1999), *This Life* (1997), *Hetty Wainthropp Investigates* (1996), *Heartbeat* (1995), *Prime Suspect* (1991), *All Creatures Great and Small* (1989) and *Auf Wiedersehen Pet* (1986). Eugene Washington has been seen in *Star Hyke* (2005), *Attack* (2005), *Doctors* (2005) and *Judge John Deed* (2005). Heather Cameron has been featured in *The Bill* (2005), *Red Cap* (2004), *A Touch of Frost* (2003), *Murder in Mind* (2002) and *Holby City* (2001). Benjamin Smith can be seen in *Hustle* (2006), *Teachers* (2003), *Only Fools and Horses* (2002) and *Second Sight* (2001). Clem Tibber was in *Robin Hood* (2006), *Doctors* (2004) and *Holby City* (2002). Lucinda Dryzek has been featured in *Vital Signs* (2006), *Casualty* (2005), *Help! I'm a Teenage Outlaw* (2004), *Pirates of the Caribbean: The Curse of the Black Pearl* (2003), *Silent Witness* (2002) and *Micawber* (2001). Caroline Berry has been seen in *Dad* (2005), *People Like Us* (1999), *Peak Practice* (1998), *The Lifeboat* (1994), *Birds of a Feather* (1993) and *Inspector Morse* (1993).

Toby Whithouse is the creator of the Channel 4 drama series *No Angels* (2004) and has penned scripts for *Torchwood* (2006), *Hotel Babylon* (2006), *Attachments* (2000) and *Where The Heart Is* (1997). He is also an accomplished television actor; his credits include roles in *Holby City* (2004), *Bridget Jones' Diary* (2001), *The Last Musketeer* (2000), *RKO 281* (1999), *Goodnight Sweetheart* (1999), *The House of Eliott* (1993), *Shadowlands* (1993) and *Mrs 'arris Goes to Paris* (1992).

TECHNICAL GOOFS: In the closing shot, as Sarah and K-9 head down the path, one of the crew (in a yellow shirt) is visible at far right. In some shots, the door to the Headmaster's office is solid, while in others it has a window; it's possible that these are separate entrances, but the interiors look quite different. When Mickey disconnects the Krillitane computers from the power supply, the students are all wearing headphones, but in the next shot, as they get out of their seats, they aren't wearing them anymore.

INTERNAL CONSISTENCY: The episode takes place in 2007; Sarah refers to the events of 'The Christmas Invasion', which took place at the end of 2006. Since the children are in school, it's likely to be some time in the spring (as the trees are in bloom; it's certainly not the autumn).

The episode takes place over two days.

TARDISODE #3: Mickey (Noel Clarke) is in an Internet café investigating UFO sightings on the British government's website ('Defence Special Projects'); his browsing is interrupted by a screen showing: 'Torchwood – Access Denied', leading him to believe he's on to something. He leaves a message for Rose on her mobile phone that there's something out there she needs to investigate...

REVIEWS

A story that would once have remained in the category of fan fiction is now canon, and by God it's about time! The return of Sarah Jane is one of the most triumphant and melancholy moments in the history of *Doctor Who*, and it's handled beautifully. A still preternaturally stunning Lis Sladen returns to the role that made her a 1970s childhood icon, bringing with her the bane of the '80s *Who* production crew – K-9, the super-intelligent robot dog that travelled with the Doctor for several years and later joined Sarah Jane. The nostalgia factor here is off the scale, but there's something that rings a bit odd. I can't quite buy that Sarah Jane ever felt for Tom Baker's bizarre alien in the way we're meant to believe. Maybe it's just that the old show was always so asexual and innocent, but it's strange to learn that she saw in that googly-eyed, curly-headed genius the love of her life. Despite the plethora of continuity touches, there were hiccups. The big one of course is that Sarah repeatedly refers to their last meeting as her departure in 1976, completely ignoring the fact that she saw several Doctors again in 1983's twentieth anniversary special, 'The Five Doctors'. Still, behind those bits and the Krillitane plot to unlock the secrets of the universe *à la* 'Logopolis' lies the new series' most powerful character study since 'Father's Day'. Sladen and David Tennant have a wonderful rapport – their scenes are charged with equal parts tension and affection – and by finally exploring both Sarah's true feelings for the Doctor and his unspoken love for her and Rose, the episode opens up new but exciting emotional territory for the series. But one can only imagine what Rose and new viewers would make of the hand-puppet Skarasen if they saw him today. Once again, though, Billie Piper is marginalised. Although this was touted as a story about Rose – the realisation of what her fate might one day be when she leaves the TARDIS – she's reduced to a sulking, bitchy child. The two women reconcile in a wonderful scene and their final farewell is touching, but Rose is ill-served by the episode, not least by her final tantrum when the Doctor allows Mickey to officially join the TARDIS crew. While the production team have obviously tried to give Sarah Jane's part in the proceedings real weight, Rose becomes as much the tin dog as Mickey. This doesn't bode well. The Krillitane creatures have a lot of potential as future foes, with their ability to adapt their appearance; cross those Raxicoricofallapatorians off the recurring monsters roster permanently, but add the Krillitanes to the top, please. And in Anthony Stewart Head's Finch, we have everything the Doctor's old arch-nemesis the Master used to be when Roger Delgado played the role. Finch is suave, seductive, animalistic, and well deserving of another appearance; he even offers the Doctor a share in the universe as the Master might have done (as in the 1971 story 'Colony in Space'). In fact, it's in his confrontations with Finch that Tennant's Doctor really begins to sparkle. The story is filled with eloquent dialogue and a propulsive score by Murray Gold. K-9 even gets to be the hero! This was simply magic. Welcome back... my *Doctor Who*! Or wait, was it *Buffy the Vampire Slayer* with a dash of 'Remembrance of the Daleks'? Oh well. – *Arnold T Blumberg*

It really is true what they say... you never forget your first love. When I started watching *Doctor Who* as a teenager, Sarah Jane Smith was the companion alongside Tom Baker's Doctor. I have to admit I was really worried I was going to discover in 'School Reunion' that Elisabeth Sladen was an actress of a particular era; and I did indeed feel that her style of performance was a little more mannered than that typically seen in today's TV. But, no, in the end, she was wonderful in this latest return appearance, and I remembered precisely why I loved her so much as a teenager: she has her own unique charisma and charm. I loved the scene with Sarah and the Doctor talking in the café, where she asks that question everyone who was ever dumped unceremoniously asks: was it me? Was there something I could have done? The fact that Lis Sladen can pull off the sort of emotional scene that was never at the core of her era of *Doctor Who* impresses me more than I can say. This story, to my mind, also features David Tennant's best performance in the series to date. My big problem with Tennant this season isn't really to do with the actor at all, but with the characterisation of his Doctor in the scripts. Watch *Secret Smile* or *Blackpool* and there is no question that as Tennant is just as capable of doing intense gravitas as is Christopher Eccleston, if not more so. But, if 'The Christmas Invasion' provides the template for the tenth Doctor's character, then the writers keep giving him far too many hyper flourishes of the 'Now when I see a great big button' and 'What kind of a man am I?' variety and not nearly enough of the quiet, brooding moments like 'No second chances, I'm that kind of a man' and 'Six words'. The former trait has been evident in pretty much every script; the latter only really on display in this story (and to a lesser extent in 'The Satan Pit' and 'Doomsday'). Watch the quiet but wonderful way he opens his soul to both Sarah and then Rose at the café, and then marvel at the glorious intensity of the scene with Finch by the pool: *that's* what David Tennant could be doing as the Doctor ever week, if only the writers would give him the material. In some ways, the story is just a vehicle to give us the emotional fireworks of what happens when Rose and the current Doctor meet a past companion. As in 'Rose', the plot is a sort of shorthand, comic book story to frame the character drama within (though Anthony Stewart Head is wonderful as the villain). And that's okay, because I thought the central conceit of treating a past companion as an ex-wife was a brilliant one. (I loved the scene where Sarah and Rose argue, and then bond over the adventures with, and quirks of, the Doctor.) And the story offers a great insight into the reality of the Doctor's emotional attachments to his companions and how hard he must find it when they part company. In some ways, though, I wish the production team could have succeeded at giving a brilliant adventure story *and* a great emotional drama. But to expect them to do that in the space of 45 minutes is a tall order. And I must concede that any story that can make the death ('You're a good dog') and resurrection of K-9 so emotionally powerful has to be doing something right.
– *Graeme Burk*

I honestly approached 'School Reunion' with the presumption that it could never work. Appearances by past cast members are always tricky, and more so when they never actually starred with the current cast, something about which *Star Trek* and its many succeeding series should know a good deal. *Doctor Who*, however, has (the odd exception aside) seen only earlier versions of the Doctor himself show up for a visit; an idea any viewer who's seen regeneration should be able to grasp. This is different. Here we have two companions from 30 years ago associated together by an aborted spin-off (*K-9 and Company*) that the general public will never remember. The entire story hinges on the idea that your average viewer – or, more likely, your average viewer's dad – has some hazy memory of the Tom Baker era. It shouldn't work. It really, really shouldn't. And yet, somehow, it does. Sarah Jane Smith was one of the very rare companions to the Doctor who started as an assistant and became something... more. That's not to say she fell in love with the Doctor, but that they became best friends, something easily seen in the performances of Tom Baker and Elisabeth Sladen. By the time they parted, they really knew what made each other tick. This serves as a brilliant counterpoint to the relationship between Rose and the Doctor, which is certainly more romantic but no less devoted, and the comparison comes across easily on-screen. The Doctor has been a vital part of Sarah's life, and he is now a vital part of Rose's. You really don't need to know much more; that's why it works. The main Sarah storyline, as good as it is, does overwhelm the actual alien invasion, which probably would have been better served by a two-part story. Despite a witty script, the editing is a little clunky, and there are several places – such as Rose and Sarah's quick turnaround from argument to laughter – where things seem to happen with an unusual abruptness. Thanks to Anthony Head's downright alien performance as Mr Finch, however, you never feel like you're losing out. He oozes evil out of every pore, and does tremendous work with a villain that could so easily have been sidelined. Quick tip to the production team: bring him back soon. The mechanics of the Krillitane invasion and the Skasas Paradigm are as daft as the time paradox of 'Father's Day', but at least they're standard *Doctor Who* daft, and actually back up the points of the more emotional plotline. There's a theme emerging of evolution and change that I can't help thinking is going to be important to the overall season: here, Sarah realises her life must change, Rose realises her life will change, and the Doctor is given the chance to change everyone's lives. Earlier, in 'The Christmas Invasion', he literally did change – and since then, so have Cassandra, the plague farm humans, a werewolf/alien entity, and dear old K-9. Even the Krillitanes thrive on evolution, and we all know what the Cybermen are like. If last year's theme was 'Everything dies', is this year's 'Everything changes'? I didn't like 'Father's Day' last year because I felt it was emotionally heavy at the expense of all else, and you could perhaps make the same point about 'School Reunion'. What can I say, though? I really enjoyed it. Maybe it's just because I have more attachment to Sarah than I ever would to Rose's father, but still... everyone does change... – *Sarah Hadley*

'School Reunion' manages the impressive feat of being both a pretty dreadful *Doctor Who* story and a wonderful episode of *Doctor Who*. It's the former because, sadly, the plot isn't really up to scratch. An awful cliché of a science-fiction story, a big secret powerful code to be cracked, wouldn't normally be a problem in the hands of a good writer, but here perhaps Toby Whithouse suffers from simply having too much else to do with the episode. The Doctor's sudden leaps – 'They're allergic to their own oil!' – seem to come out of nowhere, and the adding on of one of the pupils helping to save the day seems like a bit of an awkward attempt to engender audience identification amongst teenage viewers, which the show normally avoids and with good reason. Its case for being a wonderful episode comes from the return of Sarah Jane Smith and K-9, providing some great moments of nostalgia for the fans and emotional resonance for all viewers, young and old; and it's in these sequences that Whithouse's writing abilities come through. The scene in which the Doctor first sees Sarah and his gleeful, almost disbelieving reaction is my personal favourite, although all their scenes together are excellent and Tennant and Sladen really spark off each other. I wasn't quite as sold on the scenes between Sarah and Rose – Piper is as good as ever, and their trading of names of monsters they have encountered is great fun, but they seem to make up and become friends at breakneck speed. On the whole though the script does suffer under the weight of the emotion it's trying, and admittedly mostly succeeding, to convey, and you can't help but feel that other writers on the new series have managed to combine emotion, character and storytelling in equal measure, so why not here? On the visual side, James Hawes' direction doesn't shine quite as much as previously, although he is still up to a pretty good standard even on his average days. You do get the impression, however, that he'd perhaps been watching rather too much *EastEnders* when he came to the scene of the Doctor revealing who he is to Sarah. The Doctor stepping from the shadows with the words 'Hello Sarah Jane' is eerily reminiscent of the return of 'Dirty' Den Watts to the BBC's flagship soap opera back in 2003, stepping into a similar scene with his now infamous greeting of ''ello princess'. Other echoes come from 1990s BBC fantasy dramas set in schools, a particular sub-genre they seemed quite keen on back then, with *The Demon Headmaster* and particularly Davies's own 1991 serial *Dark Season*, the computers-controlling-minds element of which is repeated very strongly here. A touching episode, and great to see Elisabeth Sladen and K-9 again, and the strong scenes they provide are just about enough to stop this feeling too much like rather an underwhelming affair. – *Paul Hayes*

This could have been a car crash of an episode. A wreck, tarnishing the memory of two beloved characters and showing that *Doctor Who* can't vanish up its own fundament any more. But it wasn't. From the pre-title sequence – 'You poor... *thin*... child' – we all know who the big bad is this week, but the Doctor as a teacher? I wish my classes sat there that quietly! But all this is foreplay: we old-timers are waiting for one single moment, and when that happens, the Doctor is reduced to a tongue-tied teenager. We've just started to come to terms with a Doctor capable of romantic emotion, but his first meeting with Sarah Jane Smith – a Lis Sladen seemingly frozen in amber – demonstrates that the emotions were always there. It's a platonic love, but as deep as time itself. How companions react to being 'dumped' has been addressed within the various novels and spin-offs: with the Virgin and BBC novels they were seemingly only a call away, with Ace's semi-regular appearances, Benny popping back, and even the Brigadier rejuvenating. But in the TV series, there are many moments when you realise that the Doctor misses his companions when they leave. At the end of 'The Massacre of St Bartholomew's Eve' (1966), the Doctor, alone in the TARDIS, says: 'Now they're all gone. All gone. None of them could understand. Not even my little Susan, or Vicki.' 'School Reunion' is that sentiment writ large. Unfortunately, there has to be a sci-fi subplot to underpin the emotion, but we're reasonably well-served by the concept of a race of body-snatchers trying to solve the Godmaker equation. While this has echoes of 'Logopolis' with the power of Block Transfer Computation, the spin-off *Downtime* with young people being used as adjuncts to a computer program, and indeed my own novel *Millennial Rites* with the Millennium Codex, it's still a fascinating idea, and Murray Gold's wonderfully driving music – 'Carmina Burana' on speed – actually aids the storyline for once, rather than drowning it out. Both Anthony Head and Eugene Washington are delightfully evil, with the former recreating his persona from the Big Finish *Excelis* trilogy as slime incarnate. As for the moment when he offers the Doctor godhood... well, this is clearly becoming one of the themes of the series, and this time round, the Doctor is clearly tempted. Only Sarah Jane's impassioned plea brings him round... what happens next time? But all of this is nothing more than background. 'School Reunion' is, as Mickey says, about 'the missus and the ex'. While the bitch-fest between Rose and Sarah Jane might not be up there with the face-offs between *Dynasty*'s Krystle and Alexis, the emotion is written all over the screen: Rose thinks she's the first, and now she discovers she's nothing more than the latest in a long line of companions. Sarah Jane, meanwhile, has effectively wasted her life waiting for the Doctor to return, only to discover that he's moved on – and she couldn't. But the Doctor's explanation to Rose – that he can't bear to see his companions wither and die – is possibly one of the most moving scenes in the series. He's been our teacher and our guide for so long... but did it ever occur to us that we're nothing more than mayflies in his Time Lord life? Once the Krillitanes are wiped out – return visit for Hector Finch, anyone? – along with K-9, who was sadly reduced to a cipher in this story, it's time for the goodbye. We all saw it coming, but I challenge anyone who grew up with Sarah Jane to deny that they cried at this point. 'My Sarah Jane'... well, she's our Sarah Jane, and this was our goodbye. Tapping *Doctor Who*'s rich history is an addictive and ultimately fatal temptation, but done like this... sheer, sheer class. – *Craig Hinton*

Certainly the best David Tennant *Doctor Who* yet, though there's still as much to argue with as enjoy. Writer Toby Whithouse takes an unusual but workable approach by having the thwarted alien conspiracy, which would normally be the upfront action, play as a B story, with the Doctor's relationships with past and present companions dominating the episode. Actually, the premise (aliens disguised as schoolteachers using children to crack a cosmic code that will make them all-powerful) is solid, Anthony Head makes a good, slightly offbeat evil mastermind antagonist (filed away for future reuse) and starting off in mid-plot with the Doctor already on site undercover and investigating is so effective you wonder why the approach hasn't been used more often. However, the CGI bat-creatures show why computer-images are becoming the rubber suits of the 2000s – the monsters look like refugees from a shot-in-Bulgaria SciFi Channel film premiere, and flap about evilly like a purely notional threat. In the end, this episode is about catching up with Sarah Jane Smith, and Rose wondering about her position as the Doctor's companion: it's full of relishable, affecting bits of business, which Tennant, Piper and Elisabeth Sladen leap on with delight. The strength of the 2005 *Doctor Who* was its ability to connect emotionally, and this is the first time in the new season that the show has worked on that level. A cavil is that Whithouse further sets in stone the notion that the relationship between the Doctor and his companion is primarily romantic: the set-up between Rose and Sarah is explicitly labelled as the 'every bloke's nightmare' combination of 'the missus and the ex'. The initial hostility/eventual bonding between the women is funny, has a feeling of reality and reflects interestingly on the Doctor and Mickey. (Noel Clarke comes off surprisingly well in this episode, which is a turning point for a character threatening to become surplus.) There's even credible continuity with 'The Hand of Fear' 30 years ago, though a look at the Doctor's past relationships suggests companions almost invariably leave him rather than getting dumped. Initially, the Doctor's companions were surrogate children (or grandchildren) rather than love interest – which makes the assumption he had at least a romantic and probably a physical relationship with Sarah, and presumably others, rather a murky area. As for K-9 – I'm on record as saying I'd rather see Bonnie Langford back on the series than this mechanised Scrappy-Doo, but for the most part its reappearance was well-handled, touching and funny, the emphasis being on the way Sarah has kept this useless hunk of tin around as a reminder of what she's lost. When back in action, the dog still defaults to a plot device with a laser-nose, cutely exterminating monsters to get the human characters out of trouble. – *Kim Newman*

In the new *Who*, women represent adulthood, whereas the Doctor is a little boy who will never grow up. He lives in a strange little world of his own, where he is enormously responsible on the one hand – making huge moral decisions, saving planets and the universe – and totally irresponsible on the other. He leaves a trail of crumbled civilisations, shattered lives and broken hearts behind him, and races on, almost never having to confront the results of his actions. He does not look back. Sarah Jane forces him to look back at her. Sarah's life has not been on pause since Aberdeen – certainly her adventurous career hasn't – and there's no reason to assume she's been celibate. But she has never found another partner who could compare. Every bit of three decades' bottled bitterness comes pouring out, almost from the moment she recognises him. Perhaps he has let her 'sleep in his mind'. But for her, there was no closure; she was ripped loose. It's not as though the Doctor, as an alien, doesn't have the emotions of a mere human. When he encounters Sarah, he looks as though he's about to weep with happiness. But there's something immature, something clueless: it doesn't occur to him that he'll have to deal with Sarah's anger and hurt. When she tells him 'You *were* my life', he looks a bit scared. He cannot pretend, this time, that it isn't goodbye and that it doesn't hurt: she won't let him. What would happen if he let those feelings in each time, again and again, over centuries? Would he become inured to them? Would it be simply unbearable? What will this mean for Rose's inevitable departure? Arguably, out of our four heroes, Sarah is the only real grownup. The Doctor – who after nine centuries really ought to know better – is deeply tempted to resurrect his own people even at the cost of a schoolful of souls. Rose keeps quiet. Only Sarah sees how the Skasas Paradigm would destroy them: she sees the offer of eternal youth for what it is, an offer of eternal childhood, of eternal immaturity, eternal stasis. Now, the word 'jealousy' is often misused – it refers not to your feelings about your rival, but to those about your loved one. Rose is jealous of the Doctor. She confronts both him and Sarah as she tries to reorientate herself. This climaxes in a very funny, bitchy exchange between the two – but much more importantly, in the moment where they catch themselves at it. They recognise themselves in each other: they identify with each other as women, rather than squabbling like girls. There's been no malice in the Doctor's treatment of his past companions, only carelessness, but he's earned their anger. As well as hysterics at his expense. Manslaughter is scary, as the old saw goes, but not nearly as scary as woman's laughter. – *Kate Orman*

Voila! In my review of 'The Christmas Invasion', I said I'd give Tennant until episode four to win me over. Well, I think he's done it – and one episode early! I had already written-off 'School Reunion' – in fact as soon as I heard that K-9 was returning (I was never a great fan of the little tin doggie) – and I'd placed the episode second to last in my predictions for the season order. Just goes to show how much I know! I'm going to have to revise that placement now: 'School Reunion' was quite simply fabulous. (I wanted to say 'correctamundo', but that wouldn't make sense!) My initial reaction when I heard about this one was that it would be the season's 'Father's Day' – an emotionally charged story with the companion (in this case Sarah, not Rose) facing a crossroads in their life, people trapped in a building, under siege by naff flying monsters; the story that everyone loves but for all the wrong reasons. Would it be a triumph or an opportunity wasted? I'm pleased to say it is definitely the former. For once, this is a story in which all the disparate elements actually work in tandem. Everything serves a purpose and is not just there for the sake of looking good on screen. The moment everyone was waiting for was Sarah meeting the Doctor. A beautifully played out scene in the darkness of the gymnasium. Hands up anyone who didn't shed a tear or hold back a sniffle. (You there in the back, you liar!) I've probably played and replayed that one scene about five or six times now. Usually I wait four or five days before I give an episode another viewing, but 'School Reunion' had a second outing the very next day. It's been simply ages since I smiled so much while watching an episode of *Doctor Who*. It's also been quite a number of years since I was at school – we never had computers for one thing! – but I recall several teachers were thought of as slobbering monsters. Anthony Head is quite chilling as the headmaster – a role that could have been played OTT but is handled at just the right level. We don't see him die, so I wouldn't be surprised if Finch returns... And every big-boned, ginger-haired kid with glasses must be whooping in delight as Kenny saves the day! (Though I'm a bit at a loss as to what caused the final explosion.) So, I'm happy to say my preconceptions were all wrong. 'School Reunion' now occupies a place near the top of my season rankings list. Significantly, the story marks the start of a seven week run of non-Davies-scripted episodes. It will be interesting to see what impact this will have in the weeks to come... – *Jon Preddle*

I must admit that when details of 'School Reunion' were initially announced, for the first time since *Doctor Who* returned to our screens I had some serious conceptual misgivings about an avenue being followed by the production team. The inclusion of not one but two elements from the series' past seemed so grossly at odds with the stridently 'new' direction that the first season had established. Worse, their inclusion appeared, at the time, an almost cowardly fannish gesture designed to do nothing more than please a few fortysomething men with beards. See, I've never been particularly fond of either Sarah Jane or K-9 as characters. I always found the former to be a curiously limited example of a bunch of well-intentioned but hopelessly wrong-headed middle-aged, middle-class men's idea of what a feminist icon should be. I did in 1975 and still do today. And, as for the latter... nah, sorry. Tin dogs also just don't do it for me like they once did. Thankfully, the episode came out much better in execution than I had feared it might. Toby Whithouse's script combined skilful and acute character interplay (the Rose/Sarah confrontation), some sharp social observation ('Happy-slapping hoodies with ASBOs') and, in many places, a quasi-sage-like wisdom far beyond its rather limited boundaries ('I used to have so much mercy'). This was especially true of David Tennant's chilling 'I don't age' speech, one of several mature and dignified moments that directly challenged my own preconceptions. Though the episode's key theme – the effect of the passage of time on relationships – was handled in a curiously sterile way, a seemingly dispassionate sideways glance in a episode about, well, passion, there remained plenty to admire here. The concept of loneliness – a recurring theme this season, which would be taken to some logical extremes in the following episode; an amusingly slimy and eye-rolling performance by Tony Head; a pointed critique of the 2005 debate on youth obesity in Britain (something nasty in them there chips!); Joy Division on the soundtrack; the beautifully poised question, 'Who can you talk to about having walked on other worlds?' These, and other, superb moments completed something that, for once, *was* the sum of all parts. Yes, Lis Sladen's presence still seems desperately out of place in new-*Doctor Who* to me and, yes, the plot was *very Dark Season* – even down to the fat kid saving the day. But 'School Reunion' managed, without any inherent pretentiousness, to speak to the constituent groups in its audience on many different levels and work on pretty much all of them. I don't *do* re-evaluation often or well but, here, it was a necessary thing to do, and I'm delighted about that. – *Keith Topping*

EDITOR'S REVIEW: There's been quite a bit written on the Internet complaining about the shallow story in 'School Reunion', or the gaping plot holes, and that's fine. I say that none of it really matters. Television is supposed to entertain us; those who watch any given TV series expecting to be impressed on a literary basis every week are going to be seriously disappointed, and viewers of *Doctor Who* should know by now that much of this isn't supposed to be taken that seriously anyway. But television often rewards us, the viewer, as well, with anything from a subtle wink to a full-on continuity extravaganza that succeeds even for those who aren't fully in on the joke.

'School Reunion' is such a beast, and is exemplary in its complete conviction that everyone's along for the ride. Far too often we get our moments of reward but the emotional heart of the experience just isn't there. Not here; we know that there are people out there for whom the words 'Sarah Jane Smith' and 'K-9' mean absolutely nothing. Yet the story tries to engage them anyway, ultimately showing us that it really doesn't matter when they were on the show or what they did or which Doctor they travelled with. The simple fact is that they're part of this character's past, and if we want to know the Doctor, we need to know that there *was* a past, rich and wild and full of adventure. We can see it on David Tennant's face that the Doctor recognises Sarah, and her robot dog.

When one carefully examines the story structure of 'School Reunion', it's obvious that it's only skin-deep; there's a group of nasties, and they're eating children or doing something equally bad to them, and they want what they want and it's up to the Doctor to stop it. Been there, done that. We get our moment with Anthony Head, a welcome addition to the *Doctor Who* mythology not for what he does here but for the fact that he's here at all (*Buffy* fans, take note). We have our special effects in the Krillitanes and the computer-generated technobabble that's supposed to elevate them to godhood. There are conflicts and laser shots and explosions and, hey, a 12 year old gets to blow up the school (fulfilling, no doubt, lifelong dreams for so many).

But that's not what 'School Reunion' is about, not aliens or invasion plots or mysterious yellow goo. It's about finding your place in life, and what to do when you've gone over the rainbow and come back home to Kansas. Sarah Jane Smith hasn't exactly wasted the decades since she left the Doctor – she's an investigative journalist for *The Sunday Times*, not a bad feat – but she still pines for the days facing the Loch Ness Monster and mummies and even those pesky Daleks. (If the Doctor had taken me out into space and time for several years and then dropped me back square in the middle of some dumpy Earth city, I'd probably be pretty *laissez-faire* about normal life, too.) She's moved on, to an extent, but never had the moment she needed with the Doctor, to really say goodbye once and for all. Here, Elisabeth Sladen steps into the role as if she never left it all those years ago, and we never doubt for a second that she's our Sarah Jane, changed by the Doctor into the woman she is today. (Special kudos must also be given to John Leeson; K-9 would just never have been the same without that remarkable voice.)

Rose and Mickey each learn a similar lesson; they're special, but so very, very ordinary at the same time. Intellectually, Rose has always known that she won't be around forever, whereas her friend the Doctor will be, but could never stand to admit it to herself until she met someone from the Doctor's past. Mickey had a hard time placing himself in this structure of the Doctor and the people he's come to rely upon, until realising that even the 'tin dog' can be the hero. By the end of this story, Mickey isn't asking the Doctor if he can come with them, he's telling him he will; and Rose is now quite comfortable in her role as the Doctor's friend, for as long as she can be.

'School Reunion' is just that, a blessing for those of us who have followed *Doctor Who* through good times and bad. The emotional depth and satisfaction of the reunion between the

Doctor and Sarah Jane Smith might be lost on the newcomers, but in the end, the important thing is not to understand what the relationship is, but to focus on the why: every good hero needs his sidekick(s), as foil, as conscience, as a window to the hero's soul. And, more than anything, it's about saying goodbye, on your own terms – Rose and Mickey are the present, Sarah Jane and K-9 were the past – and that even though the players in one's life might vary, the bonds we form never, ever do. – *Shaun Lyon*

204: THE GIRL IN THE FIREPLACE

On a derelict spacecraft in a distant part of the universe, the Doctor, Rose and Mickey discover a series of windows into history, all leading back to 18th Century France. But the terrible secret behind them involves mysterious Clockwork Men... and a stranger who once appeared to the young girl Reinette from inside an antique fireplace in her bedroom.

FIRST TRANSMISSION: UK – 6 May 2006. US – 20 October 2006. Canada – 30 October 2006. Australia – 5 August 2006. New Zealand – 3 August 2006.
DURATION: 44'41"
WRITER: Steven Moffat
DIRECTOR: Euros Lyn
CREDITED CAST: David Tennant (The Doctor), Billie Piper (Rose Tyler), Noel Clarke (Mickey Smith), Sophia Myles (Reinette), Ben Turner (King Louis), Jessica Atkins (Young Reinette), Angel Coulby (Katherine), Gareth Wyn Griffiths (Manservant), Paul Kasey (Clockwork Man), Ellen Thomas (Clockwork Woman), Jonathan Hart, Emily Joyce (Alien Voices)

WHERE AND WHEN: Paris and Versailles, France, in various years from 1727 to 1764. Also, the SS Madame de Pompadour, the 51st Century – roughly 3,000 years later – in deep space.

THE STORY UNFOLDS: Deep in a remote part of space called the Dagmar Cluster, circa the 51st Century, the spacecraft SS Madame De Pompadour was damaged by an ion storm, with 82% systems failure. The crew of 50 were unable to stop the ship's repair droids from taking their orders literally; with no parts to repair the ship, they instead turned against the crew, slaughtering them and harvesting their organs to use in the ship's reconstruction: a real human eye used as a camera lens, and a human heart wired in presumably as a pump. They are now in need of one more part to repair the ship, the brain of Reinette, later known as Madame de Pompadour; they consider the ship and the woman after whom the ship is named to be the same. There's a fire extinguisher on the ship that Mickey thinks is an ice gun; the Doctor later uses it to freeze one of the droids.

The repair droids are ornate clockwork constructions with egg-shaped plastic heads and make ticking sounds, and dress in period camouflage (with attention to needlework) to blend into French history. They have knives and stunners embedded in their mechanical arms and are equipped with short-range teleports. They believe the young Reinette to be 'incomplete' and have been scanning her brain to tell her age (her 'milometer', says the Doctor); when Reinette is 37, the same age as the ship, her brain will be a compatible component for the one part of the ship they've not yet repaired: its computer.

The Doctor uses multi-grade anti-oil (which looks like wine in a glass) to stop the droids. ('If it moves, it doesn't.') One of the droids refers to itself as Repair Droid 7.

According to the Doctor, the Dagmar Cluster is 'two and a half galaxies' away from Earth. While the ship is deserted and in a state of disrepair, the warp engines are going at full capacity, with enough power to 'punch a hole in the universe'. Aboard the ship are holes in time; the Doctor first calls the phenomenon a spatio-temporal hyperlink (a term he makes up because he doesn't want to call it a 'magic door'). The manifestations of the holes are time windows, gateways into history, specifically into pre-revolutionary France; some doorways exist as mirrors, others as actual doorways into such places as the gardens of a country estate, and one as an 18th Century original double-sided French fireplace. (Rose notes that the fireplace is backed up against the outer hull of the ship.) All the doorways lead to various points in the life of Reinette; through the doorways the Doctor travels into the past, as do the Clockwork Men. Time moves at different speeds on either side of the fireplace, passing far quicker (relatively) in France than it does on the ship.

The windows are controlled from a central console; because the Clockwork Men couldn't accurately pinpoint the right time in Reinette's life, they've opened many windows ('trial and error', the Doctor calls it) throughout her life. These include her childhood (aged seven) in Paris, late 1727; months later when the Clockwork Men are scanning her brain; when she is a young woman prior to meeting the King; and at age 37, possibly the night of her birthday celebration.

On the fireplace is a clock, which wasn't working when Reinette was a child; it's later repaired (as seen when Rose visits her). The Doctor names the horse that escapes into the ship Arthur (saying this is a 'good name for a horse') and compares keeping it to Rose keeping Mickey around. The mirror is made of hyperplex on the future side.

THE DOCTOR: He originally persuades the young Reinette that he's doing a routine fire check on her fireplace. 1727 is one of his favourite years (though he describes August as 'a bit rubbish'), and he thinks France is a 'different planet' but that the French know how to party. He can tell that the ticking sounds in Reinette's room come from something the size of a man (six feet tall, perhaps), because of their resonance. He admires the Clockwork Men, but their elaborate construction won't stop him from doing what he has to. He has telepathic ability (but doesn't make a habit of using it) and ventures into Reinette's head to find out what it is the droids are looking for; she also sees into his mind during this, and discovers that he was a lonely little boy and is still lonely today. He's always been 'a bit vague' about money. He says monsters have nightmares about him; Reinette says that he's worth the monsters. He knows the name of every star in the sky.

While in France (and pretending to be very drunk) the Doctor may have invented the banana daiquiri a few centuries earlier than he should have; he says the French have never seen a banana, and a banana helps in being popular at a party.

ROSE TYLER: Typically, when the Doctor tells her not to look for the clockwork droid, she goes off (with Mickey) and looks anyway. She's later captured by the droids and nearly chopped up for replacement parts for the ship. When she nags him, the Doctor tells her she's just like her mother. Rose goes back in time through a portal to warn Reinette, five years before her 37th birthday, about the droids coming for her. She's apparently fine with the idea of Mickey travelling with her and the Doctor now, despite having been less than enthusiastic about it at the end of 'School Reunion'.

CHARACTER BUILDING: *Reinette* – The future Madame de Pompadour (see 'Reality Bites'). The ship has made a connection with the fireplace in her bedroom at her home in Paris; at age seven, in 1727, she's baffled to see the Doctor on the other side. She first believes her encounters with the Doctor have been dreams about an imaginary friend, but when she sees him as an adult for the first time, she realises it was all true and kisses him. She calls the Doctor 'fireplace man' and her 'lonely angel'; she discovers his name – and his identity as a Time Lord – after touching his mind. She is not unhappy when Madame De Chateauroux, the King's mistress, is close to death; she's an ambitious woman, with designs on being the King's mistress herself. She later meets the King on the night of the Yew-Tree Ball (when she is 23), moves to Versailles and becomes his new mistress (although, according to the Doctor, she gets on well with the Queen). She visits the ship in the future, briefly, hearing her own voice in her future, and doesn't like the Doctor's 'world'. Reinette understands the nature of the windows, calling herself the 'weary traveller' who lives out her life normally while the Doctor (and the droids) visit her life like stepping through the pages of a book; she also wouldn't have what's happened to her any other way. Reinette nearly joins the Doctor on a trip into time and space, but when he finally returns for her, she has died, and her body is *en route* to Paris for burial.

Mickey Smith – Having made his first trip into outer space (and possibly his first trip in the TARDIS anywhere at all; see 'Scene Missing'), Mickey is spellbound by how 'realistic' it seems when he looks out the porthole of the ship, and considers everything to be a grand adventure (until he and Rose are captured by the droids). He hasn't seen much of the TARDIS yet beyond the console room.

King Louis XV – He obviously loves Reinette a great deal, and is devastated when she dies. He apparently didn't believe her when she told him the Doctor never aged, but finally has the chance to see it for himself.

Katherine – Reinette's friend, who strolls with her in the gardens and comments on her ambitions to become the King's mistress.

TORCHWOOD: No references in this episode.

BODY COUNT: Madame de Pompadour, who dies at the end of this episode, aged 43; also, the 50 crewmembers of the spacecraft that bears her name, who die prior to the episode's start. The clockwork droids are all deactivated. (It is possible that there were casualties in Paris as well at the hands of the droids, but we do not know for certain.)

THE DOCTOR'S MAGICAL SONIC SCREWDRIVER: The Doctor uses the screwdriver to see if the fireplace on the ship is a hologram, and later in Reinette's bedroom to scan for the source of the ticking noise. He also uses it later to repair the mechanism on the fireplace to get back to the future.

REALITY BITES: Jeanne-Antoinette Poisson, Madame de Pompadour, was born in Paris on 29 December 1721 and died on 15 April 1764. Former wife of Charles-Guillaume Le Normant d'Etoilles, with whom she had two children (a boy, who died a year after birth, and a girl, born 1744), she replaced the Duchess of Chateauroux as mistress of King Louis XV after meeting the King on 25 February 1745 at the Yew Tree Ball. Madame de Pompadour wielded enormous power within the French monarchy, and bore the brunt of criticism for France's involvement in the Seven Years War. The Doctor calls her an 'actress, artist, musician, dancer, courtesan, fantastic gardener' and delights in the fact that he's 'snogged' her.

Rose compares Reinette to Camilla Parker-Bowles, Duchess of Cornwall and second wife of Prince Charles. (This does, however, pose another continuity problem; as with 'The Christmas Invasion', it appears to contradict the assertion in the story 'Battlefield' that there was a King on the throne in the late 1990s.)

Reinette decries against commotion and distressing noise. This is very appropriate for the particular era in France and that country's notions of civility.

Rose wears a T-shirt with the name Wichita Falls on it; this city is located in Texas in the United States. Mickey, meanwhile, wears a shirt with the logo of the Famicom (more commonly known in the West as the Nintendo Entertainment System) on it, this due to the fact that the actor, Noel Clarke, is a Nintendo fan. Mickey's 'You looking at me?' line pays homage to the Robert de Nero film *Taxi Driver* (1976), while the Doctor's 'Thickania' tirade is possibly an homage to *Blackadder the Third* (1987), although a similar line appeared in the episode 'The Girl with One Heart' from Moffat's series *Coupling*.

LINKING THEMES: The Doctor and Rose remind Mickey that the TARDIS translates languages for its crew, in this case French to English; this notion has been used in several of the series' episodes, dating back to 'The End of the World' in the current series. The Doctor's twin hearts are referenced. Mickey mentions their recent meeting with Sarah Jane Smith and also refers to the Doctor knowing the famous Egyptian queen Cleopatra. (He's mentioned her only once, but called her 'Cleo'.) Rose refers to the Daleks and their name for the Doctor ('The Oncoming Storm,' previously mentioned in 'The Parting of the Ways'). There is also a reference to Zeus Plugs, a type of tool mentioned in 'The Hand of Fear' (1976); the Doctor says he has just been using them as castanets.

The Doctor's telepathic abilities are brought to the forefront here. These abilities had been alluded to earlier in the series, but rather more obliquely. In 'The Three Doctors' (1972/73) and 'The Five Doctors' (1983), various incarnations of the Doctor had made 'contact' with each other without touching. The Doctor had also placed Sarah into a state of 'suspended animation' through the use of either telepathy or hypnotism in 'Terror of the Zygons' (1975) – perhaps the closest precedent to what he does in 'The Girl in the Fireplace' – and had communicated with the Time Lords by projecting his thoughts into a makeshift contact device (created with the six sides of a cube) in 'The War Games' (1969). His granddaughter Susan had demonstrated telepathic abilities too, in 'The Sensorites' (1964), and the Doctor had told his then companion Ian Chesterton that sometimes he knew what he was thinking. The TARDIS, of course, has telepathic circuits.

The Doctor says he can't dance with Reinette, obviously because on the night she asks him, she's supposed to dance with the King for the first time. However, this also recalls 'The Doctor Dances', where 'dancing' was used as a metaphor for sex; Reinette says that the Doctor must learn to dance, despite the fact that he did so in that earlier episode.

Reinette asks the question, 'Doctor? Doctor who?', a play on the series' title. The Doctor refers to the old superstition of enduring seven years of bad luck for breaking a mirror, and says, 'Talk about seven years bad luck, try three thousand' – an allusion to the amount of time he'd need to get back to the TARDIS, Rose and Mickey without time travel.

The Doctor describes Reinette as 'fantastic' – his previous incarnation's catchphrase.

SCENE MISSING: There are issues with the continuity of time in this episode. The fireplace, for one thing, poses problems. Several years pass by in Reinette's timeframe between the Doctor's visits, but on some occasions time on her side of the fireplace seems to be moving at the same 'speed' as time on the spaceship. For instance, while the Doctor talks to young Reinette through the fireplace, and later while he promises the older Reinette that he will be right back for her, the timeframes are in sync, and the same is true when he uses the fireplace's rotation mechanism to traverse the time window. This *could* make sense if time moves at the same 'speed' on both sides very near to the fireplace. But later, Reinette herself travels through the window into the future, and yet returns to what must surely be almost the exact same time she left (or her disappearance would have caused considerable problems).

Why do the droids create time windows that link to specific eras, but then also create one, the fireplace, that never seems to link to the same period twice? If it's broken, why haven't they repaired it? This is never explained.

Why, also, is the Doctor surprised when he returns the last time and finds that years have again passed and Reinette is dead? On each occasion he's passed through the fireplace, he's found that a considerable period of time has passed in Reinette's timeframe. So why promise he'll be back in two minutes? (Could he be that smitten that he's just forgotten?) One must also wonder why the Doctor is content just to accept that the answer to why the droids were after Reinette will remain an enigma; it's not in his nature to accept a mystery at face value and not pursue it.

Still on the subject of the fireplace, if the young Reinette can see the Doctor through the flames, then surely she can see the interior of the station through the hole? Why does she not comment about *that*? If Reinette moved the fireplace from Paris to Versailles, presumably brick by brick, did she have the part of the floor that rotates moved as well? (Viewers can see that the rotation mechanism incorporates part of the patterned floor on both sides. But surely, if the fireplace is simply the location of the temporal gateway, it shouldn't have any moving parts? Why do the fireplace and the window have to rotate at all?) Since none of the other portals has a duplicate façade in the spaceship – e.g. there is no mirror corresponding with the one in the ballroom – then why is the fireplace double-sided in the first place? Also, at the start of the episode, the fireplace clock is broken on the spaceship side, and yet the clockwork droid is already under Reinette's bed... so shouldn't the broken clock be the one on the other side? And if the fireplace had been taken apart and reassembled in Versailles, and was technically offline when the mirrors went out, then how did Reinette hear the screams and her own voice calling for the Doctor while she was on the spaceship?

The droids are a mystery in themselves. Why would a 51st Century spacecraft with advanced warp drive technology employ repair droids that operate on technology several thousand years old? (K-9 was, after all, a product of the same century, and although the retro look was in, as the Doctor said, he was still an advanced device.) Why would the crew have allowed the repair droids to get to the point where they were even *capable* of harming them? And how would the body parts of the crew serve as useful repair parts for the ship? The episode demonstrates three technologies (organic, futuristic and clockwork), none of which is remotely compatible with the others by today's understanding.

(It should be noted that this episode's TARDISode intimates that all electronics were knocked offline by the ion storm; theoretically this explains why droids would be used instead. It does *not* explain why they're there in the first place.)

Where did the costumes and masks the droids use in France come from? They don't appear to have hands or fingers, only retractable blades and other tools, so they can't have made them, given that this would have required a sewing machine for the 'fine needlework' the Doctor comments on. (They couldn't have had replicator machines, otherwise they'd have made the spare parts the ship needed in the first place!) Also, the masks and costumes were obviously created as a disguise for the costume ball when Reinette was 37 years old; how did they know they'd need them when they couldn't pinpoint when she would be 'compatible'? Why would they otherwise have needed to wear the masks and costumes? Why did they wear the masks on the ship? Why are there both male-voiced and female-voiced robots, and why do they dress according to that gender?

Why, when the teleporter is used, does the beam go upwards? Why did the late crew of the *SS Madame De Pompadour* or the people who designed the ship give repair droids the capability of teleportation in the first place?

The purpose of the ship is never clearly defined, although one must ask why a deep space scout ship in the 51st Century would be named after an obscure 17th Century French aristocrat.

If this *is* Mickey's first trip in the TARDIS (and there is every indication that it is, given his enthusiasm when they arrive and his rookie attitude toward the whole thing), and if they left immediately after saying goodbye to Sarah Jane Smith at the end of 'School Reunion'... when did Rose have time to stop off and get her hair done?

Finally, why does the Doctor *not* use the TARDIS to get back into history at the end? Let's face it, the Doctor is *always* part of events, but that's never stopped him before.

ALTERED STATES: The working titles for this episode, according to writer Steven Moffat as revealed to *Doctor Who Magazine*, were at various times 'Madame de Pompadour', 'Every Tick of My Heart' and 'Reinette and the Lonely Angel'. Davies called it 'Madame de Pompadour' in his series summary document to the BBC. It was originally scheduled as the second episode of the season; on that plan, 'Rise of the Cybermen' and 'The Age of Steel' would have been aired as episodes four and five respectively.

BEHIND THE SCENES: Much of 'The Girl in the Fireplace' was recorded inside the BBC's Newport studios. Dyffryn Gardens, an estate on the outskirts of Cardiff, was used for the outdoor sequences in the garden, and a building at the site was used to record interior sequences in Reinette's bedroom. The main ballroom of the palace at Versailles was actually Ragley Hall in Alcester, Warwickshire, while Reinette's studio was created inside a room in Tredegar House, Newport (also used for 'Tooth and Claw').

The horse jump was recorded on location at the David Broome Event Centre, Crick, near Chepstow, Monmouthshire. The recording of the jump involved two horses (one named Bolero, the other one actually named Arthur), and the sequence was placed into the action via CGI, with the head of David Tennant substituting that of the stunt rider.

There is no reference to Torchwood in this episode, because writer Steven Moffat was not told ahead of time to drop the word into the script. According to Moffat, he had not read the end of the script for 'School Reunion' prior to writing this story; hence Rose's positive reaction to Mickey being in the TARDIS at the outset, in contrast to the negativity she evidenced in the prior episode. Mofatt revealed in an instalment of *Doctor Who Confidential* that the droids were inspired by the Turk, a famous hoax from the 18th Century, which appeared as a clockwork chess player but was in fact a chess master hiding inside, operating the mechanism. Moffat also clarified the line about the 'secret' around the Doctor's name; since he doesn't even tell his travelling companions his real name, there must be some sort of big secret he's keeping.

Actor Noel Clarke noted on *Doctor Who Confidential* that the fire extinguishers really *were* fire extinguishers, modified to appear like guns on screen and labelled with the warning, 'Do not use to cool drinks, freeze food, win arguments, or create Christmas grotto decorations'. The portrait of Madame de Pompadour seen at the end of the episode was painted by Cardiff-based artist Amanda Clegg.

David Tennant and Sophia Myles began dating after the recording of this story. The two previously met on the set of *Foyle's War* (2002).

DULCET TONES: As the Doctor stumbles into the control room of the spacecraft while apparently drunk, he sings 'I Could Have Danced All Night'. This song was written for and made famous by the 1956 stage musical *My Fair Lady* and the subsequent 1964 film adaptation starring Audrey Hepburn and Rex Harrison. It was the work of Frederick Loewe (music) and Alan Jay Lerner (lyrics) and was first sung on stage by actress Julie Andrews. Versions of the song were later recorded by many artists including Sylvia Syms, Rosemary Clooney, Dinah Shore, Frank Sinatra and Jamie Cullum.

OFF THE SCREEN: Sophia Myles portrayed Erika in *Underworld* (2003) and its sequel *Underworld: Evolution* (2006) as well as the female lead title character in *Tristan & Isolde* (2006); she's also been seen in *Art School Confidential* (2006), *Marple: 'Sleeping Murder'* (2005), *Thunderbirds* (2004), *Out of Bounds* (2004), *Foyle's War* (2002), *Heartbeat* (2001) and *Oliver Twist* (1999). Angel Coulby was also seen in *Hustle* (2006), *Vincent* (2005), *The League of Gentlemen's Apocalypse* (2005), *MIT: Murder Investigation Team* (2005), *Holby City* (2004), *As If* (2004), *Manchild* (2003) and *Casualty* (2002). Gareth Wyn Griffiths has appeared in *Duplicity* (2004). Ben Turner was also seen in *Love Soup* (2005) and *Casualty* (2005). Ellen Thomas was in *Basic Instinct 2* (2006), *Casualty* (2005), *The Bill* (2002), *Teachers* (2001), *Ultraviolet* (1998) and *The Lenny Henry Show* (1987). Emily Joyce is a regular in the series *My Hero* (2000-) playing the role of Janet Dawkins, and was also seen in *Midsomer Murders* (2002), *Grafters* (1998), *Casualty* (1997) and *Cracker* (1995). Paul Kasey returned to *Doctor Who* after appearing in five Series One episodes in various roles. Writer Steven Moffat's other credits were listed in the first *Back To The Vortex*.

TECHNICAL GOOFS: The Doctor meets Reinette in 1727, but says she's aged seven; the historical figure was born on 29 December 1721 and could not have been seven years old by 1727. Also, the nickname Reinette ('little queen' in French) was not in fact given to her until 1730.

When the Doctor launches through the mirror on the horse, the stuntman's wig is too big. Certain words (such as 'monsieur' and 'de Pompadour') stay in the original French, contradicting the claim that the TARDIS always translates all languages. Or perhaps it's cleverer than that and can be selective as appropriate.

CONTROVERSIES: Perhaps more so than any other this season, this episode received significant criticism from some fans concerned that *Doctor Who* had entered the realm of the romance, specifically in the relationship between the Doctor and Reinette. The media also wondered why the Doctor, portrayed as nearly asexual throughout the prior four decades, was all of a sudden cock-a-hoop over 'snogging' Madame de Pompadour. There were rumblings, too, over the developing relationship between the Doctor and Rose, which was generally felt to be rather less subtle than during the series' first year. As Davies told the *Independent*, this episode is: '... practically a love story for the Doctor... It's very understated, very beautifully done, but it's nonetheless a Time Lord falling in love and Rose's reaction to him falling in love with someone else.' Generally overlooked in all this was the fact that the first Doctor (William

Hartnell) had had a similar, albeit more understated, romance in his very first season, in 'The Aztecs' (1964).

INTERNAL CONSISTENCY: The episode appears to take place immediately after 'School Reunion', as Mickey notes that he 'got a spaceship on [his] first go'.

Writer Steven Moffat says on the BBC online commentary that while the subtitle after the opening credits states '3,000 years later', it is actually about 3,400 years after the scenes in Paris; it's merely 3,000 years after Rose's (and the viewers') present.

TARDISODE #4: Aboard the SS *Madame de Pompadour*, two crewmembers witness an explosion in space that develops from an ion storm. One of the crew sends out a mayday signal. Later, the viewer sees something unidentified (one of the droids, no doubt, given the ticking noise) approach the woman, who lies on the ground. She screams as it draws close to her, obviously intent on harming her. Then the clock on the mantelpiece of the fireplace shatters.

REVIEWS

This fairy tale of an episode may be as close to a masterpiece as the new series has yet achieved, transcending our expectations of what *Doctor Who* is and offering a lovely piece of emotionally-charged science-fiction storytelling. Classic *Who* rarely delved into the complexities of time itself, but this is an intricate time-travel-fuelled romantic adventure in which the logic is precise, the narrative seamless, and the characterisation mesmerising. The surrealism reaches a stylistic high point when Mickey just sweeps aside a tapestry to step from the deck of the 51st Century ship to an 18th Century mansion. There are too many beautiful elements to list – *that* kiss, David Tennant's (finally!) nuanced performance; Reinette's table-turning insight into the Doctor's lonely existence; the monster under the bed scene; and of course the show-stopping (albeit not technically polished) nick-of-time arrival of the Doctor on horseback. From the pre-credits sequence set during the story's climax to the final shot that resolves the mystery of why the droids were after Reinette in the first place, the entire episode alternately elicits chills or tears. The tale's childlike innocence is reflected in Murray Gold's evocative music box score and the myriad literary influences from J M Barrie to L Frank Baum to C S Lewis, to say nothing of its debt to one of the few intellectually experimental *Who*s of the classic era, 'Warriors' Gate'. Sophia Myles completely convinces as a woman of allure and intellect, exactly the kind of individual you could imagine being worthy of the Doctor's love. While Rose is all well and good, she's a child, while Reinette would be the closest thing to an equal for the Doctor since Romana left ages ago. What's this?, I hear you ask. You're praising the notion of a romantic, sexually active Doctor? Oh hell, why not? Hasn't the man earned it by now? My blessing, Doctor, you deserve it; time to dance. But what of Rose? With 'The Girl in the Fireplace', the sense that Billie Piper's Rose is being cast off with every progressive episode, underscored by her realisation in 'School Reunion' that she's not the only companion and now by the Doctor's willingness to find 'true love' with another, is starting to feel less like unfortunate scripting and more like a calculated arc. Her sense of her true place in the Doctor's vast history is doubtless going to become more and more profound for Rose as time goes on, perhaps even leading to her inevitable departure. Strangely though, after Rose's petulant fit about taking Mickey along last week, she now seems delighted that he's there, hanging all over him and giving him the veteran's tour of the universe. They make a nice team, but it feels incongruous given her past behaviour, as does her muted reaction to the Doctor's relationship with Reinette. As for Mickey, Noel Clarke doesn't have too much to do, but he does it well. In an early interview for Series One, Christopher Eccleston said of the Time Lord: 'He's got two hearts. They can both be broken.' 'The Girl in the Fireplace' is the profound realisation of that idea crafted by a production team working at the height of its powers. Given that four episodes of the first series received Hugo nominations, it will surely be a crime if this one doesn't get a nod in next year's awards. – *Arnold T Blumberg*

I suspect that many of my fellow reviewers will be raving about Steven Moffat's script, so first I thought I'd spend some time raving about the other excellent contributions that made 'The Girl In The Fireplace' so outstanding. First of all, Murray Gold's score is among his best for the entire series, particularly the music for the last five minutes, which is so haunting it stays with you for weeks afterward. Then there's David Tennant's final scene in the TARDIS, where he tells Rose 'I'm always all right', and then wordlessly toys with the console, demonstrating a whole universe of pain without saying a single word. And if I'm praising performances, I cannot say enough about the wonderful work of Sophia Myles, who plays to perfection someone you can believe the Doctor would totally fall in love with in the space of a few hours. All this is ignoring the sublime design – the clockwork robots are gorgeous to look at. And the practical and effects work – I had no idea the horse wasn't in the ballroom!

It is hard for me to limit myself on what I loved about Steven Moffat's script, but let me briefly highlight a few key points. The story is really quite cerebral and experimental in style and tone (in fact the closest analogue for it would not be in any previous TV story but rather the stories in the *Doctor Who Annual*), but Moffat makes sure all the pieces are there so the viewer can put the picture together in a satisfying way. More than that, Moffat gets Davies' mandate that emotions are the cornerstone for any *Doctor Who* adventure, and so the Doctor's growing feelings for Reinette make what could have been a sub-par *Sapphire and Steel*-type episode into something really meaningful. And then there are the little touches. While Rose is left out of most of the adventure (a shame, really), her question to the Doctor at the end, 'Why her?', is about much more than the motivation for the robots stalking Reinette, which is staggering in its subtlety. And while the story is clearly about the Doctor falling in love, Moffat is still nice enough to cut away from any actual action so that the Doctor need not be boringly heterosexual like other heroes, if that's how we prefer it. It's staggering the way all these things contribute to the success of 'The Girl In The Fireplace', but they're all tiny little miracles, each of them, and they create a broader work that is both engrossing and deeply affecting emotionally. Powerful stuff, to be sure. – *Graeme Burk*

Once upon a time, there was a hero – not like every other hero, but a one-of-a-kind adventurer who stood for justice, peace and harmony throughout time and space. He stood for everyone, everywhere... And then he kissed a girl. If I've made you think of the Doctor from 'The Girl in the Fireplace', you're right – or are you? The hue and cry of this week's kiss is a throwback to the controversy almost *exactly* ten years ago with the TV movie, and the arguments are the same: 'The Doctor is an alien / a non-sexual being / above that stuff.' When we have these conflicts, though, we're rarely talking about the Doctor as a character. We're talking about ourselves as viewers. Who we are – male or female, young or old, gay or straight – informs our point of view as to what kind of people our heroes should be. One could argue that in the earlier series, the Doctor was never categorised or forced to represent one point of view over the other. Yet you might also say he was a patronising, misogynistic member of the upper class.

Attitudes change over time, and wide-eyed child viewers grow up to become cynical adults. The television of 2006 is driven by different commercial concerns than the television of 1966. Most importantly, however, we should remember that 'The Girl in the Fireplace' is an anomaly. Back in the old days, *Doctor Who* would, every once in a great while, try a story that pushed the envelope of what was both technically possible and logically reasonable, taking the series so far into the realm of the fantastic that whatever it was, you could be sure it wasn't normal *Doctor Who*. 'The Mind Robber', 'Warriors' Gate' and 'Enlightenment' are all examples of truly unusual tales that both divide fans and stand as some of the most imaginative instalments in the show's history. They are also among my personal favourite stories. Steven Moffat carries on the tradition with a story that is part childhood fantasy, part 18th Century historical and part time travel romance. Superficially, it seems precisely like the sort of thing an American series starring Paul McGann would have come up with every week: slick drama, jumping from the past to the future, with a love interest of the week and a tidy story told in 45 minutes. But this is not an American series, nor is it trying to be. This is Moffat and the production team pushing the envelope to see how we'll react – and boy, have we ever snapped at the bait. Right now, 'The Girl in the Fireplace' feels a bit out of place in this year's line-up. It's not the cleanest of follow-throughs from 'School Reunion' (Rose seems to have dropped her grudge against Mickey), and the second half is notably weaker than the first, with a rather surprising lapse in logic from the Doctor. (Doesn't he remember how time works differently in Reinette's world?) Give it a few years, though, and I'm willing to bet fans will look back and cherry-pick this episode as one of the most fresh and innovative this era of *Doctor Who* had to offer. Euros Lyn's direction is absolutely sumptuous, Tennant and Myles have excellent chemistry, and the basic concept – whether the resolution works or not – is extremely smart. I don't love it unreservedly, but I have found myself wanting to go back to it again and again. I think other fans will, too. Kiss or no kiss, this one's going to stand the test of time. – *Sarah Hadley*

In the previous episode the Doctor was telling Rose about how distressing it is to see human beings he cares about wither and die while he lives on. In 'The Girl in the Fireplace' we get a glimpse of this aspect of the Doctor's world in microcosm. Riffing off a similar basic idea to Audrey Niffenegger's wonderful novel *The Time Traveller's Wife*, it shows us what it's like for the Doctor to pop back and forth into and out of the life of one person in the space of a few minutes, something he usually does on a larger scale and over a longer period of time. The key difference being, of course, that the Doctor doesn't usually end up falling in love with those whose paths intersect with his. Yes, it's a *Doctor Who* love story, not something I ever would have hoped or expected to see in the series – I am not generally a fan of stories of romance. But with Steven Moffat's skill as a scriptwriter and two superb central performances from Tennant and Myles, I was utterly sold on it, and 'The Girl in the Fireplace' immediately ranks for me as by far and away the strongest episode of Series Two so far. Like last week's episode it packs a hefty emotional punch, but unlike 'School Reunion', the affecting scenes aren't let down by other areas of the script. Moffat is always a very strong plotter, as evidenced both in his sitcoms and in his previous *Doctor Who* episodes last year, and he has created an intricate but never over-complex story where everything works, everything makes sense and there is a pay-off that gives you a sense of satisfaction and completeness. That is, if you're not still left bereft by the rather achingly haunting and sad conclusion to the episode. Production-wise too, everyone is firing on all cylinders, with one of the best *Doctor Who* spaceships yet seen, typically lavish BBC period design in the 18th Century scenes, and of course the *pièce de résistance*, the horse-through-the-mirror stunt that by all accounts nearly didn't make it into the final episode, but was clearly worth every penny they spent on it. A word of praise too for Murray Gold's excellent score, which occasionally and perhaps unsurprisingly evokes his work on last year's Russell T Davies period drama *Casanova*, which also placed David Tennant in an unconventional 18th Century setting. You wouldn't want *Doctor Who* to be like this every single week, and indeed the episode would have been far less affecting if that were the case. But as a change of pace from the typical action, adventure and thrills and spills of even the new series, thoughtful and layered though it often is, it's a welcome addition to the pantheon of styles and themes *Doctor Who* now explores so confidently. Magnificent stuff, a great piece of television, and I cannot wait for the next time that Steven Moffat graces *Doctor Who* with one of his scripts. – *Paul Hayes*

Ooh, posh frocks and big hair! Not *Dynasty*, but time to play in the dressing up box again. Beginning the story *in media res* is something of a departure for *Doctor Who*, which, surprisingly for a series that concerns time travel, has always preferred a linear narrative. But there's no doubt that it immediately drags the viewer in. How does this woman know who the Doctor is? What are the tick-tocking killing machines? And why on Earth is she shouting into a fireplace? The rationale is set up quite quickly, allowing the audience to buy into the concept of two space/time zones linked together. The idea that time flows at different rates in different places is nothing new in science-fiction, but it takes a steady hand to ensure that it works properly... and sadly, the usually reliable Steven Moffat – who has played around with this non-linear narrative form in his sitcoms *Joking Apart* and *Coupling* – drops the ball here. For such a stretch of imagination to be believable, it has to be self-consistent, and here time on Reinette's side of the fireplace seems to move as required by the plot rather than according to any internal logic. But 'The Girl in the Fireplace' isn't really dependant on hard-core physics. At its centre is the one thing that is anathema to far too many fans: this is a story about the Doctor falling in love. By now, it must be obvious to even the most cynical viewer that the tenth Doctor is even more passionate than his predecessor, but passion has never really been a stranger to the series except to those too blind to actually see it. Watch the end of 'The Green Death' and tell me that the Doctor's not just been dumped! To be honest, the plot is nothing more than window dressing: the clockwork robots, the wonderful horse, the beautiful set pieces... they're just there to highlight the Doctor falling in love. And why not with Madame de Pompadour? The woman was a genius – the uncrowned queen of France, but responsible for so very much more. If ever there was a human female equal to the Doctor, she is it. And they both know it. She sees his loneliness, and he sees her brilliance and compassion. A match made in heaven, played to perfection by Tennant and Sophia Myles. Even once all the clockwork nonsense is over and it looks like he's stranded in the past, he doesn't mind – if anything, he seems to relish the thought. But why doesn't he realise that, once he's fixed the fireplace, the time differential will mean her death? Has love clouded his reason? But forget the logic, the sidelining of Rose and Mickey, the lapses in reason in the script and in the Doctor's actions. All of it is worth overlooking for that single moment when the Doctor reads her letter. Has he ever looked so sad, so old, so *alone*? I confess to weeping buckets at that moment, which is truly one of the classic scenes in the whole canon. While the revelation of the name of the ship resolves some of the narrative problems, it's really rather irrelevant. This is a story that can be told only once. True, the background plot could have been better, but it is nothing more than a frame for *that* moment. And therefore worth its weight in gold. – *Craig Hinton*

All credit to writer Steven Moffat – presumably drawing on Davies' big sheaf of *Casanova* research notes – for doing a story that fits in (just) with *Doctor Who* but is structurally and tonally unlike anything else the show has attempted. Writers used to be prohibited from using time travel as a plot motor (or get-out clause) – but here it's handled, *without* recourse to the TARDIS, in a fresh manner with a series of 'windows' between a spaceship in the future and rooms inhabited by Madame de Pompadour at points in her life in 18th Century France. As in Moffat's last season two-parter, the McGuffin is a broken-down spaceship, while malign-seeming monsters (clockwork robots in period finery, vaguely reminiscent of 'The Robots of Death' without being imitations) cause panic and threaten atrocities but turn out to be mindlessly attempting to fulfil their original programming. Threats to cut off heads grow thin when they never lead to anything: we find out what's been done to the human crew of the ship from a smell of cooking, and an eye and a heart used as spare parts, but – at 7.00 pm on BBC1 – obviously aren't going to get real grue. It's a refreshing change that this is a story actually about the Doctor (Tennant's enthusiasm is starting to be a workable reading of the role) rather than his companions, with a guest star turn for Sophia Myles (hitherto mostly the best thing in irredeemably terrible films with 'under' in the title) that amounts to 45 minutes of historical footnotes and the refreshing, well-written point that Reinette intellectually (and emotionally) grasps the situation rather than gawps in stereotypical thickie-from-past-takes-science-for-sorcery manner. The theme of 'The Doctor Dances' is explicitly invoked as the Doctor dances again in the show's first lovers-across-time romance. This sub-genre comprises of works like *The Portrait of Jennie* (in which the hero similarly encounters the girl at different periods of a too-brief life, meeting her first as a child, then a grown woman) or the novel *Time and Again* (by Jack Finney, who did a few short stories on the theme). 'The Girl in the Fireplace' is a novel variation, though the hectic pace of a 45-minute show means we don't quite get the sense of time crawling by for Reinette as the Doctor nips in and out of her life at crisis points even as we realise (and suspect the Doctor does too) what'll happen at the end when he nips back to the ship promising to return instantly for the girl who's dead by the time he gets back. (He knew enough about her life to realise when it would end and might surely have scruples about snatching a well-known historical character from the timeline.) It's probably going to be more controversial that the Doctor seems to be in love with Reinette, though there are qualifiers that strike me as breaking with established character far less than, say, the Paul McGann TV movie: it's clear that Reinette loves the Doctor – she kisses him rather than the other way round – and he feels deeply for her, but raises a fine character point that he can become more involved with a woman whose life he fast-forwards inside an hour (from the Doctor's POV, the episode takes place in real-time) than the girl who's been right next to him for a season and a half and might be wondering whether or not she'd be better off with Mickey (who, at this rate, will cop off with a Cyberman next week and give Rose even more complexes) after all. – *Kim Newman*

What is romantic love? Underneath all the leather and lace there seem to be two basic assumptions: that it's between just two people; that it lasts for the rest of their lives. Underpinning those assumptions is an even deeper one: this is a matter of sex, of children. We mate for life. The original series assiduously avoided romance. The moment the new *Who* began to deal with this long-missing element, it ran up against a basic problem in the show's premise. The Doctor, whether you imagine he keeps his trousers on or no, is a serial monogamist. It's not by choice. Sarah Jane was unusual in that she was left behind: more often, his companions leave him of their own accord. But even the most devoted companion would eventually 'wither and die'. So what's the Doctor going to do when he meets the perfect match? Because, whatever he thinks or Reinette hopes, *they are not compatible.* Everything in the episode warns us that they can never be together: the ticking of clocks, the 'loose connection', even the way the Doctor is just beginning to hold Reinette when she breaks off her kiss and leaves. It takes the greatest human geniuses to approach the Doctor's mental level – think of Liz Shaw with her jillion degrees – and Reinette has the added advantage of actually having been inside his thoughts, something even Rose hasn't done. They are part of each other's childhoods. So their minds may be compatible – but their bodies aren't. Even with a happy ending, Reinette's life would have flashed before the Doctor's eyes. He is effectively an immortal. They make bad lovers. With plenty of familiar fictional precedents, of course, we can imagine the Doctor staying with Reinette until she dies. Her being the perfect mate is not enough. There also needs to be an impenetrable wall between him and his former life aboard the TARDIS – or so he thinks. Part of Reinette must know that she is giving him up forever when she shows him the way back – that he would wither and die on the slow path. The story implies a horrifying image of immortality for Reinette: her brain transplanted into the metal 'body' of the SS *Madame de Pompadour*. This would not be Reinette in any way we could recognise; she may be brilliant, but she is not simply a brain. Perhaps none of us can become part of the Doctor's world forever without losing some crucial part of ourselves – even Rose. There's a wall between these two worlds, and we can't break it down. – *Kate Orman*

Even though I'd seen the enticing trailers, I knew very little about this story beforehand, so I couldn't form many preconceptions. It was certainly another enjoyable and solid production from director Euros Lyn, but I found it lacked the 'wow' factor that the previous three stories had, despite the clever surprise twist at the end (which was like a similar moment with the 'Mary Celeste' in 'The Chase'). This story had a number of parallels with Moffat's 'The Empty Child': the 51st Century [check], bananas [yep], and the Doctor dancing [present]. Rose's first trip in the TARDIS was to a space station; Adam's first trip in the TARDIS, a space station; Mickey's first trip – guess what, it's a space station! The main difference here is that in the two previous examples, the viewer joined in as the new TARDIS crew member explored with a sense of wonder and excitement, but in Mickey's case there was very little in the way of Mickey/viewer exploration. More frustratingly, both Rose and Mickey were somewhat redundant – they had very little to do apart from getting captured and tied up, although Rose did get to share a lovely scene with Reinette. Mickey on the other hand was once again simply the comic relief (though it must be said Noel Clarke has great comic timing). It makes me wonder what the point was of bringing in Mickey as a regular – but of course the producers' grand plan for Mickey presumably will play out in subsequent episodes... The clockwork robots were a neat, typically *Doctor Who* idea, but one that didn't seem quite... right. I mean, I find it hard to accept that clockwork robots would be used in the 51st Century. This is, after all, the time period the original K-9 is from! The robots themselves were a fantastic design concept, with so much detail in the clock mechanism, but all for so little screen time. It's a great waste that we saw more of the costumed robots than we did of them, er, naked. Which brings me to the lovely Sophia Myles. No doubt many fans will get all up in arms about the French kissing. But it made perfect sense in the context of the story (as did the kiss in 'New Earth'). I have no problem with this whatsoever. Besides, we know the Doctor has previously had an attraction to historical France – for instance the Reign of Terror – and he knew Marie Antoinette quite well, so his affection for Reinette could quite likely be just another notch in a long line of French aristocratic dalliances! 'The Girl in the Fireplace' was both scary ('The Reinette of Terror'?!) and heart-wrenchingly sad, but also a *joie à cœur*. And I love it to bits! Oh, and I've noticed that 'The Christmas Invasion' had hints of Arthurian imagery (Guinevere, the sword in the stone, some lines of dialogue taken from 'Battlefield'); and now we get Arthur the horse! Coincidence? – *Jon Preddle*

Charming, witty, mature, touching, beautiful and containing a sense of both wonder and *magnificence*. 'The Girl in the Fireplace' was all these things and many, many others. Steven Moffat had already demonstrated his mastery of dramatic conceits, wry irony and cunning allegory in the previous year's masterpiece 'The Doctor Dances'. 'The Girl in the Fireplace' was a perfect reminder – if any reminder were needed – that his skill at making an audience laugh with, and care about, characters has not diminished in the slightest. The man is a star, and his scripts are white-peppered with scattergun golden moments. That the intricate and multi-layered plot worked as well as it did – one is tempted to say 'like clockwork' at this point – is a tribute to Moffat's vision. That the episode progressed beyond mere conceptual cleverness and into some genuinely groundbreaking areas of human insight required the help of a pair of quite dazzling performances from Sophia Myles and David Tennant. This was the *Doctor Who* that finally – after 42 years – gave the lie to the idea that the series cannot ever portray its central character as an inherently tragic figure. And the loneliness at the Doctor's core, of which Reinette was given a caustic taste, helped to explain so many odd and disquieting moments from the series' past. The electricity between the pair was tangible – which for once meant that Billie Piper was relegated to some pithy quips from the sidelines in an amusing double act with Noel Clarke. The dialogue was just about as good as in any *Doctor Who* script I can remember ('I mean this from the heart. And, by the way, count these'; 'Became the imaginary friend of a future French aristocrat. Picked a fight with a Clockwork Man. And I met a horse'; 'You're Mr Thick-Thick-Thickety-Thick-Face from Thicktown, Thickania... and so's yer dad!'; 'One may tolerate a world of demons for the sake of an angel'). There were also great music and costumes and design to go with the extraordinary performances and outrageous conceits. 'The Girl in the Fireplace' was the moment when, for one fan at least, *Doctor Who* finally and irrevocably grew-up. A seriously mature and knowing story with depth, weight and soul. It was a defining statement, a genius move, a thing of outstanding, terrible beauty. It is, quite possibly, my favourite *Doctor Who* episode ever, and it deserves to be praised again and again for daring, *daring*, to be different. 'I'm not winding you up.' Wonderful. – *Keith Topping*

EDITOR'S REVIEW: There comes a point when a fan must accept that whatever he (or she) has seen transpire before is old news, and today will instead bring something different. *Doctor Who* fans are no exception to this; throughout the series' long history, we've been witness to events that seem far fetched (or even flat out *wrong*) when compared to earlier times. The stagnant, antiquated lore of the Time Lords comes to mind; who could have predicted back in 1963 that the Doctor's people would turn out to be a bunch of old-time bankers patting themselves on the back, drinking cosmic brandy and smoking the intergalactic equivalent of cigars to pass the time? Drama is about a lot of things – characters, story development, atmosphere, morality, justice – but the truly exciting thing about it is *change*. Change is good; change demonstrates progress; which in turn is why we care about characters and watch what they do.

In the case of 'The Girl in the Fireplace', there are changes galore, both germane to the story and its production, and tangential to the mythos that *Doctor Who* established so long ago. When we met the Doctor for the first time, we knew he had a granddaughter and therefore was probably capable of physical love at some point, but it wasn't what we wanted to think about; so many of us preferred to view him as the archetypal wanderer, the rogue with the heart of gold setting wrongs to right and never forming permanent attachments with the people he saves. This time, however, we are confronted with the basic concept that the Doctor can love – that he has loved, and will love, and does love, and it might not in fact be with any of the people he's travelling with at the time. At first in the young Reinette, the Doctor finds a juxtaposition of innocence and strength; she is naïve but spirited, a young girl with no sense of the history to be placed upon her, yet unflinching in her defiance of the mysterious Clockwork Man who appears at her bedside. (She also seems to trust the Doctor unswervingly; perhaps an insight into her sense that she, and he, are both part of something larger.)

The irony lies in the fact that when we watch the Doctor fall for Reinette – no review or critic can change my mind about that – we may not be able to see what he sees in her. Viewers are left with the pieces to a puzzle; that's a fact of life, as we are seeing only the bits that are relevant to the story. Yet he obviously finds in her something that we the viewers may not; it is a credit to writer Steven Moffat that he subtly reminds us of just what it is that the Doctor might find attractive, whether it's her telepathic connection to him and her ability to step through the doors that he's unlocked, or perhaps her sensibility that the universe is a far larger place than the Earth, or Versailles, or her bedroom and its mysterious fireplace. It isn't because of her beauty, or her smile or charm or grace; the Doctor has, in essence, fallen in love with her mind. Which, in turn, makes Rose more uncomfortable than she wants to admit... and we're suddenly watching a different series than we've watched all these years.

For *Doctor Who*, which tells tales of adventure and high drama, seldom resorts to poetry. And lyrical poetry is what we've witnessed in 'The Girl in the Fireplace'; perhaps the most atypical *Doctor Who* tale to date, performed with the presence and sensibility of a two-act stage play – no fancy trappings, just a few rooms in a French chateau and a lonely spaceship corridor, the villains masked in fancy dress, the words substituting for the action we would otherwise expect from the programme. There are no sword fights, no grand poignant speeches from the Doctor about the nature of evil – in fact, there's really no evil to be found here at all, if you consider that the repair droids are simply broken pieces of clockwork. All we have are characters on a stage, speaking meaningfully, pondering the nature of love and the meaning of eternity, and how these windows to reality have torn down the barriers between star-crossed lovers separated by three thousand lonely years.

'The Girl in the Fireplace' isn't the best story ever told by *Doctor Who*, but it might just be the most beautiful. I think we can all do with a bit of that in our lives, now and then. – *Shaun Lyon*

205: RISE OF THE CYBERMEN

A malfunctioning TARDIS sends the Doctor, Rose and Mickey into a parallel universe whose Earth stands on the brink of disaster: a brilliant but ruthless man has unlocked the secrets of cyborg technology. Now, a new variety of enemies the Doctor has faced for centuries stands ready to achieve domination over another reality – the Cybermen are once again on the move.

FIRST TRANSMISSION: UK – 13 May 2006. US – 27 October 2006. Canada – 6 November 2006. Australia – 12 August 2006. New Zealand – 10 August 2006.
DURATION: 46'03"
WRITER: Tom MacRae
DIRECTOR: Graeme Harper
CREDITED CAST: David Tennant (The Doctor), Billie Piper (Rose Tyler), Camille Coduri (Jackie Tyler), Noel Clarke (Mickey Smith), Shaun Dingwall (Pete Tyler), Roger Lloyd Pack (John Lumic), Andrew Hayden-Smith (Jake Simmonds), Don Warrington (The President), Mona Hammond (Rita-Anne), Helen Griffin (Mrs Moore), Colin Spaull (Mr Crane), Paul Antony-Barber (Dr Kendrick), Adam Shaw (Morris), Andrew Ufondo (Soldier), Duncan Duff (Newsreader), Paul Kasey (Cyber-Leader), Nicholas Briggs (Cyber-Voice)

Cybermen originally created by Kit Pedler and Gerry Davis
With thanks to Marc Platt

WHERE AND WHEN: London, Earth in an alternate universe, 1 February 2007.

THE STORY UNFOLDS: On an alternate dimension Earth, where Zeppelins rule the skies, Cybus Industries, created and owned by reclusive businessman John Lumic, is a global conglomerate that owns just about every company in Britain including the Cybus Network (a mobile phone network), International Electromatics (a dummy company established to do Lumic's dirty work) and Vitex (a health drink brand, bought from Pete Tyler). Their main work involves sustaining the brain indefinitely within 'a cradle of copyrighted chemicals' inside a metal exoskeleton body – in effect, the 'ultimate upgrade'. The company has a plant in Battersea, South London, where the upgrades are taking place – test subjects are being converted into Cybermen.

The Doctor says these Cybermen have 'had all their humanity taken away', a living brain jammed inside a cybernetic body: '... with a heart of steel. All emotions removed.' The Cybermen describe themselves as the next level of mankind, human point two. Upgrading is compulsory for humanity, or so they believe; the alternative is to be 'deleted'. The Cybermen have gone through several prototypes; their designer, Dr Kendrick, is killed after demanding that Lumic submit to ratification of the design by Geneva, because as a new form of life, they contravene the bio-convention.

Lumic and Cybus Industries have created a system of earpods worn by most of the people in Great Britain (and presumably the entire world). The earpods plug the wearer into Cybus Industries' global communications network, allowing the wearer access to news and information. Sometimes the downloading of information is so intense that the wearer stops in mid-stride while it takes place. The earpods also allow Cybus to access the wearer's brain –

either to read the subject's mind or take it over completely. Lumic uses them to gain details of security arrangements, passwords and encryption services for Jackie's birthday party directly from her brain. Mr Crane later demonstrates that, by grafting them into the ears of some homeless men, he can use them to control their minds.

In the alternate London, technology has enabled interactive adverts and billboards. Instead of a Prime Minister, Great Britain has a President. London is under a 10.00 pm curfew. The marriage of Pete and Jackie is on the rocks. They have no children, but a Yorkshire terrier named Rose. Rose's mobile phone receives the Cybus Network, including its televised news broadcasts. There is a country called New Germany. Whiskey here seems to be a black-market item.

A group of people – including Ricky Smith, Jake Simmonds and Mrs Moore – have been drawn together to investigate Cybus and the mysterious disappearances all over London. They call themselves the Preachers (named for their quest for the 'gospel truth'). They have a hideout, and initially Jake and Mrs Moore are under the missaprehension that Ricky is dead. There is an operative called Gemini inside Cybus Industries, though they don't know his true identity.

The Doctor says that when the Time Lords were in power, people could travel between realities, but when they died, this became impossible; as he says, 'The walls of reality closed, the worlds were sealed.' The TARDIS cannot receive power from the alternate universe; the Doctor compares it to being like 'diesel in a petrol engine' and tells Mickey that they can't just hook up the ship to the national energy grid. However, the TARDIS still has one power cell remaining; the Doctor gives it some of his life so it can grow and eventually replenish the TARDIS within 24 hours. The Doctor's TARDIS is apparently the last one in the universe (or his universe, at any rate).

The security details for the Tyler estate displayed on Lumic's screen read as follows: 'Tyler Residence. Zone/Unrestricted. Security Status: Total Lockdown. Perimeter Active: Cybustech Omega 2 Epsilon. Access: Coded Invite/Full Bodyscan. Security Detail: CybusSecure – 5 Units (Armed). ****Presidential Override: UKDev. 10 Units (Armed) Moving**** Gemini Suppression: Total. Airspace Restriction: Presidential One. No Fly Zone.' This possibly indicates that Cybus is aware of the existence of the spy Gemini, though obviously they don't know his identity.

The Doctor and Rose once went on an adventure on an asteroid where they met a strange munchkin lady with big eyes who breathed fire. Ricky's grandmother knows a 'Mrs Chan' who told her about the friends her grandson hangs out with. One of the waitresses at the party is named Lucy; she's the one carrying the salmon pinwheels. One of the Cybermen platoons that Crane supervises is called Platoon Zero-L-Two.

THE DOCTOR: He believes it would be incredibly foolish for Rose to go after her father in this universe. Blowing on the small power unit in the TARDIS causes him to lose ten years of his life. He hurts himself on the console (kicking it out of frustration). He feels a bit guilty for never having got to know anything about Mickey (and yet, given the opportunity, he chooses again not to get to know Mickey, but to follow Rose instead). He and Rose use the psychic paper as identification so that they can be servants at Jackie's party, and he thinks the fact that the Tylers named their dog Rose is funny.

ROSE TYLER: She's unhappy she was never born here and resents the fact that the Tylers are rich and seem happy without her. She wants desperately to see her father in the parallel universe. She had enough of 'serving' back home – perhaps a reference to her former job in Henrik's department store, or to her brief spell as a dinner lady in 'School Reunion'.

CHARACTER BUILDING: *Mickey Smith* – His parents both left when he was young; his mother couldn't cope, and his father, Jackson Smith, who had worked at the key cutters in Cliffton's Parade, went to Spain and never came back. His grandmother Rita-Anne raised him. He feels responsible for the accident that took her life. He's convinced that the Doctor forgets him, thinks of him as a 'spare part' and has begun to resent his presence in the TARDIS. He has the insight to be able to realise they are stuck in a parallel universe, and that when both he and Rose go off to see their respective family members, the Doctor will always chase her and not him. He has a tattoo on his right arm.

Ricky Smith (Alternate) – Leader of the group investigating Cybus Industries, a wannabe hard man filled with anger and paranoia. With the arrest of someone named 'Thin Jimmy', he now claims to be London's Most Wanted. His grandmother doesn't like his new friends.

John Lumic – Head of Cybus Industries, lives aboard a Zeppelin flying above the world. He was born in Great Britain and is the inventor of high-content metal. Now dying – possibly as a result of which, he needs to use a wheelchair – he has been ruthless in his pursuit of cyborg technology in order to extend his life... but at some point decided to start playing god as well. He considers the Cybermen to be his 'children' and believes he has saved the homeless people he has had murdered by 'elevating' them and giving them 'life eternal'.

Pete Tyler (Alternate) – Here, Pete Tyler never died in a car accident and is still alive; he's taken his crazy ideas about marketing (see last season's 'Father's Day') and turned them into reality, having created a Vitex corporation and become a millionaire. He and Jackie have been married for 20 years, but their relationship has gone sour; while publicly they live together in a huge mansion, in fact he moved out a month ago. He took Jackie to a pub called The George for a pint of cider for her twenty-first birthday. He says Rose feels 'just sort of... right' when he meets her. He thinks that Lumic is brilliant and clever, but not insane. He drives a car with the licence plate PETE 1. Rose says that her version of Pete died when she was six months old.

Jackie Tyler (Alternate) – A shrill, self-important version of Jackie from the Doctor's universe. While Rose says that her mother always loves a party, here Jackie is unhappy with plans for her fortieth birthday celebration, because according to her official biography she's only 39. (The banner stating it's her fortieth particularly upsets her.) Her birthday is 1 February. She's had hand-sculpted floral arrangements by Veronica of Reykjavik brought in for her party and wants Pete to give her a Zeppelin. She receives diamond studded earpieces (which can pick up signals from as far away as Venezuela) as a present from John Lumic.

The President – Elected leader of Great Britain. Some say that he's a puppet of Cybus Industries, but he proves this wrong by denying Lumic permission to engage in cybernetic research in Britain. He thinks Vitex tastes like pop (which, of course, it is) and that Lumic might be insane; he also considers Lumic's plan to be unethical and obscene. At Jackie's birthday party, one of the Cybermen murders him after he attempts to stop them from running roughshod over the party guests.

Jake Simmonds – A member of the Preachers. He spots Crane and his people snatching the homeless off the street, and later brings Mickey back to their hideout.

Dr Kendrick – Technician involved in creating the Cybermen. Because he insists on proper procedures (through Geneva), Lumic has him electrocuted by a Cyberman.

Mr Crane – Lumic's right-hand man. He supervises the operations to pick up homeless people off the streets to be used as guinea-pigs in Lumic's experiments.

Mrs Moore – One of the members of the Preachers; an older woman with light blonde hair. She obviously has a grudge against Lumic.

Rita-Anne – Ricky's grandmother; she's blind, and nervous about the disappearances of which she's heard rumours (though there's been nothing on the official downloads). The Rita-Anne of the Doctor's universe raised Mickey, but five years ago tripped over a torn piece of carpet (that Mickey apparently forgot to fix) and fell down the stairs and died. Rose, who was still in school at the time of the accident, says she was a great woman, but she used to slap Mickey. The alternate universe Rita-Anne obviously never had the same accident, but the carpet is still torn.

Morris – A homeless man that Jake knows in the Blackfriars area of London. He hesitates when Crane offers him and the other homeless men a chance to eat for free, but becomes one of the test subjects when captured, and is turned into a Cyberman.

TORCHWOOD: The newscaster on the IE24 News broadcast on Rose's mobile phone refers to the Torchwood Institute. Pete Tyler asks someone named 'Stevie' how it's going at Torchwood.

BODY COUNT: Extensive, if the test subjects are considered no longer among the living. (The group rounded up in Blackfriars appears to be only one of many.) The President is assassinated at the Tyler Estate, and a number of party guests are killed. Lumic has his scientist Dr Kendrick murdered.

THE DOCTOR'S MAGICAL SONIC SCREWDRIVER: The screwdriver doesn't appear in this episode.

REALITY BITES: Cuba Gooding Jr, namechecked by Jackie Tyler, is an American actor who won the Academy Award for Best Supporting Actor for *Jerry Maguire* (1996).

Mickey refers to Tony Blair's election as Prime Minister as something that potentially may not have happened in the alternate universe (but see 'Scene Missing' below).

The Doctor says that the Cybus earpods are like Bluetooth attachments, referring to the wireless radio standard and communications protocol named after the Viking King Harald Bluetooth. Pete mentions The George, obviously referring to one of the many pubs of that name in London.

The army soldier refers to the people in the Zeppelins as 'toffs'; toff is a British slang term (considered by some to be offensive) for a member of the upper class.

LINKING THEMES: The (original) Cybermen debuted in the 1966 *Doctor Who* serial 'The Tenth Planet', William Hartnell's last as the Doctor, and subsequently appeared opposite all the other Doctors (if one counts their encounter with the third Doctor in 'The Five Doctors') in a succession of televised adventures. They have also featured in comic strip adventures, novels, and audio adventures – most recently a four-part spinoff series called *Cyberman*, produced, written and directed by Nicholas Briggs for Big Finish Productions. Jackie's fortieth birthday in this episode was noted in *Doctor Who Confidential* to be an acknowledgement of the fortieth anniversary of the Cybermen's creation.

International Electromatics was the name of the company run by Tobias Vaughn in the 1968

Doctor Who story 'The Invasion' starring Patrick Troughton as the Doctor. There is also a shot of St Paul's Cathedral in the episode, a further homage to 'The Invasion', where, in a famous sequence, the Cybermen marched down the steps of St Paul's Walk across from the Cathedral. In general, 'Rise of the Cybermen' owes a considerable debt to 'The Invasion', which established several of the themes that the story plays with.

Rose saw her father's death (in her universe) in 'Father's Day'. Vitex is the 'healthy' beverage that Pete Tyler originally tried to market (as seen in 'Father's Day'); here, it's been a success for him. (We see a poster with 'cherry flavour' on it.) Vitex's slogan, as used by Pete, is 'You can trust me on this.'

The name Ricky may be a wink to the Doctor's constant winding-up of Mickey by calling him by that name.

Rose chastises the Doctor over his choice of secret identities for them as servants at the party; they could have been anyone, she points out, including celebrities or nobility such as 'Dame Rose' and 'Sir Doctor'. These were the titles Queen Victoria gave them in 'Tooth and Claw'.

The name 'earpod' might be a reference to Apple's iPod technology. Jake Simmonds mentions 'the child catcher', a reference to *Chitty Chitty Bang Bang* (1968).

SCENE MISSING: The Doctor seems to realise and accept that this is a parallel world simply on account of seeing the Zeppelins in the sky, even before he and his companions see the poster of Pete. How did he leap to this conclusion so quickly? (And from a plotting point of view, wouldn't it have been better to have kept the 'mystery' longer, and then used the poster in a big reveal moment?)

What exactly is the point of Lumic's attack on the party? It might perhaps be designed simply to dispose of the President – but surely that could have been achieved when the man was leaving Lumic's Zeppelin? There is no logic in Lumic attempting to destroy Pete Tyler (who is supposed to be his ally) or Jackie Tyler, so why are they threatened? (In the following episode, it is revealed that Tyler is Gemini; this is potentially the reason for the attack, though there is no indication at any time that Lumic knows who Gemini is.) Why are the Doctor, Rose, Pete, Ricky, Jake and Mickey all immediately deemed 'incompatible' for conversion to Cybermen? Also, if Ricky doesn't trust Mickey, then why does he bring him along to the party?

Why does the Cyberman who speaks to the Doctor exclaim 'Delete' four times in succession? Why doesn't he just *delete* him and be done with it? And while we're about it, what is 'maximum deletion', and how does it differ from standard deletion? How can the Cybermen actually *weld* a brain to the circuitry around it – and why are the test subjects not completely anaesthetised before the traumatic work's done on them?

Just as Rose had her hair permed between 'School Reunion' and 'The Girl in the Fireplace' when there shouldn't have been any time for her to do so, Mickey gets his hair cut before this episode. (It's implied that this episode follows immediately on from 'The Girl in the Fireplace', but it seems the TARDIS must have stopped off somewhere with a barber in between.)

Jackie says she has the exact same date of birth as Cuba Gooding Jr. However, Gooding's date of birth is 2 January 1968, whereas Rose says that Jackie's birthday is on 1 February (the date of the episode). It's possible that Gooding was born a month earlier in the alternate universe, but most likely this is simply an error – either on the production team's part or, perhaps, on Jackie's. (Gooding's birthday would be written '1/2/68' in standard American notation, where the month precedes the day, but '2/1/68' in standard British notation, where these are reversed.)

Torchwood is apparently more widely known in this universe than in the Doctor's; the mobile phone newsreader discusses it openly. And if this *is* a parallel world with a Torchwood, presumably there is also an equivalent of UNIT. If so, didn't the Cybermen invade in 1969? Probably not, considering International Electromatics is merely a small dummy company here and not the multinational global corporation it was in 'The Invasion' during the earlier *Doctor Who* series. And if there is a Torchwood in this universe (which we later discover there is), then is there also an alternate Doctor who met Queen Victoria in the equivalent of 'Tooth and Claw'?

What's going on with the UK's Prime Minister? We know that Harriet Jones is the current Prime Minister, according to 'The Christmas Invasion'; however, Mickey namechecks Tony Blair. Was Blair the *previous* Prime Minister, and therefore the one who was killed when the Slitheen attacked Earth in 'Aliens of London'? If not, then when was Blair Prime Minister? (If you consider the books to be canon, there was someone else in the job prior to Jones, according to 'The Dying Days'... and in 'Tooth and Claw', the Doctor refers to Margaret Thatcher.)

Why does the Doctor take the recharging unit out of the TARDIS? Is it so that it can be near him and feed off him, like it does when he breathes on it? If so, how many more years of the Doctor's life are fading rapidly?

In the original series, in the stories 'Inferno' and 'Mawdryn Undead', it is noted that different versions of the same person meeting would be disastrous. This is echoed in 'Father's Day'. Here, however, Mickey and Ricky meet with no apparent issue – although they are never seen to actually make physical contact with each other.

When everyone comes to a standstill in order to receive a news dowload through their earpods... does that happen all over the world? What happens then to all the machine operators and drivers and so on? Surely if the earpods have the power to stop people dead in their tracks, then at least those in the emergency services shouldn't be wearing them? – and yet we see a policeman stop in the crowd.

The Cybermen refer to 'free upgrades'. So far they seem to have been following Lumic's plans, and yet he seems to be a businessman first and a man trying to save his own life second – why the sudden change in objective to world domination?

Finally... Rose says 'We're surrounded!' as the escapees from the party all stop and very *slowly* let the Cybermen surround them. Why give the Cybermen the opportunity to capture them? Shouldn't they be running as fast as they can in another direction?

ALTERED STATES: Director Graeme Harper notes in this episode's online commentary that the pre-credits sequence was written by executive producer Russell T Davies, who was unhappy with the one as originally scripted. Guest actor Roger Lloyd-Pack injured himself only days prior to the start of production, breaking his leg. Though writer Tom MacRae stated in an interview in *Doctor Who Magazine* that the episode would not need to be rewritten – as the Lumic character was already in a wheelchair – Lloyd-Pack told the *Sun* that the scripts did indeed require a rewrite. This episode was originally referred to, along with the following one, as 'Parallel World', and was slated to air in fourth position in the new season.

BEHIND THE SCENES: 'Rise of the Cybermen' and the subsequent episode, 'The Age of Steel', were partly inspired by 'Spare Parts', written by Marc Platt for the *Doctor Who* audio drama range produced by Big Finish. Originally it was intended that they would be more closely based on 'Spare Parts' – just as Series One's 'Dalek' had been effectively an adaptation of the audio drama 'Jubilee' (although in that case both were the work of the same writer, Rob Shearman) – but ultimately the story was taken in a different direction as scripting progressed. As writer Tom MacRae told *Doctor Who Magazine*, 'My story isn't the same; it's got a different setting, different themes, and different characters, because once we started talking, the whole thing developed in a very different direction. But as Russell says, we wouldn't have started this whole line of thinking if he hadn't heard 'Spare Parts' in the first place.' Writer Platt was paid a fee and received a credit on the end titles. Mickey's reference to being a 'spare part' in this episode pays homage to the original story. Sequences for this episode were recorded at the Riverfront Arts Centre in Newport, which doubled as the bank of the Thames in the outdoor scenes with Tennant, Piper and Clarke; the Southside Roath Dock within Cardiff Docks, which functioned as the homeless camp; and the Cardiff heliport, Veritair, where the President met the Cybus Zeppelin. Mount Stuart Square in Cardiff Bay was the busy street where the passers-by suddenly stop due to the news transmission, while Sanatorium Road was the location of the army checkpoint that stops Mickey. Compton Street, Grangetown, was used for the sequence outside Mickey's grandmother's home when he's picked up by the Preachers. A private residence within the Vale of Glamorgan was used for the Tyler Estate. Shots of the 'Battersea Power Station' chimneys and a variety of interiors were recorded at Uskmouth Power Station in Newport.

The two episodes of this story were recorded alongside 'Army of Ghosts' and 'Doomsday', the final two episodes of the season, in a single production block. This was done for ease of scheduling, in view of the fact that some cast members were appearing in all four episodes. To that end, Graeme Harper was engaged to direct all four episodes.

Guest star Roger Lloyd-Pack told the *Daily Mirror* that he had based his performance as Lumic on the US Defense Secretary: 'Who is a power-hungry mad person who believes he is completely right and has a lot of control? Donald Rumsfeld came to mind.'

The Cybermen were redesigned for their appearance in the show. Director Graeme Harper states in the episode's online commentary that he wanted an 'art deco' look, both to the Cybermen and to much of the other design seen in the parallel universe. A choreographer was engaged to work with the actors playing the Cybermen to ensure that they presented a consistent image on screen, and that they came over as an effective and scary army; the *Doctor Who Confidential* episode 'Cyberman' detailed the work undertaken in this area. Talk show host Jonathan Ross claimed in his 9 December 2005 television show that he would be appearing as a Cyberman in the series, although this was most likely a case of Ross joking with his audience, as he is wont to do. Early drafts of the script featured 'body shops' where the rich would willingly replace their organic limbs with Cyber-technology – use of the 'body shop' description was even cleared by the production team with the owners of the real-life Body Shop brand – but this aspect was dropped in the course of rewrites.

According to a Sci-Fi Wire interview with Davies, he instructed the writer to downplay differences between the familiar characters and their alternate-universe counterparts. 'I think it was one of those great lessons about the freedom of SF,' he said, 'as well as its greatest dangers, because when you're creating a parallel world, you suddenly get excited by saying everyone can wear eyepatches.'

The BBC produced several spin-off websites for the two-part story. cybusindustries.net was established as the 'home page' for Cybus Industries, complete with fake downloads for earpods, and a passworded intranet. The password 'Gemini12' leads to a game related to the episode, and there is also a game involving a Cyberman invasion of Paris; the latter game was, for a time, accessible only by entering the passcode featured in 'The Age of Steel'. The site features an interview with John Lumic (the interviewer being writer Tom MacRae). It also includes links to posters and videos seen in the episode, available for download, and a reference to a music festival called 'The Pod'. Vitex also features in a sub-site off this main page, referring to the soft drinks sold by Pete Tyler and all their beneficial health claims. Another site, cybusfitness.co.uk, refers to the 'personal fitness' division of Cybus Industries; it's presumed that this might have originally been intended to tie in with the 'body shops' in earlier drafts of the episode, as one of the slogans on the site is 'We can give you a perfect body'.

Another site, internationalelectromatics.co.uk, features a brief corporate biography of the company, stating 'From the transistors in the Magic Merlin toaster to the Cushion 8 thermostats, IE's products have made life easier', and noting that it has bases in Bournemouth, London and Aberdeen. There is a space on the 'product support' page for code entry, although this produces only brief flashes of text; one of the codes includes the numbers 23, 6 and 801, a long-running in-joke on the part of the team at BBC Online, who featured these numbers across various spinoff sites and used photo manipulation to add them to images of various props in the first series.

One of the earliest known spinoff sites for this episode wasn't a BBC one; cybuscorporation.com was long thought to be an official creation but turned out to be the work of a fan, although it was of exceptional quality and professionalism. The site's owners eventually placed a disclaimer on the site to this effect. The site later was replaced with a page stating that it had been suspended by order of the Torchwood Institute, and with a password protecting further content.

The episode featured no trailer for the concluding half of the story, 'The Age of Steel', due to its extended running-time. The closing credits featured a remix of the theme, blending the opening title music and the new arrangement of the closing theme created for this series by the BBC National Orchestra of Wales; it has been speculated that this was done because of the lack of a 'next time' trailer.

Transmission of 'Rise of the Cybermen' was rescheduled to 7.23 pm on the night of its UK debut, due to the extended run-time of the FA Cup Final football match; and it actually began a few minutes later still than that rescheduled time.

DULCET TONES: 'The Lion Sleeps Tonight' – A song from South Africa first written in 1939 that later became a pop hit in the English-speaking world, originally recorded by Solomon Linda and the Evening Birds. There have allegedly been over 140 cover versions of the song, including those by Pete Seeger of The Weavers (under the title 'Wimoweh') in 1952, The Tokens in 1961, and They Might Be Giants (in an altered version, called 'The Guitar') in 1992. The song was also used in the 1994 Disney film *The Lion King*, where it gained international recognition. It is used by Mr Crane to muffle the screams emerging from the Cyberman conversion area in the factory; he asks his subordinate to play 'track 19'. The version heard on screen is by Tight Fit and spent three weeks at number one in the UK charts in March 1982.

OFF THE SCREEN: Roger Lloyd-Pack (credited on these *Doctor Who* episodes without the hyphen in his second name) is well known for playing the character Trigger in the long-running comedy series *Only Fools and Horses* (1981-2003), Owen Newitt in *The Vicar of Dibley* (1994-2005) and Barty Crouch in the film *Harry Potter and the Goblet of Fire* (2005). In his lengthy career, Lloyd-Pack has also been seen in *Poirot* (2005), *Vanity Fair* (2004), *The Bill* (2002), *Born and Bred* (2002), *2point4 Children* (1996), *Heartbeat* (1996), *Princess Caraboo* (1994), *Mr Bean* (1990), *Inspector Morse* (1987), *Dixon of Dock Green* (1976) and *The Avengers* (1965). Andrew Hayden Smith is best known as one of CBBC's weekday presenters, a job he left in early July 2006; he also appeared for years as Ben in the series *Byker Grove* (1989-). Don Warrington has appeared in *Holby City* (2003), *Manchild* (2003), *The Crouches* (2003), *Believe Nothing* (2002), *CI5: The New Professionals* (1999), *Lovejoy* (1993) and *Rising Damp* (1974) and as the hologram Binks in the 'Holoship' episode of *Red Dwarf* (1992). Colin Spaull played Lilt in the *Doctor Who* story 'Revelation of the Daleks' (1985), which was also directed by Graeme Harper, and has been seen in *The Bill* (1989), *Holby City* (2004), *Down To Earth* (2003), *Casualty* (2005) , *Dixon of Dock Green* (1965) and *The Secret Garden* (1960). Mona Hammond played Blossom Jackson in *EastEnders* from 1994 to 1997, and has also appeared in *Doctors* (2006), *The Crouches* (2003), *Babyfather* (2002), *Holby City* (2001), *Randall & Hopkirk (Deceased)* (2001), *Juliet Bravo* (1985) and *Softly, Softly* (1968). Helen Griffin has been seen in *Little White Lies* (2006), *Holby City* (2004), *Life Force* (2000), *Solomon and Gaenor* (1999) and *Wycliffe* (1998). Paul Antony-Barber was in *V For Vendetta* (2005), *MIT: Murder Investigation Team* (2005), *55 Degrees North* (2004), *Casualty* (1998), *Press Gang* (1993) and *Auf Wiedersehen, Pet* (1986). Adam Shaw's credits include roles in *The Bill* (2002), *Footballers Wives* (2002) and *Saving Private Ryan* (1998). Duncan Duff has been in *Broken News* (2006), *Rosemary & Thyme* (2006), *The Bill* (2005), *Casualty* (1991) and *In Dreams* (1992).

Director Graeme Harper first worked on *Doctor Who* in 1971, as an assistant floor manager on the story 'Colony in Space', and later directed two stories: 'The Caves of Androzani' (1984) and 'Revelation of the Daleks' (1985). He had been scheduled to direct a story within the series' original twenty-third season, which ultimately fell through when *Doctor Who* was put on hiatus for 18 months, and later was to have directed 'The Dark Dimension', a thirtieth anniversary special, which was also aborted before production commenced. Harper originally began his career as a child actor. His other directorial credits include episodes of *Angels* (1975), *Juliet Bravo* (1984), *Bergerac* (1985), *Star Cops* (1987), *Boon* (1989), *Stay Lucky* (1990), *Heartbeat* (1995), *Casualty* (1997), *Wycliffe* (1997), *Grange Hill* (2000), *Custer's Last Stand Up* (2003) and *The Royal* (2004).

Writer Tom MacRae is the creator of *Mile High* (2003) for Sky One and *As If* (2001) for Channel 4, and has written for *Mayo* (2006), *No Angels* (2004), *Nine Lives* (2002) and *School's Out* (2002), for the latter of which he was nominated for a BAFTA in 2002. MacRae also wrote the children's book *The Opposite* and is currently scripting *Marple* for ITV.

TECHNICAL GOOFS: Rose's mobile phone is different from the one seen in previous episodes. (She could have changed it, but it's implied that it's the same one.) The mobile phone screen says 'Cybus Network' and yet the Doctor immediately refers to the parent company Cybus Industries, with no apparent way of him knowing this name. The camera crew can be seen reflected in the glasses worn by Mona Hammond in the role of Rita-Anne. Mr Crane continues his 'come and get yer lovely hot food' spiel even when (in a shot change) it's clear that only one homeless man and Jake remain – and Jake runs off without any reaction from Crane. Just before the download that the Doctor and Rose witness, a man with long hair walking behind them disappears in a shot change. A woman at Lumic's party (visible left-frame just after the Cybermen crash through the windows and behind the President when he dies) seems to be laughing through the invasion. A bad edit in the end credit music that's been present all season is now clearly audible due to the omission of a 'Next time ...' sequence.

CONTROVERSIES: There could have been major controversy arising from this episode concerning the creation of the Cybermen. In the original series, they had once been humans from the planet Mondas, a twin planet to Earth but with its own culture and history. Mondas' orbit took it away from the Sun, and in order to survive, its people started to replace parts of their bodies with cybernetics until they had become almost completely replaced. These new 'Cyber-men' then returned to Earth to try to claim it and its peoples as their own. Neatly sidestepping all this back history, however, the Cybermen here are created on a parallel Earth as effectively identical robots, each of which has a human brain surgically implanted into its skull case. Although Paul Kasey is credited as playing the Cyber Leader, this character is not seen in the episode. (A Cyber Leader is normally distinguished by having black 'handles' on the sides of its head.)

INTERNAL CONSISTENCY: Mickey says the date in London is 1 February of 'this year'; 'School Reunion' took place in early 2007, so that's certainly the correct timeframe. (The year would also be that of Cuba Gooding Jr's thirty-ninth birthday, even if the day and month of his birth are not those given on screen.) The episode takes place over the daytime and evening of 1 February, as it ends on the night of Jackie's party (her birthday being the same day).

TARDISODE #5: A 'report' from the Gemini operative to the Preachers features a profile of John Lumic, his creation of Cybus Industries and its profit margins. It states that Cybus Industries was established in 1982, its profits were $78 billion in 2001, and that a South American State has reported 265,000 people missing – presumably because of Cybus. The directive asks for all Preachers to mobilise immediately against Cybus and their 'ultimate upgrades'. We see that Ricky is listening intently to the broadcast.

REVIEWS

The Daleks had a glorious rebirth last year, but this year's resurrection of another classic monster proves a bit... stiff. What's more, this isn't a triumphant return for the Cybermen we knew, but an alternate origin that replaces the proto-Borg zombies of the earlier stories with big tin cans that house only human brains. Parallels with our modern fascination with Bluetooth headsets and upgrades are nice, but this new conception of the creatures takes away the horror that made the Cybermen so chilling; previously, you knew there was flesh in there under all that wiring and metal. And if all they need is to extract the brain, then what is that whole slice-and-dice scene with the homeless people about? Are they cutting them up for fun? As for the aesthetic qualities of the Cybusmen, the puffy gloves, boots and steel bell bottoms make them comical rather than nightmarish. They should be giant steel juggernauts; they often look like big plastic dolls. But if the Cybermen leave something to be desired, perhaps the cast can raise the bar. For me, the stand-out performance comes from Colin Spaull, playing Mr Crane with the right weary efficiency. Here is an old-school classic *Who*-style character that feels right, even if he is working for the scenery-chewing cartoon Lumic as played by Roger Lloyd-Pack. Pack is the perfect counterpoint to the suave understatement of Anthony Stewart Head's Finch from 'School Reunion'. Where Finch exuded evil with every soft-spoken word and gaze, Lloyd-Pack gruffly expels every line of dialogue with a wide-eyed stare, chewing the scenery and apparently loving every minute of it; I couldn't always say the same.

And the regulars? Noel Clarke seems to think that all he has to do as alternate Ricky is deliver his lines through clenched teeth. This guy is Britain's most wanted? For what, bad acting? He's in good company if his fellow revolutionaries are anything to go by. And isn't it a little late to introduce some emotional back story for Mickey? Tennant and Piper aren't given a lot to do themselves, although the Doctor seems to be channelling his second incarnation pretty well in the episode's cliff-hanger. The three do share a satisfying opening TARDIS scene, and the Doctor's sacrifice of ten years of his life to save the TARDIS is also well handled. The whole dystopian setting is hackneyed and convenient, relying on standard clichés like army check points, the inevitable rebel movement and a vague sense of totalitarianism. There are also an amazing series of coincidences, chief among them that Rose's dad is not only alive in this other reality but so amazingly successful that he rubs shoulders with both Lumic and the President of Great Britain. After a couple of episodes that emphasised relationships and the emotional impact on our leads, maybe it's just jarring to downshift back into straightforward action-adventure mode. Director Graeme Harper tries to ramp things up with low angle shots, handheld camera work and the clever touch of a camera mounted on Lumic's chair, but he stages a weak cliff-hanger with everybody staring just a bit too long while the Cybermen reach for their victims and repeat 'Delete' over and over as if waiting for the director to yell 'Cut'. I hope the story experiences a total upgrade in its final chapter. – *Arnold T Blumberg*

This is the first episode in the whole of new *Who* that feels completely off to me. Giving the parallel Earth Cybermen a Davros figure as creator is a disastrous idea – one of the chief strengths of 'Spare Parts' (the Big Finish audio play to which this story ultimately bears no resemblance, except in a scene in the next episode) is the notion that Cybermen were sort of created by committee, a banal soulless collection of people consigning themselves to cybernetic oblivion because of the condition of the planet they lived on. Okay, I appreciate adding the 2000s satire of 'upgrading' to the mix, but there's nothing actually *attractive* about becoming a Cyberman in the same way that one gets the latest iPod or Bluetooth peripheral device. There is no advantage to becoming a Cyberman, and there's no compelling need for it in the society they're in. You could believe in Davros in 'Genesis of the Daleks', because he was trying to find a way to ensure his own species' survival, and furthermore Michael Wisher was utterly compelling portraying someone who was almost a Dalek anyway. Lumic has no moral or scientific argument for the Cybermen, and what's more *he hasn't cybernised himself*, which kind of belies any point that this is to ensure his own survival. What's worse is that, as a character, he's a cartoon. There's nothing remotely scary or compelling about him, and Roger Lloyd-Pack is quite happy to cackle like an anaemic Valentine Dyall. Which brings up the biggest problem I have with 'Rise of the Cybermen'. Something's grossly wrong with the tone of the story. It should be scary, off-kilter and emotional – not unlike last season's story 'Dalek' – but instead it's cartoony and overplayed. Lloyd-Pack's Lumic is bad enough, but every character is played in a similar way – Noel Clarke distinguishes Ricky from Mickey by sneering like an 11 year-old, Colin Spaull effects a generic camp minion and Shaun Dingwall has jettisoned all the subtlety that made us love Pete Tyler in 'Father's Day'. Even David Tennant and Billie Piper can't pull it out of the fire – the Doctor is overbearing and ineffectual and Rose is supposed to be moody but generally isn't. The really frustrating thing here is that this is a story I really want to like. The parallel Earth is an interesting idea (although woefully underdeveloped) and I like the new-style Cybermen, and that they've enhanced the body-horror element of the characters. The storming of the Tylers' house is a wonderfully effective sequence that reminds me why I loved Graeme Harper's episodes so much. But the overall story is too two-dimensional to find its heart. – *Graeme Burk*

Each week, the BBC's *Doctor Who* website previews the next episode by running edited highlights of comments from their 'fear forecasters': a family of four kids, ages five to 13, whose telly-watching opinions are supposed to be representative of those of the average *Doctor Who* audience in the UK. For this episode, Harry – aged seven – was quick on the draw, opining that every person to appear onscreen with Cybus earpods was 'a Cyberman'. But it wasn't until 33 minutes in, with Lumic's new army loading up for a little ride, that his excitement reached its zenith: '*Real Cybermen!*' I wish I was seven again. I wish I could be Harry. I wish I had seen real Cybermen. The Cybermen are my very favourite *Doctor Who* villains, and that's a testament not so much to the stories in which they appeared – after the '60s, most of them were pretty terrible – but to the very creepy and disturbing ideas on which they were built. Few people are comfortable with the thought of invasive surgery, of replacement body parts and of people being kept alive by artificial means. Even today, it's one of the fundamental ethical debates of humanity versus technology. *Star Trek* spent ten years mining the same territory for the Borg, arguably their single most effective adversaries. So what happened? What's become of the Cybermen? Probably as a concession to inevitable comparison with those same *Star Trek* baddies, the Cybermen have been reduced to the puppet army of a mad genius, just like the Daleks of the '70s, or *The Avengers*' Cybernauts. There, at least, you had the benefit of good actors as their insane inventors, somehow raising the concept above its inherent limitations. In contrast, Roger Lloyd-Pack spends this episode defining the very term 'chewing scenery'. If he was instructed to act like that, I can only assume director Graeme Harper has fallen very far since his '80s *Who* ventures. Sadly, that might just be the case; for the first 40 minutes of 'Rise of the Cybermen', his direction is serviceable at best. Things only really pick up with an exciting final five minutes, and even then, the script doesn't quite hold up its end of the bargain. (I mean, come on, 'You will perish under maximum deletion'?) It's not that 'Rise of the Cyberman' is really bad *Doctor Who*. It's merely rather boring and cold, trapped under the weight of expectations and the feeling that nothing much is all that new. The Doctor delivers his same dire warnings to no avail, Rose is insufferably self-absorbed, and as usual, the old sci-fi cliché of the parallel universe depends on extreme coincidence to get by. Mickey's scene with his gran is probably the best part of the episode – intriguing that he's gone from utterly disposable to someone with whom we can actually empathise – and there are a few other nice set pieces, such as the 'destruction' of the TARDIS and the use of 'The Lion Sleeps Tonight' when the homeless people are being converted. Unfortunately, those little details are most notable because they at least feel original: all the major stuff has already been done before on *Doctor Who*, mostly in the stories 'The Invasion' and 'Inferno'. There's simply no comparison. While I'm glad to see the Cybermen back, and largely admire their redesign, I question whether they've returned as anything but a publicity stunt. Frankly, I'd have rather lost them to the annals of *Who* history than see them as just another set of robots. There's still a lot of potential for next week, though; now that the Cybermen have established themselves, perhaps the story will ramp up and really get original and interesting. Perhaps, then, I'll finally see some real Cybermen. – *Sarah Hadley*

'Rise of the Cybermen' has a lot of good material in it, but as an episode it never seems to gel cohesively together into one satisfying whole. That may well be because it's only the opening half of a two-part adventure, and it's always difficult to make judgements about a story until you've seen all of it. It may also simply be that the episode's premise doesn't really do a great deal for me personally – I have never been a particular fan of either parallel universe stories in science-fiction generally or the Cybermen in *Doctor Who* specifically, so this wasn't an episode of the new series that I was looking forward to with any great degree of anticipation. And once it starts, it doesn't do much to sell itself – a real Children's BBC-style pre-titles sequence doesn't bode very well, and the first TARDIS scene after the credits, as it falls into the parallel world, is simply odd. The Doctor's mocking of Mickey seems rather unfair, but all the more strange is his rather muted reaction to the apparent death of the TARDIS. 'She's perished', we're told, but even though we know he's an expert at concealing what he's really thinking, he doesn't seem overly upset about it. Tennant, in fact, seems rather quiet throughout the whole episode, and his Doctor doesn't dominate proceedings nearly as much as he has done in previous adventures, which is either a good or a bad thing depending on how much of a fan of number ten you are. Things do improve as we get out and about in the parallel world. It's good that we don't have too many exact doubles running around, with only Noel Clarke having to play two different characters – or different versions of the same character, depending on how you look at it – in the same scene. Clarke does well in these scenes, and you can tell he enjoys being able to do something a bit different for a change while playing Ricky. Elsewhere, the whole parallel Earth with its technological gizmos and shiny, slightly-different London is rather reminiscent of *Bugs*, the BBC's Saturday evening technological sci-fi show of the 1990s. It's the supporting cast who come out of all this the best – Roger Lloyd-Pack is absurd but oddly fitting as Lumic, while Colin Spaull probably shared the honours for best performance of the episode with Don Warrington, both of them bringing good things to relatively small parts, and it's a shame we look unlikely to see more of Warrington in episode two. While I'm not a fan of the creatures, the Cybermen's attack on the party at the end of the episode is realised very well, and the cliff-hanger is a good 'un – a real old-fashioned 'How are they going to get out of *that* one?', with no next time trailer to let any cats out of the bag as to who survives. Nonetheless, overall I have to say that this is probably the weakest Series Two episode so far for me, and I hope for an improvement in the concluding instalment. – *Paul Hayes*

It's almost impossible not to feel sorry for this two-part story. Almost, but not quite. It came with all the hype and build-up that the BBC could muster: *Radio Times* cover, massive trails, press coverage... But however much RTD and co try to convince us that the Cybermen are second only to the Daleks in popularity, the truth is that they're a pretty distant second. Not only are they not as iconic (jug ears versus pepperpots – I think not), but their very *raison d'etre* has been both rendered moot by society's willing acceptance of spare part surgery, and blatantly co-opted by the Borg. To make them relevant today, Tom MacRae has been forced to give these alternate universe Cybermen a new meaning and origin. Although the premise he's come up with is hardly unique in the annals of the series... From the atrocious pre-titles sequence – what was RTD thinking when he wrote this? – it is clear that 'Rise of the Cybermen', while claiming its provenance from Marc Platt's Big Finish audio 'Spare Parts', owes rather more to 'Genesis of the Daleks'. Did they really think that putting the creator of the Cybermen in a wheelchair wouldn't invite negative comparisons with Davros? Oh come on! Especially given Lloyd-Pack's dreadful performance, which, like a cheap sandwich, is a combination of cardboard and ham, and makes one fondly pine for David Gooderson's interpretation of Davros in 'Destiny of the Daleks' – not a proud achievement. That's not to say that 'Rise of the

Cybermen' isn't a visual treat, packed to the gills with pyrotechnics and spectacle. The TARDIS explosion is amazing, and alternate London, with its Zeppelins and 'just slightly off', feels both impressive and disturbing. Auteur Graeme Harper doesn't disappoint with top-notch direction, especially in his decision to keep the Cybermen a blurred yet looming presence throughout. The 'Lion Sleeps Tonight' scene is possibly one of the most chilling sequences in the whole series, helped by superb work from the SFX people. The story also benefits from excellent characterisation of both the regulars and the guests, with the bitchy alternate Jackie Tyler a true delight. Especial kudos to Colin Spaull's thuggish Mr Crane and the gutsy Mrs Moore, courtesy of Helen Griffin. No, the problem with this episode lies in the script. After a first viewing to savour the visceral pleasures, subsequent screenings make it quite clear that the plot is a hodge-podge of ideas seemingly thrown together in the vain hope that they might somehow cohere. Alternate Earth never really convinces. Is it a fascist dictatorship? Why is the world 'sick'? And Lumic's reasons for cybernising the population don't make sense. Does he want immortality? If so, for whom? Himself or his 'children'? What is the point of the massacre in the Tyler mansion if Lumic needs bodies for conversion? Given the 'International Electromatics' reference, are these Cybermen any relation at all to the 'real' ones? I wanted to love this story. I wanted to believe the hype. But despite all the positives – and there are many – the weak and shoddy scripting and suck-it-and-see approach to the storyline make part one a crushing disappointment. I'm hoping that part two will redeem matters, but with the same writer, I'm not holding my breath. – *Craig Hinton*

This opens (presumably in the spirit of irony) with a roaring cliché that dates back to the Bela Lugosi-Lionel Atwill phase of mad science: a cringing minion who has assisted the mastermind throughout a succession of unethical experiments suddenly grows a conscience but is stupid enough to tell his megalomaniac boss that he intends to alert the authorities – with predictably fatal results. It's silly stuff, but fun – and a good introduction to Roger Lloyd-Pack's John Lumic, crippled creator of the Cyber-race. Though Lumic simultaneously evokes monster-creating Davros ('Genesis of the Daleks') and cyber-quisling Tobias Vaughn ('The Invasion'), the reliable Lloyd-Pack gives him an edge of his own. The TARDIS shows up in a contemporary London, but the Zeppelins reveal this is one of those alternate universes last seen on *Doctor Who* in 'Inferno' – and not the twin Earth (Mondas) in our universe implied by 'The Tenth Planet'. We assume we aren't in a 'Genesis of the Cybermen' situation but visiting the beginning of the story in a parallel world, which could turn out differently than established (and hard-to-follow) Cyber-continuity. *Doctor Who* has made surprisingly little use of alternate realities, which Mickey is familiar with from comics: here it's used to bring on different versions of Rose's parents (richer, but not much happier) and temporarily kill the TARDIS (it gets better) rather than play with different history (this Britain is liberal enough to have a black President but oppressive enough to have a militarily-enforced curfew). Tom MacRae's script is the most deftly-plotted of the season so far, juggling the regulars' personal lives (Mickey and Rose both encounter loved ones lost in their reality) with the gradual takeover of the country by Lumic's cyborg stormtroopers. *Who* has been worried about communications technology since 'The War Machines' – and Lumic's earpieces, downloading information into paused citizenry, are credible extrapolations from those modern irritating earplug phones, while the use of computer jargon (talk of upgrades, compatibility and deletion) fits the Cybermen even if they mostly make an impression with stamping steel jackboots and regimented crashing-through-windows. The long-lasting monsters have rarely featured in top-quality *Who*, so this might be their best outing yet – though the overtly menacing metal skull-look is slightly less eerie than the simple blankness of earlier incarnations. David Tennant rushes about enthusiastically and gets some good material – it's affecting and effective when Mickey skewers the Doctor's priorities in obsessing over Rose's family while never asking about his, leading to an unusual moment as the maturing Mickey starts to gain high ground over this more childish, less arrogant Doctor, only to be turned back into comic relief by his more heroic rebel leader doppelgänger. Camille Coduri and Shaun Dingwall aren't overused as alternate Jackie and Pete, and a neat reversal of expectations has Rose, disguised as a waitress, briefly bonding with a father who doesn't know her (the Tylers are childless in this reality) as in 'Father's Day', then trying the same on her mother only to be rebuked for her upstart impudence ('You're staff') and fired. – *Kim Newman*

Imagine if 'upgrading' was strictly voluntary. Who might choose to become a Cyberman? The paralysed? The traumatised? The terminally ill, like Lumic himself? No-one? The President refuses to back Lumic's research because it's 'obscene', but arguably, so is growing human neurons inside a mouse's brain. There's no suggestion that the public have been consulted, or someone would have brought up the results of an opinion poll for or against the process. The President doesn't refuse because of Lumic's unethical experiments on human beings – he doesn't know about them, and in fact Lumic will need to carry out properly monitored experiments on volunteer subjects before his process can be legally put to use. What is it that makes Lumic's creation 'obscene'? I myself have multiple chronic illnesses and take at least five different medications each day, and the thought of becoming a brain in a robot body gives me the screaming horrors. No thank you. Interestingly, one anti-suicide website suggests that what a suicidal person seeks is *relief*. You cannot feel the delicious, blessed feeling of relief from pain if you are dead. Nor can you feel it if you are a Cyberman. Oddly, I find the thought of becoming some sort of artificial intelligence – all robot – intriguing, rather than horrifying. I wonder if the Cybermen are 'obscene' in part because they violate the boundary between machine and organic, dead and living, 'working' and 'alive'. If Lumic was transplanting brains into, say, clone bodies, it would be little more gruesome than any operation. Instead he talks about 'skin' that isn't skin and 'bodies' that aren't bodies. The question boils down to whether even volunteers would find their new existence so painful that they would need their emotions switched off – whether they might be trading one hell for another. Or is the ability to switch off one's emotions the very appeal of the process? For victims of savage depression or trauma, a life without feelings could appeal. Imagine an offshoot of Lumic's technology that allowed someone to stop a terrifying flashback or a suicidal bout of depression at the flick of a switch – an artificial calm not really different from taking a tranquilliser. It's interesting to see a science-fiction story in which the brain is acknowledged as the seat of the emotions. To his cost, Lumic disregards this as an inconvenience with a technological fix. 'The brain is what makes us human,' he argues, but he brushes aside the role of emotion in even the most rational thought. A Cyberman could solve a cryptic crossword clue without ever experiencing the 'Aha!' jolt of pure brain pleasure. But then, for all his rhetoric, Lumic is not trying to cure human suffering. It's chilling to imagine who the rejects were who went into his ovens: most likely the brain damaged, the intellectually disabled, the mentally ill, the autistic... anyone whose central nervous system did not live up to the standards of human point two. I would have burned: would you? – *Kate Orman*

Déja vu... I get the distinct impression this two-parter came about for one reason and one reason alone: the production team's desire to work with Shaun Dingwall again. Not that I have a problem with that, as I liked Dingwall's performance. But to justify his resurrection, all they've done is remake the best bits from 'Father's Day'. Rose gets all anxious about meeting Pete, Pete senses he 'recognises' Rose, Jackie is a total bitch, yada, yada, yada... But Rose has (and so have we) already gone through all that torment in 2005, so why repeat it, and why stretch it out over two episodes?! And as the Doctor keeps reminding her, Pete and Jackie in this parallel universe are not Rose's parents, so why should she or we care about them? When they discover the Jackie upgrade in part two (sorry, I'm jumping ahead a bit here) it is supposed to be a heart-wrenching moment, but as we have no real emotional attachment to her, the expected impact lands with a dull thud. Parallel worlds are an SF convention that *Doctor Who* has only ever dealt with once before – back in 1970's 'Inferno'. But these TV 'through the looking-glass' glimpses into the 'what if' are usually done as an excuse to allow a regular cast to play OTT and/or exaggerated versions of their usual roles and to dress up in wacky costumes – one only has to view *Stargate: SG-1* and the various *Star Treks* for examples of how it does and doesn't work. In these mirror worlds, it's highly unlikely that the same characters would ever meet / be married / know each other / have the same names (delete where applicable) as in the 'real' world, given that the political, social, economical, and geographical environments should be completely different. To me, there simply isn't enough difference between Cybus Earth and the 'real' Earth, so why didn't the production team just decide to set the story on an Earth-like colony, or even on near-future Earth itself? In fact, the episode (and overall story) would have been so much better if they'd jettisoned the whole parallel world subplot altogether! I found it a rather bizarre scripting decision to have the Doctor deduce that he and his companions are in a parallel universe so early on, based just on the presence of the Zeppelins, rather than build up the mystery of where/when they are, the function of the earpods etc, with the shock sting reveal being the discovery of the Pete Tyler poster. Yes, it is great to see finally some major character development for Mickey; we've not really known much about his background before now, and it helps to make him a fully rounded character rather than just 'the idiot' comic relief he was in the last two episodes. But it's a pity this all comes now, when we know Mickey's days could be numbered. For an episode that was greatly anticipated by every fan, that promised so much and is visually impressive, 'Rise of the Cybermen' is just dull, dull, dull. And please don't get me started on the Cybermen! I'll save the vitriol for my review of part two! – *Jon Preddle*

After the velvety-with-silk-lining 'The Girl in the Fireplace' comes something considerably more... stompy. Well, that's the modern world for you – *Vorsprung durch Technik*, dare one suggest? 'Rise of the Cybermen' returns to the traditional *Doctor Who* core-values of 'School Reunion' by including a whole raft of crowd-pleasing gestures at the expense of, perhaps, more imaginative concepts. In and of itself, that's perfectly fine, and writer Tom MacRae can be forgiven many of the story's less-successful ideas if only for the episode's one genuinely nerve-shredding line of dialogue: 'After that, everything became that little bit *less kind*.' But, beautiful design and some knowing glances and winks aren't entirely enough to overshadow the episode's more disappointing aspects. First, the whole thing comes over as a kind of potted history of the Cybermen for those who missed it all the first time around, taking a few random elements from 'The Tenth Planet', 'The Tomb of the Cybermen', 'The Invasion' and 'Earthshock' and using them, sad to say, to equally random effect. There's also a staggering lack of suspense in places, something not helped by Roger Lloyd-Pack's performance. A fine comedy actor, undeniably, but here he seems to be as out of place as a jester at a wake, and the way he solemnly intones ... *from beyond the grave!*' in the pre-credits sequences gives this generation of *Doctor Who* fans their first, honest-to-God '*Nossing in ze verld can schtop me now!*' moment. I also think it was a big mistake to bring back an alternate-universe Pete Tyler – not because Shaun Dingwall is anything less than terrific but because the character's resurrection isn't even remotely earned and rather cheapens the impact of 'Father's Day' last year. However, it's not all bad news. One would really have to be a card-carrying po-faced misanthrope not a crack a smile when 'The Lion Sleeps Tonight' gets played to drown out the screams of the soon-to-be-Cybermen. 'Rise of the Cybermen' is built on such dichotomy – for every great performance (Don Warrington's understated gem of an innings), there's a weak cliff-hanger never more than 45 minutes away. Big ideas, small and insecure delivery. Something of a contradiction then – too ambitious to be entirely dismissed but far too shallow to fully engage the viewer. – *Keith Topping*

EDITOR'S REVIEW: The parallel world scenario is one of the most overused clichés in science-fiction. These stories can be very satisfying if done correctly, but sadly few writers do more than take the easy way out. It's one thing to show the development of a society on legitimate, unexpected lines; it's quite another to say there's a doppelgänger of this character or that character, plonk them down in the middle of a busy city and say 'It's Earth, but not quite the Earth you remember.'

Sadly, the latter seems to be the case with 'Rise of the Cybermen'; but it's not the bigger of the two major problems I had with this episode. I'm rather fond of parallel world scenarios, but if you're going to do it, there are more critical stories to tell than 'This one's different because a mad scientist is about to take over the world.' That can be done on *our* Earth, see, and if you're going to tell the story of a parallel Earth, it should be *about* that world. Instead, it seems to be nothing more than a cipher, a way to bring Shaun Dingwall back to play Pete Tyler and allow Noel Clarke and Camille Coduri to play alternate versions of their now-familiar characters. I'm fond of all three, mind, but I think we've moved on to the point where *Doctor Who* can take a few risks rather than play to the low road. Based as this was on Marc Platt's far superior Big Finish audio play 'Spare Parts' (and, let's face it, it was an adaptation), there were ways around all that: for starters, the setting could have been, say, 2015 on the Earth we know and recognise, and it would have made a bit more sense. (Granted, Pete would still have been dead...)

That was only the dissatisfying aspect of the episode; the thing that *really* irritated me was the fact that the Cybermen were, to be honest, not *the* Cybermen. When one speaks of the metal nasties that the Doctor encountered for decades, returning with all the triumph one would expect, just as the Daleks did a year earlier, there's a caveat: these aren't the same creatures at all. They look (fairly) similar, sound (fairly) similar, and act in a (fairly) similar manner... but they're not the same. *Doctor Who* fans know that the Cybermen have an established history; they're from Mondas, they've attempted to conquer the Earth, and so forth. These 'cyber men' have no direct relation to the Cybermen we know and love. Now, you're probably asking yourself, what does it matter? It doesn't, in the larger scheme of things; but when you're going to spend all that money hyping the return of a famous villain, you should actually give the viewers the villain they expect.

The script isn't a bad one; there's plenty to like, including the nature of the Doctor's discomfort with having Mickey along for the ride, and Mickey's guilt over what happened to his own grandmother, and Rose's displeasure at being able to reach out and touch her father, only to find that the man wants nothing to do with her. There are some decent performances in there as well; for the first time, you can see that much of Mickey is in Noel's performance rather than an accidental happenstance, and Dingwall is superb in bringing back Pete touched with worldliness and a sense of the unstoppable juggernaut sailing toward his doorstep. On the other hand, I can't quite watch Roger Lloyd-Pack as John Lumic without expecting him to reach up and twirl some imaginary moustache; it's not just over-the-top, it's Richard-Briers-over-the-top without the fun.

Simply put, I think the problem is that *nothing* feels right in this story. We want Cybermen and we're given something entirely new that just happens to look like them. We want a parallel world story and instead we have an Earth where the only *major* differences are that big corporations run everything, the major media are controlled by one man and humanity is gradually losing control of its own technology. Hmmm... come to think of it, that is pretty much the same as our Earth. Best to wait then, until the story's finished, before passing judgement. – *Shaun Lyon*

206: THE AGE OF STEEL

On an alternate Earth, Cybus Industries has created the Cybermen, a new 'race' of ruthless cyborgs with designs on upgrading every last human being in the world. Can the Doctor, Rose and Mickey stop them at their genesis, or will the events that changed the course of human history in their universe happen here as well?

FIRST TRANSMISSION: UK – 20 May 2006. US – 3 November 2006. Canada – 13 November 2006. Australia – 19 August 2006. New Zealand – 17 August 2006.
DURATION: 45'52"
WRITER: Tom MacRae
DIRECTOR: Graeme Harper
CREDITED CAST: David Tennant (The Doctor), Billie Piper (Rose Tyler), Camille Coduri (Jackie Tyler), Noel Clarke (Mickey Smith), Shaun Dingwall (Pete Tyler), Roger Lloyd Pack (John Lumic), Andrew Hayden-Smith (Jake Simmonds), Helen Griffin (Mrs Moore), Colin Spaull (Mr Crane), Duncan Duff (Newsreader), Paul Kasey (Cyber-Leader), Nicholas Briggs (Cyber-Voice)

Cybermen originally created by Kit Pedler and Gerry Davis
With thanks to Marc Platt

WHERE AND WHEN: London, Earth in an alternate universe, the evening of 1 February 2007.

THE STORY UNFOLDS: John Lumic initiates the massive processing required to turn all the inhabitants of London into Cybermen. London is placed under martial law and sealed off, and people are asked to remove their earpods... if it's not too late. Removal of the earpods after they're activated will cause a brainstorm.

The control signal being used by Cybus to control the population is coming from Lumic's Zeppelin resting on the top of the Battersea Power Station. The Battersea plant has cooling tunnels underneath – one is called Deepcold Six – that are big enough for a person to walk through. Lumic notes that he has factories waiting on seven continents.

The Preachers have a mole called Gemini inside Lumic's organisation who feeds them information twice weekly; this includes details of Lumic's private files, his South American operations and so forth. According to the evidence, Pete Tyler has been working for Lumic since 2005. However, Pete Tyler in fact *is* Gemini; to prove it, he tells the Preachers he's been sending them information on encrypted wavelength six-five-seven using binary nine. Pete, however, thought he was broadcasting data to the security services, not to the Preachers.

The Cybermen, by their own account, are uniform and feel nothing. There are at least 12 chambers used for upgrading at the processing plant. They incinerate the reject human stock and store already-converted specimens in the cooling ducts below the power station. At least 6,500 people have been turned into Cybermen. One of them, a woman named Sally Phelan, who was shortly to be married to a man named Gareth, provides the Doctor with the answer he seeks – the emotional inhibitors can be turned off, causing the Cybermen to lose their force of will, so long as he has the cancellation code.

The transmitter controls inside the Zeppelin are sealed behind a casing; Mickey suggests that he and Jake need something like oxyacetylene to get through it. Jake carries a bottle of high-potency chemicals, like smelling salts but stronger, enough to knock out the guards; he says it's one of Mrs Moore's 'little tricks'. Mrs Moore herself uses an electromagnetic bomb to take out a Cyber suit. The Doctor uses remnant energy in the one remaining TARDIS power cell to neutralise the Cybermen; by discharging it, he sends it into a revitalising loop, and it will charge back up in about four hours. It then has five minutes' power to get the TARDIS back into the 'real' universe.

The TARDIS closes the crack in time between parallel realities when it leaves the alternate universe, shutting it off, supposedly forever. Mickey and Jake are apparently off to Paris to continue their fight to liberate the world from Cybus Industries.

THE DOCTOR: He thinks the human race are very susceptible to being controlled; sometimes he thinks they actually like it that way. He acknowledges that he makes up the solutions to his problems as he goes along, but thinks that he does it brilliantly. He believes he has the whole weight of the world on his shoulders. The Cybermen detect his 'binary vascular system' (i.e. his two hearts). Lumic tells him that, in his new world, doctors are no longer needed. The Doctor counters by telling him that he'd call Lumic a genius, but he himself is in the room. He thinks the one thing that makes Earth so alive is ordinary, stupid people.

ROSE TYLER: She can't stop wanting the Pete Tyler of this universe to be her father, and holds his hand at one point. She is relieved to discover he is not a traitor. She kisses Mickey when the Cybermen start their invasion, showing that there is still a spark there. She is devastated when Pete won't accept her, and later when she has to say goodbye to Mickey when the TARDIS leaves this reality. She gives Mickey her mobile phone.

CHARACTER BUILDING: *Mickey Smith* – He decides to go with Ricky, obviously enticed by the opportunity to make a difference, to stop the Cybermen. He thinks Ricky is braver than him. ('Ten times,' Ricky replies.) He still can't quite let the Doctor's relationship with Rose go. He is again referred to by the Doctor as an idiot, only this time it's a clue that the Doctor needs his help. He learned how to fly a Zeppelin by playing on a PlayStation; he calls the ship 'Mickey Smith Airlines'. When the Cybermen are stopped, for the time being, Mickey decides to leave the Doctor and Rose and stay in this reality, to reunite with his grandmother and to carry on the fight in Ricky Smith's name.

Ricky Smith (Alternate) – He's London's Most Wanted, all right, but that's for parking tickets; he was 'Fighting the system! Park anywhere, that's me.' He has a sense of admiration for his other universe counterpart. He is killed by electrocution from a Cyberman after trying to escape over a chain link fence.

John Lumic – He started the Cyberman project to keep himself (or, rather, his brain) alive at any cost. He still believes he's doing the right thing for humanity, the 'upgraded' forms of which he believes are his 'children'. Crane attempts to kill him by destroying his breathing apparatus; the Cybermen then forcibly 'upgrade' Lumic, removing his pain forever. The Lumic 'unit' is later designated Cyber-Controller; he calls this the 'age of steel'. The Lumic Cyber-Controller later climbs the Zeppelin ladder, and then falls to his (apparent) death.

Pete Tyler (Alternate) – He wants to go back for Jackie, but the Doctor tells him that whoever's left in the house is dead. He mentions (again) that Rose is his dog's name. He and

Rose use fake earpods to get into the Battersea station through the front door. He later discovers Rose is his daughter from the other universe, and can't handle it; he leaves to continue the fight.

Jackie Tyler (Alternate) – Affected by the control signal, she goes to the processing plant and is converted into a Cyberman. She recognises Pete later, but is lost among the countless Cyberman copies.

Jackie Tyler – Back in the real universe, 'our' Jackie has no idea what happened in the alternate reality. The Doctor tells her Mickey's 'gone home'.

Mrs Moore – The 'brains' of the Preachers, she knows the computer systems and drives the van, and has 'a device for every occasion', be it electronic or chemical. Her real name is Angela Price (she got the name Mrs Moore from a book), and she was married and had children before circumstances took her away; her family believe she's dead, a way to keep them safe. She worked at Cybus Industries in 1995, until she found a file she wasn't supposed to look at in the mainframe and was subsequently attacked by Cybus guards and sent on the run. She's taught herself all of her technical knowledge. A Cyberman at the plant surprises her and kills her by electrocution.

Jake Simmonds – He's very upset by the death of Ricky, but grudgingly comes to accept Mickey's help, and eventually to accept Mickey as a partner in the quest to stop all the other Cybermen. The Doctor asks him to find Mrs Moore's family, to let them know about the sacrifice she made.

Mr Crane – He removes his earpods when the signal begins; Lumic later thinks it's because he's not 'one of the faithful'. Instead, Crane attempts to kill Lumic, though his attempt is short-lived and he's electrocuted to death.

TORCHWOOD: There are no references in this episode.

BODY COUNT: Massive; at least 6,500 people are turned into Cybermen, including Jackie Tyler, and all are presumably dead after the Doctor destroys their emotional inhibitor chips. John Lumic, himself turned into a Cyberman, falls from the Zeppelin ladder, apparently to his death; and Ricky, Crane and Mrs Moore are all electrocuted.

THE DOCTOR'S MAGICAL SONIC SCREWDRIVER: The Doctor uses it to disable Pete's earpods, and again to send the Cybermen away from the rubbish bins he and his friends are hiding behind. He also uses it to seal the door in the underground tunnel, then to deactivate the Cyberman whose emotional inhibitor he breaks. Pete Tyler uses it to cut the rope on the Zeppelin ladder, sending the Cyber-Controller plunging to the ground.

REALITY BITES: Pete calls the Preachers 'Scooby Doo and his gang', referring to the long-running American children's animated programme *Scooby Doo Where Are You?* (and its various re-formatted spin-offs); this featured four teenagers – Shaggy, Velma, Fred and Daphne – and an overly intelligent dog called Scooby Doo, travelling around in a van, solving mysteries; Pete also mentions that the Preachers even have their own van.

The Doctor asks Mrs Moore if she has a hot dog in her pack, calling the item (which she thinks is 'mechanically recovered food') the 'Cyberman of food – but it's tasty!' When Mrs Moore tells the Doctor she took her name from a book, this is possibly a reference to *Mrs Moore in Space* by Gertrude Moore, the mother of astronomer Sir Patrick Moore (who himself was referred to in Series One's 'Aliens of London'), or perhaps to E M Forster's *A Passage to India* in which Mrs Moore is one of the main characters.

In addition to his love of Nintendo ('The Girl in the Fireplace'), Mickey is apparently an adept on the PlayStation, a video game console released by Sony in 1995, that by the early 21st Century had become the most widely-used home gaming system in the Western world.

LINKING THEMES: Rose refers to the Cyberman head she saw in Van Statten's museum ('Dalek'). The Doctor tells her that the Cybermen of their universe started on an 'ordinary world just like this', referring (though not by name) to Mondas, the Cybermen homeworld. He says the Cybermen then swarmed across the galaxy, while the Cybermen of this parallel world are starting in quite the same manner, but on Earth, and will do the same. Cybermen have been kept in cold storage before ('The Tomb of the Cybermen', 'The Invasion'). Their aversion to gold is never mentioned (although it is briefly noted on the Cybus Industries tie-in site that earlier models did show this trait). The use of the phrase 'above, between, below', is an homage to the twentieth anniversary story 'The Five Doctors'.

The Cyber-converted Jackie's knowledge of her previous identity and the awareness demonstrated by Sally Phelan as the Doctor and Mrs Moore deactivate her emotional inhibitor chip echo plot elements in 'Spare Parts'.

Mickey once again refers to himself being considered 'the tin dog', an allusion to K-9 in 'School Reunion' and his fears of being thought of as useless. He says he's not an idiot; the Doctor called him 'Mickey the idiot' in 'World War Three'. He also says that he once saved the universe with a big yellow truck, referring to the maintenance truck he used in 'The Parting of the Ways' to help open a panel on the TARDIS console. Mickey is the first TARDIS companion in the new series to leave voluntarily (Adam Mitchell having been forcibly evicted in 'The Long Game', and Jack Harkness having been left behind at the end of 'The Parting of the Ways'). Noel Clarke notes in this episode's online commentary that the phrase Mickey uses, 'I'm coming to get you', is the same one the Doctor uses when promising to rescue Rose at the end of 'Bad Wolf'.

SCENE MISSING: This episode raises the interesting concept of Cyber upgrade rejection; why would the Cybermen make Lumic their Controller when it's more likely he would be deemed a reject? If it was because they still acknowledged he was their creator, then why did they force him into it? Why, in fact, was Lumic so opposed to the process for himself if it was the reason he started it in the first place? (If he wasn't ready then, what was he waiting for?) Why is the Cyber-Controller attached to a mobile chair; wouldn't he have lost the disabilities that confined him to the chair in the first place? Why does he have glowing eyes (an unnecessary waste of energy)? Why is his brain left visible (making a ready target for any enemies with a gun)? And why does he have a different voice from the other Cybermen?

Why are the Cybermen susceptible to remote deactivation of the emotional inhibitors, if it's key to their design? Why does Lumic not have one, if he's forcibly upgraded by the Cybermen? (He did, after all, go after the Doctor and Rose at the end.) Why did the Cybermen not detect the Doctor's dual heart signature in the first episode of the story? How, given that they walk around with their boots making loud 'clomp clomp' noises, can one sneak up behind the Doctor and Mrs Moore without them hearing it?

If the transmitter is disabled by Mickey and Jake, then how does the emotion chip deactivation signal get broadcast? How does the sonic screwdriver not only activate the 'transmitter' on the Zeppelin but send a signal strong enough to reach it from the distant hilltop where the Doctor is standing? How does the Doctor know that Mickey is watching and listening via the TV monitor? (Sure, it could be a lucky guess... but it is also something of a coincidence.) Also, regarding the Zeppelin, why are the guards a pair of humans instead of Cybermen? Wouldn't they want to run like crazy at the first available opportunity? (It is later established in 'Army of Ghosts' that humans can be under complete Cyber-influence just through wearing the earpods, but at this point that's not explained.) Why does the second rope on the rope ladder suddenly snap at the same time Pete cuts through the first one?

Lumic says he's got production plants on seven continents. Assuming they're the same seven continents identified on our own Earth, that would include Antarctica... inhabited in our reality by a few hundred scientists who could be flown over to South America or Africa for processing. Who are the potential upgrades in Antarctica?

There is a very strange form of computer technology evident here. Following the Doctor's instructions (which the Doctor somehow manages to 'act' to the right security cameras), Mickey seems to become au fait with Lumic's system remarkably quickly, tapping into Cybus using just a keyboard (and, we should add, no mouse!). However, he seems to be simply punching away at random on the keyboard. How does he find the access codes? Why do the access code numerals magically appear on what is merely a CCTV screen? And isn't it far too convenient that the Doctor can affect everything just by plugging Rose's mobile phone, which isn't even a part of this universe, into an outlet?

Regarding the earpods, if Lumic is able to control the population of London with them, why did he attack Jackie's party and not just start controlling everyone? How is Crane able to overcome the signal? And when Crane goes to attack Lumic, why, of all the possible ways to do it, does he simply try and rip the computer monitor from his wheelchair?

How can the Battersea station be the only processing plant for the Cybermen? It would take months, if not years, for the entire population of London and the surrounding areas to pass through it to be converted.

How did the Jackie of 'our' universe know Mickey was with the Doctor and Rose in the first place? (One can only assume that, at some point between the end of 'School Reunion' and the end of this episode, she has been contacted by them, but the inference is that the episodes are contiguous.)

If it was an accident that the TARDIS moved between universes in the first place – something the Doctor even says in this episode is 'impossible' – then how does it do it a second time to make the return trip? And how does the Doctor subsequently repair the fabric of space and time?

ALTERED STATES: One of the original ideas for this and the preceding episode, according to interviews with Russell T Davies and actor Andrew Hayden Smith, was that Jake Simmonds and Ricky Smith were gay, and in a relationship; this would explain Jake's deep sadness over Ricky's death. There was still subtext to this effect in the episodes themselves, but all mention of it was abandoned.

This episode – originally simply known as the second half of 'Parallel World' – was slated to air fifth in the season; the sixth slot would have been taken by an episode entitled 'The Runaway Bride'. As Davies later told *Doctor Who Magazine*, that episode was moved to Series Three's production schedule to become the 2006 Christmas special.

EPISODE 206

BEHIND THE SCENES: Recording on this episode took place at a variety of locations including Mount Stuart Square in Cardiff (the scenes where Londoners are stopped by the earpod broadcasts), Newport Docks (the industrial alley where Ricky is killed), Grangemoor Park (the overlook where the Doctor's group spy on the Battersea plant), Brackla Bunkers near Bridgend (the interiors of the access corridor), a brewery in Magor (the Cybermen conversion tanks), the Uskmouth Power Station (the exterior of the factory) and the Veritair heliport in Cardiff (the 'rooftop' of the factory). Footage from 'Rose' was reused for this episode, specifically in the destruction of the Battersea facility, which was taken from the destruction of the Nestene lair in the earlier episode, although additional material was shot at the Cardiff papermill used in that first episode. *Blue Peter* presenter Gethin Jones played a Cyberman in this episode, uncredited.

OFF THE SCREEN: See 'Rise of the Cybermen' for details about members of the cast.

INTERNAL CONSISTENCY: The entire episode takes place over a couple of hours on the evening of 1 February 2007; it's still the night of the party at the start of the episode. When it ends, it's either before or just after midnight, as it couldn't have taken *too* long for everything to fall apart for the Cybermen.

TARDISODE #6: An order broadcast from John Lumic instructs all locations to start their conversion and upgrade of humans. We see shots of the Cybermen activating and going on the march. Incompatible versions, the order states, should be deleted.

REVIEWS

Now we're talking! After a lacklustre first part, the Cybusmen debut concludes with an episode that wraps up the story with as close to a big-screen action-adventure feel as anything the new series has yet achieved. Character is at the heart of what distinguishes 'The Age of Steel' from the flat 'Rise of the Cybermen'. From the conversation the Doctor has with Mrs Moore to Mickey's interaction with Ricky's friend Jake to Rose's tentative words with Pete Tyler, everyone is fleshed out with feelings that define who they are and why they matter. When faced with the dehumanising threat of Cyber-conversion, it's our feelings that separate us from the metallic juggernaut trying to transform us, and it's this crucial characterisation that makes us care about what happens to everyone on screen. The guest cast deliver this time around, but I still stick by my choice of Colin Spaull as the stand-out in the tale; he gets one of the best scenes in the entire story as he heroically defies Lumic with tragic results. As for the regulars, Tennant is electric in his most Doctorish performance yet as he faces down the Cyber-Controller with glib charm, while Piper rises to the occasion and finds her inner Rose again. Noel Clarke bows out as Mickey, choosing the life of an alternate universe resistance fighter over the position of TARDIS 'tin dog'. But is he really gone for good? I find it hard to believe we've seen the last of Rose's on-again off-again boyfriend, but time will tell... While this is a story that showcases the new series' high production values, there are still those jarring indications of cost-cutting here and there that sometimes push you out of the story. For example, given all the wonderful CGI shots the series has already employed, why is it that we're *told* about the Cyber-army marching along the Thames, but we never get to see it? In fact, it's a bit conspicuous when we see only four Cybermen marching together in some shots – are the larger group shots the result of some computer work? If so, why stop there? And did we really have to see the same shots of the exploding Nestene lair standing in for the destruction of Lumic's Battersea base? Do they think a television viewer's memory is really that short? Hmm, maybe they do. Also in the area of counting every penny, there's the music. Now I've enjoyed Murray Gold's work on the show, particularly his creation of several ongoing themes tied to various characters and situations that recur throughout the series, but by now the music is starting to sound less like unique episodic scores and more an edited patchwork of Gold's Greatest Hits. It makes sense to create some additional emotional resonance by repeating familiar melodic strains, I grant you, but surely we can hear a little more variation in the score instead of just an obvious replay of precisely the same recordings? While all these budget-minded elements grate on my nerves a bit, they're a small price to pay for the series being otherwise well crafted. 'The Age of Steel' is not only a rousing conclusion to Series Two's first two-parter, but it's an episode that almost completely redeems its previous instalment. Almost. – *Arnold T Blumberg*

Most of the set-up having been got out of the way, albeit clunkily, in 'Rise of the Cybermen', 'The Age of Steel' can get on with just being a full-on thrill ride. And it mostly succeeds in that goal – the Doctor and Mrs Moore walking through a tunnel with inactivated Cybermen is a particularly creepy sequence. But, like 'Rise of the Cybermen', 'The Age of Steel' undermines the potential it develops at every turn. A clear case in point is Ricky, who is established as the leader of a resistance network (or at least one cell of that network) and London's Most Wanted... but it turns out his only crime is unpaid traffic fines. Ho ho ho, we're supposed to laugh; but in fact it makes the character (and the Preachers) look weak and ineffectual. Pete's sudden conversion to the side of the angels similarly seems to be for dramatic convenience more than anything. Lumic's conversion to Cyber-Controller should be the crowning moment, the reveal of the big baddie, but he's got Roger Lloyd-Pack's voice and he's behaving as much like a cartoon character as ever. (His whole function in the plot is to gloat, get mad and fall off a ladder.) The body horror of the Cybermen is nicely touched on in two scenes – the Doctor and Mrs Moore talking to the now cybernised bride-to-be, and Pete and Rose losing the converted Jackie to a room full of Cybermen – but it too is undermined by a climax that glosses over the full horror and mass murder taking place. And then there's Mickey. In 'Rose', there's a clear moment where Rose makes a choice and helps the Doctor, even though she has nothing on her side, and it proves she's better than her lot. We should have a moment like that for Mickey... except we don't here. Mickey whines about how he's undervalued and then, hey presto, he gets to be the hero without actually doing much. Overall, the Cybermen two-parter feels dreadfully underdeveloped. The script keeps on suggesting the possibility of real emotions and scary moments, but either undermines or underdevelops them. Even my theory of 'at least the kids will like it' doesn't seem to hold here, as my goddaughter didn't like it very much. It's not that bad a story, about say a 6 or 7 out of 10, but sadly that's well below average for the new *Doctor Who* up until this point. – *Graeme Burk*

There's a major difference between the *Doctor Who* of 2005 and the *Doctor Who* of 2006 – and I'm not talking about David Tennant. Last year, the series went out of its way to avoid the past; the few elements from the show's history were either large-scale public icons (the Daleks, the TARDIS, regeneration), or tiny, fleeting touches no-one but a fan would ever notice. As a critic, I felt compelled to judge the new series on its own merit, referring to the old show as little as possible. This year, there are references *everywhere*, in every episode, and I find myself forced to acknowledge their existence. This is true of no episode more than 'The Age of Steel'. It's better than 'Rise of the Cybermen' by far, but not because it's really got anything new to say or offer. It's full of visual references that try to evoke the Cybermen classics of the past: the 'empty' Cyber-suit from 'The Tomb of the Cybermen'; the Cybermen in the sewer from 'The Invasion'; the conversions from 'Attack of the Cybermen'. It presses all the right buttons, but any fan of the series has had them pressed before. To its credit, the episode is better at presenting the Cybermen themselves. The disturbing element of their existence is in full force; the death of the cybernised bride-to-be is easily the finest scene in the episode, one that's going to show up in clip shows, I feel sure. Again, however, there's something missing. Conversion is scary – but the horror presented here is less that of technology and surgery gone wrong and more that of fascism and Nazi ethnic cleansing. The latter's something we're far more used to associating with the Daleks, and frankly, it's a bit too easy. As a friend of mine is fond of saying, 'Everyone already *knows* Nazis are bad.' Mickey's development, and the whole solution to the story, is similarly lazy. Mickey has gone from a complete idiot to a computer genius, and back, and forth, without any consistency. Now, *Scooby Doo*-style, he can just jump right in and save the day with a few simple keystrokes (and a mobile phone that magically syncs up with Cybus technology). Then, he stays behind in the parallel world to be with his gran... and immediately suggests liberating Paris. What *is* it with this guy? I've enjoyed Mickey's development as a character, but I personally feel he deserved a better departure – or at least one that made a touch more sense. And what's with the Doctor? I found Tennant's Bertie-Wooster-on-speed performance less than appealing this week, with him hopping around like a mad rabbit in front of the Cyber-Controller – right after he's decided to commit mass murder. (Can it really be termed 'euthanasia' if the victims die of intense shock and pain?) Add to that the curious fact that the Cybermen don't even *try* to stop the escaping humans, and I can only wonder where the script editors were this week. Characterisation is simply poor. Very, very poor. Now that I've ragged on 'The Age of Steel', I do feel it's necessary to add that there are some great moments, if comparatively tiny ones: the Cybermen watching Mickey from the other side of a fence; the Cyberman staring into the mirror as it realises its fate; and the realisation that Jackie has been cybernised. But for every great moment, there's at least one that seems badly thought-out, or simply done better nearly 40 years ago. This Cybermen two-parter isn't a complete failure, but I certainly don't feel compelled to revisit it anytime soon. If I want those great memories of classic Cyber terror, I'll simply slip in a DVD – and enjoy television that will stand, and already has stood, the test of time. – *Sarah Hadley*

'The Age of Steel' gets off to a disappointing start with an incredibly disappointing cliff-hanger resolution, which is a particular let-down given how strong the set-up was last week. While it's fair to say that the Doctor having the TARDIS crystal on him was established in part one and doesn't come out of nowhere, basically it's the Doctor zapping the Cybermen with a big energy gun, when I was expecting him to do something clever and interesting. And the episode never really recovers from that, which is a shame as it has some nice moments to it here and there and some good performances. As a whole, I'm sorry to say that, like last year, I found the first two-parter of the season rather weak. It just never really engages very consistently. The best moments for me come with the Doctor and Mrs Moore moving through the tunnels under the power station, with their dark corridors of dormant Cybermen gradually coming to life. This sequence is superbly creepy and very well done, and really classic *Doctor Who* stuff. Mrs Moore being killed off is a nice surprise, too – the new series doesn't actually make a great habit of killing off sympathetic characters, so it is good that they were prepared to do that.

Once again it is the supporting characters who succeed more than the regulars, which seems a shame, particularly given that this is supposed to be Mickey's send-off. Aside from the excellent Helen Griffin as Mrs Moore, it is a pity there isn't more of Colin Spaull again as Mr Crane, as he gets only a couple of very brief scenes before being killed. Lots of death around this week, at least, which usually makes for very good *Doctor Who*, although here it almost seems to be *too* much – Mrs Moore, Mr Crane and then Jackie, which means that the alternate Mrs Tyler's death, or at least Cyber-conversion, doesn't have quite the impact that it otherwise might. If it were just one or two of them, it might have been better. We also have Sally the Cyberwoman, soon to be married, relating her sad, cold story in a scene that sways between being almost touching and completely and utterly ridiculous, and never quite settling on one or the other. I'm not sold on the emotion behind Mickey wanting to stay behind in the parallel world, either – particularly given that he seems to want to stay there because his grandmother is alive, but then he ups and leaves for Paris with Jake as soon as the Doctor and Rose have gone. (Maybe he's discovered in the interim that his gran's been killed or Cyber-converted?) All of this sounds rather picky and makes it seem as if I didn't enjoy the episode. I did – there's no doubt it's entertaining television – but by the very high standards that have thus far been set by the Russell T Davies era of *Doctor Who*, it falls some way short. – *Paul Hayes*

Well, at least the Cybermen look good. Have they ever been so well directed, with their choreographed movements and CGI-multiplied ranks really convincing you that they are an army of steel capable of taking over the world? Sadly, they can convince all they like, but they're about the only thing that does. All my criticisms of 'Rise of the Cybermen' are also applicable to part two, 'The Age of Steel', but magnified ten-fold. Everything is sacrificed for plot convenience, from the Doctor's magic Cyber-destroying crystal, to Rose's super-phone (nice to see that while phones often struggle to talk to one another in this universe, they have no problem talking to a parallel world's computer network). The sonic screwdriver's 'contrivance' setting is used again, mysteriously diverting the Cybermen at one point but not used again for this purpose even at times when it would be life-savingly useful. Such things might be overlooked if the rest of the story were stronger, but it simply isn't. Things happen simply because they have to happen to move the storyline along. Pete Tyler is Gemini because... well, just because. The Cybermen have emotional inhibitors that can be overridden because... well, just because. And when the override is used, things blow up, because... well, you get the picture. Even the good ideas fizzle out: why is Mrs Moore's true identity important? What is the significance of Vitex? Why didn't anyone read this script before making it? Perhaps my expectations were pitched too high and I'm being over-picky. As with part one, 'The Age of Steel' *looks* good, and possibly the type of detailed post mortem that we fans undertake with all the brutality of the Cyber-conversion pointy-things isn't really necessary when we're presented with a story that just screams 'epic' through its visuals, if not its narrative. There is definitely much to commend 'The Age of Steel', if you ramp down the critical facilities: the central concept that the Cybermen are trapped inside their new bodies and will go mad if they realise this is chillingly reinforced by the 'cold... cold ...' scene as well as by the horrific discovery that Jackie is a victim; the sight of queues of people waiting to be converted or burnt in the incinerators; the senseless death of Mrs Moore (Wasn't she just pure class? Has she an alternate version in *this* universe?). Indeed, three scenes stand out as being amongst the best in the entire new series: the Doctor's verbal assault on the newly cybernised Lumic; the Doctor and Mrs Moore's creepy tunnel experience; and, of course, Mickey's decision to stay in the parallel universe. If braver heads had prevailed, the revelation of the gay relationship between Ricky and Jake would have been there as well, but sadly that never made it off the script. There is a good story to be made out of the basic concept. With a better writer, or stricter script editing, imagine what that two-parter could have been under the luscious guidance of Harper. But while this may blow you away visually on first viewing, it cannot stand repeated scrutiny. Still, it has got the kids going 'Delete, delete' in the playground, so mission accomplished. Just not in the most satisfying of ways. – *Craig Hinton*

A very satisfying part two – though, as with much of the more epic-scale modern *Who*, it could often do with a few more minutes to dwell on plot and character points. One of the touchstones of this two-parter, and the revival series as a whole, is 'The Dalek Invasion of Earth' (which, come to think of it, may be where Russell T Davies picked up his recurring character name 'Tyler' in the first place) – the earplugged humans marching zombie-like towards the Cybus factory to be converted are reminiscent of the Robomen from the 1964 story; there's another mutation of Battersea Power Station (its chimneys sheared in the old show, belching smoke here – note to Americans: in reality, the place hasn't smoked in decades); and the emotional climax involves one of the TARDIS crew staying behind with a victorious rebel to help in the reconstruction of a world freshly-rid of cyborg menaces. Given the show's frequent nods to omnisexuality, one wonders if Mickey even notices that the doppelgänger he stays behind to replace – the presumably departing Noel Clarke's finest acting hour comes as Mickey watches his counterpart die – seems to have been gay; in a universe without Rose and with his protective/abusive Gran, Ricky has hooked up with a blond Geordie freedom fighter.

Having 'done' Daleks in Series One, there must have been pressure of the production team to come up with a Cyberman story for Series Two – which, the Master being at least doubly dead, pretty much uses up all the *Who* villains who have entered pop culture outside the show's fandom. Again, we get to explore sides of the villains the old show didn't get to – notably, the concept that individual Cybermen used to be actual individuals (not all of them men, which answers a long-standing question about where the Cyberwomen were... or, indeed, the females of many other monster races; being evolved lizards, the Ice Warriors we saw probably *were* female, with feeble but fertile males back on Mars) and that restoring their emotions would drive them to self-destruction. The most controversial moment comes when the Doctor uses the sonic screwdriver to mercy-kill a fallen Cyberman. Tennant plays it marvellously, as he does the later scene when he empathises with the mental agonies of the awakened human brains in the robot bodies, but there's something human-centric and 'off' about the casual assumption that life as a disembodied brain isn't worth living. Surely, the Doctor would consider other options before taking such a drastic action? As an alien, he might even have a broader view of what constitutes life. The series has always been conservative about this: from the Daleks through Morbius to Lady Cassandra, there's a revulsion at post-human lifeforms that probably needs to be balanced by an episode or two putting another point of view. What 'The Age of Steel' really adds to the canon is its regimented, stamping, clanking, tech-jargon-spouting versions of the Cybermen: we mostly had build-up last week, but here the steel creatures are *everywhere*. I expect the playgrounds of the nation to be full of kids doing that Cyber-march (it reminds me of those kabuki dances with samurai armour) and making metallic percussion noises. – *Kim Newman*

It was Disney's 1987 feature *The Brave Little Toaster* that brought it home to me that male is the default gender. Maybe it's an English language thing? In French and German, a lamp is female. In the movie, a lamp is male, and so is the toaster, a blanket, a radio, a vacuum cleaner and an air conditioner. Come to think of it, in English, all those things are *neuter*. Yet somehow they're also all male. The same is true of Cybus Industries' final product. There is no race or gender, no age or sexuality; the victims of the 'upgrade' are identical, mass-produced machines. They are sexless, therefore they are male. They are not Cybernauts or Metaltrons, they are Cyber*men*. This is why we get such a jolt when a dying Cyberman tells us his name is Sally. At that instant, she snaps from being a neuter monster to a female human being – an individual. And a human being at a moment when the flesh comes to the fore: the night before her wedding. With lasers and scalpels, Sally has been cut off forever from sex, from children, from whatever future she had hoped for. She's like the victim of a car crash or a bomb, snipped off without warning. Lumic would argue she's been rescued from the thousand shocks that flesh is heir to. As one of his 'everlasting children', she will never be sick, never die. She will never catch her husband with someone else, never grieve over a stillborn baby. Lumic wouldn't know Sally from Eve, of course; he's not interested in her. For one thing, he has 'cut out the one thing that makes [her] human' – by which Mrs Moore means her heart. For another, all Lumic really wants are soldiers: identical, obedient, deadly. Only he will retain a form of identity, as the Cyber-Controller. In the end, he doesn't even want that. Looking death in the eye, perhaps Lumic suddenly remembers he's *alive*. Which means sex, which means the endless shuffling of the genetic deck, which means individuality and variation and a chance for the species to survive. His cookie-cutter corpses, in their 'everlasting peace and unity', would never compete or bicker or fight stupid little wars with each other. Nor would they debate or innovate. If one of them is wrong about something, all of them will be wrong about it, and they will never be able to adapt to change. It's this lack of living variation that destroys them: the same code affects every Cyberman equally, like a virus wiping out a monoclone crop of spuds. Lumic's triumph would have achieved only what Justice Robert Jackson called 'the unanimity of the graveyard'. – *Kate Orman*

The Cyber technology is from a crashed Cyber-ship... Mickey dies, stays or gets left behind... Oh, no, no! No! And I'm not crying over spilt Mickey (yeah, right, as if no-one saw that coming). This would have to be one of the worst 45 minutes of *Doctor Who* I've ever sat through. It was also one of the loudest – Clomp! Clomp! Clomp! Never before has an episode of *Doctor Who* given me a headache. Clomp! Clomp! Clomp! Is that a marching theme or the actual foot-thuds of the Cybermen? Actually, I refuse to call them Cybermen, because that's not what they are. John Lumic, the creator, calls them 'Upgrades', so surely that's what they should be called? And just as Pete2 and Jackie2 are not Rose's parents, these monstrosities are not *the* Cybermen! They are Upgrades... As for the design, they look okay from the waist up, but what's with the Robocop legs and cartoon Mickey Mouse feet? Okay, maybe the synchronised Cyber-clomp-a-thon movement was designed with 'kids can imitate it in the playground' in mind, but it just looks (and sounds) ridiculous. No, damn-near irritating is the term. 'Riverdance of the Cybermen'?? Whirrr! That's the sound of Kit Pedler and Gerry Davies rotating in their graves. I was so hoping there would be a revelation that Lumic had found a crashed Cyber-ship and had cannibalised the technology to make his Upgrades. Now, *that* would have been far more acceptable as an 'origin' than that with which we were presented here. If the Upgrades were not passed off as Cybermen, I'd probably have enjoyed this so much more. (Note to self – *stop* calling them Cybermen!) But I do reckon the Cyberman (arrg!) that got zapped by the

TARDIS crystal at the start of part two was blasted into the 'real' universe, so setting in motion the course of events leading to the season finale. At least I *hope* that's what happened, as it would make sense of an otherwise unforgivable *doctor ex machina* (sic) cliff-hanger resolution... There were so many potentially good ideas on display in this as well as last week's instalment (although just how much is Tom MacRae, and how much is executive interference?) but the whole shambles is poorly conceived and executed. (In fact, I said exactly the same about the 'Aliens of London'/'World War Three' two-parter in the first *Back to the Vortex*.) Breaking it down, 'The Age of Steel' is a greatest hits compilation of moments from last year – the radio transmitter sending an activation signal ('Rose'); all the Pete/Jackie/Rose stuff ('Father's Day'); a hybrid creature feeling the heat/cold before dying ('Dalek'). Worst of all is the way in which Mickey the Idiot saves the day (again!) by hacking easily (what, has Cybus never heard of passwords, encryption and firewalls?) into the computer systems (*à la* 'World War Three'). I could say I loathed and detested this episode, but that's way too harsh a criticism; however, this highly anticipated two-parter gets my vote for worst of the season to date. And given that the rumour mill indicates the Upgrades will be back at the end of the season, I for one am not particularly looking forward to that rematch. – *Jon Preddle*

Action-packed, if a tad hollow, 'The Age of Steel' clunks through the gears with a nicely self-aware piece of *deus ex machina* – the resolution to the previous episode's cliff-hanger. Thereafter, as with the previous episode, it's something of a game of two halves. Again, the design is elegant in an austere kind of way and the dialogue is witty and engaging ('At least I've got the catering staff on my side'; 'He will be rewarded. By force!'). The episode exudes a nice – and very human – *faux-Quatermass* feel, with some decent ethical questions being asked, a very sober line in abattoir imagery and, a few visual clichés aside, some assured quality direction by Graeme Harper. The latter, in particular, leads to a quite spectacular pyrotechnic climax before the episode ends on something of a downbeat (and rather contrary) coda. In relation to the latter, there's also a very well-observed double performance by Noel Clarke, who manages to bring Mickey's story full-circle with a lot of humour and not a little dramatic insight. Indeed, the only aspects of 'The Age of Steel' that in any major way disappoint are a few seemingly arbitrary bits of plot and characterisation that appear to be there purely to fill in a ten minute gap in the middle when pretty much nothing happens. The episode, of course, turns on a wonderfully realised 'Genesis of the Daleks' moment with the Doctor questioning whether he has the right to use the Cybermen's greatest weakness – emotion – powerfully and painfully against them. That dilemma doesn't last for long however. This is, after all, a very 21st Century *Doctor Who* story, in which a mobile phone call saves the world. Which, for all of the two-parter's traditionalist minimalism, is a reassuringly forward-looking step. – *Keith Topping*

EDITOR'S REVIEW: It's cheesy, it meanders quite a bit, and it's not exactly a fully satisfying wrap-up to 'Rise of the Cybermen', but for some reason, 'The Age of Steel' works on a basic level. Despite itself. I'm not sure, exactly, if this has something to do with my lowered expectations – I have a very hard time with science-fiction stories that attempt to take the macro-view, in this case the fate of an entire planet, and wrap it up in the course of 90 minutes – or if it's simply that there's a lot of heart present here. Despite the plot holes (and there are some doozies), the parallel world scenario I was talking about, and the fact that the Cybermen are pretty much unimportant doppelgängers in the larger scheme.

For all his blusterous theatrics, here the Doctor actually presents ideas that work, with the human element so strong within them; obviously the writer, Tom MacRae, presented with the fact that here we have the whole planet ready to take a jump off the proverbial cliff, has focused instead on the personal stories, leaving us only to imagine what's happened to the rest of the world. In fact, this works well when we have no clue... We know Jackie Tyler is a Cyberman, but she wanders off, and we can only assume that she dies horribly when the Doctor sabotages the control codes.

There's a tremendous canvas of heartbreak in 'The Age of Steel', and it's knowing that the people who die are people who were actually cared about by someone; they're not nameless faces being shot at with laser beams. Ricky Smith loved his grandmother; Mrs Moore had a family she wanted to get back to one day, when this was all over; Pete Tyler, despite the separation, truly did care about Jackie. While Lumic's actual motives for what he's done are pretty pointless – hey John, if you really want to save your own life, do you have to take millions of people with you in the process? – in his own twisted way he might have even cared about the upgrades he was bringing to fruition, calling them his children, as if shepherding in a new and quite twisted age of humanity for the record books. 'The Age of Steel', then, is really about death and loss, and having to pick up the pieces when it's all over.

What's interesting here is that, for the first time this season, Billie Piper's Rose is really moved to the back burner – ironic, in a story that revolves (once again) mostly around her own family – in order to bring us other personalities. While Andrew Hayden-Smith as Jake Simmonds is given the short end here, Helen Griffin has time to bring pathos to her character Mrs Moore, and make us truly sad that she dies. Shaun Dingwall has presented us with fully another side of Pete Tyler; knowing what he did with the role last season, it's quite a shock to watch the lackadaisical man who gave up his life for his newborn daughter turn his back on her when presented with her for the first time.

But this episode really belongs to Noel Clarke. I confess that I was no fan of Clarke's after seeing only the first episode, 'Rose', and it was a relief to find out much later that he wasn't a fan of himself there, either; he does have a range and experience, and given the right material, he can truly shine. Here, Clarke gives a heartfelt, and ultimately heartbreaking, performance as Mickey; one can feel that he's genuinely upset by the 'idiot' and 'tin dog' appellations, and those aren't exactly crocodile tears in his eyes at the end. As out of place as the character felt in the TARDIS, especially in 'The Girl in the Fireplace' where he was really nothing more than a sounding board so that Rose had someone to talk to besides herself, Mickey's ultimate fate here seems so right, so obvious, and yet never forced; he has a chance here to do some good, like he's watched the Doctor and Rose do so many times, and perhaps make peace with his own role in the tragedy that took his grandmother away from him.

It is a pity that such a moving moment this series as Mickey's departure – far more moving, to my mind, than the protracted, drawn-out farewell sequence in 'Doomsday' at the end of this season – is somewhat cheapened by events still to come. It would have been nice to see Mickey ride off with Jake toward Paris, never knowing what was really going to happen, but imagining that the Earth of this universe is safe, and it's all because Mickey Smith was there, and did some good, and really made a difference. Again. – *Shaun Lyon*

207: THE IDIOT'S LANTERN

The Doctor and Rose visit London in 1953, as the country is captivated by the impending Coronation of Queen Elizabeth II. But someone's selling television sets cheaply, people are disappearing off the streets, and then there's the matter of the Connolly family... and grandma, who's missing her face entirely.

FIRST TRANSMISSION: UK – 27 May 2006. US – 10 November 2006. Canada – 20 November 2006. Australia – 26 August 2006. New Zealand – 24 August 2006.
DURATION: 45'08"
WRITER: Mark Gatiss
DIRECTOR: Euros Lyn
CREDITED CAST: David Tennant (The Doctor), Billie Piper (Rose Tyler), Maureen Lipman (The Wire), Ron Cook (Magpie), Jamie Foreman (Eddie Connolly), Debra Gillett (Rita Connolly), Rory Jennings (Tommy Connolly), Margaret John (Grandma Connolly), Sam Cox (Detective Inspector Bishop), Ieuan Rhys (Crabtree), Jean Challis (Aunty Betty), Christopher Driscoll (Security Guard), Marie Lewis (Mrs Gallagher)

WHERE AND WHEN: Florizel Street, Muswell Hill, North London, 1 and 2 June 1953

THE STORY UNFOLDS: A lightning strike on the television antenna of Magpie Electricals, an electronics shop in London, proves to be anything but lightning... an alien lifeform, calling itself the Wire, escaped execution by its own kind by taking the form of an electrical pattern. Now a being of pure energy, the Wire manifests itself via television sets, taking on the visage of a female BBC presenter to communicate with the outside world. It feeds off the electrical activity of the brains of its victims, sending them into complete neural shutdown, using bolts of energy spewed forth from the television sets that Magpie has been selling; a side effect is that the victims' faces are completely wiped away, leaving blank skin where their eyes, noses and mouths should be.

The Doctor and Rose were expecting to arrive in New York in the 1950s, to see Elvis Presley perform on *The Ed Sullivan Show*, but they're years early and in Britain. In the same neighbourhood as Magpie's shop, Florizel Street in the Muswell Hill area of North London, the Connolly family is one of many that have bought new televisions and have been subsequently affected by the Wire. The police find out and take the victims, such as the Connolly's neighbour Mr Gallagher, from their homes. The police are using unmarked black cars to snatch the 'victims' and drive off; the investigator, Detective Inspector Bishop, has rounded them up at an empty warehouse. The affliction has been spreading out from North London but is most concentrated in Florizel Street. Everyone in the Connollys' neighbourhood has started getting television sets, including Mr Gallagher and the Bells 'at number 67'.

The Wire is planning to use a portable television, constructed by Magpie, to hijack the broadcast of Queen Elizabeth II's Coronation, in order to steal the energy from millions of people's minds and regain corporeal form. To stop it, the Doctor redirects the energy from the transmitter and puts it onto a videotape where it can do no harm. (The Doctor says he will use his knowledge of 'trans-temporal extirpation methods to neutralise the residual electronic pattern'; in other words, he'll tape over it.)

The Doctor owns a blue Vespa motor scooter (registration YWV 140) – albeit from a time period somewhat after 1953 – which he uses to drive himself and Rose around. He later gives it to Tommy as a present (but asks him to garage it for a few years). He and Rose were hoping to watch Elvis sing 'Hound Dog' on *The Ed Sullivan Show*. He says that 1953 is a 'brilliant' year with the invention of Technicolor (see 'Technical Goofs'), the climbing of Mount Everest and the country coming off rations. He says (referring to the police kidnapping) that 1953 is supposed to be Churchill's England and not Stalin's Russia.

According to the BBC announcer (which Magpie's television is turned to at the start of the episode), *What's My Line* has just aired; the programme's music was orchestrated by Sir Rodrey Fenning, and Dame Evelyn Glish is a member of the Kingsland Players. The announcer's broadcast originates from Alexandra Palace.

Bishop uses 'Operation Market Stall' (basically, driving into a building and having a makeshift market stall erected at the entrance to thwart pursuers) to fool the Doctor. The warehouse where the faceless victims are held has a sign that reads 'Offices to Let' from the 'Gardiner Lawton' firm at 27 Maddox Street, 6969. 'B Clacy and Son' is seen on the rubbish haulage truck.

THE DOCTOR: Using his psychic paper for credentials, he masquerades as a British official (with Rose his associate) in the Connolly household, and later as the King of Belgium to an official at Alexandra Palace. Rose wonders if he's actually passed his motor scooter driving test. He tells Rose that he likes 'the domestic approach' about her (which may or may not be an insult). He knows that you can't wrap your hand around your elbow and make your fingers meet, and he swears by rubber soles on shoes (which can't be affected by electrical impulses). The Wire says that he's 'smart as paint'. He knew Jackie Tyler would be a Cliff Richard fan and he loves television.

ROSE TYLER: She'd been hoping the TARDIS would arrive in Elvis Presley's Vegas era (the late 1960s-1970s) instead of the '50s. She knows the lingo from the 1950s; Rose and her mother watched Cliff Richard movies every bank holiday Monday. Her nan said that televisions were so rare in the early 1950s that everyone had to pile into one house to watch events like the Coronation. She knows about the Union Flag name controversy because her mother used to go out with a sailor. She always accidentally tapes over videos.

CHARACTER BUILDING: *Mr Magpie* – He owns Magpie Electricals, and is practically giving away television sets ('Magpie's Marvellous Tellies', he calls them) for only five pounds a box. The Wire first contacted him when it got to Earth. He's £200 overdrawn on his bank accounts and needs some sort of miracle, which the Wire ostensibly provides. The Wire doesn't take his face; instead it makes a deal with him, but it's still in his mind (he says that he hurts behind his eyes), and it's implied that it's stolen his soul as well. He says that 'pomp and circumstance' are what the British do best. The Wire destroys him after using him to reach Alexandra Palace.

Eddie Connolly – Head of the Connolly household, a deeply patriotic man but also a bully who intimidates his family. He is himself intimidated by the Doctor, who masquerades as a public official. In fact, Eddie has been informing the police of the victims on his block, ostensibly to protect his reputation within the community. Rita kicks him out of the house, but he remains defiant and proud.

Tommy Connolly – Connolly's teenaged son. He's scared of what's happened on their street, and thinks the people are turning into monsters. He wants to go to college, but his father wants him to work alongside him in a shop. He reads the magazine *Radio Enthusiast*. He discovers what his father's been up to and turns his back on him, and then helps the Doctor stop Magpie. Later, Rose persuades him to go after his father as he leaves, and to try to salvage what's left of their relationship.

Rita Connolly – Wife of Eddie, kept in what her husband believes is her place until she discovers Eddie's role in the disappearances, after which she kicks him out of the house. Her mother is one of the victims.

Grandma Connolly – Rita's mother. She's heard that televisions rot your brains to soup and that your brains then pour out of your ears. Her mind and her face are later stolen by the Wire. She owns the Connollys' house.

Detective Inspector Bishop – He heads up the investigation into the neighbourhood affliction... or rather, the hush-up of the problems in the community, for the sake of the Coronation day. He's rather irritated that he can't spend more time on the case because he doesn't have the man power. He's been on the force 20 years. His name is written inside his shirt collar (which the Doctor, naturally, notices).

Aunty Betty – Eddie Connolly's aunt; he calls her Beth. Regarding Tommy supposedly being a 'mummy's boy', she tells Eddie he ought to beat that out of him.

TORCHWOOD: As Bishop speaks in the background to a policeman, he says, 'Heaven help us if something happens in public tomorrow for the big day, we'll have Torchwood on our back.'

BODY COUNT: Magpie dies when the Wire disintegrates him, but apart from that, it appears everyone survives; the victims have their faces and personalities returned to them.

THE DOCTOR'S MAGICAL SONIC SCREWDRIVER: The Doctor uses this to break the lock on the door leading into the police warehouse, and again on the gates keeping the Wire's victims inside. He also uses it to detect the power source in Magpie's shop, and then to stop the Wire from stealing his face.

REALITY BITES: There are references galore in this episode to Elvis Presley, the American singer considered to be the 'king' of rock-and-roll music. The Doctor's hairstyle mimics Presley's and he occasionally adopts a similar type of slang ('You goin' my way, doll?') The 1950s, the Doctor says, are the period when they called Elvis 'the Pelvis' ('while he still had a waist').

Florizel Street, the name of the road in which much of the action takes place, is fictional. In fact, Florizel Street was the working title for the British soap *Coronation Street*, which began in 1960 and still runs on ITV today.

Alexandra Palace, built in 1873 in Muswell Hill, became the site of transmission of BBC television in 1936. It was used as the BBC's main transmission centre until 1956, but was still used for news, Open University course broadcasts and other occasional radio and television broadcasts thereafter; today 'Ally Pally', as it is affectionately known, is a national landmark.

'Are you sitting comfortably? Then I'll begin' was the opening phrase used on the BBC Radio series *Listen with Mother* (1950-1982). (Incidentally, it was also used by the Doctor himself in 'School Reunion'.) 'Goodnight children, everywhere' was a catchphrase used by BBC

Children's Hour presenter 'Uncle Mac', real name Derek McCulloch.

The Union Flag, Rose claims, is properly referred to as the Union Jack only when it's flown at sea. This most likely comes from the flying of the flag off the jack staff on British ships; the name Union Jack has actually bred controversy over the years, but remains in popular use.

The Doctor says he has invented the home video 30 years early, and refers to the Betamax format. Betamax was a videotape standard that was sent into relative obscurity (at least in home consumption format) by the advent of VHS.

The Doctor namechecks Australian singer-songwriter Kylie Minogue, quoting her as saying 'It's never too late'; this is based on her song 'Never Too Late', released on her second album, 'Enjoy Yourself' (1989). Singer Sir Cliff Richard OBE is also namechecked.

Period television references in the episode include a brief clip from *Muffin the Mule*, a children's programme broadcast from 1946 to 1955 on BBC Television; a mention of *What's My Line*, a game show originating in the US that ran in the UK from 1951 to 1963, again on BBC Television, and was revived decades later in several incarnations; and actual footage from the BBC's coverage of Queen Elizabeth II's Coronation on 2 June 1953.

The Ed Sullivan Show was a variety series that ran every Sunday night on CBS Television in America from June 1948 to June 1971. The show featured many musicians in their nationwide debuts, and the appearance of the Beatles in 1964 permanently changed the country's pop culture. Presley made the first of three appearances on 9 September 1956; it drew nearly 60 million viewers. American media treated Presley as an enigma; his appearances on *The Ed Sullivan Show* and elsewhere caused considerable ire because of his gyrations, and the show received many complaints at the time.

'Idiot's lantern' was a colloquial term for a television set in Britain during the 1940s and 1950s. Pye television sets at the time cost about £70, including installation; the £5 Magpie was charging was all but giving sets away. Bakelite is a hard but brittle plastic made from synthetic polymers and was used to make radio and television casings, amongst many other things; the Doctor tastes the substance on the device he finds in Magpie's shop and can detect a bakelite residue.

LINKING THEMES: The Queen made a brief appearance (played by actress Mary Reynolds) in the *Doctor Who* 25th anniversary story 'Silver Nemesis' in 1988. Another story, 'The Faceless Ones', dealt with a race of aliens who had lost their identities and become 'faceless'.

A few of the scribblings on the label of the Betamax tape resemble the Gallifreyan 'language' (convoluted circular patterned designs) used in some of the marketing and design for the series.

SCENE MISSING: At the beginning of the episode, Mr Magpie is £200 (around £13,000 in modern terms) overdrawn on his bank account. How, then, is he able to get enough television sets to distribute to the entire neighbourhood at only five quid each? With such a small enterprise, how would he distribute hundreds, if not thousands, of such televisions to people all over London in such a short amount of time? Moreover, why does the Wire actually *need* him to distribute cheap televisions, if all we're talking about is a few hundred people; why can't it feed off the minds of those who already have television sets (obtained elsewhere than from Magpie Electricals), and therefore avoid arousing the suspicion that brought Bishop, and then the Doctor, into this whole business in the first place? Also, how does the Wire know Magpie's name the moment it enters his television set?

When the Doctor and Rose first arrive, how do they miss all the Union Flags adorning the street before they see the bus that clues them in to the fact that they're *not* in New York?

Magpie describes the Wire as 'one of these modern programmes' – but in the early '50s, all TV was modern!

The police are trying to keep information about the victims quiet, but they have a collection of photos of them up in the room where they interrogate the Doctor.

If the Wire's energy steals the electrical impulses from the brain, why does this remove the physical features – eyes, nose and mouth – from the victim's face? (Not to mention, *how* does it do it?) But more importantly, if their noses and mouths are gone, how do the victims breathe? Presumably these are still flesh and blood creatures whose cells need the nourishment of oxygen, and they don't look like they've died by the episode's end. (Also, how do they take in water or food, presuming some of these victims have been missing for weeks?)

How do all the victims get their faces back the minute the Wire is defeated?

If the Wire has no corporeal form and is using the television set as a way to contact Magpie, how can the picture turn from black and white to colour? In 1953, television sets did not contain the components needed to generate a colour image.

The Doctor and Tommy get to Alexandra Palace only a few minutes behind Magpie, yet he was in his van and they were (apparently) on foot and had to collect the equipment necessary to stop the Wire. How did they get there so quickly? Also, in the shop, why does the Wire steal Bishop's face but not the Doctor's or Tommy's?

Why do all the faces appear on the television sets in the shop?

Why is it that when millions of people's lives are in danger the Doctor considers it merely a mystery to be solved, but when Rose's life is in danger he says that *nothing in the world* can stop him? Since when did the the the Doctor rate his companion's safety so much more highly than the greater good? In the earlier series, the greater good seemed to be his principal concern, and frequently the Doctor would risk sacrificing his travelling companion if necessary to prevent history from being altered or lives being lost; witness the death of Adric in 'Earthshock', or Ace's life being manipulated in 'The Curse of Fenric'.

ALTERED STATES: A line cut from the original script had the Doctor mentioning his fear of falling off transmitter towers (a reference to 'Logopolis', in which just such a fall led to him regenerating). The original title for the episode submitted to the BBC in the second series brief was 'Mr Sandman'; it was originally slated to air ninth after 'The Satan Pit' two parter.

BEHIND THE SCENES: The episode was recorded mostly on location in and around Cardiff. A house in Blenheim Road was used, heavily redressed, as the storefront for Magpie Electricals, while Florentia Street was redecorated as the fictional Florizel Street, and the rear of the Cardiff Royal Infirmary substituted as the base of the Alexandra Palace transmitter station (with a room inside the infirmary doubling for the control station). The Veritair heliport in Cardiff was used for the sequences on top of the transmitter tower. The South Dock of Newport Docks was used as Bishop's headquarters, while other scenes were recorded in studio.

For many scenes during this episode, director Euros Lyn employed a type of camera angle called a Dutch angle (or Dutch tilt), which utilises a diagonal camera axis to offset the scene. This is often used by directors to create an atmosphere of tension, unease or outright fear.

The official BBC *Doctor Who* website featured a game, called 'Magpie's Online Archive', based on this episode. The user needed to search various television clips from BBC history in order to detect clues left by the Wire. These included scenes from *Red Dwarf*, *Fawlty Towers*, *The Flowerpot Men*, *Muffin the Mule* (the clip used in this episode) and *Blake's 7*. Kylie Minogue's song 'Never Too Late' was also heard.

DULCET TONES: The national anthem of the United Kingdom, 'God Save the Queen', was heard during the Coronation; of course, up until the year prior, during the reign of George VI, it had been known as 'God Save the King'.

Also of note in this episode is the reuse of certain movements from 'Song for Ten', the song written for 'The Christmas Invasion', over the end of the episode when Tommy goes to help his father. Composer Murray Gold also mimicked 1950s era music in his incidental score elsewhere in the story.

OFF THE SCREEN: Maureen Lipman CBE is an actress, comedian and columnist best known for her role as Jane Lucas in *Agony* (1979) and a series of television advertisements for British Telecom; she's also appeared in *The Fugitives* (2005), *Jonathan Creek* (2003), *The Pianist* (2002), *Oklahoma!* (1999), *Carry On Columbus* (1992), *About Face* (1991), *A Little Princess* (1986) and *Educating Rita* (1983). In addition, Lipman has written for *Good Housekeeping* magazine, has a weekly column in the *Guardian* and has hosted several television programmes on design. Ron Cook has been seen in *Casanova* (2005), *The Merchant of Venice* (2004), *Thunderbirds* (2004), *Hornblower* (2003), *24 Hour Party People* (2002), *Quills* (2000), *Topsy-Turvy* (1999), *Secrets & Lies* (1996) and *The Cook, The Thief, His Wife and Her Lover* (1989). Jamie Foreman has been in *My Family* (2006), *Oliver Twist* (2005), *Layer Cake* (2004), *High Stakes* (2001), *Sleepy Hollow* (1999), *Casualty* (1999), *Bugs* (1997), *Inspector Morse* (1992) and *Dempsey & Makepeace* (1985). Debra Gillett was seen in *Spooks* (2004), *Dalziel and Pascoe* (2002), *Cold Feet* (2001), *Coogan's Run* (1995) and *The Witches* (1990). Rory Jennings has been in *Brief Encounters* (2006), *Jericho* (2005), *All About George* (2005), *Tom's Midnight Garden* (1999), *The Fast Show* (1995) and *Casualty* (1994). Margaret John appeared as Megan Jones in the *Doctor Who* story 'Fury From the Deep' (1968), and has also been in *High Hopes* (2005), *Eyes Down* (2003), *Lovejoy* (1993), *International Velvet* (1978), the pilot episode of *Blake's 7* (1978), *Emmerdale Farm* (1972), *Doomwatch* (1970), *Dixon of Dock Green* (1967), *Z Cars* (1967) and *Suspense* (1963). Sam Cox has been in *Holby City* (1999), *Crime Traveller* (1997), *Prime Suspect* (1995) and *Bergerac* (1989). Ieuan Rhys was in *High Hopes* (2005), *A Mind to Kill* (1996) and *The Englishman Who Went Up a Hill But Came Down a Mountain* (1995). Jean Challis was in *The Bill* (2003), *One Foot in the Grave* (1992), *Goodnight Sweetheart* (1993), *She Wolf of London* (1990), *Only Fools and Horses* (1988), *Are You Being Served?* (1985) and *Hi-De-Hi* (1981). Christopher Driscoll was seen in *Murder in Mind* (2001), *A Touch of Frost* (1996), *Mr Bean* (1994), *Casualty* (1989), *Quatermass* (1979) and *Born and Bred* (1978). Marie Lewis was also in *Rocket Man* (2005). Writer Mark Gatiss's credits were listed in the first *Back To The Vortex* book.

TECHNICAL GOOFS: It rained in London on 2 June 1953 during the Coronation, but it's sunny in this episode. During the Coronation party, Rita's hair covers her ears, but when she goes outside (when the Doctor and Detective Inspector appear at the door), it is behind them. At the end of the story when the Doctor and Rose clink their glasses together, in the close up the level of the liquid is significantly lower than it is in the wide shots. The BBC 'bat wings' ident seen on the television screens in Magpie's shop did not actually appear on BBC television until December 1953. Also, Muswell Hill has never had rows of houses like those featured in the episode, and although Alexandra Palace can be seen from there, the view is quite different from that depicted.

The Doctor's reference to 1953 being the year of the invention of Technicolor is not strictly correct; the initial Technicolor process was used between 1934 and 1954. In 1953, Eastman Kodak introduced a higher quality colour negative film capable of storing colour for longer periods without degradation. It's also possible that the Doctor is referring to the introduction of colour television itself; in March of 1953 the NTSC (National Television System Committee) in the USA adopted the first colour broadcast standard in the world. However, this really would never have been called 'Technicolor'. The standard has come to be known as NTSC, colloquially.

CONTROVERSIES: The 'soap opera' quality of the Connolly story was disliked by some fans. The character of Tommy was also considered by some to be a 'Mary Sue' – a term used to describe a character loosely based on the author, who is inexplicably able to save the day – although Mark Gatiss was in fact born in the 1960s rather than the 1940s.

INTERNAL CONSISTENCY: The Queen's Coronation takes place on 2 June 1953. Much of the climax of the episode is set on that date, and the Doctor and Rose arrive the day before (1 June), as that evening at Magpie's shop, Rose mentions that the Coronation is 'tomorrow'. However, the first two scenes are obviously set a considerable time earlier; the Wire's arrival predates the disappearances of many people in the neighbourhood, and there would have to have been ample time for Magpie to distribute his television sets far and wide. Bishop mentions that the Wire's victims first started appearing 'about a month ago', so it's as least as long as that, and perhaps longer.

TARDISODE #7: A delivery man unpacks a Magpie Electricals television set for Grandma Connolly. Later, she succumbs to an attack by the Wire, as we learn that the Coronation of Queen Elizabeth II is imminent.

The TARDISode is set somewhere between the first appearance of Grandma Connolly in the episode and the sequence where we discover that she's been locked up in her room.

REVIEWS

For an episode that blends elements of classic *Who* stories like 'Logopolis' and 'Delta and the Bannermen' with equal parts *Sapphire and Steel*, *Twilight Zone: The Movie*, and *Shocker*, 'The Idiot's Lantern' proves to be surprisingly inconsequential and forgettable. For all its charm in the choice of setting and some really nice isolated touches, the episode commits the sin of aspiring to be nothing but a run-of-the-mill adventure; it achieves this goal with no particular distinction and blends in with most of the typical fare one might expect from the titular device. This story, as with a lot of average television, is mildly diverting, occasionally surprising, but ultimately disposable. The 1950s time period is squandered by limiting the episode to a single street, with no chance to explore the era in any significant way. The guest cast is generally serviceable but not stellar, although Ron Cook is excellent as the tormented Magpie. As for the evil alien Wire's plot to manifest itself by sucking brain energy from 20 million humans, it rests at the centre of a threadbare, inconsistent story filled with numerous logic holes. Why does leeching energy involve physically removing the victims' faces? Why do these faces appear on the television sets in Magpie's store? Why do the zombie-like (enough already with the zombies!) victims clench their fists? How do they continue to exist at all when they cannot breathe or eat and, as the Doctor himself points out, exist as blank slates with totally empty minds? What is the device that the Doctor throws together for the nonsense tech solution at the end? What's all that about the big tower being able only to transmit or to receive at any one time? And how many more times will the Doctor only *really* get motivated to save the day when Rose is directly affected? Threaten millions of innocent lives and he'll do what he can to help them, but go after Rose, and my Lord you'd better plan to run to the furthest ends of time and space and hide in the deepest, darkest hole in existence, because this guy will tear you to pieces with his bare hands! I mean, I love the relationship between the two of them more than I ever expected I would, but this single-mindedness is getting a bit annoying. Surely the Doctor is intelligent enough to see beyond Rose's captivating eyes, her silky hair, her full, pouting... sorry. I said there were some highlights. The atmospheric music is one very nice touch, as is the fantastic direction. Almost every single shot in the episode is pitched at a severe angle, recalling the off-kilter charm of the old *Batman* TV series but also nicely evoking the feel of a comfortable setting tilted off its axis by the bizarre events taking place in an otherwise normal neighbourhood. Or maybe they just forgot to straighten the camera; but let's give them the benefit of the doubt. Tennant and Piper have some strong moments – the Doctor's interview with the detective for one, and Rose's determined investigation of the TV shop for another – but despite these bits and pieces the episode as a whole just feels like mindless filler that doesn't bear close scrutiny. But what do you expect from the tube? – *Arnold T Blumberg*

As readers of the last *Back to the Vortex* volume will be aware, I was probably the only reviewer who didn't like 'The Unquiet Dead', feeling it was traditional in all the ways that traditional *Doctor Who* stories *shouldn't* be: safe, recalling past glories but doing nothing terribly interesting and, worst of all, rendering the series' best asset , the new Doctor, useless in the resolution of the plot. I'm happy to say that those are not my feelings about 'The Idiot's Lantern', which I think is traditional in the best sense of the term: fun, inventive and entertaining. The great thing about 'The Idiot's Lantern' is how wonderfully charming it all is. Tennant and Piper get some great (and much needed) comedy scenes – it is delightful watching the Doctor and Rose put Mr Connolly in his place; and the Doctor literally turning around his interrogation by the police detective (as the other officer in the background attempts to touch his own elbow!) is one of the funniest scenes this season. The premise is delightfully off-kilter – a being that lives in television that literally rips your face off – and the Wire is a wonderful idea for a villain. What better menace could *Doctor Who* have than a 1950s continuity announcer? Maureen Lipman plays the character perfectly – upper-middle class, received pronunciation, all perfectly coiffured and yet concealing great misery beneath. Which pretty much sums up life in both the Muswell Hill community the story is set within and the 1950s in general. Mark Gatiss loves creating grotesques, but the wonderful thing about his grotesques (both here and in *The League of Gentlemen*) is that they're rooted in a real sense of pathos – Mr Connolly is a jerk but ultimately he's a character to be pitied, not sneered at. All the same, you can't help but cheer for Mrs Connolly when she shows him the door. I harbour no illusions that 'The Idiot's Lantern' is the best story of the season. But it's hugely entertaining, and I finished it with a great smile on my face having been delivered some scares, some comedy and great characters. After the debacle of the Cybermen two-parter, it's a return to form for the series and I couldn't be more delighted. – *Graeme Burk*

The most basic statement I can make about this week's *Doctor Who* is that it's brilliant. Really, really brilliant. It's so much better than the Cybermen episodes that I actually feel a sense of relief. 'The Idiot's Lantern' is classic *Doctor Who* in ways that the last two-parter could only hope to mimic: it's both funny and eerie, with memorable imagery and a solution that, if a bit contorted, is very much in the spirit of the show. What could be more *Doctor Who* than a creature that steals your identity by sucking off your face? It's completely ludicrous, but hey – raise your hand if you remember 'Pyramids of Mars'. Now, how many folks call that one of the best, if not *the* best, of the original series? I rest my case. For my money, this was one of the best episodes this year, if not my actual favourite. It harks back to a lot of classic, scary TV – *The Twilight Zone* and *Sapphire and Steel* come immediately to mind – as well as Gatiss's own *Doctor Who* novel *Nightshade*. I think what I like best about it is that it has a 'point' to make, as many of the new series episodes do (in this case, that individuality is important), but it carries the idea through as an homage to early television. It's entirely in keeping with the period it celebrates. But it's also extremely funny, especially in the first half, and for the first time since 'Tooth and Claw', Billie Piper's really back in a big way. She's been sidelined for most of this year, and sad as I am to finally admit it, her chemistry with David Tennant isn't anything close to what it was with Christopher Eccleston. (One friend of mine commented that she and Tennant are like 'a couple of girls'.) This episode, though, shows a much wittier, 'best friends' sort of dynamic for Rose and the Doctor. She steals several of the early scenes, and I wouldn't say no to more of this kind of relationship at all. The regulars are very ably supported by a solid secondary cast, chiefly Maureen Lipman and Ron Cook; the whole thing clips along at a great pace; and Euros Lyn – man, Euros Lyn just *loves* his job, doesn't he? He has quickly become the powerhouse director of new *Who*, slipping into historical periods as cleanly as a knife through butter. Although I found his direction solid last year, this year he's truly come into his own. 'The Idiot's Lantern' features what must be his most showy direction – look at those angled shots! – but, to my mind, it adds tremendously to the atmosphere. There are a couple of weak moments – Jamie Foreman and David Tennant are both a bit too shouty for their own good – but otherwise, this is an utterly entertaining little metaphorical tale, something that would fit in with nearly any era of *Doctor Who*, and completely enjoyable from beginning to end. Maybe it isn't particularly modern in approach, maybe it isn't the most important episode in the series, but 'The Idiot's Lantern' works for me. Sometimes, simple is just plain better. – *Sarah Hadley*

'The Idiot's Lantern' does not occupy a particularly enviable position within the second series of *Doctor Who*, squashed as it is in between a pair of two-part stories, and thus somewhat in danger of being rather overlooked and undervalued. This would be a shame, as while it is never going to imprint itself upon the minds of the general public in the pantheon of 'the one with ...' episodes and lacks the epic qualities to make it a fandom treasure, it is an entertaining – if slightly rough-around-the-edges – episode, and a welcome lightening of the tone after some rather more emotionally fraught adventures of late. The early history of British television has long been a great passion of mine, so I was always looking forward to this tale once I heard it included such touchstones as Alexandra Palace, the near-legendary televising of the Coronation of Queen Elizabeth II and various actual archive television clips. Gatiss engages with and uses this history in a manner that, while perhaps not startlingly original, makes for a cracking little *Doctor Who* plot, and sets up a nice conclusion on the transmission tower of the

Palace itself. It is true to say, however, that the central villain of the piece, the Wire, is a tad under-explained, and personally I was also very disappointed with Maureen Lipman's performance in the role. The Wire becomes a stock cackling villainess that seems to go way over the top, even for *Doctor Who*, at times. I felt a more restrained and sinister performance would have been far creepier and more effective. Fortunately the other major guest star of this episode, the ever-reliable Ron Cook, supporting actor in many a great film and television production, more than makes up for Lipman's shortcomings, and as he is an actor I have long admired, I was very pleased to see him at last pop up in *Doctor Who*. Rory Jennings is also very good as Tommy, the Doctor's new pseudo-companion for this episode while Rose is out of action due to the lack of a face. While I wasn't entirely sold on the sub-plot with Tommy's abusive father, Jennings makes a great job of the enthusiastic teenager gradually coming out of his shell, and you wouldn't believe that the actor is really in his early twenties. Once again the production departments have come to the fore on a historical episode, giving a sense of the distilled memories and pop culture impression of a time rather than how it strictly was, but it makes for a great television vision of Britain in the early '50s. The BBC has done a lot of this feel-good period drama stuff, *Born and Bred* being the example that readily springs to mind, although 'The Idiot's Lantern' is a more knowing and rather more fun production than that series. Euros Lyn's direction is for the most part up to his usual high standard, although I found some of his slanted camerawork a little excessive. A good episode, and a solid instalment of a generally excellent season; but you do very much get the sense of it being a pause for breath before the trials to come. – *Paul Hayes*

After last year's 'The Unquiet Dead', I had high hopes for this one. I'm well aware of Mark Gatiss's love of 1950s television, and was fully expecting his favourite themes and tropes – and *Quatermass* in particular – to be given full rein here. Add to that the setting – distant enough in time to be different, near enough to resonate – and I was sure that 'The Idiot's Lantern' was going to be another classic horror-fest. So what the hell went wrong? First, it's just too familiar a story. Bodiless alien intelligences living in the utilities, turning people into zombies... Didn't Gatiss write this one last year? And why does the Wire steal its victims' faces? How can they breathe without noses or mouths? Why do they clutch their hands? And how do they miraculously get their faces back at the end? This is almost 'The Doctor Dances' lite, but with none of the charm or wit. I'm tempted to say that Gatiss wrote the *Doctor Who* story he wanted to write with 'The Unquiet Dead'; 'The Idiot's Lantern' feels as if he's simply going through the motions, with a checklist of plot elements that have to be included. I can't fault the period feel in the slightest: the production evokes 1950s London perfectly, and my mother, who is old enough to remember the Coronation, confirmed its veracity. But the high-handed social commentary on the Connolly family just grates. Gatiss is applying 21st Century morals to a completely different era: his aim in breaking up the family by emancipating the wife and son from the bullying father is a noble one, but there is nothing unusual in a strong, stern, shouty patriarch in the 1950s. As for Tommy's shoe-horned-in diatribe on fascism... dreadful, down there with Ace's drivel about wind in 'The Curse of Fenric'. Glossing over the Wire/Gelth similarities, Maureen Lipman is superb as the villain, and her 'Are you sitting comfortably?' will chill anyone of a certain age who remembers Children's Hour. She falls down only when channelling Audrey from *The Little Shop of Horrors* (or, less charitably, Kroagnon from 'Paradise Towers') with her OTT exclamation: 'Hungry!' All this makes it sound as if I hate 'The Idiot's Lantern', but I don't. To be honest, it didn't make enough of an impact on me to rouse any strong emotions. While not as bland as last year's 'The Long Game', it just tells a straightforward story in a straightforward way, with few of the flourishes we have come to expect from RTD's re-imagining. There are a few nice touches – a background mention of Torchwood, the swastika TV aerials, a Kylie name check – but overall, this story wouldn't have been out of place in McCoy's last two seasons. Ironically, one of this story's real strengths lies in Murray Gold's music. As this season has progressed, his reuse of old themes and failure to exercise control over the volume button have rendered a lot of the incidental music both intrusive and repetitive, but here it all works perfectly, especially his wonderful reinterpretation of 'Song for Ten' at the end. I just hope he rediscovers the subtlety setting on his synthesiser for the rest of the series! 'The Idiot's Lantern' is the ultimate in 'trad' *Doctor Who* seen so far in the new series. But it must be a sign of how much more we expect from this series that 'trad' simply isn't enough any more. I just hope Gatiss's next story, if there is one, isn't more ghosts hanging around the utilities. – *Craig Hinton*

This sort of episode is the sign of a series settling in for a long run: it's the first *Doctor Who* in a while in which the TARDIS materialises somewhere, the Doctor and companion meet people they've never met before and tackle a problem they resolve before leaving. No continuing arcs, exploration of the main characters' baggage, reprises of old friends or foes (though we presume Mark Gatiss remembers 'The Faceless Ones') or tinkering with the basic premise of the show. It's one of the few recent episodes that can be watched as a standalone, and that's probably a good thing. This is a script that, with a little rejig, could have done for any of the previous Doctors in any era of the series' history – which is why it feels a little on the bland side, as if it could have been rushed into production with Sylvester McCoy as one of the 'living memory' serials of the original show's declining years. There's nothing exactly wrong here, but it is bog-standard *Doctor Who*. The device of the Doctor promising to take Rose somewhere exciting (Elvis's appearance on *The Ed Sullivan Show*) but landing somewhere different (Muswell Hill in 1953) is probably being overused, but doesn't get dwelled on too long. Three solid guest actors (Maureen Lipman, Ron Cook and Jamie Foreman) are employed, but only Lipman as an evil alien impersonating a cut-glass-accent period BBC announcer gets much material to play with, and quibblers might note that her catch-phrases ('Are you sitting comfortably?' and 'Hello children, everywhere') come from BBC radio rather than television. David Tennant, with a 1950s quiff, continues to develop his wide-eyed and determined reading of the role – gushingly enthusiastic over even the most deadly technology, drawing moral lines and taking strident stands, and clambering up Alexandra Palace's aerial in a finale that wouldn't be out of place in a Dick Barton adventure. There is a sense of trying to wring a science-fiction story, with a soap sub-plot, out of the British folk memory of crowds gathered around tiny, black and white TV sets to watch the Coronation, but not quite making all the connections. The police angle, with faceless victims bundled away in big black cars, is underdeveloped, and surprisingly nothing is made of the TARDIS finally appearing at a time and place when it would fit in. – *Kim Newman*

Is Rose right to encourage Tommy to say goodbye to his father? This depends on just how badly Mr Connolly has been mistreating his family. He's clearly a bully, who's put his own reputation ahead of their well-being, and they're better off without him. But is he a monster? I think the answer is no – but as the story progresses, he is on his way to becoming one. When we first see the Connollys, in a warmly-lit evening scene, there's no hint of fear or tension.

Grandma calls him 'Our lord and master', almost affectionately. Everything is different when we see them the next morning, *sans* Gran: the tilted camera angles, the dim blue lighting (as it's dark inside even though it's daylight outside). The house that was cozy the previous night is cramped this morning. And Mr Connolly, who has been secretly turning over the faceless victims to the police, is terrified to have one under his own roof. 'I said stop it!!!' he shrills at Rita. It's pretty clear Mr Connolly has always been the 'lord and master' in this household – but there's no suggestion that he's ruled with an iron fist. He has often been disobeyed, suggesting that there are more 'warnings' than actual punishments. Tommy convinces him to buy a TV (largely by pointing out that everyone's getting one). The argument over whether or not Tommy will go to college has obviously been going on for some time. But now Mr Connolly has an ugly secret to keep, and therefore a powerful motive to stop his son and wife questioning him or talking to outsiders. Unlike the Wire, a bully whose threats are backed up by a vicious power, all Connolly has to offer is shouting, 'I am talking!!!' The Doctor and Rose instantly recognise him as a blustering idiot, and use his own bullying tactics to get him out of the way so they can talk to Rita and Tommy. As the pressure on Mr Connolly worsens, so do his tactics. When Tommy threatens to reveal Grandma's absence to Aunty Betty, Connolly immediately retaliates by branding Tommy a 'mummy's boy' and promising to 'beat it out of him'. Tommy looks shocked. I think that, if Tommy and Rita had not taken their chance to stand up to Connolly, his tactics would only have continued to worsen. He might well have become as monstrous as the Wire, backing up the power of his voice with the power of his fists. At that moment, Rita and Tommy reveal his secret and break his power over them. It's an act of simple human heroism, and it saves the world as well as them. Exposed and shamed, Mr Connolly is no danger to his family. Told to leave, he leaves without an argument. An abusive husband or father would have used at least insults and threats to try and regain control of his family, but this bully has been thoroughly deflated. Tommy is quite safe to say farewell to him. Mr Connolly is a bully and an 'idiot', but a monster he is not. – *Kate Orman*

Coronation Street meets *Quatermass* meets *Muffin the Mule* meets *Nightshade*. Being a Mark Gatiss script (full of wonderful dialogue, grotesque characters, a twisted sense of the macabre), and directed with skilful attention to detail by Euros Lyn, a combination that made 'The Unquiet Dead' a highlight last year, 'The Idiot's Lantern' is by far one of the better productions of this (so far) pedestrian 2006 series. There are three standout aspects. The first of these is the Wire, a rarity among *Doctor Who* monsters: one that the Doctor hasn't met before and doesn't know everything about, and whose origins are never fully revealed. While a simplistic 'creature' in its on-screen realisation, the concept is made all the more effective by the warped 'from inside the TV' POV angles and Maureen Lipman's pitch perfect performance. A 2-D creation, made absolutely effective through 3-D technology! The second standout aspect doesn't really make much sense, but is the talking point of the story. The revelation of the faceless ones (and yes, the fact that 'Tooth and Claw''s Pauline Collins was in the Patrick Troughton adventure of that title hasn't escaped me!), whilst admittedly being a 'huh?' moment, is also the 'wow' moment of the episode. Yes, *Sapphire and Steel* and *Twilight Zone: The Movie* have done this already, but it is still a spine-tingling image. A loss of face is something everyone has fears about. The third aspect is the reconstruction of 1950s London. Although I'm from a different country and generation, I can see that much time and effort have gone into ensuring everything looks right. Remember, *Doctor Who* itself made its debut only some ten years after the 1953 setting of this episode. While we are now spoiled with

EPISODE 207

VidFIREd DVDs, I can't possibly imagine what it must have been like to view '100,000 BC' all those years ago on such primitive televisions! Being a New Zealander, I was delighted to hear the Doctor's reference to Everest being conquered (by New Zealander Edmund Hillary). This was brought even closer to home by the fact another New Zealander had only just reached the summit in the weeks prior to the broadcast of this episode. The final confrontation on the broadcast tower is effectively created, and until the illusion was shattered by *Doctor Who Confidential* I had no idea that it was really just a mock-up only a few feet off the ground. (It's a pity the line about the Doctor having a fear of such towers was cut, as it would have provided a nice link with the original series.) In fact the production is as slick as one expects now from the BAFTA award winning (yay!) BBC Cardiff. In my 'School Reunion' review I said I was warming to Tennant in the lead role, but, although I hate to say it, I'm now beginning to find the tenth Doctor a bit irritating. In 'The Idiot's Lantern' he shows little concern or interest in what's going on around him, and it takes Rose getting her face sucked for him to leap into action. And then he gets all shouty and unpleasant to everyone around him. But I must say the image of the Doctor racing to save the day on a Vespa seems just so typically *Doctor Who*! It's a pity he gives the bike to Tommy, as I'd love to seen him roaring to the rescue by that means again! – *Jon Preddle*

Snap-shot perception is often a key indicator of basic human weakness. It can let one down so very easily. This is particularly true regarding the folly of instantaneous critique. Who can forget the *Guardian* journalist who, after viewing the first episode of *Coronation Street* in 1960, confidently predicted that the show was 'doomed'? Or the reviewer who described *Citizen Kane* as 'the worst film ever made'? Sometimes it just pays to shut your mouth and wait for a while before one gives a reaction to pretty much anything. Which brings us to 'The Idiot's Lantern', an episode of *Doctor Who* that currently enjoys a somewhat low reputation in the show's fandom. Regardless of the episode's more outlandish foibles (guest villain Maureen Lipman going-so-far-over-the-top-she's-down-the-other-side notwithstanding), 'The Idiot's Lantern' was a story containing, for me anyway, an awful lot of truth. Although I was born roughly a decade after the year in which the episode was set and three hundred miles distant from its location, this landscape was, quite disturbingly, an England that I recognised from my own childhood. A slightly more innocent world than today's; a less cynical time, certainly. An era of community spirit and shared identity, implicit trust in the voices of authority and a wistful nostalgia for the hardships of the recent past. These elements were evocatively captured in Mark Gatiss' script, which spoke, on several levels, with an honesty often missing in *Doctor Who*'s more otherworldly conceits. Today we can view the 1950s as something akin to a sepia-tinted photograph seen in someone else's family album. Something that is both alien and yet unnervingly familiar to us at the same time. Gatiss's use of aspects of TV iconography (both visual and conceptual) was another masterstroke. As virtually the only constant in all of our lives, television serves here as both the narrator of the text and, chillingly, the device through which the menace attacks. 'Men in Black? Vanishing police cars? This is Churchill's England, not Stalin's Russia,' says the Doctor incredulously at one point. The difference between the two is, perhaps, not as clear-cut as it would once have been in the minds of the intended audience. Therein, I would suggest, lies one of the reasons for the disproportionately negative reception that the episode received. I may be alone within *Doctor Who*'s 2006 audience here, but give me something like this, an episode with both heart and soul, over cold and obvious concepts like returning Cybermen and ex-companions any day. – *Keith Topping*

EDITOR'S REVIEW: One of the complaints I've heard about today's *Doctor Who* is that it's taken the form of a soap opera. Now, soap operas of all types tell continuing stories; there's nothing wrong with that, and indeed genre television has started to recognise and adapt the serial format into its own style of storytelling. (Some of the most lauded science-fiction and fantasy productions of the past 15 years – *Buffy The Vampire Slayer*, *Babylon 5* and *Deep Space Nine* among them – were pioneers of the genre's return to its serialised origins in the pulp magazines of a century ago.) But the references to soap opera here are mostly pejorative, as people use the term to describe the descent into the more personal Earth-bound character tales of the Jackie Tyler/Mickey Smith variety. With 'The Idiot's Lantern', there was another vociferous cry that *Doctor Who* had once again entered into soap opera territory, as we looked in on the squabbles of the Connolly family.

Now, I ask you, what's more interesting: nameless, faceless (no pun intended) armies of slobbering aliens killing one another senselessly, or character drama showing how the common man reacts to uncommon situations? (Perhaps I shouldn't ask the question; I think I'd shudder at some of the responses.) Armies waging war and space battles have their place, but *Doctor Who* has never been that show; the truth and beauty within the series have come from the interpersonal moments. Ask viewers what they'll most remember from this season, and it might not be those Dalek-Cyberman battles, but rather the relationship between the Doctor and Rose, or the reunion of the Doctor and Sarah Jane. In 'The Idiot's Lantern' we are witness to another one of those relationship studies: the dysfunctional Connolly family, a product of their time, with an overbearing (yet unmistakably well-meaning) father, a put-upon wife who is looking for a way out, and a son who worships his dad yet recognises the man's shortcomings at the same time. (And let's not forget poor grandma, superstitious, gullible and, of course, later missing her face. How any of these victims manage to breathe after losing their nostrils and mouth, I'll never know.)

There is another oft-aired complaint, which is that *Doctor Who* has strayed too far from what brought it its popularity in the first place – 'traditional', fast paced stories with a villain, problems to solve, a heroic Doctor who solves them, and a definite end with a moral conviction. How ironic, therefore, that in two seasons, it falls to this mid-season, quite unpretentious little tale to represent the series' fall-back to traditional storytelling. Writer Mark Gatiss, obviously, knows *Doctor Who* well; he's been a fan for many years, and has written (in book and audio play form) stories that develop the characters and situations from the classic show. But 'The Idiot's Lantern' *feels* like it could have been written by Terrance Dicks, the series' former script editor and one of its stalwarts, whose stories define the very term 'traditional *Doctor Who*' for many fan. That, I think, is a rather high compliment (and I mean it as such), for Gatiss brilliantly captures the essence of what I have enjoyed about *Doctor Who* for years: there's an alien problem, on Earth or wherever, it doesn't matter; said evil alien is trying to do something nasty; the Doctor arrives with his companion and, as if by pure accident, stumbles upon the mystery; he solves it; he battles the alien nasty and saves the day. What, might I ask, is wrong with that?

After seven episodes of David Tennant's Doctor doing things very much out of keeping with traditional *Doctor Who* (and I don't mean that in a bad way; some of it's been downright wonderful), it's simply *refreshing* to see him settle down and crack a mystery. Sure, Rose is sidelined for part of the action – but then again, for 40 years the companion's been the one to get into trouble and we've never really batted an eye before, so why quibble? And then there's the Wire, a delightfully different form of alien nasty, and here so wonderfully played by

EPISODE 207

Maureen Lipman (making probably one of the most memorable contributions to the second series, with her devilishly down-home *Mommie Dearest* attitude). Without actually being there to kidnap the people themselves, rend their innards to gelatine or launch hyperthermonucleaowhatsit missiles at London, Lipman's Wire gives us a definite, menacing presence – and how nice that there's a reason for her doing what she does, too. The rest of the cast also do a terrific job, with Jamie Foreman pulling off the traditional father-who-needs-to-join-the-20th-Century ethos with flair, and Debra Gillett putting in an understated but still very rich portrayal of the haggard housewife who's suddenly discovered there's a world outside her door.

Put it all together in a clean package that looks like we're in the 1950s instead of in someone's backyard, and it's striking. Sure, there are questions that aren't answered and issues that arise, but this is one of those times that I can put the issues behind me, because it all works beautifully. 'The Impossible Planet' may be the season's most quality production, to my mind, but 'The Idiot's Lantern' is my favourite episode of the year. – *Shaun Lyon*

208: THE IMPOSSIBLE PLANET

Deep beneath the surface of a planet circling a black hole – a planet that shouldn't exist – a dark intelligence is about to awaken... and the Doctor and Rose, cut off from the TARDIS and trapped along with the small population of a science outpost, are seemingly powerless against it.

FIRST TRANSMISSION: UK – 3 June 2006. US – 17 November 2006. Canada – 27 November 2006. Australia – 2 September 2006. New Zealand – 31 August 2006.
DURATION: 45'19"
WRITER: Matt Jones
DIRECTOR: James Strong
CREDITED CAST: David Tennant (The Doctor), Billie Piper (Rose Tyler), Danny Webb (Mr Jefferson), Shaun Parkes (Zachary Cross Flane), Claire Rushbrook (Ida Scott), Will Thorp (Toby Zed), Ronny Jhutti (Danny Bartock), MyAnna Buring (Scooti Manista), Paul Kasey (The Ood), Gabriel Woolf (The Voice of the Beast), Silas Carson (The Voice of the Ood)

WHERE AND WHEN: Sanctuary Base Six on a nameless world (nicknamed 'the Bitter Pill') orbiting black hole K 37 Gem 5, some time in the future

THE STORY UNFOLDS: Sanctuary Base is a deep space exploration dwelling on the surface of an unnamed planet. The Doctor says that the base is most likely built out of a kit and is put together like a flat-pack wardrobe, only bigger (and easier). The doors are numbered; door 1 leads to the control room, door 19 opens into the central canteen, while door 16 is the stopgap from the damaged sections of the base. Food at the base ranges from reasonable to poor; Scooti tells Rose not to have the green, or the blue, food. Protein one ('with a dash of three') is a form of food.

The planet is in a perpetually-stable geostationary orbit around black hole K 37 Gem 5 – an orbit the Doctor describes as impossible. The remnants of solar systems and stars whip by the base, pulverised into dust... but for some reason this planet remains in orbit.

According to the scriptures of the Veltino, the planet is called Krop Tor, or 'the Bitter Pill'; their legend has it that the black hole was a mighty demon tricked into devouring the planet, which it spat out because it was poison. The planet generates a gravity field that locks it into place, and a funnel-shaped gravity well that reaches out into space and allowed the expedition to arrive in the first place. The expedition's original captain was killed in the landing attempt and Zach was put in charge. The Doctor notes that such a gravity field would take phenomenal amounts of power to maintain... specifically, a power source with an inverted self-extrapolating reflex of six to the power of six every six seconds. The power source is ten miles below the surface through solid rock (giving off readings of over 90 Statts on the Blazen scale), so the expedition is drilling down to find it, as it offers a revolution in science, massive power... or the capability for war. The planet apparently supported life long ago, before humanity had learned to walk; the expedition has found artefacts covered with a strange script unearthed by the drilling.

The Ood are a servitor race bred by humanity; everyone's got one, as Danny says. They have no titles (although they seem to have official designations like 'Ood 7 Gamma 10', 'Ood 7

EPISODE 208

Gamma 11' etc) and consider themselves 'as one'; they're empathic, with a low level telepathic field connecting them, but are a herd race, like cattle. The Ood work the mine shafts and do maintenance at the base. While they are slaves, Danny tells Rose that they offer themselves for their tasks and 'pine away and die' if they aren't given orders. There is a group out there (official or not) that calls itself the 'Friends of the Ood', the members of which are unhappy with this situation. Electromagnetics interfere with the Ood's speech systems. Their gender differences are unclear. In the telepathic scale, the Ood usually register level Basic 5. The Beast within the planet increases their telepathy; at Basic 30 they are 'shouting, screaming inside their heads... or something is shouting at them.' They later reach Basic 100, where they *should* experience brain death.

The TARDIS is a bit queasy on arrival (the Doctor likens it to indigestion). It later disappears when a landslide caused by a surface storm is deflected by Zach onto Storage 5 through 8 – which also includes Habitation 3, where the TARDIS materialised. After the impact, oxygen holds in the base and internal gravity is 56.6, which is normal.

Deep within the bowels of the planet lurks an alien Beast. The first real indication that something is amiss comes with non-sequiturs; one of the Ood tells Rose, 'The Beast and his Armies shall rise from the Pit to make war against God', though it later appears to have said something else. The temperature in the Ood habitat appears to be rising. Toby hears voices, Zach nearly catches a glimpse of the Beast in the hologram projector, and Danny hears the computer say 'He is awake'. The alien possesses Toby; it causes the alien writing to appear first on his palms and then all over his body, and makes his eyes glow red.

Humanity currently rules an Empire. The base is at least 500 light years from Earth. Rose's mobile phone is out of range of Earth (but not out of range of the Beast). One of the planetary systems swallowed by the black hole is the Scarlet system, formerly home to the mighty Pallushi civilisation, which lasted a billion years. The Doctor says that TARDISes aren't built, they're grown, and with his home planet gone there's no way to grow another. Jefferson uses stock 15 ammo, which affects only 'organics'. Condition Red authorises him to shoot his weapon at the Beast, which takes possession of the Ood as a new army to do its bidding.

The drill bit is cutting to create a mineshaft, into which a lift will be lowered (eventually carrying the Doctor and Ida downward). The drilling progress is marked by various 'point' levels; drill point zero is the end of the line, meaning they've punched through. The chamber below is beyond the base's oxygen field. Ida uses a gravity globe to illuminate the ancient chamber, which contains statues and ancient buildings, the remnants of an ancient civilisation. An energy signature to the north-northwest of the lift interferes with visual signals, while a giant seal (which the Doctor calls a 'trap door') covered with the ancient symbols, 30 feet in diameter, is discovered and soon starts to open of its own volition. The event also breaks the gravity field, pushing the planet ever closer to the black hole ...

THE DOCTOR: He admires the expedition, and humanity, for braving the elements to come here and find the source of the mystery, but also thinks they're completely mad. He's not sure he could ever settle down in a proper house with doors and carpets... and a mortgage. Perhaps with Rose. He's unhappy that he can't honour his promise to always take Rose back home. He volunteers to go down the mineshaft (despite the fact that it breaks 'every protocol' known to Zach). It's been ages since he's worn a spacesuit. He's soon trapped below with Ida in the Pit.

ROSE TYLER: She knows better than to suggest the Doctor go somewhere else if there's trouble. She is shocked at the fact that these humans have a slave race, and sympathises with the Ood; she notes that they have nothing else in life, she says that she used to feel that way herself. She laments that she can't call her mother, although even if she could, she doubts she could tell Jackie she's stuck in this time period forever. She's disappointed that space travel isn't all 'whizzing about and teleports and anti-gravity'. She's worried about the Doctor going far below, but later has more important things to worry about when the Ood, possessed by the Beast, start to come for her ...

CHARACTER BUILDING: *Ida Scott* – The base's science officer. She's introspective but seems somewhat fearless and inquisitive, and knows the history surrounding the planet. She accompanies the Doctor down to the chamber opened by the drill bit.

Zachary Cross Flane – Acting captain of the expedition; he took the job when the previous captain died, and is reluctantly serving in it. He learns to trust the Doctor but still resists his interference.

Toby Zed – He's the archaeologist for the base, and has begun hearing voices that are calling his name. The Beast chooses to take over his body, although at times he doesn't know this. Rose asks him if his job is chief dramatist after he comments that the power source is buried in the darkness, waiting for them. He doesn't think checking on the rocket link after the storm is his department.

Mr Jefferson – Head of security at the base, a no-nonsense man who believes in rules of order. He knows his British poetry. He isn't sure if his wife ever forgave him for something he did to her; the Beast tells him she never did.

Danny Bartock – The ethics committee representative at the base (which is 'not as boring as it sounds'); he's in charge of Ood operations, supervising the creatures on their workshifts. He doesn't believe the Ood have minds of their own, but is persuaded otherwise later by their eerie platitudes and shift upward on the telepathic scale. He orders the Ood to respond only to his voice.

Scooti Manista – Trainee in maintenance at base; 'Scooti' is short for her full name, Scootori. She bears the designation PKD. She discovers Toby's disappearance, and dies after witnessing his transformation as an observation post window is cracked. Her bio chip says she's in Habitation 3, but it's her corpse, in fact, floating above it. She's logged in as dead at age 20.

The Beast – An ancient alien presence, its spirit possesses the body of Toby Zed and murders Scooti Manista, but it needs to open the barricade (or seal) in the ancient chamber below to release itself. Upon manifestation in Toby it calls itself 'The heart that beats in the darkness... the blood that will never cease. And now he will rise.' The possessed Ood legion say that the Beast has woven itself into the fabric of humanity since the dawn of time; some call it Abaddon, others Krop Tor, and others Satan or Lucifer, the Deathless Prince, the Bringer of Night. It says it has been imprisoned for eternity, and will now take charge of its legions to conquer the universe.

TORCHWOOD: No references in this episode.

BODY COUNT: Scooti Manista is murdered by the Beast in Toby's body, as it breaks the window, blowing her into the vacuum outside. The Ood, possessed by the Beast, electrocute one of the crew members working with Danny.

EPISODE 208

THE DOCTOR'S MAGICAL SONIC SCREWDRIVER: The Doctor uses it in an attempt to hold the Ood at bay upon his and Rose's arrival.

REALITY BITES: The Doctor explains to Rose that a black hole is a dead star, which has collapsed in on itself and has become so dense that it pulls everything in with it; nothing can escape, not even light, gravity or time. This is the generally accepted definition of a black hole in modern scientific understanding.

Upon discovering Scooti's dead body, Mr Jefferson quotes 'Horatius', the most famous of the ballads of Thomas Babington Macaulay's *Lays of Ancient Rome*: 'And how can man die better than facing fearful odds, For the ashes of his fathers, and the temples of his gods.' (Jefferson gets the words slightly wrong, substituting 'should' for 'can' in the first line and using the singular 'father' instead of 'fathers'.) The poems were written in the early 1840s by Macaulay, also known as the first Baron Macaulay, a poet, historian, essayist and politician. Other lines referenced in the episode are straight out of Biblical mythology.

The Doctor is obviously fond of *EastEnders*: his line, 'This is going be the best Christmas Walford's ever had,' refers to the fictional London borough of Walford, the setting for the long-running series. (This will also not be the sole reference to *EastEnders* this year; see 'Army of Ghosts'.)

LINKING THEMES: The name of the base, Sanctuary Base Six, is not mentioned until the following episode, 'The Satan Pit'.

The Doctor wonders if they're in some sort of 'moonbase, seabase, spacebase... they build these things out of kits.' In fact the Doctor *has* travelled to a moonbase ('The Moonbase') and a seabase ('Warriors of the Deep') before.

Rose refers to having been a dinner lady ('School Reunion'). Previous references to the Earth's Empire have been made in stories such as 'Frontier in Space', 'The Long Game' and 'Bad Wolf'.

The Doctor says that TARDISes are grown, not built, and implies that no more can be grown now because his planet is gone. This accords with continuity established in the BBC Books range of original novels. However, in the story 'Warriors' Gate' (1980), K-9 remarks that he has all the specifications to build a duplicate of the TARDIS.

Rose appears to have picked up a new mobile phone somewhere; the one seen in this episode is of a different design than her previous one. Presumably the Doctor went out and bought her a new one or has a supply in the TARDIS.

SCENE MISSING: The Doctor's explanation of the impossibility of the planet existing here doesn't hold up. Why is it impossible? (See 'Controversies' below.) How can the planet be locked in a 'geostationary' orbit when this term refers to an orbit around the Earth, and when it would anyway be impossible to determine a precise point on the black hole for the world to lock on to?

Why are the crew of the base not more surprised by the arrival of the Doctor and Rose, given the inaccessibility of this planet?

Why is the Doctor express no outrage about the Ood being enslaved by humanity? He has fought against slavery, amongst countless other evils, for centuries, yet here he merely accepts it and moves on. Also, why does the Ood translation device hover next to them? How can there be a wind across the surface of an airless planet? How does the Beast, in Toby's mind, prevent his body from being fatally injured in the vacuum on the planet's surface (even allowing for the fact that it is a popular myth that a body will explode in such circumstances)?

Why does Ida say the trap door is 30 feet wide, when it's obviously no more than twice her height in diameter?

If the TARDIS is so valuable to the Doctor, why does he merely give up without going after it? There are spacesuits and ten-mile-long cables and such; surely he would tie off a cable to his suit and go down looking for it? Rose wouldn't exactly sit on the sidelines, either ...

ALTERED STATES: The working title for this episode was 'The Satan Pit'; both it and the follow-up episode bore this title, ostensibly with 'part one' and 'part two' attached, until they went into production. The same situation had occurred the previous year on the first two-parter, which for a long time had been collectively known as 'Aliens of London', with individual sub-titles for the episodes. The two episodes would have been aired in the season's seventh and eighth slots, respectively, had the original plan submitted to the BBC been followed.

In both the episode's online commentary and the *Doctor Who Magazine: The Doctor Who Companion: Series Two* issue, it is noted that the Slitheen were to have featured in this episode at one stage. Instead of the Ood, a far-future version of the Slitheen would have been the alien race enslaved by humanity in the 43rd Century; they would have been waiting for the Beast to awaken to free them from their servitude. This was changed when it was decided to focus less on the slave race and more on the humans and their predicament. The planet was originally called 'Hell' in the scripts.

BEHIND THE SCENES: *Doctor Who* returned to recording in a British quarry for the first time since its relaunch; this episode featured night recording at Wenvoe Quarry, which substituted for the underground cavern (and was lit by an enormous arc light). The episode also featured recording at the Johnsey Estates in Mamhilad Park Industrial Estate South at Pontypool, which became the drilling room and Ood chambers, and at the underwater stage at Pinewood Studios, where the floating body of Scooti (rather, actress MyAnna Buring) was recorded to later be inserted digitally into space over the base. The remainder of the production was shot at the soundstages in Newport.

Davies noted that the Ood were reminiscent of the Sensorites in 'The Sensorites' (1964), and said in *Doctor Who Confidential* that they were likely to be from a planet near the latter's Sense Sphere. Ten Ood masks were created by Neill Gorton and the prosthetics team, though they left the actors playing them virtually blind.

A game tie-in to this episode was featured on the official *Doctor Who* website, involving the player attempting to navigate gravity wells down to a planet. There was, however, no actual tie-in website for the story.

DULCET TONES: 'Boléro' by Maurice Ravel (1875-1937) was originally composed as a ballet and premiered in 1928, and is the composer's most famous composition. The piece has been featured in countless films and television series, and is familiar to many as the music to which Jayne Torvill and Christopher Dean figure skated when they won perfect artistic impression scores of 6.0 from every judge at the 1984 Winter Olympic Games. It is heard in this episode during the transition to the night shift.

OFF THE SCREEN: Danny Webb played Morse, the only survivor of *Alien3* (in which he appeared alongside *Doctor Who*'s eighth Doctor Paul McGann), and was also seen in *Lewis* (2006), *Life Begins* (2005), *Emmerdale Farm* (2004), *Cutting It* (2004), *Dalziel and Pascoe* (1999), *Space Precinct* (1995), *Cardiac Arrest* (1994), *The Young Indiana Jones Chronicles* (1992) and *Brookside* (1982). Shaun Parkes was in *Casanova* (2005), *Things To Do Before You're 30* (2004), *Randall & Hopkirk (Deceased)* (2001), *The Mummy Returns* (2001), *Casualty* (1999) and *Heartbeat* (1996). Claire Rushbrook has been seen in *Carrie & Barry* (2004), *Linda Green* (2002), *Spaced* (1999), *Spice World* (1997), *Touching Evil* (1997) and *Secrets & Lies* (1996). Will Thorp took part in several episodes of *Strictly Come Dancing* and *Strictly Come Dancing: It Takes Two* (2005) and appeared in *Casualty* (2005) and *Holby City* (2005) in the regular role of Paul 'Woody' Joyner, and in *The Courtroom* (2004). Ronny Jhutti has been seen in *Ideal* (2005), *Cutting It* (2003), *Where The Heart Is* (2001), *Always and Everyone* (2001) and *EastEnders* (1985). MyAnna Buring was in *The Omen* (2006), *The Descent* (2005), *Casualty* (2004) and *Murder Prevention* (2004). Silas Carson returns to *Doctor Who* after providing the voice of the Adherents of the Repeated Meme in Series One's 'The End of the World'.

Gabriel Woolf played the hellish alien warlord Sutekh in the *Doctor Who* story 'Pyramids of Mars' (1975), a role compared by many fans to that of the Beast in this episode. He recently returned to voice Sutekh in Magic Bullet Productions' two Faction Paradox audio plays written by Lawrence Miles, 'Coming to Dust' and 'The Ship of a Billion Years'. He has also appeared as Governor Rossiter in the Big Finish *Doctor Who* audio plays 'Arrangements for War' and 'Thicker Than Water', and in 1981 recorded readings of three *Doctor Who* novelisations as talking books for the Royal National Institute for the Blind. He also appeared in extra features on two *Doctor Who* DVD releases, 'Pyramids of Mars' and 'City of Death'.

Writer Matt Jones was script editor on *Queer as Folk* (1999), created by Russell T Davies, as well as the sequel series *Queer as Folk II* (2000), *Love in the 21st Century* (1999), *Clocking Off* (2000) and *Linda Green* (2001). Later, he was producer of *Serious and Organized* (2003) and executive producer of *POW* (2003) and *Shameless* (2005). Besides writing for those series, he has also written for *Children's Ward* (2000) and *Now You See Her* (2001). In 1995 he wrote a regular column entitled *Fluid Links* in *Doctor Who Magazine*. He went on to pen the *Doctor Who* novel *Bad Therapy* for Virgin Publishing's New Adventures line and the novel *Beyond the Sun* for their Bernice Summerfield spin-off range, as well as several *Doctor Who* short stories for both Virgin and BBC Books.

CONTROVERSIES: Controversy erupted over this episode's cavalier attitude toward science, specifically in relation to the black hole. According to current scientific evidence, an object is in danger of being pulled into the gravity well of a black hole only if it passes beyond the event horizon (the limit of its overwhelming gravitational pull); stars observed in range of black holes do appear to co-exist with them, while it is also theorised that a supermassive black hole lies at the centre of our Milky Way galaxy and the rest of the galaxy rotates around it. It is unlikely that even such a massive black hole would be able to pull apart entire neighbouring star systems.

INTERNAL CONSISTENCY: The dating of this episode is unclear; the action obviously takes place in the far future, and while the clothing designs and vernacular are similar to today's, the production has been known to make a mockery of that (setting 'The Long Game' 200,000 years in the future, for example). The 'date' given in dialogue is 43 K 2.1 – perhaps the 43rd Century, early in the year? The episode takes place over the course of no more than one day, as the strange events that occur seem to happen in rapid succession. However, no indication of 'day' or 'night' is ever made.

TARDISODE #8: In a futuristic office, a bureaucrat identifies black hole K 37 Gem 5 and sends Captain Walker off on a mission to investigate why the planetoid is in perfect orbit above it. Walker leaves the office armed with some local lore and legends in a book, while an Ood watches him go, obviously already under the influence of the Beast.

Walker is the captain of the expedition later killed, as noted in the episode proper (although in the episode he is never identified by name). The book is from the effects of the Geddes expedition.

REVIEWS

It's very difficult for the first part of a two-part story to hit the ball out of the park with a perfect balance of exposition, suspense, characterisation, music and design, but by all that's unholy, 'The Impossible Planet' achieves the... well, the impossible! This is just beastly! 'Cinematic' is the best way to describe this episode; it's undeniably as polished and epic as this series has ever looked so far, with stunning set and costume design that completely immerse the viewer in a realistic, lived-in futuristic base where the sight of the sky above can drive men mad. We've all too rarely ventured out into space in the new series, but for this trip, the production team have pulled out all the stops, and it shows in every nook and cranny. As for the creepy but subservient Ood, they are simply the most grotesque and convincing creatures that *Doctor Who* has ever featured. And when the Doctor gets a glimpse of what lies beneath the planet's surface, we're in *The Lord of the Rings* territory. It's just breathtaking. The Doctor and Rose have been rather glib and unconcerned about the consequences of their actions through most of this series, but they get the wind taken rather satisfyingly out of their sails early on in this episode, and their subsequent interaction is very thoughtful and touching. Tennant is settling in very well at this point, curtailing his tendency to overplay and delivering a much more modulated performance. His impromptu hug of the base captain to express his love of that ol' indomitable human spirit is a welcome touch that feels nicely Tom Bakerish (although Baker probably wouldn't have done it), while Piper's Rose is also on target, sympathising with the Ood and daring to voice some of her aspirations about a (romantic?) future with the Doctor. And once again we meet a guest cast of characters who feel real and react to the newcomers with a pleasant mix of bewilderment and trust. It's no accident that this episode arrives around 6/6/06, as the story clearly touches on demonic themes that will doubtless become more pronounced next week. 'The Impossible Planet' also does what classic *Who* always did best – paying homage to genre films, in this case *Alien*, *The Omen*, *Event Horizon*, and *Prince of Darkness* among others. As if all this wasn't enough, the episode also boasts an adrenalin-fuelled score by Murray Gold that punctuates the ancient alien subplot with atmospheric strings and shifts into bombastic fervour just in time for the cliff-hanger. Sure, there are still a few reused musical cues in there from 'The Christmas Invasion' and elsewhere, but why quibble when everything is clicking this well? One real complaint – the show *should* have ended with a hide-behind-the-sofa reveal of the Big Bad instead of stopping just short of it. In fact, in a rare show of restraint, the preview for next week's conclusion didn't include even a glimpse of what was about to emerge from the depths of this hellish world. But whatever it is, surely next to such a being, the Doctor will be nothing but an ant, a termite! We'll know for sure in a few days, but until then, I kneel before the might of a production team that can craft such exciting entertainment. – *Arnold T Blumberg*

In the first *Back to the Vortex* volume, I wrote regarding 'The Empty Child', 'It's been said over and over that *Doctor Who*'s purpose is to scare kids. And yet, until "The Empty Child", the series had only *hinted* at terrifying children without actually *doing* it.' Now, substitute 'The Impossible Planet' for 'The Empty Child' and change 'children' to 'adults' and you pretty much have my take on 'The Impossible Planet'. I'm 36 years old and this episode scared the willies out of me. I finished watching it around 7:45 pm – about the same time the broadcast ended in Britain and a generation of frightened British kids emerged from whatever piece of furniture they hid behind – and I had to go for a walk afterward, thankful that the summer allowed me an extra hour or two of daylight. But what's really amazing about 'The Impossible Planet' is that it succeeded in being the first *Doctor Who* story to seriously creep me out by using some of the oldest tricks in the book. The scariest scene in the whole 45 minutes is the one where the Voice of the Beast (Gabriel Woolf, in what must be the most inspired reuse of one of the original series actors ever) tells Toby not to turn around. At its core, everything that's so scary and/or great about 'The Impossible Planet' has been done before in *Doctor Who*: possession, an ancient civilisation, the gloomy base under siege and the TARDIS being seemingly lost (indeed I've just described practically the entirety of seasons 12-14 of the original series!) But what makes it all work so magnificently here is that the script, the direction and the actors are not afraid to connect with it all with very real emotions. Thus, the possession is genuinely creepy, the ancient civilisation is hugely ominous, the gloomy base under siege is populated by people with real hopes and fears (played by a superb cast) and the Doctor and Rose are given a wonderfully touching moment where they discuss the possibility of having to settle down with a mortgage. Plus the Ood are brilliant looking monsters. As a result, 'The Impossible Planet' pushes the envelope of new *Doctor Who* in so many ways. I don't know if we'll ever see a story this smart or this brave again, but I hope we will. – *Graeme Burk*

If there's one thing I've really appreciated about this year of *Doctor Who*, it's that it has routinely and effectively been quite scary. I'm not saying that kids need to be absolutely terrorised every week, but a little thrill is always a good thing. It's something I thought was sadly lacking from about half of last year's episodes, but now every episode has something eerie or creepy or just plain weird. This week, though... this week is just plain *tense*. And that's entirely new territory. 'The Impossible Planet' is both the sort of thing *Doctor Who* never attempts and, at the same time, the type of story it goes for again and again. The whole angle of a mysterious pit that releases telepathic commands of violence is just about as old as original sin – or Nigel Kneale, at least. But the angle of a 'realistic' outer space story is quite rare, and makes the whole thing seem like a new, fresh concept. For an episode that is little more than extenuated set-up, 'The Impossible Planet' is quite solid, rarely slacking off and managing to really ratchet up the tension during the last few minutes. And unlike most episodes in the new series, it strongly resembles the old by being almost entirely geared around plot – the characters, even the Doctor and Rose, are easily the weakest part. At times it does feel a little out of place amongst its fellow episodes, because it seems to follow such a completely different beat, but that's okay – 'The Impossible Planet' still succeeds on its own merit. The Ood – and what a great name 'the Ood' is – are a splendid realisation, cleverly walking the line between humorous and sinister. The gag involving them in the opening teaser is a bit forced, but Rose's moment with one at the lunch counter is absolutely priceless. They are perhaps the most overt success of the episode, particularly when the human characters are just a tiny bit bland, and it's hard to peg down precisely why. Their design just *works*; they seem like the product of far more confident designers than the Slitheen, the Krillitanes or the various guests to Platform One. James Strong's direction is similarly assured – surprising, for a newcomer to the show – and with the exception of one terrible effect (unfortunately, the one on which the production team seems to have spent the most time) the visual element of the episode is extremely strong. The sound aspect is the one that impressed me the most, however. I mean, Murray Gold's music is actually *quite good*. It's something I noticed last week, too, especially in the little theremin bits, but frankly I was prepared to write it off as a fluke. Here, it's even more understated, cinematic and very atmospheric. The cue of Toby on the surface of the planet may take a substantial page from Joss Whedon's *Firefly*, but it doesn't really matter. We're far from the overkill choir of 'School Reunion'. The real star of 'The Impossible Planet', of course, is a voice. One scary, evil voice. The voice of Gabriel Woolf. I can think of no other voice that simply drips 'menace' as his does, without any additional effect or treatment. And it's his voice that ushers us into the best parts of the episode, as well as, ultimately, to the first truly brilliant cliff-hanger of the new series. I was absolutely on the edge of my seat from the moment he started to speak through Toby's mouth. How the hell did the kids make it through this? Of course, the real testament to a great set-up is a great resolution, and that remains to be seen. What we have here, though, is so inviting I can hardly wait for next week. What can possibly be in that pit? – *Sarah Hadley*

For the second time this season we have an episode in which the Doctor is confronted with the apparently permanent loss of the TARDIS, and even though in 'Rise of the Cybermen' a convenient solution presented itself more or less at once, he still seemed pretty underwhelmed about the loss. In 'The Impossible Planet' his bereavement seems far more apparent and believable, although that may have something to do with the fact that this time, rather than on a parallel Earth, he and Rose find themselves stranded on a less than hospitable planet that resembles a big budget version of the industrial zone from *The Crystal Maze*. This episode starts off as a bit of a roller coaster ride, as we begin with an excellent little pre-titles teaser – even if it does rely somewhat on the cliché of monsters merely repeating their threats over and over again as they walk slowly closer rather than actually doing anything – which is then completely ruined by the immediate resolution after the titles. While there is an argument for saying it's an amusingly cheeky way of fooling the audience, to me it felt more as if the situation was manufactured completely artificially because Matt Jones knew he had to stick in a pre-titles cliff-hanger somehow or other. To give Jones his due, however, it's just about the only misstep he makes with this script, which for the rest of the episode is pretty much superb, a wonderfully creepy sci-fi thriller and by far and away my favourite episode since 'The Girl in the Fireplace'. The mysteries of the planet, its very existence and what secrets it may hold hidden deep beneath its surface are all very well set up; the Ood are a suitably unsettling presence even when they're not proclaiming the rising of the devil; and the oozingly malevolent 'voice of the Beast' is one of the darkest menaces we have encountered in *Doctor Who* yet, particularly in the wonderfully-played scene in which he is telling Toby not to look around. With Shaun Parkes leading the guest cast it's a bit of a *Casanova* reunion, as he played David Tennant's right-hand-man in that production, and they work very well with each other again here. As usual, however, the entire guest cast is pretty much spot on – I was particularly pleased to see Danny Webb making an appearance in the show, as I've been a fan of his work ever since I first saw him in one of the supporting roles in *Our Friends in the North* on BBC2 back in 1996. The cliff-hanger build-up perhaps goes on for a shade too long, as it did with 'Aliens of London' last year, but it leaves you very much wanting more, and after such a terrifically strong opening instalment, I cannot wait to see how the conclusion of this story pans out. – *Paul Hayes*

I have to say up front that this episode and the second part, 'The Satan Pit', are the closest that *Doctor Who* has ever come to a big budget movie. Even the grandeur of 'The Parting of the Ways' falls short of the sheer scope of this epic, despite the fanboy's wet dream of the great Dalek fleet and hordes of Daleks. I think this is because this two-parter, while lacking the climax of a regeneration or the presence of the Daleks, manages to blend spectacle, drama and emotion seamlessly: more of a puree than the delicious yet chunky soup of 'The Parting of the Ways'. The pre-titles don't bode well, I admit: the smugness that seems to have possessed the Doctor and Rose so far this series reaches its zenith – or is that nadir? – with their self-satisfied giggling, which actually made me want to give them both a good slapping. This is further exacerbated by the Doctor's reaction to the admittedly creepy Ood, which are like some mutant offspring of H P Lovecraft and 'The Robots of Death', waving his magic wand around like a talisman. But once we're in the episode proper, things improve exponentially. Series Two has been cursed with more than its fair share of ciphers and stereotypes, all front and no substance – yes, Mr Connolly, I'm talking about you. And I haven't forgotten you, John Lumic. I only wish I could. But Matt Jones' and Russell T Davies' script (I say that speculatively, but it definitely seems more like a Davies script than the ones his usual showrunner rewrites result in) is replete with characters who are fully-formed, with the hint of back-stories coming from their words and acting, rather than from leaden hammers of exposition: Zack's inexperience, Jefferson's world-weariness and Ida's compassion all shining through. Even the rather lacklustre Danny Bartok soon gains a bit of substance. Of course, long-time viewers will begin to recognise certain elements of the storyline. It's a classic base-under-siege, with lots of lovely red herrings – the TARDIS's behaviour, the writing, the Ood's lapses into near-Biblical rant and the loss of the TARDIS – but one definitely made for the 21st Ccentury: and infinite kudos to the design team for a truly realistic-looking Sanctuary Base. The tension is ramped far higher with Toby's encounter with pure evil, especially since Gabriel Woolf's chilling tones are coming from right behind him! Parts of fandom understandably predicted Sutekh's return, but of course, this was another Davies curve ball, and all the better for it. Other stand-out moments have to be the Doctor's admiration for humanity – not up there with Tom Baker's 'homo sapiens, such an inventive, invincible species' from 'The Ark in Space', but not far off – and the chat about mortgages, which, while light relief on the surface, show his fears of outliving Rose as clearly as in 'School Reunion'. But 35 minutes have passed, and it's time to build up to the cliff-hanger. All the pieces are put seamlessly and logically into place, in contrast to the cack-handed manipulation of 'Aliens of London', with the tension building to a real triple peril with the possession of the Ood, the planet hurtling into the black hole, and the Doctor and Ida above the Pit as the Beast announces that he is free... – *Craig Hinton*

For understandable reasons of budgeting and conceptual timidity, *Who* has been avoiding alien worlds these past two seasons – we've had 'New Earth' (i.e.: not too new to be a strain on the minds of those who want the show to take place entirely on a council estate) and a few grimy spaceships or space stations, but 'The Impossible Planet' goes further in presenting a proper alien environment even as it covers itself by making sure most of the guest cast play human beings from Earth. It's a pleasant throwback to the days of BBC space opera, where the universe is colonised by a variety of Brits with a variety of accents and there are no Yanks in earshot. Again, we get echoes of old *Who* – the apparently contented slave race (the vaguely Cthulhoid Ood, who have impressive masks that somehow still look like masks) obviously due to rebel against their human masters ('The Ark'), the trapped alien villain (the Beast, voiced by veteran Gabriel Woolf) who is the source of Earthly devil myths and due to be released to spread general havoc ('The Dæmons'), the squabbling and decimated group of far-flung space explorers cooped up in a base and suffering casualties as the trouble gets worse (too many old stories to list), the slightly-wearing-thin device of putting the TARDIS beyond use (we're supposed to think it's lost forever) for the course of the action – as if the Doctor would consider skipping out while there's a crisis (on which point there's even a good joke in the teaser). It may be derivative, but it's fun: the use of caves to represent outer space reminded me of, besides 'Revenge of the Cybermen', endearingly low-rent British science-fiction films like *Inseminoid*. Even if the old fulfilled-prophecy and opening-pit business is whiskery, it's at least done here with some fine old hysteria and mind-stretching bits with the black hole; and by counting down to a big, cataclysmic event we get a natural cliff-hanger. David Tennant continues to be *very enthusiastic*, and prone to slightly patronising weepy-huggy fits when admiring human endeavour, and Billie Piper is here a more traditional tagalong sidekick. MyAnna Buring, who doesn't make it through *The Descent* either, is appealing as the script's sacrificial victim – the cannon fodder we vaguely care about before the casualties start racking up so fast we won't get time to mourn (my guess is that we'll see some death scenes next week) – and Claire Rushbrook works hard on the heavy expository speeches. – *Kim Newman*

When living things emerged from the ocean, we were obliged to bring the ocean with us, in the form of blood. Going into space, we have to bring the Earth's atmosphere with us – not only oxygen, but also the pressure that stops us from freeze-drying on the spot, and the shielding that stops us roasting in radiation. To live on land, we had to build bodies that could hold the ocean in; to live on the impossible planet, human beings need a new kind of body: the Sanctuary Base. Multicellular bodies are so useful that they've evolved on Earth at least 16 different times, resulting in everything from sponges to Russell T Davies. The crew members of the Sanctuary Base are loosely analogous to the different types of cells in a body. Only loosely, mind you – I suppose Zach is like the brain, but I don't mean that Toby is the kidney, Scooti is the elbow, and so on. What I mean is that they all have different jobs, but work together, combining their abilities so they can all survive and accomplish their mission. Into this cheerful story of cooperation comes the Beast. It takes over not only human and Ood bodies, but the Base itself, affecting its electromagnetic 'nervous system'. This gives it physical power: for example, to keep Door 40 closed despite Scooti's desperate pleas. More usefully to the Beast, it also allows it to go to work as a 'good psychologist'. Via the comms system, it whispers in Toby's ear like a terrifying auditory hallucination. Presumably, it gets into the computers and reads everyone's personnel files, diaries, letters and everything else – gathering together titbits of information about the crew and all their fears and sins. (Perhaps it reads Rose's obituary in a database.) With this power, plus its psychokinetic abilities, the Beast could easily kill the crew and the Doctor and Rose. But of course, it needs them to carry its mind safely away from the black hole. Like a virus, the Beast will be most successful if it doesn't kill at least some of its victims, so that it can be passed on to others. But it does have to kill the Sanctuary Base itself: to damage it so much that the crew are forced to evacuate. Poor Scooti is murdered only because she happens across the possessed Toby. When she won't be lured outside, the Beast kills her by cracking the glass of the viewing port, like cracking an egg and killing the chick inside. 'The Base is open!' – like a body bleeding to death. Cells in a body have to do two things – they have to communicate with each other, and they literally have to stick together. The Beast and the Doctor both recognise that the crew's only chance is to combine their skills. Rose may not be a scientist or a soldier, but – acting as the Doctor's lieutenant – she is able to motivate and organise the others. Trapped far from home, in the ultimately hostile spot, she does what life forms have always done to survive: she adapts. – *Kate Orman*

Is this the 'Planet Zog' story that Davies has been threatening us with since Series One?... This story was hyped as being the first venture to a true alien world (the new Earth in, er, 'New Earth', and the parallel universe Earth apparently don't count). In the past, *Doctor Who* rarely got down and dirty to deliver 'at the edge of space' sagas complete with space-suits and helmets. The closest we got was perhaps 'Frontier in Space' (1973). But even though the oil, dirt, automatic doors and airlocks imagery is really old hat, it seems so fresh and welcome in this new series of *Doctor Who*. Yes, we've had space-stations a couple of times this and last year, but those have been of the *Star Trek*-y, clinically sterile variety. After so many Earth-bound stories a proper space story is a welcome breath of fresh air – if you'll excuse the oh-so witty pun. With the Ood, the producers have created an alien species with yet more playground-quotable catchphrases ('Feed me', 'The Beast awakes') to sit alongside 'Exterminate', '<D-E-L-E-T-E>' and 'Are you my mummy?' If ever there were a live-action version of *Futurama*, I'm sure the animatronic Ood would be perfect for bringing to life Zoidberg! There are some characteristic similarities between the Ood and the Monoids of 1966's 'The Ark'; specifically they are likewise a slave race of identical creatures with numerical names who use communication voice boxes and who take over the control of a human space vessel on the far fringes of space. The supporting cast take it all very seriously, thankfully! In a claustrophobic setting such as this, one can't help but place bets on who will and who won't survive to the end. I'm sure I could hear all the shouts of protest when Scooti was killed off! Why do all the cute girls have to be the first to die?! I noted that the gravity wave formula was 6-6-6, and I doubt it was a coincidence that the episode aired the week of 6 June 2006. It seems the producers might however have missed the 'once in a century' opportunity of using this unusual date as an overall theme across the season rather than the oh-so-forced Torchwood references. 'The Impossible Planet' has a remarkably cinematic quality about it, and a gritty realism in the vein of *Outland* and *Alien*. I couldn't even tell whether the Pit cavern was a CGI–enhanced set or a location. (This was before the revelation in *Doctor Who Confidential* that it was actually a quarry!) Interestingly, 'The Impossible Planet' occupies the same position in the running order as 'The Empty Child', my favourite episode from last year. And they say lightning won't strike the same place twice. Okay, so it's another crap pun, but 'The Impossible Planet' is impossibly g-Ood... – *Jon Preddle*

A critical summation of a huge chunk of *Doctor Who*'s past, 'The Impossible Planet' takes various iconic Innes Lloyd-and-Peter Bryant/Philip Hinchcliffe-and-Bob-Holmes 'base under siege' ideas and, in effect, retools 'The Ice Warriors' or 'The Robots of Death' for a whole new generation. Whilst throwing in a slab of *Alien* and *Buffy the Vampire Slayer* for good measure. So, not the most *original* idea the series has ever attempted, that's undeniably true. Yet this is yer actual 'proper' *Doctor Who*, this is. A group of nicely characterised people thrown together in a confined space by circumstance and facing an uncertain future as well as dark forces. It's archetypal stuff and, in *Doctor Who*'s case, it rarely fails to at least entertain. Where 'The Impossible' Planet' scores, hugely, over numerous similar conceits is in its casting. Fabulous performances by most of the guest cast (Danny Webb and Claire Rushbrook one would expect little else from, but a special word of praise for Shaun Parkes and Will Thorp too). And who, honestly, didn't get a little fanboy (or fangirl, for that matter) shudder when Gabriel Woolf spoke his first line – that was something I certainly didn't expect. There were also excellent jokes ('What's your job, chief dramatist?'), clever dialogue moments ('The Beast and his armies shall rise from the Pit to make war against God') and an impressive example of one of the new Doctor's most interesting facets. I love how Tennant, like Eccleston before him, is being given genuinely sad lines of apology to some of those whom he is unable to save. His plaintive 'I'm sorry' as Scooti floats off into space is one of the most touchingly-played moments I can remember. Matt Jones's script reminds us that the Doctor's lifestyle, whilst a right good laugh in many ways (see the opening scene) is riddled with potential danger – a necessary restating of some series basics. – *Keith Topping*

EDITOR'S REVIEW: Brilliant. That's just about the best word to summarise 'The Impossible Planet', because that's exactly what it is – a brilliant piece of writing, what *Doctor Who* should always be like on television, and arguably the best single episode of the two-year-old series revival. While 'The Idiot's Lantern' edges this out for my personal favourite episode of the season by a notch (only because of the nostalgic feel, and this comes in second by literally a hairline), I want to stress that 'The Impossible Planet' should be the template for future *Doctor Who* stories, and there are many reasons why.

This is, to emphasise the point, not your typical children's *Doctor Who* story. It is a tale with adult themes and situations, yet safe enough for the family to enjoy. It demonstrates the oncoming battle between good and evil, in a way that emphasises the metaphors and mythology of religion without denigrating those sacred beliefs. It's poignant where it needs to be – I thought I was going to shed a tear for a moment, listening to Jefferson quote 'Horatius' – and gets silly (in fact, resorts to what has become standard *Doctor Who* touchy-feely silliness these days) in only one place, when Tennant's Doctor calls out for his hug. The monsters work exceptionally well; we're terrified of them because of their appearance, realise our basic prejudices are working against us when we find out the Ood aren't so bad, and then start fearing them again when we recognise them for what they are, weapons in a long struggle. There's the standard *Doctor Who* technical gobbledygook alongside mention of other worlds and civilisations without any additional exposition, it *finally* takes us off Earth to an actual space-based setting, and its guest cast is perhaps the best ensemble of the season to date. And Tennant and Piper are wonderful.

Why is *Doctor Who* not this good *every* week, one must ask? I'm beginning to think that Davies and Gardner and their team, while determined to make the best show they possibly can – and quite often succeeding – have failed to understand that the science-fiction of *Doctor Who was* part of the show's success, rather than merely the trappings of a show about a funny man in funny costumes. Far too often this year we see the Doctor and Rose pining away for one another or making witty repartee while saving Earth from this or that, all the while forgetting the days of 'Frontier in Space' or 'The Face of Evil' or 'The Caves of Androzani' when it was *about* the hard science-fiction, about the universe and its vast array of wonders. By setting the show on Earth, both before and, sadly, immediately after this tale, they've limited it to the comforts of home... it's as if the only adventure out there is the adventure that lies immediately beyond one's doorstep.

Of course, it's only part one of two and there's the chance that the second episode won't live up to the first (just as last season's 'The Doctor Dances', while exceptional, was a bit of a letdown after 'The Empty Child'). It's hard to give 'The Impossible Planet' accolades simply on its own merits – like rating a book having read only the first half – and I think that's why I actually prefer 'The Idiot's Lantern' on a simple gut-feeling basis. But 'The Impossible Planet' is what, in my mind, *Doctor Who* should be, going forward: the Doctor and his companion(s) facing the *universe* rather than their own backyard, seeking adventures far and wide. Just... brilliant. – *Shaun Lyon*

209: THE SATAN PIT

On the doomed planet nicknamed the Bitter Pill, Rose and the crew of Sanctuary Base Six fight for their lives, while far below the surface, the Doctor comes face to face with an ancient evil, imprisoned for an eternity, now looking to escape ...

FIRST TRANSMISSION: UK – 10 June 2006. US – December 2006. Canada – December 2006. Australia – 9 September 2006. New Zealand – 7 September 2006.
DURATION: 47'11"
WRITER: Matt Jones
DIRECTOR: James Strong
CREDITED CAST: David Tennant (The Doctor), Billie Piper (Rose Tyler), Danny Webb (Mr Jefferson), Shaun Parkes (Zachary Cross Flane), Claire Rushbrook (Ida Scott), Will Thorp (Toby Zed), Ronny Jhutti (Danny Bartock), Paul Kasey (The Ood), Gabriel Woolf (The Voice of the Beast), Silas Carson (The Voice of the Ood)

WHERE AND WHEN: Sanctuary Base Six on the planet nicknamed 'the Bitter Pill', the far future

THE STORY UNFOLDS: As the seal in the chamber far below the surface opens, so a massive earthquake rocks the planet, during which the Ood – under the complete control of the Beast – begin attacking the remaining base crew members. The planet has shifted to the very edge of the black hole's gravitational reach; as Zach notes, 'one more inch' and the planet will fall in. The Doctor and Ida, stranded with less than an hour of air left (55 minutes, according to the readout on Ida's suit control), are in the cavern attempting to discover what lies within the Pit. The Doctor likens the area below the seal to a 'prison', but says that they haven't yet unlocked the 'cell'. He decides that he, instead of Ida, will descend into the Pit.

The base is identified in this episode as Sanctuary Base Six. There are 50 Ood on the base, and they have somehow managed to convert their interface devices (the sphere-shaped translators) into weapons. The base has only ten miles of cable attached to the mining lift, with no backup cable in case of a problem. There is one escape craft, a rocket, which the crew – including the possessed Toby – use to try and escape.

The Beast is an alien trapped in an underground chamber on this world. It was imprisoned when 'the Disciples of Light' rose up against it and chained it there for all eternity; this apparently happened before the 'Big Bang' created the universe, which the Beast describes as 'before time'. The creature plays on basic fears, including childhood nightmares and guilt, and considers the darkness to be its domain. It isn't interested in making a deal; it believes the planet to be the humans' grave. The Doctor says that there are representations of the Horned Beast in myths and legends of a million worlds across the universe, including Earth, Draconia, Vel Consadine and Dæmos. The Kaled god of war is one example. The same image recurs over and over. The Beast may, in fact, be merely an idea rather than the actual Devil.

At the bottom of the Pit is a large chamber, decorated with pictographs of a horned beast being defeated and imprisoned. There are two vases, made of a translucent yellow crystal, on pedestals next to a large cavern, in which the massive Beast is held by chains... or, rather, the physical form of the creature, lacking the Beast's intelligence, which has been released into

Toby. The Beast is trapped here, as if it breaks free, the planet will fall into the black hole. The Doctor realises that if he destroys the vases, this will destroy the prison and kill the Beast ... but will also stop the rocket's escape, potentially causing the deaths of Rose and its other human occupants. He goes ahead and does it anyway, destroying the Beast's physical body while Rose aids in killing its mind – inside Toby – when she shoots a hole in the rocket's window, blowing him out with the air.

Strategy 9 is an emergency backup plan executed by Zach. It consists of opening the airlocks of the base.

The Neo Classic faith has no devil as such, just 'the things that men do'. Religions of the universe include the Arkiphets, Quoldonity, Christianity, Pash Pash, Neo-Judaism, San Claar, the Church of the Tin Vagabond and others.

The episode is set at time frame 43 K 2.1, which is not explained but probably follows a dating convention of the far future. (Perhaps it is the 43rd Century, which is what was originally intended by the writer?)

THE DOCTOR: He thinks he's getting old when he listens to his intuition to go into the Pit and decides to retreat instead. The Beast says he's 'the killer of his own kind', intimating that the Doctor is responsible for the destruction of his people (though the Doctor chooses not to acknowledge this). He is forced to recognise that his understanding of the universe is merely a belief when the Beast confronts him with the fact that it existed before the universe was created; it doesn't fit his rule. He thinks psychologists, like the Beast, play on people's fears, and that humans are amazing. He takes a huge risk by dropping into the Pit without the rope. He's seen 'fake gods and bad gods and demi gods and would-be gods' but believes in Rose.

ROSE TYLER: The Beast calls her 'the lost girl, so far away from home' and 'the valiant child who will die in battle so very soon', terrifying her that she will lose her life in the near future. She defends Toby against Jefferson's attack and inspires everyone to come up with a solution to their situation – she has clearly developed from the shop-girl in 'Rose' to someone far more like the Doctor. Zach sedates her when she refuses to leave the base, insisting she will wait for the Doctor; and later she threatens to shoot him if he won't take her back. She knows their escape doesn't make sense – the Beast could have stopped them – and kills Toby (and the Beast's intelligence) in the rocket. The Doctor tells her the Beast lied when it said she would die in battle.

CHARACTER BUILDING: *Ida Scott* – She doesn't want to withdraw from the underground chamber, as she is consumed by its secrets; she wanted to discover things and thinks the ruins are beautiful. She is apparently 'still running from daddy', according to the Beast. She thinks the urge to jump is genetic heritage, from humanity's era as primates in the trees. She was raised in the Neo Classic congregational faith, and she misses her mother. She doesn't want to die alone in the Pit, but thinks there is no way for anyone to reach her. The Doctor later rescues her with the TARDIS.

Zachary Cross Flane – He is scared of command and feels helpless when alone in the command centre. Jefferson tells him that he's made a very good captain under the circumstances. He's later devastated by Jefferson's death and by having to leave Ida behind. Zach pilots the rocket ship away from Sanctuary Base Six along with Danny, Rose, the doomed Toby and, later, Ida.

Toby Zed – He doesn't comprehend what's happening to him; he's genuinely terrified when Jefferson threatens to shoot him. All he can remember is fury and rage, and death. He believes the beast to be the Devil. Rose assumes that when the markings vanished and the black mist passed to the Ood, Toby was released; this is not the case, however, as it's later revealed he still carries the Beast inside him. The Beast reveals that Toby's a virgin. Toby dies when Rose destroys the spacecraft's window. His full name was Tobias Zed, and he's declared deceased with honours.

Mr Jefferson – His full name is John Maynard Jefferson (with the title/acronym PKD). He is 'haunted by the eyes of his wife' and believes he's the only line of defence between the Ood and the humans. He misses getting through the closing bulkhead in the tunnels while defending himself (and the others) from the rampaging Ood, and asks for Zach to make his unavoidable death quick by explosive decompression. Zach reports him deceased with honours.

Danny Bartock – He apparently maintains guilt over something in his past, as the Beast refers to him as the 'little boy who lied'. Rose says his bum is not his 'best angle'. He survives, along with Ida and Zach, on the rocket ship.

TORCHWOOD: Zach reveals that he and, presumably, the entire base's staff are working for the Torchwood Archive.

BODY COUNT: Mr Jefferson, Toby Zed, all the Ood (identified as Ood 1 Alpha 1, Ood 1 Alpha 2, etc) and the other unnamed personnel of Sanctuary Base Six... as well as the Beast.

THE DOCTOR'S MAGICAL SONIC SCREWDRIVER: Not seen in this episode.

REALITY BITES: The Doctor refers to the universal religious concept of the Devil, and how it has appeared across the universe. Christianity is mentioned, although the Jewish faith has now apparently developed a 'New Judaism'.

Ida volunteers that she and the Doctor abseil into the Pit; the term abseiling refers to the process of roping down or descending on a rope. Rose refers to the popular convenience store chain Tesco. Jefferson's solo stand against the Ood – and the trip through the tunnels – is clearly inspired by the sequence leading up to Vasquez's and Gorman's deaths in James Cameron's 1986 film *Aliens* (ironically, considering that Danny Webb, who plays Jefferson, was in the sequel, *Alien3).*

LINKING THEMES: The Beast's revelation that the Doctor is somehow responsible for the deaths of his Time Lord brethren has been foreshadowed as far back as 'Rose', in which the Doctor demonstrated his guilt at not being able to save the planets allied against the Daleks, and in 'The End of the World' when Jabe expressed her deep sorrow for the Doctor's civilisation. Presumably the Doctor had to make a fateful decision at some point that somehow resulted in the sacrifice of his own people. This echoes a key aspect of a lengthy story arc in the BBC Books *Doctor Who* novel range, which saw the eighth Doctor choose to sacrifice his people rather than see them corrupted by a voodoo cult called Faction Paradox (a storyline somewhat revised at the end of the novel series in order to mesh with the Time Lords' existence and subsequent fall in the Time War, as referred to in the new series). The Doctor's mention that his people invented black holes may refer to their creation of the Eye of Harmony, the black hole from which the Time Lords derived their power, as established in the 1977 story

'The Deadly Assassin'; the 1996 *Doctor Who* TV movie implied that each TARDIS might have its own black hole powering it, and the *Doctor Who* novels have gone even further to say that the Time Lords did indeed create *artificial* black holes as power sources. However, they've never referred to the Time Lords actually creating black holes in the first place, as the Doctor's comments here seem to imply.

The Doctor refers to the planets Draconia and Dæmos and to the Kaled god of war. Draconia is the home of the Draconian race, a civilisation that engaged in a war with, and later became allied to, Earth, as seen in the story 'Frontier in Space'. Dæmos is the homeworld of the Dæmons, a race of satanic-looking aliens, one of which crashed on Earth and terrorised Britain in 'The Dæmons'. The Kaleds, rivals of the Thals on the planet Skaro, were later mutated by the scientist Davros to become the Daleks, as established in 'Genesis of the Daleks'.

While the Doctor states that nothing existed before the universe, the Virgin and BBC Books *Doctor Who* novel series suggested that some of the series' monsters – such as the Great Intelligence ('The Abominable Snowmen'), the Animus ('The Web Planet') and the Nestene Consciousness ('Spearhead from Space', 'Rose') – were originally Great Old Ones. This drew on the myths popularised by the writer H P Lovecraft in the first three decades of the 20th Century. Even the televised series made references to events 'before time' – Light ('Ghost Light') and Fenric ('The Curse of Fenric') both supposedly existed at this point, and indeed Fenric was trapped in a flask similar to those that were holding the Beast in captivity.

The rocket resembles one seen in 'The Sensorites', further tying this and the previous episode into that story (see 'The Impossible Planet'). The TARDIS tractor beam has been seen before, in 'The Creature from the Pit' and 'Delta and the Bannermen'.

SCENE MISSING: How does the TARDIS end up in the cave at the bottom of the Pit? In 'The Impossible Planet', it fell down into the bowels of the planet during an earthquake. (There is one explanation – the HADS, or Hostile Action Displacement System, as seen in 'The Krotons', was used to move the ship to safety. But this is not referred to at all.)

What has happened to the 'Disciples of Light' who brought the Doctor down into the chamber (cushioning his fall)? It could have been an automated system that kicked-in to save anyone who managed to get to the prison chamber (like, for example, the Osiran pyramid in 'Pyramids of Mars' and the Kastrian base in 'The Hand of Fear'), but how could it have helped him so thoroughly? This is never made clear.

A black hole will crush and destroy the Beast. This begs the question, then: why not just throw him into the black hole aeons ago and be done with it? Also, since the Beast was so well imprisoned behind the seal, how did its intelligence get out in the first place – and why is it so critical that it should stay in Toby for the entire episode?

Toby's death sequence presents a problem. Rose shoots the window; it's a relatively small cockpit and space is a vacuum, so the air should have been sucked out almost instantaneously... killing Rose and the rest of her party. And yet they all survive, and Rose still has the brainpower during the rush of oxygen from the capsule to unbuckle Toby's belt. Why does Rose shoot the window and not Toby directly? How could anyone hear Zach speaking if there is little to no air in the capsule?

Why does the Doctor not go back for the Ood? The TARDIS does, after all, travel in time as well as space. (There are precedents for such inaction in the series, usually explained by reference to laws of time, but it still doesn't make it any easier to bear; we're talking about at least 50 lives here.)

What about the other crew members of the Sanctuary Base? We don't get their names, but they were obviously human beings someone cared about. Yet Zach jumps from his report of Toby's death to the Ood. (He'd already entered Scooti's and Jefferson's deaths in the log.)

Other questions: why are there grilles between the chambers in the supposedly airtight service ducts? Why does a forced evacuation of the air in various sections of the base (Strategy 9) require 100% power and total base lockdown? And why, when the gravity field fails and traps the rocket, does the ship *turn around* before heading toward the black hole?

BEHIND THE SCENES: Much of this episode was recorded in the studios in Newport, although the scenes with the Doctor in the Beast's lair were recorded at Clearwell Caves in Gloucestershire, the same location used for the Sycorax ship interiors in 'The Christmas Invasion'. The Sanctuary Base corridor set was later used in *Totally Doctor Who*.

The look of the Beast was inspired by the paintings of comics artist Simon Bisley. Davies noted in the commentary that the destiny of Rose to 'die in battle' was a foreshadowing of the season finalé. He also notes that one of the unused ideas originally conceived for this episode will show up in a Series Three story.

OFF THE SCREEN: See 'The Impossible Planet' for details about members of the cast.

CONTROVERSIES: A major controversy ensued over the fate of the Ood. Fifty living, breathing souls from this slave race die, and even though they're possessed by the Beast, no-one seems to care about this. (It's also mentioned that they're 'not true life forms' and don't show up on the scanner.) The Doctor raises an eyebrow when Ida tells him about 'Strategy 9', but there doesn't seem to be any further consideration for the hapless slaves. He later becomes somewhat melancholy that he couldn't rescue any of the Ood, but it's a momentary blip and it's then easily passed off in the relief of survival from their battle. The story implies heavily (but doesn't come right out and say it) that the Ood are a genetically engineered race made specifically to serve humans, which itself brings up many controversial issues such as cloning, stem cell research, the creation of artificial life and the rights and wrongs of subsequently killing such life. Quite topical at the time of this book's publication, but still quite messy.

INTERNAL CONSISTENCY: The episode takes place over the course of no more than an hour or two; Ida's oxygen supply is sufficient for about an hour when they reach the Pit, and she can't have been out cold for long when the Doctor rescues her.

TARDISODE #9: At Sanctuary Base Six, a crewman and an Ood are going over the belongings of the deceased Captain Walker when the computer says 'He shall awake' and the monitor screen notes 'He shall rise from the Pit'. The crewman attempts to flee. Later, a female crewman comes in and sees her colleague, upset, with strange markings on his face.

It's unlikely that this TARDISode could take place in the continuity of the episode, because other than the Captain being dead from the crash, we're not given any indication that there has been anything amiss at the Sanctuary Base. The base ID code 'SB6' on the monitor changes quite quickly to '666', which is a generally accepted symbol of the Devil.

REVIEWS

Okay, so it wasn't Sutekh, but damn it all, it should have been, and that's just one of many irritating things about this episode. In most cases, the series' two-part stories have suffered from poorly paced, overly expository opening instalments with concluding chapters that manage to ratchet up the excitement and redeem the story as a whole. Traditionally, the reverse is true, with powerhouse openers leading to lacklustre conclusions that squander the promise of the first segment. That tradition now continues. The opening sequence paying off last week's cliff-hanger is a major cheat. The final shot of 'The Impossible Planet' deliberately played up the idea that the Beast himself was rising out of the hatchway, but surprise! There's nothing there but an endless pit that the Doctor will contemplate for another 20 minutes! Not an opening that inspires confidence. A large part of the episode is wasted in crawling through featureless ventilation ducts, and when at long last we finally get to see the Doctor meet the Beast, we're robbed of the sharply-written confrontation scene that typifies stories of this kind. This Beast is just a mindless monster, with Tennant left to rant and rave rather embarrassingly at a roaring chained CGI effect. A clever subversion of expectations? No, I think it's just a waste of a powerful dramatic opportunity. The problems don't end there. Rose's objections to the Oods' slave status seemed like a secondary plot thread set-up last time, but it never really goes anywhere; even the Doctor seems pretty comfortable with sending the poor cattle-like aliens to their doom with just a momentary sense of regret. And yet, although there's a lot to be disappointed about, the superb guest cast give it their all and infuse the characters with a natural warmth and loyalty to one another that rings true and makes their deaths all the more moving. The high production values are also a saviour here, with the shot of the TARDIS towing the rocket away from the black hole a punch-the-air highlight. I can't figure Tennant out though. At times he's commanding and heroic, and at others he's so over the top with goggle-eyed, mouth-twisting lunacy that he's physically uncomfortable to watch. But Tennant's acting is just one troubling aspect of this Doctor; another is his relationship with Rose. Never before has the Doctor been so single-mindedly devoted to his companion to the exclusion of all else. While the Doctor still does what he must to save the universe, it's interesting that his dilemma comes down to one question: can he sacrifice Rose? When mulling it over (out loud), he doesn't even mention the other three people in the rocket with her, or the one who might still be alive at the Pit opening. This is love all right, but it's also rather selfish for a hero of the universe, isn't it? For an episode that borrows liberally from *Who* stories like 'The Robots of Death' and 'Pyramids of Mars', 'The Satan Pit' suffers in comparison with its source material. On its own, 'The Satan Pit' is a slowly-paced misfire, but with 'The Impossible Planet', the story is a qualified success that offers solid character, brilliant visual design, and some thought-provoking moments marred only by poor plotting and some glaring missed opportunities. – *Arnold T Blumberg*

Given the brilliance of 'The Impossible Planet', 'The Satan Pit' probably never stood a chance at bettering it, but it certainly comes within a hair's-breadth of equalling it. Here we have base-under-siege, 2006 style, where Rose's party needs to get from point A to point B (through ventilation ducts no less!) to stop the monsters. It sounds like episode three of just about any *Doctor Who* story in 1975, but describing it that way doesn't begin to capture how brilliantly it actually works (or how incredible a moment Toby gesturing to the Ood to be quiet really is!) All the set-up of the characters in 'The Impossible Planet' pays off here – the death of Mr Jefferson, a character who in the 1980s would have been grim, cynical monster-fodder, is utterly heartbreaking; Zach coming to terms with being a leader is equally uplifting. But it's what's happening beneath the planet that makes this episode so compelling. The image of the

Doctor abseiling into blackness is an unforgettable one, but to combine it with the Doctor and Ida discussing faith (and the Doctor quietly converting, in many respects, from an atheist to an agnostic) is sheer brilliance. David Tennant is wonderful here, demonstrating the amazing power that can come out of a quiet, minimal performance. I'm sure others will quibble about the giant Beast and the Doctor finding the TARDIS so handily; I'm not one of them, as I loved the climax of the story where everything topside and underneath all came together. There are so many other elements of this story that are worthy of mention: Murray Gold's score is among his best – that lonely violin strain is absolutely perfect; Claire Rushbrook is awesome as Ida – I hope the Doctor keeps his promise and visits her again in a future season; and it's wonderful to see the Doctor and Rose have some emotional, even sexual chemistry, after it taking a long holiday earlier this season. Indeed, while this season has been missing the emotional arc between the Doctor and Rose that defined last season, 'The Impossible Planet' and 'The Satan Pit' exemplifies the fact that at the same time the quality of storytelling is actually far, far higher. – *Graeme Burk*

I think one of my biggest problems with the two-parters in the new series is that while the two separate halves may be very good individually, they often don't mesh together as a particularly cohesive whole. 'Bad Wolf' and 'The Parting of the Ways' were particularly guilty of this last year, with only about ten minutes of the former having any real bearing on the latter, and I'm sad to say that 'The Impossible Planet' and 'The Satan Pit' have a strangely similar relationship. A large part of the disconnected feel is down to the two episodes serving very, very different purposes. I noted last week that 'The Impossible Planet' was almost entirely plot-based; well, 'The Satan Pit' takes the other approach, focusing on characters. And that works great – at least, until we're required to have a plot again. And then it all goes, well, pretty much to hell. To its credit, the first half is really involving stuff. The tension from last week is kept up with considerable aplomb, but there's still time for little quiet moments. The Doctor's discussions with Ida are actually the highlight of the episode, and for a series that has uniformly either dismissed or simply ignored religion, the reflections on the nature of faith are startlingly effective. I like the idea of a Doctor who must realise he doesn't know *everything*; too often, particularly toward the end of the 1989 series, the Doctor is not only knowledgeable to the point of redundancy, he's smug. The tenth Doctor seemed to be heading in a similar direction up to this episode. I, for one, am glad to see his confidence shaken just a bit. Unfortunately, in its bid to keep questions unanswered and excitement high, the episode makes a couple of really poor choices. One is to leave the Doctor spouting pure exposition at the bottom of the Pit. The computer-generated devil is *magnificent* – in fact, it may be the single greatest special effect we've yet seen from the new series – but when you come back to the episode a second or third time, the surprise is gone, and you're left watching the Doctor go through the motions with himself. Christopher Eccleston might actually have been able to pull it off (the speech seems pitched more to his brand of intensity), but for some reason, Tennant simply can't. The other, bigger mistake of the episode is to offer, in lieu of some actual answers, a pathetically silly action finalé. Not even Gabriel Woolf's voice can save the spectacle of Toby suddenly breathing flame, and while I recognise the lead of a family show can't shoot someone in the head, couldn't a better reason have been found to get Rose to shoot out the rocket's view screen? Unnecessary suicide doesn't strike me as the brightest 'how to save the day' option, and that's not even touching on the idea that *everyone should be instantly and totally dead*. But then, it seems there's a bit of a breeze in this version of space... Honestly, I want to like 'The Satan Pit' more than I do. It's got some great concepts in there, a good cast and largely confident direction, but it simply doesn't stand up to 'The Impossible Planet'. What I thought might well turn out to be an instant classic has now become merely very good, and while that's not the end of the world, it is a bit disappointing. – *Sarah Hadley*

British television dramas do not often tend to go in for tackling big theological or philosophical ideas such as the existence or otherwise of the devil, or where the evil that lurks at the heart of men may come from. The occasional big, prestigious one-off drama production might feel brave enough to take on the potential religious ire that exploring any such issue could provoke, Russell T Davies's own *The Second Coming* with Christopher Eccleston from 2003 being a good example. But a more populist continuing drama series such as *Doctor Who* would not normally be expected to come face-to-face with the concept of Satan. There was an episode of *Holby City* several years back – in its very first series, I seem to remember, when it was still a drama rather than a soap opera – that featured a character who may or may not have been an angel of some kind, but that's the only other occasion I can remember a prime time popular drama straying into such territory. *Doctor Who* has always shied away from such issues in the past, any possible brushing up against religion being very quickly backed away from lest it offend or cause controversy. There was a rejected Hartnell-era storyline pitch, 'The Face of God', and Chris Boucher's original title for 'The Face of Evil' was 'The Day God Went Mad', but I think that's about it. Here Matt Jones goes straight for the jugular by sticking Satan right into the episode's title, although the nature of the Beast in the episode itself is skirted around just enough to avoid inciting any angry Christians to write angry letters to the BBC, I think. The existence of the Devil in the traditional form is debated but never explicitly confirmed or denied, and by the end of the episode even the Doctor can't be sure what exactly the Beast was. This could seem like ducking the issue and chickening out, but I think it actually works well, because preserving the mystery and enigma of the Beast makes it all the more interesting a creature, and it makes a nice change for the series to present us with an evil that even the Doctor cannot fully comprehend or explain. This is also a very strong episode for Billie Piper as Rose, who actually gets to do something proactive for a change as she basically takes charge of the Sanctuary Base survivors as they fight against the onslaught of the ever creepily effective Ood. Rose taking a commanding role shows a bravery and resourcefulness to her character, although it does have to be admitted that the fact she has to delegate tasks to everyone else shows that she doesn't actually seem to have any terribly useful specific skills herself. One of Murray Gold's best musical scores and some fantastic special effects work – I was convinced the Beast was an enlarged image of a man in a prosthetic suit until I saw this week's *Doctor Who Confidential* episode showing how it was created in CGI – help to boost the atmosphere, and together with Jones's serious and sensitive script, create one of the best episodes Series Two has provided to date. – *Paul Hayes*

And then it's all over. The Ood are shut behind a door, the planet stops its descent, and the Pit just sits there like pits tend to do. Just as at the start of 'World War Three', any tension built up at the last week's cliff-hanger is lost within seconds. We all know about the classic 'W' shape of drama and the three acts, but this plunges from cliff-hanger to quarry floor faster than an old Flash Gordon serial. Still, if you can overlook this – like an unpleasant *amuse bouche* before a sumptuous main course – there's nothing but delight ahead (including dessert!) As the Beast continues to speak through the Ood, the Doctor is left to wonder about its true nature. In a scene reminiscent of the his reverse ego trip in 'Planet of the Spiders', the Doctor decides to face his fear of the unknown and descend into the Pit. But the unknown isn't the darkness of the chasm. It's the darkness of not knowing. Here we see the first signs that the irritating smugness is about to be seriously dented. Because in the Doctor's science, the Beast simply cannot exist. In the original series, the closest *Doctor Who* ever came to addressing the concept of pure evil was in 'The Curse of Fenric', with the Doctor waxing metaphysical about shards of evil from the dawn of time. But even that was dressed in semi-scientific terms, with faith reduced to a psionic barrier. All other 'pure evils' have been dismissed out of hand by the Doctor's near-arrogant belief in the supremacy of science: Azal, the Chronovores, the Black Guardian... This time, the Doctor has no such glib explanations. The Beast is evil from *before* the dawn of time – totally beyond the Doctor's comprehension. Meanwhile, the Beast is messing with everyone else's minds. Like a demented Frasier Crane, it identifies each person's weak spot and exploits it. For Toby, it is his virginity – a nice twist on the virgin sacrifice – but his prediction for Rose is more than enough to wipe that self-satisfied grin off her face. However, the way that this galvanises Rose, then she the rest of the crew, serves to validate the Doctor's statement about humanity in part one. While the beloved ventilation shaft makes a welcome return to the series in scenes reminiscent of *Alien* (Why not borrow from the best? It's what *Doctor Who does*), the narrative does get a bit confusing from hereon in. It's all there up front – no *deus ex machina* here – but like a fittingly devilish crossword, it does require the viewer to really think about it, and I do wonder if one viewing is sufficient. Naturally, the answer to the conundrum has been obvious since the Doctor's descent into the Pit. Faith in Rose. But this isn't the seventh Doctor's cod-science psionic barrier, this is real faith. Because, at the end, that's what this story is all about: people's belief in each other. Before we all start a group hug and have dessert – the TARDIS as a tugboat – it's only fair to note some of the rum notes. The science of the black hole just doesn't hold water – they don't work like that, and the maths is all wrong (geek alert here!). And Jefferson's noble self-sacrifice seems to be for plot rather than logical reasons. But this is not enough to spoil a true hard-SF *Doctor Who* classic. Indeed 'the stuff of legends'. – *Craig Hinton*

This might be the most thoroughly ordinary *Doctor Who* in decades – it does all it's supposed to do and is for the most part perfectly satisfactory television. But... it's essentially just a lot of running (or falling or crawling or flying) around, with a Big Ultimate Evil figure who doesn't really seem to be all that much in the universal malign entity stakes, and plucky characters who sacrifice or survive as required. The Doctor is literally dropped down a hole for most of the story until he comes across the mighty plot get-out clause of the TARDIS and effects a happier ending. A problem of using the device of the chained Evil God is that it's hard to see how it being loose would make things any worse than the show has generally made them out to be, and no-one wants to ponder the possibility that banishing it to beyond a black hole will bring about a more benevolent universe, because it would mean the End of All Stories. It may well be a mistake for the show to get into the area of religion, since it is forced to weigh its usual default position that all the gods you've heard of are actually interfering aliens against the possibility that there might be a One True Real Deity (and we can guess which one the BBC would prefer) out there somewhere, which the Doctor ums and ahhs about invoking. If he were an Anglican Time Lord called the Vicar, he couldn't be more woolly when it comes to the sermonising about faith that writer Matt Jones gives him as he drops himself off a rope into the dark or gets close to the horned, zombie-faced roaring giant at the bottom of the well. Now, the series could do with a jolt or two if it wants to rev up towards the end of the season. – *Kim Newman*

At the end of 'The Impossible Planet', the Pit opens dramatically, with the Doctor and Ida (and me) on tenterhooks to see what emerges. Nothing does emerge, leaving us staring into a blank space. If this seems anticlimactic, that was probably the very intention of the Beast's jailers: the Doctor and Ida's curiosity is only inflamed by the deliberate tease. I think that intelligent beings across the universe, however wildly varied, will probably still have certain things in common. Useful things like eyes, which (like multicellular bodies) have evolved again and again on Earth. But also more abstract things like curiosity, and language, and a complex social structure. The tools you need to build a civilisation – and a technology capable of reaching a black hole at the edge of space. Even if I'm wrong, those ancient jailers knew that anyone who arrived at the Beast's eternal prison would be as nosy as heck. It's curiosity that gets the crew of the Sanctuary Base, as well as the Doctor and Rose, onto the impossible planet in the first place – the curiosity of explorers to see, and the curiosity of scientists to *know*. I cringed at the Doctor's delighted 'And you came' speech, waiting for a sarcastic punchline, with him berating Zach and company for their foolish meddling. But of course, he's completely sincere; after all, the Doctor himself is about as curious as a cat on uppers. Despite his bursts of contempt for 'stupid apes', the Doctor admires humans – perhaps because he sees his own curiosity reflected in us. Of course, at least some other civilisations must know about the impossible planet, to have given it names. Perhaps some others have sought Kron Tep's secret, but didn't succeed – or didn't survive. Perhaps still others, like the Time Lords, have given up both seeing and learning new things. In that respect, the Doctor is more like a human being than a Time Lord. (This could explain why he puts a positive value on sickness and suffering in 'The Age of Steel': he sees how it drives us to learn and invent.) Confronted with the tantalising Pit, the Doctor puts his curiosity aside with an almost physical effort. He suspects the Beast is relying on curiosity to lure them in. Ida talks about the primate urge to jump, which no doubt we've all felt on a balcony or a cliff edge, but the Doctor redefines it as a more universal 'urge to fall': to throw yourself into the dark and find out what's there. When he reaches the end of his rope, he literally falls the rest of the way. But it's not the Beast, but the Beast's jailers who are relying on inquisitiveness. Anyone curious enough to visit the planet will surely be curious enough to make a leap of faith – or a fall of faith – into the Pit. – *Kate Orman*

The planet is Gallifrey... Featuring the return of Sutekh? Azal? The Great Vampire? The Dæmons? Kronos? Okay, so it wasn't Sutekh! When Gabriel Woolf was announced as guest voice artist, everyone (including me) thought the Beast had to be Sutekh. But that would have been far too much – we've already had K-9, Sarah and the Cyber... oops, almost caught me there! We certainly don't need the Osirans (or any other returning evils from the dawn of time, for that matter) thrown into the mix. And I'd also heard suggestions that the impossible planet in question was the remains of post-Time War Gallifrey. Enough of the silly suggestions, already! Indeed, most of the predictions I made before the series started have not come true. Maybe it's time to give up that game. Even my Gun 'n' Rose theory (see 'New Earth') looks like it's going to be wrong. But there are still four episodes to go; the tide may still turn in my favour! Given that this was the last episode they recorded together (is this significant?), Tennant and Piper are on fine form; Piper seems to enjoy the chance of taking command of the situation and ordering the crew around! And Tennant thankfully holds back on his usual shouty, boggle-eyed loon in the beautiful moment of philosophical reflection as the Doctor ponders his options while trapped in the Pit, a moment very like the one where Ed Harris is caught in a similar predicament in James Cameron's *The Abyss*. In fact, this two-parter seems very much like a Cameron film, with further visual influences from *Aliens*. And as with all Hollywood blockbusters, it is easy to guess which characters are going to be cannon-fodder (or is that f-Ood-er?). No real surprises then, that one sacrificial lamb would be Pat Gorman look-alike Danny Webb (who was in *Alien3*!). I couldn't tell at first whether the 'devil' creature was fully CGI or a CGI-enhanced man in a rubber suit. I recall the rather cheap-looking and featureless Nestene Consciousness from last year's 'Rose'. The Mill certainly deserves an award for this latest achievement. Wonderful stuff. So, the big revelation is that Rose will die. Didn't the Face of Boe have a big revelation as well? Is there a connection? No doubt this shocking event will occur in episode 13, probably the season finale cliff-hanger that RTD and co keep mentioning. This might explain Piper's evasive answers when asked if she'll be returning in Series Three... And on that note, is Rose perhaps redundant? I mean, she worked wonderfully as a character with the ninth Doctor, but Tennant might actually need a different type of companion, one better suited to his Doctor. A truly superb set of episodes, the best of the best. I can't fault them at all. More space sagas like this next year please! Unless episodes 12 and 13 turn out to be incredible, 'The Impossible Planet'/'The Satan Pit' must be the season poll winner. If not (oh, please don't let it be 'Rise of the Cybermen'/'The Age of Steel'!), then there's simply no justice in the world... – *Jon Preddle*

Primal fears and temptations are the key metaphors in this quite thrilling conclusion. The Doctor's musings on the nature of Ultimate Evil, existence and belief ('Call it an act of faith') provide an element of precise *realpolitik* alongside more traditional and expected dialogue references (his stirring speech about the brilliance and ingenuity of humanity echoes a similar moment in 'The Ark in Space' 30 years ago). Indeed, for some old fans, the episode, complete with continuity references to 'The Dæmons' and 'Genesis of the Daleks', reinforces the notion that this two-parter represent the more traditional and unchallenging part of the season – a safe haven to return to after flights of fancy with French noblewomen and two-dimensional aliens. Which couldn't be further from the truth. 'The Satan Pit' – its gorgeous special effects and witty throwaway moments ('the Church of the Tin Vagabond') aside – is a startlingly realised meditation on all aspects of the ceaseless quest for knowledge. When the Doctor notes 'That's why I keep travelling, to be proved wrong', he is voicing a universal truth about the series that, in theory at least, its fans should recognise as part of the reason why they continue to watch the show. Because *Doctor Who* asks the questions that other dramatic texts wouldn't *dare* to. After a few weeks of stagnation in terms of character development, Rose finally gets another opportunity to display her courage and feisty-but-impulsive attitude to hopeless situations by taking charge when the Doctor is trapped in the Pit. The hint, voiced by the Beast, of what the future may hold for her is merely one other brilliant moment in an episode, literally, full of them. – *Keith Topping*

EDITOR'S REVIEW: I've read with great interest reviews that state that 'The Satan Pit' doesn't live up to the promise of the first episode, and I can't help but find myself at a loss. 'The Impossible Planet' was breathtaking science-fiction and gorgeous *Doctor Who*, and the entire task of 'The Satan Pit' was to get the Doctor and Rose and their new friends out of the jam they were in and solve the problem. Oh, and make sense of this whole Beast thing. By and large,

'The Satan Pit' does exactly what it says on the tin (to borrow Captain Jack's phrase from last season). It might not be pretty, and in one particular respect it might be a bit of a disappointment, but it certainly manages to tie up all the loose ends and do it well.

Except for that whole disappointment thing, which has to do with the Beast itself. The Doctor and Ida spent the better part of last episode and much of this one descending further and further into the planet, opening up the seal before the Doctor makes his plummet into the depths. Fine, except that it's all a great big red herring; the Beast is already on the loose, and we should have gathered that from last week. (If Toby's inhabited by the Beast, then why would it matter if he could escape or not?) This ties in, to an extent, with one of the questions we've asked in 'Scene Missing': why in the world would the Disciples of Light strand the Beast on a captive planet in the shadow of a black hole that could do him in instead of just taking care of business in the first place? Someone's *obviously* going to wander by when they discover a planet that shouldn't be there, and it seemed like the humans weren't doing much when they just happened to release the Beast's intellect, plopping itself into Toby's head without so much as a by-your-leave. The Doctor, meanwhile, goes through all that rigmarole for... what, exactly? To watch helpless as the Beast takes off into the universe? Talk about the intergalactic equivalent of a fake out ...

So yes, fine, that's a bit of a strangeness, but horses for courses; if plot holes weren't so common in *Doctor Who*, the series would probably lose some of its charm. Beyond this simple fault in the logic, and despite the fact that the Doctor isn't the one to actually face off against the Beast (that would be Rose, after all), there's still a tremendous amount that's good in 'The Satan Pit' to make it a winner. The acting on the part of its supporting cast is top notch:. Danny Webb makes Mr Jefferson entirely believable and tragic, and it never feels forced when he makes the ultimate sacrifice; Claire Rushbrook, Shaun Parkes and Ronny Jhutti all do a tremendous job with their roles, displaying the range of emotions their characters would probably face in a fit of terror; and Will Thorp manages to convey both the sense of frustration and panic in Toby and the cold malevolence of the Beast with skill. The actors are complemented by a great sense of style in the set design, good effects and a striking musical score that firmly cement this into the annals of great Saturday night science-fiction television.

One thing that bothers me, though, is the sense of moral ambiguity surrounding the Ood. As I've noted in the 'Controversies' section, I can't help but be astonished that there's very little lip service paid to the Ood after their mass slaughter. This isn't the first time, either, that I've had trouble with the moral sensibilities of the series or its characters; I had a lot of trouble last season with the Doctor's (now thankfully absent) comments about humans being 'stupid apes'. In fact, I'm bothered by the fact that many don't seem bothered by it; I'm bothered by the fact that I barely remembered it while writing this review. The Ood are scary, interesting, strikingly well crafted... and ultimately forgettable. That's a bit of a shame.

Still, what a dynamic duo 'The Impossible Planet' and 'The Satan Pit' make. There have been instances elsewhere where conventional wisdom adhered to by the production team has been proved wrong: the notion that the Doctor works best with only one companion was disproved when Captain Jack joined the TARDIS crew; and the belief that referring back to the original series, beyond a few clever monster updates, would alienate modern viewers was nullified the moment Elisabeth Sladen showed up in 'School Reunion'. Likewise, it's easy to see here that the notion that *Doctor Who* must be Earth-bound to teach us all a lesson or give us something to relate to is ultimately flawed; it's the quality of the story that matters, Earth-bound or not. Lesson learned here, in the course of a brilliant two-parter, to stunning effect. – *Shaun Lyon*

210: LOVE & MONSTERS

Elton Pope is an ordinary Londoner with a rather ordinary life. But a chance encounter with a mysterious stranger called the Doctor leads him to a group of people who have had the same experience. When the ebullient Victor Kennedy joins them, Elton's life becomes *anything* but ordinary ...

FIRST TRANSMISSION: UK – 17 June 2006. US – December 2006. Canada – December 2006. Australia – 16 September 2006. New Zealand – 14 September 2006.
DURATION: 45'05"
WRITER: Russell T Davies
DIRECTOR: Dan Zeff
CREDITED CAST: David Tennant (The Doctor), Billie Piper (Rose Tyler), Camille Coduri (Jackie Tyler), Peter Kay (Victor Kennedy), Marc Warren (Elton Pope), Shirley Henderson (Ursula Blake), Simon Greenall (Mr. Skinner), Moya Brady (Bridget), Kathryn Drysdale (Bliss), Paul Kasey (The Hoix), Bella Emberg (Mrs Croot)

Abzorbaloff created by William Grantham

WHERE AND WHEN: London, 2007.

THE STORY UNFOLDS: London resident Elton Pope narrates a video diary, describing in detail the events that led him to encounter the Doctor. The experience has brought him into contact with four other people with an interest in the Doctor – Ursula Blake, Colin Skinner, Bridget and Bliss. Originally referring to themselves as the 'inner sanctum', the group meet weekly underneath the old library on Macateer Street; they later name themselves the London Investigation 'n Detective Agency, LINDA for short. LINDA soon becomes more than just a group investigating the paranormal; the five bond and become close friends, even forming a small band. Their group is joined, one Tuesday night in March, by Victor Kennedy, a businessman. He comes to LINDA with video footage of the Doctor and Rose and soon takes over the group, pushing its members to pursue all leads to locate the Doctor. Then members of LINDA start disappearing – Bliss first, then Bridget.

Kennedy teaches the members of LINDA some skills in basic surveillance and espionage; step one is to 'engage your target', step two is to 'get on first name terms' without provoking suspicion, step three is to 'ingratiate yourself' with a joke, and step four is subtly to integrate oneself into the household. Elton attempts to use these techniques on Jackie, all the while oblivious to the fact that she's actually using similar ones on him in an effort to flirt with him. There's a step five, infiltration, but he's having second thoughts. Elton thinks a local sub station is shorting out the fuses in Jackie's flat (although she's actually sabotaging them to get him to come over). She later spills wine on his shirt to keep him around.

The Abzorbaloff is a creature that lives by absorbing other life forms; it took the guise of Victor Kennedy in order to locate and absorb the Doctor, to ingest his knowledge and experience and hijack the TARDIS. It's from Clom, the twin planet of Raxacoricofallapatorius, homeworld of the Slitheen family; it thinks the denizens of that planet are 'slime'. The name 'Abzorbaloff' is made up by Elton; the creature doesn't actually have a name, but says that it

283

likes that one. (Elton also offers 'Abzorbathon' and 'Abzorbaling', and the Doctor suggests 'Absorbatrix' and 'Absorbaclon', but it likes the other one better.) It thinks its true form is better than its human visage, and in this form it absorbs people with only one touch. The absorption process is irreversible. It likes to read the *Daily Telegraph* and thinks Ursula tastes 'like chicken'. The Abzorbaloff is held together by a limitation field; when Elton breaks this, the creature is liquefied and absorbed by the Earth, taking its victims along with it.

Jackie Tyler (and Rose) live at Bucknell House number 48, presumably their address on the Powell Estate. People think they're a nice family but 'a bit odd'. When the Internet goes into 'meltdown' from all the theories about the aliens from space, Elton's computer literally sparks and melts down (although this is possibly one of Elton's exaggerations). He later asks Ursula to join him for a Chinese meal at the Golden Locust. The basement under the library doesn't have a toilet; the group members have to use the one in the pub on the corner.

While LINDA is hunting the Doctor, the Doctor and Rose are pursuing a creature called a Hoix. The Hoix appears to be only semi-sentient; while it's dressed in a space travel suit, it's easily distracted by a pork chop. Rose douses it with the contents of a blue bucket (which is a mistake; the Doctor protests that he specifically said 'not blue!'). She later grabs a red bucket and throws the contents at the creature.

THE DOCTOR: He recognises Elton while fighting the Hoix. The Doctor claims to be sweet and innocent, but no-one should ever mistake that for nice. He later tells Elton what happened the night Elton's mother died.

ROSE TYLER: Elton recognises her accent as being a London one. She gets angry with Elton when he upsets her mum, but later comforts him.

CHARACTER BUILDING: *Elton Pope* – A Londoner with an obsession about the Doctor. When Elton was three or four years old, he went downstairs in the middle of the night – awakened by the sound of the TARDIS materialising – and saw the Doctor in his living room. He's been remembering parts of that night, but the full realisation of what actually happened comes to him only when the Doctor tells him. An elemental shade, a living shadow, had escaped from the Howling Halls, and the Doctor had tracked it to Earth, to Elton's home. While he was able to stop it, the Doctor was too late to rescue Elton's mother, who died. Elton then blocked out the memory of what had happened. With Victor's help and encouragement, Elton gets to the Doctor through Jackie Tyler, but eventually realises that his heart belongs to Ursula Blake. When he left school, he got a job as a transport manager for retail logistics at a small haulage company. He says he needs to get a remote control zoom for his video camera (which he later does). He likes football, drinking, prawns, Spain and is a huge fan of Jeff Lynne and the Electric Light Orchestra. He thinks the TARDIS materialising is the most beautiful sound in the world. Kennedy says he's a stupid man for freezing when he met the Doctor, and Elton thinks he has good ideas with his shirt off. He feels guilty for betraying Jackie, and wonders how long it will be until she and Rose will pay the price for knowing the Doctor. He thinks the world is much stranger and darker than the normal lives people lead... and so much better.

Ursula Blake – A friend whom Elton met through her website. She's run a blog site about the alien invasions of the past few years, and lived only a half mile away from Elton. On Christmas Day, while in Trafalgar Square celebrating being alive with her friends, she started taking photographs of people, and caught the Doctor in one of them (probably soon after the closing scene of 'The Christmas Invasion'). She plays the tambourine and bass guitar. Kennedy says that she's 'most likely to fight back'. She is absorbed by the Abzorbaloff, but as she was the last victim, when the creature is dissolved, the Doctor is able to key into the absorption matrix and free her – although, because it's not a complete reconstruction, she finds herself trapped as a face and with her consciousness inside a concrete slab.

Victor Kennedy/The Abzorbaloff – A hideous creature disguised as a rather repugnant, pushy man, Victor claims he suffers from eczema (mispronouncing it *ec-ZEEma*), his hand blistering to the touch, in order to avoid body contact; he says he doesn't like to be touched literally *or* metaphorically.

Mr Skinner – His first name is Colin. A very literal-minded man, rather like a school instructor, he's been writing a novel (about someone named Johnny Fransetta) and starts reading it to the group. He can play the drums. He has a crush on Bridget, and gives her a kiss shortly before she disappears. He becomes the third victim absorbed by Victor.

Bridget – An amateur photographer who's noticed the TARDIS cropping up all throughout history, she lives in the north but travels down to the LINDA meetings. She loves to cook, and soon starts cooking for the club. She isn't really sure if she believes in the Doctor; in fact, she joined the group because her daughter disappeared, most likely due to drug abuse, and she comes to London looking for her. She plays the piano, and is the second person absorbed by Victor.

Bliss – An artist and sculptor, she plays the guitar and is the first one absorbed by Victor Kennedy, who explains to the others that she left the group to get married.

Jackie Tyler – People think she and Rose are a bit odd. She tells a friend she'll meet her at the Spinning Wheel, a local pub. She does her laundry at the Wash Inn right now because her washing machine is broken (actually it's just the fuse); she invites Elton up to fix it after flirting with him at the launderette... and calls him back on several occasions thereafter, ostensibly to fix things. She misses Mickey, who she says is 'gone now... bless him', and thinks that Rose doesn't call enough; she gets sad when she does, because she feels helpless that Rose is off on some faraway adventure. She can't bear the television being silent, and sometimes uses it to annoy the woman next door. She feels betrayed by Elton when she finds a photo of Rose in his pocket and realises he was after the Doctor the whole time.

TORCHWOOD: Victor Kennedy uses the 'Torchwood files' to look at old databases – presumably of information about the Doctor – in a 'completely new light'. The Torchwood files, he says, are strangely lacking in information about the Doctor's companion.

BODY COUNT: The Abzorbaloff is destroyed, and Mr Skinner, Bridget and Bliss are all killed when the absorption field breaks. Ursula Blake survives, but not quite in the way she's used to.

THE DOCTOR'S MAGICAL SONIC SCREWDRIVER: The Doctor uses his screwdriver to key into the absorption matrix and save Ursula inside a slab of pavement.

REALITY BITES: The acronym LINDA was previously used by the television series *Why Don't You?* The series (also known as *Why Don't You Just Switch Off Your Television Set and Go and Do Something Less Boring Instead?*) was a children's programme broadcast on the BBC from 1973 to 1995; late in its run, Davies was one of its producers and directors. The series featured the 'Liverpool Investigation 'n' Detective Agency', to which the LINDA group in this episode pays homage. (Perhaps Elton took inspiration from the earlier television programme?)

Popular UK singer/entertainer Elton John is name checked (and a brief clip of him playing the piano is used). Peter Kay's 'Avante!' to get the LINDA members to leave recalls the phrase ''ave it!' that he coined for use in a series of commercials for John Smith's Bitter. The runaround with the Hoix recalls the madcap chases of *The Benny Hill Show* (on which Bella Emberg, a brief guest star in this episode, was a regular) and the American cartoon series *Scooby Doo, Where Are You?*. Elton also name checks reggae act Chaka Demus & Pliers.

Elton quotes famed horror novelist Stephen King: 'Salvation and damnation are the same thing.' This is a line from *The Dark Tower, Volume 1: The Gunslinger*, a novel that combined several short stories in 1982 to launch the author's seven-part *Dark Tower* series.

Elton also manages to end the teaser with 'Oh boy!', a possible reference to *Quantum Leap* (1989-1993), which featured those words at the end of almost all its pre-credit sequences.

LINKING THEMES: The episode features flashbacks to the events of 'Rose' (the Auton attack on the shopping mall – though it could be a different venue than Queens Arcade where Jackie was shopping during that episode), 'Aliens of London' (the crash of the fake Slitheen ship) and 'The Christmas Invasion' (the arrival of the Sycorax mothership). In all three cases, new footage was recorded to include Elton reacting to these events. Elton carries a Henrik's department store shopping bag with him (the logo for the store can also be seen on a taxi), and his windows shatter when the Sycorax ship creates the sonic boom that breaks glass throughout much of London.

The fact that Torchwood lacks information on the Doctor's companion, as stated by Victor Kennedy, will come up again in 'Army of Ghosts', where Yvonne mistakes Jackie for Rose. Victor Kennedy also notes that the files are corrupted by something called the 'Bad Wolf virus', referring to the 'Bad Wolf' story arc from last season. Photographs of Rose from 'Rose' and 'Aliens of London' are seen (along with a brief glimpse of the back of the ninth Doctor).

Rose mentions Raxacoricofallapatorius, the homeworld of the Slitheen ('Aliens of London'), when she notices that the Abzorbaloff looks a little like them. Elton predicts that Jackie and Rose will one day pay for their association with the Doctor; this echoes what the Beast said about Rose in 'The Satan Pit'.

SCENE MISSING: The episode seems to suffer from a slight case of selective amnesia. The only Doctor that most of the members of LINDA seem to recognise is the tenth, yet two of the events that drew Elton into the Doctor's world – the Auton attack and the Slitheen ship crash – involved the previous incarnation. Since Elton meets Ursula shortly after the Christmas Day invasion of the Sycorax, it's likely that the Doctor she had been following before that was the ninth... so, then, why no mention of his other face? Or other faces, given that the Doctor's influence on human history has been so vast? Bridget at one point does mention 'different forms of the Doctor' but this is brushed aside.

How much of the episode takes place entirely within Elton's memories of the events? The staggering coincidences, the fact that nobody realises Bliss and Bridget haven't just up and left but have run into some harm (not to mention the screams that followed their absorption), the computer explosion, and even the malevolence of Victor Kennedy going unchecked... It all leads one to speculate that Elton isn't exactly being truthful. Why does Skinner, who's in love with Bridget, so blindly accept that she's just disappeared, when he'd already begun a relationship with her? (He had her phone number, after all; why did he believe Kennedy's statement that he had another number that Skinner didn't?) Why does no-one disbelieve the claim that Bliss is off to get married? Surely the other members of the group would have been invited!

Why does the Abzorbaloff need a limitation field? Is it a gaseous or liquid creature, kept in this form by the device? If so, why does it need to revert to the absorbing form instead of just staying human? (Why does the Abzorbaloff not change back to regular human form when it pursues Elton? Surely the idea is for it to stay *unseen* ...) Why does it need to digest the Doctor and steal his TARDIS? There are other ways to travel ...

Who is Victor Kennedy, really? How did he amass the power to be able to create a fortune? (If we are to believe the TARDISode, he has a maid and a nice home!) Did he digest the real Victor Kennedy, or did he create this appearance for other reasons? There seems to be no explanation as to his identity, his other life, how long he's been on Earth, and so forth.

How do the Doctor and Rose find Elton and show up in the nick of time before he's killed? How does Rose know Elton's the man who upset her mother? How does the Doctor recognise Elton in the first place? Elton was only three years old when they last encountered each other, but somehow the Doctor seems to realise that they have met before. Most importantly, why does the Doctor allow Rose to have a go at Elton when, as even he says, there's a big green absorbing monster from outer space standing next to him?

Why does the compassionate Doctor allow Ursula to live on in the form of a paving slab? How does she breathe? Talk? Eat or drink? Carry on a love life, as Elton says? Perhaps it's better that we don't know... Ursula mentions that she'll never age, which means she will outlive Elton, seemingly condemning her to the fate the Doctor tries to avoid with his companions as mentioned in 'School Reunion'.

ALTERED STATES: The original title for this episode was 'I Love the Doctor'. Davies mentions in the online commentary that it started life as an idea for a potential *Doctor Who Magazine* comic strip.

BEHIND THE SCENES: This episode was recorded in a variety of locations around Cardiff, including Cargo Road in Cardiff Docks (which doubled as Woolwich, where the TARDIS lands at the opening), the impounding station on Newport Docks (the derelict warehouse where the Hoix is trapped), Heol Pentwyn Road in Whitchurch (Elton's old family home), Llandaff Fields (the park where Elton meets Ursula), the Jacob's Antiques store on West Canal Wharf (LINDA headquarters), the Wash Inn (a launderette in Cardiff that doubled as the same), Taff and Garth Street (the Abzorbaloff's final confrontation with the Doctor) and St Peter's Sport and Social Club on Minster Road (the flashback sequences in the field with Elton's mum). The production crew also returned to The Hayes in downtown Cardiff to recreate the sequences from 'Rose' featuring the Auton attack, and to St David's Market, site of Elton's hunt for Rose, which was also used in the closing moments of the very first episode.

The Abzorbaloff was created by William Grantham, a nine-year-old fan in Colchester, as the winning entry in *Blue Peter*'s 'Design a *Doctor Who* Monster' competition. Grantham originally envisioned the monster to be the size of a double-decker bus, and was reportedly disappointed with the outcome. Nevertheless, he was excited to visit the set and meet the production team, cast and crew; his visit was documented in the accompanying episode of *Doctor Who Confidential* and in *Blue Peter* itself.

In an earlier draft of the script, Davies notes, Elton was also witness to some events from the series, including a Dalek invasion of Shoreditch ('Remembrance of the Daleks'), the death of his mother via plastic daffodil ('Spearhead From Space') and the Loch Ness monster rising from the Thames ('Terror of the Zygons'). The name of the Hoix was not used in the episode; it was coined by Davies after production was completed as producer Phil Collinson felt that the creature should be named.

Several behind-the-scenes photos from the making of *Doctor Who* are actually used as the 'evidence' Victor Kennedy shows the LINDA team. Kennedy was played by popular comedian Peter Kay, who requested the chance to be in the series via a letter sent to Davies at his home address. Barney Harwood, presenter on *Totally Doctor Who*, appears as an extra in the recreation of the 'Aliens of London' sequence.

DULCET TONES: The songs of the group Electric Light Orchestra play heavily into the narrative of this episode. Three songs are heard: 'Turn To Stone', released as a single in October 1977 and later issued on the album 'Out of the Blue'; 'Mr Blue Sky', issued as a single in January 1978 and also included on 'Out of the Blue'; and 'Don't Bring Me Down', released as a single in September 1979 and included on the album 'Discovery'. Of the three, 'Don't Bring Me Down' achieved the highest success, hitting number three on the UK pop charts and number four on the US Billboard Top Singles list. 'Mr Blue Sky' is used over the scene of Elton's improvised dancing and also woven into the incidental music score; 'Turn To Stone' is used in Jackie's flat as Elton prepares for their encounter; and the LINDA group perform 'Don't Bring Me Down'.

Also featured in this episode are: a rendition of the Toni Braxton song 'Unbreak My Heart' performed by Il Divo, issued in 2004, which is played by Jackie as she seduces Elton; a brief clip of Elton John performing his 1972 hit 'Daniel', later released on the 1973 album 'Don't Shoot Me I'm Only The Piano Player'; the traditional ballad 'I Gave My Love a Cherry', also known as 'The Riddle Song', performed by Bliss at a LINDA meeting; and Bliss and Ursula performing 'Brand New Key', also known as 'The Roller Skate Song', by Melanie (aka Melanie Sakfa), which was a 1972 number one hit in America.

OFF THE SCREEN: Celebrated actor/writer/comedian Peter Kay has been in *Wallace & Gromit in The Curse of the Were-Rabbit* (2005), *The League of Gentlemen's Apocalypse* (2005), *Max & Paddy's Road to Nowhere* (2004), *Linda Green* (2002), *24 Hour Party People* (2002), *Phoenix Nights* (2001), *That Peter Kay Thing* (2000) and *Comedy Lab* (1998) as well as several live and/or recorded specials broadcast on UK television; he is one of Britain's top comedians and is well known for a series of commercials he made for John Smith's Bitter. Kay worked on a *Comic Relief* sketch in 2001 with Simon Greenhall, who has also featured in *Modern Toss* (2006), *Hustle* (2006), *Doc Martin* (2004), *Wimbledon* (2004), *Family Business* (2004), *I'm Alan Partridge* (2002), *Holby City* (2001), *Boyz Unlimited* (1999), *The Bill* (1997), *Tomb Raider II* (1997) and *Armstrong and Miller* (1997). Marc Warren appeared in 1989 as an extra on the *Doctor Who* story 'Battlefield' and since then has been seen in *Hustle* (2006), *Hooligans* (2005), *Poirot* (2003), *State of Play* (2003), *Clocking Off* (2002), *Band of Brothers* (2001), *The Vice* (1999), *Highlander* (1997), *Ghostbusters of East Finchley* (1995) and *Heartbeat* (1993). Shirley Henderson is best known to fans as Moaning Myrtle in *Harry Potter and the Chamber of Secrets* (2002) and *Harry Potter and the Goblet of Fire* (2005); she can also be seen in *Marie Antoinette* (2006), *A Cock and Bull Story* (2005), *Bridget Jones: The Edge of Reason* (2004), *Wilbur Wants To Kill Himself* (2002), *Once Upon a Time in the Midlands* (2002), *24 Hour Party*

People (2002), *Bridget Jones' Diary* (2001), *Topsy-Turvy* (1999), *Wonderland* (1999), *Hamish Macbeth* (1997) and *Trainspotting* (1996). Moya Brady has had roles in *Mayo* (2006), *Shameless* (2005), *The Bill* (2002), *TV Burp* (2002), *My Hero* (2000), *Doctors* (2000), *Peak Practice* (2000), *Mary Reilly* (1996), *The Never Ending Story II* (1994) and *Little Dorrit* (1988). Kathryn Drysdale has been in *Two Pints of Lager (And A Packet of Crisps)* (2006), *Vanity Fair* (2004), *Mersey Beat* (2003), *Rockface* (2003) and *The Vice* (2002). Bella Emberg was seen in uncredited roles in the *Doctor Who* stories 'Doctor Who and the Silurians' (1970) and 'The Time Warrior' (1973/74), and was a regular on *The Benny Hill Show* (1971-1982); she has also been seen in *The Basil Brush Show* (2002), *The Russ Abbot Show* (1986), *History of the World Part I* (1981), *Madhouse* (1980), *Doctor on the Go* (1975), *Z Cars* (1975), *Man About the House* (1974), *The Troubleshooters* (1969) and *Softly, Softly* (1969).

Dan Zeff has directed episodes of *Ideal* (2006), *The Worst Week of My Life* (2004), *Linda Green* (2001), *Out of the Ashes* (2001), *Fat Friends* (2000), *At Home with the Braithwaites* (2000) and *Sunburn* (1999). He has also written several short films including *Sweetnightgoodheart* (2001), *Black Eyes* (1996), *Dual Balls* (1996) and *That Sunday* (1994), the latter with Alan Cumming. Earlier in his career, he was a video assist operator on the film *Blue Ice* (1992) and a camera trainee on *The Crying Game* (1992).

CONTROVERSIES: Besides the obvious – most of an episode of *Doctor Who* constructed around the notion that the Doctor is nowhere to be found – there was some controversy over Elton's revelation that, even though Ursula is confined to existence inside a piece of concrete, they've still 'got a bit of a love life'. The implications of this were considered by some to be not in keeping with a family show.

Another controversy stems from the portrayal of fandom in the episode; the LINDA group is an homage to fan clubs, including those devoted to *Doctor Who* itself, both in their youthful and enthusiastic origins and in their potential hijacking by self-interested third parties. Davies has stated that the episode is a loving tribute to fandom; however, some have seen it as passing comment on obsessive fans and the lengths to which they will go.

INTERNAL CONSISTENCY: Much of the episode takes place throughout 2007; it's obviously some time after the last full episode set in 2007 ('School Reunion') and obviously after March 2007 when Kennedy first meets LINDA. In terms of the narration, Elton states that it's been two years since the events of 'Rose', which took place in early 2005, so this is likely at that point in the year or some time later. The episode takes place over the course of many months; since LINDA meets once per week, and there are many meetings of the group seen both before and after Victor Kennedy takes over, it's very possible that nearly an entire year goes by. Thus it can be postulated that this story takes place over the period March-June 2007, with the narration to camera done possibly months later. (There's certainly a gap between Elton starting and completing the video diary, as he doesn't have a zoom control when he starts it, but does when he finishes, and Ursula is holding the camera in some of his early recordings.)

TARDISODE #10: Victor Kennedy sits in a chair in an undisclosed location using his laptop to browse the website of LINDA, subtitled 'Who Is the Doctor?' He uses a device in his briefcase to take over the computer to find the location of the LINDA people. Then, when his maid comes in with a pot of tea, she's startled to find him in some hideous form (probably his 'true' form, though we don't see him) and screams ...

The website has a sketch of the tenth Doctor along with the question 'Have you seen him?' and has links to a media page, a site map, a files page and a 'join LINDA' page. The 'join' area, when clicked, says 'Last updated... WHOOPS! Ages ago, Sorry! – ELTON'; clicking on it again brings up a page that says: 'Meetings: '...but LINDA's a secret organisation. So we can't tell you where... If you need us... You'll find us.' When Kennedy uses the device, the screen goes blank, says 'Primitive Computer Page', then features a map grid to track the source of something.

REVIEWS

Wow. Just ...wow. While there have been elements of the new show that I've found a bit grating but acceptable in order to appreciate the rest, this episode manages to distil everything that is juvenile, embarrassing and insulting about this series into one mind-numbing assault on the senses. This is without a doubt the worst thing *Doctor Who* has ever done, and I *am* including the Myrka and the Kandyman. In fact, it may be one of the worst hours of television it's ever been my misfortune to witness; and I've been forced to watch *Relic Hunter*. The first 30 minutes or so managed to lull me into a false sense of security with a relatively touching tale of a group of misfits who find each other and discover the joy of simple fellowship. It's really kind of sweet; the main problem is that it has nothing much to do with *Doctor Who*, and it's as if I've turned on another show instead, but never mind. It's a pleasant enough character study, if a bit lightweight and predictable, with some solid performances by Marc Warren as Elton, Peter Kay as the pushy cad Kennedy and Camille Coduri in perhaps her finest hour as Rose's mother Jackie. While the episode's theme of examining the Doctor's effect on people's lives has already been explored better on the show through characters like Rose, Jackie, Mickey, and even Sarah Jane Smith, it's still a subject worth returning to when you have an actor as good as Warren carrying the lead. And then it happens. The whole episode goes horribly awry when Kay drops his newspaper, and the final ten minutes are a sad, offensive attack on the audience's intelligence and emotions, destroying the dynamic of the first 30 minutes and laying waste to the good feelings inspired by a lovable cast of characters. What we're given instead is a clone of Fat Bastard from Mike Myers' *Austin Powers* movies as Kay lolls his tongue around and runs through the London suburbs in a green rubber costume, sporting a black Speedo and a Mohawk – a Mohawk, for heaven's sake! This *certainly* isn't *Doctor Who*; if anything, it plays like an appalling sketch parody of the show filled with loathing for the series and disdain for the viewers. When the Doctor and Rose do deign to show up for a few minutes at the end, Rose berates poor Elton while the Doctor imprisons a sweet girl for eternity in a slab of stone so our erstwhile central character can use her framed face for sexual gratification. It's just that disgusting. 'Love & Monsters' has been described as an experiment, a brave attempt to break format and explore the myriad possibilities inherent in *Doctor Who*'s wide-ranging structure. I'm sorry to say that the people who hail it as such have clearly lost their minds. What potential there was in removing the focus from the two leads to an observer like Elton is utterly squandered by incorporating a laughable monster and puerile humour at exactly the wrong moment. You can't expect viewers to take the revelation of Elton's tragic past seriously when we've just seen Mohawk Speedo Man absorb the scenery with abandon. In the end, this is not just *Doctor Who* at its worst – it's *television* at its worst, including *elimiDATE*. – *Arnold T Blumberg*

Dear Russell T Davies: Thank you for writing a *Doctor Who* story just for me. I know you have many thousands of others perhaps saying the same thing to you about 'Love & Monsters', but

I know you wrote it for me. (I'm sure others hate it, saying the Doctor isn't in it enough, or it is too comedic. Philistines, all of them). 'Love & Monsters' is utterly brilliant. No *Doctor Who* story this season – and believe me, I've really enjoyed everything this season – has etched itself so firmly on my psyche. I love that it's a story about *Doctor Who* fans (we've all had a Victor Kennedy in our lives, and we've all fancied ourselves to be like Elton Pope fancies himself to have, and actually often are just like Elton Pope), but it's even more a story about how the thing we're most obsessed with is both the best thing and the worst thing in our lives. That's just so perceptive. Indeed, I found the whole of 'Love & Monsters' funny and heartfelt and honest and sad and true – often all at the same time. I really can't wait to see the script for it (if you're going to put out a Series Two script book), as I'm sure I'll be amazed to find yet again that you had the rapid editing for it all in your head right from the start. (That said, I think Dan Zeff was a great director). And I absolutely adored the fact that you gave Jackie Tyler a moment to truly shine. Camille Coduri was incredible. And what a great cast – Marc Warren carried the episode brilliantly, and Shirley Henderson and Peter Kay were so deftly funny and lovely. This story should never have worked – I mean, it was made without the regular cast and it featured a monster that won a contest on *Blue Peter*, but I knew if anyone could do it, you could. What I didn't count on was that you would turn this into the story that was to *Doctor Who* what 'Jose Chung's From Outer Space' was to *The X-Files* or 'The Trouble With Tribbles' was to the original *Star Trek*: the episode that turns the very premise of the series on its head and has a load of fun doing it. But more than that, with 'Love & Monsters', you proved that *Doctor Who* can do anything it wants to do and that my favourite television series is indomitable. I always knew that. Thank you for writing this for me. Much love, *Graeme Burk.*

Chances are, if you're reading this book, you're a pretty serious *Doctor Who* fan. You've shelled out your hard-earned money for a book that collates press releases, interviews, location filming details and the opinions of fewer than a dozen fans. My point is that you are probably well acquainted with the various stereotypes associated with being a fan: obsessive collecting habits, a mind-numbingly fine-tuned ability to remember trivia from 1966 (but not your next dentist appointment), willingness to go to the mat over the validity (or not) of TV tie-in novels, and so on. Probably, you even have one or two of these little habits. I know I do. In some way or another, we are all Elton Pope. I think if 'Love & Monsters' had taken the same approach one always associates with mothers and potential girlfriends – 'Why haven't you outgrown this yet?' – I would have openly hated, even reviled it. And to be honest, that's what I was expecting. What I forgot to factor in is that Davies has not only been there with us, he *is* there still – and as a result, we have an episode that is celebratory, a little bit self-deprecating, and most of all, genuinely affectionate. Those early scenes with LINDA are my favourite, because they treat their subjects with care and humour. They are aware of what we, the viewer, already know: yeah, fans can be a bit crazy, but behind the goofy habits and obsessions there are *real people.* Maybe not the most ambitious, socially-driven people, but people all the same – people who enjoy making *Doctor Who* a constant in their day-to-day existence. What makes LINDA so tragic is that these people – Elton, Ursula and the others – clearly love life. They have found their niche in the world. When Victor Kennedy arrives, he sucks away their joy, their purpose and ultimately, their very lives. It's a great dramatic core for what is some of the most effective comedy I've ever seen in either the classic or new series. I won't deny laughing my head off at the goofy *Scooby Doo*-style chase, or smiling at Elton's bumbling attempts to find Rose. It's funny enough as is, but it all takes on a new meaning once you've seen the whole episode.

Honestly, I couldn't be bothered so much about the Abzorbaloff himself. He's a better concept than realisation, more metaphor than proper monster, and he's dealt with quickly enough. The only thing that really irks me is the final few minutes. The episode should have ended on Elton's flashback of his mother, not the peculiar 'upbeat' ending Davies attempts to form out of a situation that is, really, very sad. All problems of the Doctor performing 'magic' aside, it just goes against the entire mood of the story. I can't tell you how surprised I am to have so enjoyed 'Love & Monsters'. I expected it to be *dire*. Instead, I saw a very sweet examination of fandom, with a few great laughs, a few nice, quiet moments, and some exceptionally strong performances from Marc Warren and Camille Coduri (who, frankly, has never made any especially positive impact on me before). I would not be keen on seeing a *Doctor Who* episode like this every week, or really even every year, but as it is, it's a great experiment, both well-executed and very much worth another watch. – *Sarah Hadley*

It has been a fair old while since *Doctor Who* last attempted an episode bereft – for the most part – of any of its regular leading cast members. There can't be many other British television drama series – in fact I find it difficult to think of a single other example – that have made or would attempt to make an episode focusing entirely on a group of one-week guest characters. Such an approach is not unknown in US drama shows, particularly others in the sci-fi genre. Even then, though, with episodes such as that one in *The X-Files* that dealt with the formation of the Lone Gunmen, the focus was on characters we had at least seen before. Here it's a completely new set of characters for this week, and without the regular continuing thread of audience loyalty, it could all have gone tremendously pear-shaped. That it didn't is down to the skill of Davies in creating sympathetic, engaging characters, a talent clearly visible throughout his work on *Doctor Who* and beyond, and one that's to the fore here as he makes a welcome return to writing duties a whole eight weeks on from 'Tooth and Claw'. In production terms, an episode largely without the two lead actors was something of a necessity – they were busy recording the previous story at the time – but it is fortunate, and perhaps a good reflection on the state of British television acting talent, that Davies and the production team had a first-rate group of guest stars to call upon to help sell this mostly Doctor-less plot. There's Marc Warren as Elton Pope, the focus of the piece and best known for his roles in Paul Abbott's *State of Play* and, perhaps even more so, in the Kudos/BBC1 con trick drama *Hustle*. Playing such a comparatively ordinary character as Elton must have been a nice change of pace for Warren after the collection of weirdoes and slightly odd types he is usually cast as, and he makes a great job of it. Part of the reason that Elton is such a sympathetic character, especially for *Doctor Who* fans like us, is not just down to Warren's admirable performance, however. It is that he reflects so much of the fan in all of us: desperate to get back to that lost, faraway point in nostalgic, misty childhood when the Doctor first came into our lives; desperate to recapture the moment when we first felt the magic, when we first heard the sound of the TARDIS engines. Of course, most of the publicity surrounding the episode focused on Peter Kay as Victor Kennedy and his monstrous alter ego. I'm a fan of Kay's comedy so I was very intrigued to see how he would handle a – relatively – 'straight' role in *Doctor Who*, and I'm pleased to say that I felt he was very good in both parts. This isn't Shakespeare, of course, but for the tone the episode as a whole and director Dan Zeff seem to be aiming for, Kay does very well. If *Doctor Who* were always like this then it would crash and burn pretty quickly, you have to admit that. But as a refreshing change from the norm and an experiment at doing something new and different, it more than works, and provides one of Series Two's less obvious gems. – *Paul Hayes*

Oh dear oh dear. Has fandom ever been this polarised over a story – before it's even been aired? As for afterwards... It's fascinating how fans are capable of holding two completely opposite opinions in their heads at the same time. Orwell called it *doublethink*. When news of Gabriel Woolf's return to the series was announced, people bemoaned the lack of originality that would be demonstrated if Sutekh returned. When it turned out that Sutekh would not be reappearing after all, the same people complained of a wasted opportunity. A similar thing has happened with 'Love & Monsters': people who have previously praised the series' ability to adapt to any narrative style now have hysterics when a story displays just such flexibility. Me? I loved it. I'm old enough to remember when police boxes could still be found on the streets of London, and every time my mum and I passed the one on Platt's Corner, I'd get the same shudder of excitement that central character Elton Pope exhibits. This is *Doctor Who* showing the effects of the Doctor's interference in ordinary people's lives: something explored in the novels, but new territory for the TV series. And it's all quite delightful. We've had some wonderful directors this series, but Dan Zeff just goes completely bonkers in the most marvellous way. Elton is a real person, with real interests. We see snippets of his life, his friendships, his tangential – and not so tangential – relationship with the Doctor. True, he's socially inadequate, but – with the best will in the world – that's true of many fans. And I think that's the rub: it hits far too close to home. Yet it's not done in a nasty way. When I first joined a DWAS local group in the '80s, our shared interest in *Doctor Who* was what brought us together. Just as many members of clubs develop friendships from that point *onwards*, so did we. I still have friends of over two decades' standing, and it was *Doctor Who* that brought us together rather than kept us together. But in our fandom, as in Elton's, there's always a serpent in the undergrowth. Everyone knows, or knows of, an ˌberfan. They're the ones who told the rest of us that we weren't being serious enough about our hobby. Worship of the series had to take priority over such petty concerns as friendships or other interests, usually to allow them to pursue some hidden agenda. And, quite often, those local groups would wither and die. Indeed, the series itself did. You always hurt the one you love? Never truer. The plot is basic. But this isn't an episode that needs a plot; it's a peek into a real person's life. The potential loss of innocence, redeemed by a belief in the Doctor, and, once again, each other. Elton has it, Ursula has it, and – in a bravura performance from Camille Coduri – Jackie shows she has it in spades. Okay, it has a silly monster. It's meant to have. It has a 'magic wand' ending. That doesn't spoil anything. Because the scene of Elton's mother fading away to ELO's 'Mr Blue Sky' is pure, pure class. One last thought. It can be argued that the only 'real' scenes are those viewed through Elton's camcorder. Indeed, Ursula's slab-face is never seen apart from through Elton's eyes. Can his relationship with the Doctor have driven him bonkers? Well, he wouldn't be the first one... – *Craig Hinton*

Well... it's certainly different, and it's not all bad. To get the worst out of the way first, the villain – the Abzorbaloff, played by Peter Kay – is in design (based on the winning entry in a *Blue Peter* draw-a-monster competition!), casting, performance and effect straight from the depths of 1980s begging-for-cancellation *Who*, as if John Nathan-Turner had returned from the grave. And Davies still tends to trip up when trying to deliver an emotional situation, social realism, sit-com, ruthless horror and childish humour all at the same time. (I got horrid flashbacks to Troma Films' *Toxic Avenger* efforts.) The victim talking out of the monster's arse or the chase borrowed from a *Pink Panther* cartoon are especially jarring when much of the episode tries for a sweeter, more melancholic sense of ordinary life trying to go on in the universe where the

Doctor lives. Given that the whole idea of reviving an old show is to trade on history while making it new, it's probably unfair to carp that the second season is too early to get as self-referentially hung up on its story-so-far as this does, though in stepping back through the events of 'Rose', 'Aliens of London' and 'The Christmas Invasion' (all Davies-scripted shows) and privileging those episodes as the public face of the Doctor's adventures, 'Love & Monsters' does suggest Davies has become the real absorbing being, with the faces of other creators screaming out through greenish skin. As I said in my notes on 'The Satan Pit', the show needed a shake-up to get into the home stretch of this season – and this is a welcome experiment, making the regular characters guest stars while concentrating on lesser folks in a world where wonders are increasingly common. The best stretches are the simplest, as Elton Pope (Marc Warren) talks about the coming-together of his little group of dignified saddos, with concise, deft, understanding character sketches from Davies (contrast with the cruel, lazy stereotyping of Nigel Kneale's *Kinvig*, which is about similar folk) and fine performances. Shirley Henderson – pound for pound, the best actor working in Britain today – is the most welcome addition to the series this season, even if she does get fused with a paving stone. The way the group's vague purpose changes as they form relationships and turn into a (terrible) ELO tribute band is the sort of spot-on, worthy-of-its-own series drama that makes the let-down when the monster turns up to ruin everything all the more depressing. Partially, this is what the story is about – but Kay (or 'comedian Peter Kay' as all the blurbs call him) is still the Maxwell's Silver Hammer of the episode, bringing on trite dramatics that require characters who had more *nous* to turn into disposable total idiots and playing everything with that talk-down-to-the-kiddies-and-the-fans-still-watching tone too common among *Who* gimmick guest stars of the Colin Baker-Sylvester McCoy years. A few of the speeches – notably, Jackie's umpteenth whine about those left behind, and the final turn about Elton's dead mother – seem a touch rote, but again Davies saves deep feelings for unexpected moments, as when the TARDIS appears as a monster is threatening humanity only for Rose to upbraid Elton for upsetting her mother. – *Kim Newman*

Jon here, double-banking this review while Kate's doing her piece on 'The Satan Pit'. Which works, 'cause now I can comment to camera about her and me, befitting the style, story structure and tone of this week's *Doctor Who* episode. It's not often someone spends a million-odd dollars to make a TV episode all about your life. Let's set the scene: I watched the episode (as a blotchy download not unlike Victor's pirate footage) with my wife and co-author, whom I met through fandom, and a couple of old fannish friends... who we were visiting for one of our weekly amateur jam-sessions. A few weeks earlier, Kate, a long-time ELO fan, had even suggested playing 'Don't Bring Me Down' at one of them. So yeah, now I know what the bullseye on a target feels like. And it's astonishing that 'Love & Monsters' hits so many of the un-obvious targets in fandom, while avoiding all the obvious ones. For once, fandom is centre stage as a community. Even in something fairly sympathetic like *Spaced*, the somewhat-fannish audience-identification characters are kept on the margins of fandom, as opposed to the true obsessives who are defined as Fans. But in this story, fandom *is* the home of people with lives, and interests beyond their fannish interactions too – the obsessives are the interlopers. LINDA's only rose-tinted in its members' absolute lack of bitchiness and cynicism – not just towards each other, but about their shared interests. At no point do the characters sneer at the object of their affection, or think they know better than the Doctor. Only Kennedy is seen as being out to profit from his obsession – the others are creative not for profit, but for creativity's sake. (But rather than splitting fandom into simple types of Good Fans and Bad Fans, these characters are more representative of aspects lurking in all of us. I may have bent double in agonies of recognition when Mr Skinner explained about the Doctor as a collection of archetypes, but I know I've been a Victor Kennedy too sometimes, brandishing my cane online.) Not only does the story dodge the hopeless-nerd image, it also avoids the more treacly tributes to fandom. There's none of the 'you guys make this story possible' stuff that fandom loves to hear – *Doctor Who* isn't *Firefly*, which was literally brought back because of DVD sales. (Our series was revived not because a few people loved it a lot, but because a *huge* number of people loved it a *bit*.) And this isn't a *Galaxy Quest*-esque wish-fulfilment tale where the fans serve to save the Doctor. Instead the fans save the *fans*. At least for a little while. And as it's a fan's personal story, it's fitting to use television as a way into Elton's mind. Whereas in *Casanova*, RTD set stylised and period-busting flashback sequences inside a straightforward, realistic framing story, here the narration plays funky-chicken with reality as well. Because think about it... the whole thing's presented as a video, including the flashbacks he recorded previously. Then what about the flashbacks he *didn't* record? Elton's intercutting his memories directly with his videotape evidence. Crikey, I want that plug-in for Final Cut Pro. (I've seen neat theories about how only the video footage necessarily 'really' happened – and we never see Ursula's face on the paving slab 'on camera', only in what looks like a view from Elton's point of view. Could he just be mad, and fantasising that she survived? Erm, no, actually, we hear her voice in the previous video-camera shot. So instead, she could be standing behind the camera, perfectly fine and normal-bodied, just like she was in the video shot outside Elton's house, and this whole thing is an elaborate gag they're playing together on the viewers of this video... namely, us. *That* sounds like something the fans I know would do.) The clever bit is how the rest of this story picks up on the way blurry, subjective memories coexist uneasily with 'evidence', and can even be more true. Elton's interest in the Doctor stems from a fuzzy primal memory, and he learns that the codified, quantified evidence that Victor dangles in front of them isn't the path to understanding it. If anything, LINDA's creativity is inspired by the fact that all they have are their personal, subjective responses to this unknown... concrete evidence even gets in the way of real connections, such as when a photograph destroys the bond developing between Elton and Jackie. Did Davies think of this consciously when he was writing? I have no idea. It's possible this is just instinctive – he certainly makes the transitions between 'real' and fantasy clips look effortless. But ideas like that unite the episode into a thematic whole. And indeed the season, since the story sums up the year's real primary themes of connection and disconnection, loneliness and loss. This whole episode is 'The Girl In The Fireplace' redux, from Reinette's point of view – a character on the slow path, only touching the Doctor for a few moments, but through him going from innocence to understanding. Just a taste of what his world can do to you... days like crazy-paving indeed. 'Love & Monsters' is a lovely little bow that ties the season together. The only thing that could have made it more elegant, in connecting the human-scale loves and losses with the huge mad life of the Doctor... would have been if Elton's mother was named Linda. – *Jonathan Blum (filling in for Kate Orman)*

Russell T Davies returns after a seven episode break and delivers a script for *Little Britain*! At times I thought I was watching a bizarre parody of Peter Kay look-a-like Matt Lucas's characters from that twisted comedy series. Given that it's told in 'flashback', there are two ways we can perceive 'Love & Monsters': it all happened exactly as depicted on screen, or it's mostly

Elton's exaggerated to-camera account of what really *did* happen. If you take the former approach, then not a lot of it makes sense – for instance, the *Scooby Doo* corridor chase scene is a narrative/visual trick only, while Ursula's fate as a slab of crazy paving is just plain nuts. So, yes, it's definitely the latter option, as far as I'm concerned. After all, who is Elton making the video diary for if not for himself? The biggest clue that it's an embellishment of the real events comes in the final scene: the 'face' on the concrete slab is never seen by Elton's camera (therefore by 'us'), and is visible only from Elton's perspective shots – therefore he's *imagining* Ursula is still alive. Go on, have a look if you don't believe me! The ever-reliable Marc Warren is perfect as Elton, whose life crumbles around him all thanks to the Doctor. At its heart, 'Love & Monsters' is about consequences. It's rare for the series to depict what happens following a crossing of paths with the Doctor. The ripple effect of the Doctor's well-intentioned actions was seen in 'Bad Wolf' last year, whereas 'Love & Monsters' shows what the impact of this effect can be on just one man. (But how many others like Elton are there out there?) The 'flashbacks' to previous episodes was a fabulous idea, but surely some *Forrest Gump*-style insertions of Elton into classic episodes wouldn't have gone amiss? (Was anyone else hoping for a cameo appearance from Christopher Eccleston?) One missed opportunity was a mention of Clive from 'Rose'; surely fellow Doctor-website junkie Ursula would have known him? The much-anticipated Abzorbaloff was a cross between Sil, a *Hitchhikers Guide to the Galaxy* Vogon and the Collector from 'The Sun Makers', but with a Northern accent. Peter Kay is an unknown to us here in New Zealand. My only previous exposure to him was on an instalment of the interview show *Parkinson* in which he wouldn't (couldn't?) stop talking! It is somewhat disappointing that the costume is of the standard man-in-a–rubber-suit variety rather than a CGI creation. Still, I'm sure every *Doctor Who* fan is extremely envious of William Grantham! There is much to laugh at in this comedy romp: methinks someone's been watching far too many Hanna Barbera cartoons! There's the aforementioned *Scooby Doo* bit, while musical LINDA brought to mind *Josie and the Pussycats* and *Butch Cassidy and the Sundance Kids*. ELO there! As a television production, episode 10 is funny, clever, sad and moving, demonstrating Davies's talents as a comedy writer. An interesting experiment in first person narratives, but it's an experiment that shouldn't be repeated *too* often... – *Jon Preddle*

'Love & Monsters' is silly. Daft, in fact. Silly and daft. And funny. And sweet, charming and lots of other things that TV viewers with an ounce of imagination and wit about them should find laudable. That many did enjoy this episode is great. That a proportion of the more vocal end of online *Doctor Who* fans *really* didn't tells you everything you need to know about both what the episode was trying to say and, indeed, about those who just couldn't see it. A bit close to home? Next door neighbour. I just thought it was *sweet* – especially the first half-hour. There was a really good story in there about how the 'organisation' of activities takes most of the fun out of them. The obvious allegory here was to *Doctor Who* fandom itself. Like LINDA, we are all – to greater or lesser degrees – a bunch of socially inadequate, but essentially harmless, misfits. We meet up and become friends with others because of a shared obsession. And we subsequently have our creativity sparked by it (expressed in fan fiction, art, music). Then somebody with a beard comes along and says: 'No. You don't do it *that* way, you do it *my* way ...' Blessed with a clever (video-diary-style) structure, the early scenes of 'Love & Monsters' greatly resembled parts of the *Buffy the Vampire Slayer* episode 'The Zeppo'. Like the latter, 'Love & Monsters' saw the fantastical events that surround the titular character through another's eyes – in this case, obsessive-but-harmless ELO-anorak Elton. Those who complained about the *Scooby Doo*-style opening sequence completely missed the point that this was reality as seen, and told, by a storyteller. Along the way, we get Jackie Tyler's finest moments and some very fine comedy (the revelation that the twin planet of Raxacoricofallapatorius is named Clom, for instance!). Peter Kay does a stunning Orson Welles impression before turning alien and slipping back into his normal accent. Although, as has been noted elsewhere, lots of planets have a Bolton. Probably. For an episode in which the main villain – the Abzorbaloff – was designed by a child, there was quite a bit of adult content as well. Ultimately, some charming performances (Marc Warren and Shirley Henderson, especially), a cute *Life on Mars* influence, touching lines ('I had this nice little gang once ...') and yet another bit of foreshadowing about Rose's future add up to a very worthwhile experiment. It ran out of steam a bit towards the end, but one of the main things that fans of *Doctor Who* have been saying for 43 years is that it's the flexibility of the show's format that makes it unique. How ironic that, when presented with something a bit different, a bit challenging, some of those fans should turn their back on it. Sad – in the original, rather than the modern, meaning of the word. – *Keith Topping*

EDITOR'S REVIEW: I must confess to a small amount of amusement (well, maybe more than a small amount) at seeing the hand grenade that was 'Love & Monsters' thrown into the field of *Doctor Who* fandom. I don't recall ever seeing a more controversial episode of the series in the two decades I've been around in this milieu, and that includes last year's 'Aliens of London' with its flatulent aliens, and even the couple of nonsensical stories featured during the latter years of the original show.

As a piece of drama, 'Love & Monsters' has nothing wrong with it. The dilemma here is whether or not it's a good piece of *Doctor Who*, and on that score I'm simply left with the sense that the jury is still out. I spent a good 40 minutes looking at the clock wondering when the Doctor was *finally* going to make his appearance in 'The Christmas Invasion', and I'll be darned if I'm going to go back on my previous assertion that the series is, and always should be, *about* the Doctor. Yet 'Love & Monsters' *is* about him, even without his presence on screen, and barring the appearance of Jackie Tyler (with perhaps the strongest performance yet by Camille Coduri, who's really become a welcome part of this universe), we're left with what's essentially an unwritten book. We, the viewer, are placed with pen in hand on page one, and left to piece together the events and situations that Elton Pope relays to us, in order to understand the nature of what is to come.

Perhaps that's the truth about 'Love & Monsters': it shows us who *we* are, rather than who the Doctor is. Do any of us doubt that we wouldn't love to be swept up and taken across the stars in the TARDIS? (If you really don't want that... well, why are you *watching* this show?) We have to relate to the situation through Elton's eyes, and setting aside all the extraneous parts of his life – the ELO fascination for starters – we realise that Elton's the Everyman, serving as our Mary Sue (to borrow a phrase from fan fiction), our avatar in this other universe of Time Lords and Daleks. The episode draws quite substantially from the fan world; LINDA is the representation of *Doctor Who* fans and their experiences, and the nature of what they share (and believe me, I've known a couple of those local power-hungry attention seekers in my day). I think I empathise most with the group as a whole, rather than with any individual; as Elton recalls the good old days, when they were happy, singing with their little band, sharing potlucks and professing their love for the Doctor – for *Doctor Who* itself – I find myself longing for days just like that, when we were innocent, when we looked forward to the next episode of our humble little show.

And yet, even though it strikes me as a handily crafted tale, a fun and spirited romp featuring some terrific actors and fun set pieces, I still can't tell you if I truly *like* it or not. Part of me surely does; I admire 'Love & Monsters' for taking the chances with the story, exploiting its own necessities (particularly the double-banked recording schedule) to play on the sensibilities of the *Doctor Who* viewer. At the same time, part of me is simply dumbfounded that when there are only 13 episodes in any given season, an entire episode has been allowed to go by with less than five minutes of David Tennant and Billie Piper, ostensibly the true stars of the show. Don't get me wrong... I love that *Doctor Who* is no longer afraid to take risks. (In fact, I'd like Davies and Gardner to take a few more in the next season than they did this year; much of Series Two has played it far too safe.) I love that there is a sense that *Doctor Who* has transcended its science-fiction roots and children's TV themes and actually become a rich and proper *drama*. I'm just a bit sorry that depth and development and risk-taking and all that drama have to come at the expense of the one thing I'm really tuning in to see each week: the Doctor saving the universe.

Still, you have to love an episode that causes the entirety of fandom to splinter and factionalise and get its knickers in a galaxy-sized knot. Conflict is at the heart of drama, and *Doctor Who* fans sometimes create enough drama to spare. I shudder to think what will happen when certain fans read the largely positive reviews of the episode in this book; will they burn their copies? Kick in their television screens? Post lengthy treatises on the Internet shaming it for expressing an opinion? As Paul Cornell has said, drama isn't comfortable or convenient; it's there to shock you and kick you in the pants and make you think. *Drama.* Maybe Davies has done his job better than he knows, and in the process made *Doctor Who* – like Elton said of life – so much stranger, so much darker, so much madder... and so much better. – *Shaun Lyon*

211: FEAR HER

In London, 2012, a lonely little girl named Chloe Webber has a secret: whenever she draws the children of her neighbourhood, they go missing, but they seem to take on a life of their own in her drawings. The Doctor and Rose piece together the mystery, but there may be more than just a few missing children at stake... the entire world may soon be in jeopardy!

FIRST TRANSMISSION: UK – 24 June 2006. US – December 2006. Canada – December 2006. Australia – 23 September 2006. New Zealand – 21 September 2006.
DURATION: 43'51"
WRITER: Matthew Graham
DIRECTOR: Euros Lyn
CREDITED CAST: David Tennant (The Doctor), Billie Piper (Rose Tyler), Nina Sosanya (Trish), Abisola Agbaje (Chloe), Edna Doré (Maeve), Tim Faraday (Tom's Dad), Abdul Salis (Kel), Richard Nichols (Driver), Erica Eirian (Neighbour), Stephen Marzella (Police Officer), Huw Edwards (Commentator)

WHERE AND WHEN: Dame Kelly Holmes Close, Stratford, East London, 27 July 2012.

THE STORY UNFOLDS: The quiet suburban neighbourhood of Dame Kelly Holmes Close has been disrupted recently by a series of disappearances of children. Ten-year-old Jane McKillen has been missing for some days, as has a boy named Danny Edwards who cycled into an alley and never emerged. Another boy, 11-year-old Dale Hicks, disappears on 27 July while playing football with his friend Tommy – right under the watchful nose of the latter's father and despite the warnings of the elderly Maeve.

England is preparing for the thirtieth Olympiad, being celebrated in London in 2012; the Opening Ceremonies are taking place on the day of the Doctor and Rose's arrival. The Doctor has brought Rose here for the Olympics, but Rose notices a 'missing' poster on a telegraph pole and the two become suspicious of a young girl called Chloe Webber whose room is full of crayon pictures. The Doctor notices a drop in temperature in the area and a metallic smell; he concludes that whatever is causing the problem has used a lot of power to do it. The smell is iron residue; whatever is taking the children (and a small cat) uses huge reserves of ionic power.

Despite the road having been resurfaced five times by Kel, a local council employee fixing potholes in anticipation of the runner carrying the Olympic Torch passing by the end of the block that evening, cars seem to stall over a particular spot.

The Doctor discovers that a 'scribble monster' that Rose inadvertently releases from the garage of Chloe's house is made of graphite, the same material as found in an HB pencil, and also created with ionic energy; he uses an eraser on to neutralise it. Chloe has been snatching the children and holding them in her drawings using the ionic energy; she can also create things in her drawings, such as the scribble monster and the version of her father from her nightmares.

Chloe has inadvertently swallowed a member of the Isolus, a gestalt of empathic beings of intense emotions from deep space. The Isolus Mother, a flower-shaped being from what it calls the Deep Realms, jettisoned many millions of fledgling spores – its 'children' – into space; the children, each inside a pod, ride the heat and energy of solar tides, travelling with their brothers and sisters in a journey taking thousands of years. The Isolus beings cannot bear to be alone; they need to be together, as their empathic link is what keeps them alive. While they mature, they use ionic power to create make-believe worlds in which to play ('in-flight entertainment', as Rose calls it). This particular Isolus, the one that is manipulating Chloe, was caught in a solar flare that scattered the Isolus pods; its own pod crashed on Earth and it found Chloe to keep it company. The Isolus has been snatching the children to create a family in a place where it is no longer alone.

The Isolus pod – a two-inch-across dull grey device that looks like a gull's egg – is buried in the pavement where the cars have been stalling. The Doctor uses his psychic paper to 'prove' he's a policeman, and says that he's got a colleague called Lewis (while pointing at Rose) whom he's training. 'Lewis' apparently had a choice of either being a police officer or a hairdresser.

The Isolus kidnaps all 80,000 spectators out of the Olympic stadium as well as 13,000 athletes and at least one of the commentators (named Bob); they're returned, as well as all the children and the Doctor and his TARDIS, when the Isolus gets back to its pod. An horrific image of Chloe's abusive father also comes to life, feeding on Chloe and her mother Trish's fear. Disaster is averted when the Doctor takes the Olympic Torch from the torchbearer, who has been affected by the release of energy from the Isolus pod, and himself lights the Olympic flame – the heat from the flame releasing the pod and setting it on its way home.

Dame Kelly Holmes Close is in an East London borough. The neighbourhood is in the Stratford area of East London, according to the missing children's posters. Chloe makes a ginger-coloured cat disappear. Trish talks to a friend named Kirsty on the phone. The Olympic Torch route takes it along the Mall, next to Buckingham Palace, then east along the Thames, via the Embankment, toward where the Olympic stadium is. Papua New Guinea *may* surprise everyone in the shot-put in the 2012 games.

THE DOCTOR: He accidentally materialises the TARDIS between two storage containers, blocking the doors, and has to reorientate it, by dematerialing and then materialising again, in order to get out. He thinks humans are geniuses for creating 'edible ball bearings'. He's good at squash and at Snakes and Ladders. He says he's experimenting with back-combing his hair. He's not a cat person (anymore; see 'Linking Themes'). He sticks his finger in a jar of orange marmalade in Trish's kitchen, and Rose shakes her head at him for being so rude. He puts Chloe in a trance just by touching her temples. He sympathises with the Isolus, knowing what it's like to travel on one's own. He says he was a dad once, to Rose's surprise.

ROSE TYLER: She used to have a cat just like the one she finds (which soon vanishes after entering a box). She has a bad feeling about Chloe, which the Doctor likens to a 'copper's hunch'. She has cousins and knows what it's like when they have temper tantrums. She realises that all the drawings have come to life and that Chloe needs to calm down in order to stop it.

CHARACTER BUILDING: *Trish Webber* – A single mother who lives in Dame Kelly Holmes Close; she has one daughter, Chloe, and was married to an abusive husband who mistreated both of them. She knows something is amiss with her daughter but can't figure out what it is, or simply doesn't want to; talking to Chloe, she says, is like talking to a brick wall. However, she still thinks Chloe is a great kid, and worries about her. She has seen the drawings move out of the corner of her eye, but she dismisses what she can't understand. She later accepts the

Doctor and Rose's help.

Chloe Webber – Trish's daughter, a lonely 12-year-old girl obsessed with drawing. Her father died a year ago, and she has nightmares, some of them about him. She gets As and Bs at school and is in the choir. She talks about 'us' staying together, when she's actually referring to the Isolus inside her. She returns the Doctor's Vulcan salute from *Star Trek*. Chloe's father was an alcoholic and the girl usually got the brunt of his temper. He died in a car crash and Trish thought they were free of him. The Isolus frees Chloe when it goes back to join its siblings.

Maeve – An elderly woman of the neighbourhood who knows something is seriously amiss and has grown suspicious of Trish's daughter Chloe. She doesn't care who solves the mystery, she just wants someone – especially the Doctor – to help.

Kel – A worker for the local Council, he's resurfacing the road and knows something is odd about one part of it where cars always stall. He demonstrates usual male bravado in front of Rose, telling her he's able to push a car when he's obviously struggling. (But to his credit, he's willing to lend a hand while he's meant to be working.) He says he'll report Rose to the Council when she takes a Council axe from his Council van and starts digging a hole on his Council road to find the spaceship. ('Not a Council spaceship, I'm afraid.')

TORCHWOOD: A very brief, almost inaudible, reference to Torchwood is made by BBC News 24 commentator Huw Edwards after he remarks about the disappearance of the spectators in the Olympic Stadium. It's possible that what he actually says is ... torch would ...', referring to the Olympic Torch.

BODY COUNT: To borrow a phrase used in last year's 'The Doctor Dances', 'everybody lives!' (Well, except the scribble monster!)

THE DOCTOR'S MAGICAL SONIC SCREWDRIVER: The Doctor uses the screwdriver to stop the scribble monster by shrinking it.

REALITY BITES: At the start, a banner proclaiming 'London 2012' is shown. This uses part of the official logo of the London Organising Committee of the Olympic Games and Paralympic Games; the Olympic rings, a tradition shared by all the various Olympic Games, is cut off, so only the words 'London 2012' with the multicoloured ribbon running through them are seen. However, it's possible that the 2012 event will have a different logo and a different Torch design; the logo seen in the episode was used for the London bid for the Games. The main events of the 2012 Olympic Games are due to be held in Stratford, East London, near the location where this episode is supposed to take place; the main Olympic Park will be built here for the event.

The Doctor shows Chloe that he can do something with his hand... a V-shape between the first two and last two fingers. The sign is the Vulcan 'Live Long and Prosper' salute from *Star Trek* (1966-1969). The Doctor's reference to Rose as 'Lewis' is an homage to Detective Sergeant Lewis of *Inspector Morse* (1987-2000) and the spin-off *Inspector Lewis* (2006), while his 'Keep 'em peeled' was a catchphrase used by presenter Shaw Taylor on the series *Police 5* and *Junior Police 5*. Kel name checks *Snow White and the Seven Dwarfs*.

The footage shown of the Olympic Torch run and the opening ceremonies is stock material taken from BBC News 24. The neighbourhood's namesake is Dame Kelly Holmes, the retired distance runner from Britain who won two gold medals at the 2002 Olympic Summer Games in Athens, Greece; she was made a Dame Commander of the Order of the British Empire in the New Year's Honours List of 2004. (The production team attempted to enlist Dame Kelly Holmes to appear in this episode, but she was busy at the time on *Dancing on Ice*.) The Doctor recalls the torchbearer of the 1948 Olympic Summer Games, also held in London, saying he was a lovely chap with 'legs like pipe cleaners... strong as a whippet', but can't remember if his name was John or Mark; in fact, the torchbearer's name was John Mark.

Posted bills on the fences show singer Shayne Ward, ostensibly advertising his *Greatest Hits* album; Ward was the winner of the 2005 series of ITV talent show *The X Factor*, and his single 'That's My Goal' was subsequently number one in the UK charts over Christmas 2005. The Doctor's 'edible ball bearings' are actually dragees, silver-coloured coated sugar balls used in cake decoration. Chloe has pages from the BBC magazine *Girl Talk* on her wall.

Huw Edwards plays himself as a BBC News 24 commentator. His career began in earnest when he presented the BBC's *Six O'Clock News* from 1999 to 2003.

In keeping with this episode's setting in 2012, a number of steps were taken to try to make things seem slightly futuristic. These included the use of a 19-digit telephone number in the TARDISode, the suggestion of a change in local law enforcement arrangements (reference is made to an 'East London Constabulary' – at present the area is covered by the Metropolitan Police), and the placing on the trailer of the licence plate UY61 LJW, implying a vehicle registered in the second half of 2011.

LINKING THEMES: The Doctor seems to have precision manoeuvres in the TARDIS well in hand, seeing as he can correct its position when it lands between two metal crates with the door blocked; it was generally the case before that the Doctor's control over the ship was somewhat limited. He says he's not a cat person, referring to his encounter with the Cat People in 'New Earth', he says:.'Once you've been threatened by one in a nun's wimple, it kinda takes the joy out of it.' Some of his earlier incarnations, however, displayed a fondness for cats; especially the sixth Doctor (Colin Baker), who wore a succession of cat badges on his lapel. Even in his ninth incarnation (as played by Christopher Eccleston) he picked up a cat in 'The Empty Child'. (In the *Doctor Who* novels published by Virgin in the 1990's, the Doctor travelled for a time with a cat named Wolsey in the TARDIS.) It would appear therefore that his aversion to cats is a very recent development, perhaps arising specifically from his encounter with the Cat People in 'New Earth'.

The Doctor requests parley with the creature inside Chloe 'in compliance with the Shadow Proclamation'. He last made a similar request of the Nestene Consciousness in 'Rose'; obviously it is a demand for diplomatic engagement between otherwise warring life forms. Rose herself tried to use the same line in 'The Christmas Invasion', but to no avail. The Isolus says it cares nothing for shadows or parley (though it says 'parlezes', using the proper French term for discussion.)

The Doctor says he was a dad once. For decades, questions surrounding the Doctor's family have constituted one of the great controversies of *Doctor Who* fandom. At the very outset of the original series, the Doctor was accompanied by his granddaughter Susan, which naturally implied that he must have had at least one child of his own. However, it has since been suggested – for instance in the novel *Lungbarrow* – that he may have been using 'granddaughter' essentially as a term of affection, and/or that Susan was not strictly his blood relation. The Doctor referred to his family, without going into further details, in the 1967 story 'The Tomb of the Cybermen'; and he also mentioned his father, and implied that his mother was human rather than Gallifreyan (making him half-human), in the 1996 TV movie. The *Doctor Who* novels at one point even gave him an adopted daughter named Miranda, who subsequently had her own comic-book spin-off series (that was discontinued before reaching its conclusion). In 'Fear Her', he fails to elaborate on his reference to being a father.

The Doctor mentions Club Med, the spa company that operates vacation destinations across the world.

This is the second episode to be set in 2012; the first was 'Dalek', although that took place entirely under the ground in Utah. BBC News 24 broadcasts were previously featured in 'Rose', 'Aliens of London', 'World War Three' and 'The Christmas Invasion'.

The Doctor's ominous feeling that 'a storm is coming' prefaces the two-parter to follow, and harkens back to the Beast's comment in 'The Satan Pit' that Rose would die in battle. To follow on from this, the trailer for the next episode ('Army of Ghosts') begins with narration from Rose that suggests she is about to die.

SCENE MISSING: Something never explained in the episode is why Chloe needs to draw in order to capture children to be the Isolus' 'friends'. The Isolus is capable of morphing over 80,000 people into ionic energy, so why does Chloe need to draw them first? Her drawings obviously don't have to be exact – the drawing of the Olympic stadium shows at most a couple of hundred people. If Chloe had completed the drawing of the Earth, wouldn't she and the Isolus have vanished too? And what would have happened to everyone already in the drawings? (One must also ask... what about the drawing of the massive solar flare?)

How do the drawings actually move? Why is the only glimpse of something moving seen in the teaser, whereas later in the episode Rose happens to catch a picture of Dale with a different expression on his face? Wouldn't the Doctor have walked in and seen all the drawings moving, if it were possible for them to do so?

Is there a national epidemic of missing children, or is it just confined to this street? There are more than three children in the drawings on Chloe's wall... so where did the others come from?

Have the British media – and the public – gone completely mad? Eighty thousand people vanish out of the stadium, along with thousands of athletes and even the BBC's own commentators, and yet the torchbearer keeps running toward it? Why would all of the people watching not suddenly start panicking? What about the massive repercussions worldwide of yet another unexplainable, possibly alien, phenomenon? (These are the people who faced down a Sycorax ship a few years earlier – and, of course, rampaging Daleks and Cybermen... see 'Army of Ghosts'!)

How did the Doctor get into the stadium? Assuming he was returned to where he had been standing, off the railroad tracks next to the TARDIS, how did he get all the way to the stadium and past what is obviously the worst Olympic security in history (remembering that Olympic security is usually among the strongest in the *world*) *with* the most celebrated object associated with the Games, the Olympic Torch. Where were the police? (There was more security on Dame Kelly Holmes Close than it appears there was at the stadium!) Is everyone still reeling from the fact that over 100,000 people just suddenly popped back into existence? Wouldn't the Olympics officials – if not the police or the security services – have simply closed the whole thing down pending an investigation as to why over 100,000 people just vanished into thin air and then reappeared? Isn't the Doctor doing everything possible *not* to keep a low profile?

Why did Trish tell Rose it was okay to use the loo but not where it was? Since she didn't, why is she so upset when she subsequently finds Rose in Chloe's room... obviously it's possible she got lost!

Why is it dark at the Olympic stadium but perfectly light outside in the scenes at Dame Kelly Holmes Close near the end of the episode (when Rose cheers after the Isolus finds the torch)? The locations are right next to each other!

It's fair enough that Chloe's drawing of her dad comes to life, but why, then, does its sudden manifestation glow red and cast a shadow and *cause the door to slam shut and lock!?* Why does singing to Chloe stop the apparition, when the only thing that saved Rose from the 'squiggle creature' was the Doctor's sonic screwdriver?

Finally... if 'Fear Her' is set in 2012, but 'Army of Ghosts' and 'Doomsday' are set in 2007, how could the Doctor feel a storm approaching when the event took place five years prior? Wouldn't the Doctor know that everything turns out all right in the closing two-parter if, in 2012, the world is safe and people are happily enjoying the Olympics? (Time on this show is a bit funny ...)

ALTERED STATES: The original intention was that this story by Matthew Graham would form part of Series Three; it was put on the back burner. When the episode previously intended for this slot, writer/actor Stephen Fry's contribution, had to be postponed to Series Three (and then cancelled), 'Fear Her' was brought forward. Fry's story would have been an aliens-on-Earth tale set in the 1920s and possibly involving the legend of King Arthur. According to *Doctor Who Magazine*, working titles for this episode were 'Chloe Webber Destroys the Earth' and 'You're a Bad Girl, Chloe Webber', while some reports gave the title as 'Fear Me' (which may or may not have been officially used).

BEHIND THE SCENES: Most of this episode was recorded on location in Page Drive and Blenheim Road in the Pengam Green area of Cardiff, with sequences shot outdoors around the area or inside an empty house. Parts of Trish and Chloe's home – most notably Chloe's bedroom – were then created inside the studios in Newport. The Champan's Removals & Storage Yard at Rhymney River Bridge Road in Cardiff was used for the railway area where the TARDIS lands.

The Olympic opening ceremonies shown on BBC News 24 are actually recordings from the 2002 Commonwealth Games in Manchester, with the City of Manchester stadium modified by computer graphics to show the London skyline. However, the brief scene of the commentators' box (as the two reporters are shown missing) was taped at the box inside Cardiff's Millennium Stadium, where many other episodes of the series have been recorded. The exterior of the Olympic stadium was shot at St Albans Rugby Club in Tremorfa Park.

The episode was recorded during winter, and the actors' freezing breath is visible in some of the exterior shots. In order to explain this, given the summer setting of the action, a line of dialogue indicates that there has been a drop in temperature locally due to the ionic energy signature.

While actress Abisola Agbaje is shown drawing, the actual artwork was done by someone else; a hand double was used in the scenes where she is seen drawing up close (and obviously sped up considerably).

DULCET TONES: 'Kookaburra Sits in the Old Gum Tree' is a popular Australian nursery rhyme originally written by Marion Sinclair. It was brought to music in the mid 1940s by composer Janet Tobitt. Chloe and Trish sing this song several times during the episode.

Two memorable musical cues from earlier episodes are heard briefly: the sequence first heard in conjunction with the 'Bad Wolf' situation the previous year is used to underscore the 'approaching storm' at the end of the episode, and the 'action' sequence, originally heard over the opening of 'Rose' and when the Doctor and friends ascended the Mayor's stairs in 'Boom Town', is used immediately after Trish and Chloe defeat the 'dad' creature with song and Rose pines over the Doctor's absence.

OFF THE SCREEN: Nina Sosanya featured in *Casanova* (2005), *People Like Us* (2001), *Much Ado About Nothing* (2005), *Sorted* (2006), *No Angels* (2005), *Nathan Barley* (2005), *Love Actually* (2003), *Serious and Organised* (2003), *The Jury* (2002), *Teachers* (2001), *Urban Gothic* (2000) and *Jonathan Creek* (2000). Abisola Agbaje made her television debut in this episode as Chloe. Edna Doré is best known for her four-year role as Mo Butcher in *EastEnders* (1988-1992) and has also been seen in *Doctors* (2006), *The Bill* (2006), *My Family* (2004), *Shane* (2004), *Time Gentlemen Please* (2002), *Peak Practice* (2000), *Men Behaving Badly* (1997), *Casualty* (1997), *Love Hurts* (1992), *Tenko* (1984), *The Duchess of Duke Street* (1976), *Dixon of Dock Green* (1968) and *Z Cars* (1963). Tim Faraday has been in *The Bill* (2006), *Secret Smile* (2005), *My Dad's the Prime Minister* (2004), *Murphy's Law* (2004), *Casualty* (2004), *MIT: Murder Investigation Team* (2003), *Gangs of New York* (2002), *Bad Girls* (2001), *Bugs* (1998) and *Touching Evil* (1997). Abdul Salis was seen in *Sahara* (2005), *Love Actually* (2003), *Trevor's World of Sport* (2003) and *The Hidden City* (2002). Richard Nicholas was in *My Family* (2004) and *Lucky Bag* (2001). Erica Eirian was also seen in *The Magic Paintbrush: A Story from China* (2000). Stephen Marzella was in *Belonging* (2002), *Game On* (1995) and *Bad Girl* (1992).

Journalist Huw Edwards, who plays himself as the announcer on BBC News 24, is one of the UK's chief news presenters for BBC News, anchoring the BBC *Ten O'Clock News* on BBC1 and the daily 5.00 pm news slot on BBC News 24. He formerly presented the BBC *Six O'Clock News*, was the chief political correspondent for BBC News 24 and has spent 20 years as a political reporter, including as BBC Wales's Parliamentary Correspondent.

Writer Matthew Graham is the creator, executive producer and principal writer of the critically acclaimed BBC series *Life On Mars* (2006) and creator of the ITV drama *The Last Train* (1999). He has also written episodes of *Hustle* (2004), *POW* (2003), *EastEnders* (2002), *Spooks* (2002), *The Gentleman Thief* (2001), *Reach for the Moon* (2000), *This Life* (1996), *Thief Takers* (1996) and *Byker Grove* (1989).

TECHNICAL GOOFS: The TARDIS is passed by a train run by Central Trains, which runs nowhere near Stratford (and may even be out of working order by 2012 – although on the other hand there may be a restructured rail network by this point.) When the Doctor scoops out the marmalade, in the long shot he has one finger in his mouth but in close shots he has two. The colour of Dale's trousers in Chloe's drawing is different from that of the ones he wears in the show.

INTERNAL CONSISTENCY: The episode is set in London on 27 July 2012; Dale Hicks goes missing on that day according to the poster. The Doctor notes that the three children (Dale on 27 July, Jane on 23 July, and Danny on an unspecified day) have been missing for six days; this implies that Danny disappeared on 21 July. The end-July timing fits in with the Olympic time frame; the opening of the Olympic Games traditionally takes place in late July or early August in Northern hemisphere countries, and the London Olympiad is currently scheduled to kick off on that date.

TARDISODE #11: A segment of the television programme *Crime Crackers* is investigating disappearances of children off the street. Dale Hicks and Jane McKillen are among the missing... have they run away or joined gangs? The reporter makes a pitch for viewers to help investigate the disappearances; meanwhile, a closet door opens somewhere and there's something with glowing red eyes inside.

The phone number given by the reporter is 0301 566-9155-76544891. *Crime Crackers* was an authentic BBC initiative in the early part of the decade and the production team had to request clearance to use it in this episode.

REVIEWS

If *The X-Files* featured a spiky-haired Time Lord and his spunky, sexy sidekick instead of a spiky-haired FBI agent and his spunky, sexy sidekick, it would look a lot like 'Fear Her'. What's more, for a series that does stick around modern-day Earth a heck of a lot, this episode of *Doctor Who* is rather more down-to-Earth than usual and feels as contemporary and 'outside your front door' as anything the series has done, and that's despite the near-future setting. With a thin plot that barely stretches to cover half the length of this episode, a nondescript score with only a few notable melodic strands, and minimal effects, it's up to character and performance to make or break this simple suburban thriller. Fortunately, that's exactly where it excels. In a rare reversal from the norm, the guest cast is unremarkable and only just adequate to requirements. No-one is strictly bad, least of all Abisola Agbaje as 12-year-old Chloe, who carries much of the episode's weightier material and does a decent if not impressive job. That the episode is as fun to watch as it is, however, is entirely down to the two leads, both of whom deliver performances that never waver an inch from delightful. David Tennant, who has made me uncomfortable on countless occasions with his tendency to veer way too heavily into way-out wackiness, does a superb job here as a Doctor equally as inquisitive about ionic energy snatching away children as he is about a jar of marmalade. Billie Piper gives us a Rose who has become more and more the Doctor's investigative equal. It's a shame that now, when this pair have clicked into exactly the right dynamic, we're about to see the team break up. Some complaints: while it flirts with serious subject matter like child abuse and depression, the episode only scratches the surface. And in a series where everything from massive spaceships to blubbery face-absorbing monsters is paraded on screen in full view, the shadowy suggestion of the monstrous father figure feels like a missed opportunity. Dispatching the creature plays like an anticlimactic afterthought meant to pad out the proceedings for a few more minutes. More padding comes in the form of a couple of TARDIS scenes – conspicuous only because the new show has for the most part avoided that classic episode-extending manoeuvre from the old days – but I was actually happy to see the Doctor and Rose hanging out in the console room. It is home for them, after all. Tennant even channels third Doctor Jon Pertwee as he tinkers with a makeshift piece of technology while dropping a tossed-away bombshell on Rose and the audience concerning his former status as a parent. Good stuff; so does this mean Susan is his *real* granddaughter? This'll keep the message boards lively for a long time to come. There's a silly but satisfying triumphant ending that makes me want to watch the Olympic coverage in six years' time to see if the Doctor does indeed light the ceremonial flame. The episode's final lines of dialogue seem a bit too awkwardly tacked on to create a bit of foreboding for the upcoming two-part finale. Still, if the trailer is anything to go by, things are about to become a lot more exciting. – *Arnold T Blumberg*

One of the most puzzling, and intriguing, things about Daviess' original pitch document for the new *Doctor Who* that was reprinted in Panini's *Doctor Who Magazine : The Doctor Who Companion: Series One* was the notion that 'Father's Day' was originally meant to be a '*Twilight Zone*-sort of story' with no monsters. That fascinated me – the idea of a series as grand and operatic as *Doctor Who* doing something as small-scale and nuanced as a typical episode of *The Twilight Zone* was quite novel. Well, now we have 'Fear Her', which has pretty much fulfilled that brief. And, as with all good *Who*, the roots are definitely showing – the basic story is a variation of the classic *The Twilight Zone* episode 'It's a Good Life' – the scary child with god-like powers that most people are afraid of – with touches of 'The Monsters Are Due on Maple Street' (paranoia on an ordinary street) and 'Little Girl Lost' (children lost to another dimension) for good measure. Does it work? I feel like I should be David Tennant tilting his head and saying 'Eehhhh ...' It sort of does. I think the *idea* of Chloe Webber drawing people out of existence with her crayons is actually scarier than what we actually see on screen. And one gets the sense watching it that there was a far darker story there before it had all the edges sanded off in rewrites. I'm amazed that they kept so much of the subtext of past child abuse of Chloe, but the real issue to confront was Tricia's own denial of the effect of the abuse on her daughter, and her gaining the strength and insight to stop it from happening again by standing up to the Isolus that was possessing Chloe. That all this was sidestepped by having them fend off the menace by singing 'Kookaburra Love' together indicates how gutless this story really became. Add to this the discordant touches like the annoying on-air announcer for the Olympics coverage and you have a right old mess. At least Rose returns the favour the Doctor did her in 'The Idiot's Lantern' by rescuing him after he's been taken out of play for about 15 minutes. Billie Piper is charming and delightful in the spotlight – 'That's not a Council spaceship' – and David Tennant's Doctor is at his quirkiest here – his 'Fingers on lips!' line is brilliant. I'll even go on record to say I'm probably the only *Doctor Who* fan in the world not annoyed by the Doctor carrying the Torch. But the problem is that the story should be focusing on Tricia and Chloe and better developing that relationship instead of artificially infusing the Doctor and Rose's with a sense of coming danger. All I can say is, Rod Serling would have pulled off something more effective. – *Graeme Burk*

What to say about 'Fear Her'? Well, it sucked. Hmm. Nope, not enough words... Generalisations aside, I really don't feel like there is all that much to say about the episode. I knew almost nothing about it going in – certainly, nothing more than was revealed in the trailer – and I think I can pinpoint why. The end result is so disposable, so inconsequential, it very nearly goes in one ear and out the other. What is there to reveal? 'In this episode, you'll believe a child can draw really, *really* fast'? In the days of 1960s *Who*, it might have worked – and you can tell from the accompanying *Doctor Who Confidential* episode that the production team are trying to sell it to us in exactly that way. 'Fear Her' has a simplistic, '60s sort of feel to it, but it's actually let down by modern aesthetics. A child drawing at inhuman speed isn't scary; nor is an animation of another child trapped in a drawing, or a big red light coming down the stairs. None of these things would have been seen in a Hartnell- or Troughton-era version of the story. The fear would have come from what was implied, but never seen. You would have had a *teenager* playing Chloe, and underplaying the role, to boot. And, honestly, even then it might not have been brilliant – but I'm sure it would have been better. A lot of people are likening this to 'The Idiot's Lantern', and I agree that there are similarities between the two, but I think 'Fear Her' pales by comparison. 'The Idiot's Lantern' understood the sensibility of '50s and '60s TV, because although the effects it used were modern, they were an update of what surely would have been used had the story been made at that time – at no point did it use effects where a '50s production wouldn't, at the very least, have tried to convey something similar. That episode also had the sense to remain focused on a small neighbourhood, where the fear was tangible because everyone was afraid of each other. There's some of that at the beginning of 'Fear Her', but then we go to the Olympics, which feel like they've been thrown into the story at the last possible second. There is no reason why the Doctor should run with the Olympic Torch except, by gum, someone on the production team thought it would make a brilliantly iconic image. It's incredibly hard to engineer 'iconic', though, and the moment just falls flat on its face. Perhaps the biggest let-down of the episode is the element that might have saved it from being a total mess – Chloe herself. Possessed kids can be a really scary concept, and even the most blatant rip-off of *The Exorcist* can work if it's pitched right and cast appropriately: the *Angel* episode 'I've Got You Under My Skin' is a great example. I hate to rag on any child actor, particularly one just starting out, but Abisola Agbaje simply can't carry this role. The whispery possessed voice is not only hard to hear, it's ridiculous. I could never be sure if I was honestly expected to be frightened of her; if so, it certainly wasn't working. I'm sorry to say it, but this is almost certainly my least favourite episode of the season thus far (and hopefully, at this point, it won't be trumped). 'New Earth' made me chuckle once or twice, and the Cyberman two-parter had some exciting moments. 'Fear Her' didn't give me anything to work with at all. For once, I really can say the best thing about it was the trailer for next week's episode. – *Sarah Hadley*

It is an interesting coincidence – or perhaps not quite so much of a coincidence, given how meticulously everything about the series seems to be planned by the current production team – that 'Fear Her', an episode that takes place against the backdrop of one of the world's biggest and most popular sporting events, was originally broadcast in the UK slap bang in the middle of the other, football's World Cup. The pride and the passion that sport can provoke in a nation is perhaps most notably demonstrated by the Olympics and the World Cup, and although some might find it a little mawkish, it's a feeling that's nicely tapped into by Matthew Graham in his script. Graham was justly lauded earlier in 2006 for his work in co-creating and writing several episodes of BBC1's other time travel drama, *Life on Mars*, and one of the key themes he brought to his episodes of the show was the nature of lead character Sam Tyler's relationship with his parents. Parent-and-child interactions appear to be a key interest of Graham's as they surface again here, and I'm afraid that, as with *Life on Mars*, I did find the touch of over-sentimentality regarding parenthood that he brought to proceedings proved to be the weak link. Nonetheless, the central idea of the lonely child alien was a good one, and the concept behind children being trapped in drawings was suitably creepy. Top marks as well must go to the nightmare vision of the father in the wardrobe – one of the simplest and best ideas we've seen in the second series so far. It's very *Sapphire & Steel*, which is never a bad thing. As he did with Shaun Parkes in 'The Impossible Planet' and 'The Satan Pit', David Tennant here gets the opportunity to play opposite one of his *Casanova* co-stars, in this case the ever-excellent Nina Sosanya, a familiar face from many British television productions of recent years. She's as good as ever here, and I was also particularly impressed with the performance of young Abisola

Agbaje as Chloe. The whispering voice she adopted when speaking with the voice of the Isolus was an excellent choice by director Euros Lyn, and worked far better than overlaying some alien voice audio effect onto Agbaje's performance would have done. 'Fear Her' is not, however, a perfect episode by any stretch of the imagination. While peeking ahead six years to see what the London Olympics might look like is a very good idea, having the Doctor light the Olympic flame is a little too over the top for my tastes, particularly as it comes along with a ludicrously performed voiceover from Huw Edwards. Getting real people to play themselves in *Doctor Who* can work well, as we saw in Series One, but here getting an actor to perform the part would have been far better. Mind you, even a professional might have had trouble with the rather trite voiceover dialogue. – *Paul Hayes*

A lonely little girl who can capture people in drawings and who can create terrible monsters from her pictures. A girl whose own reality is finally unleashed and threatens to destroy her and those closest to her... Yes, I remember watching the film *Paperhouse*. And the TV series *Escape into Night*. Indeed, I remember reading the book *Marianne Dreams*. Sadly, all of them did it better. Part of the problem with 'Fear Her' is the Louis Vuitton baggage that writer Matthew Graham brings with him. With his *Life on Mars* capturing some of the *Doctor Who* zeitgeist and becoming one of the sleeper hits of 2006, much was expected of his foray into our series. *Life on Mars* explored many of the same themes and tropes as *Doctor Who*, but effectively from the viewpoint of the sceptical companion, with a gritty realism that seemed a perfect match with Russell T Davies' vision of the series. Unfortunately, what he delivers is an ultra-clean, ultra-suburban cul-de-sac populated from central casting that has all the menace of a plastic cup and all the depth of a puddle in high summer. If we extract the main narrative – lonely little girl meets lonely little alien but their symbiosis threatens everything – I'm sure it would be possible to redress it with all the chills and bed-wetting horror of the original *Escape into Night*. Indeed, even *Star Trek* has managed it at least once a spin-off. Graham's initial intention, as discussed in an interview in *Doctor Who Magazine*, was to create a story of gut-wrenching terror from the premise of 'The Doctor comes to *Brookside*'... Well, no, he doesn't. He lands in an idealised suburbia in which Margot and Jerry Leadbetter wouldn't appear out of place. There are no dark corners, and, as good as the acting from Nina Sosanya and Abisola Agbaje is, they are totally incapable of generating any: Mum gawps like a fish and Chloe lacks the slightest trace of menace, even in her *The Exorcist* scene. Into this bland Barratt Homes estate come the Doctor and Rose, playing at TV detectives and doing some 'deducting' (nice use of English, Doctor – translator on the blink?), playing with teleporting cats (and look where that got us the last time!), getting menaced by a scribble, and making gargantuan leaps of intuition that would cause Sherlock Holmes to blush. Indeed, it's almost a relief when the Doctor turns into a drawing. Unfortunately, just as we are almost comatose in this barbiturate nightmare, we get a sugar rush that would send the best of us hyperglycaemic. Two weeks earlier, it was faith that saved the day. Now we are expected to believe that it is luuuurve. In a stomach-churning finale with the Doctor carrying the Olympic Torch, Huw Edwards apparently seeing the script for the first time, and a disco going on upstairs at Chloe's house as Desperate Dan boogies on down, the whole thing just degenerates into a nauseating mess. The only – and I mean *only* – redeeming features of 'Fear Her' are the TARDIS's landing and the Doctor's mention of being a father. And the chilling ending, where, against a dark yet celebratory backdrop, the Doctor senses that something is coming that will well and truly wipe the smile off their faces. *That*, Mr Graham, is how to make kids wet the bed. – *Craig Hinton*

One thing that *Doctor Who* has got the knack of this season is the stand-alone 45-minute story that *doesn't* feel like a cut-down of a serial and can afford to take a slightly different storytelling approach. Like 'The Girl in the Fireplace' and 'Love & Monsters', 'Fear Her' fits into this category: these shows remind me of the original brief that editor David Howe gave for Telos Publishing's series of *Doctor Who* novellas; relatively limited space can be used creatively and the flow of product means the occasional experiment is encouraged. Though it doesn't do anything as tricky as 'The Girl in the Fireplace' or 'Love & Monsters', 'Fear Her' limits the action to a London street (Dame Kelly Holmes Close, one of surprisingly few near-future gags to key into the 2012 setting) and a claustrophobic situation, with the Doctor (impersonating a police officer) as a detective/exorcist figure. Matthew Graham's script is influenced by Bernard Rose's movie *Paperhouse* (based on Catherine Storr's novel *Marianne Dreams*, which was done earlier on UK TV as a well-remembered serial *Escape into Night*) without being an imitation. The scary Daddy drawing that serves as a bogeyman threat is an element of *Paperhouse*, as is the compulsively-scribbling, lonely little girl protagonist; but Graham takes the story in a different direction. Following several recent *Who* stories (notably 'The Doctor Dances'), 'Fear Her' delivers 30 minutes of quality child-scaring horror, with a possessed kid (Abisola Agbaje, who is very good at being unreasonably evil) doing terrible things to friends and neighbours (and a cat), then pulls that old Gene Roddenberry switch of having it all be down to an unimaginably powerful alien who is just a child and needs to be helped rather than destroyed. (All credit to Mark Gatiss for sticking to the old *Who* formula of aliens who pretend to be nice but turn out to be evil bastards.) Graham gives Rose a couple of lines that blur the situation, suggesting that just being a kid is really no excuse for appalling behaviour, but that gets swept aside. As a Council Tax-paying Londoner who was hoping Paris would get the Olympics in 2012, I'm also not buying into that big rush of love focused around the Games, which is supposed to save the planet at the end. If the Doctor were depending on most of the folks I know to add to the outpouring of goodwill, then the world would be doomed. A certain amount of fuss has been made about the Doctor's casual aside that he was a dad once, but it's hardly a major revelation that someone who had a granddaughter when we first met him must have had at least one child – though I suspect that further delving into this back story would be an encumbrance on the continuing series (we've not heard anything of the Doctor's human mother since the TV movie, with good reason) rather than a fruitful dramatic avenue. – *Kim Newman*

Human beings: compared with other animals, not big, not strong, not fast. We survive because we're smart and, even more, because we communicate and cooperate. We readily form groups to share our day-to-day lives. Most Australians live in some kind of family – although Mr and Mrs Connolly might find the variety bewildering: two million couples with no kids, two and a half million couples with kids, eight hundred million single parents. Gay and lesbian parents, blended families, grandparents raising grandkids; all variations on the same basic human theme. And the Doctor? Since families and children will be watching, 'Fear Her' treads carefully when it comes to a real-life nightmare. It's established immediately, in the teaser, that the children are unharmed. We are never shown a distraught mother or father: Dale Hicks disappears not in front of his own parents, but in front of his friend Tom and Tom's dad (who later interrogates the Doctor). The extent of Chloe's father's abuse is not made explicit, though we can guess at it. We don't even see the investigating police; only happy parents reuniting with their children once it's all over. The nightmare here is not that children are being hurt or killed, but that families are being broken apart. This is, of course, heavy foreshadowing for the events of 'Doomsday'. With Rose all too passive for much of the season – possibly because it was unclear how many stories Billie Piper would appear in – this story gives her a chance to operate without the Doctor, a test she passes with flying colours. It's a little like growing up, the fledgling leaving the nest. Like her ability to motivate the frightened characters in 'The Satan Pit', this bodes well for her career in the alternate Torchwood. Jon and I handed our census form to a volunteer today; it's funny to think that, if the Doctor and Rose filled one in, they'd presumably also be counted as a family, a couple without children. In 'Doomsday' she will be giving up one sort of family for another. The Doctor will be left with neither. No more Christmas dinners with the Tylers for him. Blood ties and/or a shared home aren't enough to make a real family, as Chloe's dad demonstrates. Nor do the miserable kidnapped children make a family. The Isolus, a child itself, tries to force the entire population of the planet into the mould of the only kind of family it knows. 'We need to stay together,' it tells Chloe's mother. 'No. Not you. *Us*.' The Webbers' home should be a sanctuary. It wasn't one when Chloe's father was alive. With the arrival of the Isolus, it becomes a lair. The Close itself should be a sanctuary, closed to danger; instead, it's wide open. In the next story, 'Army of Ghosts', another widow will be confronted with a daughter who is changing into something other than human. What's more, the image of the Doctor as Prometheus – running with the Torch, giving fire to the human race – will be paid off, as the Doctor is imprisoned by Torchwood: direct payback for all his interference in human affairs. He doesn't remain their prisoner long, but his *hubris* is what prompts their *hubris* – their meddling in things they don't understand; and that's what eventually costs him Rose. With the advent of mass media, the human race experiences great events as a sort of enormous family. Millions of us watched the Twin Towers fall – and watched the opening ceremony of the Sydney Olympics. I'm uninterested in sports and athletics, but in 2000 it was impossible to miss the friendly buzz in Sydney – and the fact that most of the planet was peacefully cooperating, for a change. This is the 'hope' and even 'love' that the Olympic Torch comes to represent in 'Fear Her' – the world has watched together the awful emptying of the stadium, now it watches the Torch. 'Doesn't that make you feel part of something?' says Chloe's mum. The Olympics prove we can do it – we can play like children, billions of us. And the Doctor? We're reminded here that, although often so childlike, he is an adult: 'I was a dad once.' It's almost difficult to reconcile that with his boyish looks and behaviour: David Tennant is not the youngest actor to play the Doctor, but his character seems more childlike than any of them. At the very moment he drops his bombshell, he is tinkering with a bit of junk like a kid playing with a 75-in-1 Electronic Project Kit. He absently sucks marmalade from his fingers, and gets to light the Olympic flame, roaring with delight like a boy whose childhood dream has come true. He will always be running, always be playing out in space – always be stealing friends for himself away from their families. 'There's a lot of things you need to get across this universe... you know the thing you need most of all? You need a hand to hold.' – *Kate Orman*

Weird kids with strange or alien powers are a staple of SF and fantasy. Surprisingly, *Doctor Who* has rarely ventured into that territory; Susan Foreman, the Sylvest twins of 'The Twin Dilemma' and the creepy girl in 'Remembrance of the Daleks' are the only examples that immediately spring to mind. But having recently seen *The Omen* remake (on 6/6/06 no less!), I think Chloe Webber doesn't come anywhere close when it comes to creepy kids. As an, er, older person, I found little to fear in this episode, but it did have everything to give younger viewers sordid nightmares: a monster in the closet (we've already had a monster under the bed in 'The Girl in the Fireplace', so why not do *Monsters Inc* as well!); drawings coming to life; kids vanishing; and a scary old lady. But this sort of thing has been done to death – usually in horror anthologies like *The Twilight Zone*. 'Fear Her' was a close cousin to 'Survival', the last regular serial of the original series, which dealt with ordinary people (and cats!) from ordinary suburban streets vanishing into other dimensions. It also worked as a tale that dwelt on loneliness and isolation (the origin for the name Isolus, perhaps?); and even the Doctor was not immune to this. With the imminent loss (death?) of Rose, can we expect that the Doctor – he's the sole survivor of the Time War, remember – will again come to terms with always being alone? Maybe loneliness is a new theme to emerge from this season – remember the Doctor's reflections in 'School Reunion'? This is one of the few stories about which I knew absolutely nothing about beforehand, which meant I could watch it comfortably without any fear (!) of expectations being shattered. There even seemed to be much confusion in advance about the cast list – several online episode listings mistakenly placed a number of the cast of 'The Idiot's Lantern' or of the final two-parter under 'Fear Her'. Bizarre as it may seem, one memorable moment from this episode was the 'Kookaburra' song – a little tune I remember singing in kindergarten way back in the late 1960s! Tennant gives his most Doctor-ish performance here (I love the Troughton-esque finger in jam bit!), but despite some good performances by the supporting cast (and some wonderful sight gags!), 'Fear Her' unfortunately must take my vote for the weakest of the episodes so far this year. – *Jon Preddle*

The suburban, small-scale nature of 'Fear Her', with its Little England iconography (MG Minis, Union Flags, witty *Inspector Morse* references) fits in perfectly with the humanist nature of much of the rest of the season. Here is a *Doctor Who* story fashioned to be wholly a part of Davies's 21st Century vision of the show. One that takes place in a small cul-de-sac at an only marginally significant moment in history (the opening night of the 2012 Olympics). Perhaps it's that compacted, squeezed nature of the text that somewhat undercuts part of the inherent drama. Put simply, if you've got the whole universe to explore, why bother with Dame Kelly Holmes Close, London? Then again, why not? Influenced by, again, *Buffy the Vampire Slayer* (specifically the episodes 'Nightmares' and 'Restless') and by Catherine Storr's classic novel of somnambulist menace, *Marianne Dreams*, the central themes of 'Fear Her' – empathy and symbolism (beautifully summed up by Rose's parting line to the alien pod that it should 'feel the love') – benefit from some gorgeous verbal and visual allegory. Unfortunately, the weak point in the episode is the performance of the little girl, which, sadly, never quite hits the required mixture of innocence and dread. That, and the fact that BBC newsreader Huw Edwards is given a series of thoroughly, woefully rotten lines of exposition in his role as a TV commentator ('It's a beacon of hope!'). An essentially interesting little idea (with some really disturbing avenues therein – abuse monsters not least among them) is, as a consequence, almost fatally derailed by one askew performance and, admittedly, also by aspects of a somewhat meandering plot. For once, David Tennant's *faux*-Mockney act serves to irritate rather than to charm as it usually does. There's some great dialogue on display, however (the 'I was a dad once' moment is a genuinely revealing one), and the terrific 'Fingers on lips!' scene, which shows *Doctor Who* as its most cheeky. Ultimately, that's a key summation of the episode – pretty enjoyable, but somewhat lightweight. – *Keith Topping*

EDITOR'S REVIEW: Apparently, all you need is love. Or something; I can't quite tell if that's the moral of 'Fear Her' or the actual solution to the problem, because it's left unclear. All I know is, despite this being a well-intentioned story with a moral message and a good heart, some good acting and great dialogue, I feel underwhelmed. Perhaps it's the fact that the TARDIS came back to Earth in 'Love & Monsters' and here we are again in beautiful suburban London, but I think it has more to do with a good idea let down by what is ultimately a lack of conflict. We know Chloe isn't going to destroy the world, so there's really no danger there for the viewer; instead, I found myself waiting for the episode to get to the point.

I will say that there are many positives about 'Fear Her', starting with some of the actors. Abisola Agbaje does a very good job for someone whose first appearance in front of the television cameras this was (apparently the director picked her out of a play), and manages to convey the creepiness, sadness and loneliness necessary for Chloe without breaking. Nina Sosanya, given a limited amount of work to do, plays the fearful mother well; and Abdul Salis is priceless with his sitcom 'Council' dialogue and has a great rapport with Billie Piper. The Olympic trappings – nothing substantial, just a torch runner, shots of the stadium and the banner at the onset – do manage to give the viewer at least a passing sense that something wonderful is coming, without being obtrusive. The art design in Chloe's bedroom, the blend of coloured papers and crayon drawings, is stunning.

But it still feels like it was recorded in someone's backyard – it was, after all, recorded on location, and goes no further than portraying its ordinary setting in an only-slightly-less-ordinary manner. And that, combined with virtually the same ambience as 'Love & Monsters', gives me this unshakeable feeling that both episodes were afterthoughts, space-fillers between the vastly superior 'The Impossible Planet'/'The Satan Pit' and the bombastic two-part season finale to follow. Afterthoughts, rather inconsequential... which is a shame because Matthew Graham's script does have a few pearls of wisdom. (The aforementioned 'Council' sitcom dialogue had me chuckling, and some of the Doctor/Rose dialogue is lovely.)

So why does this story ultimately prove forgettable? Perhaps because it's just so plainly, exasperatingly *ordinary*. We waited 15 years for *Doctor Who* to come back, the *Doctor Who* we remember with flashing lights and aliens and spaceships and real science-fiction heroes and villains and all of it... and this week we get a simple detective story. Which isn't necessarily a problem, because the Doctor is, to all intents and purposes, a detective; the problem lies in the fact that he's not *just* a detective. I'm not sure the writer grasped that; you could do this story on any other series – call it possession by a ghost, if you will (we have a series called *Medium* in the US, and honestly, this was more like an episode of *that*!). When you realise that, in fact, the Doctor was on to the problem but didn't really solve it – unless you count an oh-so-lucky glimpse at a piece of paper by Rose, who then did the leg work – and when ultimately the point comes down to the fact that a tantrum-throwing alien child had the ability to leave all along, but was willing to sacrifice an entire planet in the meanwhile... by that time, does it really matter?

And then, all you need is love. It's love that enables the Isolus to leave – never mind the fact that it was about to destroy our entire planet, we need to love it and send it on its way. I'm a bleeding heart, and even for *me* that's a bit too sappy. Ultimately, that's where 'Fear Me' stumbles; it has a really good heart, but about halfway through, the brain stopped writing the story and the heart took over. That sometimes makes for great drama... but *Doctor Who* is also not *just* a drama. *Doctor Who* works best when the drama, comedy, science-fiction, morality play and adventure are all blended into something that is vastly superior to the sum of its parts; here, we just get a bit of a filler. Nice little story, well acted, but ultimately, sadly, forgettable. – *Shaun Lyon*

212: ARMY OF GHOSTS

Earth has been overrun by spiritual apparitions that appear and disappear like clockwork. The mysterious Torchwood Institute seems to be behind it; there's a portal in their office tower block above London that they keep opening, and a mysterious sphere in their science lab that registers as not being there at all. The Doctor and Rose soon discover that Torchwood's projects pose immense danger to the entire world... as enemies from their past finally catch up with them.

FIRST TRANSMISSION: UK – 1 July 2006. US – January 2007. Canada – December 2006. Australia – 30 September 2006. New Zealand – 28 September 2006.
DURATION: 43'18"
WRITER: Russell T Davies
DIRECTOR: Graeme Harper
CREDITED CAST: David Tennant (The Doctor), Billie Piper (Rose Tyler), Camille Coduri (Jackie Tyler), Noel Clarke (Mickey Smith), Tracy-Ann Oberman (Yvonne Hartman), Raji James (Dr Rajesh Singh), Freema Agyeman (Adeola), Hadley Fraser (Gareth), Oliver Mellor (Matt), Barbara Windsor (Peggy Mitchell), Hajaz Akram (Indian Newsreader), Anthony Debaeck (French Newsreader), Takako Akashi (Japanese Newsreader), Paul Fields (Weatherman), David Warwick (Police Commissioner), Rachel Webster (Eileen), Kyoko Morita (Japanese Girl), Maddi Cryer (Housewife), Derek Acorah (Himself), Alistair Appleton (Himself), Trisha Goddard (Herself), Paul Kasey (Cyber Leader), Nicholas Briggs (Dalek/Cybermen Voices), Barnaby Edwards, Nicholas Pegg, Stuart Crossman, Anthony Spargo, Dan Barratt, David Hankinson (Dalek Operators)

Daleks originally created by Terry Nation.
Cybermen originally created by Kit Pedler and Gerry Davis.

WHERE AND WHEN: London, England, late 2007, including the Powell Estate and Canary Wharf Tower... home of the Torchwood Institute. On a bus in London prior to the events of 'Rose', before 5 March 2005 (or 18 August 2004). Flashback to a scene from 'Rose', 5 March 2005 (or 18 August 2004). Tenth Doctor in TARDIS. Running down a street with the tenth Doctor. On an alien planet with the tenth Doctor, with stingray-like creatures wheeling overhead. Beach at Dårlig Ulv Stranden, or Bad Wolf Beach, in an alternate-universe Norway.

THE STORY UNFOLDS: The world has been captivated by the sudden appearance of ghosts at certain times each day (which people have called 'ghost-shifts'). The ghosts started appearing two months earlier, out of the blue; the world panicked, but slowly came to accept them as real. Jackie believes one in her home is her father, Rose's Granddad Prentice; she says it feels like him, with the smell of old cigarettes she was familiar with. The ghosts can walk through things, and through people; the Doctor is chilled when one walks through him. The ghosts can be seen everywhere, though seem to be gathering around Westminster Bridge; reporters in other countries discuss the presence of large numbers of ghosts in Paris, at the Taj Majal in India, and in Japan, where young girls delight at wearing t-shirts with ghost logos on them. The Doctor believes the ghosts have a psychic link; whatever they're doing, people believing it's their long-lost relatives is helping them enter this reality from wherever they've been, and although they look like people, they may be as different from them as footprints are from the boots that make them.

The Torchwood Institute is headed up by Yvonne Hartman, who knows all about the Doctor, his TARDIS and his long history fighting alien invaders of Earth. The Torchwood logo is a collection of hexagons arranged to form a 'T'. Their motto is 'If it's alien, it's ours'; what they capture, they strip down and use 'for the good of the British Empire'. Torchwood considers the Doctor to be the enemy, and a prisoner, albeit a welcome and honoured one; he was named in the Torchwood Foundation Charter of 1879 as an enemy of the Crown. Hartman says that Queen Victoria created Torchwood for the express intention of keeping Britain great and fighting the 'alien horde'. The Torchwood central warehouse contains a Jathaa Sun Glider, which was shot down and crashed off the Shetland Islands ten years earlier. They have a particle gun, which took eight years to make functional, and magna-clamps, found in a spaceship buried at the base of Mount Snowdon, that cancel the mass of an object and allow the bearer to lift as much as two Imperial tons. (Torchwood refuses to go metric.) Also in the warehouse are an Egyptian sarcophagus and hundreds of boxes and crates.

Torchwood's science department is headed up by Dr Rajesh Singh, who has been charged with finding out about a mysterious dark sphere that recently appeared there. At a loss to find anything significant, Singh allowed the R&D department in, and they came up with a new invention that could detect the heat from a single protozoa through half a mile of steel. They have failed to obtain any readings from the sphere, which their equipment says cannot exist, doesn't age, emits no heat or radiation and has no atomic mass. Singh cannot even touch the sphere; somehow it won't let him. The Doctor looks at it through a pair of blue-red anaglyph 3-D glasses and determines that it's a void ship – an impossible vessel designed to exist outside time and space, travelling through the timeless dark space between dimensions and parallel universes. The Time Lords called it the void; the Eternals called it 'the howling', and some people, the Doctor says, call it Hell.

The void ship appeared on Earth through a giant interdimensional hole; the ghosts followed in its wake. Torchwood are responsible for the ghost-shifts; they use particle engines controlled by massive levers fired at the hole to open up the breach, which brings the ghosts into our reality. Years of warning signs, including a radar blind spot 600 feet over London, led the group to build Torchwood Tower – or, as it's publicly known, Canary Wharf Tower – to reach the anomaly. The excuse for them continuing to open the breach is that it's a massive source of power, enough to stop Britain's dependence on Middle Eastern oil. The Doctor thinks whatever built the sphere aimed it at this dimension and shot it through the breach like a cannon ball.

The Doctor uses a triangulation system to capture a ghost; he references the TARDIS's deep scan, while Rose takes readings on the scanner (and establishes that the ghost pattern resonates at delta 1-6). The Doctor wears 3-D glasses while watching the ghost appear. Torchwood detect the attempted capture and shut down the ghost shift early; the 'specific excitation of the ghost field' makes it easy for them to pinpoint it to the Powell Estate in the London post code area SE15 7GO. The Doctor's suspicions about the source of a signal controlling some of Torchwood's staff are confirmed when he discovers that an 'advance guard' of Cybermen have come to Earth from the parallel universe he and Rose visited earlier. The Cybermen increase the ghost-shift to 100 percent, which brings back the ghosts all over Earth... ghosts that, true to the Doctor's fears, suddenly coalesce into Cybermen. The Cybermen say the void-ship –

which isn't theirs – broke down the barriers between universes; the Cybermen followed whatever is inside the sphere through the breach.

While the interdimensional doorway continues to open, the sphere in the lab becomes active, achieving mass and energy, and opens – revealing four Daleks!

At some point, the Doctor has taken Rose to a rocky planet with massive, flying stingray-like creatures. Rose has also picked up from an asteroid bazaar for Jackie a small trinket made of bazoolium; when the trinket gets cold, it means it's going to rain, and when it's hot, it's going to be sunny. Referring to Jackie as Rose, the Doctor says that she's not the best companion he's ever had, a bit 'too blonde', deluded, and talks too much, but very good at making tea. He also claims that the previous week she stared into the heart of the time vortex and aged 57 years. A BBC weather programme predicts 'very strong ghosts from London through the north and up into Scotland.' When the ghost energy is measured at 5,000 gigawatts, it's cause for celebration. EctoShine is an aerosol spray that supposedly brightens up ghosts from being pale and grey. According to the papers, a ghost has been elected to Parliament as an MP for Leeds. Torchwood has a guard named Sebastian. (Yvonne thinks it's important to know everyone's name.)

THE DOCTOR: He doesn't believe the ghosts are benign and thinks that there is something else at work here. When Jackie asks him if he agrees that people's deceased families coming back is beautiful, he replies, 'I think it's horrific.' He says he's never heard of Torchwood (despite evidence to the contrary); the fact that the Torchwood people have guns and he doesn't make him the better person; they can shoot him but he keeps the moral high ground. He asks Yvonne not to include the fact that he's travelling with Rose's mother in Torchwood's official history.

ROSE TYLER: She thinks nothing happened to her during the first 19 years of her life, and wants to stay with the Doctor 'forever'. She doesn't use her mobile phone (to call home to her mother) as often as Jackie would like, but brings home her washing. Jackie thinks she's changed and that she's even started to look like the Doctor; she thinks Rose will keep changing after she's gone and won't have any reason to return home.

CHARACTER BUILDING: *Jackie Tyler* – She's 40 (though the Doctor jokes that she's older). She has become very fond of the Doctor, kissing him squarely on the lips to welcome him back. (She does the same to Rose.) Her father died about ten years ago when his heart gave out; now she thinks the ghost that keeps visiting her is him. She's amused that she knows more about the ghost-shifts than the Doctor does. She's unhappy that her daughter is growing away from her. Upon her first trip in the TARDIS, she tells the Doctor that if the TARDIS ends up on Mars, she'll kill him. The Doctor takes her with him into Torchwood, explaining to Hartman that she's Rose, while Rose herself is safely hidden inside the TARDIS. She thinks the sphere 'feels weird'.

Yvonne Hartman – Head of the Torchwood Institute. She's responsible for the project involving the ghost-shifts, and is pleased and astounded when she captures the Doctor and the TARDIS. Even though he's a prisoner, she treats him as an honoured guest, applauding when she first meets him. She is fiercely patriotic; she says there isn't a British Empire at present but will be one day. She thinks the key to success is having people skills; because she knows the guard's name, she thinks she's a people person. She also has disdain for the Doctor's superior attitude about the interdimensional breach, yet is persuaded to stop the ghost-shifting – temporarily.

Rajesh Singh – Torchwood's chief scientist; he's also called Raj. He's at his wit's end regarding the sphere in the science lab. (Instead of trying to crack it, he plays Sudoku and is on book 509.) The sphere has got 'into his head', like it's staring at him. He is a fan of the Doctor.

Mickey Smith – Having faced the Cybermen in the parallel universe ('The Age of Steel'), he's come here to help defend the Earth; 'We've beaten them before,' he says, 'we can beat them again.' Having infiltrated Torchwood, he's posing as Singh's assistant Samuel. He says it's good to see Rose, but is obviously more preoccupied by the contents of the sphere. He has a huge gun with him, hoping to blast whatever comes out of the sphere into hell.

Gareth Evans, Matthew Crane, Adeola Oshodi – Employees in the Torchwood control room (whose surnames are seen on their computer screens). Gareth and Adeola are in a relationship (which they believe no-one else knows about, even though in fact it's common knowledge). Yvonne asks Matt to contact Torchwood's 'hospitality' department to send Rajesh Singh something to keep from going mad from the monotony. ('Not alcohol,' she says.) Yvonne calls Adeola 'Adi'. The three become controlled by the Cybermen using communications equipment altered to be hard-wired directly into their brains. After they return from the Cyberman-controlled construction area with earpods on both ears, and start opening the breach, the Doctor is forced to 'deactivate' them (he says that they're already dead) by deactivating their earpods.

TORCHWOOD: At last... Torchwood becomes a vital part of the storyline, as much of the action in this episode takes place in the Torchwood Institute. (See 'The Story Unfolds ...')

BODY COUNT: Employees of Torchwood, including Gareth, Matthew, Adeola and at least two others in the control room, are killed by the Cybermen. *Ghostwatch* host Alistair Appleton is strangled and houses are invaded by the Cybermen as they go on a planet-wide rampage. While not seen on screen, a massive number of casualties can be expected at the episode's end.

THE DOCTOR'S MAGICAL SONIC SCREWDRIVER: The Doctor gives it to Rose to make adjustments on the triangulation devices; he tells her to use setting B for 8 seconds. The Doctor cracks a glass panel in Yvonne's office with it to demonstrate the side effect of the ghost-shift. He also uses the screwdriver to deactivate Adeola's earpod – which in turn does the same to Matt's and Gareth's – and then attempts to locate the remote transmitter controlling the ghost-shift.

REALITY BITES: The Doctor, Jackie and Rose watch a sequence from *EastEnders*, in which the character Peggy Mitchell, landlady of the Queen Victoria pub, tells a ghost – which she believes is the spirit of another character, Den Watts – to get out. Mitchell, played by *EastEnders* actress Barbara Windsor, has worked on the series since 1994; in this episode, she says 'Get out of my pub!', a catchphrase she regularly uses on the show. She says the only spirits she'll serve are gin, whiskey and vodka. Den Watts, a character played in the series by Leslie Grantham, is not seen in this episode.

A clip from *The Trisha Goddard Show* is also seen. Entitled 'I Married a Dead Man!', the sequence features the host interviewing a panellist, Eileen, who says she's in love with 'her' ghost. Psychic medium Derek Acorah appears briefly in a television interview saying, 'Well, no-one needs me anymore' in reaction to the ghosts' appearance. Presenter Alistair Appleton also appears on a series called *Ghostwatch*; this is implied to be an updated, current-events version of the infamous ghost-hunting documentary spoof broadcast by the BBC in 1992, though now it's supposedly the genuine article.

The Doctor and Rose refer to the 1984 film *Ghostbusters* starring Bill Murray, Dan Aykroyd and Sigourney Weaver; after the Doctor dons some technical equipment to track the ghosts, the two use the catchphrases, 'Who ya gonna call? Ghostbusters!' and 'I ain't afraid of no ghosts!' The Doctor can't get the name Alonzo out of his head, after sharing the French joke '*Allons-y Alonzo!*' ('Let's go, Alonzo'); he asks Yvonne if anyone by that name works at Torchwood.

The equipment in the Torchwood science bay includes items manufactured by Spectron Laser Systems; Spectron Lasers, owned by GSI, is a real company and the logo seen is authentic.

Rose says that a ghost has been 'elected MP for Leeds'. In the real world, Leeds has five constituencies – Leeds Central, Leeds East, Leeds North East, Leeds North West and Leeds West. Presumably either in the *Doctor Who* world Leeds has only one constituency, or – perhaps more likely – Rose is merely simplifying the report she is reading.

LINKING THEMES: Once again, as at the beginning of both 'Rose' and 'The Christmas Invasion', a panoramic shot of space that rolls over Earth and descends down into London is used. Christopher Eccleston, the Series One incarnation of the Doctor, is seen for the first time since the 'story so far' section of the *Children in Need* special (in a recap of his first scene in 'Rose').

Yvonne refers to the weapon that shot the Sycorax ship down on Christmas Day, saying that Torchwood was responsible; Torchwood was referred to in 'The Christmas Invasion' when it happened. She also references the events of 'Tooth and Claw', including the Doctor's encounter with Queen Victoria and the werewolf, and refers to the events at the end of that episode, when Queen Victoria announced to Lady Isobel that she would create an institute at the site of Torchwood House.

Rose narrates the opening of the episode, saying that Earth is where she was born and where she 'died', talking about the 'army of ghosts', Torchwood and 'the war'. A brief scene of her standing on a beach presumably takes place shortly after her final scene in 'Doomsday' in Norway. (She's wearing the same jacket as from that episode.)

The Doctor's adventures in 'Rise of the Cybermen' and 'The Age of Steel' are recalled by the appearance of the Cybermen, the use of the makeshift earpods (standard communications earpieces, here modified with Cyber-technology that goes into the ear canal and connects directly to the brain) and the reappearance of Mickey Smith, who left the TARDIS at the end of the two-part story.

Yvonne Hartman's name is very similar to that of Yvonne Hartley, one of the characters who was turned into a Cyberman (but remembered her own name) in Marc Platt's *Doctor Who* audio 'Spare Parts' for Big Finish. Platt's script was used as the basis for the earlier Cybermen two-parter. When the character was first announced in the media, it was as appearing in this production block, and – as it was presumed at the time that only episodes five and six were being recorded, not the season finale as well – this led to the belief that she would be in the episodes adapted from Platt's material, adding fuel to the (ultimately mistaken) idea that MacRae's story was a close adaptation of the audio play.

The Doctor previously said he didn't believe in ghosts in the 1996 *Doctor Who* TV movie starring Paul McGann. When he uses the triangulation devices to try to capture one of the ghosts, Rose mentions the Gelth ('The Unquiet Dead'). According to the episode's online commentary, the Egyptian sarcophagus was placed deliberately as an homage to the story 'Pyramids of Mars'. The sequence of the Cybermen breaking through the plastic sheets is an homage to similar sequences in 'The Tomb of the Cybermen', 'The Invasion' and 'Earthshock'. Jackie's maiden name, Prentice – which she mentions here in conjunction with her late father – was first learned in 'Father's Day'.

This story marks the first appearance of a Cyber Leader – with traditional black-handled headpiece – and the first of a black Dalek in the new series.

The SE15 7GO London postcode was first given in the 2006 *Doctor Who Annual*, and was based partly around the initials of script editor Helen Raynor's boyfriend.

SCENE MISSING: The Doctor seems to know a lot about the void ship. He initially thinks it's an impossibility but quickly realises that this is not the case. He says that someone could sit inside, survive the Big Bang and the beginning of the next universe, and sit outside all creation. Yet in 'The Satan Pit', he considered it impossible that the Beast could have existed prior to the creation of the universe. Why did he have such an intellectual problem with the Beast's explanation when here, in 'Army of Ghosts', he readily accepts the idea and even buys into it?

The Torchwood concept continues to play havoc with *Doctor Who* timelines... and common sense. Where have they been during all the previous alien invasions seen in the series? Were they waiting in the wings during 'Rose'? Investigating the Slitheen? Yvonne doesn't seem to know who the Cybermen are; where was Torchwood during the Cybermen attacks of 'The Tenth Planet' and 'The Invasion'? (One could argue that the past is fluid and things change... but in 'School Reunion', Sarah Jane Smith still knew of all the things that had happened to her in the past.) Why is the Doctor still an enemy of the 'British Empire'; in fact, why would anyone be so rude to him if they know he's saved the Earth so many times? Why didn't Torchwood pick him up when he was UNIT's scientific advisor for all those years – in the incarnation played by Jon Pertwee, during whose era Sarah Jane was introduced? Torchwood also seems to be incredibly visible – with the name of the organisation printed on windows, and a logo everywhere! Why is that the case if this is a top-secret organisation that not even the Prime Minister is supposed to know about ('The Christmas Invasion')? (Russell T Davies, in an interview for *Doctor Who Confidential*, likened the lack of interaction between UNIT and Torchwood to a lack of cooperation between the FBI and CIA in the United States; however, everyone knows that the latter two organisations exist, whereas the Doctor has apparently never heard of Torchwood!)

How does the psychic paper, which Rose uses to give her credentials (however foolhardily) to Singh, manage to fool the electronic lock? (We've seen in the past that the writing on psychic paper doesn't actually appear and is only in the minds of the readers – the notable exception to this rule being in 'New Earth', where we presumably see the paper from Rose's point of view.) How did Torchwood move the sphere – which its people cannot even touch! – to the science lab? Why does Yvonne wear sunglasses for the ghost-shift early in the episode, yet nobody (including Yvonne) seems to need them later?

Why have the Cybermen been operating, apparently, out of a construction area in the Tower? Was there something there that they were doing? In fact, how did the Cybermen that attack the three employees get there in the first place, if it was the final ghost-shift that brought the Cybermen over from the parallel universe? Why do the ghosts walk like normal people, until we discover they're supposed to be Cybermen at the end of the episode, when they suddenly start stomping in unison like Cybermen? Why were they grinding and drilling into Matt, creating a lot of sparks in the process, if all they were doing was sticking a tube through his ear and into his brain?

How did the Daleks – even the Daleks of the other universe – get their hands on a void ship? Why didn't Van Statten know what a Dalek was in 2012 in 'Dalek' if they invaded Earth here in 2007?

Why didn't the TARDIS translate the Doctor's amusing (yet only to himself) '*Allons-y*' joke from French to English? (It's not a proper name, after all ...) Perhaps it telepathically realises he's joking and leaves the phrase untranslated for that reason – there are certainly precedents in the show for the TARDIS's translation to be that intelligent. What's more unusual is that the TV stations the Doctor flips between are untranslated. How did Eileen get the ghost to come to the *Trisha Goddard* studio. Similarly, how did the *EastEnders* production team get their ghost into the scene with Peggy Mitchell? (Perhaps it was just a visual effect.) It's also difficult to see how, in reality, a ghost could have been elected as the new Leeds MP.

If Jackie is such a big *EastEnders* fan, why doesn't she remark on Yvonne Hartman's resemblance to the soap's Chrissie Watts, or Singh's startling resemblance to Ash Ferreira? (Okay, so we quibble ...)

ALTERED STATES: At one point during the writing of this episode, it was called 'Torchwood Rises' (with episode 13 called 'Torchwood Falls'). The script that was circulated to most of the cast and crew omitted the final scene with the Daleks. Preview copies of the episode distributed to the press had Rose's opening monologue replaced with a slightly different one in which she talks about 'war on Earth' and omits to refer to the fact that she is to 'die', and also had the final shots revealing the Daleks omitted.

BEHIND THE SCENES: Many parts of the episode were recorded on location in an aircraft hangar at RAF St Athan in the Vale of Glamorgan in Wales, which doubled as the Torchwood Tower central hangar and warehouse. Corridor scenes in Torchwood Tower were recorded at the Brackla Bunkers near Bridgend. The sequence with Rose on the bus was shot in a London bus transported to St Mary Street in Cardiff, while the Southerndown beach in the Vale of Glamorgan was used for both the opening beach sequence (shot concurrently with the ones seen in 'Doomsday') and as the alien planet. The crew returned to Loudoun Square, Butetown, Cardiff (where 'The Parting of the Ways' was recorded the previous year) to shoot the playground sequences, and used a private home in Canton for the Cyberman break-in. Sequences were also shot on the Brandon Estate in Kennington – which has been used as the Powell Estate in episodes past – and at the studios in Newport.

The view of One Canada Square (the Canary Wharf building) seen in the episode is a reused shot from the opening sequence of *The Apprentice* (UK version). The *BBC Wales Today* set is seen, redressed to represent the French news station.

The BBC's *Ghostwatch* tie-in website was created for this episode. It includes games, a 'ghost report' and details of viewer sightings of ghosts around the country. Also started at around this time was the website www.torchwood.org.uk, ostensibly to tie into the forthcoming debut of the *Torchwood* TV series, but at the time of broadcast presenting just an 'Access Denied' message.

The episode was broadcast with a thanks credit to the Canadian Broadcasting Corporation. This credit had not been included before on a UK broadcast of a new series episode; it is, however, part of the standard credits seen on some internationally-distributed copies, and is also present on the DVD releases.

DULCET TONES: Moments before the Daleks' appearance, viewers with good ears can guess what's coming, as choral elements from the previous season's Dalek episodes, 'Dalek' and 'The Parting of the Ways', are reused.

OFF THE SCREEN: Tracy-Ann Oberman is best known for playing Christine Watts in *EastEnders*, and has also appeared in *Sorted* (2006), *Murder in Suburbia* (2004), *The Last Detective* (2004), *Big Train* (2002), *The Bill* (2000), *Kiss Me Kate* (1998), *Casualty* (1998) and *Loved By You* (1997). Raji James was in *Nina's Heavenly Delights* (2006), *Doctors* (2006), *EastEnders* (2003), *Waking the Dead* (2003), *The Bill* (2000), *Coupling* (2000) and *Cry Wolf* (2000). Barbara Windsor is one of the leads on the long-running *EastEnders*, playing Peggy Mitchell from 1994-2003 and again from 2005 onwards; she's also been seen in *One Foot in the Grave* (1995), *You Rang, M'Lord?* (1991), *Filthy Rich & Catflap* (1987), *Worzel Gummidge* (1979), *Carry On Laughing* (1975), *Up Pompeii* (1970), *Dad's Army* (1968) and many of the *Carry On...* films series. Hajaz Akram was seen in *Casualty* (2005), *Lara Croft Tomb Raider: The Cradle of Life* (2003) and *Murder in Mind* (2003). Anthony Debaeck appeared in *Love Soup* (2005). Takako Akashi was in *Jonathan Creek* (2003). Paul Fields was in *Love Soup* (2005) and *Down to Earth* (2003). Maddi Cryer appeared in *You Gotta Be Jokin* (1991).

Freema Agyeman's previous television experience includes roles in *The Bill* (2006), *Silent Witness* (2005), *Casualty* (2004) and *Crossroads* (2001), in the latter of which she played the regular Lola Wise. Agyeman was originally signed on to do this episode and then auditioned for the role of Martha Jones, the replacement for Rose Tyler. On 4 July 2006, the BBC announced that Agyeman would join Tennant as the new series companion starting in the first regular episode of Series Three, to be transmitted in the spring of 2007.

David Warwick previously appeared as Kimus in the *Doctor Who* story 'The Pirate Planet', opposite Tom Baker and Mary Tamm, and later played two roles in *Doctor Who* audio plays for Big Finish, David Garnier in 'The Harvest' with Sylvester McCoy, and Erich in 'Gallifrey: A Blind Eye', in which he starred alongside his wife, former *Doctor Who* companion Louise Jameson (Leela). Warwick has also been seen in *All About Me* (2002), *Peak Practice* (1994), *Keeping Up Appearances* (1991), *The Bill* (1990), *Yes Minister* (1984), *The Fall and Rise of Reginald Perrin* (1976) and *Z Cars* (1972).

Derek Acorah (real name Derek Johnson) is a popular television psychic medium in Britain, the author of six books about contacting the world of the dead, the star of many television specials and a celebrity spokesman. He came to prominence as a medium as one of the team of investigators on *Most Haunted* (2002-2005), and his own series include *Derek Acorah's Ghost Towns* (2005).

Alistair Appleton is a television presenter whose roles include *Hot TV* on Sky, *House Doctor* (1999) for Five, *Travel On* on the Travel Channel, *Garden Invaders* on BBC1, *Stately Suppers* (2006) for BBC Food and *Cash in the Attic*. He has also featured in guest spots on *Footballers' Wives* (2002) and *Rhona* (2000).

Trisha Goddard is the host of *The Trisha Goddard Show* (2005) for Five; for the previous seven years, she hosted ITV's flagship chat show, *Trisha*. She has hosted programmes in

EPISODE 212

Australia as well, and has appeared as herself in *The Second Coming* (2003), *Shaun of the Dead* (2004) and *Little Britain* (2005).

INTERNAL CONSISTENCY: The episode takes place some time after 'Love & Monsters', which was set in the spring of 2007, when there has been no sign of the ghosts. Jackie says that they started appearing two months ago (which would just be consistent with a ghost appearing in *EastEnders* – usually recorded six to eight weeks in advance of broadcast); assuming they didn't appear as soon as the Doctor left Earth in 'Love & Monsters', that would place the episode in at least October, perhaps later (though the dry weather doesn't suggest it takes place too much later!)

TARDISODE #12: An investigative reporter for a major newspaper is attempting to find out information about Torchwood and the Doctor. The reporter has pictures of the Doctor, and is searching through files in a filing cabinet bearing the Torchwood logo; he's come to think that they're both connected to the ghosts that have suddenly appeared. The reporter is suddenly captured in his editor's office by representatives of Torchwood, who have pressurised the editor into cooperating. The reporter is dragged away in a straitjacket.

REVIEWS

I thought the return of Sarah Jane and K-9 in 'School Reunion' was a seismic shift in the balance between fan fiction and official canon, but I had no idea what was coming at the end of this series. A massive Cyber-invasion of modern day Earth is exciting enough, with thrilling shots of steel giants materialising around the world and threatening people in their very homes, but Daleks??! With a brand-new black Dalek leading the charge? The show's classic Big Two monsters are finally brought face to face (or eyestalk to faceplate) with humanity caught in the middle. Just two years into *Doctor Who*'s revival and with an understandable sense that perhaps continuity should be doled out sparingly, we now stand on the brink of the first-ever Dalek-Cyber war. I can't help but say it's about time – talk about a payoff to beat them all! Of course, this kind of malevolent match-up would never fly if it wasn't fun and thrilling for all viewers, not just eager fans, but it most assuredly is. As with all good first parts, this episode does a great job of slowly ratcheting up the tension until the final minutes, when Murray Gold's percussive score propels us toward what may be one of the show's most breathtaking cliff-hangers ever. And as if we don't have enough to worry about, we know that Rose is about to depart. Her opening monologue suggests – despite reports and fan theories – that she will not die in a physical sense, but how exactly she will bow out has naturally been the subject of plenty of speculation. What could possibly make her leave the Doctor's side? We'll know soon enough... Guest star Tracy-Ann Oberman is spot on as the slimy yet slightly seductive head of Torchwood, Yvonne Hartman, giving us a person to loathe even as the endless Torchwood references throughout the series finally get a dramatic pay-off. I'm still wondering though – what happened to UNIT? Real world explanations aside, wouldn't the Brig's troops be knee-deep in Cyber-guts with these familiar foes turning up all around the world? It just doesn't ring true that UNIT has so quickly vanished as a major alien-battling presence and Torchwood is now the only game in town. Surely Benton himself would drop his car dealership and grab an Uzi if he saw the ol' handlebar heads materialising out of thin air? As for other guest performers, Raji James makes Dr Singh just likeable enough that you know he isn't long for this world. Some of the cutesy TV-bound cameos are nicely handled; a *Ghostbusters* joke less so.

But Tennant is mostly under control, completely inhabiting the Doctor in a wonderful intellectual stand-off with Hartman. Camille Coduri's Jackie even gets to be a companion for a little while, and she does a fine job of it too. And look who's working with Dr Singh in the sphere room – Mickey! It just keeps getting better and better. 'Army of Ghosts' is a superb opener for what looks like a spectacular – and heart-rending – Series Two conclusion. One can only hope that 'Doomsday' delivers on the enormous promise of this instalment, and one wonders how the production team can top this next year for Series Three! – *Arnold T Blumberg*

Over the years, I have become increasingly convinced that the episode to watch in a season is not the finale, but the penultimate episode. Season finales are high-octane rides into the abyss; penultimate episodes often have the meatier character and plot aspects, as the goal is to get everything into place so the fireworks can happen the following episode. 'Army of Ghosts' is a case in point. We have some wonderful moments with Rose, the Doctor and Jackie that bring out some long-needed development in the relationship between the Doctor and Rose and a culmination of the Torchwood thread. Rather like in 'Bad Wolf' last season, Davies starts out with a deliciously satirical premise: what if we could suddenly see ghosts as a regular everyday occurrence? Well, we'd make them plotlines on *EastEnders* and fodder for talk TV and dodgy advertising... but mostly we'd put all our misplaced faith in them, even if there's really no proof. Which is rather the point you'd expect from the author of *The Second Coming*. This might have made a lovely 45 minute story all its own, but it's actually just the first seven or so minutes, because subverting expectations is what 'Army of Ghosts' is all about. We get our first glimpse into Torchwood, but instead of it being run with military precision by a Picard-like figure we have Yvonne Hartmann, who acts more like a life coach than the director of a super-secret organisation – which is why she's so utterly perfect (and played to perfection by Tracy-Ann Oberman). And then, just when you think you're headed into a Cybermen invasion story, we have... *that* cliff-hanger. It's a testament to 'Army of Ghosts' that even though I had heard the rumour of an appearance by the Daleks (and even thought that I had noticed a Dalek extermination effect in the preview at the end of 'Fear Her') I had completely put it out of my mind while I was watching, and the occupants of the sphere became a total surprise. I've never wanted more badly for a week to pass... which says to me Davies has done his job exceedingly well. – *Graeme Burk*

It's 'Bad Wolf' all over again. We get a penultimate episode that reveals the meaning to the year's catchphrase, leads into a massive alien invasion, spends a lot of time on explanations and only actually starts the story proper about ten minutes before the end. Once again, I enjoyed the episode on its own merits, but I find myself wondering just how much of it will actually impact on 'Doomsday'. Again, as in 'Bad Wolf', the fake-out plot-line is actually pretty interesting. I like the idea of the Doctor worrying about a situation where he finds everyone too *happy*; and although the ghosts bring up a lot of unanswered questions – How do they influence people to believe they're meeting dead relatives? And why don't they walk like Cybermen? – they're certainly an effective image. Best of all, the ghosts allow Camille Coduri to come into her own again. Why is it that, like Mickey, Jackie has become a truly interesting character only in her final appearances? She is, in turn, both touchingly sad and an unflinching reminder of how flippant the Doctor and Rose have become. After half a dozen episodes, we are finally returning to the themes of change and responsibility that were so important to 'Tooth and Claw' and 'School Reunion'. Torchwood itself is an interesting concept, a sort of

Area 51-type group who both oppose the Doctor's methods and believe themselves the authority in all things extra-terrestrial. As interesting as their moral grey area is, however, that's not enough to hang a series on long-term. The actual *Torchwood* series is going to have to broaden the concept and make it something we're actually interested in from week-to-week. Which brings up another point – am I the only one who's just a little bit skittish about using the show to indirectly promote an adults-only spin-off? You can't convince me your average *Who*-loving kid won't look up the schedules some months from now, see *Torchwood* advertised, and not want to watch it. Returning to *Doctor Who*, though – well, it's hard to come up with a lot of concrete opinion, because this episode is such complete and total set-up for part two (as seems to be the pattern). It's certainly very pacey, and the shots of Cybermen appearing all over the Earth go some way toward upping the excitement. There are a few cringe-worthy moments – the horrible *Ghostbusters* gag, Tracy-Ann Oberman's peculiar 'Superb! Happy day!' welcome speech, and the Cybermen actually attacking the populace ('They're metal *men*!') – but overall, this is solid stuff. I just wish Graeme Harper's direction was a touch more creative. His two stints on the original series are unforgettable, but here, as with the earlier Cyberman story, he seems largely content to point and shoot. Finally, I suppose I should discuss the cliff-hanger. It's a good cliff-hanger, sure enough, but I'm afraid I already knew what was coming. All the way back around the time of 'School Reunion', someone spoiled the return of the Daleks for me, so I've had a very long time to come around to the idea. I'm not sure it will work – it's one of those 'ultimate' concepts that seems like it's never been done for a reason – but I am certainly excited to see a proper, all-out invasion of Earth, which is what I had hoped 'The Parting of the Ways' would be like all those months ago. No matter what they do next week, it's got to be better than watching continents melt like butter on a computer screen. Davies has, for better or worse, set himself quite the challenge for this year's final episode. He's got a Cyberman/Dalek war, he's brought back Jackie, Mickey, Pete and Jake, and somehow he's got to write out Rose before it's done. All this in 45 minutes! How he'll do this, I don't know, but I can't wait to see... – *Sarah Hadley*

It's perhaps difficult to judge 'Army of Ghosts' on its own merits as an episode, given that probably more so than any other first episode of a two-parter so far in the new series, it feels like a set-up for what's to come, getting all the players into their positions on stage before the curtain comes up on the main attraction next week. That's not to say that it's a bad episode in any way – I certainly found it entertaining, which is no mean feat considering I, like many other English viewers, had to watch it hot on the heels of seeing our team crash out of the World Cup! Just that it is in a certain way frustrating, as we see so much that is good or has the potential to be exciting wheeled into place and have to wait with it all left there for a week before we see how it turns out. The mystery of the ghosts is quite nicely handled, and just as Jackie herself feels, it is nice to see her having a spot of superior knowledge to the Doctor, just for a change! The ghost special effect is very well done, and although I could do without the Doctor and Rose bursting into snatches of the *Ghostbusters* theme tune, I enjoyed the rather ramshackle way in which the Doctor tracked the creatures down. When the majority of the action switches to Torchwood, it is hard, however, not to find the place just a smidgen disappointing after all the build-up it's been given over the rest of the series. The white look, especially, puts you in mind of the misguided Initiative from season four of *Buffy the Vampire Slayer*, something Joss Whedon himself has admitted they never had the money to make look good. 'Army of Ghosts' gets away with it though on the strength of the performance from

Oberman as Yvonne, as well as the intriguing mystery of the sphere. Davies's script is pretty top-rate as well, the Welshman as always managing to combine the humorous – such as the Doctor's attempt to pass off Jackie as Rose – with the horrific, such as the Cyber implant Yvonne removes, taking part of one of her employee's brains with it. But of course, the cliff-hanger is the part of this episode that will always be remembered, probably as one of the greatest there has been in the history of the show. Personally I have never liked the Cybermen, so I could take or leave their presence, and seeing them and the Daleks combined in one story could be considered a cynical audience-grabbing move... But hooray for cynicism and audience grabbing, I say, if it leads to another episode as thrilling as the last few moments of 'Army of Ghosts'. Because as those Daleks sweep down from beyond oblivion and into our world, you just know that something epic is about to unfold. – *Paul Hayes*

If 'Rise of the Cybermen' came with hype, 'Army of Ghosts'/'Doomsday' comes with expectations so stratospheric that you'd have to be either insane or a genius to even attempt it. Especially given the no-way out, doom-laden pre-title sequence. Once again, Davies shows that he has a more finessed approach to plotting and pacing his stories than in Series One, which adds more credence to his input on 'The Impossible Planet'/'The Satan Pit' as the styles are so similar. In contrast to the stop-start narrative of 'Aliens of London'/'World War Three', 'Army of Ghosts' starts with two mysteries – the so-called ghosts and the mysterious Torchwood – and then proceeds to intertwine these plot strands tighter and tighter until, with a satisfying 'aaah' from the audience, it all starts to make sense as the parallel Earth and Queen Victoria from earlier in the series enter the mix. Unlike the info-dump of 'Bad Wolf', this really is a pay-off for the diligent viewer; the sort of arc that so delighted fans of *Babylon 5* and its ilk. Throughout this, both adding and serving as a delightful counterpoint to the tension, the story is healthily scattered with Davies's trademark humour, from Rose's fears that her mum has lost the plot, to the Doctor's passing off of Jackie as her daughter. Everything feels *real*, which is vitally important when you are being asked to accept both an Earth living in harmony with dead relatives and the existence of a top secret organisation (despite being mentioned virtually every week!) that exists only because of the Doctor. They even have Sutekh's sarcophagus! I admit to a personal bias concerning secret organisations based in Canary Wharf Tower, having set one of my novels there, but it's such an iconic – and TARDIS-like – building that it begs for inclusion. Unlike UNIT, Torchwood exists to appropriate alien technology to defend the Earth, which can be done with callous and deadly efficiency as we saw in 'The Christmas Invasion'. How far a step is it from that until mankind becomes the very monsters that the Doctor has always fought? Deep questions with no black or white answers: we are far, far from the days of 'If it's ugly, kill it', which too often characterised the early series. You'd have to have overdosed on 'Fear Her' not to know that the Cybermen were the ghosts, but even so, their actual manifestation is realised superbly. We love you, Graeme Harper! Elegant CGI creates armies of them across the world, and, for the first time ever in *Doctor Who*, you really do believe that the Earth is being invaded. They even break into a family's home, and are waiting on the landing! (I didn't want to mention 'Fear Her' again, but ...) Meanwhile, Davies has been spinning another conundrum: the void ship. It comes from Hell, it threatens reality, and it has allowed Mickey to return. And it's active! Common sense dictates that this is the fault of the Cybermen, but in a scene similar to the Doctor's questioning of the Emperor Dalek last year (although far less clumsy), we learn it isn't. And then we learn whose fault it is. *Doctor Who* really hasn't had any other cliff-hanger that has ever come close to this. Madness or genius? Pure fan indulgence or the bravest move since Sydney Newman appointed Verity Lambert? Only 'Doomsday' will tell... – *Craig Hinton*

In only two seasons, *Doctor Who* seems to have hit on a pattern of interleaved 'arc' and standalone episodes, with a continuing thread (last season, Bad Wolf; this year, Torchwood) mentioned in almost every story, the highly-publicised revival of a major foe (Daleks, Cybermen), developments with Rose's supporting characters (who come and go), ominous foreshadowings, and a two-parter written by RTD to cap things off, built around the departure of a leading cast member (then, Christopher Eccleston; now, Billie Piper) with a slightly-guessable cliff-hanger reveal of the big baddies who'll rampage next week (actually, the *same* big baddies both times). So 'Army of Ghosts' slots into the model of 'Bad Wolf', with a lot of UK TV in-jokes and a general sense of entertaining wheel-spinning before a very tasty set-up for the series finale. It opens with Rose alone on a beach and her voice-over, explaining that this is the story of how she dies – the pictures and the words contradict each other, but we trust that there's a clever get-out in the offing, especially since Rose proceeds not to get that much to do in the rest of the episode. Then, picking up on the thoughts about the passing nature of the Doctor's companions from 'School Reunion' and the shuttle through the story-so-far from 'Love & Monsters', we get up to speed on where we are two seasons into the revival and plunge back to a contemporary Earth, plagued with a large-scale supernatural manifestation. One of the canny things Davies has done since 'Rose', which was set in essentially our world, is establish that the London to which we keep returning is now an imaginary setting, altered by major alien incursions that can't be ignored. The witty montage of ghost-related TV programmes, from weather reports to a very funny soap snippet (with Barbara Windsor – this could have been a dreaded frame-breaking moment, but was brief and clever), is much less liable to date in future than the laboured gags about game shows in 'Bad Wolf'. The matter of the episode, which doesn't have much more plot than Cybermen leaking in from the neighbouring universe of 'Rise of the Cybermen'/'The Age of Steel', is getting to know the often-mentioned Torchwood Institute, which comes across as UNIT run by New Labour, an idea that is funny and scary at the same time. Tracy-Ann Oberman's mumsy-but-fanatical Yvonne Hartman has a lot of potential, as heroine and/or villain, and David Tennant's scenes with her are wonderful, with the Doctor cheerfully appalled at the ethos and methods of Torchwood but also responding with weird admiration for the lunatic enterprise. As for the kicker, and the trailer for next week's finale, it isn't quite up there with the subtler, more inspiring finish of 'Bad Wolf' but still managed to make a demoralised and dejected nation (the show had the misfortune to be broadcast to an audience who had just watched England kicked out of the World Cup!) want to tune in again next week. – *Kim Newman*

The new *Who* is populated by women with power and/or authority. Even the sexually ambiguous villains, Cassandra and the Wire, have female forms. Jackie Tyler is arguably the only woman the Doctor fears. Queen Victoria, Empress of India, has her modern equivalent in Yvonne Hartman, would-be empire-builder. Appropriately for a modern empire, her Torchwood is a corporation. You just know they have a mission statement, probably something about enhancing outcomes in terms of border protection. Hartman's Torchwood may be imperialists – down to their units of weight! – but next to the Cybermen and the Daleks, they're small beer. Superior military technology was one reason Britain held out against Hitler, but Hartman's Torchwood has barely begun to scavenge alien tech. They're easily lured by the promise of power – literally power, a new form of energy – and not only allow the Cybermen to invade, but actually help them along by shooting particles at the 'hole in the world'. They poke at the Sphere like children playing with an unexploded bomb. Faced with their enemies, Torchwood are pretty much useless: as in Wells' *War of the Worlds*, 'It's bows and arrows against the lightning.' But unarmed, of course, is not the same as helpless. The ultra-professional Torchwood compare poorly to the amateur Doctor. As Dr Singh explains that they've scanned the mysterious Sphere with 'every device imaginable', the Doctor whips out his cardboard 3D glasses and identifies it instantly as a void ship. Torchwood are all white coats and military uniforms and schedules; the Doctor throws together a ghost trap with what appear to be alien traffic cones hooked together by speaker leads, powered by a novelty student backpack. Throughout this season – and throughout *Doctor Who*, old and new – ordinary people have collided with the Doctor's extraordinary world and lost loved ones to it, or got them back changed – a new K-9, Mickey instead of Ricky, Ursula the paving slab. Like Trish Webber, Jackie sees her daughter in danger of losing her humanity. That might seem a small thing, in the face of so much alien wonder, not to mention so much human-centric SF cliché. But it's ordinary human courage, not super science or a massive budget, that allows Torchwood to retain some grace: Dr Singh offering himself for Dalek interrogation, Yvonne Hartman clinging to her loyalties even as her empire starts to crumble. In this show, individual improvisation beats corporate hubris every time, whether it's Satellite 5, the Cybus Corporation, or the universe's worst monsters. – *Kate Orman*

Hmmmm. Well, I got that bit wrong! The Upgrades destroyed at the start of episode six *didn't* 'transfer' across the dimensions. Indeed, looking over my wish list for the season, both 'Army of Ghosts' and 'Doomsday', were the two episodes this season that had the greatest number of my wish list items attached to them, and sadly few of those were fulfilled. I was so sure the ghosts were the counterparts of 'dead' people in the real world, crossing over from the parallel universe. One problem with coming up with elaborate theories like this is I'm often disappointed when the episodes fail to deliver along the same lines! (Note to self: don't do wish lists!) I've already expressed my dislike for the new Cybermen. What's been done to them has totally castrated the impact of the originals. For an analogy, imagine the worldwide reaction should four young Liverpudlian musicians form a band this year and call themselves the Beatles. While they might look and sound like J, P, G and R, they aren't J, P, G and R! And no matter how good they are, and how often they or others say it, *we know they aren't* the Beatles. So while it's all good and well the BBC calling, designing and publicising them as Cybermen, the Lumic Upgrades *are not* Cybermen. Lumic's monstrosities call themselves Cybermen, but this is not the same as them *being* Cybermen in 'our' universe. They don't share the same history, and that's a huge difference, in my book. But the *proper* Cybermen are still out there somewhere, so maybe next time we'll have *real* Cybermen -v- the Upgrades! Thankfully the Upgrades were on screen for only a short time (we have more Cyber-stomping next week to look forward to – not), so this episode really belonged to Torchwood. But after all the scattered (and sometimes unbelievably forced – hello 'The Satan Pit'!) references to it throughout this season, it was a let-down that the organisation turned out to be nothing more than a group of Men In Black wannabes. And I still find it hard to fathom how the Doctor could have remained totally ignorant of their existence all this time, especially when in the far, far futures of 'The Satan Pit' and 'Bad Wolf' its existence will apparently be known to mere civilians. It was a clever idea to have the Canary Wharf building as their HQ. I remember the updated *The*

EPISODE 212

Tomorrow People did something similar. But using yet another London landmark (cf the London Eye in 'Rose' and the Tower of London in 'The Christmas Invasion') as the location of a secret base was stretching the tease just a tad too far. What next – Buckingham Palace is an alien spaceship? Oh, but isn't Yvonne Hartman adorable! ('Oh, I should say. Hooray!') Please don't kill her off! The opening narration and Next Time clips intimate that 'Doomsday' is going to be a blood bath. Who will survive and who won't? Despite the presence of the Upgrades, I'm absolutely looking forward to seeing what happens next! – *Jon Preddle*

The funereal pace and tone of the opening scenes of 'Army of Ghosts' suggest that what we'll be getting afterwards will be something like a wake. Instead, the much publicised return of the Cybermen is casually trumped in the episode's final scenes by the super secret return of the Daleks. Next to those big hitters, the arrival of some flesh on the Torchwood bones that a season of allusions and implications have fashioned goes almost unnoticed. Beautifully directed, with pace and vision, by Graeme Harper, 'Army of Ghosts' combines many clever TV and movie industry in-jokes, a deliciously vampish performance by Tracy-Ann Oberman and two of Jackie Tyler's most perfectly realised moments; her sad little conversation with Rose about change and her criticism of the Doctor at reducing every vainglorious flight of fantasy to unwanted scientific reality. Typical Jackie – show her a Cyberman and she'll see the ghost of her dear old dad! Conceptualised as a, literal, doorway to Hell, the void works as a terrific device with which to tie up the loose ends left over from 'The Age of Steel', bringing back Mickey Smith and those stompy metal men from their alternate universe. Again, the dialogue is frequently fantastic ('They can shoot me dead but the moral high ground is mine!'). The episode also sees the Doctor at his most demonstrative and bossy and wise – particularly in his knowing scenes with Yvonne. This is the *Doctor Who* that the British public have embraced in 2005/06. As loud, flashy, abrasive and camp as its detractors would argue, but with a core goodness (in all its forms) that transcends the harsh and spiteful words of negativity. – *Keith Topping*

EDITOR'S REVIEW: 'Army of Ghosts' is a study in contrasts. On the one hand it's very exciting; full of fun and entertaining moments and great dialogue; manages quite a few shocking revelations; and never takes itself too seriously. On the other, it's about 30 minutes of preamble followed by another ten minutes of rapid, forceful escalation (exacerbated by more Murray Gold dramatic incidental music stings than in the rest of the series combined) and a denouement that comes out of left field. The end effect is of an episode that seems chaotic and all over the map.

Not that that's a complaint, because I really enjoyed 'Army of Ghosts'... especially on repeat viewing. I think the first time I watched it, the build-up-build-up-build-up-Daleks! was a bit much to appreciate, since the entire episode amounts to the television equivalent of sensory overload; suddenly everything's starting to connect, we're finally seeing Torchwood for the first time after being hit over the head with it as early as 'The Christmas Invasion' (not to mention the rumours that circulated after the throwaway mention in 'Bad Wolf'), and it's all non-stop Doctor-Fearful Yvonne-Arrogant and Jackie-Cheapshot in rapid succession. When I found myself taking it apart for this book, suddenly a lot of it made more sense and I began to appreciate it even more. If anything, Davies knows how to create drama out of what is basically nothing but false drama: the ghosts really aren't a threat until the Doctor gets busy; Torchwood aren't threatening to shoot him, because they seem to love him so much; and Mickey's there to prevent anything bad from happening to Rose.

Of course, much of the drama we infer from 'Army of Ghosts' lies in the *expectation* of what's coming in the following, final episode – with Daleks and Cybermen present together, you know there's going to be trouble. Daleks versus Cybermen. It's likely that most *Doctor Who* fans and viewers have awaited this ultimate showdown for four decades, even the ones that won't admit it. Of course, we're only treated to a glimpse of Daleks in the final seconds, as they arrive from within their mysterious spaceship – and one has to ask, if the Daleks are so powerful as to have created a void ship, why haven't they blown the TARDIS to kingdom come before now? – while the Cybermen are really treated as more of a secondary threat, even though they're the ones who are brainwashing the pretty, manicured executive-types and holding vigil in a construction area. (Didn't those construction guys even *notice* there were big silver suits of armour behind the sheets of plastic?)

The plot holes aside – and there are quite a number ('Scene Missing' could have gone on and on) – 'Army of Ghosts' succeeds in a number of ways. Tracy-Ann Oberman is probably one of the most refreshing 'villains' in recent *Doctor Who* memory, certainly for this season; she's cold and calculating and seems to be drunk in her own nationalism, and yet you can't help but like her when she calls herself a 'people person' and smiles her toothy smile. (One almost feels that the Doctor has a genuine camaraderie with her at times as well; here's someone he actually respects a little.) At first I thought seeing Noel Clarke as Mickey again would be a cheat, but it feels like an old friend coming home, and on second viewing it was a surprising real-world anchor in a situation gone terribly mad. And I must say, this is Camille Coduri's best work on *Doctor Who* to date – not that she's been anything but enjoyable throughout, but her line, 'If we end up on Mars, I'll kill you,' had me laughing out loud.

David Tennant, by the way, seems to be having a better time of things in the twelfth episode than Christopher Eccleston did last year, though I could have done with a bit less shtick on the *Ghostbusters* homage. And even though I've never seen a moment of *EastEnders*, I'd been told who the character Peggy Mitchell was; her cameo appearance, and the others, worked very well. It's nice to see a bit of pop culture in each of the two seasons we've witnessed (including the game show references last year in 'Bad Wolf'), and it's not a trend I'm anxious to be rid of any time soon.

'Army of Ghosts' has just the right amount of anticipation and excitement to lead into a proper finale... and it appears to have Daleks and Cybermen to spare. Might we also see a bit of Rose's death in the finale, perhaps, or just a muddle of metaphoric passing? Time will tell. – *Shaun Lyon*

213: DOOMSDAY

The interdimensional doorway between universes has been opened; the Cybermen have invaded Earth, while the void ship has revealed four Daleks carrying the mysterious Genesis Ark. Earth has become a battleground between the two most powerful enemies the Doctor has ever known; to stop them, he must make some very difficult choices. But in doing so, will he lose Rose Tyler forever?

FIRST TRANSMISSION: UK – 8 July 2006. US – January 2007. Canada – December 2006. Australia – 7 October 2006. New Zealand – 5 October 2006.
DURATION: 46'23"
WRITER: Russell T Davies
DIRECTOR: Graeme Harper
CREDITED CAST: David Tennant (The Doctor), Billie Piper (Rose Tyler), Camille Coduri (Jackie Tyler), Noel Clarke (Mickey Smith), Shaun Dingwall (Pete Tyler), Andrew Hayden-Smith (Jake Simmonds), Tracy-Ann Oberman (Yvonne Hartman), Raji James (Dr Rajesh Singh), Paul Kasey (Cyber Leader), Nicholas Briggs (Dalek/Cybermen Voices), Barnaby Edwards, Nicholas Pegg, Stuart Crossman, Anthony Spargo, Dan Barratt, David Hankinson (Dalek Operators), and introducing Catherine Tate as the Bride

Daleks originally created by Terry Nation.
Cybermen originally created by Kit Pedler and Gerry Davis.

WHERE AND WHEN: The Torchwood Tower, London, England, late 2007. Dårlig Ulv Stranden, or Bad Wolf Bay, in Norway. On board the TARDIS.

THE STORY UNFOLDS: Torchwood is at the centre of two invasions: The four Daleks that have come to Earth in the void ship are carrying with them something called the Genesis Ark, a device they are sworn to protect. The Cybermen begin a systematic takeover of the planet, telling the world they will remove fear, sex, class, colour and creed. They are impervious to guns, but not to shoulder-launched missiles.

The Cybermen offer an alliance with the Daleks; the latter consider the former an inferior species and want no part of it, and destroy them with ease ('This is not war, this is pest control'). The Daleks believe just one of them could destroy all five million Cybermen on Earth, as the Cybermen's only superiority is at dying. The Daleks are, however, afraid of the Doctor. Daleks have no concept of elegance. When a Cyber Leader is killed, the information required to lead is simply downloaded into another unit, which is then upgraded.

The four Daleks – named Thay, Caan, Sec and Jast – are members of the Cult of Skaro, something the Doctor previously thought was just a legend. The Cult of Skaro is a secret order reporting to no-one, not even the Emperor; its task was to imagine, to think as the enemy thinks, to find new ways of conquest. The four have brought the Genesis Ark to Earth; the Ark is not Dalek technology but in fact is the only artefact from the homeworld of the Time Lords that survived the Time War: a prison ship carrying millions of Daleks inside it. One touch from a time traveller will cause the Genesis Ark to activate; when it does, legions of Daleks pour out across the skies of London.

There is a Torchwood Institute in the alternate dimension, also in the Canary Wharf Tower; it developed the devices (small yellow badges worn around the neck) that allow Mickey, Jake and their soldiers to hop between realities. The other Torchwood is a shambles, but is controlled by the People's Republic (possibly the name of the new world government there). Pete Tyler works with the group. One of the soldiers Jake leads is named Chrissy.

When the Doctor left the other universe at the end of 'The Age of Steel', Pete and the Preachers sealed the factories with the Cybermen inside; a debate ensued about the fact that the people inside the Cybermen suits were still alive. While the people debated, the Cybermen infiltrated the other Torchwood, mapped themselves onto the Doctor's universe and vanished; it took the Cybermen three years to cross the void (due to the mass of five million Cybermen being carried over). The alternate Earth was left with a new golden age. However, the interdimensional breach is having a side effect on the other Earth – temperatures have risen by two degrees in six months, and the ice caps are melting. If this continues, the planet will eventually boil. The Doctor once told Rose that travellers in the TARDIS soak up harmless 'background radiation' as they move through the time vortex; the Daleks evolved so that they could use this radiation as a power supply.

The Doctor's 3-D glasses are actually a device enabling him to see the 'void stuff', a different type of background radiation caused by interdimensional travel between universes; he and Rose have it, as do Pete, Mickey and Jake. Closing the door to the other universe (which he nicknames 'Pete's World') will allow the others to survive there while he opens this universe up to the breach, sucking everything that has crossed through the void back inside.

The TARDIS orbits a supernova (the Doctor says he's 'burning up a sun') to use a tiny hole in the universe to contact Rose in the alternate dimension. She, Pete, Mickey and Jackie travel to Norway, to a spot about 50 miles outside Bergen where the Doctor is able to talk to her. Rose says the place is called Dårlig Ulv Stranden, which translates as 'Bad Wolf Bay' in Norwegian. When the breach closes, the transmission ends, leaving the Doctor alone in the TARDIS... but a woman wearing a wedding dress is suddenly there with him!

The black Dalek manages to escape via an emergency temporal shift before it can be drawn into the void with the others.

THE DOCTOR: He is shocked to discover the presence of the Daleks. He recognises that he's proof that emotions can be one's downfall, but he thinks hope is a good emotion too. He survived the Time War by fighting on the front lines and regrets the fall of Arcadia, which he hasn't come to terms with yet. He is heartbroken when Rose becomes trapped in the other universe, but is able to say goodbye to her... even though he can't tell her he loves her.

ROSE TYLER: She confronts the Daleks with her knowledge of their name and the existence of the Time War, demanding they keep her alive if they want to know how she knows. Jackie said Rose told her she was terrified of the Daleks. She chooses to remain behind with the Doctor when he sends the others into the alternate universe, but she's nearly sucked into the void – until Pete saves her. In the other universe, she hears the Doctor calling to her in her dreams, and takes a trip to a faraway place to talk to him again, allowing her one last chance to say goodbye. She intends to work for Torchwood in the other universe, to help defend the Earth; in her own universe, she's listed among the dead.

CHARACTER BUILDING: *Jackie Tyler* – She tells the Doctor he promised to save Rose and he's let them down. She later sees the alternate universe Pete for the first time; she doesn't care about the reason behind it, she's just glad to see him. She says there was never anyone else besides him. (Mickey and the Doctor exchange a sceptical look.) She's pregnant again (by Pete) at the end of the episode, and is expecting soon.

Yvonne Hartman – Her organisation defeated, she is led to the processing chamber and converted into a Cyberman. However, some part of her still remains; later, she stops the other Cybermen from approaching the Torchwood executive suite, buying the Doctor time.

Rajesh Singh – The Daleks extract information from his brain by applying their suction arms to his head, desiccating his body and killing him in the process.

Mickey Smith – Rose says he's the bravest human she's ever met. He accidentally opens the Genesis Ark by touching it. At the end of the story, he's back with Rose as part of her 'family' in the alternate universe.

Jake Simmonds – Having worked with Mickey in the alternate universe to defeat the Cybermen there, he now leads a squadron of soldiers back to this universe. Later he leads some Cybermen in an attack against the Daleks.

Pete Tyler (alternate) – Leading the fight in the other reality, he is persuaded by the Doctor to come to this universe to stop the Cybermen and Daleks. He says the daft little plans he used to work on in his universe made him rich (which we saw in 'Rise of the Cybermen').

TORCHWOOD: The episode takes place inside the Torchwood Institute, and there is a Torchwood in the alternate universe (as we learned in the mid-season two-parter).

BODY COUNT: Massive; there is widespread death and destruction on Earth as the Daleks and Cybermen open fire on people. Most of the Torchwood survivors are turned into Cybermen or killed; among the casualties are Yvonne Hartman and Rajesh Singh. One could always argue that Rose also died; she's listed among the dead back home, and feels in her heart as if a part of her has died ...

THE DOCTOR'S MAGICAL SONIC SCREWDRIVER: The Doctor brandishes his screwdriver (the Daleks call it a probe) to blow open the doors into the science lab. He also uses it to adjust the TARDIS console, allowing his projection to solidify a bit more to say goodbye to Rose.

REALITY BITES: Mickey says that the initial encounter between the Daleks and Cybermen – where neither will identify themselves first – is like Stephen Hawking arguing with a speaking clock. Professor Stephen Hawking is the Lucasian chair of mathematics of Cambridge University, renowned as one of the world's leading theoretical physicists and author of the famed book *A Brief History of Time*. Since undergoing a tracheotomy in 1985 he has spoken with the aid of an electronic voice synthesiser. The speaking clock is the 'TIM' service launched in the UK by British Telecom in 1936 and currently voiced by Brian Cobby. To access it in the UK you dial '123'.

The Doctor refers to *Mutt and Jeff*, a popular American newspaper comic strip, and *Shiver and Shake*, a British comic from the mid-1970's about a mischievous ghost (Shiver) and an elephant (Shake). (The Doctor says he's Shake.)

Pete Tyler's jeep drives all the way to Norway. Presumably they would have ferried over the jeep since there are no roads connecting the British Isles to Scandinavia.

LINKING THEMES: The opening of the episode features the same beach as seen in 'Army of Ghosts'. It is used once more at the end of the episode. Rose again states in the opening narration: 'This is the story of how I died.'

A clip of Rose touching the Dalek in the Series One episode 'Dalek' is seen, demonstrating how she brought it back to life, with the overlaid vortex effect first employed in 'Boom Town' used again here. Rose also tells one of the Daleks that the Emperor survived the Time War ('The Parting of the Ways') until it met her. She greets the Doctor again in Bad Wolf Bay, a reference to the previous year's Bad Wolf storyline.

In the alternate universe, Harriet Jones (from 'Aliens of London', 'World War Three' and 'The Christmas Invasion') has become President.

Dalek casings are made out of polycarbide, as previously referred to in the *Doctor Who* story 'Remembrance of the Daleks' in 1988 (though they were made from Dalekanium in 'The Dalek Invasion of Earth' in 1964). Their homeworld, Skaro, is named for the first time in the new series; it was well known in the original. ('The Parting of the Ways' featured references to the Dalek home planet, but it was never named.) The Cult of Skaro represents the latest in a long line of Dalek attempts to understand their enemies (or to find what they refer to as the 'human factor', as originally established in 'The Evil of the Daleks' in 1967). This is not the first time Daleks have had names: 'The Evil of the Daleks' saw the Doctor give names to three Daleks implanted with the human factor. He called them 'Alpha', 'Beta' and 'Omega'. The Daleks unit of time is the 'rel'; this is the first reference to it in the television series, though the term was used in the 1960s cinema films *Dr Who and the Daleks* and *Daleks – Invasion Earth 2150 AD* and in various comic strips and in audios produced by Big Finish.

This is the first time in televised *Doctor Who* that the Daleks and the Cybermen have encountered each other... although these are not really the Cybermen from the Doctor's universe.

The Doctor repeats Jackie's full name, Jacqueline Andrea Suzette Tyler; he learned this in 'Father's Day'. He tells the alternate Pete that he was at their wedding (in this universe), where Pete got her name wrong during the ceremony.

A planet called Arcadia was previously mentioned in the *Doctor Who* novel *Deceit* by Peter Darvill-Evans, published in 1993 by Virgin; there is no indication, however, that there is any connection between the two.

As in the other Cybermen episodes this year, the presence of a partially Cybernised female recalls both the Big Finish story 'Spare Parts' and 'Real Time', a BBCi online serial made by Big Finish.

SCENE MISSING: The closing scenes of 'Doomsday' are rife with unanswered questions... How *does* the Doctor close the breach between universes when all he seems to do is open the void to suck the Daleks and Cybermen in, and close it when it's done? How is Pete able to come over and save Rose if the breach on the side of the alternate universe is closed off? How does Pete know *exactly* where and when to arrive in order to save Rose's life before she's taken into the void, and how does he manage to stand right by the void for several seconds without getting sucked in himself?

It doesn't end there... What's happened to the Cybermen? We see Daleks fly into the void breach, but no Cybermen are seen to enter it, although they do get lifted off the ground. Are they sucked in as well and we just don't see it? If so, how do they get there so quickly from their various locations all over the world? Or perhaps they, like the Daleks, return to the void the way they came, passing through smaller fissures (like the cracks in the pane of glass as demonstrated by the Doctor) and materialising between worlds. (This was Russell T Davies's intention, as recounted in the episode's online commentary, but it was not explained in the episode itself.) Why do all the Daleks get sucked in through a small hole in an office window in the Torchwood Tower instead of being sucked in from all sides, breaking the walls on their way? How do the Doctor and Rose survive with thousands of Daleks coming at them; doesn't even one of the Daleks collide with them on the way in? Moreover, the event doesn't appear to have damaged anything inside the control room: not the side walls (despite several Daleks bouncing off them), the lighting panel or the steel conduits in front of the wall on which the void breach opens up. Just what are Torchwood's walls made of?

How does Rose remember defeating the Dalek Emperor? She didn't have any memory of the experience when she absorbed the time vortex. The Doctor could have told her about it, but she appears here to have more confidence and conviction about it than would be consistent with that. Why does the Yvonne-Cyberman cry? (It appears to be some sort of metallic fluid or oil, but still ...) Why does she speak with a modified version of her own voice when all the other Cybermen speak with the familiar male metallic voice? Although it's possible hers was a 'rushed' part-Cybernisation, why do we not see more of these?

If the void needs to be closed permanently in order for both universes to be safe, then why does the Doctor – who supposedly champions the cause of everyone, not just his companion – open it again to talk to her? By sacrificing a star, no less. (Perhaps this is simply hyperbole and he is just using the energy of a star that has already gone supernova). We have previously been told by the Doctor that travel between universes is impossible ('Rise of the Cybermen'). Here, however, it becomes commonplace with the aid of the yellow disc devices that everyone in the alternate reality Torchwood appears to have...

What happens to the Dalek void ship? It appears to fold in upon itself, but is never referred to again.

Why do the Daleks not detect the mayday signal being sent by the Dalek eventually captured and taken to van Statten's museum in 2012? Why, in 'Dalek', do van Statten, Adam and everyone else at the base not recognise the 'Metaltron', as they call it, when the Daleks very visibly invaded London *en masse* in 2007? Is this perhaps more evidence of the theory first suggested by 'The Unquiet Dead' that (maybe as a consequence of the Time Lords' downfall?) the course of history can be changed? In other words, is it possible that the people the Doctor and Rose meet in 2012 in 'Dalek' and 'Fear Her' would recall, for example, the Auton attack of 2005, but know nothing of the Dalek/Cybermen invasion of 2007, because history has yet to be changed (by virtue of the Doctor's later involvement in the events of 'Army of Ghosts'/'Doomsday') to 'incorporate' that?

How do the two universes operate at different speeds? Pete says it's been three years since the Cybermen left, while it can't have been very long since 'The Age of Steel' took place; it's still 2007 in 'our' universe. Are Pete, Mickey, Jake, *et al* travelling in time as well as space?

How does the Doctor contact Rose to tell her to come to the beach in Norway? How would she know where to look for him, if all she's heard is his voice... in dreams, no less? How do the Doctor's 3-D glasses work when he's looking at a monitor – a digitised display of what's actually happening? Unless Torchwood's security cameras are set up to see the void-stuff and encode them in such a way that the Doctor would be able to see them with his glasses ...

How do the Daleks identify the Doctor as an enemy without even knowing who he is? (This is before Rose tells them.) Also, for someone who's never seen the Cybermen before, Yvonne seems to know exactly what upgrading means. How does she know that the Cybermen are metal casings with human brains?

BEHIND THE SCENES: As for 'Army of Ghosts', scenes for this episode were recorded at RAF St Athan in the Vale of Glamorgan in Wales (the Torchwood warehouse), Brackla Bunkers near Bridgend (various corridor and stairwell scenes), the Southerndown beach in the Vale of Glamorgan (the beach sequences at the end) and at the studios in Newport.

Davies notes in the online commentary that, while Rose says she is to die in both 'Army of Ghosts' and 'Doomsday', this was never really considered as an option as it would have been inappropriate in such an upbeat television series. Most copies of the script that were circulated to the cast and crew omitted the final few scenes of the episode (everything after Rose is trapped in the other universe). This was in order to protect the secrecy of the ending. Davies was unsure until a late draft who would save Rose: Mickey or Pete.

The episode ends with a note that the series will return at Christmas in 'The Runaway Bride'. The bride's name is unmentioned in this episode; Davies notes in the online commentary that her name is Donna. Catherine Tate's guest appearance was kept quiet prior to transmission and was not reported in the press until after the episode had aired.

The episode was cut by six minutes prior to transmission, for timing reasons. Much of the deleted footage consisted of exterior shots of the Cybermen attacking London.

DULCET TONES: A similar version of the music originally played when Rose entered the TARDIS for the first time in 'Rose' is used during her farewell sequences. The piece here in 'Doomsday' is accompanied by rhythm and speeded up a bit.

TECHNICAL GOOFS: At various points during the climactic battle, scenes of widespread damage and fires are seen through the windows of Torchwood, but are missing in exterior shots.

INTERNAL CONSISTENCY: The episode takes place over a couple of hours at most, from the time of the Daleks' and Cybermen's arrival to their demise in the void at the end. It is unclear how much time then passes for the Doctor until he arrives at the supernova; for Rose and her family, it has obviously been several months, because Jackie is expecting a child and they have all settled into their new lives.

TARDISODE #13: An emergency broadcast from the British government includes footage of Cybermen firing on the population. Suddenly the studio is attacked by Daleks and the reporter is exterminated.

REVIEWS

If you thought last year's 'The Parting of the Ways' was a phenomenal series conclusion, you had no idea. 'Doomsday' is a sublime mix of action, suspense and intense emotion that can't help but move viewers to tears, whether they're witnessing two lonely people rediscovering their long-lost spouses from across time and space or watching the tragic and touching departure of Rose. It's never a cheery occasion when a companion says goodbye, but this is a special case given the way the new show has crafted the Doctor/Rose relationship into one of absolute love if not physical consummation. The poignant final goodbye between Rose and the

Doctor on a wintry beach in Norway will cause even the most hard-hearted anti-'shipper' fan to reach for the Kleenex. And there are Daleks and Cybermen! In the same story! What more could you ask for? That this is Billie Piper's last episode as Rose is well documented, but it's worth noting that this also means the departure of Noel Clarke's Mickey and Camille Coduri's Jackie Tyler as recurring characters. For fans who began with the new series of *Doctor Who*, this is a far more profound change than the loss of Christopher Eccleston's ninth Doctor last year. Then we were simply losing the weird alien that Rose had grown to love; this time we're losing the emotional heart and soul – the human touchstone – of the series. Never mind what the Doctor is going to do without Rose; will the series *itself* survive? Hopefully it will, but it might take a while to adjust to a new person in the Doctor's life. The Doctor/Rose story is beautifully handled, with both Tennant and Piper giving their finest performance to date. But there are a few flaws, most likely due to the justifiable weight given to the emotional side of the story. For one thing, the much-hyped Dalek-Cyber war winds up lasting a very short time, with only a few limited shots of Dalek swarms over London and a couple of dozen marching Cybermen to indicate that a worldwide conflict is taking place. Then there's the apparent ability of Torchwood head Yvonne Hartman to retain her personality after Cyber-conversion and shed tears of oil; oh please. But there are delightful touches for continuity buffs as well, like the first mention of the Dalek's home world Skaro in the new series, to the Daleks' use of 'rels' for measurement, to the flawless interaction between these two classic monster races as they verbally spar for the first time. Is it any surprise that the pepperpots easily get the upper... um, plunger? Another thrilling addition is Rose's taunting of the black Dalek; five million Cybermen don't scare the creature at all, but one mention of the Doctor makes this heartless war machine back up in terror. Excellent. But it all comes down to the Doctor and Rose. In the end, the lonely Time Lord almost admits his true feelings for the young woman who restored his soul, and we last see her standing alone on that beach with her family waiting to comfort her, knowing that it will be a long time before she can leave her love for the Doctor behind. Who can blame her? As for Rose, Eccleston's Doctor said it best – she was just 'fantastic'. And she'll be missed... – *Arnold T Blumberg*

Was it all a dream? It almost seems like it now to me. Daleks and Cybermen in the same story, bitchily smacking down each other; Pete Tyler's return; Rose's heart wrenching departure... it all seems so much for one story, and yet there it was: 45 minutes of non-stop action, emotion, poignance, drama, apocalypse (in so many ways). So many wonderful moments: the Cyber-Oberman's tear; the Daleks declaring that exterminating the Cybermen would be 'pest control'; Jackie and Pete reuniting; the Doctor's gut-wrenching scream as Rose falls toward the void; the Doctor pressing his face against a blank and empty wall. Was it all a dream? No it wasn't. These were moments of greatness: David Tennant delivering an awe-inspiring performance, full of restraint but all the while hinting at powerful emotion; Billie Piper glorious in her last hurrah; the rest of the cast – particularly Shaun Dingwall and Camille Coduri – being simply glorious. (Was it a dream? Was this not shot at the same time as the unbelievably risible Cyberman two-parter earlier this season?) Graeme Harper's direction is pitch-perfect – it was brilliant to have the Doctor almost entirely in close-up on the beach – and Murray Gold captures the devastation of the loss of Rose with a superb musical cue. And then there's the ending. Imagine being able to have a two minute conversation with a person you love more than anything who has died in an untimely fashion, and this is the only chance you have to say anything... That's the situation Rose and the Doctor are in here. The emotion of it feels absolutely real. (I watched in a room full of hard-bitten *Doctor Who* fans, mostly male, and I don't think there was a dry eye in the room afterward.) What I love most about 'Doomsday' is that in the midst of all the cosmic drama going on, it still knows that the real drama lies in the Doctor being separated from the companion who defined this new series, and the five minutes it takes to do that is final but fitting, tying up everything (even 'Bad Wolf'!) but also acknowledging that this is *Doctor Who*, and life must go on for the Doctor... Was it all a dream? It could have been. 'Doomsday' is in some ways the finale that the second season doesn't really deserve to have, bringing thematic unity to a season that lacked the cohesiveness of the previous one (even though it did, overall, have better stories). But it's so good, you're grateful that it did. Was it all a dream? If it was, I hope to have an even better one soon. Roll on 2007! – *Graeme Burk*

'Doomsday' is everything 'The Parting of the Ways' should have been – and then it's a little bit more. Somehow, almost impossibly, Davies has managed to pull together all the necessary strands and elements and connect them in a story that is very, very satisfying. There are a few tiny little casualties here and there – the various implications of last week's 'ghosts' have been completely forgotten – but they're not the sort of issues you're going to remember until long after the episode's done. And once that's happened, you'll need time to get a handkerchief, wipe your eyes and let it all soak in. What impressed me most is how densely packed 'Doomsday' really is. I didn't notice what time of night I started watching the episode, so when Rose looked set to fall into the void I was, quite literally, on the edge of my seat: surely we had now reached the end of the 45 minutes? Even on second viewing, it still felt an extraordinarily long episode, but in no way badly paced. The story does stop dead on occasion for little, emotional moments, but they seem needed when the stakes are so high and we, the audience, already know the Doctor will walk out of this adventure alone. Admittedly, my favourite villains, the Cybermen, get completely *owned* by the Daleks, but they have some great lines along the way. (The much-trailed Cyber broadcast is especially effective.) In fact, the entire face-off between the two enemies works far better than I ever expected, even if the Cybermen don't manage to destroy one single Dalek! It's a terse and appropriate backdrop for Rose's last stand and, for once, a companion's departure actually feels like it *means* something. Okay, Billie blubs on so long it's embarrassing, and her much-heralded 'death' is swept under the carpet with an offhand line, but... how can anyone not be moved by that final goodbye? I do find it interesting that we got such a climactic finale for what was, by and large, an anti-climactic season. This is not to say I disliked this year's *Doctor Who*; in fact, it felt more like 'real' *Doctor Who* to me than last year's. I admired the fact it didn't aim for an obvious plot arc, although that may end up costing it American viewers this autumn. And I was perfectly satisfied with the fairly steady run of above-average stories, as opposed to the extreme highs and lows of the first year. But the truth is, it all doesn't really add up to anything bigger. A modern television season tends to be one where you can look back at the end and see a 'bigger picture', and aside from some vague recurring themes in the early episodes, there's little of that to be found here at all. So where can *Doctor Who* go from this point onward? Is it on a slow but steady decline? Well, even with another traditionally-structured set of stories, there are a couple of elements that could potentially lead to a very strong third year. To be honest, David Tennant still hasn't quite found his feet – and as much as I tend to prefer his Doctor, his performance lacks the gravity and range of Christopher Eccleston's, some of which may be down to freshman jitters. He also, quite desperately, needs a new companion who suits him better. Maybe he'll find her in Freema Agyeman. For all my little reservations, I'm very much looking forward to the next year of

Doctor Who. It could have gone so wrong, but 'Doomsday' is hardly a cataclysmic end to the show. Instead, it is a prelude to a whole new range of possibilities. – *Sarah Hadley*

Most science-fiction series make at least a notional effort to convince the viewer that they take place in the 'real' universe. They do this by such methods as being set so far ahead in the future as to make it impossible to contradict them, for the moment at least, or by taking place on such a scale or under such supposed secrecy that the rest of the world never really notices. No such half-measures for Davies's *Doctor Who*. With its Daleks bringing down terror from the skies of London and armies of Cybermen marching the streets of the world, 'Doomsday' divorces itself completely from any tenuous connection with reality and sees out Series Two in fairly spectacular fashion. This doubtless creates all sorts of continuity errors – not least in relation to episodes such as 'Dalek' last year – but on the whole, as an excuse to insert a massive great battle between the Daleks and the Cybermen, the show's two most iconic alien races, you'd have to say it's worth it. As should always be the case, the Daleks lord it over the Cybermen, both in cutting dialogue and in literally cutting the pathetic tin soldiers to pieces. I know there are some die-hard fans of the Cybermen, and doubtless they will have been disappointed that they were so weak as to barely even scratch a single Dalek – hey, even humanity managed to down at least one Cyberman – but I for one have never liked the silver giants and was cheering every Dalek ray-gun shot. But this episode was about more than simply spectacular set-tos between alien monsters, as good as they were. The departure of Rose Tyler, indeed her whole family and her sometime boyfriend too, marks the end of an era for *Doctor Who*, after just two series. Although it does seem a little too convenient perhaps that Pete popped up just in the nick of time to rescue her from being sent to Hell – a very *Buffy the Vampire Slayer* fate – what would action-adventure be without last-minute rescues against all odds? The final farewell scene on the beach is a fine little coda to Rose's time in the TARDIS, but for me the real wrench of the ending is the Doctor's scream as Rose was sucked towards the breach – a great piece of raw emotional acting from David Tennant. He's not been perhaps quite as impressive in the role as Christopher Eccleston was, but those are very big shoes to fill, and on the whole he's done a fine job this year of creating the new character of the tenth Doctor in his own right. With a year's experience under his belt and lessons learned, he can only get better as time passes, I feel. But Billie Piper is gone, her contribution to the new series having been a massive one, and again a large gap has been left to be filled. But such changes have always been the bedrock of *Doctor Who*'s success, and I feel sure the viewers will be coming back at Christmas after such a fine, dramatic, exciting episode. Especially given *that* brilliant cliff-hanger. – *Paul Hayes*

So it is Daleks versus Cybermen after all. Unlike at the start of 'The Satan Pit', Davies doesn't let up with the tension or the black humour. Okay, so we all know where this could be heading, and, at the risk of sounding churlish, 'Doomsday' does roll out logically with few left-field surprises. But is that a bad thing? After all the criticism he came in for in Series One, Davies has eschewed virtually all plot contrivances in favour of inevitability, irrevocability and a mounting sense of desperation from everyone, but especially the Doctor. This both is and isn't just about the Doctor: whole universes are in danger. But he's the lonely god, and after lording it over all and sundry for the last 13 weeks with a knowing smugness, he realises that, with his people gone, all this is his responsibility. He finally has to pay the price for his arrogance. This is why 'Doomsday' works so well. Daleks versus Cybermen is inherently boring. The

Cybermen may be terrifying to humans, but to the Daleks they are merely cannon fodder. We know from 'Dalek' that just these four are sufficient to wipe out the entire Cyber-army, so when the Genesis Ark finally spews forth millions, it really is 'game over'. But this is merely the backdrop, however apocalyptic (and beautifully done!). No, the real drama is where it has to be, where it's been building since 'Rose'. Rose's journey is coming to an end, and the pieces have been fitting into place for two years. Davies once said that the Doctor brings out the very best in people, and nowhere is that more true than with the extended Tyler clan: Jackie, belying her initially sluttish persona, has been transformed into someone who puts others first; Mickey has bloomed into a fearless resistance fighter; and Pete is not only alive, but successful. The perfect nuclear family, all waiting for Rose while the Doctor and the truly magnificent Cyber-Yvonne logically – and, ironically, not so logically – defeat the baddies and save two universes. Except Rose chooses the Doctor. That was inevitable: he's her (platonic) lover, her best friend, the person who is worth all the monsters. And we feel his pain as her grip slips... and then, in a beautiful reversal of 'Father's Day', she is saved by her father. But saved in what way? The Doctor and Rose are separated by an entire universe. She might as well be dead. They really do pay the price for their superiority in the highest personal coin. But if there's been one theme throughout this series, it's that love, faith and perseverance will always shine through. Only the Doctor could burn up a star to say goodbye! Rose now has all she ever wanted way back in 'Rose', but she has lost her soul mate. And, with the unspoken words and the single tear, so has the Doctor. In my review of 'The Girl in the Fireplace', I asked 'Has he ever looked so sad, so old, so *alone*?' Now, he really is. For now... Davies said he wanted an epic, a war in heaven between the bronze and silver gods. In the wrong hands, this could have been gratuitous nonsense. But by using it – and almost all of the other stories this series – as a backdrop to personal dramas and character development, Series Two has, overall, been a resounding success. – *Craig Hinton*

Two big things happen in 'Doomsday', as is appropriate for a season finale that tries valiantly to match 'The Parting of the Ways' from last year even as it evokes 'Flashpoint' (the last episode of 'The Dalek Invasion of Earth' all the way back in 1964). The show has to wrap up an epic-scale event – the fanfic-like war between the Cybermen and the Daleks – almost as a B story, while devoting much of the episode to the departure (ie: the writing-out) of Billie Piper's Rose. First off, she doesn't die – and all that 'This is how I died' stuff is arrant writer's puffery that doesn't square with the character at all – but she does wind up, along with her entire supporting cast, shunted into a parallel universe we're promised the Doctor can never visit again and rewarded with a new-made happy family that we assume will in time balance the loss of her travelling life with the Doctor. Given that there has been so much stress on the Doctor-Rose relationship throughout the series, it's no surprise that Davies goes for all-out tear jerking and declarations of undying love. However, in a case of crying (bad) wolf too often, when the final parting comes, it's after two seasons' worth of misty-eyed moments and is just another one rather than a really big blub. In this particular show, I was more moved by the trickling fluid from the teardrop Cyber-eye of the transformed Yvonne Hartman and the clinch between Jackie and Parallel World Pete as they decide they don't care if they really are who they think they are. As leavings from the series go, I think the understated finish of 'The Green Death', with the Doctor quietly slipping out unnoticed from a companion's engagement party, worked a lot better. The void-hopping and the Cyberman-Dalek conflict business still feel to me like the kind of contrivances necessary to get a crossover going, and that big sucking chasm in reality that pulls in both evil races at the end is no more credible or workable than the magnetic effect in 'Flashpoint' – but there's still room for good stuff in the dissing session between the named Daleks and the Cyber-Leader and the zapping battle between the two armies. David Tennant, after very shaky beginnings, has been finding his character lately – and it's possible that losing Rose, a holdover from the Christopher Eccleston Doctor, will allow him to become the actual star of his own show, which is probably a good thing. It strikes me that the Doctor seems less bereft than relieved in his quiet moment before the hook that sets up the Christmas special. – *Kim Newman*

When did Rose know that she would never leave the Doctor? Was it when she essentially proposed to him in 'The Impossible Planet'? Or when he asked her how long she would stay with him, while they watched the manta rays flying overhead? If there was one specific moment when it clicked into place in her head, I think it was in 'The Satan Pit', when she would not leave him alone, even if she could only be with him in death. Loneliness is what this season of *Doctor Who* has been all about. Cassandra, long ago the life of the party; widows and widowers, Victoria, Isobel, Pete, Jackie; the abandoned Sarah Jane; Chloe and the Isolus. Even the Daleks, 'Locked inside a cold metal cage – completely alone.' And loneliest of all, the Doctor, homeless, nationless, peerless. When 'Doomsday' arrives, Rose chooses the Doctor over her patchwork family – if it comes to it, she'll take dying with him over living with them. But the Doctor is not her mate, her lover, her husband, her family, and can never be; this is 'the one adventure [he] can never have', or, like Peter Pan, 'the one joy from which he must be forever barred'. I think Rose knows this, deep down, and knows she will lose her humanity if she stays with him – like any visitor to Fairyland. But she simply cannot leave him. And as in 'The Satan Pit', I don't think it's because she's clinging to a naïve, girly dream of sex and babies. Her hopeless dream is of a Doctor who never has to be alone again. 'He does it alone, Mum. But not any more.' Rose has come light years since we first met her. She defies the Daleks; once again, she saves the Earth. Her experience and her ability to lead and inspire will, with Torchwood, no doubt help save it again. Of course she is shattered to lose the Doctor; that only reminds us she is very young, with adventure ahead of her (and I'll bet lots of sex and babies too). When the wall is shut between them, Rose doesn't turn to her family. Before she can accept what's happened, she needs the closure of that final conversation with the Doctor. It's the sort of talk every mourner must wish, with all their heart, that they could have. When their last words are said, that's when she runs to her mum, back to her family. Rose, at least, will never be alone. And the Doctor? 'I'll just have to hold on tight. I've been doing it all my life.' – *Kate Orman*

Oomvay iff von da vool... vad a diffill... um, let me just take my foot out of my mouth. 'Doomsday' is wonderful! What a visual feast. And I thought it would be awful. I was overly critical of 'Rise of the Cybermen', as I can now see how the whole Cyber-saga fits into RTD's grand scheme of things. (In fact you could call this Cyber-quartet 'The Four to Doomsday'!) While I still think the synchronised Cyber-Stomp was a bad move, and the Upgrades should have been built from salvaged Cyber-technology from the real universe, the Cyber-clompers managed to be not so irritating this time around. But only just. So, Daleks -v- Cybermen – a clash of the titans long-desired by many fans, this 'hard to please' one included. But now that it's been and gone, it was a bit of a let down. I mean, we wanted Daleks and Cybermen blowing the crap out of each other right across the universe, not just shooting at close range inside one building in London! We (and they) deserve better than that! But the cop out 'black Dalek escapes to fight another day' shot no doubt means more Daleks in Series Three! So, this was it – the emotionally-charged departure for Rose, and what a shock/surprise/shock/surprise ending (although having the Doctor separated from Rose and then contacting her via a 'hologram' was done before in 'The Parting of the Ways': that's one gripe I have about Series Two – so many of the themes and so much of the imagery were repeated from last year). I had a cold when I saw 'Doomsday', so I had good reason to be sniffing at the end – or at least, that's my excuse! More was said about the relationship in that wonderful shot of the Doctor and Rose separated on either side of the wall (*à la* the Doctor and the werewolf in 'Tooth and Claw') than they said to each other later at Bad Wolf Bay. And what's astonishing is that Tennant and Piper recorded this episode halfway through the production schedule. After completing her departure scenes, Piper still had another five more episodes to record. I loved Tennant in this episode. There have been a couple of episodes where I've nearly cringed at his overacting, but when he holds back, as he does here, he's simply superb. Um, my Gun 'n' Rose theory (see my 'New Earth' review) was rubbish, I thought Rose and the Doctor would end up doing a body-swap at the end of the season. But at a pre-'Doomsday' fan get-together I did guess correctly the fates of Rose, Pete, Jackie and Mickey! Yay! I got one right! What do you mean there's no prize? Spoilsports... 'Doomsday' was the perfect ending to the season and a satisfying denouement to Rose's story. It was also a satisfactory conclusion for Jackie and Mickey. It's only proper that Mickey and Rose ended up together again. (But what of poor Sarah Jane Smith, left maybe waiting for Rose to get in touch ...?) So, bye bye Billie, Camille and Noel. Thanks for the joy-ride! You will be missed! – *Jon Preddle*

Shockingly, 'Doomsday' almost doesn't work. For 37 minutes it's a non-stop rollercoaster of thrillingly realised set-pieces; fast, furious, manic, helter-skelter. It's also witty and gregarious, touching and breathless, full of humanity; and even the one great cop-out in it – Pete saving Rose from an eternity in Hell – is *perfect*. And then, it's followed by a slightly disappointingly dragged-out (albeit necessary) final six or seven minutes. Not that there's anything specifically wrong with most of the sequences in that latter part of the episode; they just feel as though they belong in another show. Though it must be said, 'I'm burning up a sun to say goodbye' is one hell of a parting line! And yet, in that essential conundrum, we have the episode's reason for existence – this is the end of a 27 episode arc – not just Rose's story, but Jackie's, Mickey's and Pete's too. That it achieves, some considerations like love aside, a mostly happy ending is to the episode's, and to the series', ultimate credit. Television has so little time for small victories these days. Raspberry-rippled with continuity references, the laugh-out-loud funny bitching between the Daleks and the Cybermen ('This is not war, this is pest control!'), trauma and, as so often this year, humanity ('Five million Cybermen, easy. One Doctor, now you're scared!'), 'Doomsday' hurtles towards its inevitable, signposted conclusion. And then, like Rose, it hits a well. What we're left with, thereafter, are a few minutes where the episode sags, sighs for lost friends and lovers, before giving Billie and David a moment to shine like the stars they are, and then, an odd (and oddly realised) coda that suggests a confusing, if not necessarily unamusing, immediate future for the Doctor. – *Keith Topping*

EDITOR'S REVIEW: Oh dear. I'm afraid the jury is still out on this one, because there's much to admire about 'Doomsday' and yet so much to be concerned about, and I would hate to think that I'm still too lost in the fray of what is undoubtedly one of the biggest events of the British television year to paint an accurate picture. Yes, there are parts of 'Doomsday' I really like, and yes, there are parts I truly loathe; as with last year's season finale, I found myself somewhat let down at the end – though I was frankly far more unhappy with some of what I saw on first viewing than I am now, having watched the episode a number of times and taken in more of the bigger picture.

Russell T Davies is an adventure man. There's no doubt in my mind that he could one day pen an adventure series to rival *Star Wars* or *Indiana Jones*; he knows how to take the pieces of the puzzle and mix them up to create something to amaze the audience, frighten the children and win award after award. What disappoints me about 'Doomsday' – and I think disappoints is the word I'd use, rather than saying I dislike it – is that it's like a wading pool, wide and inviting but only six inches deep. Far be it from me to say that's a problem; some of my favourite films and television series have rated far higher on the flash-factor scale than they have on intricate, sophisticated storytelling, and I like a good old action-adventure like the next guy. The problem is that *Doctor Who* is supposed to be brilliant and insightful, with those moments of crystal clarity when everything fits. I remember sitting in my car on a long drive one weekend listening to one of the early *Doctor Who* audio plays by Rob Shearman and having a moment where I suddenly exclaimed, to no-one in particular, 'Brilliant!' That's the *Doctor Who* I crave... but with so many holes in the logic in 'Doomsday', I find myself a bit let down. The Cybermen just gave up and moved to our world? Mickey's here, when it was supposedly impossible to cross the gap in the first place? Pete shows up to save Rose *exactly* where and when it's necessary, and a great big whirlpool sucking the life out of the universe doesn't affect either of them?

These are story quibbles, yes, but they add up, and thinking about them doesn't make things any more enjoyable. It's the little things that get you, although I will say that I *loathed* the Dalek's line about this being 'pest control' at first and managed to smile the last time I watched it, so that's progress. Maybe like 'Army of Ghosts', this will grow on me further, much in the same way that 'The Parting of the Ways' has over time. But I *would* like the series to focus less on the melodrama next year – the 'I did my duty'-insert-metallic-tear-here, the long weepy shots of Rose – and more on the edgier science-fiction we thought we might see when *Doctor Who* was brought back.

I recognise that many people love the final scenes between Rose and the Doctor, and I won't quibble with that. I argued in *Back to the Vortex* that Billie Piper was the best thing to happen to *Doctor Who* since the announcement that Davies was taking the lead, and I'm going to miss her terribly next year. The farewell does go on far too long, and I do have to wonder about the deep devotion the Doctor has to Rose, beyond any relationship ever experienced in the original series, even though from what we've seen there's no reason to think that it should be that deep. But no matter; the emotional heart of the series has been Rose Tyler since it came back, and if that's the way things need to play out here, so be it. I must confess I was greatly amused that the TARDIS signal brought them all to Bad Wolf Bay ...

One thing I would like to say: I *loved* the ending. Unlike most of you reading this, probably, I hadn't the slightest idea who Catherine Tate was, until I heard she would be appearing as the series finale's last big twist. It comes out of nowhere, it's surprising and disconcerting and it's absolutely a brilliant way to end the season.

It's been quite a journey, these long months... we've had great episodes and not-so-great episodes, key character scenes and defining *Doctor Who* moments. The programme has come into its own, not just as a continuation of a series from yesteryear but as a contemporary drama series in its own right, setting a tone for today's television programming. While there have been missteps and a few obstacles, *Doctor Who* still has a marvellous leading man (David Tennant, you're fabulous; I'd only ask you to tone down the hypertheatrics a *bit!*), a great formula and capable people at the helm who know how to make the public happy. If these past 27 episodes have been any indication of what BBC Drama is capable of, then *Doctor Who* shouldn't just enjoy a long and healthy future; it should bring about a renaissance in British adventure television we'll all benefit from. One might call that a bonus; I call it the *real* trip of a lifetime. – *Shaun Lyon*

APPENDICES

APPENDIX A:
CAST AND CREW INDEX

The following is an index of *credited* cast and crew associated with the first two series of *Doctor Who*. It does not include anyone not specifically credited to a role or position. The roles played by actors are in **boldface**, crew positions are *italicised*; the numerals match the episode number.

Note: Ranges of episodes presented refer only to the 27 televised episodes of *Doctor Who* to date, but do not include the BBC digital special 'Attack of the Graske'; credits for this production are indicated separately by its number, 200A. Since there are were no credits presented onscreen for the *Children in Need* special (199) other than the two leads during the opening sequence, it is not included in this index.

Acorah, Derek: **Himself** (212)
Adams, Christine: **Cathica** (107)
Adams, Jamie: *Assistant Editor* (109, 110)
Agbaje, Abisola: **Chloe** (211)
Agyeman, Freema: **Adeola** (212)
Ahearne, Joe: *Director* (106, 108, 111-113)
Aitken, Paul: *Props Chargehand* (201-206); *Assistant Props Master* (207-213)
Akashi, Takako: **Japanese Newsreader** (212)
Akram, Hajaz: **Indian Newsreader** (212)
Allan, Lucy: *Stunt Performer* (103)
Allison, Jonathan Marquand[1]: *Art Dept Production Manager* (200-213)
Anderson, Paul: **Jason** (200)
Andoh, Adjoa: **Sister Jatt** (201)
Anscombe, Adrian: *Standby Props* (101-105); *Property Master* (106-213)
Antony-Barber, Paul: **Dr Kendrick** (205)
Any Effects: *Special Effects* (101-106, 109-213)
Appleton, Alistair: **Himself** (212)
Armesto, Sebastian: **Broff** (112)
Armory, Beccy: **Raffalo** (102)
Arthur, Rod: **Mr Parsons** (203)
Arundel, Howard: *First Assistant Director* (111)
Arya, Sagar: **Newsreader 2** (200)
Ashmore, Ben: *Special Effects Co-ordinator* (204-207, 210-213)
Atkins, Jessica: **Young Reinette** (204)
Audouard, Jean: *3D Artist* (202, 203, 208, 209, 211)
Austin, Ben: *Design Assistant* (200, 201, 203, 204)
Badland, Annette: **Margaret Blaine** (104, 105, 111)
Baker, Bob: *K-9 originally created by* (203)
Baker, Matt: **Himself** (104)

---

1 Credited as Jonathan Allison on 200

---

2 Credited as Jack Harkness in 109, as Jack in 110, and as Captain Jack in 111-113

3 Listed during broadcast for 101, but credit omitted on DVD release; credited as Ailsa Altena-Burk on 101-112

Busser-Casas, Astrid: *2D VFX Artist* (102, 103, 107, 109-113)
Butler-Adams, Melissa: *2D Artist* (200-203, 207-209, 211)
Cacciato, Serena: *3D Artist* (207-209)
Callis, Sam: **Security Guard** (112)
Callow, Simon: **Charles Dickens** (103)
Cameron, Heather: **Nina** (203)
Carl, Lachele: **Reporter** (104, 105); **Newsreader 3** (200)
Carlsen, Sean: **Policeman** (200)
Carpenter, Jana: **De Maggio** (106)
Carson, Silas: **Alien Voices** (102); **The Voice of the Ood** (208, 209)
Cartwright, Katy: *Production Co-ordinator* (200A)
Cassey, Zoë: *On Line Editor* (109, 110)
Cater, Wayne: **Stage Manager** (103)
Challis, Jean: **Aunty Betty** (207)
Challis, Julia: *Standby Scenic Artist* (210)
Chester, Peter: *Best Boy* (101-213)
Chowdhry, Navin: **Indra Ganesh** (104)
Chung, Basil: **Bau** (104)
Clarke, Matthew[4]: *On Line Editor* (101-204, 207-213)
Clarke, Noel[5]: **Mickey Smith** (101, 104, 105, 111, 113-201, 203-206, 212, 213)
Clarke, Stuart: *Stunt Performer* (106, 112, 113)
Clayton, Sean: *Second Assistant Director* (106, 108)
Clissold, Bonnie: *A/Production Accountant* (200, 201, 204-206, 210, 211, 213)
Coduri, Camille: **Jackie Tyler** (101, 102, 104, 105, 108, 113-201, 205, 206, 210, 212, 213)
Cohen, Will: *Visual FX Producer* (101-213, 200A)
Collins, Abbi: *Stunt Co-ordinator* (205, 206, 212, 213)
Collins, Pauline: **Queen Victoria** (202)
Collinson, Phil: *Producer* (101-213)
Constantine, Susannah: **Voice of Zu-Zana** (112)
Cook, Ron: **Magpie** (207)
Cope, Martha: **Controller** (112)
Cordory, Mark: *Specialist Prop Maker* (200-213)
Cornell, Paul: *Writer* (108)
Costelloe, Mike: *Camera Operator* (101-105)
Cottle, George: *Stunt Performer* (111)
Coulby, Angel: **Katherine** (204)
Courtis, Joseph: *2D Artist* (201-204, 207-209, 211)
Cox, Sam: **Detective Inspector Bishop** (207)
Coxon, Glen: *Production Runner* (210)
Cresswell, David: *Editor* (205, 206, 212, 213)
Croll, Dona: **Matron Casp** (201)
Crossman, Stuart: **Dalek Operator** (212, 213)
Crowley, Mike: *Special Effects Supervisor* (204-207, 210-213)

---

4 Credited in the role of On Line Editor to 204, the Online Editor from 207

5 Credited as Mickey on 111 and 113, and as Mickey Smith in all other appearances

English, Rick: *Stunt Performer* (202)
Eniola, Abi: **Crosbie** (112)
Evans, Anna: *Production Runner* (113)
Evans, Clive: *Location Manager* (101-105)
Evans, Daniel: **Danny Llewellyn** (200)
Evans, Dathyl: *Production Co-ordinator* (101, 104, 105)
Fante, Sophie: *Producer* (200A)
Faraday, Tim: **Tom's Dad** (211)
Fergison, Cheryl: **Mrs Lloyd** (109, 110)
Fernandes, Bob: *Lighting Gaffer* (200A)
Fields, Paul: **Weatherman** (212)
Finnigan, Neil: *Stunt Performer* (106)
Fitzgerald, Michael: **Duke of Manhattan** (201)
Foreman, Jamie: **Eddie Connolly** (207)
Forman, Dave: *Stunt Co-ordinator* (202, 204, 207, 211)
Fort, Alex[6]: *Digital Matte Painter* (101, 102, 106, 107, 109, 110, 112, 113-204, 211); *Digital Matte Artist* (208, 209)
Fost, Elizabeth: **Auton** (101); **Slitheen** (104, 105)
Foster, Dean: *Stunt Performer* (200, 201)
Foster, Glen: *Stunt Performer* (202)
Franzl, Sarah: *Stunt Performer* (102, 207)
Fraser, Hadley: **Gareth** (212)
Fraser, Simon: *Sound Recordist* (200-207, 211-213)
Friend, Dorothy: *Continuity* (111)
Gadd, Phil: *Online Editor* (200A)
Gallagher, Sean: **Chip** (201)
Gammon, Lee: *Standby Art Director* (202, 204, 207, 211)
Garcia, Adam: **Alex** (200)
Gardner, Julie: *Executive Producer* (101-213, 200A)
Garnett, Elli: **Caroline** (101)
Gatiss, Mark: *Writer* (103, 207)
Gerwitz, George: *First Assistant Director* (101, 104, 105)
Gilder, Sean: **Sycorax Leader** (200)
Gillett, Debra: **Rita Connolly** (207)
Glover, Jo: *Prosthetics Technician* (204-210, 212, 213)
Goddard, Trisha: **Herself** (212)
Gold, Murray: *Music* (101-213, 200A)
Goodhart, Rose: *Costume Supervisor* (210)
Gorton, Neill: *Prosthetics* (200, 201, 204-210, 212, 213)
Grainer, Ron: *Original Theme Music* (101-213, 200A)
Grant, Brian: *Director* (107)
Grantham, William: *Abzorbaloff created by* (210)
Graham, Matthew: *Writer* (211)
Green, Crispin: *Editor* (202, 204, 207, 211)

---

6 Credited as Alex Ford on 200

7 Credited as Michael Harison on broadcast for 102, corrected on DVD release

8 Credited as Nicolas Hernandes on 108

Hodgson, Martin: **Jenkins** (110)

Holden, Simon C[9]: *2D VFX Artist* (101-113); *2D Artist* (200-204, 207-209, 211)

Hollingbery, Vilma: **Mrs Harcourt** (110)

Holmes, Robert: *Autons Originally Created By* (101)

Holt, Judy: **Adam's Mum** (107)

Hope, Anna: **Novice Hame** (201)

Hopkins, Dai: *Grip* (210)

Hopkins, Morgan: **Sergeant Price** (105)

Horth, Russell: *2D Artist* (200, 207-211)

Houghton, Dave: *Visual FX Supervisor* (101-213)

Howarth, Penny: *Prop Maker* (200-213)

Howe, Gary: *Casting* (200A)

Howell, Andy: *3D VFX Artist* (101, 102, 104-110, 112, 113); *3D Artist* (200, 201)

Howell, Trystan[10] *Standby Props* (106-206, 212, 213)

Hughes, Non Eleri: *Continuity* (102, 103, 109, 110, 112, 113, 202, 204-209, 211-213)

Hughes, Tony: *Electrician* (210)

Humphreys, Pam: *Continuity* (106-108)

Humphries, Pam: *Script Supervisor* (200A)

Hutchings, Mark: *Gaffer* (101-209, 211-213)

Hywel-Davies, Matthew: *Construction Manager* (200-213)

Isaac, Mark: *Focus Puller* (101-201, 203)

James, Albert: *Practical Electrician* (204-206, 210, 211, 213)

James, Anna: *Camera Assistant* (102, 103)

James, Raji: **Dr Rajesh Singh** (212, 213)

James, Rhian: **Suzie** (108)

Jefferies, Paul: *Sound FX Editor* (101-213, 200A)

Jeffreys, Peter: *Dubbing Mixer* (106)

Jennings, Rory: **Tommy Connolly** (207)

Jhutti, Ronny: **Danny Barlock** (208, 209)

John, Margaret: **Grandma Connolly** (207)

Johnson, Clive: *Electrician* (205, 206, 211-213)

Johnson, Corey: **Henry van Statten** (106)

Johnson, Noah: **Voice of The Empty Child** (109, 110)

Jones, Allen: *Construction Chargehand* (201-213)

Jones, Ceris: **Policeman** (104)

Jones, David: *Camera Assistant* (102, 103)

Jones, Davy: *Make-Up Designer* (101-113)

Jones, Harriet: *Standby Props* (210)

Jones, Jennie: *Post Production Supervisor* (200A)

Jones, Matt: *Writer* (208, 209)

Jones, Mike: *Editor* (101, 104, 105, 208, 209)

Jones, Natalie: **Sarah** (108)

Joseph, Paterson: **Rodrick** (112, 113)

9 Credited as Simon Holden (no middle initial) on 207-209

10 Credited as Tristan Howell on 106, 108

Marzella, Stephen: **Police Officer** (211)
Maskell, Tina: *Stunt Performer* (111)
Matthews, Jeff: *Sound Recordist* (210)
Maxwell-Martin, Anna: **Suki** (107)
Mayor, Rob: *Prosthetics Supervisor* (204-210, 212, 213)
McCall, Davina: **Voice of Davinadroid** (112)
McCann, Fiona: *Costume Assistant* (210)
McCoy, Adam: **Clive's Son** (101)
McDowall, Sian: **Sandra** (200)
McFadden, Paul: *Dialogue Editor* (101-113); *Sound Editor* (200-213)
McGarrity, Kim: *Stunt Performer* (109-111, 200, 201)
McKinney, Matt[11]: *3D VFX Artist* (102, 109-113); *3D Artist* (200-204, 208, 209, 211)
McKinstry, Peter: *Design Assistant* (202, 204-213); *Concept Artist* (200A)
Meire, Chad: *2D VFX Artist* (113)
Meire, Joel: *3D VFX Artist* (102, 111)
Meldrum, Debbie: *Production Runner* (113-201, 203)
Mellor, Oliver: **Matt** (212)
Meredith, Robin: **Granddad** (200A)
Miles, Peter: *Stunt Performer* (202, 204)
Mill, The: *Visual Effects* (101-213, 200A)
Millennium Effects: *Prosthetics* (101, 102, 104-107, 109-201, 204-210, 212, 213, 200A)
Miller, Brandon: **Alf** (109)
Milne, Ruthie: **Flora** (202)
Mitchell, Charlotte: *Costume Assistant* (210)
Moffat, Steven: *Writer* (109, 110, 204)
Mohammed, Jason: **Newsreader 1** (200)
Montana, Joe: **Commander** (106)
Montanes, Alberto: *2D VFX Artist* (101-103, 107, 109)
Mori, Naoko: **Doctor Sato** (104)
Morison, David: *Standby Art Director* (111, 210); *Set Decorator* (202, 204, 207, 211)
Morita, Kyoko: **Japanese Girl** (212)
Morris, Simon: *Second Assistant Director* (210)
Morris, Steffan: *Second Assistant Director* (101-105, 107, 109-201, 203, 205-209, 211-213)
Morus, Llyr: *Unit Manager* (106-108); *Location Manager* (109, 110, 112, 113)
MTFX: *Special Effects* (107)
Muir, Lynsey: *Third Assistant Director* (200, 201, 203, 205-209, 211-213); *Second Assistant Director* (202, 204)
Mullins, Matt: *Assistant Editor* (208-210)
Mumford, Dan: *Third Assistant Director* (102, 103, 106-113)
Murphy, Cathy: **Mum** (200)
Murphy, Jordan: **Ernie** (109, 110)
Myles, Eve: **Gwyneth** (103)
Myles, Sophia: **Reinette** (204)
Nation, Terry: *Daleks originally created by* (106, 112, 113, 212, 213)

---

11 Credited as Matthew McKinney on 200-204

Nayar, Nisha: **Female Programmer** (112, 113)
Nicholas, Stephen: *Supervising Art Director* (101-213)
Nichols, Richard: **Driver** (211)
Nicholson, Clare: *First Assistant Director* (205, 206)
North, James: *A/Supervising Art Director* (200-213)
North, Matthew: *Forward Dresser* (202-206, 212, 213); *Standby Props* (207, 211); *Art Department Co-ordinator* (208-210)
North, Russell: *2D Artist* (201-204)
Nott, Roger: **Older Man** (200A)
O'Dee, James: *Stunt Performer* (205, 206, 212, 213)
Oberman, Tracy-Ann: **Yvonne Hartman** (212-213)
Older, Jon: *First Assistant Director* (109, 110, 200, 201, 203)
Olding, Catherine: **Young Woman** (200A)
Oliver, Ben: **Urchin** (200A)
Omambala, Chu: **Major Blake** (200)
Ormiston, Marine: *Costume Supervisor* (205, 206, 212, 213)
Otway, Helen: **Auton** (101)
Page, Louise: *Costume Designer* (200-213)
Palfrey, Lisa: **Mum** (200A)
Parkes, Shaun: **Zachary Cross Flane** (208, 209)
Parry, Dafydd Rhys[12]: *Third Assistant Director* (101, 104, 105)
Pearce, Jo: *Producer* (200A)
Pearce, Roger: *Camera Operator* (205, 206, 212, 213)
Peart-Smith, Yolanda: *Wardrobe Supervisor* (101-113)
Pedler, Kit: *Cybermen originally created by* (205, 206, 212, 213)
Pedrick, Aled: **Idris Hopper** (111)
Peel, Bean: *Stunt Performer* (108)
Pegg, Nicholas: **Dalek Operator** (112, 113, 212, 213)
Pegg, Simon: **The Editor** (107)
Perrott, Porl[13]: *3D VFX Artist* (101, 102, 104, 105)
Perry, Dian: **Computer Voice** (109, 110)
Perry, Luke: **Timothy Lloyd** (110)
Petts, Chris: *3D VFX Artist* (101-110, 112, 113); *3D Artist* (200-204, 207-211)
Petty, Gweneth: **Grandma** (200A)
Phelan, Kim: *2D Artist* (200); *Visual Effects Co-ordinator* (201-204, 207, 208, 210-213)
Pickley, Joe: **Kenny** (203)
Piper, Billie: **Rose Tyler** (101-213)
Platt, Marc: *With thanks to* (205, 206)
Plowman, Anna-Louise: **Goddard** (106)
Potts, Eric: **Oliver Charles** (104)
Povey, Meic: **Driver** (103)
Prince, Marcus: *Production Manager* (202, 204, 207, 211)

12 Credited as Dafydd Parry on 104
13 Credited as Paul Perrott in transmitted versions of 101, 102; corrected for DVD release

Pritchard, Claire: *Make-Up Artist* (103[14], 106-113, 210)

Prockter, Colin: **Head Chef** (107)

Prosser, Sian: *Continuity* (101, 104, 105)

Pryor, Andy, CDG: *Casting Director* (101-213)

Pryor, Will: *3D Artist* (202, 203, 208, 209, 211)

Pugsley, Richard: *Business Manager* (101-105); *Finance Manager* (106-213)

Raynor, Helen: *Script Editor* (103, 106, 109, 110, 112, 113, 200, 203-206, 212, 213)

Rees, Gill: *Make-up Artist* (210)

Rees, Steve: *Focus Puller* (202, 204, 207, 210, 211)

Reid, Emma: *Unit Manager* (102, 103)

Rezard, Martin: *Prosthetics Technician* (204-210, 212, 213)

Rhys, Huw: **Redpath** (103)

Rhys, Ieuan: **Crabtree** (207)

Richards, John: *Editor* (102, 103, 107)

Richardson, Damian: *Boom Operator* (101-113)

Richardson, Ian: *Sound Recordist* (101-113)

Ricketts, Tim: *Dubbing Mixer* (101-105, 107-213, 200A)

Riddell, Derek: **Sir Robert** (202)

Roach, Sandra: *2D Artist* (207-210)

Roberts, Al: *Design Assistant* (204-213)

Roberts, Claire: *Production/Script Secretary* (201-213)

Roberts, Gareth: *Writer* (200A)

Roberts, Richard: *2D VFX Artist* (113)

Robertson, Kirsty: *Casting Associate* (101-113)

Robinson, Anne: **Voice of Anne Droid** (112, 113)

Robinson, John: *Grip* (101-213)

Robinson, Lucy: **Frau Clovis** (201)

Roche, Neil: *3D Artist* (200-203, 208, 209, 211)

Rodger, Struan: **Face of Boe** (201)

Rogers, Seon: *Stunt Performer* (108)

Rowlands, Elwen: *Script Editor* (101, 102, 104, 105, 107, 108, 111)

Rozelaar-Green, Frank: **Sonny** (108)

Rumbelow, Joelle: *Production Buyer* (111, 202, 204, 207, 211)

Ruscoe, Alan: **Auton** (101); **Slitheen** (104, 105, 111); **Android** (112, 113)

Rushbrook, Claire: **Ida Scott** (208, 209)

Russell, Jenna: **Floor Manager** (112)

Salis, Abdul: **Kel** (211)

Samuel, Catherine: *Production Buyer* (101-110, 112-201, 203, 205, 206, 208, 212, 213); *Set Decorator* (111, 210)

Samuels, Damian: **Mr Lloyd** (109, 110)

Sant, David: **Auton** (101)

Savage, Matthew: *Design Assistant* (200-203, 205, 213)

Schwab, John: **Bywater** (106)

Seed, Gordon: *Stunt Performer* (207)

---

14 Listed during broadcast for 103, but credit omitted on DVD release

Shaw, Adam: **Morris** (205)

Shearman, Robert: *Writer* (106)

Shellard, Phill: *Standby Props* (101-209, 211-213)

Sheward, Lee: *Stunt Co-ordinator* (102, 103, 106-110, 111)

Shipton, Penny: *Camera Assistant* (204, 206, 211)

Silva, Tony: *Stunt Performer* (202)

Simpson, Tracie: *Production Manager* (101-201, 203, 205, 206, 208-210, 212, 213)

Sinclair, Doug: *Sound Editor* (200-213)

Sives, Jamie: **Captain Reynolds** (202)

Skelding, Gareth: *Location Manager* (200, 201, 203, 205, 206, 208-213)

Sladen, Elisabeth: **Sarah Jane Smith** (203)

Slocombe, Stephen: *Electrician* (212, 213)

Smith, Andrew: *Construction Manager* (101-113)

Smith, Benjamin: **Luke** (203)

Smith, Steve: *Make-up Artist* (200-209, 211-213)

Smith, Tom: **The Host** (202)

Sosanya, Nina: **Trish** (211)

Spargo, Anthony: **Dalek Operator** (212, 213)

Spaull, Colin: **Mr Crane** (205, 206)

Speirs, Steve: **Strickland** (104, 105)

Stephens, Martin: *Camera Operator* (101-113)

Stewart, Sara: **Computer Voice** (102)

Stone Fewings, Jo: **Male Programmer** (112, 113)

Strong, James: *Director* (208, 209)

Tarlton, Jack: **Reporter** (104, 105)

Tate, Catherine[15]: **The Bride** (213)

Taylor, Rocky: *Stunt Performer* (207)

Taylor, Rory: *Director of Photography* (202, 204, 207, 210, 211, 200A)

Tennant, David[16]: **Doctor Who** (113); **The Doctor** (200-213, 200A)

Thomas, Bryn: *Boom Operator* (205, 206, 210, 213)

Thomas, Edward: *Production Designer* (101-213, 200A)

Thomas, Ellen: **Clockwork Woman** (204)

Thomas, Lowri: *Location Manager* (101, 104-108, 200, 201, 203, 205, 206, 208-210, 212, 213);
Unit Manager (111)

Thomas, William: **Mr Cleaver** (111)

Thomson, Moira: *Make-up Artist* (200-209, 211-213)

Thorne, Zoë: **The Gelth** (103)

Thorp, Will: **Toby Zed** (208, 209)

Tibber, Clem: **Milo** (203)

Tramontin, Alf: *Steadicam Operator* (200A)

Tremain, Joseph: **Jim** (109, 110)

Tucker, Chris: *3D VFX Artist* (101, 103); *3D Artist* (200-203, 207-209, 211)

Tucker, Mike: *Model Unit Supervisor* (101, 104, 105, 107, 113, 200, 203, 208, 209)

---

15 Credited as 'and Introducing Catherine Tate as The Bride' on 213

16 Credited as 'and introducing David Tennant as Doctor Who' on 113

Turner, Ben: **King Louis** (204)
Tyler, Peter: *Model Unit DOP* (113)
Ufondo, Andrew: **Soldier** (205)
Valentine, Albert: **The Child** (109, 110)
Vallis, Helen: *Associate Producer* (101-206)
van Beers, Kai: *Colourist* (101-108)
van Niekerk, Jess: *Production Co-ordinator* (106—213)
Vansittart, Rupert: **General Asquith** (104, 105)
Vee, Jimmy: **Graske** (200A)
Vee, Jimmy: **Moxx of Balhoon** (102); **Alien** (104)
Verrey, David: **Joseph Green** (104, 105)
Vincent, Mick: *Colourist* (200-204, 207-213)
Vincze, Ernie, BSC: *Director of Photography* (101-201, 203, 205, 206, 208, 209, 212, 213)
Walker, Graham: *Editor* (106, 108, 111-113)
Wallman, Mark: *3D VFX Artist* (101 104-108, 110, 112, 113); *3D Artist* (201-204, 208, 209, 211)
Walpole, Peter: *Set Decorator* (101-105)
Walters, Dawn: *Associate Producer* (200A)
Walters, Gavin: *Electrician* (210)
Wanamaker, Zoë: **Cassandra** (102, 201)
Warren, Marc: **Elton Pope** (210)
Warrington, Don: **The President** (205)
Warwick, David: **Police Commissioner** (212)
Washington, Eugene: **Mr Wagner** (203)
Watson, Philip: *Interactive Team* (200A)
Way, Ashley: *Director* (200A)
Webb, Danny: **Mr Jefferson** (208, 209)
Webber, Nick: *3D VFX Artist* (102, 107, 109, 112, 113); *3D Artist* (200, 201, 203, 207-210)
Webster, Rachel: **Eileen** (212)
Welch, Jeff: *Boom Operator* (200-209, 211-213)
Wells, Sheelagh: *Make-up Designer* (200-213)
Wey, Tom: *Interactive Team* (200A)
Wheel, Victoria: *Production Runner* (205, 208, 211)
Whitehouse, Andrew: *Producer* (200A)
Whithouse, Toby: *Writer* (203)
Whitmey, Nigel: **Simmons** (106)
Wilkinson, Jamie: *Colourist* (109, 110)
Wilkinson, Kirsty: *Costume Assistant* (207-209, 211)
Williams, Endaf Emyr: *Production Accountant* (101-213)
Williams, Gareth: *First Assistant Director* (106-108, 208, 209)
Williams, Shaun: *Storyboard Artist* (204-213)
Williams, Silas: *Standby Carpenter* (200, 201, 204-206, 211, 213)
Williams, Steve: *Make-Up Artist* (106-113)
Wilson, Richard: **Dr Constantine** (109, 110)
Wilson, Sarah: *Make-Up Artist* (101-105)
Wilton, Penelope: **Harriet Jones** (104, 105, 200)
Winchester, Karren: **Fitch** (112)

Windsor, Barbara: *Peggy Mitchell* (212)
Winstone, Simon: *Script Editor* (201, 202, 207-211, 200A)
Wollman, Mark: *3D Artist* (200)
Woodall, Trinny: **Voice of Trine-E** (112)
Wooddisse, Stuart: *Props Storeman* (200-213)
Woodruff, Rod: *Stunt Co-ordinator* (101, 105)
Woolf, Gabriel: **The Voice of the Beast** (208, 209)
Wright, Lucinda: *Costume Designer* (101-113)
Wyn Griffiths, Gareth: **Manservant** (204)
Wyn Jones, Arwel[17]: *Standby Art Director* (102, 103, 109, 110, 200, 208, 209, 212, 213);
    Supervising Art Director (200A)
Wyn Jones, Llinos: *Continuity* (200, 201, 203)
Yeoman, Rhydian: *Boom Operator* (201, 203, 204, 208, 209)
Young, Mal: *Executive Producer* (101-113)
Zeff, Dan: *Director* (210)

---

17 Credited as Arwel Jones in 109, 110 and 200A

APPENDIX B:
DOCTOR WHO CONFIDENTIAL

For a second year, BBC Wales commissioned the documentary series *Doctor Who Confidential* to air on BBC3. Once again produced by Gillane Seaborne and Adam Page, *Doctor Who Confidential* took an inside look at the making of each episode of the series.

Writer Mark Gatiss narrated the 13 episodes, replacing first season narrator Simon Pegg (who had also narrated a special nine-minute production, *Backstage at Christmas*, produced by the *Confidential* team and issued on the first series DVD release). In addition, a special episode, 'One Year On', was produced for the *Doctor Who* Night broadcast a week prior to the start of Series Two; this was introduced by Corey Johnson, who had played Henry van Statten in the episode 'Dalek' during the first season.

In addition to clips and behind-the-scenes footage of *Doctor Who* in production, *Confidential* once more presented a wide variety of specially-conducted interviews. The interviewees included series stars David Tennant and Billie Piper; executive producers Russell T Davies and Julie Gardner; producer Phil Collinson; writers Steven Moffat, Mark Gatiss, Matthew Graham and Toby Whithouse; directors James Hawes, Graeme Harper, James Strong and Euros Lyn; and actors Elisabeth Sladen, John Leeson, Noel Clarke, Camille Coduri, John Barrowman, Maureen Lipman, Peter Kay, Tracy-Ann Oberman, Marc Warren, Will Thorp, MyAnna Buring, Jamie Foreman, Shaun Parkes, Ian Hanmore, Eve Myles, Ron Donachie, Nicholas Briggs and Sophia Myles.

As with the first season, shortened *Doctor Who Confidential Cut Down* versions (ranging from nine to 13 minutes in length) were also prepared for BBC3; these ran in repeat slots. The scheduling of repeats varied widely; most episodes were repeated on the Sunday after transmission, sometimes in the *Cut Down* version and sometimes the full edition, while further repeats also aired during the week, often on the Friday.

A complete list of credits for the entire two-series run, including the various specials, is included below. Each episode listing includes date and time of transmission and duration.

BC BACKSTAGE AT CHRISTMAS
Released: *Doctor Who: The Complete First Series* DVD set (BBC Video)
A special nine-minute presentation produced by the *Doctor Who Confidential* team, shot on location during the recording of 'The Christmas Invasion', this feature was produced as a teaser/preview for the Christmas special and released on the first series DVD boxed set. Simon Pegg, narrator of the first series of *Confidential*, narrated the special.

2.0 ONE YEAR ON
Transmission: 9 April 2006, 7.00 pm, BBC3 (55'31")
An hour-long feature special looking back at the production of *Doctor Who* from the first series to the end of the second, featuring glimpses into the season to come and a selection of clips and interview segments to bring the viewer up to speed. The episode was aired as part of the BBC3 *Doctor Who* Night strand.

2.1 NEW NEW DOCTOR
Transmission: 15 April 2006, 8.00 pm, BBC3 (28'31")

The first regular episode of the series goes on location to the Gower Peninsula as well as into the studio for the recording of the first episode, 'New Earth', featuring interviews with cast and crew. Russell T Davies and Julie Gardner talk about the casting of David Tennant, with clips from Tennant's past work, as well as the creation of the tenth Doctor's new wardrobe. The subject of the Doctor's regeneration is addressed, with a look back into *Doctor Who* history at how the programme previously dealt with the change in lead actor.

2.2 FEAR FACTOR

Transmission: 22 April 2006, 8.00 pm, BBC3 (27'17")
The production of 'Tooth and Claw' is highlighted in an episode about the horror elements of *Doctor Who*, in both the classic and the new series. The visual effects process is discussed, including details of the creation of computer-generated creatures such as the episode's werewolf, and of how the recording with human subjects is transformed into the finished product. Werewolf sound effects, the dangers of shooting on location and the making of the martial arts fight sequence that opens 'Tooth and Claw' are also analysed.

2.3 FRIENDS REUNITED

Transmission: 29 April 2006, 8.05 pm, BBC3 (28'06")
The reunion of *Doctor Who* past and present is highlighted as the series discusses the return of Elisabeth Sladen as Sarah Jane Smith in 'School Reunion'. The history of the character is highlighted, as is the relationship between Sarah Jane and Rose – and how they relate to the Doctor. *Buffy the Vampire Slayer* star Anthony Head's appearance in the episode is also covered, as is the history of K-9 and the contribution of voice actor John Leeson.

2.4 SCRIPT TO SCREEN

Transmission: 6 May 2006, 7.45 pm, BBC3 (28'26")
The creative process involved in the construction of a *Doctor Who* story – in this case, 'The Girl in the Fireplace' – is analysed, from the writing to the script breakdowns and brainstorming, as well as the construction of the sets and costumes, and the process of shooting in historic buildings on location. The relationships between the actors, the romantic entanglements involved in the plot, and the editing to assemble the finished programme are all highlighted.

2.5 CYBERMEN

Transmission: 13 May 2006, 8.05 pm, BBC3 (27'23")
The return of another classic monster from *Doctor Who* lore is the subject of this episode, which focuses primarily on the metal monsters and the episode 'Rise of the Cybermen'. As well as a look into the history of the Cybermen on television, this show focuses on the design elements involved in their recreation and update for a new generation. Director Graeme Harper is interviewed.

2.6 FROM ZERO TO HERO

Transmission: 20 May 2006, 7.25 pm, BBC3 (27'58")
Mickey Smith is the subject of this episode, from his origins in 'Rose' through the to making of the latest episode, 'The Age of Steel', in which he confronts his double. Actor Noel Clarke is interviewed, discussing his thoughts on bringing the character to life. The making of the

APPENDIX B

episode, including Mickey's departure sequence, is also covered.

2.7 THE WRITER'S TALE
Transmission: 27 May 2006, 7.45 pm, BBC3 (27'06")
Confidential narrator Mark Gatiss gets a chance to tell his story, about the making of his episode 'The Idiot's Lantern'. Recreating '50s London, both on location and in studio with such sets as the Connolly living room, is discussed, as Gatiss describes the writing process and how his words are brought to life. Actors and crewmembers are interviewed as well.

2.8 YOU'VE GOT THE LOOK
Transmission: 3 June 2006, 7.45 pm, BBC3 (28'53")
'The creative talents behind the look of *Doctor Who*' are profiled in this episode, as *Confidential* looks at the techniques and prosthetics involved in the creation of monsters such as the Ood in 'The Impossible Planet'. Creating an entire world in the studio is also discussed, from the Sanctuary Base to the interiors in the rest of the series. The episode also visits the underwater stage at Pinewood Studios for the filming of Scooti's death sequence, and the Wenvoe Quarry where the massive underground chamber was realised.

2.9 MYTHS AND LEGENDS
Transmission: 10 June 2006, 7.45 pm, BBC3 (27'46")
The limits of the Doctor's knowledge, and the mythology of the series, are discussed, as David Tennant reflects on the character and his all-too-human limitations. The make-up work on Will Thorp and Toby's death sequence are highlighted, as well as the location work done for 'The Satan Pit' and the CGI creation of the Beast. Satanic and sinister villains from the history of the series are also featured.

2.10 THE NEW WORLD OF WHO
Transmission: 17 June 2006, 7.45 pm, BBC3 (27'33")
The technological developments of the 21st Century and how they relate to *Doctor Who* are discussed in an episode about the atypical story 'Love & Monsters'. The *Blue Peter* Design-a-Monster competition is featured, including the selection of the Abzorbaloff and Tennant's participation in the process. Also discussed is the world of the Internet, including the creation of 'Attack of the Graske' and the various *Doctor Who* websites, including the official spinoffs. The appeal of the series to women is also noted, as is the makeover of the *Doctor Who* theme by the BBC National Orchestra of Wales.

2.11 THE FRIGHT STUFF
Transmission: 24 June 2006, 7.45 pm, BBC3 (28'03")
What makes *Doctor Who* so scary? That's the focus of this episode, in which the making of 'Fear Her' is discussed and the history of frightening and suspenseful elements in the show is profiled. The earliest years of *Doctor Who* are used to exemplify the rich history of terrors in the show. The ending of 'Fear Her', in which the Doctor and Rose confront the 'approaching storm', is also discussed.

2.12 WELCOME TO TORCHWOOD
Transmission: 1 July 2006, 7.45 pm, BBC3 (27'14")

The introduction of the Torchwood Institute, the return of the Daleks and their long-awaited battle with the Cybermen... it's all covered in this episode, which features an analysis of the production of 'The Age of Steel'. Also in this episode, a first look at the production of the new spinoff series *Torchwood*.

2.13 FINALE

Transmission: 8 July 2006, 7.45 pm, BBC3 (28'30")

'Doomsday' has arrived and *Confidential* goes behind the scenes for the making of the second series finale, including the Dalek battle against the Cybermen and the future of Earth in multiple universes. But this episode focuses primarily on the departure of Billie Piper, looking at the impact she has made on *Doctor Who* through two years playing Rose Tyler. Piper and other cast members are interviewed about the actress's departure from the series and comment about its future.

CREDITS

The combined credits index below includes: the initial special 'Doctor Who: A New Dimension' (ND); Series One, comprising episodes 1.1 to 1.13; the first season finale special 'The Ultimate Guide' (UG); the DVD special 'Backstage at Christmas' (BC); the *Doctor Who* Night special 'One Year On' (2.0); and Series Two, comprising episodes 2.1-2.13.

Ablett, Dan: *Editor* (2.7)
Allen, Mark: *Edit Producer* (2.0, 2.10)
Appleby, Tom: *Editor* (1.10, 1.11, 1.13, ND); *Programme Editor* (UG); *Colourist* (2.12)
Aranha, Rheea: *Titles* (ND, UG)
Arwel, Rhian: *Runner* (2.0, 2.5-2.13)
Baker, Paul: *Sound* (1.2-1.4, UG, 2.0, 2.2)
Barlow, Stewart: *Editor* (1.4)
Bianco, Alia: *Runner* (2.0, 2.5-2.10, 2.12, 2.13)
Binding, Lee: *Countdown Graphics* (ND)
Brailsford, James: *Editor* (2.0, 2.6, 2.9)
Brereton, Stuart: *Camera* (2.7-2.9, 2.12)
Britz, Nic: *Runner* (1.7-1.13, UG)
Brooks, Sven: *Editor* (1.1, ND, 2.10); *Insert Editor* (UG)
Bruce, Robert: *Copyright Contracts* (1.1, 1.13, UG)
Bryant, Mat: *Camera* (1.1, 1.3, 1.4, 1.8-1.13, UG, 2.0, 2.6, 2.9-2.13)
Budd, Jenny: *Camera* (2.0)
Buers, Lee: *Editor* (1.12, ND)
Chappell, Cat: *Researcher* (2.0, 2.8-2.13)
Cole, Simon: *Sound* (1.5, 2.9)
Coles, Andy: *Title Music Arrangement* (ND)
Collins, John: *Camera* (2.0, 2.2, 2.8)
Cossey, Mark: *Executive Producer* (All)
Cox, Paul: *Camera* (1.10, 1.11, UG)
Dalby, Tim: *Editor* (2.2, 2.4)
Davies, Dewi: *Camera* (2.0-2.2, 2.4-2.6, 2.10)
Davies, Russell T: *Executive Producer for Dr Who* (All)

Davies, Sarah T: *Edit Producer* (2.12)
Dawson, Tim: *Editor* (1.2, 1.3, 1.6); *Insert Editor* (UG)
Dimitroff, Danny: *Camera* (1.10, 1.11)
Doel, Richard: *Colourist* (1.1, 1.5)
Eason, Peter: *Sound* (1.8, 1.10, 1.11, UG)
Evans, Bethan: *Cyfle Trainee* (1.7); *Runner* (1.10-1.13, UG); *Production Team Assistant* (2.1-2.7)
Evans, Geoff: *Researcher* (1.1-1.11, 1.13, ND, UG); *Assistant Producer* (1.12, 2.0-2.6, 2.8-2.13);
    Edit Producer (2.7); *Producer* (2.11); *Director* (2.11)
Everett, Jon: *Colourist* (1.2-1.4, 1.7-1.13, 2.1, 2.2, 2.9, 2.10, 2.12, 2.13)
Ferda, Mark: *Dubbing* (1.4, 1.5, 1.13, 2.1, 2.7-2.11)
Foakes, John: *Sound* (2.7)
Found, Mark: *Sound* (2.0, 2.2, 2.8)
Gardner, Julie: *Executive Producer for Dr Who* (All)
Gaster, Joe: *Sound* (2.0)
Gatiss, Mark: *Narrator* (2.0-2.13)
Gerallt, Deian: *Sound* (2.0, 2.10)
Gold, Murray: *Title Music Arrangement* (ND)
Goldsmith, Si,n: *Runner* (2.12, 2.13)
Gosling, Catherine: *Production Manager* (1.1-1.13, ND)
Gratton, Alexander: *Junior Researcher* (1.1-1.13, UG); *Researcher* (2.0-2.13)
Hacking, Nick: *Edit Producer* (2.13)
Hacking, Nick: *Edit Producer* (2.9)
Hall, Simon: *Edit Producer* (2.2, 2.4)
Harris, Caroline: *Production Co-ordinator* (1.1-1.7, ND)
Hart, Stephen: *Camera* (2.0, 2.2)
Hickman, Clayton: *Thanks to* (1.1, 1.13)
Hodge, Steve: *Sound* (2.11-2.13)
Hoy, Steve: *Sound* (1.1, 1.4, 1.9-1.11, 1.13, UG, 2.0-2.8, 2.11-2.13)
Hudson, Steve: *Dubbing* (ND); *Dubbing Mixer* (UG)
Hughes, Maxine: *Runner* (1.1-1.13, ND, UG)
Hunt, Ian: *Editor* (1.2, 1.3, 1.5, 1.6, ND); *Insert Editor* (UG)
Hunt, Tim: *Sound* (2.12, 2.13)
Huyton, Eric: *Camera* (All)
Jardine, Nick: *Camera* (1.1, 1.2, 1.4, 1.8, 1.10, 1.11, ND, UG, 2.0)
Jeffreys, Peter: *Dubbing* (1.1-1.3, 1.6-1.12, 2.2-2.6)
Jenkins, Aled: *Camera* (1.4, 1.8, 1.12, 1.13, UG, BC, 2.0, 2.4-2.13)
Jones, Claire: *Production Team Assistant* (2.0, 2.3-2.13)
Jones, Sara: *Editor* (1.7, 1.10, 2.2, 2.4, 2.11); *Insert Editor* (UG)
Lee, Tony: *Producer* (1.4, 1.9, 1.11); *Director* (1.4, 1.9, 1.11); *Insert Director* (UG)
Liquid: *Titles* (1.1)
Longhurst, Lesley: *Artist Contracts* (1.1, 1.13, UD, 2.1)
Lutman, Lucy: *Runner* (1.7-1.13, UG, BC, 2.0-2.5)
Lynch-Blosse, Caroline: *Editor*: (1.4, 1.9); *Insert Editor* (UG)
Mansell, Rob: *Editor* (1.2-1.6, 1.8, ND, BC, 2.0-2.6, 2.8, 2.13); *Insert Editor* (UG)
Maxwell, Richard: *Sound* (1.1, 1.2, ND, UG, 2.0)

McCombie, John[1]: *Sound* (2.0, 2.2, 2.5, 2.6, 2.8-2.10, 2.13)
Meek, Simon: *Colourist* (1.4, 2.3-2.8, 2.11)
Meredith, Kevin: *Sound* (All)
Monaghan, Kate: *Researcher* (2.0, 2.8-2.13)
Mowbray, Les: *Sound* (1.2-1.7, 1.10-1.13, UG)
Owens, Gareth: *Colourist* (1.6)
Packman, Chris: *Colourist* (ND, UG, 2.0)
Page, Adam: *Producer* (1.2-1.6, 1.8, 1.12, ND, BC, 2.0-2.4, 2.6-2.13); *Director* (1.2-1.6, 1.8, 1.12, ND, BC, 2.1, 2.3); *Insert Director* (UG)
Pain, Chris: *Camera* (1.6, 1.7, ND, 2.0, 2.3)
Pegg, Simon: *Narrator* (1.1-1.13, UG, BC)
Pitch, Ian: *Editor* (1.2, 1.3, 1.6, ND)
Pixley, Andrew: *Thanks to* (1.1, 1.13)
Podpadec, John: *Camera* (1.2-1.5, UG, 2.0)
Powell, Nigel: *Dubbing* (2.0)
Procter, Mark: *Edit Producer* (2.6)
Ricketts, Tim: *Dubbing* (2.12, 2.13)
Rodgerson, Keith: *Sound* (2.0, 2.1)
Rogers, Johnny: *Camera* (1.5, UG, 2.0-2.6, 2.9)
Rose, Polly: *Editor* (BC, 2.2, 2.4)
Ross, Graham: *Sound* (1.1, 1.2, UG)
Rowland, Griff: *Producer* (1.7, 1.10); *Director* (1.7, 1.10) *Insert Director* (UG)
Rudomino, Phoebe: *Camera* (2.8)
Rushton, Zoë: *Researcher* (1.1-1.3, 1.5-1.13, ND, UG); *Assistant Producer* (1.4, BC, 2.0-2.4, 2.6, 2.7, 2.9-2.13); *Producer* (2.5); *Director* (2.5); *Edit Producer* (2.8)
Sanderson, Rebecca: *Insert Director* (UG)
Scott, Zoë: *Production Manager* (1.7-1.13, ND, UG, BC, 2.0-2.13)
Seaborne, Gillane: *Series Producer* (1.2-1.12, BC, 2.0-2.13); *Producer* (1.1, 1.13, ND, UG); *Director* (1.1, 1.13, ND, UG)
Short, Tim: *Editor* (2.0)
Simpson, Hannah: *Production Secretary* (1.1-1.7); *Production Co-ordinator* (1.8-1.13, ND, UG, BC, 2.0-2.13)
Smith, Andy: *Camera* (1.1-1.7, 1.9-1.13, UG, 2.0-2.13)
Stevens, Hannah: *Runner* (2.0)
Street, Natalie: *Production Manager* (2.0, 2.6-2.13)
Tajiki, Maz: *Sound* (1.4, UG)
Tennant, David: *Narrator* (ND)
Thomas, Stephen: *Assistant Producer* (2.10)
Thomas, Steve: *Researcher* (1.1-1.13, UG, 2.0)
Thompson, Mark: *Camera* (2.0)
Turner, Phil: *Sound* (1.1, 1.3, 1.4, 1.8-1.13, UG, 2.0)
Ullah, Brian: *Sound* (2.4)
Van Koningsveld, Roger[2]: *Sound* (1.1, 1.3, 1.6-1.8, 1.10-1.13, ND, UG, 2.0)

1 Credited as John McCombi on 2.5
2 Credited as Roger van K on all but 1.1, ND, UG

Weeks, John: *Runner* (2.0)

Westergaard, Mike: *Tities Music* (1.1)

Williams, Hannah: *Runner* (1.1-1.11, 1.13, ND, UG); *Edit Assistant* (2.1-2.4); *Researcher* (2.0, 2.5-2.13)

Windley, Ryan: *Sound* (1.8, 1.9, UG, 2.0, 2.6, 2.9-2.13)

Young, Mal: *Executive Producer for Dr Who* (1.1-1.13, ND, UG)

Zafar, Joe: *Camera* (2.11-2.13)

APPENDIX C:
TOTALLY DOCTOR WHO

Doctor Who Confidential was not the only series made to accompany the second season of *Doctor Who*... *Totally Doctor Who*, aimed at the legions of children who were now following the adventures of the Doctor and Rose, was commissioned by the BBC's children's channel, CBBC.

The weekly episodes, transmitted on successive Thursdays, were presented by Liz Barker and Barney Harwood and featured in-studio guests (listed below), behind the scenes looks at the making of the series and special competitions. Other regular items included: a trivia quiz to find the 'Who-ru' (or *Doctor Who* trivia guru); 'Companion Academy', a reality-show-format competition judged by motivational coach and actor Jeremy Milne, *Doctor Who* stunt coordinator Abbi Collins and *Doctor Who Magazine* editor Clayton Hickman and ultimately won by young fan Louise Delmege; the 'Filing Cabinet', featuring submissions from viewers; and a sneak-preview of the upcoming episode of *Doctor Who*.

All episodes had a scheduled start time of 5.00 pm; the first 11 had their debut transmission on BBC1, but (in order to accommodate coverage of the Wimbledon tennis tournament) the last two aired on BBC2. The date of initial broadcast and duration are listed below. Each episode was repeated a day later (on Friday) at 6.30 pm, then on Saturday at 6.30 pm and the following Monday at 1.00 pm. All repeats were on the digital channel CBBC. Small edits were made to some of the repeats to correct errors spotted by viewers on the original transmissions. (Most notably, on one episode, the names of third and fifth Doctor actors Jon Pertwee and Peter Davison were misspelt in captions – as 'John Pertwee' and 'Peter Davidson' respectively; this was corrected for the repeats.)

T1	Episode 1	13 April 2006	26'47"	Noel Clarke
T2	Episode 2	20 April 2006	27'31"	David Tennant
T3	Episode 3	27 April 2006	26'19"	Noel Clarke
T4	Episode 4	4 May 2006	27'39"	David Tennant, Joe Pickley
T5	Episode 5	11 May 2006	27'58"	Sheelagh Wells, Jessica Atkins, Camille Coduri
T6	Episode 6	18 May 2006	27'38"	Camille Coduri, Andrew Hayden Smith
T7	Episode 7	25 May 2006	27'30"	Paul Kasey, Rob Mayor (prosthetics), Julie Ankerson (foley artist)
T8	Episode 8	1 June 2006	27'11"	Rory Jenkins
T9	Episode 9	8 June 2006	27'03"	Charlie Bluett (Prosthetics), Paul Kasey, MyAnna Buring, Mike Valentine (underwater cameraman)
T10	Episode 10	15 June 2006	26'08"	Ronny Jhutti, Kevin McCurdy (fight coordinator)
T11	Episode 11	22 June 2006	23'59"	Russell T Davies
T12	Episode 12	29 June 2006	27'02"	Edward Thomas, Abisola Agbaje
T13	Episode 13	6 July 2006	26'59"	Camille Coduri, Nicholas Briggs, Paul Kasey, Raji James, Elisabeth Sladen, Mat Irvine (visual effects designer)

CREDITS

Ablett, Dan: *VT Editor* (T1)
Archer, John: *Studio Cameras* (All)

Attille, Ros: *Producer* (T6-T13)
Ayers, Catherine: *Studio Sound* (T5-T8, T12, T13)
Baker, Tim: *Title Music* (T2-T13)
Barker, Liz: *Presenter* (All)
BDH: *Graphics* (All)
Bradley, Nigel: *Location Cameras* (All)
Brailsford, James: *VT Editor* (T1); *Offline Editor* (T2, T3, T9)
Burt, Tony: *Studio Sound* (All)
Chappell, Catherine: *Researcher* (T1, T2)
Coles, Simon: *Location Sound* (T13)
Cooper, Joe: *Location Cameras* (T11)
Cossey, Mark: *Executive Producer* (All)
Dan, Hong: *Location Sound* (T11)
Davies, Carolyn: *Vision Mixer* (T1-T6)
Davies, Dewi: *Location Cameras* (T2, T9-T11)
Davies, Jonathan: *Aston Operator* (T3)
Davies, Russell T: *Executive Producer for Doctor Who* (All)
Dicks, Angela[1]: *Script Supervisor* (T5, T6, T9, T10)
Doleman, Mark: *Location Cameras* (T3, T12)
Ellyn, Eirios: *Make Up* (T2-T4, T6-T12)
Evans, Carrie: *Researcher* (All)
Evans, Robert: *Offline Editor* (T7)
Gardner, Julie: *Executive Producer for Doctor Who* (All)
Gerrard, Catherine: *Researcher* (T1-T10, T12, T13)
Goodman, Mike: *Studio Cameras* (All)
Hall, Simon: *Producer* (All)
Hannington, Mark: *Location Sound* (T4-T6)
Hart, Stephen: *Location Cameras* (T3)
Harwood, Barney: *Presenter* (All)
Hatcher, Chris: *Studio Cameras* (T9-T13)
Heard, Tony Andrew: *Studio Sound* (T1-T4)
Hicks, Sian: *Make Up* (T5-T8, T13)
Honeybill, Catrin: *Production Team* (All)
Hopkins, Mike: *Offline Editor* (T3)
Hoy, Steve: *Location Sound* (T6)
Hubbard, Steve: *Location Sound* (All)
Hunt, Sarah: *Location Sound* (T5, T8)
Huyton, Eric: *Location Cameras* (T2, T8)
Jackson, Simon: *Studio Cameras* (T1-T8, T10-T13)
Jameson, Jack: *Assistant Producer* (All)
Jenkins, Glenn: *Studio Sound* (T9-T11)
Jenkins, Sian Eleri: *Script Supervisor* (T2-T4, T7, T8, T12, T13)
Johnson, Ian: *Studio Sound* (All)
Jones, Darren: *Dubbing Mixer* (T7-T9, T12, T13)

---

1 Credited as Angie Dicks on T10, T11

Jones, Dave: *Assistant Producer* (T1, T3, T5, T12, T13)

Jones, Sara[2]: *Offline Editor* (T2, T4, T5)

Keogh, Donovan: *Assistant Producer* (T1)

King, Jason: *Aston Operator* (T1, T2)

Knight, Emily: *Researcher* (T1-T11, T13)

Lutman, Lucy: *Production Team* (T1-T8); *Researcher* (T9-T13)

Mansell, Rob: *Online Editor* (T1, T2)

Mastafa, Rahim: *Offiline Editor* (T6-T8, T11)

McCombie, John: *Location Sound* (T7, T11)

Meredith, Kevin: *Location Sound* (T2, T3, T8-T10)

Millard, Ross: *Location Cameras* (T1, T8, T10, T13)

Miller, Steve: *Dubbing Mixer* (T1-T6, T10, T11)

Moss, Richard: *Online Editor* (T3-T13)

Newman, J.P.: *Location Cameras* (T4, T5, T8)

Nouss, Reem: *Executive Producer for CBBC* (All)

Parry, Alan: *Location Sound* (T3, T12)

Payne, John: *Studio Director* (T9-T11)

Payne, Sarah: *Production Team* (T12)

Procter, Mark: *Edit Producer* (T1, T2)

Protheroe, Iola: *Floor Manager* (T1-T8)

Quigley, Simon: *Assistant Producer* (T2-T8, T13)

Roberts, Alys: *Production Team* (T9-T13)

Roberts, Gwyndaf: *Studio Director* (T1-T9, T12, T13)

Rogers, Johnny: *Location Cameras* (T7, T13)

Ross, Gordon: *Location Cameras* (T9)

Scott, Zoe: *Production Manager* (All)

Seaborne, Gillane: *Series Producer* (All)

Shevki, Jacqui: *Production Team* (T1); *Production Co-ordinator* (T2-T13)

Smith, Dean: *VT Editor* (T1); *Offline Editor* (T2-T13)

Smith, Iain: *Location Cameras* (T1, T6)

Thomas, Ann: *Vision Mixer* (T7-T13)

Thomas, Edward: *Set Design* (All)

Thomas, Jeff: *Studio Cameras* (T1-T9)

Thompson, Mark: *Location Cameras* (T4-T7)

Thomson, James: *Location Sound* (T4)

Tozer, Dave: *Location Sound* (T1, T2, T8, T10, T13)

Udall, Susannah: *Assistant Producer* (All)

Walton, John: *Lighting Director* (All)

Windley, Ryan: *Location Sound* (T1, T7)

Woodward, Simon: *Location Sound* (T9)

Wyn Jones, Richard[3]: *Floor Manager* (T9-T13)

Zikking, Andrew: *Offline Editor* (T3-T5)

---

2 Credited as Sarah Jones on T2

3 Credited as Richard Jones on T9, T10

APPENDIX D:
WINNING THE RATINGS WAR

After the ratings success of Series One, the big question was whether or not the advent of a new Doctor so soon into the show's revival would adversely affect *Doctor Who*'s popularity with the general audience. A third series had been guaranteed by the BBC's Controller of Drama, Jane Tranter, at a preview screening of 'The Parting of the Ways' in June 2005, but audience response to Christopher Eccleston's replacement remained uncertain. Could the programme maintain the strong performance of its first year as it entered its second?

INTRODUCTION

At the heart of BBC1's 2005 Christmas Day schedule, 'The Christmas Invasion' not only won in its time slot but finally managed to outdo the ratings phenomenon of ITV1's *Coronation Street*, coming a close second to BBC1's *EastEnders* later that evening. Earlier in the year, Series One had been consistently beaten by both soaps, and usually by a third – ITV1's *Emmerdale* – but 'The Christmas Invasion' marked the start of a new phase in *Doctor Who*'s ratings success.

For most of Series Two, the show was the top-rated show each Saturday evening (though it did come a close second to the television 'event' *The Eurovision Song Contest*). A pattern was quickly established: *Doctor Who* edged up from almost always being in the week's top 20 to frequently being in the week's top ten. The Time Lord was starting to equal the soaps for popularity – consistently outdoing *Emmerdale* and rivalling both *EastEnders* and *Coronation Street* – a situation that became only more pronounced as the series' later start in the year took it into the summer months. As the weather improves, television ratings generally go down – *Doctor Who*'s figures briefly seemed to be following this expected trend around the middle of its run, yet recovered strongly toward the end, while the soaps' audiences continued to decline. By the end of the series, more people were watching the fate of Rose Tyler than almost anything else on TV.

The exception was the football World Cup coverage, which can still deliver audience numbers beyond the reach of ordinary programming. With certain England matches attracting absolutely huge audiences, *Doctor Who* was like every other programme – not in the same league. But the series did end its run with more than a million more viewers than had the Series One finale, despite the seasonal changes that were driving down the ratings for the supposedly unbeatable soaps to as low as four million... And while the World Cup seemed to contribute to declining overall television audiences ('There's nothing else on!'), football, rather unexpectedly, turned out to be the Doctor's friend, as a number of episodes inherited large audiences from popular matches broadcast immediately beforehand, and managed to hold on to them.

FINAL RATINGS

The following is a detailed breakdown of the final, consolidated ratings for Series Two, including time-shifted video recordings, featuring the final reported viewing figure in millions for the initial Saturday night broadcast on BBC1, the audience share (the percentage of the total television audience in that time slot who tuned in for the broadcast), the audience Appreciation Index (or AI, an index based on a rating of 1 to 10 given by demographic samples of viewers) and the audience reach (percentage of total televisions tuned in for the broadcast), as well as, for the purposes of comparison, the viewing figure for the top competitor in the time slot. The final column gives the Series One viewing figures for the equivalent weekend in 2005.

EPISODE	VIEWING FIGURE	SHARE	AI*	REACH	COMPETITOR	SERIES ONE
'The Christmas Invasion'	9.84m	44%	84	18	6.55m (ITV1 Who Wants to be a Millonaire)	n/a
'New Earth'	8.62m	40%	85	16	5.10m (ITV1, Harry Potter and the Chamber of Secrets)	7.63m ('Aliens of London')
'Tooth and Claw'	9.24m	43%	83	17	3.48m (ITV1, Midsomer Murders)	7.98m ('World War Three')
'School Reunion'	8.31m	42%	85	15	2.64m (BBC2, Snooker)	8.63m ('Dalek')
'The Girl in the Fireplace'	7.90m	38%	84	14	3.50m (ITV1, Peter Pan)	8.01m ('The Long Game')
'Rise of the Cybermen'	9.22m	44%	86	17	3.06m (ITV1, X-Men)	8.06m ('Father's Day')
'The Age of Steel'	7.64m	38%	86	14	5.30m (ITV1, Prince's Trust 30th Birthday Concert Live)	7.11m ('The Empty Child')
'The Idiot's Lantern'	6.76m	33%	84	12	6.04m (ITV1, Soccer Aid 2006)	6.86m ('The Doctor Dances')
'The Impossible Planet'	6.32m	41%	85	11	n/k	7.69m ('Boom Town')
'The Satan Pit'	6.08m	38%	86	11	4.09m (ITV1, Who Wants to Be a Millonaire)	6.81m ('Bad Wolf')
'Love & Monsters'	6.66m	40%	76	12	2.55m (C4, Deal or No Deal)	6.91m ('The Parting of the Ways')
'Fear Her'	7.14m	41%	83	13	3.62m (ITV1, Who Wants to Be a Millonaire)	n/a
'Army of Ghosts'	8.19m	45%	86	15	n/k	n/a
'Doomsday'	8.22m	44%	89	15	3.29m (ITV1, Mrs Doubtfire)	n/a
Series average (excl TCI)	7.71m	41%	84	14	n/a	7.95m
Year-on-year average	7.68m					7.57m

Source for viewing figures: Broadcasters' Audience Research Board Ltd (BARB)
* AI figures not sourced from BARB

CHART POSITIONS

The following is a breakdown of British TV chart positions for each episode, compared to: other BBC1 programmes on the day of broadcast; other BBC1 programmes during the week of broadcast; other programmes on all other channels in the same time slot; other programmes on all channels on the day of broadcast; and other programmes on all channels during the week of broadcast.

EPISODE	BBC1 DAY	BBC1 WEEK	TIME SLOT	ALL DAY	ALL WEEK
'The Christmas Invasion'	2	5	1	2	9
'New Earth'	1	4	1	1	9
'Tooth and Claw'	1	5	1	1	10
'School Reunion'	1	5	1	1	12
'The Girl in the Fireplace'	1	6	1	1	13
'Rise of the Cybermen'	1	2	1	1	6
'The Age of Steel'	2	7	1	2	15
'The Idiot's Lantern'	1	6	1	1	18
'The Impossible Planet'	2	8	1	2	18
'The Satan Pit'	4	9	1	4	19
'Love & Monsters'	1	6	1	1	15
'Fear Her'	2	12	1	2	20
'Army of Ghosts'	3	3	1	3	7
'Doomsday'	1	5	1	1	8

Source: Broadcasters' Audience Research Board Ltd (BARB)

APPENDIX D

ANALYSIS

The first thing to note is that in 2006 every episode of *Doctor Who* achieved a top 20 position in the UK TV charts, a feat narrowly missed the previous year when 'The Empty Child' was in twenty-first place. 'Rose' had claimed seventh place at the start of Series One, but a year later five episodes of Series Two plus the 2005 Christmas special occupied positions in the top ten. As for Series One, every episode of Series Two was unbeaten in its time slot – no matter what ITV1 scheduled in 2005, the commercial channel was unable to dislodge *Doctor Who* from the top slot; in 2006, it often seemed that ITV had surrendered Saturday evenings to the BBC, generally relying on reruns of movies that rarely secured substantial audiences. ITV1 did appear to hit back briefly with a couple of pieces of 'event television' scheduled against *Doctor Who*. The show's ratings and share did slip as a result, although other factors probably played a greater part.

For BBC1, it was possibly more significant that *Doctor Who* was bucking another trend through its second run. It's frequently stated that television audiences decline in good weather, and several episodes of Series One bore witness to the effect of sunny Saturdays. In 2006, however, the show tended if not to defy the weather entirely, at least to maintain a much healthier audience than most other top shows. Significant here is the fate of BBC1's flagship soap *EastEnders*, which has been essentially unchallenged at the top of the charts (alongside *Coronation Street* on ITV1) for more than 20 years. On Christmas Day, the soap held a small lead over the tenth Doctor's debut, but by Easter 2006, its ratings were starting to slide: *Doctor Who* outrated every episode of *EastEnders* in its final two weeks, and managed higher ratings and chart positions than several other editions of the soap in several other weeks during the run. Having beaten *Coronation Street* into third place on Christmas Day, *Doctor Who* also outperformed a couple of episodes of the ITV1 juggernaut in each of its last two weeks. And ITV1's *Emmerdale*, a consistent ratings-winner in 2005, rarely challenged *Doctor Who* in the upper reaches of the charts second time around. While *Doctor Who* generally managed to hold on to or improve its ratings across the two years, in 2006 the dominant soaps were actually about two million down on their 2005 viewing figures. This reflects an overall drift downwards in the numbers watching terrestrial (non-digital/non-satellite) channels and indeed in total television audiences – there are simply fewer people watching television with each year that goes by, it seems.

All of which was overturned by the advent of the football World Cup, with several matches securing average audiences approaching 20 million, a figure that actually disguises much higher peak audiences at key stages of various matches (notably those featuring the England team). Blanket coverage of the tournament severely affected viewing figures for non-football programming, with millions of people simply giving up on watching television for its duration. The flip side of this was that healthy football audiences would often stay (slumped?) in front of the screen for the programmes that followed. *Doctor Who* benefited from this effect twice, or arguably three times: 'Tooth and Claw' and 'Rise of the Cybermen' both followed high-profile matches and apparently held on to a good proportion of the football fans, even if some of those 'casual viewers' didn't return a week later. The influence of this 'football effect' on 'Army of Ghosts' is less certain, since 'Doomsday' the next week managed a slightly higher audience without a preceding football match, and the two-part story had the advantage of much greater publicity than had been seen since the earlier weeks of the series. The World Cup also had an odd effect on the TV charts, since BARB divides the television coverage into three parts (which it does not do for other sports events) – pre-match, match and post-match. This, of course, tends to put the 15-minute segments of post-match analysis into very high positions in the charts – which is why 'Army of Ghosts' was third for the day and not second.

Also of note for Series Two are the effects of certain regular 'special' events. Like 'The Empty

Child' the year before, 'The Age of Steel' had a significantly earlier start time (and so a lower audience) than other episodes, thanks to BBC1's annual broadcast of *The Eurovision Song Contest*. On both occasions, the latter took the top spot for the night, although, intriguingly, an appreciation index in the 60s suggests that the 8.33m viewers of the contest didn't actually enjoy it that much. On the same evening, ITV1 scheduled a live concert celebrating and fundraising for the Prince's Trust charity; it's impossible to be certain if that show dented the ratings for 'The Age of Steel', although since that episode's audience figure was higher than that of 'The Empty Child' the previous year, it seems unlikely.

The other episode potentially affected by a one-off event was 'The Idiot's Lantern', with *Soccer Aid* challenging it for the top spot (and missing). While *Soccer Aid*'s audience went up as soon as *Doctor Who* finished, the charity event may not have had a significant impact – 'The Idiot's Lantern' had an almost identical rating to 'The Doctor Dances' 12 months earlier. In fact, the reason for the drop in audience figures around this time may be more easily discerned: the last weekend of May not only includes a public holiday but also falls at the end of a week-long break from school for the nation's under-16s. With millions of families away from home, nobody's there to turn on the television.

Year-on-year, Series Two enjoyed a very slight improvement in its viewing figures – a ten-episode average of 7.68m against 7.57m the year before – rising at its climax to figures similar to those it had achieved at the start of the run and confirming *Doctor Who*'s place among the most popular television shows in the UK.

BBC3 REPEATS

EPISODE	7PM SUNDAY 1 JANUARY	9PM FRIDAY 10 FEBRUARY	8PM SUNDAY 9 APRIL	SATURDAY 15 JULY	7PM THURSDAY 17 AUGUST	7PM FRIDAY 1 SEPTEMBER
'The Christmas Invasion'	0.50m	0.26m	0.50m	0.23m	0.32m	0.27m

EPISODE	SUNDAYS 7PM	FRIDAYS 9PM	DAILY 7PM (mid-season)	DAILY 7PM (end of season)	DAILY 7PM (summer)
'New Earth'	0.38m	0.46m	0.28m (a)	0.22m (c)	0.29m (e)
'Tooth and Claw'	0.56m	0.40m	0.25 (a)	0.26m (c)	0.25m (e)
'School Reunion'	0.63m	0.43m	0.27m (a)	0.36m (c)	0.22m (e)
'The Girl in the Fireplace'	0.69m	0.35m	0.24m (a)	0.31m (c)	0.29m (e)
'Rise of the Cybermen'	0.63m	0.31m	0.14m (a)	324,000 (c)	0.18m (e)
'The Age of Steel'	0.62m	0.38m	0.17m (b)	0.39m (c)	0.25m (e)
'The Idiot's Lantern'	0.64m	0.42m	0.15m (b)	0.27m (c)	0.18m (e)
'The Impossible Planet'	0.69m	0.32m	0.16m (b)	0.27m (c)	0.26m (e)
'The Satan Pit'	0.66m	0.32m	0.26m (b)	0.32m (c)	0.37m (e)
'Love & Monsters'	0.72m	0.21m	-	0.35m (c)	0.37m (e)
'Fear Her'	0.54m	0.15m	-	0.37m (c)	0.34m (e)
'Army of Ghosts'	0.76m	0.57m	-	0.23m (d)	0.31m (e)
'Doomsday'	0.70m	0.37m	-	0.43m (d)	0.33m (e)

(a) Weekday broadcasts from 22 to 26 May.
(b) Weekday broadcasts from 19 to 23 June.
(c) Weekday double/triple bills from 3 to 7 July.
(d) Double bill on 21 July.
(e) Weekday/weekend broadcasts from 19 to 31 August.

Again, these figures show *Doctor Who* reversing the expected seasonal decline (that had affected Series One) towards the end of the run, with a set of very strong and very consistent figures throughout the 13 weeks. The repeat figures tended to be higher for episodes where the BBC1 debut had reached a lower audience, although this trend was not as marked as in 2005 and seems to have been more a response to higher levels of publicity for the show in those weeks. The various weekday showings secured unspectacular but healthy figures for their time slot on digital channels.

TOTAL VIEWERS PER EPISODE, RANKED

In 2001, BARB discontinued its practice of calculating a total audience for individual television programmes from figures for debut, repeat and omnibus showings within a seven-day period. However, various studies have shown that audiences on BBC3 are composed of as much as 95 percent 'new' (rather than repeat) viewers, so there is still some validity in setting out these informal totals. As supplied in *Back to the Vortex*, the following unofficial chart is compiled by adding BARB's consolidated BBC1 ratings for each episode to the figures available for same-week BBC3 repeats. The equivalent figures for Series)ne are also included here for purposes of comparison.

EPISODE	TOTAL BBC1 + BBC3
'Rose'	11.3m
'New Earth'	10.7m
'The Christmas Invasion'	10.3m (a)
'Tooth and Claw'	10.2m
'Rise of the Cybermen'	10.2m
'Army of Ghosts'	9.5m
'Dalek'	9.4m
'School Reunion'	9.4m
'Doomsday'	9.3m
'The Unquiet Dead'	9.2m
'The Girl in the Fireplace'	8.9m
Series Two average	8.9m
'Father's Day'	8.8m
'The Long Game'	8.7m
'World War Three'	8.6m
'The Age of Steel'	8.6m
Series One average	8.6m
'The End of the World'	8.4m
'Boom Town'	8.3m
'Aliens of London'	8.2m
'The Empty Child'	8.0m
'Bad Wolf'	8.0m
'The Parting of the Ways'	7.9m
'Fear Her'	7.8m
'The Idiot's Lantern'	7.8m
'The Doctor Dances'	7.6m
'Love & Monsters'	7.6m
'The Impossible Planet'	7.3m
'The Satan Pit'	7.1m

(a) includes New Year's Day repeat, eight days after first broadcast.

These figures are of necessity approximate, with consolidated figures from BARB not available for a number of BBC3 repeats. While Series Two hit some lower 'lows' than did Series One, its average figure is once again rather higher, and it has a much higher number of episodes breaking the barrier of nine million viewers. The 'event' episode effect can be seen clearly here, with 'Rose', 'New Earth' and 'The Christmas Invasion' attracting the best audiences.

DOCTOR WHO CONFIDENTIAL

This was also a very strong year for BBC3's companion show, with its final edition being seen by more than a million viewers, a significant and very rare achievement in the multichannel world. The programme regularly appeared in BBC3's weekly top ten, taking first place four times and also featuring strongly in the overall multichannel chart throughout the series. Once again, *Cut Down* versions were broadcast in some slots. There were also late-night repeats for some editions.

EPISODE	SATURDAY DEBUT	SUNDAY REPEAT	FRIDAY CUT DOWN
'One Year On'	0.28m (a)	-	-
2.1 'New New Doctor'	0.76m	0.34m	-
2.2 'Fear Factor'	0.66m	-	-
2.3 'Friends Reunited'	0.61m	-	-
2.4 'Script to Screen'	0.73m	0.30m (b)	0.25m
2.5 'Cybermen'	0.78m	0.33m	0.17m
2.6 'From Zero to Hero'	0.63m	0.36m (b)	0.16m
2.7 'The Writer's Tale'	0.45m	0.36m (b)	0.21m
2.8 'You've Got the Look'	0.55m	0.39m (b)	0.22m
2.9 'Myths and Legends'	0.46m	0.25m (b)	0.16m
2.10 'The New World of Who'	0.77m	0.48m (b)	-
2.11 'The Fright Stuff'	0.54m	0.35m (b)	0.21m
2.12 'Welcome to Torchwood'	0.57m	0.48m (b)	-
2.13 'Finale'	1.01m	-	0.29m

(a) 7 pm Sunday 9 April.
(b) Cut Down edition.

TOTALLY DOCTOR WHO AND THE CHILDREN'S AUDIENCE

Shown each Thursday afternoon on BBC1, and repeated three times each week on the digital channel CBBC, this children's magazine show managed to attract audiences that rivalled and often exceeded those for other popular children's shows. Among children, *Doctor Who* itself was proving to be, by a good margin, the highest-rated programme on television, so there was a ready-made audience for this spin-off. Audience research revealed a high proportion of *Totally Doctor Who*'s audience to be adults, although this is in fact fairly normal for other shows like *Blue Peter* and is largely (though probably not entirely) explained by parents watching with their children. While the last two shows went out on BBC2 (thanks to sports coverage taking over BBC1), so reducing the ratings, the eleventh edition followed a football match, with spectacular results ...

EDITION	VIEWING FIGURE
1	0.8m
2	0.9m
3	0.8m
4	0.7m
5	0.8m
6	0.8m
7	0.8m
8	0.7m
9	0.7m
10	0.4m
11	1.5m
12	0.6m
13	0.5m

Totally Doctor Who performed exceptionally well against other children's television shows, but the parent series had an outstanding run amongst under-16s. In its original 26-year run, between 40% and 60% of *Doctor Who*'s audience tended to be children. This time around, that figure is much lower, but this seems largely because the show has finally achieved what its legend always claimed for it – it's become a 'family show' that is actually being watched by families. It's also become by far the children's favourite, or at least most-watched, television show, topping the under-16s' chart every week and leaving previous chart-toppers like *EastEnders* trailing it by a third of a million viewers or more. As well as achieving that increase in the size of the child audience recorded for a single programme, Series Two managed a remarkably consistent young audience, with the number of children generally holding up even in weeks where the number of adults dipped. A good example of this is the near-identical age-four-to-15 ratings for the two-part Cyber-story, unaffected by the significant drop in total audience numbers from 'Rise of the Cybermen' to 'The Age of Steel' . The biggest audience dip among young viewers came, unsurprisingly, during the schools' mid-term break in late May and early June; but all bar one Series Two episode managed to attract a larger child audience than the first-series average.

EPISODE	VIEWERS AGE 4-15	% EPISODE TOTAL AUDIENCE
'Rise of the Cybermen'	1.66m	18%
'Doomsday'	1.64m	20%
'Army of Ghosts'	1.64m	20%
'The Age of Steel'	1.60m	21%
'The Christmas Invasion'	1.58m	16%
'Boom Town'	1.54m (a)	20%
'Rose'	1.51m	14%
'Tooth and Claw'	1.48m	16%
'New Earth'	1.46m	17%
'Fear Her'	1.43m	20%
Series Two average	1.40m	18%
'Dalek' (c)	1.38m	16%
'The Parting of the Ways'	1.38m	20%
'The Unquiet Dead'	1.33m	15%
'School Reunion' (c)	1.33m	16%
'Father's Day'	1.29m	16%
'The Long Game'	1.28m	16%
'The Girl in the Fireplace'	1.26m	16%
'The Idiot's Lantern' (b) (c)	1.23m	18%
'World War Three'	1.20m	15%
'Love & Monsters'	1.20m	18%
'The Impossible Planet' (b)	1.20m	19%
'Bad Wolf'	1.16m	17%
Series One average	1.13m	15.60%
'The Satan Pit'	1.09m	18%
'Aliens of London'	1.07m	14%
'The Empty Child' (b)	1.00m	14%
'The Doctor Dances' (b) (c)	0.96m	14%
'The End of the World'	0.96m	12%

(a) There is no obvious explanation for this figure being so high!
(b) Broadcast during mid-term school holidays
(c) Broadcast during public holiday weekends (excluding Christmas/Easter)

All of which indicates that, in its second year, *Doctor Who* not only maintained but actually built on its popularity among the under-16s – a loyal and growing audience that is the foundation of the show's future success well beyond the three or four series that are often the norm in UK television...

EPISODE POLLS

Members of the Outpost Gallifrey website Forum participated in weekly discussions and rankings of each episode of Series Two; each episode was given a ranking between one and five, with five being the highest. With a wide cross-section of *Doctor Who* fans participating – typically in the region of 3,500 to 4,000 people (with a high of almost 4,400 for 'Love & Monsters', the episode that provoked the most debate) – they were a good indicator of fan reaction to the episodes. The percentage rankings below have been calculated by adding together the total number of marks received by each episode (as of 24 September 2006) and dividing by the maximum that could have been achieved if everyone who voted had given the episode a five. (The ratings for *Attack of the Graske* and the *Children in Need* special are based on much lower numbers of voters but are included for the sake of completeness.)

'Doomsday'	93%
'The Impossible Planet'	92%
'Army of Ghosts'	92%
'School Reunion'	88%
'The Satan Pit'	88%
'Tooth and Claw'	86%
'The Girl in the Fireplace'	86%
'The Christmas Invasion'	84%
'The Age of Steel'	82%
'Rise of the Cybermen'	80%
'The Idiot's Lantern'	72%
'New Earth'	69%
'Love & Monsters'	66%
'Fear Her'	65%
'Attack of the Graske'	81%
Children in Need special	62%

Comparison of these rankings with the AI figures for the general audience suggests that 'Fear Her' was relatively less well-received by fans than by most viewers, for whom 'Love & Monsters' took bottom position this year. 'Doomsday' achieved the same fan ranking – 93% – as the previous season's most popular episode, 'Dalek', but both 'Love & Monsters' and 'Fear Her' fell below the 68% achieved by Season One's least well-received episode, 'Boom Town'. This makes 'Fear Her' the least popular Russell T Davies-produced *Doctor Who* episode yet amongst fans, judging by these Outpost Gallifrey rankings.

APPENDIX E:
NOVELS, COMICS AND OTHER FICTIONS

Doctor Who is no longer just a television odyssey... in fact, it hasn't been for years, since the BBC opened up to licensees for original fiction way back in 1964 in places like *TV Comic* and the *Doctor Who Annual*. The following is a guide to the recent ninth- and tenth-Doctor-related *Doctor Who* fiction in other media.

NOVELS

BBC Books continued publishing two batches of three books a year featuring the current Doctor, and in late 2005 wrapped up their series of Eighth Doctor and Past Doctor adventures to concentrate on the Eccleston and Tennant eras.

THE DEVIANT STRAIN

WRITER: Justin Richards
PUBLICATION DATE: 4 September 2005
COVER: Design by Henry Steadman, landscape photograph by Imagebank/Getty

WHERE AND WHEN: The fictional location of the Novrosk Peninsula, Russia, in the early 21st Century (a decade after nuclear submarines had begun to be decommissioned, which was around 1994 in our history). As the TARDIS line-up includes Rose and Captain Jack, the only space for this would appear to be prior to 'Boom Town'.

SYNOPSIS: Jack pilots the TARDIS to 21st Century Russia, responding to a distress signal. When met by soldiers lead by Colon Oleg Levin, the Doctor and his companions are forced to assume the identities of Russian and American intelligence officers investigating a body that has been found suffering complete atrophy. They meet Sofia Barinska, an authority figure in an quarantine community living in the radioactive area, who believes the body to be that of Pavel Vahlen, who had snuck out to meet a girl. The team find the girl in question, alive but aged considerably. Sofia believes her to be the mythical Vourdulak – a Russian vampire – but as they investigate they discover more... including a fragment of stone that causes rapid aging and a tentacled jelly-monster. When Sofia turns on Rose and tries to use the stone to age her, the truth becomes clear: the monsters are using the stones (and influence over the locals) to recharge their crashed spaceship. Following a battle that all but destroys the village, the Doctor defeats the monsters and the tensions between the locals are relieved.

THE STORY UNFOLDS: Jack describes early 21st Century Earth as a good-for-nothing barren wilderness. The Doctor once again uses psychic paper to establish credentials for himself. Although the Russians have decommissioned 150 nuclear submarines in the past decade, all their reactors still remain intact. When the soldiers find Valeria, only Jack is unwilling to leave her behind to die. Jack fears growing old and infirm. The Vourdulak legend seems to have some historical grounds: a death in St Petersburg in 1827. The base is manned by several semi-scientists, including the 'multi-disciplinary' Klebanov, despised wannabe teacher Alex Minin and dispassionate biologist Catherine Kornilova. Although the stone affects the Doctor, and ages his hand, it quickly heals itself, unlike the more permanent effect it has on humans. Rose mentions *Frankenstein*; *Planet of the Apes*; 'Mr Spocksky', referring to the character Mr Spock in *Star Trek* (1966-69); and in a post-modern twist, BBC1's 'Trip of a Lifetime' trailers for the first season of the new *Doctor Who* (see page 135 of the novel). The code to the base's airlock is 1-9-1-7, a reference to the start of the Russian Revolution. Klebanov has been director of the base since 1947, around 60 years prior to the adventure. Fan theory has it that the monsters in the story are the Rutans (nemesis of the Sontarans, who appeared onscreen in 'Horror of Fang Rock' (1977)), although they are never specifically referred to as such in the book.

BAD WOLF: No reference. As the Bad Wolf story arc had been resolved on TV by the date of publishing, the authors felt no need to crowbar the phrase into this batch of books.

PUBLISHING NOTES: As with the previous batch of three books (covered in the first *Back to the Vortex* volume) *The Deviant Strain*, *Only Human* and *The Stealers of Dreams* were published simultaneously, and Henry Steadman provided cover designs for all. Also as with the previous batch, editor Justin Richards commissioned a title from himself, and asked friend/author/predecessor Stephen Cole to edit it. Richards himself continued to receive a Creative Director credit on all three books; Shirley Patton and Stuart Cooper were listed as Commissioning Editors; and Russell T Davies, Julie Gardner, Mal Young and Phil Collinson as representatives of BBC Wales. The font used for the main text remained Albertina, with typesetting by Rocket Editorial (Stephen Cole's own company) and printing by GGP Media. Although all new series merchandise to that point had used Lloyd Springer's Deviant Strain font for titles and product descriptions, this book was the first to credit it – as was also named after it. The 'Gallifreyan numbering' used in the chapter headers and on the book's spines continued to give a clue as to the intended reading order, and we have adopted this here. *The Deviant Strain* is thus book number four.

ONLY HUMAN

WRITER: Gareth Roberts
PUBLICATION DATE: 4 September 2005
COVER: Design by Henry Steadman

WHERE AND WHEN: Bromley, 2005 and 29,185 BC. After the brief initial sequence in 2005, Jack remains in that time alone for a month, but only two days pass for the Doctor and Rose in the past.

As with *The Deviant Strain*, this story must take place between 'The Empty Child' and 'Boom Town'. Although there is nothing specific within the text to support this, the spine numbering suggests that this follows *The Deviant Strain*.

SYNOPSIS: The Doctor, Rose and Jack arrive in London, 2005, to find a Neanderthal man has been causing havoc and been taken to Southam Hospital. Rescuing him, they discover his name is Das and he came from Wednesday 24 May 29,185 BC – the Doctor warns them that he cannot be sent back as his body is unstable from the rip engine that transported him in the first place. Jack stays in 2005 to teach Das about modern life, while the Doctor and Rose travel back to find out what happened... They find a team of researchers from the future: during a space battle in Monoceros between Kallix Grover and the Sine Wave Shrine of Shilltar, Earth got caught in the middle of a reef of magnetic energy that destroyed all computer technology – this team have travelled into the past to try and re-learn the lost secrets of man. But behind a mysterious grey door, something is killing the researchers... Rose marries a Neanderthal, and the Doctor defeats the deadly 'Hy-Bractor', leaving them free to return to the future and collect Jack, where Das has married a modern woman, and plans to name their first three children Rose, Jack... and the Doctor.

THE STORY UNFOLDS: The Doctor is taking his companions to Kegron Pluva, a planet that has an orbiting sun and nine moons, 43 seasons in a year, solid water (ice, surely?), a 'dog-plant-fungus thing' and edible metal plums. In a rare fit of poor fashion sense, Jack wears a blue and white sailor outfit for the start of the novel. A dirty rip engine is something that 'punches a hole in time'. Sky+ (a PVR service launched in 2001) interferes with the sonic screwdriver, which has 29 computers in it. In reality, there is no Southam Hospital, but as Southam is in Coventry, hundreds of miles away from Bromley, it's unlikely anyone would be taken to one place from the other. Das has no waist. When infiltrating a hospital, the Doctor suggests to Rose that she acts like she owns the place – she points out that as it's NHS, she does. The Ebola virus, first seen in humans in 1976, is cured in 2076. The Doctor subtly implies he has seen a bigger penis than Captain Jack's before. He has met a couple of Neanderthals before, and claims they died out 28,000 years ago (current science has only estimated 'roughly 30,000'). Werinoka, a nurse in Southam Hospital, is briefly caught up in the story and feels that her life will never be the same again (foreshadowing ongoing plotlines in Tennant's first year as the Doctor). Rose refers to Das as one of the Village People (a disco band that started in 1977) and makes reference to Sylvanian Families (the 1985 Epoch/Tomy toy craze) and, oddly, the Kraals from 'The Android Invasion' (1975). The Doctor mentions Coldplay (1997 onwards, British rock band), *Chitty Chitty Bang Bang* (the 1964 Ian Fleming novel, or more likely the 1968 film) and *Carry on Cleo* (1964). The Doctor keeps a flat in Bromley, and has a credit card with a £500,000 credit limit on it and the PIN number '1'. The team in the past are led by Chantal Osterberg (who in the prologue is aged seven on 2 October 483,553). They can all live to around 400 and rely on drugs to suppress emotions, except Quilley who refuses. The Doctor once wrestled a tiger. In the 46th Century everyone is bald and has at least one leg missing. Das falls in love with Bakewell tarts, mini-rolls, *Are You Being Served?* (1972-1985), *Coronation Street* (1960-), *Spider-Man* (2002), *Trisha* (1998-2004), *Celebrity Love Island* (2005-), spritzers and *Will & Grace* (1998-2006). Jack has, in the past, seduced both an Elizabethan girl and a Gloobi from 39th Century Tarsius. He also remembers that the inhabitants of the planet Celation (from 'The Daleks' Master Plan') aren't too fussy. By the 484th Century, the EU has collapsed and the Mage of Toronto has been assassinated. Crakkits is a Neanderthal game. The TARDIS translation circuit seems to give the Neanderthals 'chav' personalities, and Rose invents the manicure around 28,000 years too early. Cephalids are notorious gamblers. Das bumps into Jackie Tyler, who makes a brief cameo in the story complaining about wasps. (Given the date, this is probably during the year she spends looking for her missing daughter.) Chantal describes the Hy-Bractors as 'upgrades', and the Doctor mocks her, calling them 'human version 2.0' – foreshadowing the Cybermen's words the following year.

THE STEALERS OF DREAMS

WRITER: Steve Lyons
PUBLICATION DATE: 4 September 2005
COVER: Design by Henry Steadman, cityscape photography by Photodisc

WHERE AND WHEN: A day on Colony World 4378976.Delta-Four, in 2775 (aka Arkannis Major). When Rose calls Jackie she refers to the events of 'Boom Town', so this trip must be *en route* to Raxacoricofallapatorius just before 'Bad Wolf'. This opens up the possibility that further stories take place in this gap, although it's unlikely that they would be carrying Blon's egg with them for any longer than necessary.

SYNOPSIS: The Doctor, Rose and Jack arrive in the 28th Century on an unusual colony world where technology is out of date and the inhabitants are squeezed into just 10% of the planet's space. The Doctor goes undercover as a journalist, teaming up with local Inspector Waller. He discovers that fiction is banned and that public enemy number one is Hal Gryden, who runs the 'Static' TV channel and encourages people to use their imaginations. Rose and Jack meet Domnic Allen, a 'fiction geek' who creates his own comics and lives in fear of the Big White House, where his kind are taken to be 'cured'. Domnic runs away and Jack vows to find Gryden. He meets a tramp who reveals himself to be the very man, but is actually just a delusional who leads him into a trap. Waller and the Doctor face Arno Finch, who is threatening to blow up his workplace – and Waller sees two possible realities simultaneously... When the two go to the Big White House, the Doctor realises that Waller was there herself when she was younger. Rose, left alone, begins seeing images from Domnic's comic and goes in search of monsters, eventually meeting a fantasy version of the Doctor who leads her into a trap in the Big White House, where she teams up with the real Jack. Meeting up with Domnic, the Doctor discovers that natural micro-organisms are turning people's dreams into reality – so he kills the ones in Domnic's head, allowing him to dream safely. Finally, a civil war erupts between the thinkers and the rest of the population. The Doctor realises that Gryden is a group hallucination, but uses the concept to bring imagination back into the world safely.

THE STORY UNFOLDS: The Doctor wears a wrist-watch that displays the year. Telesales exists on the Colony World, but the operatives are completely honest. The Doctor uses the sonic screwdriver to interrupt a radio signal, but later it runs out of power. Jack tells a (possibly untrue) story about someone dressed as the Face of Boe ('The End of the World'). When the Doctor modified Rose's phone ('The End of the World') it was not only to increase its range; it also never needs recharging any more. The Doctor also has a phone, but never takes it with him. The police of this time use 'spray-cuffing', while the psychiatrists still use the Rorschach inkblot test, developed by Hermann Rorschach in the early 20th Century. The planet has a network called the Ethernet. The Doctor refers to Mickey and Adam as 'apes' who couldn't cope. When Rose realises the media are in control, she wonders if it's the Jagrafess again ('The Long Game'). The Doctor says to Domnic 'D'you wanna come with me?', echoing the line from the trailer campaign in Spring 2005. Rose says the Doctor watches *Batman* (although she doesn't specify which of the many versions).

BAD WOLF: The only reference in the September 2005 novels – on page 113, Tyko says: 'We've good reasons to be afraid of the big bad wolf.'

THE STONE ROSE

WRITER: Jacqueline Rayner
PUBLICATION DATE: 3 April 2006
COVER: Design by Henry Steadman, statue by Stone/Getty, background scene by Photolibrary.com

WHERE AND WHEN: Variously: London, early 2007 (for Jackie and Mickey, this seems to be set between 'The Christmas Invasion' and 'School Reunion'); Rome, 18-19 March 120 AD); London, two weeks after they left; 19 March 120 AD again; and 16th Century Italy (where the Doctor spends several months). For Rose, this story is set sometime after 'New Earth' (she has vague memories of experiences that Cassandra had inside her body) and before 'School Reunion'.

SYNOPSIS: Mickey takes Rose, Jackie and the Doctor to the British Museum to see an exact replica of Rose in statue form – from nearly 2000 years ago. The Doctor and Rose travel back to investigate. They meet a man, Gracilis, whose son has recently disappeared, and a fortune-telling slave called Vanessa whom Gracilis buys to help find the boy. Gracilis introduces them to Ursus, who has been creating a perfect statue of Optatus, the missing boy, but will let no-one into his studio... except Rose, whom he offers to sculpt. But Ursus is no sculptor, and is instead using powers to turn people into statues, which he does to Rose. The Doctor discovers that Vanessa is actually from Sardinia in 2375. While he is searching for statue-Rose, he hears a mysterious voice speaks from behind another statue and gives him a cure for Rose's new condition. He is then captured for having stolen a horse and thrown into an arena, where he fights a bear and then leads an escape. He transforms all the statues back to humans and then heads for 2007 to save Rose. When the statue in the museum doesn't change back, the Doctor realises it's a copy, and returns to Rome and restores the real Rose. They rejoin Vanessa, who explains that her father was researching time travel, and that she arrived in Rome when she made a wish, but doesn't understand how it could have come true. They find Ursus worshipping the goddess Minerva in human form – but when the Doctor wishes to see her in her real form, she transforms into a small dragon. Ursus turns the Doctor into stone and Rose wishes that he'd never come back for her – his stone form vanishes. The dragon is a GENIE, and everything that has happened so far has been due to people making unwise wishes. Rose resurrects the Doctor and gives an antidote phial to his past self, and the two then leave Vanessa back in her own time and set the GENIE free. Finally, the Doctor explains how the duplicate statue ended up in the British Museum – he took some time out to work with Michelangelo on a copy himself.

THE STORY UNFOLDS: Mickey's friend Vic once asked Rose to pose on a sheepskin rug in her underwear. The Doctor takes credit for a giant foot in the British Museum, saying it is the remains of the Ogre of Hyfor Three that he defeated around 200 AD. Mickey has been doing volunteer work in the British Museum. Jackie has been watching *Rome* (2005). The bed sheets in the TARDIS have Winnie the Pooh and Piglet on them. The Doctor watches Living TV (a cable channel started in the UK in 1993 as UK Living and renamed in 1997) on the TARDIS scanner. Rose remembers a time when she and her friend Shareen stole some wine from Jackie and passed out, despite intending to go to Danny Fennel's party. She likens her relationship with Ursus to the one between Clarice Starling and Hannibal Lecter in *Silence of the Lambs* (1991, based on the 1988 novel by Thomas Harris) and has memories of the events of 'Rose', 'Parting of the Ways' and (via a dream-flashback to moments when Cassandra was inhabiting her body, specifically a reference to 'petrifold regression') 'New Earth'. The Doctor knows that although Vanessa sounds like a Roman name, it was in fact invented by Jonathan Swift in the early 18th Century. The Doctor names his cellmates after '60s pop band the Beatles – John, Paul, George and Ringo. He uses the sonic screwdriver to calm wild animals. Rose plans on rampaging through Colchester (the oldest recorded town in Britain, which the Romans invaded in 43 AD), and also makes references to *AI* (2001) and *The Sixth Sense* (1999). The GENIE (Genetically Engineered Neutral Imagination Engine) was invented by Salvatorio Morretti in 2375 and (with the typical nature of human greed and envy) was responsible for the destruction of the planet. The solution humanity came up with was to return to 17 April 2375 and destroy all but the prototype. The Doctor claims that this sort of paradox is the cause of a number of 'fictional' stories actually being based on fact – apart from genies, elves, pixies and gnomes, also *The Moomins* (1945-), *Chorlton and the Wheelies* (1976-79), *SpongeBob Squarepants* (1999-), *Robocop* (1987-), 'five famous justices of the future' (*The Famous Five*, 1942-1963) and Miss Marple (1930-1971). Rose is given a copy of the book *Kitten's Garden Adventure* by Marian Golightly by the GENIE. She loved the Disney version of *Aladdin* (1992).

PUBLISHING NOTES: Two names were added to the list of credits for this latest batch of three books: Peter Hunt as Production Controller (he had this responsibility on the mainly non-fiction books *Doctor Who: Monsters and Villains* and *Doctor Who: Aliens and Enemies* as well) and Helen Raynor as Consultant Editor. Mal Young's name was removed from the production team credit. All three of these novels were read by David Tennant in abridged form for two-CD talking book sets, released in July. A short interview with the author was added at the end of the second disc of each. Tennant read the stories in his natural Scottish accent, but used his Doctor voice where appropriate.

THE FEAST OF THE DROWNED

WRITER: Stephen Cole
PUBLICATION DATE: 3 April 2006
COVER: Design by Henry Steadman, ship and background by Corbis

WHERE AND WHEN: A Friday and Saturday in London, early 2007. (This dating is based on the fact that Rose's visits to modern London are usually 'in sequence'.)

As with the prior two novels, set between 'New Earth' and 'School Reunion' for both the Doctor and Rose and also Mickey.

SYNOPSIS: Rose takes the Doctor to visit her old friend Keisha, who is mourning the death of her brother Jay, a Navy officer killed in action, but they see the ghost of Jay, beckoning them to find him before 'the feast'. Going to the wreckage of Jay's ship, they find Anne Dusty, the mother of one of Jay's crewmates, about to jump in the water – she had received a similar message. The Doctor breaks into the local Navy base and meets liaison officer Vida Swann before getting discovered and chased into the wreckage, where he finds evidence of alien technology and meets Jay briefly, before the ghostly images of a pirate and a Nazi marine drag him away. He teams up with Vida as the people of London begin suffering advanced dehydration and Anne and Keisha enter a zombie-like state and try to return to the Thames. Mickey captures Keisha, but Anne escapes and drowns herself. They all reunite at Vida's lab, where the Doctor runs tests on her, discovering that the oceans are using pheromones to control humans and eventually turn them into aliens. Swann and Mickey hack into the personnel files of the Ascendent and discover that its commander, Admiral Crayshaw, died age 55 on the Ballantine in 1759. Rose and Vida are captured, Mickey and the Doctor go after them, and Keisha and Jackie get lured to the water by a ghostly image of Rose. The Doctor defeats the aliens and everyone comes back to life.

THE STORY UNFOLDS: Rose is 19 and had a crush on Keisha's brother five years ago. Keisha believes Rose was overseas during the year she disappeared, although Mickey seems to have been telling people she moved to Nottingham. The Doctor doesn't think chips taste right unless they're wrapped in newspaper (and on the planet Jacdusta in the Dustijek nebula, they cost £10 a portion and come with no newspaper wrapping). When Rose disappeared before 'Aliens of London', Keisha had her friends attack Mickey to find out where she'd gone. The Doctor uses his old alias of John Smith twice – first as Sir John Smith, then as his son Dr John Smith Junior. He loves Norfolk. Rose refers to Admiral Crayshaw as 'Captain Bird's-Eye', a reference to Captain Birdseye, mascot of Birds Eye Frozen Foods. Jackie has an on-off relationship with a man called Dennis. The Doctor quotes *Alice in Wonderland* (1865) when he says 'curiouser and curiouser'; also, 'I'll be back' from the *Terminator* series of films (1984, 1991, 2003) and 'I'm just going outside, I may be some time' (slightly misquoting Lawrence Oates' final words, as transcribed by Robert Falcon Scott in 1912). The woman in the Powell Estate newsagents watches *Casualty* (1986-) and Rose buys a copy of the *Star* (a UK tabloid first published in 1978) from her. In reference to the terminology of the 1963-89 series, the Doctor struggles to decide whether Rose is an 'assistant' or a 'companion', but decides the latter 'sounds like something off *Crimewatch*' (1984-). The Doctor and Rose refer to the 1930s Universal *Frankenstein* films (the Doctor says 'It's alive!') and Calvin Klein fragrances (launched 1981). There was a tramp that used to hang around the Powell Estate that the locals nicknamed Old Scary. When Rose went missing initially, Keisha tried to seduce a drunken Mickey, and since then has let him believe that they went further than they actually did. The aliens refer to the legend of the Trojan Horse (from Virgil's *The Aeneid*, and as seen in the *Doctor Who* story 'The Myth Makers'). The Doctor uses the sonic screwdriver to resonate concrete, as in 'The Doctor Dances'.

TORCHWOOD: The only reference in these three novels comes on page 179 where Kelper believes they will need the organisation's help to get out of their current predicament.

APPENDIX E

THE RESURRECTION CASKET

WRITER: Justin Richards
PUBLICATION DATE: 3 April 2006
COVER: Design by Henry Steadman, ship by Corbis, background images by Photolibrary.com

WHERE AND WHEN: A couple of weeks, on and around Starfall, the far future.

Rose refers to New Earth, implying they have only recently left that planet. This batch of books is therefore probably all set immediately after that television story.

SYNOPSIS: The TARDIS crash-lands on Starfall, a planet populated by humans in a pre-industrial state – steam is used to power everything, but the technology seems to be highly futuristic, if lacking in electricity. Asking around at the local pub, the Broken Spyglass, they meet young Jimm (a wannabe pirate) and robotic barmaid Silver Sally. They are told of the zeg field, which stops all electrics from working (including the TARDIS) and of Hamlet Glint's lost treasure, which many – including the owner of Starfall, Drel McCavity – seek, but people don't talk about, lest they be attacked by the dreaded Kaspar. The Doctor meets McCavity, and learns of Glint's notoriety and of the Resurrection Casket: Glint's final haul that McCavity seeks. He is attacked by a Kaspar (aka Kevin), who he discovers is from the Black Shadow Dimension and, despite being both gentle and a genius, is forced to kill anyone that is given the mark of the black shadow. The Doctor escapes under the technicality of not having a real name. He joins up with Jimm and his friends, including Silver Sally, to sail out of the zeg field to find the Casket, where the TARDIS should also be operable once more. As they approach the edge of zeg, though, they discover that Sally (and the other robot shipmates) were Glint's old crew. During a lengthy battle, the Doctor realises that McCavity's obsession with the Resurrection Casket is due to the fact that he believes it will bring the wife he murdered back to life. They defeat the robots and McCavity, set Kevin free of his responsibilities, and discover that Glint once stepped into the Casket, and became Jimm ...

THE STORY UNFOLDS: The 'black shadow' is clearly based on the 'black spot' as used in Robert Louis Stevenson's *Treasure Island* (1883), which was placed in the hand of an accused shipmate who had been found guilty of a crime. It has since featured in a great deal of pirate literature, most recently in the second *Pirates of the Caribbean* film, *Dead Man's Chest* (2006). The Doctor uses an everlasting match, first seen in David Whitaker's novelisation *Doctor Who in an Exciting Adventure with the Daleks* (1964), this time explaining that it's made from wood from the planet Umbeka, where heat stimulates tree growth. The Doctor uses his psychic paper to pretend to be from the Intergalactic Tourist Bureau, and then later to fake the mark of the black shadow. Kevin likes kronkburgers ('The Long Game').

PUBLISHING NOTES: As with Richards' previous books, he kept the Creative Director role, but handed editing over to Stephen Cole. In a rare typographical error, Jimm is referred to as Jim on page 221.

I AM A DALEK

WRITER: Gareth Roberts
PUBLICATION DATE: 18 May 2006
COVER: Design by Henry Steadman

WHERE AND WHEN: In Berkshire, one night on a Thursday in May (probably 2007, in keeping with Rose's appearances in modern England being 'in sequence'), with a brief flashback to Durham in 1970. Likely to be set between 'New Earth' and 'School Reunion' due to the tone and the TARDIS line-up.

SYNOPSIS: Although aiming to play golf on the moon, the Doctor and Rose land in modern England, where they discover a Dalek in an archaeological dig through Roman soil, and a woman who is killed and resurrected. The Dalek begins to come back to life and explains that the woman, Kate, is carrying part of the Dalek Factor – a gene left behind when its ancestor fell to Earth in a time capsule in the final days of the Time War. The Doctor and Rose are able to convince Kate to use her connection to the Daleks against it.

THE STORY UNFOLDS: Cultural references are made to *Mary Poppins* (1934), Radio 2 presenters Terry Wogan and Ken Bruce, Anne Murray's 'Snowbird' (1970), *Brainteaser* (2002-), *The X Factor* (2004-), Kylie Minogue and the chain store Boots. The TARDIS kidnaps the Doctor near the start to take him directly to the site of the dig. The head of the dig lives in the town of Twyford, Berkshire at 15 Redlands Road, WP4 2LN, a fictional postcode. 'Never turn your back on a dead Dalek' is apparently a saying from the year 4000. The Doctor refers to himself as the Oncoming Storm, and also says 'I'm so sorry' – a catchphrase of the tenth Doctor. The Doctor uses a time ring, as first seen in 'Genesis of the Daleks'. He doesn't agree with credit cards.

PUBLISHING NOTES: This 103-page novella was printed as part of the BBC Quick Reads range – a collection of stories aimed at people who don't usually read, in association with World Books Day, 2006. They are much shorter, and with larger print, than the average novel, but do not pitch down to an especially younger age group. The recommended retail price for the Quick Reads books was £2.99 (compared to £6.99 for the full length novels at the time) with many shops running promotions making it possible to get them even cheaper. Although regular cover artist Henry Steadman was back, the typesetting and printing were sourced elsewhere by companies willing to provide their services for free.

COMING SOON...

The Art of Destruction by Stephen Cole
The Nightmare of Black Island by Mike Tucker
The Price of Paradise by Colin Brake
All published 21 September 2006

APPENDIX E

COMICS

Panini's *Doctor Who Magazine* continued to print new, nine page comic strips each month, and in June 2006 also gathered together the ninth Doctor strips (*The Love Invasion, Art Attack* – both covered in *Back to the Vortex* – *The Cruel Sea, A Groatsworth of Wit* and the *Doctor Who Annual's Mr Nobody*) into their thirteenth special edition: the 100-page *The Ninth Doctor Collected Comics*.

THE CRUEL SEA

WRITER: Robert Shearman
ILLUSTRATORS: Mike Collins (Pencils), David A Roach (Inks), James Offredi (Colours), Roger Langridge (Letters)
EDITORIAL: Scott Gray (Consulting Editor), Clayton Hickman (Editor)
PUBLICATION: *Doctor Who Magazine* issues 359-362; 21 July 2005, 18 August 2005, 15 September 2005, 13 October 2005

WHERE AND WHEN: Across one evening on a liner in the seas of early 22nd Century Mars. The Doctor and Rose have been to other alien worlds previously, setting this after the BBC Book *The Monsters Inside* (itself most probably set just before 'Dalek'). The most likely timeframe for this is after 'Father's Day', when the Doctor also takes Rose to Woman Wept (see 'Boom Town') before the arrival of Captain Jack.

SYNOPSIS: *Part One* – A woman in a wedding dress throws her ring overboard – but the red sea attacks her. Later, the Doctor and Rose try to relax on a luxury liner on the Martian seas but are captured by a woman with a gun. Meanwhile, two women tend to the sleeping body of Alvar Chambers, the widower of Susannah (the bride from the previous night). While the Doctor tries to talk his way out of their current situation, he, Rose and their captor are attacked by an image of the bride, dripping with red liquid, who then collapses on the deck. The woman with the gun forces the Doctor to go to Chambers, where he meets Drs Latimer and Godwin, who keep Chambers (barely) alive for financial purposes. Back on the deck. Rose tries to help the bride, who suddenly explodes into a puddle of cranberry juice. The Doctor is lead away from Alvar, and thrown overboard ...

Part Two – Under the Martian seas, the Doctor is surprised to find he can talk, and seems to have himself as a companion. Back on the ship, Rose is captured, but the puddle of cranberry juice forms the word 'run' before attacking. Rose befriends Chambers' fourteenth wife, Vikki, who takes her to Chambers. Rose argues with his financial adviser, but the Doctor bursts in, dripping with the red juice, warning them that they have unleashed something very old and very powerful. It transpires that this is exactly what Chambers' associates are hoping for – something that can renew Chambers' youth. The Doctor tricks Vikki into kissing Alvar, which turns her into the red liquid too – disgusted, Rose runs off. Chambers awakens, and he and the Doctor cackle – but it isn't the Doctor, it's the sea disguised. Alone, Rose stares into a bathroom mirror – her reflection leaps out and swallows her.

Part Three – Rose dreams. The Doctor didn't return for her at the end of her adventure with the Autons, she stayed behind... had Mickey's baby, Susannah... and then separated from him.

The Doctor finally returns to tell her 'It also travels in time'. He asks her to leave Susannah, but she can't, so instead he leaves, saying he can't and won't face the universe alone. In the real world, 'the Doctor' and Chambers make their way to the engine room to find the financial adviser, wife two. She willingly allows Chambers to feed on her, crawling into his gaping mouth. In the dream, the Doctor meets Rose again, years later, when she is working on a supermarket checkout. He had kidnapped baby Susannah and made her his fifty-seventh companion. Meanwhile in reality, more doppelgängers appear, as 'Rose' and one of the previous 'wives' join together. In the dream, the Doctor meets Rose again when she is elderly and in a nursing home. Throwing her zimmer frame at the Doctor, Rose smashes the walls of her dream and finds the Doctor, who instructs her to use the sonic screwdriver to destroy the images, even at the risk of his own life. She returns to the ship, and does so ...

Part Four – The sea-images of 'Alvar', 'Rose' and the 'wife' all merge with that of 'the Doctor' to regain strength. 'The Doctor' explains to Rose that the reflections have no life until they take people's bodies, which usually last only an hour. Meanwhile, in the Doctor's imagination, he talks to 'himself' and warns him that if the bodies he's absorbed wake up, things could get 'a bit messy'. On deck, Rose falls into the eyes of 'the Doctor', and finds all the dead wives, and Chambers. Chambers wants to stay in this warped reality, but Rose and the wives choose to leave. 'The Doctor' enters the TARDIS to steal it, but the real Doctor's face appears out of the walls and swallows him. The Doctor/'The Doctor' leaves the TARDIS and forces all the reflections out of himself, allowing the two travelling companions to leave Mars behind for the wives to enjoy their new lives.

THE STORY UNFOLDS: By the early 22nd Century Mars had become a pleasure planet with an artificial red sea comprised mainly of cranberry juice. Multi-trillionaire Alvar Chambers has had 19 wives, including the one who dies at the story's opening, and has made his business by owning all the air on Earth.

BAD WOLF: No reference.

PUBLISHING NOTES: The first and only ninth Doctor strip to be written by someone who had written for the TV version.

A GROATSWORTH OF WIT

WRITER: Gareth Roberts
ILLUSTRATORS: Mike Collins (Pencil Art), David A Roach (Inks), James Offredi (Colours), Roger Langridge (Letters)
EDITORIAL: Clayton Hickman, Scott Gray
PUBLICATION: *Doctor Who Magazine* issues 363-364; 10 November 2005, 8 December 2005

WHERE AND WHEN: The opening is set in the final days of Robert Greene's life – September 1592. Although the majority is set '400 years' in the future, it's clearly not literally 1992 – most likely this story is set in 2006, chronologically appropriate for Rose. The scenes at the Rose Theatre depict the premiere of *Richard III*, which is generally believed to have been in 1592 also. Modern locations include Tottenham Court Road, Charing Cross Road and Leicester

Square, all in central London. Probably set shortly after 'Father's Day' as the Doctor makes a reference to 'our big row'.

SYNOPSIS: *Part One* – Two unseen aliens look for violent thoughts in 16th Century London, and find Robert Greene, a man obsessed with his rivalry with Shakespeare. They move him 400 years into his own future, where the Doctor and Rose are drawn to him. He enters a book store and is amazed to discover that Shakespeare has been remembered, but he has not. His rage, and the power given to him by the aliens, cause him to go on a destructive streak through central London, with the Doctor and Rose following closely behind. Catching up, the Doctor tries to talk reason into Greene, explaining that creatures are using him – but the creatures leave the playwright and attack ...

Part Two – The Doctor identifies the creatures as Shadeys. He and Rose escape and travel to see the premiere of *Richard III*. Rose flirts with Shakespeare to distract him, and the Doctor takes his place as Richard. As Shakespeare begins to compare Rose 'to a summer's day', Greene (dragged back in time by the creatures) launches at him. Rose drags Shakespeare back to the theatre (where the Doctor is performing marvellously as Richard III) for a final showdown. The Doctor and Shakespeare are unable to convince Greene to back down, but Rose points out that he could be remembered for saving the world. Greene banishes the creatures, and the two leave ...

THE STORY UNFOLDS: In modern-day London, the film *Shakespeare's Shrew* (starring Ty Baxter as Petruchio) is opening. Rose is disappointed that Shakespeare doesn't look like Joseph Fiennes (referring to the 1998 film *Shakespeare in Love*).

BAD WOLF: The pub on the first page has an image of a wolf with the letters 'BW' emblazoned on it.

PUBLISHING NOTES: The final comic strip of the ninth Doctor ends with him wondering if he'll ever be forgotten – Rose promises it will never happen ...

THE BETROTHAL OF SONTAR

WRITER: John Tomlinson, Nick Abadzis (Story)
ILLUSTRATORS: Mike Collins (Pencil Art), David A Roach (Inks), James Offredi (Colours), Roger Langridge (Lettering)
EDITORIAL: Clayton Hickman, Scott Gray
Sontarans created by Robert Holmes
PUBLICATION: *Doctor Who Magazine* issues 365-367; 5 January 2006, 2 February 2005, 2 March 2006

WHERE AND WHEN: The planet Serac, during the course of one day, many years into the Sontaran/Rutan conflict. As Mickey does not appear, this is most likely set sometime prior to 'School Reunion'.

SYNOPSIS: *Part One* – On the mining rig the 'Betrothal of Sontar', Sontaran Colonel Snathe continues to battle morale problems by executing his crew, to the disapproval of his subordinate, Lerox. More morale-boosting seems to take the form of allowing the crew to kill the weak native people, the Inuk, again to Lerox's disapproval. Lerox reports to Snathe that an alien artefact has been discovered at the Noord Eisig shelf, and Snathe despatches Skagg and Krege to uncover it. The artefact is the TARDIS – Rose and the Doctor have just arrived. Seeing Skagg, the Doctor urges Rose to call him Fred from here on. Skagg believes them to be Rutans and takes them prisoner. Lerox reports to Snathe and discovers something interesting in the latter's quarters. He storms off, disgusted at his commanding officer. The Doctor and Rose have been shackled up separately, and are interrogated by Snathe and Lerox respectively – Rose getting something of an easier time. Meanwhile, Skagg and Krege are attacked by an unseen force, and Snathe, recognising the TARDIS, realises he has the Doctor in captivity. The Time Lord is released... only to be threatened with beheading by the Sontaran Colonel.

Part Two – The Doctor gains a reprieve when he recognises the symbol of Thanatos that Snathe is wearing and promises to help him fulfil his destiny. Lerox gives Rose a tour of their facilities, during which she discovers his unpopularity with the other Sontarans. Lerox fights with Corporal Stakk. The Doctor enhances some of Snathe's equipment to find Thanatos – it is in the base of the Ventraux Massif – and the two travel there to find it. Back at the rig, Lerox discovers that Snathe has deserted and explains that Thanatos is a legendary weapon. At the Ventraux, Snathe and the Doctor discover a large number of the Inuk – Snathe is not afraid, but from the Inuks' mouths comes the thing that had attacked Skagg and Krege ...

Part Three – Lerox and Rose travel to try and find Snathe and the Doctor – who has realised that the Inuk are antibodies created by Thanatos. Although Snathe wants to fight, the Doctor leads an escape... and they find Thanatos. Lenox and Rose meet them there – and Thanatos merges with Snathe. The Doctor explains that Thanatos is a judgment engine. Its merging has caused it to judge the Sontaran home planet Sontar as having no future – and the world is destroyed. Snathe escapes and goes insane, trying to kill everyone but ultimately being sucked into the machine. Back at the 'Betrothal of Sontar', Lerox takes command and the Doctor and Rose leave ...

THE STORY UNFOLDS: The Doctor reveals he once swam the English channel naked following a lost bet with Oliver Reed. References are made to the Rutans (from earlier Sontaran stories, and 'Horror of Fang Rock'), the Mitchell Brothers (from BBC1's *EastEnders*, 1985-) and Stockholm Syndrome (named after the Norrmalstorg robbery of 1973 in which hostages began to bond with their captors). In Rose's handbag is a picture of her and Mickey, and another of the ninth Doctor in a 'kiss me quick' hat.

TORCHWOOD: Unlike with the ninth Doctor strips, none of the tenth Doctor strips feature this season's 'word'.

THE LODGER

WRITER: Gareth Roberts
ILLUSTRATORS: Mike Collins (Pencils), David A Roach (Inks), James Offredi (Colours), Roger Langridge (Lettering).
EDITORIAL: Clayton Hickman, Scott Gray

APPENDIX E

PUBLICATION: *Doctor Who Magazine* issue 368; 30 March 2006.

WHERE AND WHEN: Across four days (Thursday to Sunday) in the life of Mickey Smith. Probably between 'New Earth' and 'Tooth and Claw'.

SYNOPSIS: Following an attack by some angry Lombards, the Doctor and Rose decided to pay a visit to Jackie and Mickey – the Doctor mis-set the controls, however, and after he left the TARDIS, it jumped forwards a few days. The Doctor has decided to spend those few days getting to know Mickey. He reprograms Mickey's game system to have non-violent options, adjusts the TV to pick up a broadcast of *EastEnders* from ten years hence, plays football far too well, wins at the pub quiz machines (getting the approval of Mickey's friends), intrudes on a date Mickey has with Gina (and encourages her to turn her life around), makes the Earth invisible to the aggressive Bandrigan space fleet from Mickey's bedroom and eventually causes Mickey to lose his temper. Rose finally arrives (not realising she's missed three days), and the Doctor arranges for her to be happily reunited with her boyfriend.

THE STORY UNFOLDS: The Doctor plans on taking Rose to Oxyveguramosa next. Jackie is seducing a man by the name of Alan. Mickey plays football every Saturday with Chris (from work), Karl, Big Robbo and Little Robbo. T-Mobile appears to be called Z-Mobile in the Doctor's universe, and O2 is renamed O^2.

F.A.Q.

WRITER: Tony Lee (Story)
ILLUSTRATORS: Mike Collins (Pencil Art), David A Roach (Inks), James Offredi (Colours), Roger Langridge (Letters)
EDITORIAL: Clayton Hickman, Scott Gray
PUBLICATION: *Doctor Who Magazine* issues 369-371; 27 April 2006, 25 May 2006, 22 June 2006

WHERE AND WHEN: South West London, 'today', including Kelsey Road. Most of Rose's 'London' adventures have happened in chronological order, however, so it's more likely to be early 2007 than April 2006 (publication date). Craig went missing three weeks and five days ago. The story takes place over one afternoon, probably sometime after 'The Age of Steel' as Rose makes no suggestion of visiting Mickey despite being in the vicinity.

SYNOPSIS: *Part One* – In a surreal London street, cowboys ride dinosaurs chasing ninjas on unicorns. Something isn't right. The Doctor and Rose, on their way to the Great Wall of China, arrive and find faces (which the Doctor identifies as human) engraved in trees– but that isn't all... Rose uses a branch from a tree to defeat an attacking Viking, who has three teenage girls in shackles. Following an earthquake, the girls take the travellers to the library, where they meet the manager, Laurie, and a teacher, Cathryn Lloyd. Lloyd brings their attention to the only children unaffected – Craig and Trudy. Craig and Trudy are arguing over the relative merits of their favourite comic book characters, who magically appear and begin a fight. The Doctor helps break up the battle with an ice cream van, and Trudy worries 'He's not one of us'.

Craig responds by causing Cathryn and Rose to disappear, and bringing about a storm that will end the world ...

Part Two – Trudy calms down Craig and leads him away, but not before he's caused a statue to hold the Doctor prisoner. The Doctor realises he isn't in the real world, due to the weather inconsistencies. In the real world, Cathryn and Rose appear, but Cathryn's old colleague Miss Baldwin doesn't recognise her. Miss Baldwin confirms that Craig Phillips has been missing for weeks, along with a number of other students. Meanwhile the Doctor talks to Craig, and realises that Trudy isn't real, but Trudy convinces Craig otherwise – she says they played together as children, and encourages Craig to create a bigger trap for the Doctor. Craig creates a mobile prison cell, in which he imprisons not only the Doctor but Trudy as well. In the real world, Cathryn and Rose use the psychic paper to go undercover and interview Craig's mum, who tells them he vanished after receiving a parcel. Examining this, they realise the truth about the virtual world inside a box. Meanwhile, Trudy begs for her freedom, reminding Craig of the boys in the trees that had bullied him, and describing herself as his only friend. Mrs Phillips meanwhile shows Rose and Cathryn the family album and explains that Trudy was Craig's childhood imaginary friend, based on a sister whose death at a young age created in him a self-destructive streak. Finally, inside the box, new problems abound as Craig pitches the Doctor and Trudy into an arena with his favourite comic book villains ...

Part Three – The Doctor uses the sonic screwdriver to give himself Craig's powers, imprisoning all the monsters *and* Trudy. He hacks into the game to show Craig different possible futures – all of which involve him giving up his imaginary friend. Craig accepts this, but Trudy has become more powerful... He finally defeats her when he realises that she's not his sister but a self-destructive sense of guilt. Lloyd and Rose arrive in time for the Doctor to discover the former is an alien – Cyrelleod from Happytimez Intergalactical, the game's manufacturer – and that's why Miss Baldwin didn't recognise her. She explains away the whole thing as a case of misdelivered mail (as the box was meant for the exiled king of New Fraxonia, two doors down from Craig). Everyone returns home, and Craig plans a new life as a rock star ...

THE STORY UNFOLDS: Rose refers to the London Transport region 'Zone 4' as the location of 'The Christmas Invasion' and 'Rose'. The characters all seem to be based on comic book heroes of the Doctor's fictional world, including Stegnor the Conqueror, The Shield of Truth and The Revenger. The Doctor has been a comic book fan since he was at least 900.

PUBLISHING NOTES: In the twelfth episode of CBBC's *Totally Doctor Who*, host Barney Harwood interviewed artist Mike Collins, and designed the cat pirate seen on the seventh page of *F.A.Q.* Part Two.

COMING SOON...

THE FUTURISTS

WRITER: Mike Collins
ILLUSTRATORS: Mike Collins (Art), David A Roach (Inks), James Offredi (Colours), Roger Langridge (Letters)
EDITORIAL: Clayton Hickman, Scott Gray

PUBLICATION: *Doctor Who Magazine* issues 372- (Story not completed at the time of this book going to press)

DOCTOR WHO ADVENTURES

In April 2006, BBC Magazines launched *Doctor Who Adventures*, a fortnightly magazine (initially published every other Wednesday, later switching to Thursday) aimed at six- to 12-year-olds. This included a six-page comic strip, generally split into two parts across the issue and with the cliff-hanger appearing after the fourth page. The cliff-hangers are indicated in the descriptions below. Although most of these strip stories were written by Si Spencer or Alan Barnes, BBC Books and Audios regulars Michael Stevens and Jacqueline Rayner also joined in to help launch the range. Although these stories were aimed at a younger readership than those in *Doctor Who Magazine*, John Ross's stylised art and Adrian Salmon's bold colouring ensured they were of high enough quality to attract a large number of adults to buy the magazine for the strip alone.

WHICH SWITCH?

WRITER: Michael Stevens
ILLUSTRATORS: John Ross (Artwork), Adrian Salmon (Colouring)
PUBLICATION: *Doctor Who Adventures* issue 1; 5 April 2006.

SYNOPSIS: Although aiming for Shantella Prime, the TARDIS lands on Earth. The Doctor presses a random button on the console, and discovers it's a Wraparound Hologram generator. Another enters him into the Galactic Lotto. When he thinks he's found the in-flight stereo system, it's actually a Micromodulator that makes him and Rose tiny. They use the Doctor's (full-size) tie to climb onto the console, but Rose slips on some oil (cliff-hanger). The Doctor saves her by throwing down a cord, and apologises that he'd recently oiled the Gravity Guage. The Doctor walks straight into a cobweb, but Rose finds the correct switch and returns them to normal size. She suggests that perhaps the Doctor doesn't know what all the buttons on the console really do. He's not impressed.

MIRROR IMAGE

WRITER: Jacqueline Rayner
ILLUSTRATORS: John Ross (Artwork), Adrian Salmon (Colouring)
PUBLICATION: *Doctor Who Adventures* issue 2; 19 April 2006.

SYNOPSIS: The Doctor and Rose investigate a creepy alien castle filled with mirrors. An evil fanged Rose pulls the real Rose into one of the mirrors, where she is greeted by 'the Trapped' – others who have suffered a similar fate in the last 50 years. Out in the real world, an alternate Rose has befriended the Doctor, when he runs into the local villagers, who warn him away. He listens, leaving Rose stuck in the mirror (cliff-hanger). The alternate Rose's eagerness to leave makes the Doctor realise she can't be 'his'. The Doctor returns to the castle and uses his sonic screwdriver to open portals in the mirrors, returning everyone to their homes, and the Mirrorlings to their original dimension.

UNDER THE VOLCANO

WRITER: Si Spencer
ILLUSTRATORS: John Ross (Artwork), Adrian Salmon (Colouring).
PUBLICATION: *Doctor Who Adventures* issue 3; 3 May 2006.

SYNOPSIS: The Doctor and Rose have been kidnapped by head-hunters in Indonesia, 1883 – they believe the Doctor is there to defile their Mountain God, like the 'men of flame'. The Doctor undoes the ropes (something Baden Powell taught him c 1900) and they slip away. The Doctor explains that the men of flame are probably Chalderans, silicone-based life forms with incredibly high body temperatures who mine planets for lava. They find a group of Chalderans behind a waterfall, and are captured again. The Doctor distracts the creatures by making them argue, and then uses the sonic screwdriver to enable him and Rose to escape. They run through the waterfall, which kills the Chalderans with its low temperature, and the Doctor warns Rose they must get back to the TARDIS ready for 'the fireworks' (cliff-hanger). Krakatoa explodes, taking the remaining Chalderans with it. The Doctor suggests to Rose that they visit the Mating Dance of the Fire Dragons of Ket-El or a twin supernova near Deneb Three.

THE GERM WAR

WRITER: Alan Barnes
ILLUSTRATORS: John Ross (Artwork), Adrian Salmon (Colouring).
PUBLICATION: *Doctor Who Adventures* issue 4; 17 May 2006.

SYNOPSIS: The Doctor and Rose are on the run on an empty space station from a team of robots that scream 'Sterilise and disinfect'! These robots are the Disinfectroids, and they are trying to clean up the space station. The Doctor empties his pockets of an apple core, bus tickets, a Belgian phrasebook (which he carries despite the translation circuit on the TARDIS – and despite there being, at least at present, no such thing as a Belgian language!), a bit of jigsaw, a hairy lollipop, a water pistol, a cuddly toy... and finally finds his sonic screwdriver, which he uses to effect an escape back to the TARDIS. Before the Doctor and Rose can enter the ship, however, it is sucked up by the Disinfectroid's mighty vacuum cleaner (cliff-hanger). They follow, and discover that they have been transported to a dumping planet, half a universe away. They meet up with the humans from the space station, and the natives, who are unhappy at how their planet has been treated. The Doctor finds the TARDIS and takes them all back to the station, where the aliens can take out their revenge on the robots and the Doctor can reprogram them to dump their garbage at the manufacturer's site in New Brentford.

APPENDIX E

WARFREEKZ!

WRITER: Alan Barnes
ILLUSTRATORS: John Ross (Artwork), Adrian Salmon (Colouring).
PUBLICATION: *Doctor Who Adventures* issue 5; 31 May 2006.

SYNOPSIS: As the TARDIS snack machine is out of chocolate, the Doctor takes Rose to Belgium... or so they think. They are ambushed by wartime German soldiers, and discover they are being watched by a camera... This camera is transmitting to aliens half a billion light years away. The Doctor identifies the technology as being that of the Warfreekz, aliens who watch wars from afar. The Warfreekz gleefully watch as the camera electrocutes a solider, and then predict a dangerous battle ahead (cliff-hanger). The Doctor destroys the camera, and then Rose uses the sonic screwdriver to give her the appearance of an angel, scaring off the enemy soldiers. The Doctor then uses the camera to send a feedback pulse to the Warfreekz, causing them pain and putting them off their hobby. One soldier gratefully provides Rose with his weekly chocolate ration.

PUBLISHING NOTES: John Ross chose to include Destrii, from *Doctor Who Magazine*'s eighth Doctor strips, as one of the Warfreekz.

A DELICATE OPERATION

WRITER: Si Spencer
ILLUSTRATORS: John Ross (Artwork), Adrian Salmon (Colouring).
PUBLICATION: *Doctor Who Adventures* issue 6; 14 June 2006.

SYNOPSIS: The Doctor and Rose are inside someone's bloodstream. They attack a malicious entity, and the host's immune system kicks in. Unfortunately the immune system thinks of them as the enemy, so they escape, stopping only to have an argument about Rose's shoe collection. They go inside the evil creature, which promptly explodes for no readily apparent reason (cliff-hanger). In the outside world, the Queen of Svelna is on an operating table – the TARDIS and the two travellers are extracted by syringe... The Queen thanks the Doctor for saving her life, and he asks her to sign an intergalactic peace treaty. She accepts and proposes marriage to him. He's less than thrilled – not because she's a giant, but because the Svelnoids cheat at Tiddlywinks.

BLOOD AND TEARS

WRITER: Si Spencer
ILLUSTRATORS: John Ross (Artwork), Adrian Salmon (Colouring).
SCRIPT EDITOR: Gareth Roberts
PUBLICATION: *Doctor Who Adventures* issue 7; 29 June 2006.

SYNOPSIS: In the village of the Galathos, the Doctor and Rose hear the locals' sad tale of the 'sickwind' that infects them with an illness – when markings appear on their skin, they have seven days in which to slay a beast called the Dramos in order to save themselves. Even the cute Palanth cries at the stories. The time travellers set off to find the Dramos, as the Palanth becomes ill. The Dramos finds them first, and attacks. The Doctor intercepts – but plans to set the creature free... (cliff-hanger). The Dramos is a feeble creature, who weeps at the thought of being killed by the Galathos – and her tears heal the Palanth, better than the blood ever did. The Doctor takes the Dramos back to the village, and the Galathos tell her sad stories of the sickwind to get more of her healing tears.

FRIED DEATH

WRITER: Alan Barnes
ILLUSTRATORS: John Ross (Artwork), Adrian Salmon (Colouring), Paul Vyse (Lettering)
SCRIPT EDITOR: Gareth Roberts
PUBLICATION: *Doctor Who Adventures* issue 8; 13 July 2006.

SYNOPSIS: The Doctor and Rose arrive at Terry's Cafe, near Blethering and Wardleswick (apparently on the A342, which in the real world is in Wiltshire). Sitting down to enjoy some chips, they see a nearby man explode after eating too much food. The Doctor explains that the man was a Gastronaut – their young grow inside them, and they feed until they burst. Sure enough, a younger Gastronaut emerges, and informs them that the Earth is prime territory for its species' eating needs. The cafe is then invaded by hundreds of flying saucers. Famed Gastronaut Rammzi arrives and tries to take over from Terry by pureeing his mind (something he'd previously done to rival Pukka Oliffa of Geeza-7) but is distracted by Rose and turns to do the same to her (cliff-hanger). The Doctor and Terry manage to regain control, and the Doctor passes rumours round that there is a better restaurant at Quadrant 92. The Gastronauts leave, as does Terry's waitress, who quits. Rammzi is left stranded there – but Terry offers him his waitress's job ...

PUBLISHING NOTES: Rammzi is a parody of British celebrity chef Gordon Ramsey, who rose to fame in the1998 TV series *Boiling Point* and has since had successes with *Ramsey's Kitchen Nightmares* and *Hell's Kitchen*. Pukka Oliffa is similarly based on Jamie Oliver, an Essex-born celebrity chef known as 'the Naked Chef' who has had success with shows such as *Jamie's School Dinners*.

THE BIZARRE HERO

WRITER: Stewart Sheargold
ILLUSTRATORS: John Ross (Artwork), Adrian Salmon (Colouring), Paul Lang (Lettering)
SCRIPT EDITOR: Gareth Roberts
PUBLICATION: *Doctor Who Adventures* issue 9; 27 July 2006.

SYNOPSIS: The Doctor and Rose arrive back at the Powell Estate to find that an Ice Age seems to have hit. The only person they can find is one of Jackie's neighbours, Jason Harris. Harris tells them that this all started four days ago, when some aliens came and took everyone. The ice attacks him and freezes him, and then moves to attack the time travellers (cliff-hanger, after just 3 pages – the second half is also 3 pages). The two escape, but the ice catches up with Rose, absorbs her and speaks through her – explaining that it has always been on Earth and had to attack as global warming was killing it... The Doctor shatters the ice with his screwdriver, and then melts all of it with a weather machine.

PUBLISHING NOTES: The plot of this story bore some similarities to that of the *Doctor Who* Novella *Time and Relative* by Kim Newman (Telos Publishing, 2001).

SAVE THE HUMANS!

WRITER: Alan Barnes
ILLUSTRATORS: John Ross (Artwork), Adrian Salmon (Colouring), Paul Lang (Lettering)
SCRIPT EDITOR: Gareth Roberts
PUBLICATION: *Doctor Who Adventures* issue 10; 10 August 2006.

SYNOPSIS: The Doctor and Rose arrive at the Wumba's World of Wild safari park. The Doctor explains that he doesn't like meerkats, as he 'knows what they're planning'. The park is on another planet, where humans are kept as beasts. The two friends are captured and placed with the humans, including Steve, Phoebe and Adam. The prisoners are colonists from the 41st Century, and have become used to performing for the aliens' amusement. Suddenly a stomping noise is heard (cliff-hanger). Dinosaurs attack, and the Doctor encourages them to follow him by speaking in reptilian: 'Follow me for pizza.' He uses the dinosaurs to break out of the cages and leaves Adam and Steve to ponder their new future ...

PUBLISHING NOTES: This strip caused a little controversy, as the ending – with 'Adam and Steve' walking off to begin a life together – implied a homosexual retelling of the Biblical story of Adam and Eve.

BAT ATTACK!

WRITER: Alan Barnes
ILLUSTRATORS: John Ross (Artwork), Adrian Salmon (Colouring), Paul Lang (Lettering)
SCRIPT EDITOR: Gary Russell
PUBLICATION: *Doctor Who Adventures* issue 11; 24 August 2006.

SYNOPSIS: The Doctor and Rose are in London, 1897, and have helped Inspector Lestrade solve the case of the unsuitable suitor. They head off, only to be trapped by a sudden flock of vampire bats. They end up at the Royal Lyceum Theatre where Bram Stoker is presenting a dramatic reading of his new novel *Dracula*. Suddenly Count Dracula of Transylvania arrives demanding revenge for Stoker's misrepresentation of him. The Doctor tries to calm the situation, but instead gets a crossbow bolt fired at him. Stoker's wife, Florence, transforms into a vampire creature and captures the bolt in her hand. She summons the bats, which carry the real Dracula back to Transylvania. Florence has mesmerised the people in the theatre and intends to vampirise them all. The Doctor offers an alternative – if he can destroy the man who turned her, then she will be cured. But the man who did this is Oscar Wilde, currently held in Reading gaol.

PUBLISHING NOTES: Inspector Lestrade is presumably the same character as featured in Sir Arthur Conan Doyle's Sherlock Holmes stories.

THE BATTLE OF READING GAOL

WRITER: Alan Barnes
ILLUSTRATORS: John Ross (Artwork), Adrian Salmon (Colouring), Paul Lang (Lettering)
SCRIPT EDITOR: Gary Russell
PUBLICATION: *Doctor Who Adventures* issue 12; 7 September 2006.

SYNOPSIS: The Doctor is taken to Reading gaol by the bats. He springs the vampire Wilde from the cell with his sonic screwdriver. Meanwhile Rose is attempting a distraction elsewhere in the gaol, only to find that all the staff are vampires as well. They intend to turn Rose into a vampire, but the Doctor and Wilde burst in. The Doctor realises that Wilde is the source of the vampirism and can command all those who have been infected. This Wilde does, and Rose is saved. The Doctor drinks the vampire virus they have been cultivating and burps up a curative bubble that envelops all the vampires there. He then burps up more bubbles, which head off to cure any other vampires that might be around as well.

TRISKAIDEKAPHOBIA

WRITER: Alan Barnes
ILLUSTRATORS: John Ross (Artwork), Lee Sullivan (Colouring), Paul Vyse (Lettering).
SCRIPT EDITOR: Gary Russell
PUBLICATION: *Doctor Who Adventures* issue 13; 19 September 2006.

SYNOPSIS: Escaping from an attack by the Speardroids, Rose complains that they always arrive in danger. So the Doctor plugs the randomiser into the TARDIS and they arrive at galactic coordinates 13:13:13:13:13:13 on the thirteenth moon of the thirteenth planet of the thirteenth galaxy, on the thirteenth day of the thirteenth year of the thirteenth century. The TARDIS is hit by lightning and the Doctor and Rose meet Father Tragedy of the Triskaidekaphobes (which means fear of the number 13). They walk through the rain until they find a lawn in which is a lucky four leafed clover. The Doctor tosses a coin and it comes up heads every time. Suddenly a lightning monster attacks from the raincloud (cliff-hanger). It's really a matter transporter and the Doctor and Rose are taken on board a spaceship in the cloud where Bob Kreesus is harvesting luck from the planet below. The Doctor breaks his computer and luck returns to the planet. Kreesus threatens Rose but slips on a banana skin and falls off a cliff.

APPENDIX E

PUBLISHING NOTES: The randomiser was used by the Doctor to avoid the attentions of the Black Guardian and first appeared in 'The Armageddon Factor' in 1979.

DOCTOR WHO: BATTLES IN TIME

Doctor Who: Battles in Time was a part-work that had a test run of seven issues in two UK regions in mid-2006 before being relaunched nationally that September. Each issue featured a comic strip story. The stories in the first six issues were linked in an arc, while that in the seventh and final issue of the trial run was a stand-alone adventure.

GROWING TERROR

WRITER: Steve Cole
ILLUSTRATORS: John Ross (Artwork), Alan Craddock (Colouring).
PUBLICATION: *Doctor Who: Battles In Time* issue 1; 19 April 2006.

SYNOPSIS: The TARDIS makes a clumsy landing, having been dragged to an unnamed planet. The Doctor and Rose meet Coffa and Lute, two of the Tree people they previously encountered on Platform One, who explain that the survivors of the events on Platform One are disappearing one by one. Another ship arrives, but this releases a violent robot that tries to kill the Doctor and Rose. They run and are chased, but lead the robot and its owner – an intergalactic garden centre owner who wants the intelligent Trees as stock – into a patch of 'super-evolved space dandelions' that grow quickly and engulf them. The Doctor and Rose leave, wondering what is happening to the survivors of Platform One.

PUBLISHING NOTES: The Trees Coffa and Lute appeared in the episode 'The End of the World', as did all the other characters the Doctor is looking for in this series of comic strips.

HYPERSTAR RISING

WRITER: Steve Cole
ILLUSTRATORS: John Ross (Artwork), Alan Craddock (Colouring).
PUBLICATION: *Doctor Who: Battles In Time* issue 2; 3 May 2006.

SYNOPSIS: The TARDIS arrives at a Hyper-Film studio on the planet Woldyhool, year five billion. They meet the film director Zemm Foolini and learn that the leading manbot, Cal 'Spark Plug' Macnannovich, has gone missing. Suddenly a monster Banjunx appears, having eaten all the extras and security force. It chases them all, but the Doctor creates some shadow puppets with his hands and this keeps the creature happy, as it's only a baby. Its parent arrives to collect it.

DEATH RACE FIVE BILLION

WRITER: Steve Cole
ILLUSTRATORS: John Ross (Artwork), Alan Craddock (Colouring).
PUBLICATION: *Doctor Who: Battles In Time* issue 3; 17 May 2006.

SYNOPSIS: The Doctor and Rose travel to another planet to find the brothers Hop Pyleen, more Platform One guests... They find themselves at the start of a pod race, but a spacecraft appears and swallows a pod piloted by Skip. The Doctor follows and finds many wrecked ships but no drivers. He discovers the spacecraft is piloted by Rakkonoids, the biggest techno thieves in the galaxy. And Skip is in league with them. Rose, following in another pod, loses control and smashes through the hull of the Rakkonoid ship. The Doctor locks Skip and the Rakkonoids up as he takes the ship back to base. However, the brothers Hop Pyleen are nowhere to be found. They seem to have vanished ...

THE MACROBE MENACE

WRITER: Steve Cole
ILLUSTRATORS: John Ross (Artwork), Alan Craddock (Colouring).
PUBLICATION: *Doctor Who: Battles In Time* issue 4; 31 May 2006.

SYNOPSIS: The TARDIS arrives in a space library, the University of Rago Rago's reading dome, five billion years in the future. Rose plugs in to download a book, but releases a macrobe computer virus that runs amok in the library. The virus affects living brains, and all the life forms in the library become zombified and attack the Doctor. He escapes and, with the help of an unaffected librarian, chooses all the most boring books, including *Toenail Clippings of the Ug-Raptor*, *A History of Peas* and *How to Speak Zarbi in 10,000 Steps*. They upload these books, causing all the affected life forms to fall asleep and thereby sending the macrobe virus back into the net, which the Doctor then disconnects. As Rose recovers, the Doctor explains that he wanted to meet the Chosen Scholars of Class 55, but they have disappeared. He determines that somewhere in the library of ten trillion books there must be a clue as to what is happening. Lucky he's a fast reader.

PUBLISHING NOTES: The Zarbi were giant ants that communicated by trilling wordlessly instead of speaking. They appeared in the story 'The Web Planet' in 1965.

THE HUNT OF DOOM

WRITER: Steve Cole
ILLUSTRATORS: John Ross (Artwork), Alan Craddock (Colouring).
PUBLICATION: *Doctor Who: Battles In Time* issue 5; 14 June 2006.

SYNOPSIS: The Doctor has found a book on Power Boosted Transmats, and by tracing Lectra-Energy leaks he arrives on another planet, Gameworld Gamma, owned by Mr and Mrs

Pakoo. On this world, the Pakoos hunt humans. The Doctor rescues someone, but in doing so spoils the royal hunt. He is set upon by a bird, but a group of humans rescue him and they all run. They reach a swamp, but the Doctor ignites the gases with his sonic screwdriver and the pursuing birds are driven off. The huntmasters arrive carrying the Doctor's psychic paper (which he dropped), which shows him to be the personal assistant to President Kaakaa. Mr and Mrs Pakoo have vanished... but this time the Doctor believes he can track down whoever is doing this.

PUBLISHING NOTES: In one panel of the comic, a character who appears to be the Moxx of Balhoon is seen hovering in the air as Mr and Mrs Pakoo arrive to berate the Doctor for disturbing the hunt.

REUNION OF TERROR

WRITER: Steve Cole
ILLUSTRATORS: John Ross (Artwork), Alan Craddock (Colouring).
PUBLICATION: *Doctor Who: Battles In Time* issue 6; 28 June 2006.

SYNOPSIS: The TARDIS tracks the Lectra-Energy leak. A skeletal figure appears in the TARDIS and whacks the Doctor and Rose. Rose wakes up in a prison with all the other Platform One survivors. They are prisoners of the Elth of Balhoon, identical brother to the Moxx. In accordance with Statute 7 of the Hanamacat Pel Jadrabone Convention, the Balhoons want revenge for their brother's death. The Doctor bursts in and rescues everyone – the Elth had not taken him, as his face didn't match that of the Doctor who was on Platform One. The Elth bursts out crying and the other survivors comfort him – maybe they could make a film about his brother's life, or grow a garden of remembrance? The Doctor and Rose head off.

PUBLISHING NOTES: No credits were given in the issue for the comic strip. Those listed above are assumptions.

THE GLUTONOID MENACE

PUBLICATION: *Doctor Who: Battles In Time* issue 7; 12 July 2006.

SYNOPSIS: The Doctor is repairing the TARDIS's food machine, but gets food cubes tasting of steak, chocolate, pickled gherkins, sprouts and ear wax! He takes Rose to the planet Phijax IV, where the best all-night steaks are served. However, they arrive in an arena where competitors are battling. They are chained up but take advantage of the low gravity to leap about and win the bout. Rose is then selected to be eaten by a huge blob-monster called a Glutonoid. The Doctor objects and uses his umbrella to activate the Glutonoid's travel disk, which flies into the air. He throws the Glutonoid the packet of disgusting food squares produced by the TARDIS's food machine, and the creature explodes. The Doctor and Rose head off in the TARDIS.

PUBLISHING NOTES: No credits were given in the issue for the comic strip.

THE DOCTOR WHO FILES

This range of four small hardbacked books was published by BBC Children's Books, part of the Penguin Group, on 31 August 2006. Each was devoted to a different character or race from the TV series and featured a text story at the back.

THE HERO FACTOR

WRITER: Stephen Cole
PUBLICATION: *Doctor Who Files 1: The Doctor*; 31 August 2006.

SYNOPSIS: The Doctor and Rose are enjoying a holiday at the Warp Hotel on Askenflatt Minor when they are mobbed by reporters. The Doctor is apparently the future Champion of Askenflatt in a battle against the dreaded Hasval the Destroyer. The Doctor is teleported to a TV studio where he is interviewed by famed presenter Jazami Paxxo regarding the forthcoming battle – about which the Doctor knows nothing. When he agrees to help the people of Askenflatt, Paxxo and the studio vanish – they were all a hologram. He has been captured by Hasval, who also has Rose locked up. The Doctor and Rose make Hasval slip on a banana skin, and then Rose uses the hologram device to create an image of 250 Doctors who glare at Hasval. The creature runs in terror and turns back his attack fleet. Rose and the Doctor return to the Warp Hotel to continue their holiday.

PUBLISHING NOTES: Jazami Paxxo is a parody of television presenter Jeremy Paxman (*Newsnight*, *University Challenge*).

THE STAMP OF APPROVAL

WRITER: Jacqueline Rayner
PUBLICATION: *Doctor Who Files 2: Rose*; 31 August 2006.

SYNOPSIS: Rose and the Doctor are in Bath, 1840, as the Doctor has decided to take up stamp collecting and this is where the first ever stamp, the Penny Black, was printed. At the printers' works, they find a dead body in a vat of ink and are then attacked by zombified printers. The works is the focus of an alien Hobothy, which uses hypnosis to get others to do its bidding. The creature is using the ink to take over other people. Rose is affected along with the printers, but manages to kick the Hobothy into the press, where it is squashed to death. The hypnotic control is broken and all is back to normal. Rose keeps one of the Penny Blacks as a souvenir.

PUBLISHING NOTES: This story references Rose's meeting with Queen Victoria in 'Tooth and Claw'. It is written in the form of a letter from Rose to Jackie.

APPENDIX E

NO FUN AT THE FAIR

WRITER: Jacqueline Rayner

PUBLICATION: *Doctor Who Files 3: The Slitheen*; 31 August 2006.

SYNOPSIS: The Doctor and Rose are at a funfair. While the Doctor has a go on the water slide, Rose chooses the ghost train, but inside she sees a Slitheen. Later, when the fair is closed, she and the Doctor watch as the Slitheen leaves the ghost train and attends the various stalls: ring toss, test your strength, dodgems... They discover that the creature is a scout for an invasion. Rose is spotted and chased by the Slitheen. They end up coming down the water slide, but the Doctor has put vinegar in the water and the Slitheen explodes at the bottom. As a souvenir of the day, the Doctor gives Rose a photograph of her being chased by the Slitheen, taken at the Tunnel of Love.

THE FINAL DARKNESS

WRITER: Stephen Cole

PUBLICATION: *Doctor Who Files 4: The Sycorax*; 31 August 2006.

SYNOPSIS: The Sycorax live in the wastelands of space. Their metal probes detect the planet Earth and sense it is host to many precious stones, metals and minerals. They also believe that slave traders will pay well for a supply of human cattle. The Sycorax intercept a probe as they approach Earth; it contains seeds, fluid, maps and human blood. Preparing a blood charm under the forbidden arts of Astrophia, the Sycorax leader sends a message to Earth commanding total surrender. The humans refuse, and the Sycorax attempt conquest by using blood control to compel one third of the humans to attempt suicide from tall buildings. The leader summons the skinny woman ruler of Earth, and two of her defenders are killed. But then the Sycorax detect foreign machinery and take a blue box on board their ship. A yellow-haired girl tries to scare them with the names of worthy foes, and then a stranger appears from the blue box and pulls the death whip from the Sycorax leader's hands and breaks his mighty staff over his knee. This 'Doctor' ruins everything by activating the blood control matrix, freeing the humans below. He invokes the sanctified rules of combat and stands as Champion of Earth. The fight is long but it is this 'Doctor' who triumphs, leaving the Sycorax leaderless and forbidden to scavenge the Earth for the rest of time. The Sycorax ship departs, but then there is more treachery and deception... Sensors detect energy approaching their ship. As the warriors prepare to die, they chant 'Sycorax strong, Sycorax mighty, Sycorax ...' Log terminates.

PUBLISHING NOTES: This is the plot of 'The Christmas Invasion' as told through the eyes of the Sycorax. The story is written as a journal, with entry dates starting at 23-mol-786-lassac-5 – translation copyright of UNIT Alien-English software.

THE DOCTOR WHO ANNUALS

In Autumn 2005, Panini Comics relaunched the *Doctor Who Annual* format with the *Doctor Who Annual 2006*, containing stories, puzzles and non-fiction items for young readers. The last *Annual* before this had been the one for 1986, published in 1985; although in the early 1990s Panini had also brought out a series of five *Doctor Who Yearbook* titles aimed at an older age group. In August 2006, two *Annual*-type books appeared: *Doctor Who: The Official Annual 2007* was published by BBC Children's Books, although this contained only one piece of original fiction, the comic strip story *Down the Rabbit Hole* (the other story being a reprint of the *Mirror Image* comic strip from *Doctor Who Adventures* number 2); while *Doctor Who Storybook 2007* came from Panini Books and consisted entirely of new fiction.

DOCTOR WHO ANNUAL 2006

EDITOR: Clayton Hickman
DESIGNER: Peri Goldbold

Published by the team behind *Doctor Who Magazine* , but aimed at a younger audience. The book included a piece by Russell T Davies on each of the series' two lead characters. In these, Davies revealed: that the Halldons, from the text story 'We Are The Daleks!' in the *Radio Times* special published to celebrate *Doctor Who*'s tenth anniversary in 1973, waged war on the Eternals, from the television story 'Enlightenment'; that President Romana (in the *Doctor Who* novels series and the Big Finish audio range, the Doctor's companion Romana became President of the Time Lords after leaving him) attempted to make a peace treaty with the Daleks; that the Daleks used the 'Deathsmiths of Goth', as referred to in the comic strip story 'Black Legacy' in *Doctor Who Magazine* (issues 35-38); that hieroglyphics on planet Crafe Tec Hydra predict other survivors of the Time War; and that Rose's birth date is 27 April 1987, her postcode is SE15 7GO and her friend Shareen's surname is Costello. Davies also gave a great deal more information about Rose's school days. In addition, the book contained four new short stories – all featuring the Rose/ninth Doctor line-up – and a comic strip – a ninth Doctor solo adventure. These all probably take place just prior to 'Dalek'.

DOCTOR VS DOCTOR

WRITER: Gareth Roberts
ILLUSTRATOR: Andy Walker

SYNOPSIS: The TARDIS crash-lands on Earth in 1920, after something pulls it off-course. (The Doctor tries to fix the problem, but that part of the TARDIS computer uses DOS, which he's 'useless' with.) The travellers interrupt famed detective Dr Merrivale Carr as he is about to solve his latest crime and identify the guilty party. The Doctor tells Carr he has got it wrong: invisible aliens are responsible for the murder he is investigating – they are trapped on Earth and trying to escape, but killing people by accident in the meantime. The Doctor talks to the aliens using the standard galactic code of the 455th Century and repairs their crashed ship.

PUBLISHING NOTES: The character Dr Merrivale Carr is an homage to crime fiction author John Dickson Carr (1906-1977), famous for his novels involving the solution of seemingly impossible, or even supernatural, crimes. Sir Henry Merrivale was one of Carr's most celebrated characters.

THE MASK OF MAKASSAR

WRITER: Paul Cornell
ILLUSTRATOR: Martin Geraghty

SYNOPSIS: The Doctor and Rose are guests on an alien world where the people all wear masks that allow them to share thoughts. Their leader, Makassar, reveres the Doctor as a Time Lord. That night, Rose sees a ghost of one of the aliens begging for help. The Doctor meanwhile discovers that Makassar is weak, but Makassar then forces a mask onto his 'guest'. The Doctor uses the enhanced powers he has now gained in order to create a 'haven' for himself and Rose, in the form of a virtual Powell Estate. Makassar and his followers (whom the Doctor realises are being controlled by Makassar's mask) appear in this virtual world also, but the Doctor defeats the leader and sets everyone free.

MR NOBODY

WRITER: Scott Gray
ILLUSTRATOR: John Ross (Art), James Offredi (Colours), Roger Langridge (Lettering)

SYNOPSIS: Phil Tyson, a 26-year-old employee of Cheeky Chicken in Peckham, has a boring life. At least until he's taken prisoner by aliens and tried for war crimes against the Mighty Vandos Imperium, who believe he is the reincarnation of Shogalath, a war criminal. The Doctor and Rose arrive, create a distraction and escape with Tyson. Although the people of Vandos catch up, Tyson throws his cleaning bucket, full of ammonia, at them, and they leave in the TARDIS. The aliens attack, but the Doctor has set their systems to backfire and their ship explodes. The Doctor explains to Tyson that Shogalath was actually an inspirational hero, and leaves the man to begin a new, happier life on Earth.

PUBLISHING NOTES: Judging by Tyson's age and date of birth, this story is set in 2005.

PITTER-PATTER

WRITER: Robert Shearman
ILLUSTRATOR: Daryl Joyce

SYNOPSIS: On a hostile mining world, young Andy and his parents (along with other human colonists) live in constant shelter from deadly rain. The Doctor and Rose investigate and discover that the water is alive, and it's punishing the new arrivals for drinking it. The Doctor talks to the rain and calls a temporary truce, allowing everyone time to leave.

WHAT I DID ON MY HOLIDAYS BY SALLY SPARROW

WRITER: Stephen Moffat
ILLUSTRATOR: Martin Geraghty

SYNOPSIS: While holidaying at her aunt's for Christmas, 12-year-old Sally Sparrow discovers a note beneath the wallpaper reading 'Help me Sally Sparrow, 25/12/85', along with a photograph from that Christmas of the ninth Doctor holding a sign reading 'Help me Sally Sparrow'. She finds another note telling her to think of a number and go to a tree in the garden – the tree shows the number she'd been thinking of – and then a video of the Doctor explaining that the TARDIS 'burped' forwards 20 years, and he needs Sally to retrieve it and bring it back to him. He also explains that while fighting the Sontarans in Istanbul he met a beautiful spy who gave him Sally's completed homework. That spy, he reveals, was the future Sally ...

PUBLISHING NOTES: Christmas 1985 is described as being 20 years ago, so this story is set on 22 December 2005.

DOCTOR WHO STORYBOOK 2007

EDITOR: Clayton Hickman
DESIGNER: Peri Goldbold

Judging from the tone and the TARDIS line-up, these tenth Doctor stories are all probably set between 'New Earth' and 'School Reunion'.

A LETTER FROM THE DOCTOR

WRITER: Russell T Davies

SYNOPSIS: Rose and the tenth Doctor face the Squirn from the planet Squirn in Galaxy 5.

CUCKOO-SPIT

WRITER: Mark Gatiss
ILLUSTRATOR: Daryl Joyce

SYNOPSIS: June 1975. Young teenager Jason starts a diary, telling us the story of when he met the Doctor and Rose. His friend Graham has vanished, and he finds the travellers investigating. One night, he sees Graham and follows him, finding more people who have vanished. He then realises the truth – that they are already dead, having been taken over by something. Graham attacks Jason, but the Doctor and Rose arrive at the last minute to save him.

APPENDIX E

THE CAT CAME BACK

WRITER: Gareth Roberts
ILLUSTRATOR: Martin Geraghty

SYNOPSIS: After enjoying some 'bangers and mash' in 1921 Burma, the Doctor and Rose arrive on an exploring spacecraft and find a terrified crewmember, Jonah. The three are teleported away to the planet Phostris and interrogated by Mitzi, the first cat in space who has mutated and gained powers she should never have. Rose manages to return Mitzi to normal, and they take her to the Powell Estate in the 1990s and set her free – destined to become a stray that Rose and Jackie will take in and name Puffin for the last five years of her life.

ONCE UPON A TIME

WRITER: Tom MacRae
ILLUSTRATOR: Adrian Salmon

SYNOPSIS: In a small village, young Brynn and Lissa hear mysterious music from far away. Their friends begin to hear it too, and although their parents try to keep them away, they must tell stories to keep it from their minds. Their friends, following the music, begin to disappear, and Brynn follows to investigate. He meets the Doctor, who tells him that the music is a distress signal coming from a giant ship that the villagers believed to be a mountain, that has been listening to the villagers' stories for years and has begun to crave its own 'happily ever after'. Brynn completes the story, allowing the ship to die peacefully.

OPERA OF DOOM

WRITER: Jonathan Morris
ILLUSTRATORS: Martin Geraghty (Art), Fareed Choudhry (Inks), James Offredi (Colours), Roger Langridge (Lettering)
EDITORS: Scott Gray, Clayton Hickman

SYNOPSIS: The Doctor and Rose attend an opera performed by an 'automatic orchestra' on the planet Vanezia and meet the future genius musician Frederico Gobbo. The Doctor discovers that the 'automatic orchestra' is a Rokathian device that takes its power from the minds of others, draining them of life. The owner, Magrillo, captures them, but Gobbo gives the machine indigestion by singing a very bad tune... and later discovers his talent for good quality music. The Doctor takes Rose away, off to the Cavern Club ...

PUBLISHING NOTES: 'Opera of Doom' was the supposed title of a planned *Doctor Who* story in the 1980s; it was actually fictitious, invented by a mischievous fan in an attempt to 'spoof' the fanzine *DWB* into making it the basis of a news story. The attempt was successful and the title has gone down in fan history because of this. The Cavern Club in Liverpool was the venue for some famous performances by the Beatles in the 1960s.

GRAVESTONE HOUSE

WRITER: Justin Richards
ILLUSTRATOR: Andy Walker

SYNOPSIS: While playing football, school friends Raj and Jim meet an old woman whom they believe to be a witch. The Doctor and Rose are meanwhile tracking a probe they believe to be a terraformer. (Rose knows all about these from *Star Trek*.) Raj and Jim break into the supposed witch's garden, where the TARDIS lands and is sucked into a boggy swamp that the terraforming probe has created. The Doctor and Rose meet the boys and are chased by a super evolving creature and then some skeletons, who force them inside the house where they meet the 'witch' – a lovely old lady named Ivy Henson who makes them tea. As the skeletons attack, the Doctor realises they have been animated by the probe in order to repair it – so he hands them the probe, and once fixed, it not only reverses the damage done to the house and garden but also reverts Miss Henson back to a much younger age.

UNTITLED

WRITER: Robert Shearman
ILLUSTRATOR: Brian Williamson

SYNOPSIS: The Doctor takes Rose to an art gallery on the Moon, and amongst the 17th Century masterpieces they find a picture of her screaming. Investigating, they find a collection of bodies, all with the same twisted expression, that collapse into puddles of paint. The pictures on the walls, including that of the moustached King Carl XVII, all turn into the vision of Rose. Then the paint melts from the frames and attacks. The Doctor learns the truth – that the pictures are inhabited by the soul of a painter who had put just a little too much of himself into his work. The Doctor convinces the art-monster to become a picture of some lemon cheesecake.

NO ONE DIED

WRITER: Nicholas Briggs
ILLUSTRATOR: Ben Willsher

SYNOPSIS: The Doctor and Rose visit the town of Lower Downham just prior to its mysterious disappearance in 1962 to have some Sky Ray lollies and find out what happened to the place. They then visit the town after its disappearance, and discover that space seems to have folded inwards around the area. Travelling to the day of the disappearance, they find that everyone has been placed into glass coffins by the alien Viyrans, who have come to neutralise the fallout from some intergalactic chemical weapons. They are moving the villagers elsewhere and setting up a perceptual barrier around the village to quarantine it permanently. The Doctor and Rose leave, having solved most of mystery, except why it was dark at 3 pm.

PUBLISHING NOTES: This story introduced the Viyrans, a race that Big Finish Productions' new producer Briggs plans to feature in their range of *Doctor Who* CD drama releases in 2007.

CORNER OF THE EYE

WRITER: Steven Moffat
ILLUSTRATOR: Daryl Joyce

SYNOPSIS: In an instant messaging chat, Tom asks Kathy to describe the room she's in. She finds herself unable to do so, and he tells her a story he claims he has told her many times before:

While shaving, Tom sees a small man in his bathroom mirror. Obsessing over this, he looks through all his old photos and finds the same figure in every one. He considers putting an ad in the local paper, and as he does so, the Doctor arrives, having seen the ad in the future. The Doctor explains that for the last ten years, Tom's had a Floof in the house, which has made him agoraphobic and caused his relationship with his wife to be handled by instant messenger. (This is despite Tom not even having an Internet connection.) The Doctor finds Kathy's body – the Floof killed her ten years ago. He convinces Tom to leave with him, but not before programming a virtual Tom for the virtual Kathy to talk to.

DOCTOR WHO: THE OFFICIAL ANNUAL 2007

DOWN THE RABBIT HOLE

WRITER: Davey Moore
ILLUSTRATORS: John Ross (Artwork), James Offredi (Colouring).

SYNOPSIS: The Doctor and Rose are relaxing on a world where there seems to be nothing nasty lurking. They meet a girl in a red hood. The girl is picking flowers and is off to see her grandma, who lives in the middle of the forest. An old crone appears, offering Rose an apple. The Doctor stops her taking it and deactivates the crone – she is a robot. In fact, the whole forest is robotic. Suddenly, a woodsman runs amok with an axe and the other robots start running wild as well. The Doctor gets into the forest control room, where a man is making the androids smash each other up as they did him out of a job as one of the dwarfs. Rose and the Doctor disarm him and set the system correct again.

OTHER FICTION

MONSTERS AND VILLAINS

WRITER: Justin Richards, with additional material by Russell T Davies
COMMISSIONING EDITORS: Shirley Patton and Stuart Cooper
PROJECT EDITOR: Vicky Vrint

CREATIVE DIRECTOR: Justin Richards
DESIGN: Lee Binding
PRODUCTION CONTROLLER: Peter Hunt
PUBLISHED: May 2005

SYNOPSIS: This book contained a lengthy, Russell T Davies-written sidebar on Lady Cassandra. According to this, she was born Brian Edwards Cobbs in the year 4.99/4763/A/15. Following a sex change, she married billionaire Harry Klime, who mysteriously died (having fallen on his garden rake five times). She later escaped to Sant's World to become B-Movie star Cassandra Hoots. A smaller sidebar, also written by Russell T Davies, focused on the Face of Boe, and revealed that he had many offspring, all of whom died, and that (as later described in 'New Earth') he would one day reveal his secret to a wandering traveller, and then die, leaving the sky to crack asunder. Davies also provided details of the colonisation of the Forest of Cheem (dating back to 111222/9967) and some personal information on the Moxx of Balhoon (whose favourite song is apparently 'Yap Cap Forward Bigga Toom Toom Toom'). Lastly, a page from *Jane's Book of Planets*, 'translated' by Davies, provided (some weeks before broadcast) the back-story to 'Boom Town' – including in particular the family Slitheen's disgrace and their homeworld's favoured form of capital punishment.

AUTHOR'S NOTE AND ACKNOWLEDGEMENTS

This concludes my second and final *Back To The Vortex* book; these things are incredibly difficult and time-consuming to write, and I've decided to call it quits (for now). Never fear, though... Telos Publishing will soon have you waiting at the bookstore for Stephen James Walker's definitive unofficial guide to the first season of *Torchwood*, with other wonderful *Doctor Who* books no doubt to follow.

Special thanks to the following people for being so integral to the successful publication of *Second Flight*: Paul Engelberg, for his tireless and meticulous scanning of news feeds for articles and commentaries about *Doctor Who*, providing the basis for the bulk of the 'Journey' section of the book, and to Steve Tribe for his help with the previous season; Matt Dale, Robert D Franks and Jon Preddle for their extensive notes and comments about each of the Series Two episode sections and the novels and comics section; the rest of the review team – Arnold T Blumberg, Graeme Burk, Sarah Hadley, Paul Hayes, Craig Hinton, Kim Newman, Kate Orman, and Keith Topping – for their terrific contributions to the text (along with Jonathan Blum for filling in for wife Kate for the 'Love & Monsters' review); John Molyneux, for making it all possible; John Bowman, Peter Weaver, Andy Parish, Adam Kirk, Chuck Foster, Benjamin Elliott and 'Marcus' for their tremendous help with the material incorporated into the narrative; David Howe, Stephen James Walker and Rosemary Howe at Telos Publishing for their support; Colin Baker, Rob Shearman and Paul Cornell for sage counsel, friendship and support of the book; the staff of the Outpost Gallifrey Forum community – Steve Hill, Jennifer Kelley, Michael Zecca, Karen Baldwin, Michael Blumenthal, Wil Cantrell, Neil Chester, Samantha Dings, Matt Evenden, Lindsay Johnson, Derek Kompare, Matthew Kopelke, J R Loflin, Raymond Sawaya, Mark Stevens, Garth Wilcox and Scott Alan Woodard – for keeping things running while I've been otherwise preoccupied; the Thursday night dinner crew – Scott Busman, Erik Engman, Ingrid Oliansky, Suze Campagna, Carol Loessin, Dwaine Maggart and Jill Sherwin – for listening; my friends in the Stonewall Champions guild (Proudmoore server) of *World of Warcraft* for filling up the rest of my days when I wasn't writing; my parents and my brother for their support; and Jason Knight, Nick Johnson, Nick Seidler, Greg Bakun, Jason Tucker, Jeff Ovik, Joe Cochran, Andy Shoemaker, David Grandin and Robbie Bourget for being there when needed. Also, to those of you in sensitive positions to whom I cannot offer credit because, sadly, being listed in an unauthorised book like this would give you no end of grief (and you know who you are), you have my sincerest thanks for everything.

Thanks also to the following individuals who contributed significant information, news stories or material to this book: Lee Whiteside, Michael Doran, Faiz Rehman, Ian Golden, Paul Mount, Darren Floyd, Peter Anghelides, Mark Richardson, Keith Armstrong, Paul Greaves, Scott Matthewman, John Campbell Rees, Simon Bishop, David Traynier, Joanna Pinkney, Martin Hoscik at unitnews.co.uk, Bill Albert, Scott Matthewman, Timothy Farr, Emma Sandrey, Graham Kibble-White, Matt Kimpton, everyone at david-tennant.com, Andrew Harvey, Chris Winwood, John Hutton, Paul Robinson, Philip Dore, Matt Gaynor, Stuart Ian Burns, Paul Taylor and Derek Handley at 10th Planet, Steven Scott at scificollector.co.uk, Marcus Hearn, Ian Wheeler, Chris Lane, Simon Watkins, David Shaw, Gareth Price, Kevin West, Nick Seidler, Mustafa Hirji, Richard Kirkpatrick, Matthew Kilburn, Melanie Hill, Phil Creighton, Sarah Roberts, Malcolm Prince, Luke McCullough, Roger Anderson, Richard Walter, Dan Garrett, Ruth Gunstone, Steve Gerrard, Nathan Baron, John Williams, Rob

Stickler, Steve Gray and whoniverse.org, the fine folks who keep Wikipedia's *Doctor Who* entries updated, and everyone who has contributed news articles to the Outpost Gallifrey *Doctor Who* News Page.

Best wishes and thanks to Russell T Davies, David Tennant, Billie Piper, Julie Gardner, Phil Collinson, Noel Clarke and everyone at *Doctor Who*, for another stellar year.

And, as always, my dearest thanks to my wonderful and supportive partner, Chad Jones, who puts up with all this and makes every day worth waking up for.

In memory of Mr Puck (1990-2006).

ABOUT THE AUTHOR

Shaun Lyon is the author of *Back To The Vortex: The Unofficial and Unauthorised Guide to Doctor Who 2005*, published in 2005 by Telos Publishing. Shaun has been involved in *Doctor Who* fandom for 20 years, including as editor of the popular *Doctor Who* website Outpost Gallifrey (www.gallifreyone.com) and as co-founder and programme director of Gallifrey One, North America's longest-running annual *Doctor Who* convention. He's previously authored works of licensed *Doctor Who* short fiction and spends far too much time these days playing *World of Warcraft*. He and his partner Chad Jones live in Los Angeles.

ABOUT THE REVIEWERS

Dr Arnold T Blumberg is Curator of Geppi's Entertainment Museum and has authored or co-authored *The Big BIG LITTLE BOOK Book: An Overstreet Photo-Journal Guide*, two editions of *Howe's Transcendental Toybox* and two subsequent updates, and *Zombiemania: 80 Movies to Die For*. He also contributed to the *Doctor Who* charity anthologies *Missing Pieces, The Cat Who Walked Through Time* and *Walking in Eternity*. You can find him online at www.atbpublishing.com, www.cinejunkie.com, and www.apanelwithnoborders.com.

Graeme Burk is the editor of *Enlightenment*, the acclaimed fanzine of the *Doctor Who* Information Network. He was the first Canadian to contribute to *Doctor Who* professional fiction with two stories in the *Short Trips* range of anthologies. In his spare time, he works as a freelance writer in Toronto.

Sarah Hadley lives near Nashville, Tennessee, in the United States, where she is currently concluding her education and working as a freelance journalist and writer. She is trying to finish several marketable writing projects at the time of publication, so watch this space and see what the psychic paper says in about a year's time. Her irreverent podcast commentaries for new and old episodes of *Doctor Who*, recorded with her long-time friend Michael Hickerson, can be heard online at The Millennium Effect, a *Doctor Who* research site she co-edits with Matt Dale and Kev West.

Paul Hayes was born and raised in West Sussex and currently lives in Norwich, but hopes to travel to many other such exotic and far-flung locations in the future. He has poured forth his thoughts on *Doctor Who* across various locations on the internet, such as Outpost Gallifrey and the Behind the Sofa collaborative blog. When not scribbling away at novels nobody will ever publish, he sometimes answers telephones for the BBC.

Craig Hinton was born in London in 1964, so he's just old enough to remember Patrick Troughton's Doctor! Among other things, he's been a technical author, a magazine editor and a night porter (!), and he is about to embark on a new career as a maths teacher. In what little spare time he has, he's written extensively for magazines such as *Doctor Who Magazine* and *TV Zone*, as well as penning five *Doctor Who* novels – *Synthespians*™, *The Quantum*

Archangel, GodEngine, Millennial Rites and *The Crystal Bucephalus* – for Virgin and the BBC and a number of audios and short stories for Big Finish.

Kim Newman is a novelist, critic and broadcaster whose books includes *The Night Mayor, Anno Dracula, Life's Lottery, Back in the USSA* (with Eugene Byrne), *The Man From the Diogenes Club, Ghastly Beyond Belief* (with Neil Gaiman), *The BFI Companion to Horror, Millennium Movies* and BFI Classics studies of *Cat People* and *Doctor Who*. He is a contributing editor to *Sight & Sound* and *Empire* magazines and has written and broadcast widely on a range of topics. He has won the Bram Stoker Award, the International Horror Critics Award, the British Science Fiction Award and the British Fantasy Award, but doesn't like to boast about them. His official web-site, Dr Shade's Laboratory, can be found at www.johnnyalucard.com.

Kate Orman lives in Sydney, Australia, with her husband and collaborator Jonathan Blum and their two cats, Frank and Tim. She has written or co-written 13 *Doctor Who* novels, including *Vampire Science, Seeing I, Unnatural History, The Year of Intelligent Tigers, Blue Box, Set Piece, The Left Handed Hummingbird* and *So Vile a Sin*, and is pursuing a career in original fiction. Read her blog at kateorman.livejournal.com.

Jon Preddle is a prominent figure in New Zealand fandom. He is a long-serving regular writer/researcher for the internationally highly respected fanzine *TSV* (*Time Space Visualiser*), which will celebrate its twentieth anniversary in 2007. *Timelink*, his unofficial guide to *Doctor Who* continuity, is due to be published by Telos Publishing.

Keith Topping is a Tyneside-based author/journalist/broadcaster. His work includes five *Doctor Who* novels, along with such in-depth reference guides as *Slayer, Hollywood Vampire, Inside Bartlet's White House, Do You Want to Know a Secret?, Beyond the Gate, Triquetra, A Vault of Horror* and, with Paul Cornell and Martin Day, *Doctor Who: The Discontinuity Guide*.

PHOTO CREDITS

The photographs in the colour section are copyright and courtesy of the South Wales News Service and Philip Newman.

BACK TO THE VORTEX: THE UNOFFICIAL AND UNAUTHORISED GUIDE TO DOCTOR WHO 2005
by J SHAUN LYON

Complete guide to the 2005 series of Doctor Who starring Christopher Eccleston as the Doctor

£12.99 (+ £2.50 UK p&p) Standard p/b ISBN: 1-903889-78-2
£30.00 (+ £2.50 UK p&p) Deluxe h/b ISBN: 1-903889-79-0

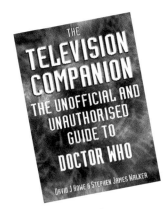

Other
Doctor Who
Telos Titles
Available

THE TELEVISION COMPANION: THE UNOFFICIAL AND UNAUTHORISED GUIDE TO DOCTOR WHO by DAVID J HOWE & STEPHEN JAMES WALKER
Complete episode guide to the popular TV show.
£14.99 (+ £4.75 UK p&p) Standard p/b ISBN: 1-903889-51-0

THE HANDBOOK: THE UNOFFICIAL AND UNAUTHORISED GUIDE TO THE PRODUCTION OF DOCTOR WHO by DAVID J HOWE, STEPHEN JAMES WALKER and MARK STAMMERS
Complete guide to the making of *Doctor Who*.
£14.99 (+ £4.75 UK p&p) Standard p/b ISBN: 1-903889-59-6
£30.00 (+ £4.75 UK p&p) Deluxe h/b ISBN: 1-903889-96-0

HOWE'S TRANSCENDENTAL TOYBOX: SECOND EDITION by DAVID J HOWE & ARNOLD T BLUMBERG
Complete guide to *Doctor Who* Merchandise.
£25.00 (+ £4.75 UK p&p) Standard p/b ISBN: 1-903889-56-1

HOWE'S TRANSCENDENTAL TOYBOX: UPDATE NO. 1: 2003 by DAVID J HOWE & ARNOLD T BLUMBERG
Complete guide to *Doctor Who* Merchandise released in 2003.
£7.99 (+ £1.50 UK p&p) Standard p/b ISBN: 1-903889-57-X

TIME HUNTER

A range of high-quality, original paperback and limited edition hardback novellas featuring the adventures in time of Honoré Lechasseur. Part mystery, part detective story, part dark fantasy, part science fiction … these books are guaranteed to enthral fans of good fiction everywhere, and are in the spirit of our acclaimed range of *Doctor Who* Novellas.

THE WINNING SIDE by LANCE PARKIN

Emily is dead! Killed by an unknown assailant. Honoré and Emily find themselves caught up in a plot reaching from the future to their past, and with their very existence, not to mention the future of the entire world, at stake, can they unravel the mystery before it is too late?
An adventure in time and space.
£7.99 (+ £1.50 UK p&p) Standard p/b ISBN 1-903889-35-9 (pb)

THE TUNNEL AT THE END OF THE LIGHT by STEFAN PETRUCHA

In the heart of post-war London, a bomb is discovered lodged at a disused station between Green Park and Hyde Park Corner. The bomb detonates, and as the dust clears, it becomes apparent that *something* has been awakened. Strange half-human creatures attack the workers at the site, hungrily searching for anything containing sugar …
Meanwhile, Honoré and Emily are contacted by eccentric poet Randolph Crest, who believes himself to be the target of these subterranean creatures. The ensuing investigation brings Honoré and Emily up against a terrifying force from deep beneath the earth, and one which even with their combined powers, they may have trouble stopping.
An adventure in time and space.
£7.99 (+ £1.50 UK p&p) Standard p/b ISBN 1-903889-37-5 (pb)
£25.00 (+ £1.50 UK p&p) Deluxe h/b ISBN 1-903889-38-3 (hb)

THE CLOCKWORK WOMAN by CLAIRE BOTT

Honoré and Emily find themselves imprisoned in the 19th Century by a celebrated inventor … but help comes from an unexpected source – a humanoid automaton created by and to give pleasure to its owner. As the trio escape to London, they are unprepared for what awaits them, and at every turn it seems impossible to avert what fate may have in store for the Clockwork Woman.
An adventure in time and space.
£7.99 (+ £1.50 UK p&p) Standard p/b ISBN 1-903889-39-1 (pb)
£25.00 (+ £1.50 UK p&p) Deluxe h/b ISBN 1-903889-40-5 (hb)

KITSUNE by JOHN PAUL CATTON

In the year 2020, Honoré and Emily find themselves thrown into a mystery, as an ice spirit – *Yuki-Onna* – wreaks havoc during the Kyoto Festival, and a haunted funhouse proves to contain more than just paper lanterns and wax dummies. But what does all this have to do with the elegant owner of the Hide and Chic fashion

chain … and to the legendary Chinese fox-spirits, the Kitsune?
An adventure in time and space.
£7.99 (+ £1.50 UK p&p) Standard p/b ISBN 1-903889-41-3 (pb)
£25.00 (+ £1.50 UK p&p) Deluxe h/b ISBN 1-903889-42-1 (hb)

THE SEVERED MAN by GEORGE MANN

What links a clutch of sinister murders in Victorian London, an angel appearing in a Staffordshire village in the 1920s and a small boy running loose around the capital in 1950? When Honoré and Emily encounter a man who appears to have been cut out of time, they think they have the answer. But soon enough they discover that the mystery is only just beginning and that nightmares can turn into reality.
An adventure in time and space.
£7.99 (+ £1.50 UK p&p) Standard p/b ISBN 1-903889-43-X (pb)
£25.00 (+ £1.50 UK p&p) Deluxe h/b ISBN 1-903889-44-8 (hb)

ECHOES by IAIN MCLAUGHLIN & CLAIRE BARTLETT

Echoes of the past … echoes of the future. Honoré Lechasseur can see the threads that bind the two together, however when he and Emily Blandish find themselves outside the imposing tower-block headquarters of Dragon Industry, both can sense something is wrong. There are ghosts in the building, and images and echoes of all times pervade the structure. But what is behind this massive contradiction in time, and can Honoré and Emily figure it out before they become trapped themselves …?
An adventure in time and space.
SOLD OUT

PECULIAR LIVES by PHILIP PURSER-HALLARD

Once a celebrated author of 'scientific romances', Erik Clevedon is an old man now. But his fiction conceals a dangerous truth, as Honoré Lechasseur and Emily Blandish discover after a chance encounter with a strangely gifted young pickpocket. Born between the Wars, the superhuman children known as 'the Peculiar' are reaching adulthood – and they believe that humanity is making a poor job of looking after the world they plan to inherit …
An adventure in time and space.
£7.99 (+ £1.50 UK p&p) Standard p/b ISBN 1-903889-47-2 (pb)
£25.00 (+ £1.50 UK p&p) Deluxe h/b ISBN 1-903889-48-0 (hb)

DEUS LE VOLT by JON DE BURGH MILLER

'Deus Le Volt!'…'God Wills It!' The cry of the first Crusade in 1098, despatched by Pope Urban to free Jerusalem from the Turks. Honoré and Emily are plunged into the middle of the conflict on the trail of what appears to be a time travelling knight. As the siege of Antioch draws to a close, so death haunts the blood-soaked streets … and the Fendahl – a creature that feeds on life itself – is summoned. Honoré and Emily find themselves facing angels and demons in a battle to survive their latest adventure.
An adventure in time and space.
£7.99 (+ £1.50 UK p&p) Standard p/b ISBN 1-903889-49-9 (pb)
£25.00 (+ £1.50 UK p&p) Deluxe h/b ISBN 1-903889-97-9 (hb)

THE ALBINO'S DANCER by DALE SMITH

'Goodbye, little Emily.'

April 1938, and a shadowy figure attends an impromptu burial in Shoreditch, London. His name is Honoré Lechasseur. After a chance encounter with the mysterious Catherine Howkins, he's had advance warning that his friend Emily Blandish was going to die. But is forewarned necessarily forearmed? And just how far is he willing to go to save Emily's life?

Because Honoré isn't the only person taking an interest in Emily Blandish – she's come to the attention of the Albino, one of the new breed of gangsters surfacing in post-rationing London. And the only life he cares about is his own.

An adventure in time and space.

£7.99 (+ £1.50 UK p&p) Standard p/b ISBN 1-84583-100-4 (pb)
£25.00 (+ £1.50 UK p&p) Deluxe h/b ISBN 1-84583-101-2 (hb)

THE SIDEWAYS DOOR by R J CARTER & TROY RISER

Honoré and Emily find themselves in a parallel timestream where their alternate selves think nothing of changing history to improve the quality of life – especially their own. Honoré has been recently haunted by the death of his mother, an event which happened in his childhood, but now there seems to be a way to reverse that event … but at what cost?

When faced with two of the most dangerous people they have ever encountered, Honoré and Emily must make some decisions with far-reaching consequences.

An adventure in time and space.

£7.99 (+ £1.50 UK p&p) Standard p/b ISBN 1-84583-102-0 (pb)
£25.00 (+ £1.50 UK p&p) Deluxe h/b ISBN 1-84583-103-9 (hb)

TIME HUNTER FILM

DAEMOS RISING by DAVID J HOWE, DIRECTED BY KEITH BARNFATHER

Daemos Rising is a sequel to both the *Doctor Who* adventure *The Daemons* and to *Downtime*, an earlier drama featuring the Yeti. It is also a prequel of sorts to Telos Publishing's *Time Hunter* series. It stars Miles Richardson as ex-UNIT operative Douglas Cavendish, and Beverley Cressman as Brigadier Lethbridge-Stewart's daughter Kate. Trapped in an isolated cottage, Cavendish thinks he is seeing ghosts. The only person who might understand and help is Kate Lethbridge-Stewart … but when she arrives, she realises that Cavendish is key in a plot to summon the Daemons back to the Earth. With time running out, Kate discovers that sometimes even the familiar can turn out to be your worst nightmare. Also starring Andrew Wisher, and featuring Ian Richardson as the Narrator.

An adventure in time and space.

£14.00 (+ £2.50 UK p&p) PAL format R4 DVD

Order direct from Reeltime Pictures, PO Box 23435, London SE26 5WU

HORROR/FANTASY

CAPE WRATH by PAUL FINCH
Death and horror on a deserted Scottish island as an ancient Viking warrior chief returns to life.
£8.00 (+ £1.50 UK p&p) Standard p/b ISBN: 1-903889-60-X

KING OF ALL THE DEAD by STEVE LOCKLEY & PAUL LEWIS
The king of all the dead will have what is his.
£8.00 (+ £1.50 UK p&p) Standard p/b ISBN: 1-903889-61-8

GUARDIAN ANGEL by STEPHANIE BEDWELL-GRIME
Devilish fun as Guardian Angel Porsche Winter loses a soul to the devil …
£9.99 (+ £2.50 UK p&p) Standard p/b ISBN: 1-903889-62-6

FALLEN ANGEL by STEPHANIE BEDWELL-GRIME
Porsche Winter battles she devils on Earth …
£9.99 (+ £2.50 UK p&p) Standard p/b ISBN: 1-903889-69-3

SPECTRE by STEPHEN LAWS
The inseparable Byker Chapter: six boys, one girl, growing up together in the back streets of Newcastle. Now memories are all that Richard Eden has left, and one treasured photograph. But suddenly, inexplicably, the images of his companions start to fade, and as they vanish, so his friends are found dead and mutilated. Something is stalking the Chapter, picking them off one by one, something connected with their past, and with the girl they used to know.
£9.99 (+ £2.50 UK p&p) Standard p/b ISBN: 1-903889-72-3

THE HUMAN ABSTRACT by GEORGE MANN
A future tale of private detectives, AIs, Nanobots, love and death.
£7.99 (+ £1.50 UK p&p) Standard p/b ISBN: 1-903889-65-0

BREATHE by CHRISTOPHER FOWLER
The Office meets *Night of the Living Dead.*
£7.99 (+ £1.50 UK p&p) Standard p/b ISBN: 1-903889-67-7
£25.00 (+ £1.50 UK p&p) Deluxe h/b ISBN: 1-903889-68-5

HOUDINI'S LAST ILLUSION by STEVE SAVILE
Can master illusionist Harry Houdini outwit the dead shades of his past?
£7.99 (+ £1.50 UK p&p) Standard p/b ISBN: 1-903889-66-9

ALICE'S JOURNEY BEYOND THE MOON by R J CARTER
A sequel to the classic Lewis Carroll tales.
£6.99 (+ £1.50 UK p&p) Standard p/b ISBN: 1-903889-76-6
£30.00 (+ £1.50 UK p&p) Deluxe h/b ISBN: 1-903889-77-4

APPROACHING OMEGA by ERIC BROWN
A colonisation mission to Earth runs into problems.
£7.99 (+ £1.50 UK p&p) Standard p/b ISBN: 1-903889-98-7
£30.00 (+ £1.50 UK p&p) Deluxe h/b ISBN: 1-903889-99-5

VALLEY OF LIGHTS by STEPHEN GALLAGHER
A cop comes up against a body-hopping murderer …
£9.99 (+ £2.50 UK p&p) Standard p/b ISBN: 1-903889-74-X
£30.00 (+ £2.50 UK p&p) Deluxe h/b ISBN: 1-903889-75-8

PARISH DAMNED by LEE THOMAS
Vampires attack an American fishing town.
£7.99 (+ £1.50 UK p&p) Standard p/b ISBN: 1-84583-040-7

MORE THAN LIFE ITSELF by JOE NASSISE
What would you do to save the life of someone you love?
£7.99 (+ £1.50 UK p&p) Standard p/b ISBN: 1-84583-042-3

PRETTY YOUNG THINGS by DOMINIC MCDONAGH
A nest of lesbian rave bunny vampires is at large in Manchester. When Chelsey's ex-boyfriend is taken as food, Chelsey has to get out fast.
£7.99 (+ £1.50 UK p&p) Standard p/b ISBN: 1-84583-045-8

A MANHATTAN GHOST STORY by T M WRIGHT
Do you see ghosts? A classic tale of love and the supernatural.
£9.99 (+ £2.50 UK p&p) Standard p/b ISBN: 1-84583-048-2

TV/FILM GUIDES

A DAY IN THE LIFE: THE UNOFFICIAL AND UNAUTHORISED GUIDE TO 24 by KEITH TOPPING
Complete episode guide to the first season of the popular TV show.
£9.99 (+ £2.50 p&p) Standard p/b ISBN: 1-903889-53-7

LIBERATION: THE UNOFFICIAL AND UNAUTHORISED GUIDE TO BLAKE'S 7 by ALAN STEVENS & FIONA MOORE
Complete episode guide to the popular TV show.
Featuring a foreword by David Maloney
£9.99 (+ £2.50 UK p&p) Standard p/b ISBN: 1-903889-54-5

THE END OF THE WORLD?: THE UNOFFICIAL AND UNAUTHORISED GUIDE TO SURVIVORS by ANDY PRIESTNER & RICH CROSS
Complete guide to Terry Nation's Survivors
£12.99 (+ £2.50 UK p&p) Standard p/b ISBN: 1-84583-001-6

TRIQUETRA: THE UNOFFICIAL AND UNAUTHORISED GUIDE TO CHARMED by KEITH TOPPING
Complete guide to Charmed
£12.99 (+ £2.50 UK p&p) Standard p/b ISBN: 1-84583-002-4

WHOGRAPHS: THEMED AUTOGRAPH BOOK
80 page autograph book with an SF theme
£4.50 (+ £1.50 UK p&p) Standard p/b ISBN: 1-84583-110-1

TALKBACK: THE UNOFFICIAL AND UNAUTHORISED DOCTOR WHO INTERVIEW BOOK: VOLUME 1: THE SIXTIES edited by STEPHEN JAMES WALKER
Interviews with behind the scenes crew who worked on Doctor Who in the sixties
£12.99 (+ £2.50 UK p&p) Standard p/b ISBN: 1-84583-006-7
£30.00 (+ £2.50 UK p&p) Deluxe h/b ISBN: 1-84583-007-5

TALKBACK: THE UNOFFICIAL AND UNAUTHORISED DOCTOR WHO INTERVIEW BOOK: VOLUME 2: THE SEVENTIES edited by STEPHEN JAMES WALKER
Interviews with behind the scenes crew who worked on Doctor Who in the seventies
£12.99 (+ £2.50 UK p&p) Standard p/b ISBN: 1-84583-010-5
£30.00 (+ £2.50 UK p&p) Deluxe h/b ISBN: 1-84583-011-3

ZOMBIEMANIA: 80 FILMS TO DIE FOR by DR ARNOLD T BLUMBERG & ANDREW HERSHBERGER
A guide to 80 classic zombie films, along with an extensive filmography of over 500 additional titles
£12.99 (+ £2.50 UK p&p) Standard p/b ISBN: 1-84583-003-2

MIKE RIPLEY

The first three titles in Mike Ripley's acclaimed 'Angel' series of comic crime novels.

JUST ANOTHER ANGEL by MIKE RIPLEY
£9.99 (+ £1.50 UK p&p) Standard p/b ISBN: 1-84583-106-3
ANGEL TOUCH by MIKE RIPLEY
£9.99 (+ £1.50 UK p&p) Standard p/b ISBN: 1-84583-107-1
ANGEL HUNT by MIKE RIPLEY
£9.99 (+ £1.50 UK p&p) Standard p/b ISBN: 1-84583-108-X

HANK JANSON

Classic pulp crime thrillers from the 1940s and 1950s.

TORMENT by HANK JANSON
£9.99 (+ £1.50 UK p&p) Standard p/b ISBN: 1-903889-80-4
WOMEN HATE TILL DEATH by HANK JANSON
£9.99 (+ £1.50 UK p&p) Standard p/b ISBN: 1-903889-81-2
SOME LOOK BETTER DEAD by HANK JANSON
£9.99 (+ £1.50 UK p&p) Standard p/b ISBN: 1-903889-82-0
SKIRTS BRING ME SORROW by HANK JANSON
£9.99 (+ £1.50 UK p&p) Standard p/b ISBN: 1-903889-83-9
WHEN DAMES GET TOUGH by HANK JANSON
£9.99 (+ £1.50 UK p&p) Standard p/b ISBN: 1-903889-85-5
ACCUSED by HANK JANSON
£9.99 (+ £1.50 UK p&p) Standard p/b ISBN: 1-903889-86-3
KILLER by HANK JANSON
£9.99 (+ £1.50 UK p&p) Standard p/b ISBN: 1-903889-87-1
FRAILS CAN BE SO TOUGH by HANK JANSON
£9.99 (+ £1.50 UK p&p) Standard p/b ISBN: 1-903889-88-X
BROADS DON'T SCARE EASY by HANK JANSON
£9.99 (+ £1.50 UK p&p) Standard p/b ISBN: 1-903889-89-8
KILL HER IF YOU CAN by HANK JANSON
£9.99 (+ £1.50 UK p&p) Standard p/b ISBN: 1-903889-90-1
LILIES FOR MY LOVELY by HANK JANSON
£9.99 (+ £1.50 UK p&p) Standard p/b ISBN: 1-903889-91-X
BLONDE ON THE SPOT by HANK JANSON
£9.99 (+ £1.50 UK p&p) Standard p/b ISBN: 1-903889-92-8

Non-fiction:
THE TRIALS OF HANK JANSON by STEVE HOLLAND
£12.99 (+ £2.50 UK p&p) Standard p/b ISBN: 1-903889-84-7

The prices shown are correct at time of going to press. However, the publishers reserve the right to increase prices from those previously advertised without prior notice.

TELOS PUBLISHING
c/o Beech House, Chapel Lane, Moulton, Cheshire, CW9 8PQ, England
Email: orders@telos.co.uk
Web: www.telos.co.uk

To order copies of any Telos books, please visit our website where there are full details of all titles and facilities for worldwide credit card online ordering, or send a cheque or postal order (UK only) for the appropriate amount (including postage and packing), together with details of the book(s) you require, plus your name and address to the above address. Overseas readers please send two international reply coupons for details of prices and postage rates.